Agatha Christie is known throug Her books have sold over a billio in foreign languages. She is the m and in any language, outsold only the author of 80 crime novels and short story collections, 20 plays, and six novels written under the name of Mary Westmacott.

Agatha Christie's first novel, *The Mysterious Affair at Styles*, was written towards the end of the First World War, in which she served as a VAD. In it she created Hercule Poirot, the little Belgian detective who was destined to become the most popular detective in crime fiction since Sherlock Holmes. It was eventually published by The Bodley Head in 1920.

In 1926, after averaging a book a year, Agatha Christie wrote her masterpiece. *The Murder of Roger Ackroyd* was the first of her books to be published by Collins and marked the beginning of an author-publisher relationship which lasted for 50 years and well over 70 books. *The Murder of Roger Ackroyd* was also the first of Agatha Christie's books to be dramatized – under the name *Alibi* – and to have a successful run in London's West End. *The Mousetrap*, her most famous play of all, opened in 1952 and is the longest-running play in history.

Agatha Christie was made a Dame in 1971. She died in 1976, since when a number of books have been published posthumously: the bestselling novel *Sleeping Murder* appeared later that year, followed by her autobiography and the short story collections *Miss Marple's Final Cases*, *Problem at Pollensa Bay* and *While the Light Lasts*. In 1998 *Black Coffee* was the first of her plays to be novelized by another author, Charles Osborne.

THE AGATHA CHRISTIE COLLECTION

Agatha Christie

1960s

OMNIBUS

·

ENDLESS NIGHT

·

BY THE PRICKING OF MY THUMBS

·

PASSENGER TO FRANKFURT

·

POSTERN OF FATE

·

HarperCollins*Publishers*

HarperCollins*Publishers*
77–85 Fulham Palace Road,
Hammersmith, London W6 8JB
www.harpercollins.co.uk

This edition first published 2006
3

Endless Night © Agatha Christie Limited 1967
By the Pricking of My Thumbs © Agatha Christie Limited 1968
Passenger to Frankfurt © Agatha Christie Limited 1970
Postern of Fate © Agatha Christie Limited 1973

ISBN-13   978-0-00-720866-1
ISBN-10   0-00-720866-9

Typeset in Plantin Light and Gill Sans by
Palimpsest Book Production Limited,
Polmont, Stirlingshire

Printed and bound in Great Britain by
Clays Ltd, St Ives plc

CONTENTS

PUBLISHER'S NOTE

This final volume in the 'decades' series, though titled *1960s*, does include Agatha Christie's final novel, *Postern of Fate*, for the sake of completeness. It was in fact written and published in 1973.

ENDLESS NIGHT

Every Night and every Morn
Some to Misery are born.
Every Morn and every Night
Some are born to Sweet Delight,
Some are born to Sweet Delight,
Some are born to Endless Night.

William Blake
Auguries of Innocence

BOOK I

....

CHAPTER I

In my end is my beginning . . . That's a quotation I've often heard
people say. It sounds all right – but what does it really mean?

Is there ever any particular spot where one can put one's finger
and say: 'It all began that day, at such a time and such a place,
with such an incident?'

Did my story begin, perhaps, when I noticed the Sale Bill
hanging on the wall of the George and Dragon, announcing
Sale by Auction of that valuable property 'The Towers', and
giving particulars of the acreage, the miles and furlongs, and
the highly idealized portrait of 'The Towers' as it might have
been perhaps in its prime, anything from eighty to a hundred
years ago?

I was doing nothing particular, just strolling along the main
street of Kingston Bishop, a place of no importance whatever,
killing time. I noticed the Sale Bill. Why? Fate up to its dirty
work? Or dealing out its golden handshake of good fortune?
You can look at it either way.

Or you could say, perhaps, that it all had its beginnings when
I met Santonix, during the talks I had with him; I can close my
eyes and see: his flushed cheeks, the over-brilliant eyes, and the
movement of the strong yet delicate hand that sketched and
drew plans and elevations of houses. One house in particular,
a beautiful house, a house that would be wonderful to own!

My longing for a house, a fine and beautiful house, such a
house as I could never hope to have, flowered into life then. It
was a happy fantasy shared between us, the house that Santonix
would build for me – if he lasted long enough . . .

A house that in my dreams I would live in with the girl that
I loved, a house in which just like a child's silly fairy story we
should live together 'happy ever afterwards'. All pure fantasy,

all nonsense, but it started that tide of longing in me. Longing for something I was never likely to have.

Or if this is a love story – and it *is* a love story, I swear – then why not begin where I first caught sight of Ellie standing in the dark fir trees of Gipsy's Acre?

Gipsy's Acre. Yes, perhaps I'd better begin there, at the moment when I turned away from the Sale board with a little shiver because a black cloud had come over the sun, and asked a question carelessly enough of one of the locals, who was clipping a hedge in a desultory fashion nearby.

'What's this house, The Towers, like?'

I can still see the queer face of the old man, as he looked at me sideways and said:

'That's not what us calls it here. What sort of a name is that?' He snorted disapproval. 'It's many a year now since folks lived in it and called it The Towers.' He snorted again.

I asked him then what *he* called it, and again his eyes shifted away from me in his old wrinkled face in that queer way country folk have of not speaking to you direct, looking over your shoulder or round the corner, as it were, as though they saw something you didn't; and he said:

'It's called hereabouts Gipsy's Acre.'

'Why is it called that?' I asked.

'Some sort of a tale. I dunno rightly. One says one thing, one says another.' And then he went on, 'Anyway, it's where the accidents take place.'

'Car accidents?'

'All kinds of accidents. Car accidents mainly nowadays. It's a nasty corner there, you see.'

'Well,' I said, 'if it's a nasty curve, I can well see there might be accidents.'

'Rural Council put up a Danger sign, but it don't do no good, that don't. There are accidents just the same.'

'Why Gipsy?' I asked him.

Again his eyes slipped past me and his answer was vague.

'Some tale or other. It was gipsies' land once, they say, and they were turned off, and they put a curse on it.'

I laughed.

'Aye,' he said, 'you can laugh but there's places as *is* cursed.

You smart-Alecks in town don't know about them. But there's places as is cursed all right, and there's a curse on this place. People got killed here in the quarry when they got the stone out to build. Old Geordie he fell over the edge there one night and broke his neck.'

'Drunk?' I suggested.

'He may have been. He liked his drop, he did. But there's many drunks as fall – nasty falls – but it don't do them no lasting harm. But Geordie, he got his neck broke. In there,' he pointed up behind him to the pine-covered hill, 'in Gipsy's Acre.'

Yes, I suppose that's how it began. Not that I paid much attention to it at the time. I just happened to remember it. That's all. I think – that is, when I think properly – that I built it up a bit in my mind. I don't know if it was before or later that I asked if there were still gipsies about there. He said there weren't many anywhere nowadays. The police were always moving them on, he said. I asked:

'Why doesn't anybody like gipsies?'

'They're a thieving lot,' he said, disapprovingly. Then he peered more closely at me. 'Happen you've got gipsy blood yourself?' he suggested, looking hard at me.

I said not that I knew of. It's true, I do look a bit like a gipsy. Perhaps that's what fascinated me about the name of Gipsy's Acre. I thought to myself as I was standing there, smiling back at him, amused by our conversation, that perhaps I *had* a bit of gipsy blood.

Gipsy's Acre. I went up the winding road that led out of the village and wound up through the dark trees and came at last to the top of the hill so that I could see out to sea and the ships. It was a marvellous view and I thought, just as one does think things: I wonder how it would be if Gipsy's Acre was *my* acre . . . Just like that . . . It was only a ridiculous thought. When I passed my hedge clipper again, he said:

'If you want gipsies, there's old Mrs Lee of course. The Major, he gives her a cottage to live in.'

'Who's the Major?' I asked.

He said, in a shocked voice, 'Major Phillpot, of course.' He seemed quite upset that I should ask! I gathered that Major Phillpot was God locally. Mrs Lee was some kind of dependent of his, I suppose, whom he provided for. The Phillpots seemed to have lived there all their lives and more or less to have run the place.

As I wished my old boy good day and turned away he said:

'She's got the last cottage at the end of the street. You'll see her outside, maybe. Doesn't like the inside of houses. Them as has got gipsy blood don't.'

So there I was, wandering down the road, whistling and thinking about Gipsy's Acre. I'd almost forgotten what I'd been told when I saw a tall black-haired old woman staring at me over a garden hedge. I knew at once it must be Mrs Lee. I stopped and spoke to her.

'I hear you can tell me about Gipsy's Acre up there,' I said.

She stared at me through a tangled fringe of black hair and she said:

'Don't have nought to do with it, young man. You listen to me. Forget about it. You're a good-looking lad. Nothing good comes out of Gipsy's Acre and never will.'

'I see it's up for sale,' I said.

'Aye, that's so, and more fool he who buys it.'

'Who's likely to buy it?'

'There's a builder after it. More than one. It'll go cheap. You'll see.'

'Why should it go cheap?' I asked curiously. 'It's a fine site.'

She wouldn't answer that.

'Supposing a builder buys it cheap, what will he do with it?'

She chuckled to herself. It was malicious, unpleasant laughter.

'Pull down the old ruined house and build, of course. Twenty – thirty houses, maybe – and all with a curse on them.'

I ignored the last part of the sentence. I said, speaking before I could stop myself:

'That would be a shame. A great shame.'

'Ah, you needn't worry. *They'll* get no joy of it, not those who buys and not those who lays the bricks and mortar. There'll be a foot that slips on the ladder, and there'll be the lorry that crashes with a load, and the slate that falls from the roof of a house and finds its mark. And the trees too. Crashing, maybe, in a sudden gale. Ah, you'll see! There's none that'll get any good out of Gipsy's Acre. They'd do best to leave it alone. You'll see. You'll see.' She nodded vigorously and then she repeated softly to herself, '*There's no luck for them as meddles with Gipsy's Acre.* There never has been.'

I laughed. She spoke sharply.

'Don't laugh, young man. It comes to me as may-be one of these days you'll laugh on the wrong side of your mouth. There's never been no luck there, not in the house nor yet in the land.'

'What happened in the house?' I asked. 'Why has it been empty so long? Why was it left to fall down?'

'The last people that lived there died, all of them.'

'How did they die?' I asked out of curiosity.

'Best not to speak of it again. But no one cared to come and live in it afterwards. It was left to moulder and decay. It's forgot by now and best that it should be.'

'But you could tell me the story,' I said, wheedlingly. 'You know all about it.'

'I don't gossip about Gipsy's Acre.' Then she let her voice drop to a kind of phoney beggar's whine. 'I'll tell your fortune now, my pretty lad, if you like. Cross my palm with silver and I'll tell your fortune. You're one of those that'll go far one of these days.'

'I don't believe nonsense about fortune-telling,' I said, 'and I haven't any silver. Not to spare, anyway.'

She came nearer to me and went on in a wheedling voice. 'Sixpence now. Sixpence now. I'll do it for sixpence. What's that? Nothing at all. I'll do it for sixpence because you're a handsome lad with a ready tongue and a way with you. It could be that you'll go far.'

I fished a sixpence out of my pocket, not because I believed in any of her foolish superstitions but because for some reason I liked the old fraud even if I did see through her. She grabbed the coin from me, and said:

'Give me your hand then. Both hands.'

She took my hands in her withered claw and stared down at the open palms. She was silent for a minute or two, staring. Then she dropped my hands abruptly, almost pushing them away from her. She retreated a step and spoke harshly.

'If you know what's good for you, you'll get out of Gipsy's

Acre here and now and you won't come back! That's the best advice I can give you. Don't come back.'

'Why not? Why shouldn't I come back?'

'Because if you do you'll come back to sorrow and loss and danger maybe. There's trouble, black trouble waiting for you. Forget you ever saw this place. I'm warning you.'

'Well of all the —'

But she had turned away and was retreating to the cottage. She went in and slammed the door. I'm not superstitious. I believe in luck, of course, who doesn't? But not a lot of superstitious nonsense about ruined houses with curses on them. And yet I had an uneasy feeling that the sinister old creature had seen *something* in my hands. I looked down at my two palms spread out in front of me. What could anyone see in the palms of anyone's hands? Fortune-telling was arrant nonsense — just a trick to get money out of you — money out of your silly credulity. I looked up at the sky. The sun had gone in, the day seemed different now. A sort of shadow, a kind of menace. Just an approaching storm, I thought. The wind was beginning to blow, the backs of the leaves were showing on the trees. I whistled to keep my spirits up and walked along the road through the village.

I looked again at the pasted-up bill advertising the auction of The Towers. I even made a note of the date. I had never attended a property sale in my life but I thought to myself that I'd come and attend this one. It would be interesting to see who bought The Towers. That is to say interesting to see who became the owner of Gipsy's Acre. Yes, I think that's really where it all began . . . A fantastic notion occurred to me. I'd come and pretend to myself that I was the man who was going to bid for Gipsy's Acre! I'd bid against the local builders! They'd drop out, disappointed in their hopes of buying it cheap. *I'd* buy it and I'd go to Rudolf Santonix and say, 'Build me a house. I've bought the site for you.' And I'd find a girl, a wonderful girl, and we'd live in it together happy ever after.

I often had dreams of that kind. Naturally they never came to anything but they were fun. That's what I thought then. Fun! Fun, my God! If I'd only known!

CHAPTER 2

It was pure chance that had brought me to the neighbourhood of Gipsy's Acre that day. I was driving a hired car, taking some people down from London to attend a sale, a sale not of a house but its contents. It was a big house just at the outskirts of the town, a particularly ugly one. I drove an elderly couple there who were interested, from what I could overhear of their conversation, in a collection of *papier mâché*, whatever *papier mâché* was. The only time I ever heard it mentioned before was by my mother in connection with washing-up bowls. She'd said that a *papier mâché* washing-up bowl was far better than a plastic one any day! It seemed an odd thing for rich people to want to come down and buy a collection of the stuff.

However I stored the fact away in my mind and I thought I would look in a dictionary or read up somewhere what *papier mâché* really was. Something that people thought worthwhile to hire a car for, and go down to a country sale and bid for. I liked to know about things. I was twenty-two years of age at that time and I had picked up a fair amount of knowledge one way and another. I knew a good deal about cars, was a fair mechanic and a careful driver. Once I'd worked with horses in Ireland. I nearly got entangled with a dope gang but I got wise and quit in time. A job as a chauffeur to a classy car hire firm isn't bad at all. Good money to be made with tips. And not usually too strenuous. But the work itself was boring.

Once I'd gone fruit picking in summer time. That didn't pay much, but I enjoyed myself. I'd tried a lot of things. I'd been a waiter in a third-class hotel, life guard on a summer beach, I'd sold encyclopaedias and vacuum cleaners and a few other things. I'd once done horticultural work in a botanical garden and had learnt a little about flowers.

I never stuck to anything. Why should I? I'd found nearly everything I did interesting. Some things were harder work than others but I didn't really mind that. I'm not really lazy. I suppose what I really am is restless. I want to go everywhere, see everything, do everything. I want to *find* something. Yes, that's it. I want to find something.

From the time I left school I wanted to find something, but I didn't yet know what that something was going to be. It was just something I was looking for in a vague, unsatisfied sort of way. It was *somewhere*. Sooner or later I'd know all about it. It might perhaps be a girl . . . I like girls, but no girl I'd met so far had been important . . . You liked them all right but then you went to the next one quite gladly. They were like the jobs I took. All right for a bit and then you got fed up with them and you wanted to move on to the next one. I'd gone from one thing to another ever since I'd left school.

A lot of people disapproved of my way of life. I suppose they were what you might call my well-wishers. That was because they didn't understand the first thing about me. They wanted me to go steady with a nice girl, save money, get married to her and then settle down to a nice steady job. Day after day, year after year, world without end, amen. Not for yours truly! There must be something better than that. Not just all this tame security, the good old welfare state limping along in its half-baked way! Surely, I thought, in a world where man has been able to put satellites in the sky and where men talk big about visiting the stars, there must be *something* that rouses you, that makes your heart beat, that's worthwhile searching all over the world to find! One day, I remember, I was walking down Bond Street. It was during my waiter period and I was due on duty. I'd been strolling looking at some shoes in a shop window. Very natty they were. Like they say in the advertisements in newspapers: '*What smart men are wearing today*' and there's usually a picture of the smart man in question. My word, he usually looks a twerp! Used to make me laugh, advertisements like that did.

I passed on from the shoes to the next window. It was a picture shop. Just three pictures in the window artily arranged with a drape of limp velvet in some neutral colour arranged over a corner of a gilt frame. Cissy, if you know what I mean. I'm not much of a one for Art. I dropped in to the National Gallery once out of curiosity. Fair gave me the pip, it did. Great big shiny coloured pictures of battles in rocky glens, or emaciated saints getting themselves stuck with arrows. Portraits of simpering great ladies sitting smirking in silks and velvets and lace. I decided then and there that Art wasn't for me. But the picture I was looking at now was somehow different. There were three pictures in the window. One a landscape, nice bit of country for what I call everyday. One of a woman drawn in such a funny way, so much out of proportion, that you could hardly see she *was* a woman. I suppose that's what you call *art nouveau*. I don't know what it was about. The third picture was my picture. There wasn't really much to it, if you know what I mean. It was – how can I describe it? It was kind of *simple*. A lot of space in it and a few great widening circles all round each other if you can put it that way. All in different colours, odd colours that you wouldn't expect. And here and there, there were sketchy bits of colour that didn't seem to mean anything. Only somehow they *did* mean something! I'm no good at description. All I can say is that one wanted terribly to go on looking at it.

I just stood there, feeling queer as though something very unusual had happened to me. Those fancy shoes now, I'd have liked them to wear. I mean I take quite a bit of trouble with my clothes. I like to dress well so as to make an impression, but I never seriously thought in my life of buying a pair of shoes in Bond Street. I know the kind of fancy prices they ask there. Fifteen pounds a pair those shoes might be. Hand-made or something, they call it, making it more worthwhile for some reason. Sheer waste of money that would be. A classy line in shoes, yes, but you can pay too much for class. I've got my head screwed on the right way.

But this picture, what would *that* cost? I wondered. Suppose *I* were to buy that picture? You're crazy, I said to myself. You don't go for pictures, not in a general way. That was true enough. But I wanted this picture . . . I'd like it to be *mine*. I'd like to be able to hang it and sit and look at it as long as I liked and know that *I* owned it! Me! Buying pictures. It seemed a crazy idea. I took a look at the picture again. Me wanting that picture didn't make sense, and anyway, I probably couldn't afford it. Actually I was in funds at just that moment. A lucky tip on a horse. This picture would probably cost a packet. Twenty pounds? Twenty-five? Anyway, there would be no harm in asking. They couldn't eat me, could they? I went in, feeling rather aggressive and on the defensive.

The inside of the place was all very hushed and grand. There was a sort of muted atmosphere with neutral-colour walls and a velvet settee on which you could sit and look at the pictures. A man who looked a little like the model for the perfectly dressed man in advertisements came and attended to me, speaking in a rather hushed voice to match the scenery. Funnily, he didn't look superior as they usually do in high-grade Bond Street shops. He listened to what I said and then he took the picture out of the window and displayed it for me against a wall, holding it there for me to look at as long as I wanted. It came to me then – in the way you sometimes know just exactly how things are, that the same rules didn't apply over pictures as they do about other things. Somebody might come into a place like this dressed in shabby old clothes and a frayed shirt and turn out to be a millionaire who wanted to add to his collection. Or he could come in looking cheap and flashy, rather like me perhaps, but somehow or other he'd got such a yen for a picture that he managed to get the money together by some kind of sharp practice.

'A very fine example of the artist's work,' said the man who was holding the picture.

'How much?' I said briskly.

The answer took my breath away.

'Twenty-five thousand,' he said in his gentle voice.

I'm quite good at keeping a poker face. I didn't show anything. At least I don't think I did. He added some name that sounded foreign. The artist's name, I suppose, and that it had just come on the market from a house in the country, where the people who lived there had had no idea what it was. I kept my end up and sighed.

'It's a lot of money but it's worth it, I suppose,' I said.

Twenty-five thousand pounds. What a laugh!

'Yes,' he said and sighed. 'Yes indeed.' He lowered the picture very gently and carried it back to the window. He looked at me and smiled. 'You have good taste,' he said.

I felt that in some way he and I understood each other. I thanked him and went out into Bond Street.

CHAPTER 3

I don't know much about writing things down – not, I mean, in the way a proper writer would do. The bit about that picture I saw, for instance. It doesn't really have anything to do with anything. I mean, nothing came of it, it didn't lead to anything and yet I feel somehow that it is important, that it has a place somewhere. It was one of the things that happened to me that *meant* something. Just like Gipsy's Acre meant something to me. Like Santonix meant something to me.

I haven't really said much about him. He was an architect. Of course you'll have gathered that. Architects are another thing I'd never had much to do with, though I knew a few things about the building trade. I came across Santonix in the course of my wanderings. It was when I was working as a chauffeur, driving the rich around places. Once or twice I drove abroad, twice to Germany – I knew a bit of German – and once or twice to France – I had a smattering of French too – and once to Portugal. They were usually elderly people, who had money and bad health in about equal quantities.

When you drive people like that around, you begin to think that money isn't so hot after all. What with incipient heart attacks, lots of bottles of little pills you have to take all the time, and losing your temper over the food or the service in hotels. Most of the rich people I've known have been fairly miserable. They've got their worries, too. Taxation and investments. You hear them talking together or to friends. Worry! That's what's killing half of them. And their sex life's not so hot either. They've either got long-legged blonde sexy wives who are playing them up with boy-friends somewhere, or they're married to the complaining kind of woman, hideous as hell, who keeps telling them where they get off. No. I'd rather be myself. Michael Rogers, seeing the world, and getting off with good-looking girls when he feels like it!

Everything a bit hand-to-mouth, of course, but I put up with that. Life was good fun, and I'd been content to go on with life being fun. But I suppose I would have in any case. That attitude goes with youth. When youth begins to pass fun isn't fun any longer.

Behind it, I think, was always the other thing – wanting someone and something . . . However, to go on with what I was saying, there was one old boy I used to drive down to the Riviera. He'd got a house being built there. He went down to look how it was getting on. Santonix was the architect. I don't really know what nationality Santonix was. English I thought at first, though it was a funny sort of name I'd never heard before. But I don't think he was English. Scandinavian of some kind I guess. He was an ill man. I could see that at once. He was young and very fair and thin with an odd face, a face that was askew somehow. The two sides of it didn't match. He could be quite bad-tempered to his clients. You'd have thought as they were paying the money that they'd call the tune and do the bullying. That wasn't so. Santonix bullied *them* and he was always quite sure of himself although they weren't.

This particular old boy of mine was frothing with rage, I remember, as soon as he arrived and had seen how things were going. I used to catch snatches here and there when I was standing by ready to assist in my chauffeurly and handyman way. It was always on the cards that Mr Constantine would have a heart attack or a stroke.

'You have not done as I said,' he half screamed. 'You have spent too much money. Much too much money. It is not as we agreed. It is going to cost me more than I thought.'

'You're absolutely right,' said Santonix. 'But the money's got to be spent.'

'It shall not be spent! It shall not be spent! You have got to keep within the limits I laid down. You understand?'

'Then you won't get the kind of house you want,' said Santonix. 'I *know* what you want. The house I build you will be the house you want. I'm quite sure of that and you're quite sure of it, too. Don't give me any of your pettifogging middle-class economies. You want a house of quality and you're going to *get* it, and you'll boast about it to your friends and they'll envy you. I don't build a house for anyone, I've told you that. There's more to it than money. This house isn't going to be like other people's houses!'

'It is going to be terrible. Terrible.'

'Oh no it isn't. The trouble with you is that *you* don't know what you want. Or at least so anyone might think. But you do know what you want really, only you can't bring it out into your mind. You can't *see* it clearly. But I *know*. That's the one thing I always know. What people are after and what they want. There's a feeling in you for quality. I'm going to *give* you quality.'

He used to say things like that. And I'd stand by and listen. Somehow or other I could see for myself that this house that was being built there amongst pine trees looking over the sea, wasn't going to be the usual house. Half of it didn't look out towards the sea in a conventional way. It looked inland, up to a certain curve of mountains, up to a glimpse of sky between hills. It was odd and unusual and very exciting.

Santonix used to talk to me sometimes when I was off duty. He said:

'I only build houses for people I *want* to build for.'

'Rich people, you mean?'

'They have to be rich or they couldn't pay for the houses. But it's not the money I'm going to make out of it I care about. My clients have to be rich because I want to make the kind of houses that cost money. The house only isn't enough, you see. It has to have the setting. That's just as important. It's like a ruby or an emerald. A beautiful stone is only a beautiful stone. It doesn't lead you anywhere further. It doesn't mean anything, it has no form or significance until it has its setting. And the setting has to have a beautiful jewel to be worthy of it. I take the setting, you see, out of the landscape, where it exists only in its own right. It has no meaning until there is my house sitting proudly like a jewel within its grasp.' He looked at me and laughed. 'You don't understand?'

'I suppose not,' I said slowly, 'and yet – in a way – I think I do . . .'

'That may be.' He looked at me curiously.

We came down to the Riviera again later. By then the house was nearly finished. I won't describe it because I couldn't do it properly, but it was – well – something special – and it was *beautiful*. I could see that. It was a house you'd be proud of, proud to show to people, proud to look at yourself, proud to be in with the right person perhaps. And then suddenly one day Santonix said to me:

'I could build a house for *you*, you know. I'd know the kind of house you'd want.'

I shook my head.

'I shouldn't know myself,' I said, honestly.

'Perhaps you wouldn't. I'd know for you.' Then he added, 'It's a thousand pities you haven't got the money.'

'And never shall have,' I said.

'You can't say that,' said Santonix. 'Born poor doesn't mean you've got to stay poor. Money's queer. It goes where it's wanted.'

'I'm not sharp enough,' I said.

'You're not ambitious enough. Ambition hasn't woken up in you, but it's there, you know.'

'Oh, well,' I said, 'some day when I've woken up ambition and I've made money, then I'll come to you and say "build me a house".'

He sighed then. He said:

'I can't wait . . . No, I can't afford to wait. I've only a short time to go now. One house – two houses more. Not more than that. One doesn't *want* to die young . . . Sometimes one has to . . . It doesn't really matter, I suppose.'

'I'll have to wake up my ambition quick.'

'No,' said Santonix. 'You're healthy, you're having fun, don't change your way of life.'

I said: 'I couldn't if I tried.'

I thought that was true then. I liked my way of life and I was having fun and there was never anything wrong with my health. I've driven a lot of people who've made money, who've worked hard and who've got ulcers and coronary thrombosis and many other things as a result of working hard. I didn't want to work hard. I could do a job as well as another but that was all there was to it. And I hadn't got ambition, or I didn't think I had ambition. Santonix had had ambition, I suppose. I could see that designing houses and building them, the planning of the drawing and something else that I couldn't quite get hold of, all that had taken it out of him. He hadn't been a strong man to begin with. I had a fanciful idea sometimes that he was killing himself before his time by the work he had put out to drive his ambition. I didn't *want* to work. It was as simple as that.

I distrusted work, disliked it. I thought it was a very bad thing, that the human race had unfortunately invented for itself.

I thought about Santonix quite often. He intrigued me almost more than anyone I knew. One of the oddest things in life, I think, is the things one remembers. One chooses to remember, I suppose. Something in one must choose. Santonix and his house were one of the things and the picture in Bond Street and visiting that ruined house, The Towers, and hearing the story of Gipsy's Acre, all those were the things that I'd chosen to remember! Sometimes girls that I met, and journeys to the foreign places in the course of driving clients about. The clients were all the same. Dull. They always stayed at the same kind of hotels and ate the same kind of unimaginative food.

I still had that queer feeling in me of waiting for something, waiting for something to be offered to me, or to happen to me, I don't quite know which way describes it best. I suppose really I was looking for a girl, the right sort of girl – by which I don't mean a nice, suitable girl to settle down with, which is what my mother would have meant or my Uncle Joshua or some of my friends. I didn't know at that time anything about love. All I knew about was sex. That was all anybody of my generation seemed to know about. We talked about it too much, I think, and heard too much about it and took it too seriously. We didn't know – any of my friends or myself – what it was really going to be when it happened. Love I mean. We were young and virile and we looked the girls over we met and we appreciated their curves and their legs and the kind of eye they gave you, and you thought to yourself: 'Will they or won't they? Should I be wasting my time?' And the more girls you made the more you boasted and the finer fellow you were thought to be, and the finer fellow you thought yourself.

I'd no real idea that that wasn't all there was to it. I suppose it happens to everyone sooner or later and it happens suddenly. You don't think as you imagine you're going to think: 'This might be the girl for me . . . This is the girl who is going to be mine.' At least, I didn't feel it that way. I didn't know that when it happened it would happen quite suddenly. That I would say: 'That's the girl I belong to. I'm *hers*. I belong to *her*, utterly, for always.' No. I never dreamed it would be like that. Didn't one of the old comedians say once – wasn't it one of his stock jokes? 'I've been in love once and if I felt it coming on again I tell you I'd emigrate.' It was the same with me. If I had known, if I had only known what it could all come to mean *I'd* have emigrated too! If I'd been wise, that is.

CHAPTER 4

I hadn't forgotten my plan of going to the auction.

There was three weeks to go. I'd had two more trips to the Continent, one to France and the other to Germany. It was when I was in Hamburg that things came to a crisis. For one thing I took a violent dislike to the man and his wife I was driving. They represented everything I disliked most. They were rude, inconsiderate, unpleasant to look at, and I suppose they developed in me a feeling of being unable to stand this life of sycophancy any longer. I was careful, mind you. I thought I couldn't stand them another day but I didn't tell them so. No good running yourself in bad with the firm that employs you. So I telephoned up their hotel, said I was ill and I wired London saying the same thing. I said I might be in quarantine and it would be advisable if they sent out a driver to replace me. Nobody could blame me for that. They wouldn't care enough about me to make further inquiries and they'd merely think that I was too feverish to send them any more news. Later, I'd turn up in London again, spinning them a yarn of how ill I'd been! But I didn't think I should do that. I was fed up with the driving racket.

That rebellion of mine was an important turning-point in my life. Because of that and of other things, I turned up at the auction rooms on the appointed date.

'Unless sold before by private treaty' had been pasted across the original board. But it was still there, so it hadn't been sold by private treaty. I was so excited I hardly knew what I was doing.

As I say, I had never been to a public auction of property before. I was imbued with the idea that it would be exciting but it wasn't exciting. Not in the least. It was one of the most moribund performances I have ever attended. It took place in a semi-gloomy atmosphere and there were only about six or

seven people there. The auctioneer was quite different from
those auctioneers that I had seen presiding at furniture sales or
things of that kind; men with facetious voices and very hearty
and full of jokes. This one, in a dead and alive voice, praised the
property and described the acreage and a few things like that and
then he went half-heartedly into the bidding. Somebody made a
bid of £5,000. The auctioneer gave a tired smile rather as one
who hears a joke that isn't really funny. He made a few remarks
and there were a few more bids. They were mostly country types
standing around. Someone who looked like a farmer, someone
who I guessed to be one of the competitive builders, a couple
of lawyers, I think, one a man who looked as though he was a
stranger from London, well dressed and professional-looking. I
don't know if he made an actual bid, he may have done. If so it
was very quietly and done more by gesture. Anyway the bidding
petered to an end, the auctioneer announced in a melancholy
voice that the reserve price had not been reached and the thing
broke up.

'That was a dull business,' I said to one of the country-looking
fellows whom I was next to as I went out.

'Much the same as usual,' he said. 'Been to many of these?'

'No,' I said, 'actually it's the first.'

'Come out of curiosity, did you? I didn't notice you doing any
bidding.'

'No fear,' I said. 'I just wanted to see how it would go.'

'Well, it's the way it runs very often. They just want to see
who's interested, you know.'

I looked at him inquiringly.

'Only three of 'em in it, I should say,' said my friend.
'Whetherby from Helminster. He's the builder, you know. Then
Dakham and Coombe, bidding on behalf of some Liverpool firm,
I understand, and a dark horse from London, too, I should say
a lawyer. Of course there may be more in it than that, but
those seemed the main ones to me. It'll go cheap. That's what
everyone says.'

'Because of the place's reputation?' I asked.

'Oh, you've heard about Gipsy's Acre, have you? That's only
what the country people say. Rural Council ought to have altered
that road years ago – it's a death trap.'

'But the place *has* got a bad reputation?'

'I tell you that's just superstition. Anyway, as I say, the real business'll happen now behind the scenes, you know. They'll go and make offers. I'd say the Liverpool people might get it. I don't think Whetherby'll go high enough. He likes buying cheap. Plenty of properties coming into the market nowadays for development. After all, it's not many people who could afford to buy the place, pull that ruined house down and put up another house there, could they?'

'Doesn't seem to happen very often nowadays,' I said.

'Too difficult. What with taxation and one thing and another, and you can't get domestic help in the country. No, people would rather pay thousands for a luxury flat in a town nowadays up on the sixteenth floor of a modern building. Big unwieldy country houses are a drag on the market.'

'But you could build a modern house,' I argued. 'Labour-saving.'

'You *could*, but it's an expensive business and people aren't so fond of living lonely.'

'Some people might be,' I said.

He laughed and we parted. I walked along, frowning, puzzling to myself. My feet took me without my really noticing where I was going along the road between the trees and up, up to the curving road that led between the trees to the moorlands.

And so I came to the spot in the road where I first saw Ellie. As I said, she was standing just by a tall fir tree and she had the look, if I can explain it, of someone who hadn't been there a moment before but had just materialized, as it were, out of the tree. She was wearing a sort of dark green tweed and her hair was the soft brown colour of an autumn leaf and there was something a bit unsubstantial about her. I saw her and I stopped. She was looking at me, her lips just parted, looking slightly startled. I suppose I looked startled too. I wanted to say something and I didn't quite know what to say. Then I said:

'Sorry. I – I didn't mean to startle you. I didn't know there was anyone here.'

She said, and her voice was very soft and gentle, it might have been a little girl's voice but not quite. She said:

'It's quite all right. I mean, I didn't think anyone would be here either.' She looked round her and said, 'It – it's a lonely spot.' And she shivered just a little.

There was rather a chilly wind that afternoon. But perhaps it wasn't the wind. I don't know. I came a step or two nearer.

'It is a sort of scary place rather, isn't it?' I said. 'I mean, the house being a ruin the way it is.'

'The Towers,' she said thoughtfully. 'That was the name of it, wasn't it – only I mean, there don't seem to have been any towers.'

'I expect that was just a name,' I said. 'People call their houses names like The Towers to make them sound grander than they are.'

She laughed just a little. 'I suppose that was it,' she said. 'This – perhaps you know, I'm not sure – this is the place that they're selling today or putting up for auction?'

'Yes,' I said. 'I've come from the auction now.'

'Oh.' She sounded startled. 'Were you – are you – interested?'

'I'm not likely to buy a ruined house with a few hundred acres of woodland land,' I said. 'I'm not in that class.'

'Was it sold?' she asked.

'No, it didn't come up to reserve.'

'Oh. I see.' She sounded relieved.

'You didn't want to buy it either, did you?' I said.

'Oh no,' she said, 'of course not.' She sounded nervous about it.

I hesitated and then I blurted out the words that came to my lips.

'I'm pretending,' I said. 'I can't buy it, of course, because I haven't got any money, but I'm interested. I'd *like* to buy it. I *want* to buy it. Open your mouth and laugh at me if you like but that's the way it is.'

'But isn't it rather too decrepit, too –'

'Oh yes,' I said. 'I don't mean I want it like it is *now*. I want to pull this down, cart it all away. It's an ugly house and I think it must have been a sad house. But this *place* isn't sad or ugly. It's beautiful. Look here. Come a little this way, through the trees. Look out at the view that way where it goes to the hills and the moors. D'you see? Clear away a vista *here* – and then you come this way –'

I took her by the arm and led her to a second point of the compass. If we were behaving unconventionally she did not notice it. Anyway, it wasn't that kind of way I was holding her. I wanted to show her what I saw.

'Here,' I said, 'here you see where it sweeps down to the sea and where the rocks show out *there*. There's a town between us and that but we can't see it because of the hills bulging out farther down the slope. And then you can look a third way, to a vague foresty valley. Do you see now if you cut down trees and make big vistas and clear this space round the house, do you see what a beautiful house you could have *here*? You wouldn't site it where the old one is. You'd go about fifty – a hundred yards to the right, here. This is where you could have a house, a wonderful house. A house built by an architect who's a genius.'

'Do you know any architects who are geniuses?' She sounded doubtful.

'I know one,' I said.

Then I started telling her about Santonix. We sat down side by side on a fallen tree and I talked. Yes, I talked to that slender woodland girl whom I'd never seen before and I put all I had into what I was telling her. I told her the dream that one could build up.

'It won't happen,' I said, 'I know that. It couldn't happen. But think. Think into it just like I'm thinking into it. There we'd cut the trees and there we'd open up, and we'd plant things, rhododendrons and azaleas, and my friend Santonix would come. He'd cough a good deal because I think he's dying of consumption or something but he could do it. He could do it before he died. He could build the most wonderful house. You don't know what his houses are like. He builds them for very rich people and they have to be people who want the right thing. I don't mean the right thing in the conventional sense. Things people who want a dream come true want. Something wonderful.'

'I'd want a house like that,' said Ellie. 'You make me see it, feel it . . . Yes, this would be a lovely place to live. Everything one has dreamed of come true. One could live here and be free, not hampered, not tied round by people pushing you into doing everything you don't want, keeping you from doing anything you do want. Oh I am so sick of my life and the people who are round me and *everything*!'

That's the way it began, Ellie and I together. Me with my dreams and she with her revolt against her life. We stopped talking and looked at each other.

'What's your name?' she said.

'Mike Rogers,' I said. 'Michael Rogers,' I amended. 'What's yours?'

'Fenella.' She hesitated and then said, 'Fenella Goodman,' looking at me with a rather troubled expression.

This didn't seem to take us much further but we went on looking at each other. We both wanted to see each other again – but just for the moment we didn't know how to set about it.

CHAPTER 5

Well, that's how it began between Ellie and myself. It didn't really go along so very quickly, because we both had our secrets. Both had things we wanted to keep from the other and so we couldn't tell each other as much about ourselves as we might have done, and that kept bringing us up sharp, as it were, against a kind of barrier. We couldn't bring things into the open and say, 'When shall we meet again? Where can I find you? Where do you live?' Because, you see, if you ask the other person that, they'd expect you to tell the same.

Fenella looked apprehensive when she gave me her name. So much so that I thought for a moment that it mightn't be her real name. I almost thought that she might have made it up! But of course I knew that that was impossible. I'd given her my real name.

We didn't know quite how to take leave of each other that day. It was awkward. It had become cold and we wanted to wander down from The Towers – but what then? Rather awkwardly, I said tentatively:

'Are you staying round here?'

She said she was staying in Market Chadwell. That was a market town not very far away. It had, I knew, a large hotel, three-starred. She'd be staying there, I guessed. She said, with something of the same awkwardness, to me:

'Do you live here?'

'No,' I said, 'I don't live here. I'm only here for the day.'

Then a rather awkward silence fell. She gave a faint shiver. A cold little wind had come up.

'We'd better walk,' I said, 'and keep ourselves warm. Are you – have you got a car or are you going by bus or train?'

She said she'd left the car in the village.

'But I'll be quite all right,' she said.

She seemed a little nervous. I thought perhaps she wanted to get rid of me but didn't quite know how to manage it. I said:

'We'll walk down, shall we, just as far as the village?'

She gave me a quick grateful look then. We walked slowly down the winding road on which so many car accidents had happened. As we came round a corner, a figure stepped suddenly from beneath the shelter of the fir tree. It appeared so suddenly that Ellie gave a start and said, 'Oh!' It was the old woman I had seen the other day in her cottage garden. Mrs Lee. She looked a great deal wilder today with a tangle of black hair blowing in the wind and a scarlet cloak round her shoulders; the commanding stance she took up made her look taller.

'And what would you be doing, my dears?' she said. 'What brings you to Gipsy's Acre?'

'Oh,' Ellie said, 'we aren't trespassing, are we?'

'That's as may be. Gipsies' land this used to be. Gipsies' land and they drove us off it. You'll do no good here, and no good will come to you prowling about Gipsy's Acre.'

There was no fight in Ellie, she wasn't that kind. She said gently and politely:

'I'm very sorry if we shouldn't have come here. I thought this place was being sold today.'

'And bad luck it will be to anyone who buys it!' said the old woman. 'You listen, my pretty, for you're pretty enough, bad luck will come to whoever buys it. There's a curse on this land, a curse put on it long ago, many years ago. You keep clear of it. Don't have nought to do with Gipsy's Acre. Death it will bring you and danger. Go away home across the sea and don't come back to Gipsy's Acre. Don't say I didn't warn you.'

'We're doing no harm.'

'Come now, Mrs Lee,' I said, 'don't frighten this young lady.'

I turned in an explanatory way to Ellie.

'Mrs Lee lives in the village. She's got a cottage there. She tells fortunes and prophesies the future. All that, don't you, Mrs Lee?' I spoke to her in a jocular way.

'I've got the gift,' she said simply, drawing her gipsy-like figure up straighter still. 'I've got the gift. It's born in me. We all have it. I'll tell your fortune, young lady. Cross my palm with silver and I'll tell your fortune for you.'

'I don't think I want my fortune told.'

'It'd be a wise thing to do. Know something about the future. Know what to avoid, know what's coming to you if you don't take care. Come now, there's plenty of money in your pocket. Plenty of money. I know things it would be wise for you to know.'

I believe the urge to have one's fortune told is almost invariable in women. I've noticed it before with girls I knew. I nearly always had to pay for them to go into the fortune-tellers' booths if I took them to a fair. Ellie opened her bag and laid two half-crowns in the old woman's hand.

'Ah, my pretty, that's right now. You hear what old Mother Lee will tell you.'

Ellie drew off her glove and laid her small delicate palm in the old woman's hand. She looked down at it, muttering to herself. 'What do I see now? What do I see?'

Suddenly she dropped Ellie's hand abruptly.

'I'd go away from here if I were you. Go – and don't come back! That's what I told you just now and it's true. I've seen it again in your palm. Forget Gipsy's Acre, forget you ever saw it. And it's not just the ruined house up there, it's the land itself that's cursed.'

'You've got a mania about that,' I said roughly. 'Anyway the young lady has nothing to do with the land here. She's only here for a walk today, she's nothing to do with the neighbourhood.'

The old woman paid no attention to me. She said dourly:

'I'm telling you, my pretty. I'm warning you. You can have a happy life – but you must avoid danger. Don't come to a place where there's danger or where there's a curse. Go away where you're loved and taken care of and looked after. You've got to keep yourself safe. Remember that. Otherwise – otherwise –' she gave a short shiver. 'I don't like to see it, I don't like to see what's in your hand.'

Suddenly with a queer brisk gesture she pushed back the two half-crowns into Ellie's palm, mumbling something we could hardly hear. It sounded like 'It's cruel. It's cruel, what's going to happen.' Turning, she stalked away at a rapid pace.

'What a – what a frightening woman,' said Ellie.

'Pay no attention to her,' I said gruffly. 'I think she's half off her head anyway. She just wants to frighten you off. They've got a sort of feeling, I think, about this particular piece of land.'

'Have there been accidents here? Have bad things happened?'

'Bound to be accidents. Look at the curve and the narrowness of the road. The Town Council ought to be shot for not doing something about it. Of course there'll be accidents here. There aren't enough signs warning you.'

'Only accidents – or other things?'

'Look here,' I said, 'people like to collect disasters. There are plenty of disasters always to collect. That's the way stories build themselves up about a place.'

'Is that one of the reasons why they say this property which is being sold will go cheap?'

'Well, it may be, I suppose. Locally, that is. But I don't suppose it'll be sold locally. I expect it'll be bought for developing. You're shivering,' I said. 'Don't shiver. Come on, we'll walk fast.' I added, 'Would you rather I left you before you got back into the town?'

'No. Of course not. Why should I?'

I made a desperate plunge.

'Look here,' I said, 'I shall be in Market Chadwell tomorrow. I – I suppose – I don't know whether you'll still be there . . . I mean, would there be any chance of – seeing you?' I shuffled my feet and turned my head away. I got rather red, I think. But if I didn't say something *now*, how was I going to go on with this?

'Oh yes,' she said, 'I shan't be going back to London until the evening.'

'Then perhaps – would you – I mean, I suppose it's rather cheek –'

'No, it isn't.'

'Well, perhaps you'd come and have tea at a café – the Blue Dog I think it's called. It's quite nice,' I said. 'It's – I mean, it's –' I couldn't get hold of the word I wanted and I used the word that I'd heard my mother use once or twice – 'it's quite ladylike,' I said anxiously.

Then Ellie laughed. I suppose it sounded rather peculiar nowadays.

'I'm sure it'll be very nice,' she said. 'Yes. I'll come. About half past four, will that be right?'

'I'll be waiting for you,' I said. 'I – I'm glad.' I didn't say what I was glad about.

We had come to the last turn of the road where the houses began.

'Goodbye, then,' I said, 'till tomorrow. And – don't think again about what that old hag said. She just likes scaring people, I think. She's not all there,' I added.

'Do you feel it's a frightening place?' Ellie asked.

'Gipsy's Acre? No, I don't,' I said. I said it perhaps a trifle too decidedly, but I didn't think it was frightening. I thought as I'd thought before, that it was a beautiful place, a beautiful setting for a beautiful house . . .

Well, that's how my first meeting with Ellie went. I was in Market Chadwell the next day waiting in the Blue Dog and she came. We had tea together and we talked. We still didn't say much about ourselves, not about our lives, I mean. We talked mostly about things we thought, and felt; and then Ellie glanced at her wrist-watch and said she must be going because her train to London left at 5.30 –

'I thought you had a car down here,' I said.

She looked slightly embarrassed then and she said no, no, that hadn't been her car yesterday. She didn't say whose it had been. That shadow of embarrassment came over us again. I raised a finger to the waitress and paid the bill, then I said straight out to Ellie:

'Am I – am I ever going to see you again?'

She didn't look at me, she looked down at the table. She said:

'I shall be in London for another fortnight.'

I said:

'Where? How?'

We made a date to meet in Regent's Park in three days' time. It was a fine day. We had some food in the open-air restaurant and we walked in Queen Mary's Gardens and we sat there in two deck-chairs and we talked. From that time on, we began to talk about ourselves. I'd had some good schooling, I told her, but otherwise I didn't amount to much. I told her about the jobs I'd had, some of them at any rate, and how I'd never stuck to things and how I'd been restless and wandered about trying this and that. Funnily enough, she was entranced to hear all this.

'So different,' she said, 'so wonderfully different.'

'Different from what?'

'From me.'

'You're a rich girl?' I said teasingly – 'A poor little rich girl.'

'Yes,' she said, 'I'm a poor little rich girl.'

She talked then in a fragmentary way about her background of riches, of stifling comfort, of boredom, of not really choosing your own friends, of never doing what you wanted. Sometimes looking at people who seemed to be enjoying themselves, when she wasn't. Her mother had died when she was a baby and her father had married again. And then, not many years after, he had died, she said. I gathered she didn't care much for her stepmother. She'd lived mostly in America but also travelling abroad a fair amount.

It seemed fantastic to me listening to her that any girl in this age and time could live this sheltered, confined existence. True, she went to parties and entertainments, but it might have been fifty years ago it seemed to me from the way she talked. There didn't seem to be any intimacy, any *fun*! Her life was as different from mine as chalk from cheese. In a way it was fascinating to hear about it but it sounded stultifying to me.

'You haven't really got any friends of your own then?' I said, incredulously. 'What about boyfriends?'

'They're chosen for me,' she said rather bitterly. 'They're deadly dull.'

'It's like being in prison,' I said.

'That's what it seems like.'

'And really no friends of your own?'

'I have now. I've got Greta.'

'Who's Greta?' I said.

'She came first as an *au pair* – no, not quite that, perhaps. But anyway I'd had a French girl who lived with us for a year, for French, and then Greta came from Germany, for German. Greta was different. Everything was different once Greta came.'

'You're very fond of her?' I asked.

'She helps me,' said Ellie. 'She's on my side. She arranges so that I can do things and go places. She'll tell lies for me. I couldn't have got away to come down to Gipsy's Acre if it hadn't been for Greta. She's keeping me company and looking after me in London while my stepmother's in Paris. I write two or three letters and if I go off anywhere Greta posts them every three or four days so that they have a London postmark.'

'Why did you want to go down to Gipsy's Acre though?' I asked. 'What for?'

She didn't answer at once.

'Greta and I arranged it,' she said. 'She's rather wonderful,' she went on. 'She thinks of things, you know. She suggests ideas.'

'What's this Greta like?' I asked.

'Oh, Greta's beautiful,' she said. 'Tall and blonde. She can do anything.'

'I don't think I'd like her,' I said.

Ellie laughed.

'Oh yes you would. I'm sure you would. She's very clever, too.'

'I don't like clever girls,' I said. 'And I don't like tall blonde girls. I like small girls with hair like autumn leaves.'

'I believe you're jealous of Greta,' said Ellie.

'Perhaps I am. You're very fond of her, aren't you?'

'Yes, I am *very* fond of her. She's made all the difference in my life.'

'And it was she who suggested you went down there. Why, I wonder? There's not much to see or do in that part of the world. I find it rather mysterious.'

'It's our secret,' said Ellie and looked embarrassed.

'Yours and Greta's? Tell me.'

She shook her head. 'I must have *some* secrets of my own,' she said.

'Does your Greta know you're meeting me?'

'She knows I'm meeting someone. That's all. She doesn't ask questions. She knows I'm happy.'

After that there was a week when I didn't see Ellie. Her stepmother had come back from Paris, also someone whom she called Uncle Frank, and she explained almost casually that she was having a birthday, and that they were giving a big party for her in London.

'I shan't be able to get away,' she said. 'Not for the next week. But after that – after that, it'll be different.'

'Why will it be different after that?'

'I shall be able to do what I like then.'

'With Greta's help as usual?' I said.

It used to make Ellie laugh the way I talked about Greta. She'd say, 'You're so silly to be jealous of her. One day you must meet her. You'll like her.'

'I don't like bossy girls,' I said obstinately.

'Why do you think she's bossy?'

'By the way you talk about her. She's always busy arranging something.'

'She's very efficient,' said Ellie. 'She arranges things very well. That's why my stepmother relies on her so much.'

I asked what her Uncle Frank was like.

She said, 'I don't know him really so very well. He was my father's sister's husband, not a real relation. I think he's always been rather a rolling stone and got into trouble once or twice. You know the way people talk about someone and sort of hint things.'

'Not socially acceptable?' I asked. 'Bad lot?'

'Oh, nothing really bad I think, but he used to get into scrapes, I believe. Financial ones. And trustees and lawyers and people used to have to get him out of them. Pay up for things.'

'That's it,' I said. 'He's the bad hat of the family. I expect I'd get on better with him than I would with the paragon Greta.'

'He can make himself very agreeable when he likes,' said Ellie. 'He's good company.'

'But you don't really like him?' I asked sharply.

'I think I do . . . It's just that sometimes, oh I can't explain it. I just feel I don't know what he's thinking or planning.'

'One of our planners, is he?'

'I don't know what he's really like,' said Ellie again.

She didn't ever suggest that I should meet any of her family. I wondered sometimes if I ought to say something about it myself. I didn't know how she felt about the subject. I asked her straight out at last.

'Look here, Ellie,' I said, 'do you think I ought to – meet your family or would you rather I didn't?'

'I don't want you to meet them,' she said at once.

'I know I'm not much –' I said.

'I don't mean it *that* way, not a bit! I mean they'd make a *fuss*. I can't stand a fuss.'

'I sometimes feel,' I said, 'that this is rather a hole and corner business. It puts me in a rather bad light, don't you think?'

'I'm old enough to have my own friends,' said Ellie. 'I'm nearly twenty-one. When I am twenty-one I can have my own friends and nobody can stop me. But now you see – well, as I say there'd be a terrible fuss and they'd cart me off somewhere so that I couldn't meet you. There'd be – oh do, *do* let's go on as we are now.'

'Suits me if it suits you,' I said. 'I just didn't want to be, well, too underhand about everything.'

'It's not being underhand. It's just having a friend one can talk to and say things to. It's someone one can –' she smiled suddenly, 'one can make-believe with. You don't know how wonderful that is.'

Yes, there was a lot of that – make-believe! More and more our times together were to turn out that way. Sometimes it was me. More often it was Ellie who'd say, 'Let's suppose that we've bought Gipsy's Acre and that we're building a house there.'

I had told her a lot about Santonix and about the houses he'd built. I tried to describe to her the kind of houses they were and the way he thought about things. I don't think I described it very well because I'm not good at describing things. Ellie no doubt had her own picture of the house – our house. We didn't *say* 'our house' but we knew that's what we meant . . .

So for over a week I wasn't to see Ellie. I had taken out what savings I had (there weren't many), and I'd bought her a little green shamrock ring made of some Irish bog stone. I'd given it to her for a birthday present and she'd loved it and looked very happy.

'It's beautiful,' she said.

She didn't wear much jewellery and when she did I had no doubt it was real diamonds and emeralds and things like that but she liked my Irish ring.

'It will be the birthday present I like best,' she said.

Then I got a hurried note from her. She was going abroad with her family to the South of France immediately after her birthday.

'But don't worry,' she wrote, 'we shall be back again in two or three weeks' time, on our way to America this time. But anyway we'll meet again then. I've got something special I want to talk to you about.'

I felt restless and ill at ease not seeing Ellie and knowing she'd gone abroad to France. I had a bit of news about the Gipsy's Acre property too. Apparently it *had* been sold by private treaty but there wasn't much information about who'd bought it. Some firm of London solicitors apparently were named as the purchasers. I tried to get more information about it, but I couldn't. The firm in question were very cagey. Naturally I didn't approach the principals. I palled up to one of their clerks and so got a little vague information. It had been bought for a very rich client who was going to hold it as a good investment capable of appreciation when the land in that part of the country was becoming more developed.

It's very hard to find out about things when you're dealing with really exclusive firms. Everything is as much of a deadly secret as though they were M.I.5 or something! Everyone is always acting on behalf of someone else who can't be named or spoken of! Takeover bids aren't in it!

I got into a terrible state of restlessness. I stopped thinking about it all and I went and saw my mother.

I hadn't been to see her for a good long time.

CHAPTER 6

My mother lived in the same street she had lived in for the last twenty years, a street of drab houses all highly respectable and devoid of any kind of beauty or interest. The front doorstep was nicely whitened and it looked just the same as usual. It was No. 46. I pressed the front-door bell. My mother opened the door and stood there looking at me. She looked just the same as usual, too. Tall and angular, grey hair parted in the middle, mouth like a rattrap, and eyes that were eternally suspicious. She looked hard as nails. But where I was concerned there was a core of softness somewhere in her. She never showed it, not if she could help it, but I'd found out that it was there. She'd never stopped for a moment wanting me to be different but her wishes were never going to come true. There was a perpetual state of stalemate between us.

'Oh,' she said, 'so it's you.'

'Yes,' I said, 'it's me.'

She drew back a little to let me pass and I came into the house and went on past the sitting-room door and into the kitchen. She followed me and stood looking at me.

'It's been quite a long time,' she said. 'What have you been doing?'

I shrugged my shoulders.

'This and that,' I said.

'Ah,' said my mother, 'as usual, eh?'

'As usual,' I agreed.

'How many jobs have you had since I saw you last?'

I thought a minute. 'Five,' I said.

'I wish you'd grow up.'

'I'm fully adult,' I said. 'I have chosen my way of life. How have things been with you?' I added.

'Also as usual,' said my mother.

'Quite well and all that?'

'I've no time to waste being ill,' said my mother. Then she said abruptly, 'What have you come for?'

'Should I have come for anything in particular?'

'You usually do.'

'I don't see why you should disapprove so strongly of my seeing the world,' I said.

'Driving luxurious cars all over the Continent! Is that your idea of seeing the world?'

'Certainly.'

'You won't make much of a success in that. Not if you throw up the job at a day's notice and go sick, dumping your clients in some heathen town.'

'How did you know about that?'

'Your firm rang up. They wanted to know if I knew your address.'

'What did they want me for?'

'They wanted to re-employ you I suppose,' said my mother. 'I can't think why.'

'Because I'm a good driver and the clients like me. Anyway, I couldn't help it if I went sick, could I?'

'I don't know,' said my mother.

Her view clearly was that I could have helped it.

'Why didn't you report to them when you got back to England?'

'Because I had other fish to fry,' I said.

She raised her eyebrows. 'More notions in your head? More wild ideas? What jobs have you been doing since?'

'Petrol pump. Mechanic in a garage. Temporary clerk, washer-up in a sleazy night-club restaurant.'

'Going down the hill in fact,' said my mother with a kind of grim satisfaction.

'Not at all,' I said. 'It's all part of the plan. My plan!'

She sighed. 'What would you like, tea or coffee? I've got both.'

I plumped for coffee. I've grown out of the tea-drinking habit. We sat there with our cups in front of us and she took a home-made cake out of a tin and cut us each a slice.

'You're different,' she said, suddenly.

'Me, how?'

'I don't know, but you're different. What's happened?'

'Nothing's happened. What should have happened?'

'You're excited,' she said.

'I'm going to rob a bank,' I said.

She was not in the mood to be amused. She merely said:

'No, I'm not afraid of your doing that.'

'Why not? Seems a very easy way of getting rich quickly nowadays.'

'It would need too much work,' she said. 'And a lot of planning. More brainwork than you'd like to have to do. Not safe enough, either.'

'You think you know all about me,' I said.

'No, I don't. I don't really know anything about you, because you and I are as different as chalk and cheese. But I know when you're up to something. You're up to something now. What is it, Micky? Is it a girl?'

'Why should you think it's a girl?'

'I've always known it would happen some day.'

'What do you mean by "some day"? I've had lots of girls.'

'Not the way I mean. It's only been the way of a young man with nothing to do. You've kept your hand in with girls but you've never been really serious till now.'

'But you think I'm serious now?'

'Is it a girl, Micky?'

I didn't meet her eyes. I looked away and said, 'In a way.'

'What kind of a girl is she?'

'The right kind for me,' I said.

'Are you going to bring her to see me?'

'No,' I said.

'It's like that, is it?'

'No, it isn't. I don't want to hurt your feelings but –'

'You're not hurting my feelings. You don't want me to see her in case I should say to you "Don't". Is that it?'

'I wouldn't pay any attention if you did.'

'Maybe not, but it would shake you. It would shake you somewhere inside because you take notice of what I say and think. There are things I've guessed about you – and maybe I've guessed right and you know it. I'm the only person in the world who can shake your confidence in yourself. Is this girl a bad lot who's got hold of you?'

'Bad lot?' I said and laughed. 'If you only saw her! You make me laugh.'

'What do you want from me? You want something. You always do.'

'I want some money,' I said.

'You won't get it from me. What do you want it for – to spend on this girl?'

'No,' I said, 'I want to buy a first-class suit to get married in.'

'You're going to marry her?'

'If she'll have me.'

That shook her.

'If you'd only tell me something!' she said. 'You've got it badly, I can see that. It's the thing I always feared, that you'd choose the wrong girl.'

'Wrong girl! Hell!' I shouted. I was angry.

I went out of the house and I banged the door.

CHAPTER 7

When I got home there was a telegram waiting for me – it had been sent from Antibes.

Meet me tomorrow four-thirty usual place.

Ellie was different. I saw it at once. We met as always in Regent's Park and at first we were a bit strange and awkward with each other. I had something I was going to say to her and I was in a bit of a state as to how to put it. I suppose any man is when he comes to the point of proposing marriage.

And she was strange about something too. Perhaps she was considering the nicest and kindest way of saying No to me. But somehow I didn't think that. My whole belief in life was based on the fact that Ellie loved me. But there was a new independence about her, a new confidence in herself which I could hardly feel was simply because she was a year older. One more birthday can't make that difference to a girl. She and her family had been in the South of France and she told me a little about it. And then rather awkwardly she said:

'I – I saw that house there, the one you told me about. The one that architect friend of yours had built.'

'What – Santonix?'

'Yes. We went there to lunch one day.'

'How did you do that? Does your stepmother know the man who lives there?'

'Dmitri Constantine? Well – not exactly but she met him and – well – Greta fixed it up for us to go there as a matter of fact.'

'Greta again,' I said, allowing the usual exasperation to come into my voice.

'I told you,' she said, 'Greta is very good at arranging things.'

'Oh all right. So she arranged that you and your stepmother –'

'And Uncle Frank,' said Ellie.

'Quite a family party,' I said, 'and Greta too, I suppose.'

'Well, no, Greta didn't come because, well –' Ellie hesitated, '– Cora, my stepmother, doesn't treat Greta exactly like that.'

'She's not one of the family, she's a poor relation, is she?' I said. 'Just the *au pair* girl, in fact. Greta must resent being treated that way sometimes.'

'She's not an *au pair* girl, she's a kind of companion to me.'

'A chaperone,' I said, 'a cicerone, a duenna, a governess. There are lots of words.'

'Oh do be quiet,' said Ellie, 'I want to tell you. I know now what you mean about your friend Santonix. It's a wonderful house. It's – it's quite *different*. I can see that if he built a house for us it would be a wonderful house.'

She had used the word quite unconsciously. *Us*, she had said. She had gone to the Riviera and had made Greta arrange things so as to see the house I had described, because she wanted to visualize more clearly the house that we would, in the dream world we'd built ourselves, have built for us by Rudolf Santonix.

'I'm glad you felt like that about it,' I said.

She said: 'What have you been doing?'

'Just my dull job,' I said, 'and I've been to a race meeting and I put some money on an outsider. Thirty to one. I put every penny I had on it and it won by a length. Who says my luck isn't in?'

'I'm glad you won,' said Ellie, but she said it without excitement, because putting all you had in the world on an outsider and the outsider winning didn't mean anything to Ellie's world. Not the kind of thing it meant in mine.

'And I went to see my mother,' I added.

'You've never spoken much of your mother.'

'Why should I?' I said.

'Aren't you fond of her?'

I considered. 'I don't know,' I said. 'Sometimes I don't think I am. After all, one grows up and – outgrows parents. Mothers and fathers.'

'I think you do care about her,' said Ellie. 'You wouldn't be so uncertain when you talk about her otherwise.'

'I'm afraid of her in a way,' I said. 'She knows me too well. She knows the worst of me, I mean.'

'Somebody has to,' said Ellie.

'What do you mean?'

'There's a saying by some great writer or other that no man is a hero to his valet. Perhaps everyone ought to have a valet. It must be so hard otherwise, always living up to people's good opinion of one.'

'Well, you certainly have ideas, Ellie,' I said. I took her hand. 'Do you know all about me?' I said.

'I think so,' said Ellie. She said it quite calmly and simply.

'I never told you much.'

'You mean you never told me anything at all, you always clammed up. That's different. But I know quite well what you are *like*, you yourself.'

'I wonder if you do,' I said. I went on, 'It sounds rather silly saying I love you. It seems too late for that, doesn't it? I mean, you've known about it a long time, practically from the beginning, haven't you?'

'Yes,' said Ellie, 'and you knew, too, didn't you, about me?'

'The thing is,' I said, 'what are we going to do about it? It's not going to be easy, Ellie. You know pretty well what I am, what I've done, the sort of life I've led. I went back to see my mother and the grim, respectable little street she lives in. It's not the same world as yours, Ellie. I don't know that we can ever make them meet.'

'You could take me to see your mother.'

'Yes, I could,' I said, 'but I'd rather not. I expect that sounds very harsh to you, perhaps cruel, but you see we've got to lead a queer life together, you and I. It's not going to be the life that you've led and it's not going to be the life that I've led either. It's got to be a new life where we have a sort of meeting ground between my poverty and ignorance and your money and culture and social knowledge. My friends will think you're stuck up and your friends will think I'm socially unpresentable. So what are we going to do?'

'I'll tell you,' said Ellie, 'exactly what we're going to do. We're going to live on Gipsy's Acre in a house – a dream house – that your friend Santonix will build for us. That's what we're going to do.' She added, 'We'll get married first. That's what you mean, isn't it?'

'Yes,' I said, 'that's what I mean. If you're sure it's all right with you.'

'It's quite easy,' said Ellie, 'we can get married next week. I'm of age, you see. I can do what I like now. That makes all the difference. I think perhaps you're right about relations. I shan't tell my people and you won't tell your mother, not until it's all over and then they can throw fits and it won't matter.'

'That's wonderful,' I said, 'wonderful, Ellie. But there's one thing. I hate telling you about it. We can't live at Gipsy's Acre, Ellie. Wherever we build our house it can't be there because it's sold.'

'I know it's sold,' said Ellie. She was laughing. 'You don't understand, Mike. *I'm* the person who's bought it.'

CHAPTER 8

I sat there, on the grass by the stream among the water flowers with the little paths and the stepping stones all round us. A good many other people were sitting round about us, but we didn't notice them or even see they were there, because we were like all the others. Young couples, talking about their future. I stared at her and stared at her. I just couldn't speak.

'Mike,' she said. 'There's something, something I've got to tell you. Something about me, I mean.'

'You don't need to,' I said, 'no need to tell me anything.'

'Yes, but I must. I ought to have told you long ago but I didn't want to because – because I thought it might drive you away. But it explains in a way, about Gipsy's Acre.'

'You *bought* it?' I said. 'But how did you buy it?'

'Through lawyers,' she said, 'the usual way. It's a perfectly good investment, you know. The land will appreciate. My lawyers were quite happy about it.'

It was odd suddenly to hear Ellie, the gentle and timid Ellie, speaking with such knowledge and confidence of the business world of buying and selling.

'You bought it for us?'

'Yes. I went to a lawyer of my own, not the family one. I told him what I wanted to do, I got him to look into it, I got everything set up and in train. There were two other people after it but they were not really desperate and they wouldn't go very high. The important thing was that the whole thing had to be set up and arranged ready for me to sign as soon as I came of age. It's signed and finished.'

'But you must have made some deposit or something beforehand. Had you enough money to do that?'

'No,' said Ellie, 'no, I hadn't control of much money beforehand, but of course there are people who will advance you money. And if you go to a new firm of legal advisers, they will want you to go on employing them for business deals once you've come into what money you're going to have so they're willing to take the risk that you might drop down dead before your birthday comes.'

'You sound so businesslike,' I said, 'you take my breath away!'

'Never mind business,' said Ellie, 'I've got to get back to what I'm telling you. In a way I've told it you already, but I don't suppose really you realize it.'

'I don't want to know,' I said. My voice rose, I was almost shouting. 'Don't tell me *anything*. I don't want to know anything about what you've done or who you've been fond of or what has happened to you.'

'It's nothing of that kind,' she said. 'I didn't realize that that was what you were fearing it might be. No, there's nothing of that kind. No sex secrets. There's nobody but you. The thing is that I'm – well – I'm rich.'

'I know that,' I said, 'you've told me already.'

'Yes,' said Ellie with a faint smile, 'and you said to me, "poor little rich girl". But in a way it's more than that. My grandfather, you see, was enormously rich. Oil. Mostly oil. And other things. The wives he paid alimony to are dead, there was only my father and myself left because his two other sons were killed. One in Korea and one in a car accident. And so it was all left in a great big huge trust and when my father died suddenly, it all came to *me*. My father had made provision for my stepmother before, so she didn't get anything more. It was all *mine*. I'm – actually one of the richest women in America, Mike.'

'Good Lord,' I said. 'I didn't know . . . Yes, you're right, I didn't know it was like *that*.'

'I didn't want you to know. I didn't want to tell you. That was why I was afraid when I said my name – Fenella Goodman. We spell it G-u-t-e-m-a-n, and I thought you might know the name of Guteman so I slurred over it and made it into Goodman.'

'Yes,' I said, 'I've seen the name Guteman vaguely. But I don't think I'd have recognized it even then. Lots of people are called names rather like that.'

'That's why,' she said, 'I've been so hedged around all the time and fenced in, and imprisoned. I've had detectives guarding me and young men being vetted before they're allowed even to speak to me. Whenever I've made a friend they've had to be quite sure it wasn't an unsuitable one. You don't know what a terrible, terrible prisoner's life it is! But now that's all over, and if you don't mind –'

'Of course I don't mind,' I said, 'we shall have lots of fun. In fact,' I said, 'you couldn't be *too* rich a girl for me!'

We both laughed. She said: 'What I like about you is that you can be natural about things.'

'Besides,' I said, 'I expect you pay a lot of tax on it, don't you? That's one of the few nice things about being like me. Any money I make goes into my pocket and nobody can take it away from me.'

'We'll have our house,' said Ellie, 'our house on Gipsy's Acre.' Just for a moment she gave a sudden little shiver.

'You're not cold, darling,' I said. I looked up at the sunshine.

'No,' she said.

It was really very hot. We'd been basking. It might almost have been the South of France.

'No,' said Ellie, 'it was just that – that woman, that gipsy that day.'

'Oh, don't think of her,' I said, 'she was crazy anyway.'

'Do you think she *really* thinks there's a curse on the land?'

'I think gipsies are like that. You know – always wanting to make a song and dance about some curse or something.'

'Do you know much about gipsies?'

'Absolutely nothing,' I said truthfully. 'If you don't want Gipsy's Acre, Ellie, we'll buy a house somewhere else. On the top of a mountain in Wales, on the coast of Spain or an Italian hillside, and Santonix can build us a house there just as well.'

'No,' said Ellie, 'that's how I want it to be. It's where I first saw you walking up the road, coming round the corner very suddenly, and then you saw me and stopped and stared at me. I'll never forget that.'

'Nor will I,' I said.

'So that's where it's going to be. And your friend Santonix will build it.'

'I hope he's still alive,' I said with an uneasy pang. 'He was a sick man.'

'Oh yes,' said Ellie, 'he's alive. I went to see him.'

'You went to see him?'

'Yes. When I was in the South of France. He was in a sanitorium there.'

'Every minute, Ellie, you seem to be more and more amazing. The things you do and manage.'

'He's rather a wonderful person I think,' said Ellie, 'but rather frightening.'

'Did he frighten you?'

'Yes, he frightened me very much for some reason.'

'Did you talk to him about us?'

'Yes. Oh yes, I told him all about us and about Gipsy's Acre and about the house. He told me then that we'd have to take a chance with him. He's a very ill man. He said he thought he still had the life left in him to go and see the site, to draw the plans, to visualize it and get it all sketched out. He said he wouldn't mind really if he died before the house was finished, but I told him,' added Ellie, 'that he mustn't die before the house was finished because I wanted him to see us live in it.'

'What did he say to that?'

'He asked me if I knew what I was doing marrying you, and I said of course I did.'

'And then?'

'He said he wondered if *you* knew what you were doing.'

'I know all right,' I said.

'He said "You will always know where you're going, Miss Guteman." He said "You'll be going always where you want to go and because it's your chosen way."

'"But Mike," he said, "might take the wrong road. He hasn't grown up enough yet to know where he's going."

'I said,' said Ellie, '"He'll be quite safe with me."'

She had superb self-confidence. I was angry though at what Santonix had said. He was like my mother. She always seemed to know more about me than I knew myself.

'I know where I'm going,' I said. 'I'm going the way I want to go and we're going it together.'

'They've started pulling down the ruins of The Towers already,' said Ellie.

She began to talk practically.

'It's to be a rush-job as soon as the plans are finished. We must hurry. Santonix said so. Shall we be married next Tuesday?' said Ellie. 'It's a nice day of the week.'

'With nobody else there,' I said.

'Except Greta,' said Ellie.

'To hell with Greta,' I said, 'she's not coming to our wedding. You and I and nobody else. We can pull the necessary witnesses out of the street.'

I really think, looking back, that that was the happiest day of my life . . .

BOOK 2

CHAPTER 9

So that was that, and Ellie and I got married. It sounds abrupt just putting it like that, but you see it was really just the way things happened. We decided to be married and we got married.

It was part of the whole thing – not just an end to a romantic novel or a fairy story. 'And so they got married and lived happily ever afterwards.' You can't, after all, make a big drama out of living happily ever afterwards. We were married and we were both happy and it was really quite a time before anyone got on to us and began to make the usual difficulties and commotions and we'd made up our minds to those.

The whole thing was really extraordinarily simple. In her desire for freedom Ellie had covered her tracks very cleverly up to now. The useful Greta had taken all the necessary steps, and was always on guard behind her. And I had realized fairly soon on that there was nobody really whose business it was to care terribly about Ellie and what she was doing. She had a stepmother who was engrossed in her own social life and love affairs. If Ellie didn't wish to accompany her to any particular spot on the globe there was no need for Ellie to do so. She'd had all the proper governesses and ladies' maids and scholastic advantages and if she wanted to go to Europe, why not? If she chose to have her twenty-first birthday in London, again why not? Now that she had come into her vast fortune she had the whip hand of her family in so far as spending her money went. If she'd wanted a villa on the Riviera or a castle on the Costa Brava or a yacht or any of those things, she had only to mention the fact and someone among the retinues that surrounded millionaires would put everything in hand immediately.

Greta, I gather, was regarded by her family as an admirable stooge. Competent, able to make all arrangements with the utmost efficiency, subservient no doubt and charming to the stepmother, the uncle and a few odd cousins who seemed to be knocking about. Ellie had no fewer than three lawyers at her command, from what she let fall every now and then. She was surrounded by a vast financial network of bankers and lawyers and the administrators of trust funds. It was a world that I just got glimpses of every now and then, mostly from things that Ellie let fall carelessly in the course of conversation. It didn't occur to her, naturally, that I wouldn't know about all those things. She had been brought up in the midst of them and she naturally concluded that the whole world knew what they were and how they worked and all the rest of it.

In fact, getting glimpses of the special peculiarities of each other's lives were unexpectedly what we enjoyed most in our early married life. To put it quite crudely – and I did put things crudely to myself, for that was the only way to get to terms with my new life – the poor don't really know how the rich live and the rich don't know how the poor live, and to find out is really enchanting to both of them. Once I said uneasily:

'Look here, Ellie, is there going to be an awful schemozzle over all this, over our marriage, I mean?'

Ellie considered without, I noticed, very much interest.

'Oh yes,' she said, 'they'll probably be awful.' And she added, 'I hope you won't mind *too* much.'

'I won't mind – why should I? – But you, will they bully you over it?'

'I expect so,' said Ellie, 'but one needn't listen. The point is that they can't *do* anything.'

'But they'll try?'

'Oh yes,' said Ellie. 'They'll try.' Then she added thoughtfully, 'They'll probably try and buy you off.'

'Buy me off?'

'Don't look so shocked,' said Ellie, and she smiled, a rather happy little girl's smile. 'It isn't put exactly like that.' Then she added, 'They bought off Minnie Thompson's first, you know.'

'Minnie Thompson? Is that the one they always call the oil heiress?'

'Yes, that's right. She ran off and married a life guard off the beach.'

'Look here, Ellie,' I said uneasily, '*I* was a life guard at Littlehampton once.'

'Oh, were you? What fun! Permanently?'

'No, of course not. Just one summer, that's all.'

'I wish you wouldn't worry,' said Ellie.

'What happened about Minnie Thompson?'

'They had to go up to 200,000 dollars, I think,' said Ellie, 'he wouldn't take less. Minnie was man-mad and really a half-wit,' she added.

'You take my breath away, Ellie,' I said. 'I've not only acquired a wife, I've got something I can trade for solid cash at any time.'

'That's right,' said Ellie. 'Send for a high-powered lawyer and tell him you're willing to talk turkey. Then he fixes up the divorce and the amount of alimony,' said Ellie, continuing my education. 'My stepmother's been married four times,' she added, 'and she's made quite a lot out of it.' And then she said, 'Oh, Mike, don't look so *shocked*.'

The funny thing is that I was shocked. I felt a priggish distaste for the corruption of modern society in its richer phases. There had been something so little-girl-like about Ellie, so simple, almost touching in her attitude that I was astonished to find how well up she was in worldly affairs and how much she took for granted. And yet I knew that I was right about her fundamentally. I knew quite well the kind of creature that Ellie was. Her simplicity, her affection, her natural sweetness. That didn't mean she had to be ignorant of things. What she did know and took for granted was a fairly limited slice of humanity. She didn't know much about my world, the world of scrounging for jobs, of race-course gangs and dope gangs, the rough and tumble dangers of life, the sharp-Aleck flashy type that I knew so well from living amongst them all my life. She didn't know what it was to be brought up decent and respectable but always hard up for money, with a mother who worked her fingers to the bone in the name of respectability, determining that her son should do well in life. Every penny scrimped for and saved, and the bitterness when your gay carefree son threw away his chances or gambled his all on a good tip for the 3.30.

She enjoyed hearing about my life as much as I enjoyed hearing about hers. Both of us were exploring a foreign country.

Looking back I see what a wonderfully happy life it was, those early days with Ellie. At the time I took them for granted and so did she. We were married in a registry office in Plymouth. Guteman is not an uncommon name. Nobody, reporters or otherwise, knew the Guteman heiress was in England. There had been vague paragraphs in papers occasionally, describing her as in Italy or on someone's yacht. We were married in the Registrar's office with his clerk and a middle-aged typist as witnesses. He gave us a serious little harangue on the serious responsibilities of married life, and wished us happiness. Then we went out, free and married. Mr and Mrs Michael Rogers! We spent a week in a seaside hotel and then we went abroad. We had a glorious three weeks travelling about wherever the fancy took us and no expense spared.

We went to Greece and we went to Florence, and to Venice and lay on the Lido, then to the French Riviera and then to the Dolomites. Half the places I forget the names of now. We took planes or chartered a yacht or hired large and handsome cars. And while we enjoyed ourselves, Greta, I gathered from Ellie, was still on the Home Front doing her stuff.

Travelling about in her own way, sending letters and forwarding all the various post-cards and letters that Ellie had left with her.

'There'll be a day of reckoning, of course,' said Ellie. 'They'll come down on us like a cloud of vultures. But we might as well enjoy ourselves until that happens.'

'What about Greta?' I said. 'Won't they be rather angry with her when they find out?'

'Oh, of course,' said Ellie, 'but Greta won't mind. She's tough.'

'Mightn't it stop her getting another job?'

'Why should she get another job?' said Ellie. 'She'll come and live with us.'

'No!' I said.

'What do you mean, *no*, Mike?'

'We don't want anyone living with us,' I said.

'Greta wouldn't be in the way,' said Ellie, 'and she'd be very useful. Really, I don't know what I'd do without her. I mean, she manages and arranges everything.'

I frowned. 'I don't think I'd like that. Besides, we want our own house – our dream house, after all, Ellie – we want it to ourselves.'

'Yes,' said Ellie, 'I know what you mean. But all the same –' She hesitated. 'I mean, it would be very hard on Greta not to have anywhere to live. After all, she's been with me, done everything for me for four years now. And look how she's helped me to get married and all that.'

'I won't have her butting in between us all the time!'

'But she's not *like* that at all, Mike. You haven't even met her yet.'

'No. No, I know I haven't but – but it's nothing to do with, oh with liking her or not. We want to be by *ourselves*, Ellie.'

'Darling Mike,' said Ellie softly.

We left it at that for the moment.

During the course of our travels we had met Santonix. That was in Greece. He had been in a small fisherman's cottage near the sea. I was startled by how ill he looked, much worse than when I had seen him a year ago. He greeted both Ellie and myself very warmly.

'So you've done it, you two,' he said.

'Yes,' said Ellie, 'and now we're going to have our house built, aren't we?'

'I've got the drawings for you here, the plans,' he said to me. 'She's told you, hasn't she, how she came and ferreted me out and gave me her – commands,' he said, choosing the words thoughtfully.

'Oh! not commands,' said Ellie. 'I just pleaded.'

'You know we've bought the site?' I said.

'Ellie wired and told me. She sent me dozens of photographs.'

'Of course you've got to come and see it first,' said Ellie. 'You mightn't like the site.'

'I do like it.'

'You can't *really* know till you've seen it.'

'But I have seen it, child. I flew over five days ago. I met one of your hatchet-faced lawyers there – the English one.'

'Mr Crawford?'

'That's the man. In fact, operations have already started:

clearing the ground, removing the ruins of the old house, foundations – drains – When you get back to England I'll be there to meet you.' He got out his plans then and we sat talking and looking at our house to be. There was even a rough water-colour sketch of it as well as the architectural elevations and plans.

'Do you like it, Mike?'

I drew a deep breath.

'Yes,' I said, 'that's it. That's absolutely *it*.'

'You used to talk about it enough, Mike. When I was in a fanciful mood I used to think that piece of land had laid a spell upon you. You were a man in love with a house that you might never own, that you might never see, that might never even be built.'

'But it's going to be built,' said Ellie. 'It's going to be built, isn't it?'

'If God or the devil wills it,' said Santonix. 'It doesn't depend on me.'

'You're not any – any better?' I asked doubtfully.

'Get it into your thick head. I shall never be *better*. That's not on the cards.'

'Nonsense,' I said. 'People are finding cures for things all the time. Doctors are gloomy brutes. They give people up for dead and then the people laugh and cock a snook at them and live for another fifty years.'

'I admire your optimism, Mike, but my malady isn't one of that kind. They take you to hospital and give you a change of blood and back you come again with a little leeway of life, a little span of time gained. And so on, getting weaker each time.'

'You are very brave,' said Ellie.

'Oh no, I'm not brave. When a thing is certain there's nothing to be brave about. All you can do is find your consolation.'

'Building houses?'

'No, not that. You've less vitality all the time, you see, and therefore building houses becomes more difficult, not easier. The strength keeps giving out. No. But there *are* consolations. Sometimes very queer ones.'

'I don't understand you,' I said.

'No, you wouldn't, Mike. I don't know really that Ellie would.

She might.' He went on, speaking not so much to us as to himself. 'Two things run together, side by side. Weakness and strength. The weakness of fading vitality and the strength of frustrated power. It doesn't matter, you see, *what* you do now! You're going to die anyway. So you can do *anything you choose*. There's nothing to deter you, there's nothing to hold you back. I could walk through the streets of Athens shooting down every man or woman whose face I didn't like. Think of that.'

'The police could arrest you just the same,' I pointed out.

'Of course they could. But what could they do? At the most take my life. Well my life's going to be taken by a greater power than the law in a very short time. What else could they do? Send me to prison for twenty – thirty years? That's rather ironical, isn't it, there aren't twenty or thirty years for me to serve. Six months – one year – eighteen months at the utmost. There's nothing anyone can do to me. So in the span that's left to me I am king. I can do what I like. Sometimes it's a very heady thought. Only – only, you see, there's not much temptation because there's nothing particularly exotic or lawless that I want to do.'

After we had left him, as we were driving back to Athens, Ellie said to me:

'He's an odd person. Sometimes you know, I feel frightened of him.'

'Frightened, of Rudolf Santonix – why?'

'Because he isn't like other people and because he has a – I don't know – a ruthlessness and an arrogance about him somewhere. And I think that he was trying to tell us, really, that knowing he's going to die soon has increased his arrogance. Supposing,' said Ellie, looking at me in an animated way, with almost a rapt and emotional expression on her face, 'supposing he built us our lovely castle, our lovely house on the cliff's edge there in the pines, supposing we were coming to live in it. There he was on the doorstep and he welcomed us in and then –'

'Well, Ellie?'

'Then supposing he came in after us, he slowly closed the doorway behind us and sacrificed us there on the threshold. Cut our throats or something.'

'You frighten me, Ellie. The things you think of!'

'The trouble with you and me, Mike, is that we don't live in the real world. We dream of fantastic things that may never happen.'

'Don't think of sacrifices in connection with Gipsy's Acre.'

'It's the name, I suppose, and the curse upon it.'

'There isn't any curse,' I shouted. 'It's all nonsense. Forget it.'

That was in Greece.

CHAPTER 10

It was, I think, the day after that. We were in Athens. Suddenly, on the steps of the Acropolis Ellie ran into people that she knew. They had come ashore from one of the Hellenic cruises. A woman of about thirty-five detached herself from the group and rushed along the steps to Ellie exclaiming:

'Why, I never did. It's really you, Ellie Guteman? Well, what are you doing here? I'd no *idea*. Are you on a cruise?'

'No,' said Ellie, 'just staying here.'

'My, but it's lovely to see you. How's Cora, is she here?'

'No, Cora is at Salzburg I believe.'

'Well, well.' The woman was looking at me and Ellie said quietly, 'Let me introduce – Mr Rogers, Mrs Bennington.'

'How d'you do. How long are you here for?'

'I'm leaving tomorrow,' said Ellie.

'Oh dear! My, I'll lose my party if I don't go, and I just don't want to miss a word of the lecture and the descriptions. They do hustle one a bit, you know. I'm just dead beat at the end of the day. Any chance of meeting you for a drink?'

'Not today,' said Ellie, 'we're going on an excursion.'

Mrs Bennington rushed off to rejoin her party. Ellie, who had been going with me up the steps of the Acropolis, turned round and moved down again.

'That rather settles things, doesn't it?' she said to me.

'What does it settle?'

Ellie did not answer for a minute or two and then she said with a sigh, 'I must write tonight.'

'Write to whom?'

'Oh, to Cora, and to Uncle Frank, I suppose, and Uncle Andrew.'

'Who's Uncle Andrew? He's a new one.'

'Andrew Lippincott. Not really an uncle. He's my principal guardian or trustee or whatever you call it. He's a lawyer – a very well-known one.'

'What are you going to say?'

'I'm going to tell them I'm married. I couldn't say suddenly to Nora Bennington "Let me introduce my husband." There would have been frightful shrieks and exclamations and "I never heard you were married. Tell me all about it, darling" etcetera, etcetera. It's only fair that my stepmother and Uncle Frank and Uncle Andrew should be the first to know.' She sighed. 'Oh well, we've had a lovely time up to now.'

'What will they say or do?' I asked.

'Make a fuss, I expect,' said Ellie, in her placid way. 'It doesn't matter if they do and they'll have sense enough to know that. We'll have to have a meeting, I expect. We could go to New York. Would you like that?' She looked at me inquiringly.

'No,' I said, 'I shouldn't like it in the least.'

'Then they'll come to London probably, or some of them will. I don't know if you'd like that any better.'

'I shouldn't like any of it. I want to be with you and see our house going up brick by brick as soon as Santonix gets there.'

'So we can,' said Ellie. 'After all, meetings with the family won't take long. Possibly just one big splendid row would do. Get it over in one. Either we fly over there or they fly over here.'

'I thought you said your stepmother was at Salzburg.'

'Oh, I just said that. It sounded odd to say I didn't know where she was. Yes,' said Ellie with a sigh, 'we'll go home and meet them all. Mike, I hope you won't mind too much.'

'Mind what – your family?'

'Yes. You won't mind if they're nasty to you.'

'I suppose it's the price I have to pay for marrying you,' I said. 'I'll bear it.'

'There's your mother,' said Ellie thoughtfully.

'For heaven's sake, Ellie, you're not going to try and arrange a meeting between your stepmother in her frills and her furbelows and my mother from her back street. What do you think they'd have to say to each other?'

'If Cora was my own mother they might have quite a lot to

say to each other,' said Ellie. 'I wish you wouldn't be so obsessed with class distinctions, Mike!'

'Me!' I said incredulously. 'What's your American phrase – I come from the wrong side of the tracks, don't I?'

'You don't want to write it on a placard and put it on yourself.'

'I don't know the right clothes to wear,' I said bitterly. 'I don't know the right way to talk about things and I don't know anything really about pictures or art or music. I'm only just learning who to tip and how much to give.'

'Don't you think, Mike, that that makes it all much more exciting for you? I think so.'

'Anyway,' I said, 'you're not to drag my mother into your family party.'

'I wasn't proposing to drag anyone into anything, but I think, Mike, *I* ought to go and see your mother when we go back to England.'

'No,' I said explosively.

She looked at me rather startled.

'Why not, Mike, though? I mean, apart from anything else, I mean it's just very rude not to. Have you told her you're married?'

'Not yet.'

'Why not?'

I didn't answer.

'Wouldn't the simplest way be to tell her you're married and take me to see her when we get back to England?'

'No,' I said again. It was not so explosive this time but it was still fairly well underlined.

'You don't want me to meet her,' said Ellie, slowly.

I didn't of course. I suppose it was obvious enough but the last thing I could do was to explain. I didn't see how I could explain.

'It wouldn't be the right thing to do,' I said slowly. 'You must see that. I'm sure it would lead to trouble.'

'You think she wouldn't like me?'

'Nobody could help liking you, but it wouldn't be – oh I don't know how to put it. But she might be upset and confused. After all, well, I mean I've married out of my station. That's the old-fashioned term. She wouldn't like *that*.'

Ellie shook her head slowly.

'Does anybody really think like that nowadays?'

'Of course they do. They do in your country too.'

'Yes,' she said, 'in a way that's true but – if anyone makes good there –'

'You mean if a man makes a lot of money.'

'Well, not only money.'

'Yes,' I said, 'it's money. If a man makes a lot of money he's admired and looked up to and it doesn't matter where he was born.'

'Well, that's the same everywhere,' said Ellie.

'Please, Ellie,' I said. 'Please don't go and see my mother.'

'I still think it's unkind.'

'No it isn't. Can't you let me know what's best for my own mother? She'd be upset. I tell you she would.'

'But you must tell her you've got married.'

'All right,' I said. 'I'll do that.'

It occurred to me it would be easier to write to my mother from abroad. That evening when Ellie was writing to Uncle Andrew and Uncle Frank and her stepmother Cora van Stuyvesant, I, too, was writing my own letter. It was quite short.

'Dear Mum,' I wrote. 'I ought to have told you before but I felt a bit awkward. I got married three weeks ago. It was all rather sudden. She's a very pretty girl and very sweet. She's got a lot of money which makes things a bit awkward sometimes. We're going to build ourselves a house somewhere in the country. Just at present we're travelling around Europe. All the best, Yours, Mike.'

The results of our evening's correspondence were somewhat varied. My mother let a week elapse before she sent a letter remarkably typical of her.

"Dear Mike. I was glad to get your letter. I hope you'll be very happy. Your affectionate mother."

As Ellie had prophesied, there was far more fuss on her side. We'd stirred up a regular hornet's nest of trouble. We were beset by reporters who wanted news of our romantic marriage, there were articles in the papers about the Guteman heiress and her romantic elopement, there were letters from bankers and lawyers. And finally official meetings were arranged. We met Santonix on the site of Gipsy's Acre and we looked at the plans there and discussed things, and then having seen things under way we came to London, took a suite at Claridge's and prepared, as they say in old world books, to receive cavalry.

The first to arrive was Mr Andrew P. Lippincott. He was an elderly man, dry and precise in appearance. He was long and lean with suave and courteous manners. He was a Bostonian and from his voice I wouldn't have known he was an American. By arrangement through the telephone he called upon us in our suite at 12 o'clock. Ellie was nervous, I could tell, although she concealed it very well.

Mr Lippincott kissed Ellie and extended a hand and a pleasant smile to me.

'Well, Ellie my dear, you are looking very well. Blooming, I might say.'

'How are you, Uncle Andrew? How did you come? Did you fly?'

'No, I had a very pleasant trip across on the *Queen Mary*. And this is your husband?'

'This is Mike, yes.'

I played up, or thought I did. 'How are you, sir?' I said. Then I asked him if he'd have a drink, which he refused pleasantly. He sat down in an upright chair with gilt arms to it and looked, still smiling, from Ellie to me.

'Well,' he said, 'you young people have been giving us shocks. All very romantic, eh?'

'I'm sorry,' said Ellie, 'I really am sorry.'

'Are you?' said Mr Lippincott, rather dryly.

'I thought it was the best way,' said Ellie.

'I am not altogether of your opinion there, my dear.'

'Uncle Andrew,' Ellie said, 'you know perfectly well that if I'd done it any other way there would have been the most frightful fuss.'

'Why should there have been such a frightful fuss?'

'You know what they'd have been like,' said Ellie. 'You too,' she added accusingly. She added, 'I've had two letters from Cora. One yesterday and one this morning.'

'You must discount a certain amount of agitation, my dear. It's only natural under the circumstances, don't you think?'

'It's my business who I get married to and how and where.'

'You may think so, but you will find that the women of any family would rarely agree as to that.'

'Really, I've saved everyone a lot of trouble.'

'You may put it that way.'

'But it's true, isn't it?'

'But you practised, did you not, a good deal of deception, helped by someone who should have known better than to do what she did.'

Ellie flushed.

'You mean Greta? She only did what I asked her to. Are they all very upset with her?'

'Naturally. Neither she nor you could expect anything else, could you? She was, remember, in a position of trust.'

'I'm of age. I can do what I like.'

'I am speaking of the period of time before you were of age. The deceptions began then, did they not?'

'You mustn't blame Ellie, sir,' I said. 'To begin with I didn't know what was going on and since all her relations are in another country it wasn't easy for me to get in touch with them.'

'I quite realize,' said Mr Lippincott, 'that Greta posted certain letters and gave certain information to Mrs van Stuyvesant and to myself as she was requested to do by Ellie here, and made, if I may say so, a very competent job of it. You have met Greta Andersen, Michael? I may call you Michael, since you are Ellie's husband?'

'Of course,' I said, 'call me Mike. No, I haven't met Miss Andersen –'

'Indeed? That seems to me surprising.' He looked at me with a long thoughtful gaze. 'I should have thought that she would have been present at your marriage.'

'No, Greta wasn't there,' said Ellie. She threw me a look of reproach and I shifted uncomfortably.

Mr Lippincott's eyes were still resting on me thoughtfully. He made me uncomfortable. He seemed about to say something more then changed his mind.

'I'm afraid,' he said after a moment or two, 'that you two,

Michael and Ellie, will have to put up with a certain amount of reproaches and criticism from Ellie's family.'

'I suppose they are going to descend on me in a bunch,' said Ellie.

'Very probably,' said Mr Lippincott. 'I've tried to pave the way,' he added.

'You're on our side, Uncle Andrew?' said Ellie, smiling at him.

'You must hardly ask a prudent lawyer to go as far as that. I have learnt that in life it is wise to accept what is a *fait accompli*. You two have fallen in love with each other and have got married and have, I understood you to say, Ellie, bought a piece of property in the South of England and have already started building a house on it. You propose, therefore, to live in this country?'

'We want to make our home here, yes. Do you object to our doing that?' I said with a touch of anger in my voice. 'Ellie's married to me and she's a British subject now. So why shouldn't she live in England?'

'No reason at all. In fact, there is no reason why Fenella should not live in any country she chooses, or indeed have property in more than one country. The house in Nassau belongs to you, remember, Ellie.'

'I always thought it was Cora's. She always has behaved as though it was.'

'But the actual property rights are vested in you. You also have the house in Long Island whenever you care to visit it. You are the owner of a great deal of oil-bearing property in the West.' His voice was amiable, pleasant, but I had the feeling that the words were directed at me in some curious way. Was it his idea of trying to insinuate a wedge between me and Ellie? I was not sure. It didn't seem very sensible, rubbing it in to a man that his wife owned property all over the world and was fabulously rich. If anything I should have thought that he would have played down Ellie's property rights and her money and all the rest of it. If I was a fortune hunter as he obviously thought, that would be all the more grist to my mill. But I did realize that Mr Lippincott was a subtle man. It would be hard at any time to know what he was driving at; what he had in his mind behind his even and pleasant manner. Was he trying in a way of his own to make me feel uncomfortable, to make me feel that I was going to be branded almost publicly as a fortune hunter? He said to Ellie:

'I've brought over a certain amount of legal stuff which you'll have to go through with me, Ellie. I shall want your signature to many of these things.'

'Yes, of course, Uncle Andrew. Any time.'

'As you say, any time. There's no hurry. I have other business in London and I shall be over here for about ten days.'

Ten days, I thought. That's a long time. I rather wished that Mr Lippincott wasn't going to be here for ten days. He appeared friendly enough towards me, though, as you might say, indicating that he still reserved his judgment on certain points, but I wondered at that moment whether he was really my enemy. If he was, he would not be the kind of man to show his hand.

'Well,' he went on, 'now that we've all met and come to terms, as you might say, for the future, I would like to have a short interview with this husband of yours.'

Ellie said, 'You can talk to us both.' She was up in arms. I put a hand on her arm.

'Now don't flare up, ducks, you're not a mother hen protecting a chicken.' I propelled her gently to the door in the wall that led into the bedroom. 'Uncle Andrew wants to size me up,' I said. 'He's well within his rights.'

I pushed her gently through the double doors. I shut them both and came back into the room. It was a large handsome sitting-room. I came back and took a chair and faced Mr Lippincott. 'All right,' I said. 'Shoot.'

'Thank you, Michael,' he said. 'First of all I want to assure you that I am not, as you may be thinking, your enemy in any way.'

'Well,' I said, 'I'm glad to hear that.' I didn't sound very sure about it.

'Let me speak frankly,' said Mr Lippincott, 'more frankly than I could do before that dear child to whom I am guardian and of whom I am very fond. You may not yet appreciate it fully, Michael, but Ellie is a most unusually sweet and lovable girl.'

'Don't you worry. I'm in love with her all right.'

'That is not at all the same thing,' said Mr Lippincott in his dry manner. 'I hope that as well as being in love with her you can also appreciate what a really dear and in some ways very vulnerable person she is.'

'I'll try,' I said. 'I don't think I'll have to try very hard. She's the tops, Ellie is.'

'So I will go on with what I was about to say. I shall put my cards on the table with the utmost frankness. You are not the kind of young man that I should have wished Ellie to marry. I should like her, as her family would have liked her, to marry someone of her own surroundings, of her own set –'

'A toff in other words,' I said.

'No, not only that. A similar background is, I think, to be desired as a basis for matrimony. And I am not referring to the snob attitude. After all, Herman Guteman, her grandfather, started life as a dockhand. He ended up as one of the richest men in America.'

'For all you know I might do the same,' I said. 'I may end up one of the richest men in England.'

'Everything is possible,' said Mr Lippincott. 'Do you have ambitions that way?'

'It's not just the money,' I said. 'I'd like to – I'd like to get somewhere and do things and –' I hesitated, stopped.

'You have ambitions, shall we say? Well, that is a very good thing, I am sure.'

'I'm starting at long odds,' I said, 'starting from scratch. I'm nothing and nobody and I won't pretend otherwise.'

He nodded approval.

'Very frankly and handsomely said, I appreciate it. Now, Michael, I am no relation to Ellie, but I have acted as her guardian, I am a trustee, left so by her grandfather, of her affairs, I manage her fortune and her investments. And I assume therefore a certain responsibility for them. Therefore I want to know all that I can know about the husband she has chosen.'

'Well,' I said, 'you can make inquiries about me, I suppose, and find out anything you like easily enough.'

'Quite so,' said Mr Lippincott. 'That would be one way of doing it. A wise precaution to take. But actually, Michael, I should like to know all that I can about you from your own lips. I should like to hear your own story of what your life has been up to now.'

Of course I didn't like it. I expect he knew I wouldn't. Nobody in my position would like that. It's second nature to make the best of yourself. I'd made a point of that at school and onwards, boasted about things a bit, said a few things, stretching the truth a bit. I wasn't ashamed of it. I think it's natural. I think it's the sort of thing that you've got to do if you want to get on. Make out a good case for yourself. People take you at your own valuation and I didn't want to be like that chap in Dickens. They read it out on the television, and I must say it's a good yarn on its own. Uriah something his name was, always going on about being humble and rubbing his hands, and actually planning and scheming behind that humility. I didn't want to be like that.

I was ready enough to boast a bit with the chaps I met or to put up a good case to a prospective employer. After all, you've *got* a best side and a worst side of yourself and it's no good showing the worst side and harping on it. No, I'd always done the best for myself describing my activities up to date. But I didn't fancy doing that sort of thing with Mr Lippincott. He'd rather pooh-poohed the idea of making private inquiries about me but I wasn't at all sure that he wouldn't do so all the same. So I gave him the truth unvarnished, as you might say.

Squalid beginnings, the fact that my father had been a drunk, but that I'd had a good mother, that she'd slaved a good bit to help me get educated. I made no secret of the fact that I'd been a rolling stone, that I'd moved from one job to another. He was a good listener, encouraging, if you know what I mean. Every now and then, though, I realized how shrewd he was. Just little questions that he slipped in, or comments, some comments that I might have rushed in unguardedly either to admit or to deny.

Yes, I had a sort of feeling that I'd better be wary and on my toes. And after ten minutes I was quite glad when he leaned back in his chair and the inquisition, if you could call it that, and it wasn't in the least like one, seemed to be over.

'You have an adventurous attitude to life, Mr Rogers – Michael. Not a bad thing. Tell me more about this house that you and Ellie are building.'

'Well,' I said, 'it's not far from a town called Market Chadwell.'

'Yes,' he said, 'I know just where it is. As a matter of fact I ran down to see it. Yesterday, to be exact.'

That startled me a little. It showed he was a devious kind of fellow who got round to more things than you might think he would.

'It's a beautiful site,' I said defensively, 'and the house we're building is going to be a beautiful house. The architect's a chap called Santonix. Rudolf Santonix. I don't know if you've ever heard of him but –'

'Oh yes,' said Mr Lippincott, 'he's quite a well-known name among architects.'

'He's done work in the States I believe.'

'Yes, an architect of great promise and talent. Unfortunately I believe his health is not good.'

'He thinks he's a dying man,' I said, 'but I don't believe it. I believe he'll get cured, get well again. Doctors – they'll say anything.'

'I hope your optimism is justified. You are an optimist.'

'I am about Santonix.'

'I hope all you wish will come true. I may say that I think you and Ellie have made an extremely good purchase in the piece of property that you have bought.'

I thought it was nice of the old boy to use the pronoun 'you'. It wasn't rubbing it in that Ellie had done the buying on her own.

'I have had a consultation with Mr Crawford –'

'Crawford?' I frowned slightly.

'Mr Crawford of Reece & Crawford, a firm of English solicitors. Mr Crawford was the member of the firm who put the purchase in hand. It is a good firm of solicitors and I gather that this property was acquired at a cheap figure. I may say that I wondered slightly at that. I am familiar with the present prices of land in this country and I really felt rather at a loss to account for it. I think Mr Crawford himself was surprised to get it at so low a figure. I wondered if you knew at all why this property happened to go so cheaply. Mr Crawford did not advance any opinion on that. In fact he seemed slightly embarrassed when I put the question to him.'

'Oh well,' I said, 'it's got a curse on it.'

'I beg your pardon, Michael, what did you say?'

'A curse, sir,' I explained. 'The gipsy's warning, that sort of thing. It is known locally as Gipsy's Acre.'

'Ah. A story?'

'Yes. It seems rather confused and I don't know how much people have made up and how much is true. There was a murder or something long ago. A man and his wife and another man. Some story that the husband shot the other two and then shot himself. At least that's the verdict that was brought in. But all sorts of other stories go flying about. I don't think anyone really knows what happened. It was a good long time ago. It's changed hands about four or five times since, but nobody stays there long.'

'Ah,' said Mr Lippincott appreciatively, 'yes, quite a piece of English folklore.' He looked at me curiously. 'And you and Ellie are not afraid of the curse?' He said it lightly, with a slight smile.

'Of course not,' I said. 'Neither Ellie nor I would believe in any rubbish of that kind. Actually it's a lucky thing since because of it we got it cheap.' When I said that a sudden thought struck me. It was lucky in one sense, but I thought that with all Ellie's money and her property and all the rest of it, it couldn't matter to her very much whether she bought a piece of land cheap or at the top price. Then I thought, no, I was wrong. After all, she'd had a grandfather who came up from being a dock labourer to a millionaire. Anyone of that kind would always wish to buy cheap and sell dear.

'Well, I am not superstitious,' said Mr Lippincott, 'and the view from your property is quite magnificent.' He hesitated. 'I only hope that when you come to move into your house to live there, that Ellie will not hear too many of these stories that are going about.'

'I'll keep everything from her that I can,' I said. 'I don't suppose anybody will say anything to her.'

'People in country villages are very fond of repeating stories of that kind,' said Mr Lippincott. 'And Ellie, remember, is not as tough as you are, Michael. She can be influenced easily. Only in some ways. Which brings me –' he stopped without going on to say what he had been going to. He tapped on the table with one finger. 'I'm going to speak to you now on a matter of some difficulty. You said just now that you had *not* met this Greta Andersen.'

'No, as I said, I haven't met her yet.'

'Odd. Very curious.'

'Well?' I looked at him inquiringly.

'I should have thought you'd have been almost sure to have met her,' he said slowly. 'How much do you know about her?'

'I know that she's been with Ellie some time.'

'She has been with Ellie since Ellie was seventeen. She has occupied a post of some responsibility and trust. She came first to the States in the capacity of secretary and companion. A kind of chaperone to Ellie when Mrs van Stuyvesant, her stepmother, was away from home, which I may say was a quite frequent occurrence.' He spoke particularly dryly when he said this. 'She is, I gather, a well-born girl with excellent references, half-Swedish half-German. Ellie became, quite naturally, very much attached to her.'

'So I gather,' I said.

'In some way Ellie was, I suppose, almost too much attached to her. You don't mind my saying that?'

'No. Why should I mind? As a matter of fact I've – well, I've thought so myself once or twice. Greta this and Greta that. I got – well, I know I've no business to, but I used to get fed up sometimes.'

'And yet she expressed no wish for you to meet Greta?'

'Well,' I said, 'it's rather difficult to explain. But I think, yes, I think she probably did suggest it in a mild way once or twice but, well, we were too taken up with having met each other. Besides, oh well, I suppose I didn't really want to meet Greta. I didn't want to share Ellie with anyone.'

'I see. Yes, I see. And Ellie did not suggest Greta being present at your wedding?'

'She did suggest it,' I said.

'But – but you didn't want her to come. Why?'

'I don't know. I really don't know. I just felt that this Greta, this girl or woman I'd never met, she was always horning in on everything. You know, arranging Ellie's life for her. Sending post-cards and letters and filling in for Ellie, arranging a whole itinerary and passing it on to the family. I felt that Ellie was dependent on Greta in a way, that she let Greta run her, that she wanted to do everything that Greta wanted. I – oh, I'm sorry, Mr Lippincott, I oughtn't to be saying all these things perhaps. Say I was just plain jealous. Anyway I blew up and I said I didn't want Greta at the wedding, that the wedding was ours, that it was just our business and nobody else's. And so we went along to the Registrar's office and his clerk and the typist from his office were the two witnesses. I dare say it was mean of me to refuse to have Greta there, but I wanted to have Ellie to myself.'

'I see. Yes, I see, and I think, if I may say so, that you were wise, Michael.'

'You don't like Greta either,' I said shrewdly.

'You can hardly use the word "either", Michael, if you have not even met her.'

'No, I know but, well, I mean if you hear a lot about a person you can form some sort of idea of them, some judgment of them. Oh well, call it plain jealousy. Why don't *you* like Greta?'

'This is without prejudice,' said Mr Lippincott, 'but you are Ellie's husband, Michael, and I have Ellie's happiness very much at heart. I don't think that the influence that Greta has over Ellie is a very desirable one. She takes too much upon herself.'

'Do you think she'll try and make trouble between us?' I asked.

'I think,' said Mr Lippincott, 'that I have no right to say anything of that kind.'

He sat looking cautiously at me, and blinking like a wrinkled old tortoise.

I didn't know quite what to say next. He spoke first, choosing his words with some care.

'There has been, then, no suggestion that Greta Andersen might take up her residence with you?'

'Not if I can help it,' I said.

'Ah. So that is what you feel? The idea *has* been mooted.'

'Ellie did say something of the kind. But we're newly married, Mr Lippincott. We want our house – our new home – to ourselves. Of course she'll come and stay sometimes, I suppose. That'll only be natural.'

'As you say, that would be only natural. But you realize,

perhaps, that Greta is going to be in a somewhat difficult position as regards further employment. I mean, it is not a question of what *Ellie* thinks of her, but of what the people who engaged her and reposed trust in her feel.'

'You mean that you or Mrs van What's-her-name won't recommend her for another post of the same kind?'

'They are hardly likely to do so except so far as to satisfy purely legal requirements.'

'And you think that she'll want to come to England and live on Ellie.'

'I don't want to prejudice you too much against her. After all, this is mostly in my mind. I dislike some of the things she has done and the way she has done them. I think that Ellie who has a very generous heart will be upset at having, shall we say, blighted Greta's prospects in many ways. She might impulsively insist on her coming to live with you.'

'I don't think Ellie will insist,' I said slowly. I sounded a little worried all the same, and I thought Lippincott noticed it. 'But couldn't we – Ellie, I mean – couldn't Ellie pension her off?'

'We should not put it precisely like that,' said Mr Lippincott. 'There is a suggestion of age about pensioning anyone off and Greta is a young woman, and I may say a very handsome young woman. Beautiful, in fact,' he added in a deprecating, disapproving voice. 'She's very attractive to men, too.'

'Well, perhaps she'll marry,' I said. 'If she's all that, why hasn't she got married before this?'

'There have been people attracted, I believe, but she has not considered them. I think, however, that your suggestion is a very sound one. I think it might be carried out in a way that would not hurt anyone's susceptibilities. It might seem quite a natural thing to do on Ellie's having attained her majority and having had her marriage helped on by Greta's good offices – settle a sum of money upon her in a fit of gratitude.' Mr Lippincott made the last two words sound as sour as lemon juice.

'Well, then, that's all right,' I said cheerfully.

'Again I see that you are an optimist. Let us hope that Greta will accept what is offered to her.'

'Why shouldn't she? She'd be mad if she didn't.'

'I don't know,' said Mr Lippincott. 'I should say it would be extraordinary if she did not accept, and they will remain on terms of friendship, of course.'

'You think – what *do* you think?'

'I would like to see her influence over Ellie broken,' said Mr Lippincott. He got up. 'You will, I hope, assist me and do everything you can to further that end?'

'You bet I will,' I said. 'The last thing I want is to have Greta in our pockets all the time.'

'You might change your mind when you see her,' said Mr Lippincott.

'I don't think so,' I said. 'I don't like managing females, however efficient and even handsome they are.'

'Thank you, Michael, for listening to me so patiently. I hope you will give me the pleasure of dining with me, both of you. Possibly next Tuesday evening? Cora van Stuyvesant and Frank Barton will probably be in London by that time.'

'And I've got to meet them, I suppose?'

'Oh yes, that will be quite inevitable.' He smiled at me and this time his smile seemed more genuine than it had before. 'You mustn't mind too much,' he said. 'Cora, I expect, will be very rude to you. Frank will be merely tactless. Reuben won't be over just at present.'

I didn't know who Reuben was – another relation I supposed.

I went across to the connecting doors and opened them. 'Come on, Ellie,' I said, 'the grilling is over.'

She came back in the room and looked quickly from Lippincott to myself, then she went across and kissed him.

'Dear Uncle Andrew,' she said. 'I can see you've been nice to Michael.'

'Well, my dear, if I weren't nice to your husband you wouldn't have much use for me in the future, would you? I do reserve the right to give a few words of advice now and then. You're very young you know, both of you.'

'All right,' said Ellie, 'we'll listen patiently.'

'Now, my dear, I'd like to have a word with *you* if I may.'

'My turn to be odd man out,' I said, and I too went into the bedroom.

I shut the two double doors ostentatiously but I opened the

inner one again after I got inside. I hadn't been as well brought up as Ellie so I felt a bit anxious to find out how double-faced Mr Lippincott might turn out to be. But actually there was nothing I need have listened to. He gave Ellie one or two wise words of advice. He said she must realize that I might find it difficult to be a poor man married to a rich wife and then he went on to sound her about making a settlement on Greta. She agreed to it eagerly and said she'd been going to ask him that herself. He also suggested that she should make an additional settlement on Cora van Stuyvesant.

'There is no earthly need that you should do so,' he said. 'She has been very well provided for in the matter of alimony from several husbands. And she is as you know paid an income, though not a very big one, from the trust fund left by your grandfather.'

'But you think I ought to give her more still?'

'I think there is no legal or moral obligation to do so. What I think is that you will find her far less tiresome and shall I say catty if you do so. I should make it in the form of an increased income, which you could revoke at any time. If you find that she has been spreading malicious rumours about Michael or yourself or your life together, the knowledge that you can do that will keep her tongue free of those more poisonous barbs that she so well knows how to plant.'

'Cora has always hated me,' said Ellie. 'I've known that.' She added rather shyly, 'You do like Mike, don't you, Uncle Andrew?'

'I think he's an extremely attractive young man,' said Mr Lippincott. 'And I can quite see how you came to marry him.'

That, I suppose, was as good as I could expect. I wasn't really his type and I knew it. I eased the door gently to and in a minute or two Ellie came to fetch me.

We were both standing saying goodbye to Lippincott when there was a knock on the door and a page boy came in with a telegram. Ellie took it and opened it. She gave a little surprised cry of pleasure.

'It's Greta,' she said, 'she's arriving in London tonight and she'll be coming to see us tomorrow. How lovely.' She looked at us both. 'Isn't it?' she said.

She saw two sour faces and heard two polite voices saying, one: 'Yes indeed, my dear,' the other one, 'Of course.'

CHAPTER 11

I had been out shopping the next morning and I arrived back at the hotel rather later than I had meant. I found Ellie sitting in the central lounge and opposite her was a tall blonde young woman. In fact Greta. Both of them were talking nineteen to the dozen.

I'm never any hand at describing people but I'll have a shot at describing Greta. To begin with one couldn't deny that she was, as Ellie had said, very beautiful and also, as Mr Lippincott had reluctantly admitted, very handsome. The two things are not exactly the same. If you say a woman is handsome it does not mean that actually you yourself admire her. Mr Lippincott, I gathered, had not admired Greta. All the same when Greta walked across the lounge into a hotel or in a restaurant, men's heads turned to look at her. She was a Nordic type of blonde with pure gold-corn-coloured hair. She wore it piled high on her head in the fashion of the time, not falling straight down on each side of her face in the Chelsea tradition. She looked what she was, Swedish or north German. In fact, pin on a pair of wings and she could have gone to a fancy dress ball as a Valkyrie. Her eyes were a bright clear blue and her contours were admirable. Let's admit it. She was something!

I came along to where they were sitting and joined them, greeting them both in what I hope was a natural, friendly manner, though I couldn't help feeling a bit awkward. I'm not always very good at acting a part. Ellie said immediately:

'At last, Mike, this is Greta.'

I said I guessed it might be, in a rather facetious, not very happy manner. I said:

'I'm very glad to meet you at last, Greta.'

Ellie said:

'As you know very well, if it hadn't been for Greta we would never have been able to get married.'

'All the same we'd have managed it somehow,' I said.

'Not if the family had come down on us like a ton of coals. They'd have broken it up somehow. Tell me, Greta, have they been very awful?' Ellie asked. 'You haven't written or said anything to me about that.'

'I know better,' said Greta, 'than to write to a happy couple when they're on their honeymoon.'

'But were they very angry with you?'

'Of course! What do you imagine? But I was prepared for that, I can assure you.'

'What have they said or done?'

'Everything they could,' said Greta cheerfully. 'Starting with the sack naturally.'

'Yes, I suppose that was inevitable. But – but what have you done? After all they can't refuse to give you references.'

'Of course they can. And after all, from their point of view I was placed in a position of trust and abused it shamefully.' She added, 'Enjoyed abusing it too.'

'But what are you going to do now?'

'Oh I've got a job ready to walk into.'

'In New York?'

'No. Here in London. Secretarial.'

'But are you all right?'

'Darling Ellie,' said Greta, 'how can I not be all right with that lovely cheque you sent me in anticipation of what was going to happen when the balloon went up?'

Her English was very good with hardly any trace of accent though she used a lot of colloquial terms which sometimes didn't run quite right.

'I've seen a bit of the world, fixed myself up in London and bought a good many things as well.'

'Mike and I have bought a lot of things too,' said Ellie, smiling at the recollection.

It was true. We'd done ourselves pretty well with our continental shopping. It was really wonderful that we had dollars to spend, no niggling Treasury restrictions. Brocades and fabrics in Italy for the house. And we'd bought pictures too, both in Italy and in Paris, paying what seemed fabulous sums for them. A whole world had opened up to me that I'd never dreamt would have come my way.

'You both look remarkably happy,' said Greta.

'You haven't seen our house yet,' said Ellie. 'It's going to be wonderful. It's going to be just like we dreamed it would be, isn't it, Mike?'

'I have seen it,' said Greta. 'The first day I got back to England I hired a car and drove down there.'

'Well?' said Ellie.

I said Well? too.

'Well,' said Greta consideringly. She shifted her head from side to side.

Ellie looked grief-stricken, horribly taken aback. But I wasn't taken in. I saw at once that Greta was having a bit of fun with us. If the thought of fun wasn't very kind, it hardly had time to take root. Greta burst out laughing, a high musical laugh that made people turn their heads and look at us.

'You should have seen your faces,' she said, 'especially yours, Ellie. I have to tease you just a little. It's a wonderful house, lovely. That man's a genius.'

'Yes,' I said, 'he's something out of the ordinary. Wait till you meet him.'

'I have met him,' said Greta. 'He was down there the day I went. Yes, he's an extraordinary person. Rather frightening, don't you think?'

'Frightening?' I said, surprised. 'In what way?'

'Oh I don't know. It's as though he looks through you and – well, sees right through to the other side. That's always disconcerting.' Then she added, 'He looks rather ill.'

'He is ill. Very ill,' I said.

'What a shame. What's the matter with him, tuberculosis, something like that?'

'No,' I said, 'I don't think it's tuberculosis. I think it's something to do with – oh with blood.'

'Oh I see. Doctors can do almost anything nowadays, can't they, unless they kill you first while they're trying to cure you. But don't let's think of that. Let's think of the house. When will it be finished?'

'Quite soon, I should think, by the look of it. I'd never imagined a house could go up so quickly,' I said.

'Oh,' said Greta carelessly, 'that's money. Double shifts and bonuses – all the rest of it. You don't really know yourself, Ellie, how wonderful it is to have all the money you have.'

But *I* did know. I had been learning, learning a great deal in the last few weeks. I'd stepped as a result of marriage into an entirely different world and it wasn't the sort of world I'd imagined it to be from the outside. So far in my life, a lucky double had been my highest knowledge of affluence. A whack of money coming in, and spending it as fast as I could on the biggest blow-out I could find. Crude, of course. The crudeness of my class. But Ellie's world was a different world. It wasn't what I should have thought it to be. Just more and more super luxury. It wasn't bigger bathrooms and larger houses and more electric light fittings and bigger meals and faster cars. It wasn't just spending for spending's sake and showing off to everyone in sight. Instead, it was curiously simple. The sort of simplicity that comes when you get beyond the point of splashing for splashing's sake. You don't want three yachts or four cars and you can't eat more than three meals a day and if you buy a really top-price picture you don't want more than perhaps one of them in a room. It's as simple as that. Whatever you have is just the best of its kind, not so much because it is the best, but because there is no reason if you like or want any particular thing, why you shouldn't have it. There is no moment when you say, 'I'm afraid I can't afford that one.' So in a strange way it makes sometimes for such a curious simplicity that I couldn't understand it. We were considering a French Impressionist picture, a Cézanne, I think it was. I had to learn that name carefully. I always mixed it up with a tzigane which I gather is a gipsy orchestra. And then as we walked along the streets of Venice, Ellie stopped to look at some pavement artists. On the whole they were doing some terrible pictures for tourists which all looked the same. Portraits with great rows of shining teeth and usually blonde hair falling down their necks.

And then she bought quite a tiny picture, just a picture of a little glimpse through to a canal. The man who had painted it appraised the look of us and she bought it for £6 by English exchange. The funny thing was that I knew quite well that Ellie had just the same longing for that £6 picture that she had for the Cézanne.

It was the same way one day in Paris. She'd said to me suddenly:

'What fun it would be – let's get a really nice crisp French loaf of bread and have that with butter and one of those cheeses wrapped up in leaves.'

So we did and Ellie I think enjoyed it more than the meal we'd had the night before which had come to about £20 English. At first I couldn't understand it, then I began to see. The awkward thing was that I could see now that being married to Ellie wasn't just fun and games. You have to do your homework, you have to learn how to go into a restaurant and the sort of things to order and the right tips, and when for some reason you gave more than usual. You have to memorize what you drink with certain foods. I had to do most of it by observation. I couldn't ask Ellie because that was one of the things she wouldn't have understood. She'd have said 'But, darling Mike, you can have anything you like. What does it matter if waiters think you ought to have one particular wine with one particular thing?' It wouldn't have mattered to her because she was born to it but it mattered to me because I couldn't do just as I liked. I wasn't simple enough. Clothes too. Ellie was more helpful there, for she could understand better. She just guided me to the right places and told me to let them have their head.

Of course I didn't look right and sound right yet. But that didn't matter much. I'd got the hang of it, enough so that I could pass muster with people like old Lippincott, and shortly, presumably, when Ellie's stepmother and uncles were around, but actually it wasn't going to matter in the future at all. When the house was finished and when we'd moved in, we were going to be far away from everybody. It could be our kingdom. I looked at Greta sitting opposite me. I wondered what she'd really thought of our house. Anyway, it was what I wanted. It satisfied me utterly. I wanted to drive down and go through a private path through the trees which led down to a small cove which would be our own beach which nobody could come to on the land side. It would be a thousand times better, I thought, plunging into the sea there. A thousand times better than a lido spread along a beach with hundreds of bodies lying there. I didn't want all the *senseless* rich things. I wanted – there were the words again, my own particular words – I want, I want . . . I could feel all the feeling surging up in me. I wanted a wonderful woman and a wonderful house like nobody else's house and I wanted my wonderful house to be full of wonderful things. Things that belonged to *me*. Everything would belong to me.

'He's thinking of our house,' said Ellie.

It seemed that she had twice suggested to me that we should go now into the dining-room. I looked at her affectionately.

Later in the day – it was that evening – when we were dressing to go out to dinner, Ellie said a little tentatively:

'Mike, you do – you do like Greta, don't you?'

'Of course I do,' I said.

'I couldn't bear it if you didn't like her.'

'But I do,' I protested. 'What makes you think I don't?'

'I'm not quite sure. I think it's the way you hardly look at her even when you're talking to her.'

'Well, I suppose that's because – well, because I feel nervous.'

'Nervous of Greta?'

'Yes, she's a bit awe-inspiring, you know.'

And I told Ellie how I thought Greta looked rather like a Valkyrie.

'Not as stout as an operatic one,' said Ellie and laughed. We both laughed. I said:

'It's all very well for you because you've known her for years. But she is just a bit – well, I mean she's very efficient and practical and sophisticated.' I struggled with a lot of words which didn't seem to be quite the right ones. I said suddenly, 'I feel – I feel at a disadvantage with her.'

'Oh Mike!' Ellie was conscience-stricken. 'I know we've got a lot of things to talk about. Old jokes and old things that happened and all that. I suppose – yes, I suppose it might make you feel rather shy. But you'll soon get to be friends. She likes you. She likes you very much. She told me so.'

'Listen, Ellie, she'd probably tell you that anyway.'

'Oh no she wouldn't. Greta's very outspoken. You heard her. Some of the things she said today.'

It was true that Greta had not minced her words during luncheon. She had said, addressing me rather than Ellie:

'You must have thought it queer sometimes, the way I was backing Ellie up when I'd not even seen you. But I got so mad – so mad with the life that they were making her lead. All tied up in a cocoon with their money, their traditional ideas. She never had a chance to enjoy herself, go anywhere really by herself and do what she wanted. She wanted to rebel but she didn't know how. And so – yes, all right, I urged her on. I suggested she should look at properties in England. Then I said when she was twenty-one she could buy one of her own and say goodbye to all that New York lot.'

'Greta always has wonderful ideas,' said Ellie. 'She thinks of things I'd probably never have thought of myself.'

What were those words Mr Lippincott had said to me? 'She has too much influence over Ellie.' I wondered if it was true. Queerly enough I didn't really think so. I felt that there was a core somewhere in Ellie that Greta, for all that she knew her so well, had never quite appreciated. Ellie, I was sure, would always accept any ideas that matched with the ideas she wanted to have herself. Greta had preached rebellion to Ellie but Ellie herself wanted to rebel, only she was not sure how to do so. But I felt that Ellie, now that I was coming to know her better, was one of those very simple people who have unexpected reserves. I thought Ellie would be quite capable of taking a stand of her own if she wished to. The point was that she wouldn't very often wish to and I thought then how difficult everyone was to understand. Even Ellie. Even Greta. Even perhaps my own mother . . . The way she looked at me with fear in her eyes.

I wondered about Mr Lippincott. I said, as we were peeling some outsize peaches:

'Mr Lippincott seems to have taken our marriage very well really. I was surprised.'

'Mr Lippincott,' said Greta, 'is an old fox.'

'You always say so, Greta,' said Ellie, 'but I think he's rather a dear. Very strict and proper and all that.'

'Well, go on thinking so if you like,' said Greta. 'Myself, I wouldn't trust him an inch.'

'Not trust him!' said Ellie.

Greta shook her head. 'I know. He's a pillar of respectability and trustworthiness. He's everything a trustee and a lawyer should be.'

Ellie laughed and said, 'Do you mean he's embezzled my fortune? Don't be silly, Greta. There are thousands of auditors and banks and check-ups and all that sort of thing.'

'Oh, I expect he's all right really,' said Greta. 'All the same, those are the people that do embezzle. The trustworthy ones. And then everyone says afterwards, "I'd never have believed it of Mr A. or Mr B. The last man in the world." Yes, that's what they say. "The last man in the world".'

Ellie said thoughtfully that her Uncle Frank, she thought, was much more likely to go in for dishonest practices. She did not seem unduly worried or surprised by the idea.

'Oh well he looks like a crook,' said Greta. 'That handicaps him to start with. All that geniality and bonhomie. But he'll never be in a position to be a crook in a big way.'

'Is he your mother's brother?' I asked. I always got confused over Ellie's relations.

'He's my father's sister's husband,' said Ellie. 'She left him and married someone else and died about six or seven years ago. Uncle Frank has more or less stuck on with the family.'

'There are three of them,' said Greta kindly and helpfully. 'Three leeches hanging round, as you might say. Ellie's actual uncles were killed, one in Korea and one in a car accident, so what she's got is a much-damaged stepmother, an Uncle Frank, an amiable hanger-on in the family home, and her cousin Reuben whom she calls Uncle but he's only a cousin and Andrew Lippincott, and Stanford Lloyd.'

'Who is Stanford Lloyd?' I asked, bewildered.

'Oh another sort of trustee, isn't he, Ellie? At any rate he manages your investments and things like that. Which can't really be very difficult because when you've got as much money as Ellie has, it sort of makes more money all the time without anyone having to do much about it. Those are the main surrounding group,' Greta added, 'and I have no doubt that you will be meeting them fairly soon. They'll be over here to have a look at you.'

I groaned, and looked at Ellie. Ellie said very gently and sweetly:

'Never mind, Mike, they'll go away again.'

CHAPTER 12

They did come over. None of them stayed very long. Not that time, not on a first visit. They came over to have a look at me. I found them difficult to understand because of course they were all Americans. They were types with which I was not well acquainted. Some of them were pleasant enough. Uncle Frank, for instance. I agreed with Greta about him. I wouldn't have trusted him a yard. I had come across the same type in England. He was a big man with a bit of a paunch and pouches under his eyes that gave him a dissipated look which was not far from the truth, I imagine. He had an eye for women, I thought, and even more of an eye for the main chance. He borrowed money from me once or twice, quite small amounts, just, as it were, something to tide him over for a day or two. I thought it was not so much that he needed the money but he wanted to test me out, to see if I lent money easily. It was rather worrying because I wasn't sure which was the best way to take it. Would it have been better to refuse point blank and let him know I was a skinflint or was it better to assume an appearance of careless generosity, which I was very far from feeling? To hell with Uncle Frank, I thought.

Cora, Ellie's stepmother, was the one that interested me most. She was a woman of about forty, well turned out with tinted hair and a rather gushing manner. She was all sweetness to Ellie.

'You mustn't mind those letters I wrote you, Ellie,' she said. 'You must admit that it came as a terrible shock, your marrying like that. So secretly. But of course I know it was Greta who put you up to it, doing it that way.'

'You mustn't blame Greta,' said Ellie. 'I didn't mean to upset you all so much. I just thought that – well, the less fuss –'

'Well, of course, Ellie dear, you have something there. All the men of business were simply livid. Stanford Lloyd and Andrew Lippincott. I suppose they thought everyone would blame them for not looking after you better. And of course they'd no idea what Mike would be like. They didn't realize how charming he was going to be. I didn't myself.'

She smiled across at me, a very sweet smile and one of the falsest ones I'd ever seen! I thought to myself that if ever a woman hated a man, it was Cora who hated me. I thought her sweetness to Ellie was understandable enough. Andrew Lippincott had gone back to America and had, no doubt, given her a few words of caution. Ellie was selling some of her property in America, since she herself had definitely decided to live in England, but she was going to make a large allowance to Cora so that the latter could live where she chose. Nobody mentioned Cora's husband much. I gathered he'd already taken himself off to some other part of the world, and had not gone there alone. In all probability, I gathered, another divorce was pending. There wouldn't be much alimony out of this one. Cora's last marriage had been to a man a good many years younger than herself with more attractions of a physical kind than cash.

Cora wanted that allowance. She was a woman of extravagant tastes. No doubt old Andrew Lippincott had hinted clearly enough that it could be discontinued any time if Ellie chose, or if Cora so far forgot herself as to criticize Ellie's new husband too virulently.

Cousin Reuben, or Uncle Reuben, did not make the journey. He wrote instead to Ellie a pleasant, non-committal letter hoping she'd be very happy, but doubted if she would like living in England. 'If you don't, Ellie, you come right back to the States. Don't think you won't get a welcome here because you will. Certainly you will from your Uncle Reuben.'

'He sounds rather nice,' I said to Ellie.

'Yes,' said Ellie meditatively. She wasn't, it seemed, quite so sure about it.

'Are you fond of any of them, Ellie?' I asked, 'or oughtn't I to ask that?'

'Of course you can ask me anything.' But she didn't answer for a moment or two all the same. Then she said, with a sort of finality and decision, 'No, I don't think I am. It seems odd, but I suppose it's because they don't really belong to me. Only by environment, not by relationship. They none of them are my flesh and blood relations. I loved my father, what I remembered of him. I think he was rather a weak man and I think my grandfather was disappointed in him because he hadn't got much head for business. He didn't want to go into the business life. He liked going to Florida and fishing, that sort of thing. And then later he married Cora and I never cared for Cora much – or Cora for me, for that matter. My own mother, of course, I don't remember. I liked Uncle Henry and Uncle Joe. They were fun. In some ways more fun than my father was. He, I think, was in some ways a quiet and rather sad man. But the uncles enjoyed themselves. Uncle Joe was, I think, a bit wild, the kind that is wild just because they've got lots of money. Anyway, he was the one who got smashed up in the car, and the other one was killed fighting in the war. My grandfather was a sick man by that time and it was a terrible blow to him that all his three sons were dead. He didn't like Cora and he didn't care much for any of his more distant relatives. Uncle Reuben for instance. He said you could never tell what Reuben was up to. That's why he made arrangements to put his money in trust. A lot of it went to museums and hospitals. He left Cora well provided for, and his daughter's husband Uncle Frank.'

'But most of it to you?'

'Yes. And I think that worried him a little bit. He did his best to get it looked after for me.'

'By Uncle Andrew and by Mr Stanford Lloyd. A lawyer and a banker.'

'Yes. I suppose he didn't think I could look after it very well by myself. The odd thing is that he let me come into it at the age of twenty-one. He didn't keep it in trust till I was twenty-five, as lots of people do. I expect that was because I was a girl.'

'That's odd,' I said, 'it would seem to me that it ought to be the other way round?'

Ellie shook her head. 'No,' she said, 'I think my grandfather thought that young males were always wild and hit things up and that blondes with evil designs got hold of them. I think he thought it would be a good thing if they had plenty of time to sow their wild oats. That's your English saying, isn't it? But he said once to me, "If a girl is going to have any sense at all, she'll have it at twenty-one. It won't make any difference making her wait four years longer. If she's going to be a fool she'll be a fool by then just as much." He said, too,' Ellie looked at me and smiled, 'that he didn't think I *was* a fool. He said, "You mayn't know very much about life, but you've got good sense, Ellie. Especially about people. I think you always will have."'

'I don't suppose he would have liked me,' I said thoughtfully.

Ellie has a lot of honesty. She didn't try and reassure me by saying anything but what was undoubtedly the truth.

'No,' she said, 'I think he'd have been rather horrified. To begin with, that is. He'd have had to get used to you.'

'Poor Ellie,' I said suddenly.

'Why do you say that?'

'I said it to you once before, do you remember?'

'Yes. You said poor little rich girl. You were quite right too.'

'I didn't mean it the same way this time,' I said. 'I didn't mean that you were poor because you were rich. I think I meant –' I hesitated. 'You've too many people,' I said, '*at* you. All round you. Too many people who want things from you but who don't really care about you. That's true, isn't it?'

'I think Uncle Andrew really cares about me,' said Ellie, a little doubtfully. 'He's always been nice to me, sympathetic. The others – no, you're quite right. They only want *things*.'

'They come and cadge off you, don't they? Borrow money off you, want favours. Want you to get them out of jams, that sort of thing. They're *at* you, *at* you, *at* you!'

'I suppose it's quite natural,' said Ellie calmly, 'but I've done with them all now. I'm coming to live here in England. I shan't see much of them.'

She was wrong there, of course, but she hadn't grasped that fact yet. Stanford Lloyd came over later by himself. He brought a great many documents and papers and things for Ellie to sign and wanted her agreement on investments. He talked to her about investments and shares and property that she owned, and the disposal of trust funds. It was all Double Dutch to me. I couldn't have helped her or advised her. I couldn't have stopped Stanford Lloyd from cheating her, either. I hoped he wasn't, but how could anyone ignorant like myself be sure?

There was something about Stanford Lloyd that was almost too good to be true. He was a banker, and he looked like a banker. He was rather a handsome man though not young. He was very polite to me and thought dirt of me though he tried not to show it.

'Well,' I said when he had finally taken his departure, 'that's the last of the bunch.'

'You didn't think much of any of them, did you?'

'I think your stepmother, Cora, is a double-faced bitch if I ever knew one. Sorry, Ellie, perhaps I oughtn't to say that.'

'Why not, if that's what you think? I expect you're not far wrong.'

'You must have been lonely, Ellie,' I said.

'Yes, I was lonely. I knew girls of my own age. I went to a fashionable school but I was never really *free*. If I made friends with people, somehow or other they'd get me separated, push another girl at me instead. You know? Everything was governed by the social register. If I'd cared enough about anybody to make a fuss – but I never got far enough. There was never anybody I *really* cared for. Not until Greta came, and then everything was different. For the first time someone was really fond of *me*. It was wonderful.' Her face softened.

'I wish,' I said, as I turned away towards the window.

'What do you wish?'

'Oh I don't know . . . I wish perhaps that you weren't – weren't quite so dependent on Greta. It's a bad thing to be as dependent as that on anyone.'

'You don't like her, Mike,' said Ellie.

'I do,' I protested hurriedly. 'Indeed I do. But you must realize, Ellie, that she is – well, she's quite a stranger to me. I suppose, let's face it, I'm a bit jealous of her. Jealous because she and you – well, I didn't understand before – how linked together you were.'

'Don't be jealous. She's the only person who was good to me, who cared about me – till I met you.'

'But you have met me,' I said, 'and you've married me.' Then I said again what I'd said before. 'And we're going to live happily ever afterwards.'

CHAPTER 13

I'm trying as best I can, though that isn't saying much, to paint a picture of the people who came into our lives, that is to say: who came into *my* life because, of course, they were in Ellie's life already. Our mistake was that we thought they'd go out of Ellie's life. But they didn't. They'd no intention of doing so. However, we didn't know that then.

The English side of our life was the next thing that happened. Our house was finished, we had a telegram from Santonix. He'd asked us to keep away for about a week, then the telegram came. It said: 'Come tomorrow.'

We drove down there, and we arrived at sunset. Santonix heard the car and came out to meet us, standing in front of the house. When I saw our house, finished, something inside me leaped up, leaped up as though to burst out of my skin! It was *my house* – and I'd got it at last! I held Ellie's arm very tight.

'Like it?' said Santonix.

'It's the tops,' I said. A silly thing to say but he knew what I meant.

'Yes,' he said, 'it's the best thing I've done . . . It's cost you a mint of money and it's worth every penny of it. I've exceeded my estimates all round. Come on, Mike,' he said, 'pick her up and carry her over the threshold. That's the thing to do when you enter into possession with your bride!'

I flushed and then I picked up Ellie – she was quite a light weight – and carried her as Santonix had suggested, over the threshold. As I did so, I stumbled just a little and I saw Santonix frown.

'There you are,' said Santonix, 'be good to her, Mike. Take care of her. Don't let harm come to her. She can't take care of herself. She thinks she can.'

'Why should any harm happen to me?' said Ellie.

'Because it's a bad world and there are bad people in it,' said Santonix, 'and there are some bad people around you, my girl. I know. I've seen one or two of them. Seen them down here. They come nosing around, sniffing around like the rats they are. Excuse my French but somebody's got to say it.'

'They won't bother us,' said Ellie, 'they've all gone back to the States.'

'Maybe,' said Santonix, 'but it's only a few hours by plane, you know.'

He put his hands on her shoulders. They were very thin now, very white-looking. He looked terribly ill.

'I'd look after you myself, child, if I could,' he said, 'but I can't. It won't be long now. You'll have to fend for yourself.'

'Cut out the gipsy's warning, Santonix,' I said, 'and take us round the house. Every inch of it.'

We went round the house. Some of the rooms were still empty but most of the things we'd bought, pictures and the furniture and the curtains, were there.

'We haven't got a name for it,' said Ellie suddenly. 'We can't call it The Towers, that was a ridiculous name. What was the other name for it that you told me once?' she said to me. 'Gipsy's Acre, wasn't it?'

'We won't call it that,' I said sharply. 'I don't like that name.'

'It'll always be called that hereabouts,' said Santonix.

'They're a lot of silly superstitious people,' I said.

And then we sat down on the terrace looking at the setting sun and the view, and we thought of names for the house. It was a kind of game. We started quite seriously and then we began to think of every silly name we possibly could. 'Journey's End', 'Heart's Delight' and names like boarding-houses. 'Seaview', 'Fairhome', 'The Pines'. Then suddenly it grew dark and cold, and we went indoors. We didn't draw the curtains, just closed the windows. We'd brought down provisions with us. On the following day an expensively acquired domestic staff was coming.

'They'll probably hate it and say it's lonely and they'll all go away,' said Ellie.

'And then you'll give them double the money to stay on,' said Santonix.

'*You* think,' said Ellie, 'that everyone can be bought!' But she only said it laughingly.

We had brought *pâté en croûte* with us and French bread and large red prawns. We sat round the table laughing and eating and talking. Even Santonix looked strong and animated, and there was a kind of wild excitement in his eyes.

And then it happened suddenly. A stone crashed in through the window and dropped on the table. Smashed a wineglass too, and a sliver of glass slit Ellie's cheek. For a moment we sat paralysed, then I sprang up, rushed to the window, unbolted it and went out on the terrace. There was no one to be seen. I came back into the room again.

I picked up a paper napkin and bent over Ellie, wiping away a trickle of blood I saw coursing down her cheek.

'It's hurt you . . . There, dear, it's nothing much. It's just a wee cut from a sliver of glass.'

My eyes met those of Santonix.

'Why did anyone do it?' said Ellie. She looked bewildered.

'Boys,' I said, 'you know, young hooligans. They knew, perhaps, we were settling in. I dare say you were lucky that they only threw a stone. They might have had an air gun or something like that.'

'But *why* should they do it to us? *Why?*'

'I don't know,' I said. 'Just beastliness.'

Ellie got up suddenly. She said:

'I'm frightened. I'm afraid.'

'We'll find out tomorrow,' I said. 'We don't know enough about the people round here.'

'Is it because we're rich and they're poor?' said Ellie. She asked it not of me but of Santonix as though he would know the answer to the question better than I did.

'No,' said Santonix slowly, 'I don't think it's that . . .'

Ellie said:

'It's because they hate us . . . Hate Mike and hate me. *Why?* Because we're happy?'

Again Santonix shook his head.

'No,' Ellie said, as though she were agreeing with him, 'no, it's something else. Something we don't know about. Gipsy's Acre. Anyone who lives here is going to be hated. Going to be persecuted. Perhaps they will succeed in the end in driving us away . . .'

I poured out a glass of wine and gave it to her.

'Don't, Ellie,' I begged her. 'Don't say such things. Drink this. It's a nasty thing to happen, but it was only silliness, crude horseplay.'

'I wonder,' said Ellie, 'I wonder . . .' She looked hard at me. 'Somebody is trying to drive us away, Mike. To drive us away from the house we've built, the house we love.'

'We won't let them drive us away,' I said. I added, 'I'll take care of you. Nothing shall hurt you.'

She looked again at Santonix.

'You should know,' she said, 'you've been here while the house was building. Didn't anyone ever say anything to you? Come and throw stones – interfere with the building of the house?'

'One can imagine things,' said Santonix.

'There *were* accidents, then?'

'There are always a few accidents in the building of a house. Nothing serious or tragic. A man falls off a ladder, someone drops a load on his foot, someone gets a splinter in his thumb and it goes septic.'

'Nothing more than that? Nothing that might have been *meant*?'

'No,' said Santonix, '*no*. I swear to you, no!'

Ellie turned to me.

'You remember that gipsy woman, Mike. How queer she was that day, how she warned me not to come here.'

'She's just a bit crazy, a bit off her head.'

'We've built on Gipsy's Acre,' said Ellie. 'We've done what she told us not to do.' Then she stamped her foot. 'I won't let them drive me away. I won't let *anyone* drive me away!'

'Nobody shall drive us away,' I said. 'We're going to be happy here.'

We said it like a challenge to fate.

CHAPTER 14

That's how our life began at Gipsy's Acre. We didn't find another name for the house. That first evening fixed Gipsy's Acre in our heads.

'We'll call it Gipsy's Acre,' said Ellie, 'just to show! A kind of challenge, don't you think? It's *our* Acre, and to hell with the gipsy's warning.'

She was her old gay self again the next day and soon we were busy getting ourselves settled in, and getting also to know the neighbourhood and the neighbours. Ellie and I walked down to the cottage where the gipsy woman lived. I felt it would be a good thing if we found her digging in her garden. The only time Ellie had seen her before was when she told our fortunes. If Ellie saw she was just an ordinary old woman – digging up potatoes – but we didn't see her. The cottage was shut up. I asked if she were dead but the neighbour I asked shook her head.

'She must have gone away,' she said. 'She goes away from time to time, you know. She's a gipsy really. That's why she can't stay in houses. She wanders away and comes back again.' She tapped her forehead. 'Not quite right up here.'

Presently she said, trying to mask curiosity, 'You've come from the new house up there, haven't you, the one on the top of the hill, that's just been built?'

'That's right,' I said, 'we moved in last night.'

'Wonderful-looking place it is,' she said. 'We've all been up to look at it while it was building. Makes a difference, doesn't it, seeing a house like that where all those gloomy trees used to be?' She said to Ellie rather shyly, 'You're an American lady, aren't you, so we heard?'

'Yes,' said Ellie, 'I'm American – or I was, but now I'm married to an Englishman so I'm an Englishwoman.'

'And you've come here to settle down and live, haven't you?' We said we had.

'Well, I hope you'll like it, I'm sure.' She sounded doubtful.

'Why shouldn't we?'

'Oh well, it's lonely up there, you know. People don't always like living in a lonely place among a lot of trees.'

'Gipsy's Acre,' said Ellie.

'Ah, you know the local name, do you? But the house that was there before was called The Towers. I don't know why. It hadn't any towers, at least not in my time.'

'I think The Towers is a silly name,' said Ellie. 'I think we'll go on calling it Gipsy's Acre.'

'We'll have to tell the post office if so,' I said, 'or we shan't get any letters.'

'No, I suppose we shan't.'

'Though when I come to think of it,' I said, 'would that matter, Ellie? Wouldn't it be much nicer if we *didn't* get any letters?'

'It might cause a lot of complications,' said Ellie. 'We shouldn't even get our bills.'

'That would be a splendid idea,' I said.

'No, it wouldn't,' said Ellie. 'Bailiffs would come in and camp there. Anyway,' she said, 'I wouldn't like not to get any letters. I'd want to hear from Greta.'

'Never mind Greta,' I said. 'Let's go on exploring.'

So we explored Kingston Bishop. It was a nice village, nice people in the shops. There was nothing sinister about the place.

Our domestic help didn't take to it much, but we soon arranged that hired cars should take them into the nearest seaside town or into Market Chadwell on their days out. They were not enthusiastic about the location of the house, but it was not superstition that worried them. I pointed out to Ellie nobody could say the house was haunted because it had been just built.

'No,' Ellie agreed, 'it's not the house. There's nothing wrong with the house. It's outside. It's that road where it curves round through the trees and that bit of rather gloomy wood where that woman stood and made me jump so that day.'

'Well, next year,' I said, 'we might cut down those trees and plant a lot of rhododendrons or something like that.'

We went on making plans.

Greta came and stayed with us for a weekend. She was enthusiastic about the house, and congratulated us on all our furnishings and pictures and colour schemes. She was very tactful. After the weekend she said she wouldn't disturb the honeymooners any longer, and anyway she'd got to get back to her job.

Ellie enjoyed showing her the house. I could see how fond Ellie was of her. I tried to behave very sensibly and pleasantly but I was glad when Greta went back to London, because her staying there had been a strain on me.

When we'd been there a couple of weeks we were accepted locally and made the acquaintance of God. He came one afternoon to call upon us. Ellie and I were arguing about where we'd have a flower border when our correct, to me slightly phoney-looking, manservant came out from the house to announce that Major Phillpot was in the drawing-room. It was then that I said in a whisper to Ellie: 'God!' Ellie asked me what I meant.

'Well, the locals treat him like that,' I said.

So we went in and there was Major Phillpot. He was just a pleasant, nondescript man of close on sixty. He was wearing country clothes, rather shabby, he had grey hair going a little thin on top and a short bristly moustache. He apologized for his wife not being able to come and call on us. She was something of an invalid, he said. He sat down and chatted with us. Nothing he said was remarkable or particularly interesting. He had the knack of making people feel at their ease. He touched quite lightly on a variety of subjects. He didn't ask any direct questions, but he

soon got it into his head where our particular interests lay. He
talked to me about racing and to Ellie about making a garden
and what things did well in this particular soil. He had been to
the States once or twice. He found out that though Ellie didn't
care much for race meetings, she was fond of riding. He told her
that if she was going to keep horses she could go up a particular
track through the pine woods and she would come out on a good
stretch of moor where she could have a gallop. Then we came
to the subject of our house and the stories about Gipsy's Acre.

'I see you know the local name,' he said, 'and all the local
superstitions, too, I expect.'

'Gipsies' warnings in profusion,' I said. 'Far too many of them.
Mostly old Mrs Lee.'

'Oh dear,' said Phillpot. 'Poor old Esther: she's been a nuisance,
has she?'

'Is she a bit dotty?' I asked.

'Not so much as she likes to make out. I feel more or less
responsible for her. I settled her in that cottage,' he said, 'not
that she's grateful for it. I'm fond of the old thing though she
can be a nuisance sometimes.'

'Fortune-telling?'

'No, not particularly. Why, has she told your fortune?'

'I don't know if you can call it a fortune,' said Ellie. 'It was
more a warning to us against coming here.'

'That seems rather odd to me.' Major Phillpot's rather bristly
eyebrows rose. 'She's usually got a honeyed tongue in fortunes.
Handsome stranger, marriage bells, six children and a heap of
good fortune and money in your hand, pretty lady.' He imitated
rather unexpectedly the gipsy whine of her voice. 'The gipsies
used to camp here a lot when I was a boy,' he said. 'I suppose
I got fond of them then, though they were a thieving lot, of
course. But I've always been attracted to them. As long as you
don't expect them to be law-abiding, they're all right. Many a
tin mug of gipsy stew I've had as a schoolboy. We felt the family
owed Mrs Lee something, she saved the life of a brother of mine
when he was a child. Fished him out of a pond when he'd gone
through the ice.'

I made a clumsy gesture and knocked a glass ashtray off a
table. It smashed into fragments.

I picked up the pieces and Major Phillpot helped me.

'I expect Mrs Lee's quite harmless really,' said Ellie. 'I was very foolish to have been so scared.'

'Scared, were you?' His eyebrows rose again. 'It was as bad as that, was it?'

'I don't wonder she was afraid,' I said quickly. 'It was almost more like a threat than a warning.'

'A threat!' He sounded incredulous.

'Well, it sounded that way to me. And then the first night we moved in here something else happened.'

I told him about the stone crashing through the window.

'I'm afraid there are a good many young hooligans about nowadays,' he said, 'though we haven't got many of them round here – not nearly as bad as some places. Still, it happens, I'm sorry to say.' He looked at Ellie. 'I'm very sorry you were frightened. It was a beastly thing to happen, your first night moving in.'

'Oh, I've got over it now,' said Ellie. 'It wasn't only that, it was – it was something else that happened not long afterwards.'

I told him about that too. We had come down one morning and we had found a dead bird skewered through with a knife and a small piece of paper with it which said in an illiterate scrawl, 'Get out of here if you know what's good for you.'

Phillpot looked really angry then. He said, 'You should have reported that to the police.'

'We didn't want to,' I said. 'After all, that would only have put whoever it is even more against us.'

'Well, that kind of thing has got to be stopped,' said Phillpot. Suddenly he became the magistrate. 'Otherwise, you know, people will go on with the thing. Think it's funny, I suppose. Only – only this sounds a bit more than fun. Nasty – malicious – It's not,' he said, rather as though he was talking to himself, 'it's not as though anyone round here could have a grudge against you, a grudge against either of you personally, I mean.'

'No,' I said, 'it couldn't be that because we're both strangers here.'

'I'll look into it,' Phillpot said.

He got up to go, looking round him as he did.

'You know,' he said, 'I like this house of yours. I didn't think I should. I'm a bit of an old square, you know, what used to be called old fogey. I like old houses and old buildings. I don't like all these matchbox factories that are going up all over the country. Big boxes. Like beehives. I like buildings with some ornament on them, some grace. But I like this house. It's plain and very modern, I suppose, but it's got shape and light. And when you look out from it you see things – well, in a different way from the way you've seen them before. It's interesting. Very interesting. Who designed it? An English architect or a foreigner?'

I told him about Santonix.

'Mm,' he said, 'I think I read about him somewhere. Would it have been in *House and Garden*?'

I said he was fairly well known.

'I'd like to meet him sometime, though I don't suppose I'd know what to say to him. I'm not artistic.'

Then he asked us to settle a day to come and have lunch with him and his wife.

'You can see how you like my house,' he said.

'It's an old house, I suppose?' I said.

'Built 1720. Nice period. The original house was Elizabethan. That was burnt down about 1700 and a new one built on the same spot.'

'You've always lived here then?' I said. I didn't mean him personally, of course, but he understood.

'Yes. We've been here since Elizabethan times. Sometimes prosperous, sometimes down and out, selling land when things have gone badly, buying it back when things went well. I'll be glad to show it to you both,' he said, and looking at Ellie he said with a smile, 'Americans like old houses, I know. *You're* the one who probably won't think much of it,' he said to me.

'I won't pretend I know much about old things,' I said.

He stumped off then. In his car there was a spaniel waiting for him. It was a battered old car with the paint rubbed off, but I was getting my values by now. I knew that in this part of the world he was still God all right, and he'd set the seal of his approval on us. I could see that. He liked Ellie. I was inclined to think that he'd liked me, too, although I'd noticed the appraising glances which he shot over me from time to time, as though he was making a quick snap judgment on something he hadn't come across before.

Ellie was putting splinters of glass carefully in the waste-paper basket when I came back into the drawing-room.

'I'm sorry it's broken,' she said regretfully. 'I liked it.'

'We can get another like it,' I said. 'It's modern.'

'I know! What startled you, Mike?'

I considered for a moment.

'Something Phillpot said. It reminded me of something that happened when I was a kid. A pal of mine at school and I played truant and went out skating on a local pond. Ice wouldn't bear us, silly little asses that we were. He went through and was drowned before anyone could get him out.'

'How horrible.'

'Yes. I'd forgotten all about it until Phillpot mentioned about his own brother.'

'I like him, Mike, don't you?'

'Yes, very much. I wonder what his wife is like.'

We went to lunch with the Phillpots early the following week. It was a white Georgian house, rather beautiful in its lines, though not particularly exciting. Inside it was shabby but comfortable. There were pictures of what I took to be ancestors on the walls of the long dining-room. Most of them were pretty bad, I thought, though they might have looked better if they had been cleaned. There was one of a fair-haired girl in pink satin that I rather took to. Major Phillpot smiled and said:

'You've picked one of our best. It's a Gainsborough, and a good one, though the subject of it caused a bit of trouble in her time. Strongly suspected of having poisoned her husband. May have been prejudice, because she was a foreigner. Gervase Phillpot picked her up abroad somewhere.'

A few other neighbours had been invited to meet us. Dr Shaw, an elderly man with a kindly but tired manner. He had to rush away before we had finished our meal. There was the Vicar who was young and earnest, and a middle-aged woman with a bullying voice who bred corgis. And there was a tall handsome dark girl called Claudia Hardcastle who seemed to live for horses, though hampered by having an allergy which gave her violent hay fever.

She and Ellie got on together rather well. Ellie adored riding and she too was troubled by an allergy.

'In the States it's mostly ragwort gives it to me,' she said – 'but horses too, sometimes. It doesn't trouble me much nowadays because they have such wonderful things that doctors can give you for different kinds of allergies. I'll give you some of my capsules. They're bright orange. And if you remember to take one before you start out you don't as much as sneeze once.'

Claudia Hardcastle said that would be wonderful.

'Camels do it to me worse than horses,' she said. 'I was in Egypt last year – and the tears just streamed down my face all the way round the Pyramids.'

Ellie said some people got it with cats.

'And pillows.' They went on talking about allergies.

I sat next to Mrs Phillpot who was tall and willowy and talked exclusively about her health in the intervals of eating a hearty meal. She gave me a full account of all her various ailments and of how puzzled many eminent members of the medical profession had been by her case. Occasionally she made a social diversion and asked me what I *did*. I parried that one, and she made half-hearted efforts to find out whom I *knew*. I could have answered truthfully 'Nobody,' but I thought it would be well to refrain – especially as she wasn't a real snob and didn't really want to know. Mrs Corgi, whose proper name I hadn't caught, was much more thorough in her queries but I diverted her to the general iniquity and ignorance of vets! It was all quite pleasant and peaceful, if rather dull.

Later, as we were making a rather desultory tour of the garden, Claudia Hardcastle joined me.

She said, rather abruptly, 'I've heard about you – from my brother.'

I looked surprised. I couldn't imagine it to be possible that I knew a brother of Claudia Hardcastle's.

'Are you sure?' I said.

She seemed amused.

'As a matter of fact, he built your house.'

'Do you mean *Santonix* is your brother?'

'Half-brother. I don't know him very well. We rarely meet.'

'He's wonderful,' I said.

'Some people think so, I know.'

'Don't you?'

'I'm never sure. There are two sides to him. At one time he was going right down the hill . . . People wouldn't have anything to do with him. And then – he seemed to change. He began to succeed in his profession in the most extraordinary way. It was as though he was –' she paused for a word – 'dedicated.'

'I think he is – just that.'

Then I asked her if she had seen our house.

'No – not since it was finished.'

I told her she must come and see it.

'I shan't like it, I warn you. I don't like modern houses. Queen Anne is my favourite period.'

She said she was going to put Ellie up for the golf club. And they were going to ride together. Ellie was going to buy a horse, perhaps more than one. She and Ellie seemed to have made friends.

When Phillpot was showing me his stables he said a word or two about Claudia.

'Good rider to hounds,' he said. 'Pity's she's mucked up her life.'

'Has she?'

'Married a rich man, years older than herself. An American. Name of Lloyd. It didn't take. Came apart almost at once. She went back to her own name. Don't think she'll ever marry again. She's anti man. Pity.'

When we were driving home, Ellie said: 'Dull – but nice. Nice people. We're going to be very happy here, aren't we, Mike?'

I said: 'Yes, we are.' And took my hand from the steering wheel and laid it over hers.

When we got back, I dropped Ellie at the house, and put away the car in the garage.

As I walked back to the house, I heard a faint twanging of Ellie's guitar. She had a rather beautiful old Spanish guitar that must have been worth a lot of money. She used to sing to it in a soft low crooning voice. Very pleasant to hear. I didn't know what most of the songs were. American spirituals partly, I think, and some old Irish and Scottish ballads – sweet and rather sad. They weren't pop music or anything of that kind. Perhaps they were folk songs.

I went round by the terrace and paused by the window before going in.

Ellie was singing one of my favourites. I don't know what it was called. She was crooning the words softly to herself, bending her head down over the guitar and gently plucking the strings. It had a sweet-sad haunting little tune.

> Man was made for Joy and Woe
> And when this we rightly know
> Thro' the World we safely go . . .
>
> Every Night and every Morn
> Some to Misery are born.
> Every Morn and every Night
> Some are born to Sweet Delight,
> Some are born to Sweet Delight,
> Some are born to Endless Night . . .

She looked up and saw me.

'Why are you looking at me like that, Mike?'

'Like what?'

'You're looking at me as though you loved me . . .'

'Of course I love you. How else should I be looking at you?'

'But what were you thinking just then?'

I answered slowly and truthfully: 'I was thinking of you as I saw you first – standing by a dark fir tree.' Yes, I'd been remembering that first moment of seeing Ellie, the surprise of it and the excitement . . .

Ellie smiled at me and sang softly:

> 'Every Morn and every Night
> Some are born to Sweet Delight,
> Some are born to Sweet Delight,
> Some are born to Endless Night.'

One doesn't recognize in one's life the really important moments – not until it's too late.

That day when we'd been to lunch with the Phillpots and came back so happily to our home was such a moment. But I didn't know then – not until afterwards.

I said: 'Sing the song about the Fly.' And she changed to a gay little dance tune and sang:

'Little Fly,
Thy Summer's play
My thoughtless hand
Has brushed away.

Am not I
A fly like thee?
Or art not thou
A man like me?

For I dance
And drink, and sing
Till some blind hand
Shall brush my wing.

If thought is life
And strength and breath
And the want
Of thought is death;

Then am I
A happy fly
If I live
Or if I die.'

Oh, Ellie – Ellie . . .

CHAPTER 15

It's astonishing in this world how things don't turn out at all the way you expect them to!

We'd moved into our house and were living there and we'd got away from everyone just the way I'd meant and planned. Only of course we *hadn't* got away from everyone. Things crowded back upon us across the ocean and in other ways.

First of all there was Ellie's blasted stepmother. She sent letters and cables and asked Ellie to go and see estate agents. She'd been so fascinated, she said, by our house that she really must have a house of her own in England. She said she'd love to spend a couple of months every year in England. And hard on her last cable she arrived and had to be taken round the neighbourhood with lots of orders to view. In the end she more or less settled on a house. A house about fifteen miles away from us. We didn't want her there, we hated the idea – but we couldn't tell her so. Or rather, what I really mean is even if we *had* told her so, it wouldn't have stopped her taking it if she'd wanted to. We couldn't order her *not* to come there. It was the last thing Ellie wanted. I knew that. However, while she was still awaiting a surveyor's report, some cables arrived.

Uncle Frank, it seemed, had got himself into a jam of some kind. Something crooked and fraudulent, I gathered, which would mean a big sum of money to get him out. More cables passed to and fro between Mr Lippincott and Ellie. And then there turned out to be some trouble between Stanford Lloyd and Lippincott. There was a row about some of Ellie's investments. I had felt, in my ignorance and credulity, that people who were in America were a long way away. I'd never realized that Ellie's relations and business connections thought nothing of taking a plane over to England for twenty-four hours and then flying back again. First Stanford Lloyd flew over and back again. Then Andrew Lippincott flew over.

Ellie had to go up to London and meet them. I hadn't got the hang of these financial things. I think everybody was being fairly careful in what they said. But it was something to do with the settling up of the trusts on Ellie, and a kind of sinister suggestion that either Mr Lippincott had delayed the matter or it was Stanford Lloyd who was holding up the accounting.

In the lull between these worries Ellie and I discovered our Folly. We hadn't really explored all our property yet (only the part just round the house). We used to follow up tracks through the woods and see where they led. One day we followed a sort of path that had been so overgrown that you couldn't really see where it was at first. But we tracked it out and in the end it came out at what Ellie said was a Folly. A sort of little white ridiculous temple-looking place. It was in fairly good condition so we cleared it up and had it painted and we put a table, and a few chairs in it, and a divan and a corner cupboard in which we put china and glasses, and some bottles. It was fun really. Ellie said we'd have the path cleared and made easier to climb and I said no, it would be more fun if no one knew where it was except us. Ellie thought that was a romantic idea.

'We certainly won't let Cora know,' I said and Ellie agreed.

It was when we were coming down from there, not the first time but later, after Cora had gone away and we were hoping to be peaceful again, that Ellie, who was skipping along ahead of me, suddenly tripped over the root of a tree and fell and sprained her ankle.

Dr Shaw came and said she'd taken a nasty sprain but that she'd be able to get about again all right in perhaps a week. Ellie sent for Greta then. I couldn't object. There was no one really to look after her properly, no woman I mean. The servants we had were pretty useless and anyway Ellie wanted Greta. So Greta came.

She came and she was a great blessing of course to Ellie. And to me as far as that went. She arranged things and kept the household working properly. Our servants gave notice about now. They said it was too lonely – but really I think Cora had upset them. Greta put in advertisements and got another couple almost at once. She looked after Ellie's ankle, amused her, fetched things for her that she knew she liked, the kind of books and fruit and things like that – things I knew nothing about. And they seemed frightfully happy together. Ellie was certainly delighted to see Greta. And somehow or other Greta just didn't go away again . . . She stopped on. Ellie said to me:

'You don't mind, do you, if Greta stays on for a bit?'

I said, 'Oh no. No, of course not.'

'It's such a comfort having her,' said Ellie. 'You see, there are so many sort of *female* things we can do together. One's awfully lonely without another woman about.'

Every day I noticed Greta was taking a bit more upon herself, giving orders, queening it over things. I pretended I liked having Greta there, but one day when Ellie was lying with her foot up inside the drawing-room and Greta and I were out on the terrace, we suddenly got into a row together. I can't remember the exact words that started it. Something that Greta said, it annoyed me and I answered sharply back. And then we went on, hammer and tongs. Our voices rose. She let me have it, saying all the vicious, unkind things she could think of, and I pretty well gave her as good as I was getting. Told her she was a bossy, interfering female, that she'd far too much influence over Ellie, that I wasn't going to stand having Ellie bossed about the whole time. We shouted at each other and then suddenly Ellie came hobbling out on the terrace looking from one to the other of us, and I said:

'Darling, I'm sorry. I'm terribly sorry.'

I went back into the house and settled Ellie on the sofa again. She said:

'I didn't realize. I didn't realize a bit that you – that you really hated having Greta here.'

I soothed her and calmed her and said she mustn't take any notice, that I just lost my temper, that I was rather quarrelsome sometimes. I said all that was the matter was that I thought Greta was just a bit bossy. Perhaps that was natural enough because she'd been used to being so. And in the end I said I really liked Greta very much, it was just that I'd lost my temper because I'd been upset and worried. So it ended that I practically begged Greta to stay on.

It was quite a scene we'd had. I think quite a good many other people in the house had heard it as well. Our new manservant and his wife certainly did. When I get angry I do shout. I dare say I really overdid it a bit. I'm like that.

Greta seemed to make a point of worrying a great deal about Ellie's health, saying she oughtn't to do this, or that.

'She isn't really very strong, you know,' she said to me.

'There's nothing wrong with Ellie,' I said, 'she's always perfectly well.'

'No, she isn't, Mike. She's delicate.'

When Dr Shaw next came to have a look at Ellie's ankle and to tell her, by the way, that it was quite all right again, just bind it up if she was going to walk over rough ground, I said to him, I suppose in rather the foolish way that men do:

'She isn't delicate or anything, is she, Dr Shaw?'

'Who says she's delicate?' Dr Shaw was the kind of practitioner that is fairly rare nowadays and was, indeed, known locally as 'Leave-it-to-Nature Shaw'.

'Nothing wrong with her as far as I can see,' he said. 'Anyone can sprain an ankle.'

'I didn't mean her ankle. I wondered if she had a weak heart or anything like that.'

He looked at me through the top of his spectacles. 'Don't start imagining things, young man. What put it into your head? You're not the type that worries usually about women's ailments.'

'It was only what Miss Andersen said.'

'Ah. Miss Andersen. What does she know about it? Not medically qualified, is she?'

'Oh no,' I said.

'Your wife's a woman of great wealth,' he said, 'according to local gossip anyway. Of course some people just imagine all Americans are rich.'

'She is wealthy,' I said.

'Well, you must remember this. Rich women get the worst of it in many ways. Some doctor or other is always giving them powders and pills, stimulants or pep pills, or tranquillizers, things that on the whole they'd be better without. Now the village women are much healthier because nobody worries about their health in the same way.'

'She does take some capsules or something,' I said.

'I'll give her a check-up if you like. Might as well find out what muck she's been given. I can tell you, before now I've said to people "chuck the whole lot in the wastepaper basket".'

He spoke to Greta before he left. He said:

'Mr Rogers asked me to give Mrs Rogers a general check-up. I can't find anything much wrong with her. I think more exercise in the open air might do her good. What does she take in the way of medicines?'

'She has some tablets that she takes when she's tired, and some that she takes for sleeping if she wants them.'

She and Dr Shaw went and had a look at Ellie's prescriptions. Ellie was smiling a little.

'I don't take all these things, Dr Shaw,' she said. 'Only the allergy capsules.'

Shaw took a look at the capsules, read the prescription and said there was no harm in that, and passed on to a prescription for sleeping pills.

'Any trouble with sleeping?'

'Not living in the country. I don't think I've taken a single sleeping pill since I've been here.'

'Well, that's a good thing.' He patted her on the shoulder. 'There's nothing wrong with you, my dear. Inclined to worry a bit sometimes, I should say. That's all. These capsules are mild enough. Lots of people take them nowadays and they don't do them any harm. Go on with them but leave the sleeping pills alone.'

'I don't know why I worried,' I said to Ellie apologetically. 'I suppose it was Greta.'

'Oh,' said Ellie and laughed, 'Greta fusses about me. She never takes any remedies herself.' She said, 'We'll have a turn-out, Mike, and throw most of these things away.'

Ellie was getting on very friendly terms with most of our neighbours now. Claudia Hardcastle came over quite often and she and Ellie went riding together occasionally. I didn't ride, I'd dealt with cars and mechanical things all my life. I didn't know the first thing about a horse in spite of mucking out stables in Ireland for a week or two once, but I thought to myself that some time or other when we were in London I'd go to a posh riding stable and learn how to ride properly. I didn't want to start down here. People would laugh at me very likely. I thought riding was perhaps good for Ellie. She seemed to enjoy it.

Greta encouraged her to ride, although Greta herself also knew nothing about horses.

Ellie and Claudia went together to a sale and on Claudia's advice Ellie bought herself a horse, a chestnut called Conquer. I urged Ellie to be careful when she went out riding by herself but she laughed at me.

'I've ridden since I was three years old,' she said.

So she usually went for a ride about two or three times a week. Greta used to drive the car and go into Market Chadwell to do the shopping.

One day Greta said at lunchtime: 'You and your gipsies! There was a terrible-looking old woman this morning. She stood in the middle of the road. I might have run over her. Just stood smack in front of the car. I had to pull up. Coming up the hill too.'

'Why, what did she want?'

Ellie was listening to us both but she didn't say anything. I thought, though, that she looked rather worried.

'Damn' cheek, she threatened me,' said Greta.

'Threatened you?' I said sharply.

'Well, she told me to get out of here. She said: "This is gipsy land here. Go back. Go back the lot of you. Go back to where you came from if you wish to be safe." And she lifted up her fist and shook it at me. She said: "If I curse you," she said, "there'll be no good luck for you ever again. Buying our land and raising houses on our land. We don't want houses where tent dwellers should be."'

Greta said a lot more. Ellie said to me afterwards, frowning a little:

'It all sounded most improbable, didn't you think so, Mike?'

'I think Greta was exaggerating a bit,' I said.

'It didn't sound right somehow,' said Ellie. 'I wonder if Greta was making some of it up.'

I considered. 'Why would she want to make things up?' Then I asked sharply, '*You* haven't seen our Esther lately, have you? Not when you are out riding?'

'The gipsy woman? No.'

'You don't sound quite sure, Ellie,' I said.

'I think I've caught glimpses of her,' said Ellie. 'You know, standing among the trees peering out but never near enough for me to be sure.'

But Ellie came back from a ride one day, white and shaking. The old woman had come out from in between the trees. Ellie had reined up and stopped to speak to her. She said the old woman was shaking her fist and muttering under her breath. Ellie said, 'This time I was angry, I said to her:

"What do you want here? This land doesn't belong to you. It's our land and our house."'

The old woman had said then:

'It'll never be your land and it'll never belong to you. I warned you once and I've warned you twice. I shan't warn you again. It won't be long now – I can tell you that. It's Death I see. There behind your left shoulder. It's Death standing by you and it's Death will have you. That horse you're riding has got one white foot. Don't you know that it's bad luck to ride a horse with one white foot? It's Death I see and the grand house you've built falling in ruins!'

'This has got to be stopped,' I said angrily.

Ellie didn't laugh it off this time. Both she and Greta looked upset. I went straight down to the village. I went first to Mrs Lee's cottage. I hesitated for a moment but there was no light there and I went on to the police station. I knew the Sergeant in Charge, Sergeant Keene, a square, sensible man. He listened to me, then he said:

'I'm sorry you've had this trouble. She's a very old woman and she may be getting tiresome. We've never had much real trouble with her up to now. I'll speak to her and tell her to lay off.'

'If you would,' I said.

He hesitated a minute and then said:

'I don't like to suggest things – but as far as you know, Mr Rogers, is there anyone around here who might – perhaps for some trivial cause – have it in for you or your wife?'

'I should think it most unlikely. Why?'

'Old Mrs Lee has been flush of money lately – I don't know where it's coming from –'

'What are you suggesting?'

'It could be someone is paying her – someone who wants you out of here. There was an incident – a good many years ago. She took money from someone in the village – to frighten a neighbour away. Doing this same sort of stuff – threats – warnings – evil eye business – Village people are superstitious. You'd be surprised at the number of villages in England that have got their private witch, so to speak. She got a warning then and so far as I know she's never tried it on since – but it could be like that. She's fond of money – they'll do a lot for money –'

But I couldn't accept that idea. I pointed out to Keene that we were complete strangers here. 'We've not had time to make enemies,' I said.

I walked back to the house worried and perplexed. As I turned the corner of the terrace, I heard the faint sound of Ellie's guitar, and a tall figure, who had been standing by the window looking in, wheeled round and came towards me. For a moment I thought it was a gipsy, then I relaxed as I recognized Santonix.

'Oh,' I said with a slight gasp, 'it's you. Where have you sprung from? We've not heard from you for ages.'

He didn't answer me directly. He just caught my arm and drew me away from the window.

'So she's here!' he said. 'I'm not surprised. I thought she'd come sooner or later. Why did you let her? She's dangerous. You ought to know that.'

'You mean Ellie?'

'No, no, not Ellie. The other one! What's her name? Greta?'

I stared at him.

'Do you know what Greta's like or don't you? She's *come*, hasn't she? Taken possession! You won't get rid of her now. She's come to *stay*.'

'Ellie sprained her ankle,' I said. 'Greta came to look after her. She's – I suppose she's going soon.'

'You don't know anything of the kind. She always meant to come. I knew that. I took her measure when she came down while the house was building.'

'Ellie seems to want her,' I muttered.

'Oh yes, she's been with Ellie some time, hasn't she? She knows how to manage Ellie.'

That was what Lippincott had said. I'd seen for myself lately how true it was.

'Do you want her here, Mike?'

'I can't throw her out of the house,' I said irritably. 'She's Ellie's old friend. Her best friend. What the hell can I do about it?'

'No,' said Santonix, 'I suppose you can't do anything, can you?'

He looked at me. It was a very strange glance. Santonix was a strange man. You never knew what his words really meant.

'Do you know where you're going, Mike?' he said. 'Have you any idea? Sometimes I don't think you know anything at all.'

'Of course I know,' I said. 'I'm doing what I want to. I'm going where I wanted.'

'Are you? I wonder. I wonder if you really know what you want yourself. I'm afraid for you with Greta. She's stronger than you are, you know.'

'I don't see how you make that out. It isn't a question of strength.'

'Isn't it? I think it is. She's the strong kind, the kind that always gets her way. You didn't mean to have her here. That's what you said. But here she is, and I've been watching them. She and Ellie sitting together, at home together, chattering and settled in. What are *you*, Mike? The outsider? Or aren't you an outsider?'

'You're crazy, the things you say. What do you mean – I'm an outsider? I'm Ellie's husband, aren't I?'

'*Are* you Ellie's husband or is Ellie *your* wife?'

'You're daft,' I said. 'What's the difference?'

He sighed. Suddenly, his shoulders sagged as though vigour went out of him.

'I can't reach you,' said Santonix. 'I can't make you hear me. I can't make you understand. Sometimes I think you do understand, sometimes I think you don't know anything at all about yourself or anyone else.'

'Look here,' I said, 'I'll take so much from you, Santonix. You're a wonderful architect – but –'

His face changed in the queer way it had.

'Yes,' he said, 'I'm a good architect. This house is the best thing I have done. I'm as near as possible satisfied with it. You wanted a house like this. And Ellie wanted a house like this, too, to live in with you. She's got it and you've got it. Send that other woman away, Mike, before it's too late.'

'How can I upset Ellie?'

'That woman's got you where she wants you,' said Santonix.

'Look here,' I said, 'I don't like Greta. She gets on my nerves. The other day I even had a frightful row with her. But none of it's as simple as you think.'

'No, it won't be simple with her.'

'Whoever called this place Gipsy's Acre and said it had a curse on it may have had something,' I said angrily. 'We've got gipsies who jump out from behind trees and shake fists at us and warn us that if we don't get out of here, some awful fate will happen to us. *This place that ought to be good and beautiful.*'

They were queer words to say, those last ones. I said them as though it was somebody else saying them.

'Yes, it should be like that,' said Santonix. 'It should be. But it can't be, can it, if there is something evil possessing it?'

'You don't believe, surely, in –'

'There are many queer things I believe . . . I know something about evil. Don't you realize, haven't you often felt, that *I* am partly evil myself? Always have been. That's why I know when it's near me, although I don't always know exactly where it is . . . *I want the house I built purged of evil.* You understand that?' His tone was menacing. 'You understand that? It matters to me.'

Then his whole manner changed.

'Come on,' he said, 'don't let's talk a lot of nonsense. Let's come in and see Ellie.'

So we went in through the window and Ellie greeted Santonix with enormous pleasure.

Santonix showed all his normal manner that evening. There were no more histrionics, he was his own self, charming, light-hearted. He talked mostly to Greta, giving her as it were the special benefit of his charm. And he had a lot of charm. Anyone would have sworn that he was impressed by her, that he liked her, that he was anxious to please her. It made me feel that Santonix was really a dangerous man, there was a great deal more to him than I had ever glimpsed.

Greta always responded to admiration. She showed herself at her best. She could on occasion dim her beauty or else reveal it and tonight she looked as beautiful as I'd ever seen her. Smiling at Santonix, listening to him as though spellbound. I wondered what lay behind his manner. You never knew with Santonix. Ellie said she hoped he was staying for several days but he shook his head. He had to leave on the following day, he said.

'Are you building something now, are you busy?'

He said no, he'd just come out of hospital.

'They've patched me up once more,' he said, 'but it's probably for the last time.'

'Patched you up? What do they do to you?'

'Drain the bad blood out of my body and put some good, fresh red blood in,' he said.

'Oh.' Ellie gave a little shudder.

'Don't worry,' said Santonix, 'it will never happen to you.'

'But why has it got to happen to you?' said Ellie. 'It's cruel.'

'Not cruel, no,' said Santonix. 'I heard what you were singing just now.

'Man was made for Joy and Woe
And when this we rightly know
Thro' the World we safely go.

'I go safely because I know why I'm here. And for you, Ellie:

'Every Morn and every Night
Some are born to Sweet Delight.

'That's *you.*'
    'I wish I could feel safe,' said Ellie.
    'Don't you feel safe?'
    'I don't like to be threatened,' said Ellie. 'I don't like anyone to put a curse on me.'
    'You're talking about your gipsy?'
    'Yes.'
    'Forget it,' said Santonix. 'Forget it for tonight. Let's be happy. Ellie – your health – Long life to you – and a quick and merciful end to me – and good luck to Mike here –' He stopped, his glass raised towards Greta.
    'Yes?' said Greta. 'And to me?'
    'And to you, what's coming to you! Success, perhaps?' he added, half quizzically with an ironic question in his tone.
    He went away next morning early.
    'What a strange man he is,' Ellie said. 'I've never understood him.'
    'I never understand half of what he says,' I answered.
    'He knows things,' said Ellie thoughtfully.
    'You mean he knows the future?'
    'No,' said Ellie, 'I didn't mean that. He knows people. I said it to you once before. He knows people better than they know themselves. Sometimes he hates them because of that, and sometimes he's sorry for them. He's not sorry for me, though,' she added meditatively.
    'Why should he be?' I demanded.
    'Oh, because –' said Ellie.

CHAPTER 16

It was the next day in the afternoon that as I was walking rather rapidly in the darkest part of the wood where the shade of the pine trees was more menacing than anywhere else, I saw the figure of a tall woman standing in the drive. I took a quick impulsive step off the path. I'd taken it for granted that she was our gipsy but I stopped in sudden recoil when I saw who it actually was. It was my mother. She stood there tall and grim and grey-haired.

'Good Lord,' I said, 'you startled me, Mum. What are you doing here? Come to see us? We've asked you often enough, haven't we?'

We hadn't actually. I'd extended one rather lukewarm invitation, that was all. I'd put it, too, in a way which made it pretty sure that my mother wouldn't accept. I didn't want her here. I'd never wanted her here.

'You're right,' she said. 'I've come to see you at last. To see all's well with you. So this is the grand house you've built, and it is a grand house,' she said, looking over my shoulder.

I thought I detected in her voice the disapproving acidity that I'd expected to find.

'Too grand for the likes of me, eh?' I said.

'I didn't say that, lad.'

'But you thought it.'

'It wasn't what you were born to, and no good comes from getting out of your station in life.'

'Nobody'd ever get anywhere if they listened to you.'

'Aye, I know that's what you say and think, but I don't know what good ambition's ever done to anybody. It's the kind of thing that turns to dead-sea fruit in your mouth.'

'Ah, for God's sake don't croak,' I said. 'Come on. Come along up to see our grand house for yourself and turn up your nose at it. And come and see my grand wife, too, and turn up your nose at her if you dare.'

'Your wife? I've seen her already.'

'What do you mean, you've seen her already?' I demanded.

'So she didn't tell you, eh?'

'What?' I demanded.

'That she came to see me.'

'She came to see you?' I asked, dumbfounded.

'Yes. There she was one day standing outside the door, ringing the bell and looking a little scared. She's a pretty lass and a sweet one for all the fine clothes she had on. She said, "You're Mike's mother, aren't you?" and I said, "Yes, and who are you?" and she said, "I'm his wife." She said, "I had to come to see you. It didn't seem right that I shouldn't know Mike's mother . . ." And I said, "I bet *he* didn't want you to" and she hesitated, and I said: "You don't need to mind telling me that. I know my boy and I know what he'd want or not want." She said, "You think – perhaps he's ashamed of you because he and you are poor and I'm rich, but it isn't like that at all. That isn't like him at all. It isn't, really it isn't." I said again, "You don't need to tell me, lass. I know what faults my boy has. That's not one of his faults. He's not ashamed of his mother and he's not ashamed of his beginnings.

'"He's not ashamed of me," I said to her. "He's *afraid* of me if anything. I know too much about him, you see." And that seemed to amuse her. She said, "I expect mothers always feel like that – that they know all about their sons. And I expect sons always feel embarrassed just because of that!"

'I said in a way that might be true. When you're young, you're always putting on an act to the world. I mind myself, when I was a child in my auntie's house. On the wall over my bed there was a great big eye in a gilt frame. It said "Thou God seest me." Gave me the creeps it did all up my spine before I went to sleep.'

'Ellie should have told me she'd been to see you,' I said. 'I don't see why she should keep it such a secret. She should have told me.'

I was angry. I was very angry. I'd had no idea that Ellie would keep secrets like that from me.

'She was a little scared of what she'd done, maybe, but she'd no call to be frightened of you, my boy.'

'Come on,' I said, 'come on and see our house.'

I don't know whether she liked our house or not. I think not. She looked round the rooms and raised her eyebrows and then she went into the terrace room. Ellie and Greta were sitting there. They'd just come in from outside and Greta had a scarlet wool cloak half over her shoulders. My mother looked at them both. She just stood there for a moment as though rooted to the spot. Ellie jumped up and came forward and across the room.

'Oh, it's Mrs Rogers,' she said, then turning to Greta, she said, 'It's Mike's mother come to see our house and us. Isn't that nice? This is my friend Greta Andersen.'

And she held out both her hands and took Mum's and Mum looked hard at her and then looked over her shoulder at Greta very hard.

'I see,' she said to herself, 'I see.'

'What do you see?' asked Ellie.

'I wondered,' said Mum. 'I wondered what it would all be like here.' She looked round her. 'Yes, it's a fine house. Fine curtains and fine chairs and fine pictures.'

'You must have some tea,' said Ellie.

'You look as if you've finished tea.'

'Tea's a thing that need never be finished,' said Ellie, then she said to Greta, 'I won't ring the bell. Greta, will you go out to the kitchen and make a fresh pot of tea?'

'Of course, darling,' said Greta and went out of the room looking over her shoulder once in a sharp, almost scared way at my mother.

My mother sat down.

'Where's your luggage?' said Ellie. 'Have you come to stay? I hope you have.'

'No, lass, I won't stay. I'm going back by train in half an hour's time. I just wanted to look in on you.' Then she added rather quickly, probably because she wished to get it out before Greta came back, 'Now don't worry yourself, love, I told him how you came to see me and paid me a visit.'

'I'm sorry, Mike, that I didn't tell you,' said Ellie firmly, 'only I thought perhaps I'd better not.'

'She came out of the kindness of her heart, she did,' said my mother. 'She's a good girl you've married, Mike, and a pretty one. Yes, a very pretty one.' Then she added half audibly, 'I am sorry.'

'Sorry,' said Ellie, faintly puzzled.

'Sorry for thinking the things I did,' said my mother and added with a slight air of strain, 'Well, as you say, mothers are like that.

Always inclined to be suspicious of daughters-in-law. But when I saw you, I knew he'd been lucky. It seemed too good to be true to me, that it did.'

'What impertinence,' I said, but I smiled at her as I said it. 'I always had excellent taste.'

'You've always had expensive taste, that's what you mean,' said my mother and looked at the brocade curtains.

'I'm not really the worse for being an expensive taste,' said Ellie, smiling at her.

'You make him save a bit of money from time to time,' said Mum, 'it'll be good for his character.'

'I refuse to have my character improved,' I said. 'The advantage of taking a wife is that the wife thinks everything you do is perfect. Isn't that so, Ellie?'

Ellie was looking happy again now. She laughed and said:

'You're above yourself, Mike! The conceit of you.'

Greta came back then with the teapot. We'd been a little ill at ease and we were just getting over it. Somehow when Greta came back the strain came out again. My mother resisted all endeavours on Ellie's part to make her stay over and Ellie didn't insist after a short while. She and I walked down together with my mother along the winding drive through the trees and to the gateway.

'What do you call it?' my mother asked abruptly.

Ellie said, 'Gipsy's Acre.'

'Ah,' said my mother, 'yes you've got gipsies around here, haven't you?'

'How did you know that?' I asked.

'I saw one as I came up. She looked at me queer, she did.'

'She's all right really,' I said, 'a little half-baked, that's all.'

'Why do you say she's half-baked? She'd a funny look to her when she looked at me. She's got a grievance against you of some kind?'

'I don't think it's real,' said Ellie. 'I think she's imagined it all. That we've done her out of her land or something like that.'

'I expect she wants money,' said my mother. 'Gipsies are like that. Make a big song and dance sometimes of how they've been done down one way or another. But they soon stop when they get some money in their itching palms.'

'You don't like gipsies,' said Ellie.

'They're a thieving lot. They don't work steady and they don't keep their hands off what doesn't belong to them.'

'Oh well,' Ellie said, 'we – we – don't worry any more now.'

My mother said goodbye and then added, 'Who's the young lady that lives with you?'

Ellie explained how Greta had been with her for three years before she married and how but for Greta she would have had a miserable life.

'Greta's done everything to help us. She's a wonderful person,' said Ellie. 'I wouldn't know how – how to get on without her.'

'She's living with you or on a visit?'

'Oh well,' said Ellie. She avoided the question. 'She – she's living with us at present because I sprained my ankle and had to have someone to look after me. But I'm all right again now.'

'Married people do best alone together when they're starting,' my mother said.

We stood by the gate watching my mother march away.

'She's got a very strong personality,' said Ellie thoughtfully.

I was angry with Ellie, really very angry because she'd gone and found out my mother and visited her without telling me. But when she turned and stood looking at me with one eyebrow raised a little and the funny half-timid, half-satisfied little-girl smile on her face, I couldn't help relenting.

'What a deceitful little thing you are,' I said.

'Well,' said Ellie, 'I've had to be sometimes, you see.'

'That's like a Shakespeare play I once saw. They did it at a school I was at.' I quoted self-consciously, '"She has deceiv'd her father and may thee."'

'What did you play – Othello?'

'No,' I said, 'I played the girl's father. That's why I remember that speech, I suppose. It's practically the only thing I had to say.'

'"She has deceiv'd her father and may thee,"' said Ellie thoughtfully. 'I didn't even deceive my father as far as I know. Perhaps I would have later.'

'I don't suppose he would have taken very kindly to your marrying me,' I said, 'any more than your stepmother did.'

'No,' said Ellie, 'I don't suppose he would. He was pretty conventional I think.' Then she gave that funny little-girl smile again. 'So I suppose I'd have had to be like Desdemona and deceived my father and run away with you.'

'Why did you want to see my mother so much, Ellie?' I asked curiously.

'It's not so much I wanted to see her,' said Ellie, 'but I felt terribly bad not doing anything about it. You haven't mentioned your mother very often but I did gather that she's always done everything she could for you. Come to the rescue about things and worked very hard to get you extra schooling and things like that. And I thought it seemed so mean and purse-proud of me not to go near her.'

'Well, it wouldn't have been your fault,' I said, 'it would have been mine.'

'Yes,' said Ellie. 'I can understand that perhaps you didn't want me to go and see her.'

'You think I've got an inferiority complex about my mother? That's not true at all, Ellie, I assure you it isn't. It wasn't that.'

'No,' said Ellie thoughtfully, 'I know that now. It was because you didn't want her to do a lot of mother stuff.'

'Mother stuff?' I queried.

'Well,' said Ellie, 'I can see that she's the kind of person who would know quite well what other people ought to do. I mean, she'd want you to go in for certain kinds of jobs.'

'Quite right,' I said. 'Steady jobs. Settling down.'

'It wouldn't have mattered very much now,' said Ellie. 'I dare say it was very good advice. But it wouldn't have been the right advice ever for *you*, Mike. You're not a settler down. You don't want to be steady. You want to go and see things and do things – be on top of the world.'

'I want to stay here in this house with you,' I said.

'For a while, perhaps . . . And I think – I think you'll always want to come back here. And so shall I. I think we shall come here every year and I think we shall be happier here than anywhere else. But you'll want to go places too. You'll want to travel and see things and buy things. Perhaps think up new plans for doing the garden here. Perhaps we'll go and look at Italian gardens, Japanese gardens, landscape gardens of all kinds.'

'You make life seem very exciting, Ellie,' I said. 'I'm sorry I was cross.'

'Oh, I don't mind your being cross,' said Ellie. 'I'm not afraid of you.' Then she added, with a frown: 'Your mother didn't like Greta.'

'A lot of people don't like Greta,' I said.

'Including you.'

'Now look here, Ellie, you're always saying that. It's not true. I was just a bit jealous of her at first, that was all. We get on very well now.' And I added, 'I think perhaps she makes people get rather on the defensive.'

'Mr Lippincott doesn't like her either, does he? He thinks she's got too much influence over me,' said Ellie.

'Has she?'

'I wonder why you should ask that. Yes, I think perhaps she has. It's only natural, she's rather a dominant personality and I had to have someone I could trust in and rely on. Someone who'd stand up for me.'

'And see you got your own way?' I asked her, laughing.

We went into the house arm in arm. For some reason it seemed dark that afternoon. I suppose because the sun had just left the terrace and left a feeling of darkness behind it. Ellie said:

'What's the matter, Mike?'

'I don't know,' I said. 'Just suddenly I felt as though someone were walking over my grave.'

'A goose is walking over your grave. That's the real saying, isn't it?' said Ellie.

Greta wasn't about anywhere. The servants said she'd gone out for a walk.

Now that my mother knew all about my marriage and had seen Ellie, I did what I had really wanted to do for some time. I sent her a large cheque. I told her to move into a better house and to buy herself any additional furniture she wanted. Things like that. I had doubts of course as to whether she would accept it or not. It wasn't money that I'd worked for and I couldn't honestly pretend it was. As I expected, she sent the cheque back torn in two with a scrawled note. 'I'll have naught to do with any of this,' she wrote. 'You'll never be different. I know that now, heaven help you.' I flung it down in front of Ellie.

'You see what my mother's like,' I said. 'I married a rich girl, and I'm living on my rich wife's money and the old battleaxe disapproves of it!'

'Don't worry,' said Ellie. 'Lots of people think that way. She'll get over it. She loves you very much, Mike,' she added.

'Then why does she want to alter me all the time? Make me into *her* pattern. I'm myself. I'm not anybody else's pattern. I'm not mother's little boy to be moulded the way she likes. I'm *myself*. I'm an adult. I'm *me*!'

'You're you,' said Ellie, 'and I love you.'

And then, perhaps to distract me, she said something rather disquieting.

'What do you think,' she said, 'of this new manservant of ours?'

I hadn't thought about him. What was there to think? If anything I preferred him to our last one who had not troubled to conceal his low opinion of my social status.

'He's all right,' I said. 'Why?'

'I just wondered whether he might be a security man.'

'A security man? What do you mean?'

'A detective. I thought Uncle Andrew might have arranged it.'

'Why should he?'

'Well – possible kidnapping, I suppose. In the States, you know, we usually had guards – especially in the country.'

Another of the disadvantages of having money that I hadn't known about!

'What a beastly idea!'

'Oh, I don't know . . . I suppose I'm used to it. What does it matter? One doesn't really notice.'

'Is the wife in it, too?'

'She'd have to be, I think, though she cooks very well. I should think that Uncle Andrew, or perhaps Stanford Lloyd, whichever one of them thought of it, must have paid our last ones to leave, and had these two all lined up ready to take their place. It would have been quite easy.'

'Without telling you?' I was still incredulous.

'They'd never dream of telling me. I might have kicked up a fuss. Anyway, I may be quite wrong about them.' She went on dreamily. 'It's only that one gets a kind of feeling when one's been used to people of that kind always being around.'

'Poor little rich girl,' I said savagely.

Ellie did not mind at all.

'I suppose that does describe it rather well,' she said.

'The things I'm learning about you all the time, Ellie,' I said.

CHAPTER 17

What a mysterious thing sleep is. You go to bed worrying about gipsies and secret enemies, and detectives planted in your house and the possibilities of kidnapping and a hundred other things; and sleep whisks you away from it all. You travel very far and you don't know where you've been, but when you wake up, it's to a totally new world. No worries, no apprehensions. Instead, when I woke up on the 17th September I was in a mood of boisterous excitement.

'A wonderful day,' I said to myself with conviction. 'This is going to be a wonderful day.' I meant it. I was like those people in advertisements that offer to go anywhere and do anything. I went over plans in my head. I had arranged to meet Major Phillpot at a sale at a country house about fifteen miles away. They had some very nice stuff there and I'd already marked down two or three items in the catalogue. I was quite excited about the whole thing.

Phillpot was very knowledgeable about period furniture and silver and things of that kind, not because he was artistic – he was entirely a sporting man – but simply because he knew. His whole family was knowledgeable.

I looked over the catalogue at breakfast. Ellie had come down in a riding habit. She rode most mornings now – sometimes alone, sometimes with Claudia. She had the American habit of drinking coffee and a glass of orange juice and nothing much else for breakfast. My tastes, now that I hadn't got to restrain them in any way, were very much those of a Victorian squire! I liked lots of hot dishes on the sideboard. I ate kidneys this morning and sausages and bacon as well. Delicious.

'What are you doing, Greta?' I asked.

Greta said she was meeting Claudia Hardcastle at the station at

Market Chadwell and they were going up to London to a white sale. I asked what a white sale was.

'Does there really have to be white in it?' I asked.

Greta looked scornful and said that a white sale meant a sale of household linen and blankets and towels and sheets, etc. There were some very good bargains at a special shop in Bond Street of which she had been sent a catalogue.

I said to Ellie, 'Well, if Greta is going to London for the day, why don't you drive in and meet us at the George in Bartington. The food there's very good, so old Phillpot said. He suggested you might come. One o'clock. You go through Market Chadwell and then you take a turning about three miles after that. It's sign-posted, I think.'

'All right,' said Ellie, 'I'll be there.'

I mounted her and she went off riding through the trees. Ellie loved riding. She usually rode up one of the winding tracks and came out on the Downs and had a gallop before returning home. I left the smaller car for Ellie as it was easier to park and took the big Chrysler myself. I got to Bartington Manor just before the sale began. Phillpot was there already and had kept a place for me.

'Some quite nice stuff here,' he said. 'One or two good pictures. A Romney and a Reynolds. I don't know if you're interested?'

I shook my head. My taste at the moment was entirely for modern artists.

'Several dealers here,' Phillpot went on, 'a couple down from London. See that thin man over there with the pinched lips? That's Cressington. Pretty well known. Not brought your wife?'

'No,' I said, 'she's not awfully keen on sales. Anyway, I didn't particularly want her to come this morning.'

'Oh? Why not?'

'There's going to be a surprise for Ellie,' I said. 'Did you notice Lot 42?'

He took a glance at the catalogue and then looked across the room.

'Hm. That *papier mâché* desk? Yes. Rather a beautiful little piece. One of the best examples of *papier mâché* I've seen. Desk rather rare too. Plenty of hand desks to stand on tables. But this is an early example. Never seen one quite like it before.'

The little piece was inlaid with a design of Windsor Castle and the sides of it had bouquets of roses and thistles and shamrock.

'Beautiful condition,' said Phillpot. He looked at me curiously. 'I shouldn't have thought it was your taste but –'

'Oh, it isn't,' I said. 'It's a little too flowery and ladylike for me. But Ellie loves the stuff. It's her birthday next week and I want it as a present for her. A surprise. That's why I didn't want her to know I was bidding for it today. But I know there's nothing I could give her that she'd like more. She'll be really surprised.'

We went in and took seats and the sale began. Actually, the piece I wanted was run up pretty high. Both the London dealers seemed keen on it although one of them was so practised and reserved about it that you could hardly notice the almost infinitesimal motion of his catalogue which the auctioneer was observing closely. I bought a carved Chippendale chair as well which I thought would look well in our hall and some enormous brocade curtains in good condition.

'Well, you seem to have enjoyed yourself all right,' said Phillpot, rising to his feet when the auctioneer completed the morning's sale. 'Want to come back this afternoon?'

I shook my head.

'No, there's nothing in the second half of the sale that I want. Mostly bedroom furniture and carpets and things like that.'

'No, I didn't think you'd be interested. Well –' he looked at his watch, 'we'd better be getting along. Is Ellie meeting us at the George?'

'Yes, she'll be there.'

'And – er – Miss Andersen?'

'Oh, Greta's gone to London,' I said. 'She's gone to what they call a white sale. With Miss Hardcastle, I believe.'

'Oh yes, Claudia said something about it the other day. Price of sheets and things are fantastic nowadays. Do you know what a linen pillow case costs? Thirty-five shillings. Used to buy 'em for six bob.'

'You're very knowledgeable on household purchases,' I said.

'Well, I hear my wife complaining about them.' Phillpot smiled. 'You're looking in the pink of condition, Mike. Happy as a sandboy.'

'That's because I've got the *papier mâché* desk,' I said, 'or at any rate that's partly it. I just woke up feeling happy this morning. You know those days when everything in the world seems right.'

'Mm,' said Phillpot, 'be careful. That's what's known as being fey.'

'Fey?' I said. 'That's something Scottish, isn't it?'

'It comes before disaster, my boy,' said Phillpot. 'Better curb your exuberance.'

'Oh, I don't believe those silly superstitions,' I said.

'Nor in gipsies' prophecies, eh?'

'We haven't seen our gipsy lately,' I said. 'Well, not for a week at least.'

'Perhaps she's away from the place,' said Phillpot.

He asked me if I'd give him a lift in my car and I said I would.

'No use taking the two of them. You can drop me here on your way back, can't you? What about Ellie, will she be bringing her car over?'

'Yes, she's bringing the little one.'

'Hope the George will put on a good meal,' said Major Phillpot. 'I'm hungry.'

'Did you buy anything?' I asked. 'I was too excited to notice.'

'Yes, you've got to keep your wits about you when you're bidding. Have to notice what the dealers are doing. No. I made a bid or two but everything went far above my price.'

I gathered that although Phillpot owned enormous quantities of land round about, his actual income did not amount to much. He was what you might describe as a poor man though a large landowner. Only by selling a good portion of his land would he have had money to spend and he didn't want to sell his land. He loved it.

We got to the George and found a good many cars standing there already. Possibly some of the people from the auction. I didn't see Ellie's though. We went inside and I looked around for her but she hadn't turned up yet. However, it was only just past one.

We went and had a drink at the bar while we were waiting for Ellie to arrive. The place was pretty crowded. I looked into the dining-room but they were still holding our table. There were a good many local faces that I knew and sitting at a table by the window was a man whose face seemed familiar to me. I was sure I knew him but I couldn't remember when and where we'd met. I didn't think he was a local, because his clothes didn't fit in with these parts. Of course I've knocked up against a great many people in my time and it is unlikely that I can remember them all easily. He hadn't been at the sale as far as I could remember, though, oddly enough, there had been one face that I thought I'd recognized but couldn't place. Faces are tricky unless you can connect up when and where you'd seen them.

The presiding goddess of the George, rustling in her usual black silk of affected Edwardian style which she always wore, came to me and said:

'Will you be coming to your table soon, Mr Rogers? There's one or two waiting.'

'My wife will be here in a minute or two,' I said.

I went back to rejoin Phillpot. I thought perhaps that Ellie might have had a puncture.

'We'd better go in,' I said, 'they seem to be getting rather upset about it. They've got quite a crowd today. I'm afraid,' I added, 'that Ellie isn't the most punctual of people.'

'Ah,' said Phillpot in his old-fashioned style, 'the ladies make a point of keeping us waiting, don't they? All right, Mike, if that's all right by you. We'll go in and start lunch.'

We went into the dining-room, chose steak and kidney pie off the menu and started.

'It's too bad of Ellie,' I said, 'to stand us up like this.' I added that it was possibly because Greta was in London. 'Ellie's very used, you know,' I said, 'to Greta helping her to keep appointments, reminding her of them, and getting her off in time and all that.'

'Is she very dependent on Miss Andersen?'

'In that way, yes,' I said.

We went on eating and passed from the steak and kidney pie to apple tart with a self-conscious piece of phoney pastry on top of it.

'I wonder if she's forgotten all about it,' I said suddenly.

'Perhaps you'd better ring up.'

'Yes, I think I'd better.'

I went out to the phone and rang. Mrs Carson, the cook, answered.

'Oh, it's you, Mr Rogers, Mrs Rogers hasn't come home yet.'

'What do you mean, hasn't come home? Home from where?'

'She hasn't come back from her ride yet.'

'But that was after breakfast. She can't have been riding the whole morning.'

'She didn't say anything different. I was expecting her back.'

'Why didn't you ring up sooner and let me know about it?' I asked.

'Well, I wouldn't know where to get at you, you see. I didn't know where you'd gone.'

I told her I was at the George at Bartington and gave her the number. She was to ring up the moment Ellie came in or she had news of her. Then I went back to join Phillpot. He saw from my face at once that something was wrong.

'Ellie hasn't come home,' I said. 'She went off riding this morning. She usually does most mornings but it only lasts half an hour to an hour.'

'Now don't worry before you need to, boy,' he said kindly. 'Your place is in a very lonely part, you know. Maybe her horse went lame and she might be walking it home. All that moorland and downs above the woods. There's nobody much in that part to send a message by.'

'If she decided to change her plans and ride over and see anyone, anything like that,' I said, 'she'd have rung here. She'd have left a message for us.'

'Well, don't get het up yet,' Phillpot said. 'I think we'd better go now, right away, and see what we can find out.'

As we went out to the car park, another car drove away. In it was the man I had noticed in the dining-room and suddenly it came to me who it was. Stanford Lloyd or someone just like him. I wondered what he could be doing down here. Could he be coming to see us? If so, it was odd he hadn't let us know. In the car with him was a woman who had looked like Claudia Hardcastle, but surely she was in London with Greta, shopping. It all floored me rather . . .

As we drove away Phillpot looked at me once or twice. I caught his eye once and said rather bitterly:

'All right. You said I was fey this morning.'

'Well, don't think of that yet. She may have had a fall and sprained an ankle or something like that. She's a good horse-woman, though,' he said. 'I've seen her. I can't feel an accident is really likely.'

I said, 'Accidents can happen at any time.'

We drove fast and came at last to the road over the downs above our property, looking about us as we went. Now and again we stopped to ask people. We stopped a man who was digging peat and there we got the first news.

'Seen a riderless horse I have,' he said. 'Two hours ago maybe or longer. I would-a caught it but it galloped off when I got near it. Didn't see anyone though.'

'Best drive home,' suggested Phillpot, 'there may be news of her there.'

We drove home but there was no news. We got hold of the groom and sent him off to ride the moorland in search of Ellie. Phillpot telephoned his own house and sent a man from there too. He and I went up a path together and through the wood, the one that Ellie often took, and came out on the downs there.

At first there was nothing to be seen. Then we walked along the edge of the wood near where some of the other paths came out and so – we found her. We saw what looked like a huddled heap of clothes. The horse had come back and was now standing cropping near that huddled heap. I began to run. Phillpot followed me faster than I'd have thought a man of his age could have kept up.

She was there – lying in a crumpled-up heap, her little white face turned up to the sky. I said:

'I can't – I can't –' and turned my face away.

Phillpot went and knelt down by her. He got up almost at once.

'We'll get hold of a doctor,' he said. 'Shaw. He's the nearest. But – I don't think it's any use, Mike.'

'You mean – she's dead?'

'Yes,' he said, 'it's no good pretending anything else.'

'Oh God!' I said and turned away. 'I can't believe it. Not Ellie.'

'Here, have this,' said Phillpot.

He took a flask out of his pocket, unscrewed it and handed it to me. I took a good deep pull at it.

'Thanks,' I said.

The groom came along then and Phillpot sent him off to fetch Dr Shaw.

CHAPTER 18

Shaw came up in a battered old Land-Rover. I suppose it was the car he used for going to visit isolated farms in bad weather. He barely looked at either of us. He went straight and bent over Ellie. Then he came over to us.

'She's been dead at least three or four hours,' he said. 'How did it happen?'

I told him how she'd gone off riding as usual after breakfast that morning.

'Has she had any accidents up to this time when she's been out riding?'

'No,' I said, 'she was a good rider.'

'Yes, I know she's a good rider. I've seen her once or twice. She's ridden since she was a child, I understand. I wondered if she might have had an accident lately and that that might have affected her nerve a bit. If the horse had shied –'

'Why should the horse shy? It's a quiet brute –'

'There's nothing vicious about this particular horse,' said Major Phillpot. 'He's well behaved, not nervy. Has she broken any bones?'

'I haven't made a complete examination yet but she doesn't seem physically injured in any way. There may be some internal injury. Might be shock, I suppose.'

'But you can't die of shock,' I said.

'People have died of shock before now. If she'd had a weak heart –'

'They said in America that she had a weak heart – some kind of weakness at least.'

'Hm. I couldn't find much trace of it when I examined her. Still, we didn't have a cardiograph. Anyway no point in going into that now. We shall know later. After the inquest.'

He looked at me consideringly, then he patted me on the shoulder.

'You go home and go to bed,' he said. 'You're the one who's suffering from shock.'

In the queer way people materialize out of nowhere in the country, we had three or four people standing near us, by this time. One a hiker who had come along from the main road seeing our little group, one a rosy-faced woman who I think was going to a farm over a short cut and an old roadman. They were making exclamations and remarks.

'Poor young lady.'

'So young too. Thrown from her horse, was she?'

'Ah well, you never know with horses.'

'It's Mrs Rogers, isn't it, the American lady from The Towers?'

It was not until everyone else had exclaimed in their astonished fashion, that the aged roadman spoke. He gave us information. Shaking his head he said:

'I must-a seen it happen. I must-a seen it happen.'

The doctor turned sharply on him.

'What did you see happen?'

'I saw a horse bolting across country.'

'Did you see the lady fall?'

'No. No, I didn't. She were riding along the top of the woods when I saw her and after that I'd got me back turned and I was cutting the stones for the road. And then I heard hoofs and I looked up and there was the horse a-galloping. I didn't think there'd been an accident. I thought the lady perhaps had got off and let go of the horse in some way. It wasn't coming towards me, it was going in the other direction.'

'You didn't see the lady lying on the ground?'

'No, I don't see very well far. I saw the horse because it showed against the sky line.'

'Was she riding alone? Was there anyone with her, or near her?'

'Nobody near her. No. She was all alone. She rode not very far from me, past me, going along that way. She was bearing towards the woods, I think. No, I didn't see anyone at all except her and the horse.'

'Might have been the gipsy who frightened her,' said the rosy-faced woman.

I swung round.

'What gipsy? When?'

'Oh, must have been – well, it must have been three or four hours ago when I went down the road this morning. About quarter to ten maybe, I saw that gipsy woman. The one as lives in the cottages in the village. Least I think it was she. I wasn't near enough to be sure. But she's the only one as goes about hereabouts in a red cloak. She was walking up a path through the trees. Somebody told me as she'd said nasty things to the poor American young lady. Threatened her. Told her something bad would happen if she didn't get out of this place. Very threatening, I hear she was.'

'The gipsy,' I said. Then, bitterly, to myself, though out loud, 'Gipsy's Acre. I wish I'd never seen the place.'

BOOK 3

CHAPTER 19

I

It's extraordinary how difficult it is for me to remember what happened after that. I mean, the sequence of it all. Up to then, you see, it's all clear in my mind. I was a little doubtful where to begin, that was all. But from then on it was as though a knife fell, cutting my life into two halves. What I went on to from the moment of Ellie's death seems to me now like something for which I was not prepared. A confusion of thrusting people and elements and happenings where I wasn't myself in control of anything any more. Things happened not to me, but all around me. That's what it seemed like.

Everybody was very kind to me. That seems the thing I remember best. I stumbled about and looked dazed and didn't know what to do. Greta, I remember, came into her element. She had that amazing power that women have to take charge of a situation and deal with it. Deal, I mean, with all the small unimportant details that someone has to see to. I would have been incapable of seeing to them.

I think the first thing I remembered clearly after they'd taken Ellie away and I'd got back to my house – our house – *the* house – was when Dr Shaw came along and talked to me. I don't know how long after that was. He was quiet, kind, reasonable. Just explaining things clearly and gently.

Arrangements. I remember his using the word arrangements. What a hateful word it is and all the things it stands for. The things in life that have grand words – Love – sex – life – death – hate – those aren't the things that govern existence at all. It's lots of other pettifogging, degrading things. Things you have to endure, things you never think about until they happen to you. Undertakers, arrangements for funerals, inquests. And servants coming into rooms and pulling the blinds down. Why should blinds be pulled down because Ellie was dead? Of all the stupid things!

That was why, I remember, I felt quite grateful to Dr Shaw. He dealt with such things so kindly and sensibly, explaining gently why certain things like an inquest had to be. Talking rather slowly, I remember, so that he could be quite sure I was taking them in.

II

I didn't know what an inquest would be like. I'd never been to one. It seemed to me curiously unreal, amateurish. The Coroner was a small fussy little man with pincenez. I had to give evidence of identification, to describe the last time I had seen Ellie at the breakfast table and her departure for her usual morning ride and the arrangement we had made to meet later for lunch. She had seemed, I said, exactly the same as usual, in perfectly good health.

Dr Shaw's evidence was quiet, inconclusive. No serious injuries, a wrenched collar bone and bruises such as would result from a fall from the horse – not of a very serious nature, and inflicted at the time of death. She did not appear to have moved again after she had fallen. Death, he thought, had been practically instantaneous. There was no specific organic injury to have caused death, and he could give no other explanation of it than that she had died from heart failure caused by shock. As far as I could make out from the medical language used Ellie had died simply as a result of absence of breath – of asphyxia of some kind. Her organs were healthy, her stomach contents normal.

Greta, who also gave evidence, stressed rather more forcibly than she had done to Dr Shaw before, that Ellie had suffered from some form of heart malady three or four years ago. She had never heard anything definite mentioned but Ellie's relations had occasionally said that her heart was weak and that she must take care not to over-do things. She had never heard anything more definite than that.

Then we came to the people who had seen or been in the vicinity at the time the accident happened. The old man who had been cutting peat was the first of them. He had seen the lady pass him, she'd been about fifty yards or so away. He knew who she was though he'd never spoken to her. She was the lady from the new house.

'You knew her by sight?'

'No, not exactly by sight but I knew the horse, sir. It's got a white fetlock. Used to belong to Mr Carey over at Shettlegroom. I've never heard it anything but quiet and well behaved, suitable for a lady to ride.'

'Was the horse giving any trouble when you saw it? Playing up in any way?'

'No, it was quiet enough. It was a nice morning.'

There hadn't been many people about, he said. He hadn't noticed many. That particular track across the moor wasn't much used except as a short cut occasionally to one of the farms. Another track crossed it about a mile farther away. He'd seen one or two passers-by that morning but not to notice. One man on a bicycle, another man walking. They were too far away for him to see who they were and he hadn't noticed much anyway. Earlier, he said, before he'd seen the lady riding, he'd seen old Mrs Lee, or so he thought. She was coming up the track towards him and then she turned off and went into the woods. She often walked across the moors and in and out of the woods.

The Coroner asked why Mrs Lee was not in court. He understood that she'd been summoned to attend. He was told, however, that Mrs Lee had left the village some days ago – nobody knew exactly when. She had not left any address behind. It was not her habit to do so, she often went away and came back without notifying anyone. So there was nothing unusual about this. In fact one or two people said they thought she'd already left the village *before* the day the accident happened. The Coroner asked the old man again.

'You think, however, that it *was* Mrs Lee you saw?'

'Couldn't say, I'm sure. Wouldn't like to be certain. It was a tall woman and striding along, and had on a scarlet cloak, like Mrs Lee wears sometimes. But I didn't look particular. I was busy with what I was doing. Could have been she, it could have been someone else. Who's to say?'

As for the rest he repeated very much what he had said to us. He'd seen the lady riding nearby, he'd often seen her riding before. He hadn't paid any particular attention. Only later did he see the horse galloping alone. It looked as though something had frightened it, he said. 'At least, it could be that way.' He couldn't tell what time that was. Might have been eleven, might have been earlier. He saw the horse much later, farther away. It seemed to be returning towards the woods.

Then the Coroner recalled me and asked me a few more questions about Mrs Lee, Mrs Esther Lee of Vine Cottage.

'You and your wife knew Mrs Lee by sight?'

'Yes,' I said, 'quite well.'

'Did you talk with her?'

'Yes, several times. Or rather,' I added, 'she talked to us.'

'Did she at any time threaten you or your wife?'

I paused a moment or two.

'In a sense she did,' I said slowly, 'but I never thought –'

'You never thought what?'

'I never thought she really meant it,' I said.

'Did she sound as though she had any particular grudge against your wife?'

'My wife said so once. She said she thought she had some special grudge against her but she couldn't see why.'

'Had you or your wife at any time ordered her off your land, threatened her, treated her roughly in any way?'

'Any aggression came from her side,' I said.

'Did you ever have the impression that she was mentally unbalanced?'

I considered. 'Yes,' I said, 'I did. I thought she had come to believe that the land on which we had built our house belonged to her, or belonged to her tribe or whatever they call themselves. She had a kind of obsession about it.' I added slowly, 'I think she was getting worse, more and more obsessed by the idea.'

'I see. She never offered your wife physical violence at any time?'

'No,' I said, slowly, 'I don't think it would be fair to say that. It was all – well all a sort of gipsy's warning stuff. "You'll have bad luck if you stay here. There'll be a curse on you unless you go away."'

'Did she mention the word death?'

'Yes, I think so. We didn't take her seriously. At least,' I corrected myself, 'I didn't.'

'Do you think your wife did?'

'I'm afraid she did sometimes. The old woman, you know, could be rather alarming. I don't think she was really responsible for what she was saying or doing.'

The proceedings ended with the Coroner adjourning the inquest for a fortnight. Everything pointed to death being due to accidental causes but there was not sufficient evidence to show what had caused the accident to occur. He would adjourn the proceedings until he had heard the evidence of Mrs Esther Lee.

CHAPTER 20

The day after the inquest I went to see Major Phillpot and I told him point-blank that I wanted his opinion. Someone whom the old peat-cutting man had taken to be Mrs Esther Lee had been seen going up towards the woods that morning.

'You know the old woman,' I said. 'Do you actually think that she would have been capable of causing an accident by deliberate malice?'

'I can't really believe so, Mike,' he said. 'To do a thing like that you need a very strong motive. Revenge for some personal injury caused to you. Something like that. And what had Ellie ever done to her? Nothing.'

'It seems crazy, I know. Why was she constantly appearing in that queer way, threatening Ellie, telling her to go away? She seemed to have a grudge against her, but how could she have had a grudge? She'd never met Ellie or seen her before. What was Ellie to her but a perfectly strange American? There's no past history, no link between them.'

'I know, I know,' said Phillpot. 'I can't help feeling, Mike, that there's something here that we don't understand. I don't know how much your wife was over in England previous to her marriage. Did she ever live in this part of the world for any length of time?'

'No, I'm sure of that. It's all so difficult. *I* don't really know anything about Ellie. I mean, who she knew, where she went. We just – met.' I checked myself and looked at him. I said, 'You don't know how we came to meet, do you? No,' I went on, 'you wouldn't guess in a hundred years how we met.' And suddenly, in spite of myself, I began to laugh. Then I pulled myself together. I could feel that I was very near hysteria.

I could see his kind patient face just waiting till I was myself again. He was a helpful man. There was no doubt about that.

'We met here,' I said. 'Here at Gipsy's Acre. I had been reading the notice board of the sale of The Towers and I walked up the road, up the hill because I was curious about this place. And that's how I first saw her. She was standing there under a tree. I startled her – or perhaps it was she who startled me. Anyway, that's how it all began. That's how we came to live here in this damned, cursed, unlucky place.'

'Have you felt that all along? That it would be unlucky?'

'No. Yes. No, I don't know really. I've never admitted it. I've never wanted to admit it. But I think *she* knew. I think she's been frightened all along.' Then I said slowly, 'I think somebody deliberately wanted to frighten her.'

He said rather sharply, 'What do you mean by that? Who wanted to frighten her?'

'Presumably the gipsy woman. But somehow I'm not quite sure about it . . . She used to lie in wait for Ellie, you know, tell her this place would bring her bad luck. Tell her she ought to go away from it.'

'Tcha!' He spoke angrily. 'I wish I'd been told more about that. I'd have spoken to old Esther. Told her she couldn't do things like that.'

'Why did she?' I asked. 'What made her?'

'Like so many people,' said Phillpot, 'she likes to make herself important. She likes either to give people warnings or else tell their fortunes and prophesy happy lives for them. She likes to pretend she knows the future.'

'Supposing,' I said slowly, 'somebody gave her money. I've been told she's fond of money.'

'Yes, she was very fond of money. If someone paid her – that's what you're suggesting – what put that idea into your head?'

'Sergeant Keene,' I said. 'I should never have thought of it myself.'

'I see.' He shook his head doubtfully.

'I can't believe,' he said, 'that she would deliberately try to frighten your wife to the extent of causing an accident.'

'She mayn't have counted on a fatal accident. She might have done something to frighten the horse,' I said. 'Let off a squib or flapped a sheet of white paper or something. Sometimes, you know, I did feel that she had some entirely personal grudge against Ellie, a grudge for some reason that I don't know about.'

'That sounds very far-fetched.'

'This place never belonged to her?' I asked. 'The land, I mean.'

'No. Gipsies may have been warned off this property, probably more than once. Gipsies are always getting turned off places, but I doubt if they keep up a life-long resentment about it.'

'No,' I said, 'that would be far-fetched. But I do wonder if for some reason that we don't know about – she was paid –'

'A reason we don't know about – what reason?'

I reflected a moment or two.

'Everything I say will just sound fantastic. Let's say that, as Keene suggested, someone paid her to do the things she did. What did that someone want? Say they wanted to make us both go away from here. They concentrated on Ellie, not on me, because I wouldn't be scared in the way Ellie would be. They frightened her to get her – and through her both of us – to leave here. If so, there must be some reason for wanting the land to come on the market again. Somebody, shall we say, for some reason wants our land.' I stopped.

'It's a logical suggestion,' Phillpot said, 'but I know of no reason why anyone should.'

'Some important mineral deposit,' I suggested, 'that nobody knows about.'

'Hm, I doubt it.'

'Something like buried treasure. Oh, I know it sounds absurd. Or – well, say the proceeds of some big bank robbery.'

Phillpot was still shaking his head but rather less vehemently now.

'The only other proposition,' I said, 'is to go one step farther back as you did just now. Behind Mrs Lee to the person who paid Mrs Lee. That might be some unknown enemy of Ellie's.'

'But you can't think of anyone it would be likely to be?'

'No. She didn't know anyone down here. That I'm sure of. She had no links with this place.' I got up. 'Thank you for listening to me,' I said.

'I wish I could have been more helpful.'

I went out of the door, fingering the thing that I was carrying in my pocket. Then, taking a sudden decision, I turned on my heels and went back into the room.

'There's something I'd like to show you,' I said. 'Actually, I was going to take it down to show Sergeant Keene and see what he could make of it.'

I dived into my pocket and brought out a stone round which was wrapped a crumpled bit of paper with printed writing on it.

'This was thrown through our breakfast window this morning,' I said. 'I heard the crash of the glass as I came down the stairs. A stone was thrown through the window once before when we first came here. I don't know if this is the same person or not.'

I took off the wrapping paper and held it out for him. It was a dirty, coarse bit of paper. There was some printing on it in rather faint ink. Phillpot put on his spectacles and bent over the piece of paper. The message on it was quite short. All it said was, '*It was a woman who killed your wife.*'

Phillpot's eyebrows went up.

'Extraordinary,' he said. 'Was the first message you got printed?'

'I can't remember now. It was just a warning to go away from here. I can't even remember the exact wording of it now. Anyway, it seems pretty certain that that was hooligans. This doesn't seem quite the same.'

'Do you think it was thrown in by someone who knew something?'

'Probably just a bit of silly cruel malice in the anonymous letter class. You get it, you know, a good deal in villages.'

He handed it back to me.

'But I think your instinct was right,' he said, 'to take it to Sergeant Keene. He'll know more about these anonymous things than I should.'

I found Sergeant Keene at the police station and he was definitely interested.

'There's queer things going on here,' he said.

'What do you think it means?' I asked.

'Hard to say. Might be just malice leading up to accusing some particular person.'

'It might be just accusing Mrs Lee, I suppose?'

'No, I don't think it would have been put that way. It might be – I'd like to think it was – it might be that someone saw or heard something. Heard a noise or a cry or the horse bolted right past someone, and they saw or met a woman soon afterwards. But it sounds as though it was a different woman from the gipsy, because everyone thinks the gipsy's mixed up in this anyway. So this sounds as though another, an entirely different woman was meant.'

'What about the gipsy?' I said. 'Have you had news of her, found her?'

He shook his head slowly.

'We know some of the places she used to go when she left here. East Anglia, that way. She'd friends there among the gipsy clan. She's not been there, they say, but they'd say that anyway. They clam up, you know. She's fairly well known by sight in those parts but nobody's seen her. All the same, I don't think she's as far away as East Anglia.'

There was something peculiar about the way he said the words.

'I don't quite understand,' I said.

'Look at it this way, she's scared. She's got good reason to be. She's been threatening your wife, frightening her, and now, say, she caused an accident and your wife died. The police'll be after her. She knows that, so she'll go to earth, as you might say. She'll put as big a distance between herself and us as she possibly can. But she won't want to show herself. She'd be afraid of public transport.'

'But you'll find her? She's a woman of striking appearance.'

'Ah yes, we shall find her eventually. These things take a little time. That is, if it *was* that way.'

'But you think it was some other way.'

'Well, you know what I've wondered all along. Whether somebody was paying her to say the things she did?'

'Then she might be even more anxious to get away,' I pointed out.

'But somebody else would be anxious too. You've got to think of that, Mr Rogers.'

'You mean,' I said slowly, 'the person who paid her.'

'Yes.'

'Supposing it was a – a woman who paid her.'

'And supposing somebody else has some idea of that. And so they start sending anonymous messages. The woman would be scared too. She needn't have *meant* this to happen, you know. However much she got that gipsy woman to frighten your wife away from this place she wouldn't have meant it to result in Mrs Rogers' death.'

'No,' I said. 'Death wasn't meant. It was just to frighten us. To frighten my wife and to frighten me into leaving here.'

'And now who's going to be frightened? The woman who caused the accident. And that's Mrs Esther Lee. And so she's going to come clean, isn't she? Say it wasn't really her doing. She'll admit even that she was paid money to do it. And she'll mention a name. She'll say who paid her. And somebody wouldn't like that would they, Mr Rogers?'

'You mean this unknown woman that we've more or less postulated without even knowing there's any such person?'

'Man or woman, say someone paid her. Well, that someone would want her silenced pretty quickly, wouldn't they?'

'You're thinking she might be dead?'

'It's a possibility, isn't it?' said Keene. Then he made what seemed quite an abrupt change of subject. 'You know that kind of Folly place, Mr Rogers, that you've got up at the top of your woods?'

'Yes,' I said, 'what of it? My wife and I had it repaired and fixed up a bit. We used to go up there occasionally but not very often. Not lately certainly. Why?'

'Well, we've been hunting about, you know. We looked into this Folly. It wasn't locked.'

'No,' I said, 'we never bothered to lock it. There was nothing of value in there, just a few odd bits of furniture.'

'We thought it possible old Mrs Lee had been using it but we found no traces of her. We did find this, though. I was going to show it to you anyway.' He opened a drawer and took out a small delicate gold-chased lighter. It was a woman's lighter and it had an initial on it in diamonds. The letter C. 'It wouldn't be your wife's, would it?'

'Not with the initial C. No, it's not Ellie's,' I said. 'She hadn't anything of that kind. And it's not Miss Andersen's either. Her name is Greta.'

'It was up there where somebody had dropped it. It's a classy bit of goods – cost money.'

'C,' I said, repeating the initial thoughtfully. 'I can't think of anyone who's been with us whose initial is C except Cora,' I said. 'That's my wife's stepmother. Mrs van Stuyvesant, but I really can't see her scrambling up to the Folly along that overgrown path. And anyway she hasn't been staying with us for quite a long time. About a month. I don't think I've ever seen her using this lighter. Perhaps I wouldn't notice anyway,' I said. 'Miss Andersen might know.'

'Well, take it up with you and show it to her.'

'I will. But if so, if it's Cora's, it seems odd that we've never seen it when we've been in the Folly lately. There's not much stuff there. You'd notice something like this lying on the floor – it was on the floor?'

'Yes, quite near the divan. Of course anybody might use that Folly. It's a handy place, you know, for a couple of lovers to meet any time. The locals I'm talking about. But they wouldn't be likely to have an expensive thing of this kind.'

'There's Claudia Hardcastle,' I said, 'but I doubt if she'd have anything as fancy as this. And what would she be doing in the Folly?'

'She was quite a friend of your wife's, wasn't she?'

'Yes,' I said, 'I think she was Ellie's best friend down here. And she'd know we wouldn't mind her using the Folly any time.'

'Ah,' said Sergeant Keene.

I looked at him rather hard. 'You don't think Claudia Hardcastle was a – an enemy of Ellie's do you? That would be absurd.'

'Doesn't seem any reason why she should be, I agree, but you never know with ladies.'

'I suppose –' I began and then stopped because what I was going to say would seem perhaps rather odd.

'Yes, Mr Rogers?'

'I believe that Claudia Hardcastle was originally married to an

American – an American named Lloyd. Actually – the name of my wife's principal trustee in America is Stanford Lloyd. But there must be hundreds of Lloyds and anyway it would only be a coincidence if it was the same person. And what would it have to do with all this?'

'It doesn't seem likely. But then –' he stopped.

'The funny thing is that I thought I saw Stanford Lloyd down here on the day of the – the accident – Having lunch in the George at Bartington –'

'He didn't come to see you?'

I shook my head.

'He was with someone who looked rather like Miss Hardcastle. But probably it was just a mistake on my part. You know, I suppose, that it was her brother who built our house?'

'Does she take an interest in the house?'

'No,' I said, 'I don't think she likes her brother's type of architecture.' Then I got up. 'Well, I won't take any more of your time. Try and find the gipsy.'

'We shan't stop looking, I can tell you that. Coroner wants her too.'

I said goodbye and went out of the police station. In the queer way that so often happens when you suddenly meet someone you've been talking about, Claudia Hardcastle came out of the post office just as I was passing it. We both stopped. She said with that slight embarrassment that you have when you meet someone that's been recently bereaved:

'I'm so terribly sorry, Mike, about Ellie. I won't say any more. It's beastly when people say things to you. But I have just – just to say that.'

'I know,' I said. 'You were very nice to Ellie. You made her feel at home here. I've been grateful.'

'There was one thing I wanted to ask you and I thought perhaps I'd better do it now before you go to America. I hear you're going quite soon.'

'As soon as I can. I've got a lot to see to there.'

'It was only – if you *were* putting your house on the market I thought it might be a thing you'd set in motion before you went away . . . And if so – if so, I'd rather like to have the first refusal of it.'

I stared at her. This really did surprise me. It was the last thing I'd expected.

'You mean you'd like to buy it? I thought you didn't even care for that type of architecture?'

'My brother Rudolf said to me that it was the best thing he'd done. I dare say he knows. I expect you'll want a very large price for it but I could pay it. Yes, I'd like to have it.'

I couldn't help thinking it was odd. She'd never shown the faintest appreciation of our house when she'd come to it. I wondered as I'd wondered once or twice before what her links with her half-brother really were. Had she really a great devotion to him? Sometimes I'd almost thought that she disliked him, perhaps hated him. She spoke of him certainly in a very odd way. But whatever her actual emotions were, he *meant* something to her. Meant something important. I shook my head slowly.

'I can see that you might think I'd want to sell the place and leave here because of Ellie's death,' I said. 'But actually that's not so at all. We lived here and were happy and this is the place I shall remember her best. *I shan't sell Gipsy's Acre* – not for any consideration! You can be quite sure of that.'

Our eyes met. It was like a kind of tussle between us. Then hers dropped.

I took my courage in both hands and spoke.

'It's no business of mine, but you were married once. Was the name of your husband Stanford Lloyd?'

She looked at me for a moment without speaking. Then she said abruptly:

'Yes,' and turned away.

CHAPTER 21

Confusion – That's all I can remember when I look back. Newspapermen asking questions – wanting interviews – masses of letters and telegrams – Greta coping with them –

The first really startling thing was that Ellie's family were not as we supposed in America. It was quite a shock to find that most of them were actually in England. It was understandable, perhaps, that Cora van Stuyvesant should be. She was a very restless woman, always dashing across to Europe, to Italy, to Paris, to London and back again to America, to Palm Beach, out West to the ranch; here, there and everywhere. On the actual day of Ellie's death she had been not more than fifty miles away, still pursuing her whim of having a house in England. She had rushed over to stay in London for two or three days and gone to fresh house agents for fresh orders to view and had been touring round the country seeing half a dozen on that particular day.

Stanford Lloyd, it turned out, had flown over in the same plane ostensibly for a business meeting in London. These people learnt of Ellie's death, not from the cables which we had dispatched to the United States but from the public Press.

An ugly wrangle developed about where Ellie should be buried. I had assumed it was only natural that she'd be buried here where she had died. Here where she and I had lived.

But Ellie's family objected violently to this. They wanted the body brought to America to be buried with her forebears. Where her grandfather and her father, her mother and others had been laid to rest. I suppose it was natural, really, when one comes to think of it.

Andrew Lippincott came down to talk to me about it. He put the matter in a reasonable way.

'She never left any directions as to where she wished to be buried,' he pointed out to me.

'Why should she?' I demanded hotly. 'How old was she – twenty-one? You don't think at twenty-one you're going to die. You don't start thinking then the way you want to be buried. If we'd ever thought about it we'd assume we'd be buried together somewhere even if we didn't die at the same time. But who thinks of death in the middle of life?'

'A very just observation,' said Mr Lippincott. Then he said, 'I'm afraid you'll also have to come to America, you know. There's a great deal of business interests you'll have to look into.'

'What sort of business? What have I got to do with business?'

'You could have a great deal to do with it,' he said. 'Don't you realize that you're the principal beneficiary under the will?'

'You mean because I'm Ellie's next of kin or something?'

'No. Under her will.'

'I didn't know she ever made a will.'

'Oh yes,' said Mr Lippincott. 'Ellie was quite a businesslike young woman. She'd had to be, you know. She'd lived in the middle of that kind of thing. She made a will on coming of age and almost immediately after she was married. It was lodged with her lawyer in London with a request that one copy should be sent to me.' He hesitated and then said, 'If you do come to the States, which I advise, I also think that you should place your affairs in the hands of some reputable lawyer there.'

'Why?'

'Because in the case of a vast fortune, large quantities of real estate, stocks, controlling interests in varying industries, you will need technical advice.'

'I'm not qualified to deal with things like that,' I said. 'Really I'm not.'

'I quite understand,' said Mr Lippincott.

'Couldn't I place the whole thing in your hands?'

'You could do so.'

'Well then, why don't I?'

'All the same, I think you should be separately represented. I am already acting for some members of the family and a conflict of interests might arise. If you will leave it in my hands, I will see that your interests are safeguarded by your being represented by a thoroughly able attorney.'

'Thank you,' I said, 'you're very kind.'

'If I may be slightly indiscreet –' he looked a little uncomfortable – it pleased me rather thinking of Lippincott being indiscreet.

'Yes?' I said.

'I should advise you to be very careful of anything you sign. Any business documents. Before you sign anything, read it thoroughly and carefully.'

'Would the kind of document you're talking about mean anything to me if I do read it?'

'If it is not all clear to you, you will then hand it over to your legal adviser.'

'Are you warning me against somebody or someone?' I said, with a suddenly aroused interest.

'That is not at all a proper question for me to answer,' said Mr Lippincott. 'I will go this far. Where large sums of money are concerned it is advisable to trust *nobody*.'

So he *was* warning me against someone, but he wasn't going to give me any names. I could see that. Was it against Cora? Or had he had suspicions – perhaps suspicions of some long standing – of Stanford Lloyd, that florid banker so full of bonhomie, so rich and carefree, who had recently been over here 'on business'? Might it be Uncle Frank who might approach me with some plausible documents? I had a sudden vision of myself, a poor innocent boob, swimming in a lake surrounded by evilly disposed crocodiles, all smiling false smiles of amity.

'The world,' said Mr Lippincott, 'is a very evil place.'

It was perhaps a stupid thing to say, but quite suddenly I asked him a question.

'Does Ellie's death benefit anyone?' I asked.

He looked at me sharply.

'That's a very curious question. Why do you ask that?'

'I don't know,' I said, 'it just came into my head.'

'It benefits you,' he said.

'Of course,' I said. 'I take that for granted. I really meant – does it benefit anyone else?'

Mr Lippincott was silent for quite a long time.

'If you mean,' he said, 'does Fenella's will benefit certain other people in the way of legacies, that is so in a minor degree. Some old servants, an old governess, one or two charities but nothing of any particular moment. There's a legacy to Miss Andersen but not a large one for she has already, as you probably know, settled a very considerable sum on Miss Andersen.'

I nodded. Ellie had told me she was doing that.

'You were her husband. She had no other near relations. But I take it that your question did not mean specifically that.'

'I don't know quite what I meant by it,' I said. 'But somehow or other, you've succeeded, Mr Lippincott, in making me feel suspicious. Suspicious of I don't know who, or why. Only – well, suspicious. I don't understand finance,' I added.

'No, that is quite apparent. Let me say only that I have no exact knowledge, no exact suspicions of any kind. At someone's death there is usually an accounting of their affairs. This may take place quickly or it may be delayed for a period of many years.'

'What you really mean,' I said, 'is that some of the others quite likely might put a few fast ones over and ball up things generally. Get me perhaps to sign releases – whatever you call the things.'

'If Fenella's affairs were not, shall we say, in the healthy state they ought to be, then – yes, possibly her premature death might be, shall we say, fortunate for someone, we will name no names, someone perhaps who could cover his traces more easily if he had a fairly simple person, if I may say so, like yourself to deal with. I will go that far but I do not wish to speak further on the matter. It would not be equitable to do so.'

There was a simple funeral service held in the little church. If I could have stayed away I would have done so. I hated all those people who were staring at me lining up outside the church. Curious eyes. Greta pulled me through things. I don't think I'd realized until now what a strong, reliable character she was. She made the arrangements, ordered flowers, arranged everything. I understood better now how Ellie had come to depend upon Greta as she had done. There aren't many Gretas in the world.

The people in the church were mostly our neighbours – some, even, that we had hardly known. But I noticed one face that I had seen before, but which I could not at the moment place. When I got back to the house, Carson told me there was a gentleman in the drawing-room waiting to see me.

'I can't see anyone today. Send him away. You shouldn't have let him in!'

'Excuse me, sir. He said he was a relation.'

'A relation?'

Suddenly I remembered the man I'd seen in the church.

Carson was handing me a card.

It meant nothing to me for a moment. Mr William R. Pardoe. I turned it over and shook my head. Then I handed it to Greta.

'Do you know by any chance who this is?' I said. 'His face seemed familiar but I couldn't place it. Perhaps it's one of Ellie's friends.'

Greta took it from me and looked at it. Then she said:

'Of course.'

'Who is it?'

'Uncle Reuben. You remember. Ellie's cousin. She's spoken of him to you, surely?'

I remembered then why the face had seemed familiar to me. Ellie had had several photographs in her sitting-room of her various relations carelessly placed about the room. That was why the face had been so familiar. I had seen it so far only in a photograph.

'I'll come,' I said.

I went out of the room and into the drawing-room. Mr Pardoe rose to his feet, and said:

'Michael Rogers? You may not know my name but your wife was my cousin. She called me Uncle Reuben always, but we haven't met, I know. This is the first time I've been over since your marriage.'

'Of course I know who you are,' I said.

I don't know quite how to describe Reuben Pardoe. He was a big burly man with a large face, wide and rather absent-looking as though he were thinking of something else. Yet after you had talked to him for a few moments you got the feeling that he was more on the ball than you would have thought.

'I don't need to tell you how shocked and grieved I was to hear of Ellie's death,' he said.

'Let's skip that,' I said. 'I'm not up to talking about it.'

'No, no, I can understand that.'

He had a certain sympathetic personality and yet there was something about him that made me vaguely uneasy. I said, as Greta entered:

'You know Miss Andersen?'

'Of course,' he said, 'how are you, Greta?'

'Not too bad,' said Greta. 'How long have you been over?'

'Just a week or two. Touring around.'

Then it came to me. On an impulse I went in. 'I saw you the other day.'

'Really? Where?'

'At an auction sale at a place called Bartington Manor.'

'I remember now,' he said, 'yes, yes I think I remember your face. You were with a man about sixty with a brown moustache.'

'Yes,' I said. 'A Major Phillpot.'

'You seemed in good spirits,' he said, 'both of you.'

'Never better,' I said, and repeated with the strange wonder that I always felt, 'Never better.'

'Of course – at that time you didn't know what had happened. That was the date of the accident, wasn't it?'

'Yes, we were expecting Ellie to join us for lunch.'

'Tragic,' said Uncle Reuben. 'Really tragic . . .'

'I had no idea,' I said, 'that you were in England. I don't think Ellie had any idea either?' I paused, waiting for what he would tell me.

'No,' he said, 'I hadn't written. In fact, I didn't know how much time I should have over here, but actually I'd concluded my business earlier than I thought and I was wondering if after the sale I'd have the time to drive over and see you.'

'You came over from the States on business?' I asked.

'Well, partly yes and partly no. Cora wanted some advice from me on one or two matters. One concerning this house she's thinking of buying.'

It was then that he told me where Cora had been staying in England. Again I said:

'We didn't know that.'

'She was actually staying not far from here that day,' he said.

'Near here? Was she in a hotel?'

'No, she was staying with a friend.'

'I didn't know she had any friends in this part of the world.'

'A woman called – now what was her name? – Hard – something. Hardcastle.'

'Claudia Hardcastle?' I was surprised.

'Yes. She was quite a friend of Cora's. Cora knew her well when she was in the States. Didn't you know?'

'I know very little,' I said. 'Very little about the family.'

I looked at Greta.

'Did *you* know that Cora knew Claudia Hardcastle?'

'I don't think I ever heard her speak of her,' said Greta. 'So that's why Claudia didn't turn up that day.'

'Of course,' I said, 'she was going with you to shop in London. You were to meet at Market Chadwell station –'

'Yes – and she wasn't there. She rang up the house just after

I'd left. Said some American visitor had turned up unexpectedly and she couldn't leave home.'

'I wonder,' I said, 'if the American visitor could have been Cora.'

'Obviously,' said Reuben Pardoe. He shook his head. 'It all seems so confused,' he said. He went on, 'I understand the inquest was adjourned.'

'Yes,' I said.

He drained his cup and got up.

'I won't stay to worry you any more,' he said. 'If there's anything I can do, I'm staying at the Majestic Hotel in Market Chadwell.'

I said I was afraid there wasn't anything he could do and thanked him. When he had gone away, Greta said:

'What does he want, I wonder? Why did he come over?' And then sharply: 'I wish they'd all go back where they belong.'

'I wonder if it was really Stanford Lloyd I saw at the George – I only got a glimpse.'

'You said he was with someone who looked like Claudia so it probably was him. Perhaps he called to see *her* and Reuben came to see Cora – what a mix-up!'

'I don't like it – all of them milling round that day.'

Greta said things often happened that way – as usual she was quite cheerful and reasonable about it.

CHAPTER 22

I

There was nothing more for me to do at Gipsy's Acre. I left Greta in charge of the house while I sailed to New York to wind up things there and to take part in what I felt with some dread were going to be the most ghastly gold-plated obsequies for Ellie.

'You're going into the jungle,' Greta warned me. 'Look after yourself. Don't let them skin you alive.'

She was right about that. It *was* the jungle. I felt it when I got there. I didn't know about jungles – not that kind of jungle. I was out of my depth and I knew it. I wasn't the hunter,

I was the hunted. There were people all round me in the undergrowth, gunning for me. Sometimes, I expect, I imagined things. Sometimes my suspicions were justified. I remember going to the lawyer supplied for me by Mr Lippincott (a most urbane man who treated me rather as a general practitioner might have done in the medical profession). I had been advised to get rid of certain mining properties to which the title deeds were not too clear.

He asked me who had told me so and I said it was Stanford Lloyd.

'Well, we must look into it,' he said. 'A man like Mr Lloyd ought to know.'

He said to me afterwards:

'There's nothing wrong with your title deeds, and there is certainly no point in your selling the land in a hurry, as he seems to have advised you. Hang on to it.'

I had the feeling then that I'd been right, everybody *was* gunning for me. They all knew I was a simpleton when it came to finance.

The funeral was splendid and, I thought, quite horrible. Gold-plated, as I had surmised. At the cemetery, masses of flowers, the cemetery itself like a public park and all the trimmings of wealthy mourning expressed in monumental marble. Ellie would have hated it, I was sure of that. But I suppose her family had a certain right to her.

Four days after my arrival in New York I had news from Kingston Bishop.

The body of old Mrs Lee had been found in the disused quarry on the far side of the hill. She had been dead some days. There had been accidents there before, and it had been said that the place ought to be fenced in – but nothing had been done. A verdict of Accidental Death had been brought in and a further recommendation to the Council to fence the place off. In Mrs Lee's cottage a sum of three hundred pounds had been found hidden under the floorboards, all in one-pound notes.

Major Phillpot had added in a postscript, 'I'm sure you will be sorry to hear that Claudia Hardcastle was thrown from her horse and killed out hunting yesterday.'

Claudia – killed? I couldn't believe it! It gave me a very nasty jolt. Two people – within a fortnight, killed in a riding accident. It seemed like an almost impossible coincidence.

II

I don't want to dwell on that time I spent in New York. I was a stranger in an alien atmosphere. I felt all the time that I had to be wary of what I said and what I did. The Ellie that I had known, the Ellie that had belonged peculiarly to me was not there. I saw her now only as an American girl, heiress to a great fortune, surrounded by friends and connections and distant relatives, one of a family that had lived there for five generations. She had come from there as a comet might have come, visiting my territory.

Now she had gone back to be buried with her own folk, to where her own home was. I was glad to have it that way. I shouldn't have been easy feeling her there in the prim little cemetery at the foot of the pine woods just outside the village. No, I shouldn't have been easy.

'Go back where you belong, Ellie,' I said to myself.

Now and again that haunting little tune of the song she used to sing to her guitar came into my mind. I remembered her fingers twanging the strings.

Every Morn and every Night
Some are born to Sweet Delight

and I thought 'That was true of you. You were born to Sweet Delight. You had Sweet Delight there at Gipsy's Acre. Only it didn't last very long. Now it's over. You've come back to where perhaps there wasn't much delight, where you weren't happy. But you're *at home* here anyway. You're among your own folk.'

I wondered suddenly where *I* should be when the time came for me to die. Gipsy's Acre? It could be. My mother would come and see me laid in my grave – if she wasn't dead already. But I couldn't think of my mother being dead. I could think more easily of death for myself. Yes, she'd come and see me buried. Perhaps the sternness of her face would relax. I took my thoughts away from her. I didn't want to think of her. I didn't want to go near her or see her.

That last isn't quite true. It wasn't a question of seeing *her*.

It was always with my mother a question of *her* seeing *me*, of her eyes looking through me, of an anxiety that swept out like a miasma embracing me. I thought: 'Mothers are the devil! Why have they got to brood over their children? Why do they feel they know all about their children? They don't. They *don't*! She ought to be proud of me, happy for me, happy for the wonderful life that I've achieved. She ought –' Then I wrenched thoughts away from her again.

How long was I over in the States? I can't even remember. It seemed an age of walking warily, of being watched by people with false smiles and enmity in their eyes. I said to myself every day, 'I've got to get *through* this. I've got to get *through* this – and then.' Those were the two words I used. Used in my own mind, I mean. Used them every day several times. *And then* – They were the two words of the future. I used them in the same way that I had once used those other two words. *I want* . . .

Everyone went out of their way to be nice to me because I was rich! Under the terms of Ellie's will I was an extremely rich man. I felt very odd. I had investments I didn't understand, shares, stocks, property. And I didn't know in the least what to do with them all.

The day before I went back to England I had a long conversation with Mr Lippincott. I always thought of him like that in my mind – as Mr Lippincott. He'd never become Uncle Andrew to me. I told him that I thought of withdrawing the charge of my investments from Stanford Lloyd.

'Indeed!' His grizzled eyebrows rose. He looked at me with his shrewd eyes and his poker face and I wondered what exactly his 'indeed' meant.

'Do you think it's all right to do that?' I asked anxiously.

'You have reasons, I presume?'

'No,' I said, 'I haven't got reasons. A feeling, that's all. I suppose I can say anything to you?'

'The communication will be privileged, naturally.'

'All right,' I said, 'I just feel that he's a crook!'

'Ah.' Mr Lippincott looked interested. 'Yes, I should say your instinct was possibly sound.'

So I knew then that I was right. Stanford Lloyd had been

playing hanky-panky with Ellie's bonds and investments and all the rest of it. I signed a power of attorney and gave it to Andrew Lippincott.

'You're willing,' I said, 'to accept it?'

'As far as financial matters are concerned,' said Mr Lippincott, 'you can trust me absolutely. I will do my best for you in that respect. I don't think you will have any reason to complain of my stewardship.'

I wondered exactly what he meant by that. He meant something. I think he meant that he didn't like me, had never liked me, but financially he would do his best for me because I had been Ellie's husband. I signed all necessary papers. He asked me how I was going back to England. Flying? I said no, I wasn't flying, I was going by sea. 'I've got to have a little time to myself,' I said. 'I think a sea voyage will do me good.'

'And you are going to take up your residence – where?'

'Gipsy's Acre,' I said.

'Ah. You propose to live there.'

'Yes,' I said.

'I thought perhaps you might have put it on the market for sale.'

'No,' I said, and the no came out rather stronger than I meant. I wasn't going to part with Gipsy's Acre. Gipsy's Acre had been part of my dream, the dream that I'd cherished since I'd been a callow boy.

'Is anybody looking after it while you have been away in the States?'

I said that I'd left Greta Andersen in charge.

'Ah,' said Mr Lippincott, 'yes. Greta.'

He meant something in the way he said 'Greta' but I didn't take him up on it. If he disliked her, he disliked her. He always had. It left an awkward pause, then I changed my mind. I felt that I'd got to say *something*.

'She was very good to Ellie,' I said. 'She nursed her when she was ill, she came and lived with us and looked after Ellie. I – I can't be grateful enough to her. I'd like you to understand that. You don't know what she's been like. You don't know how she helped and did everything after Ellie was killed. I don't know what I'd have done without her.'

'Quite so, quite so,' said Mr Lippincott. He sounded drier than you could possibly imagine.

'So you see I owe her a lot.'

'A very competent girl,' said Mr Lippincott.

I got up and said goodbye and I thanked him.

'You have nothing for which to thank me,' said Mr Lippincott, dry as ever.

He added, 'I wrote you a short letter. I have sent it by air mail to Gipsy's Acre. If you are going by sea you will probably find it waiting there on arrival.' Then he said, 'Have a good voyage.'

I asked him, rather hesitantly, if he'd known Stanford Lloyd's wife – a girl called Claudia Hardcastle.

'Ah, you mean his first wife. No I never met her. The marriage I believe broke up quite soon. After the divorce, he remarried. That too ended in divorce.'

So that was that.

When I got back to my hotel I found a cable. It asked me to come to a hospital in California. It said a friend of mine, Rudolf Santonix, had asked for me, he had not long to live and he wished to see me before he died.

I changed my passage to a later boat and flew to San Francisco. He wasn't dead yet, but he was sinking very fast. They doubted, they said, if he would recover consciousness before he died, but he had asked for me very urgently. I sat there in that hospital room watching him, watching what looked like a shell of the man I knew. He'd always looked ill, he'd always had a kind of queer transparency about him, a delicacy, a frailness. He lay now looking a deadly, waxen figure. I sat there thinking: 'I wish he'd speak to me. I wish he'd say something. Just *something* before he dies.'

I felt so alone, so horribly alone. I'd escaped from enemies now, I'd got to a friend. My only friend, really. He was the only person who knew anything about me, except Mum, but I didn't want to think of Mum.

Once or twice I spoke to a nurse, asked her if there wasn't anything they could do, but she shook her head and said non-committally:

'He might recover consciousness or might not.'

I sat there. And then at last he stirred and sighed. The nurse raised him up very gently. He looked at me but I didn't know whether he recognized me or not. He was just looking at me as though he looked past me and beyond me. Then suddenly a difference came into his eyes. I thought, 'He *does* know me, he *does* see me.' He said something very faintly and I bent over the bed so as to catch it. But they didn't seem words that had any meaning. Then his body had a sudden spasm and twitch, and he threw his head back and shouted out:

'You damned fool . . . Why didn't you go the other way?'

Then he just collapsed and died.

I don't know what he meant – or even if he knew himself what he was saying.

So that was the last I saw of Santonix. I wonder if he'd have heard me if I had said anything to him? I'd like to have told him once more that the house he'd built me was the best thing I had in the world. The thing that mattered most to me. Funny that a house could mean that. I suppose it was a sort of symbolism about it. Something you want. Something you want so much that you don't quite know what it is. But he'd known what it was and he'd given it to me. And I'd got it. And I was going home to it.

Going home. That's all I could think about when I got on the boat. That and a deadly tiredness at first . . . And then a rising tide of happiness oozing up as it were from the depths . . . I was going home. I was going home . . .

Home is the sailor, home from the sea
And the hunter home from the hill . . .

CHAPTER 23

I

Yes, that was what I was doing. It was all over now. The last of the fight, the last of the struggle. The last phase of the journey.

It seemed so long ago to the time of my restless youth. The days of '*I want, I want.*' But it wasn't long. Less than a year . . .

I went over it all – lying there in my bunk, and thinking.

Meeting Ellie – our times in Regent's Park – our marriage in the Registrar's Office. The house – Santonix building it – the house completed. Mine, all mine. I was me – me – me as I wanted to be. As I'd always wanted to be. I'd got everything I'd wanted and I was going home to it.

Before I left New York I'd written one letter and sent it off by air mail to get there ahead of me. I'd written to Phillpot. Somehow I felt that Phillpot would understand, though others mightn't.

It was easier to write than to tell him. Anyway, he'd got to know. Everyone had got to know. Some people probably wouldn't understand, but I thought he would. He'd seen for himself how close Ellie and Greta had been, how Ellie had depended on Greta. I thought he'd realize how I'd come to depend upon her also, how it would be impossible for me to live alone in the house where I'd lived with Ellie unless there was someone there to help me. I don't know if I put it very well. I did my best.

'I'd like you,' I wrote, 'to be the first to know. You've been so kind to us, and I think you'll be the only person to understand. I can't face living alone at Gipsy's Acre. I've been thinking all the time I've been in America and I've decided that as soon as I get home I'm going to ask Greta to marry me. She's the only person I can really talk to about Ellie, you see. She'll understand. Perhaps she won't marry me, but I think she will . . . It will make everything as though there were the three of us together still.'

I wrote the letter three times before I could get it to express just what I wanted to say. Phillpot ought to get it two days before my return.

I came up on deck as we were approaching England. I looked out as the land came nearer. I thought, 'I wish Santonix was with me.' I did wish it. I wished he could know how everything was all coming true. Everything I'd planned – everything I'd thought – everything I'd wanted.

I'd shaken off America, I'd shaken off the crooks and the sycophants and all the whole lot of them whom I hated and whom I was pretty sure hated me and looked down on me for being so low class! I was back in triumph. I was coming back to the pine trees and the curling dangerous road that made its way up through Gipsy's Acre to the house on the hilltop. *My* house! I was coming back to the two things I wanted. My house

– the house that I'd dreamed of, that I'd planned, that I'd wanted above everything. That and a wonderful woman . . . I'd known always that I'd meet one day a wonderful woman. I had met her. I'd seen her and she'd seen me. We'd come together. A wonderful woman. I'd known the moment I saw her that I belonged to her, belonged to her absolutely and for always. I was hers. And now – at last – I was going to her.

Nobody saw me arrive at Kingston Bishop. It was almost dark and I came by train and I walked from the station, taking a roundabout side road. I didn't want to meet any of the people in the village. Not that night . . .

The sun had set when I came up the road to Gipsy's Acre. I'd told Greta the time I'd arrive. She was up there in the house waiting for me. At last! We'd done with subterfuges now and all the pretences – the pretence of disliking her – I thought now, laughing to myself, of the part I'd played, a part I'd played carefully right from the beginning. Disliking Greta, not wanting her to come and stay with Ellie. Yes, I'd been very careful. Everyone must have been taken in by the pretence. I remembered the quarrel we'd faked up so that Ellie should overhear it.

Greta had known me for what I was the first moment we met. We'd never had any silly illusions about each other. She had the same kind of mind, the same kind of desires as I had. We wanted the World, nothing less! We wanted to be on top of the World. We wanted to fulfil every ambition. We wanted to have everything, deny ourselves nothing. I remembered how I'd poured out my heart to her when I first met her in Hamburg, telling her my frenzied desire for things. I hadn't got to conceal my inordinate greed for life from Greta, she had the same greed herself. She said:

'For all you want out of life you've got to have money.'

'Yes,' I said, 'and I don't see how I'm going to get it.'

'No,' said Greta, 'you won't get it by hard work. You're not the kind.'

'Work!' I said. 'I'd have to work for years! I don't want to wait. I don't want to be middle-aged.' I said, 'You know the story about that chap Schliemann how he worked, toiled, and made a fortune so that he could have his life's dream come true and go to Troy and dig it up and find the graves of Troy. He got his dream but he had to wait till he was forty. But I don't want to wait till I'm a middle-aged man. Old. One foot in the grave. I want it now when I'm young and strong. You do too, don't you?'

'Yes. And I know the way you can do it. It's easy. I wonder you haven't thought of it already. You can get girls easily enough, can't you? I can see that. I can feel it.'

'Do you think I care about girls – or ever have really? There's only one girl I want,' I said. 'You. And you know that. I belong to you. I knew it the moment I saw you. I knew always that I'd meet someone like you. And I have. I belong to you.'

'Yes,' said Greta, 'I think you do.'

'We both want the same things out of life,' I said.

'I tell you it's easy,' said Greta. 'Easy. All you've got to do is to marry a rich girl, one of the richest girls in the world. I can put you in the way of doing that.'

'Don't be fantastic,' I said.

'It's not fantastic, it'll be easy.'

'No,' I said, 'that's no good to me. I don't want to be the husband of a rich wife. She'll buy me things and we'll do things and she'll keep me in a golden cage, but that's not what I want. I don't want to be a tied-up slave.'

'You needn't be. It's the sort of thing that needn't last for long. Just long enough. Wives do die, you know.'

I stared at her.

'Now you're shocked,' she said.

'No,' I said, 'I'm not shocked.'

'I thought you wouldn't be. I thought perhaps already?' She looked at me inquiringly, but I wasn't going to answer that. I still had some self-preservation left. There are some secrets one doesn't want anyone to know. Not that they were much in the way of secrets, but I didn't like to think of them. I didn't like to think of the first one. Silly though. Puerile. Nothing that mattered. I had had a boy's passion for a classy wrist-watch that a boy . . . a friend of mine at school – had been given. I wanted it. I wanted it badly. It had cost a lot of money. A rich godfather had given it to him. Yes, I wanted that, but I didn't think I'd ever have a chance of getting it. Then there was the day we went skating together. The ice wasn't strong enough to bear. Not that we thought of it beforehand. It just happened. The ice cracked. I skated across to him. He was hanging on. He had gone through a hole and he was hanging on to the ice which was cutting his hands. I went across to pull him out, of course, but just as I got there I saw the glint of the wrist-watch. I thought 'Supposing he goes under and drowns.' I thought how easy it would be . . .

It seemed almost unconsciously, I think, that I unfastened the strap, grabbed the watch and pushed his head under instead of trying to pull him out . . . Just held his head under. He couldn't struggle much, he was under the ice. People saw and came towards us. They thought I was trying to pull him out! They got him out in due course, with some difficulty. They tried artificial respiration on him but it was too late. I hid my treasure away in a special place where I kept things now and then. Things I didn't want Mum to see because she'd ask me where I got them. She came across that watch one day when she was fooling about with my socks. Asked me if that wasn't Pete's watch? I said of course it wasn't – it was one I'd swopped with a boy at school.

I was always nervous with Mum – I always felt she knew too much about me. I was nervous with her when she found the watch. She suspected, I think. She couldn't *know*, of course. Nobody *knew*. But she used to look at me. In a funny way. Everybody thought I'd tried to rescue Pete. I don't think she ever thought so. I think she knew. She didn't want to know, but her trouble was that she knew too much about me. I felt a bit guilty sometimes, but it wore off, fairly soon.

And then later on, when I was in camp. It was during our military training time. Chap called Ed and I had been to a sort of gambling place. I'd had no luck at all, lost everything I had, but Ed had won a packet. He changed his chips and he and I were coming home and he was stuffed up with notes. His pockets were bulging with them. Then a couple of toughs came round the corner and went for us. They were pretty handy with the flick knives they'd got. I got cut in the arm but Ed got a proper sort of stab. He went down under it. Then there was a noise of people coming. The toughs hooked it. I could see that if I was quick . . . I *was* quick! My reflexes are pretty good – I wrapped a handkerchief round my hand and I pulled out the knife from Ed's wound and I stuck the knife in again a couple of times in better places. He gave a gasp and passed out. I was scared, of course, scared for a second or two and then I knew it was going to be all right. So I felt – well – naturally I felt proud of myself for thinking and acting quick! I thought 'Poor old Ed, he always was a fool.' It took me no time at all to transfer those notes to my own pocket! Nothing like having quick reflexes, seizing your opportunity. The trouble is the opportunities don't come very often. Some people, I suppose, get scared when they know they've killed someone. But I wasn't scared. Not this time.

Mind you, it's not a thing you want to do too often. Not unless it might be really worth your while. I don't know how Greta sensed that about me. But she'd known. I don't mean that she'd known that I'd actually killed a couple of people. But I think she knew the idea of killing wouldn't shock or upset me. I said:

'What's all this fantastic story, Greta?'

She said, 'I am in a position to help you. I can bring you in touch with one of the richest girls in America. I more or less look after her. I live with her. I have a lot of influence over her.'

'Do you think she'd look at someone like me?' I said. I didn't believe it for a moment. Why should a rich girl who could have her pick of any attractive, sexy man she liked go for me?

'You've got a lot of sex appeal,' said Greta. 'Girls go for you, don't they?'

I grinned and said I didn't do too badly.

'She's never had that kind of thing. She's been looked after too well. The only young men she's been allowed to meet are conventional kids, bankers' sons, tycoons' sons. She's groomed to make a good marriage in the moneyed class. They're terrified of her meeting handsome foreigners who might be after her money. But naturally she's keener on people like that. They'd be new to her, something she's never seen before. You've got to make a big play for her. You've got to fall in love with her at first sight and sweep her off her feet! It'll be easy enough. She's never had anyone to make a real sexy approach to her. You could do it.'

'I could try,' I said doubtfully.

'We could set it up,' said Greta.

'Her family would step in and stop it.'

'No they wouldn't,' said Greta, 'they wouldn't know anything about it. Not until it was too late. Not until you'd got married secretly.'

'So that's your idea.'

So we talked about it. We planned. Not in detail, mind you. Greta went back to America, but she kept in touch with me. I went on with various jobs. I'd told her about Gipsy's Acre and that I wanted it, and she said that was just fine for setting up a romantic story. We laid our plans so that my meeting with Ellie would take place there. Greta would work Ellie up about having a house in England and getting away from the family as soon as she came of age.

Oh yes, we set it up. Greta was a great planner. I don't think I could have planned it, but I knew I could play my part all right. I'd always enjoyed playing a part. And so that's how it happened. That's how I met Ellie.

It was fun, all of it. Mad fun because of course there was always a risk, there was always a danger that it wouldn't come off. The thing that made me really nervous were the times that I had to meet Greta. I had to be sure, you see, that I never gave myself away, by looking at Greta. I tried *not* to look at her. We agreed it was best that I should take a dislike to her, pretend jealousy of her. I carried that out all right. I remember the day she came down to stay. We staged a quarrel, a quarrel that Ellie could hear. I don't know whether we overdid it a bit. I don't think so. Sometimes I was nervous that Ellie might guess or something, but I don't think she did. I don't know. I don't know really. I never did know about Ellie.

It was very easy to make love to Ellie. She was very sweet. Yes, she was really sweet. Just sometimes I was afraid of her because she did things sometimes without telling me. And she knew things that I never dreamt she knew. But she loved me. Yes, she loved me. Sometimes – I think I loved her too . . .

I don't mean it was ever like Greta. Greta was the woman I belonged to. She was sex personified. I was made for her and I had to hold myself in. Ellie was something different. I enjoyed living with her, you know. Yes, that sounds very queer now I think back to it. I enjoyed living with her very much.

I'm putting this down now because this is what I was thinking that evening when I arrived back from America. When I arrived back on top of the world, having got all I'd longed for in spite of the risks, in spite of the dangers, in spite of having done a pretty good murder, though I say it myself!

Yes, it was tricky, I thought once or twice, but nobody could tell, not the way we'd done it. Now the risks were over, the dangers were over and here I was coming up to Gipsy's Acre. Coming as I'd come up to it that day after I'd first seen the poster on the walls, and gone up to look at the ruins of the old house. Coming up and rounding the bend –

And then – *it was then I saw her*. I mean it was then I saw Ellie. Just as I came round the corner of the road in the dangerous place where the accidents happened. *She was there* in the same place just where she'd been before, standing in the shadow of the fir tree. Just as she'd stood, when she'd started a little as she saw me and I'd started, seeing her. There we'd looked at each other first and I'd come up and spoken to her, played the part of the young man who's fallen suddenly in love. Played it jolly well too! Oh, I tell you I'm a fine actor!

But I hadn't expected to see her now . . . I mean, I *couldn't* see her now, could I? But I *was* seeing her . . . She was looking – looking straight at me. Only – there was something that frightened me – something that frightened me very much. It was, you see, just as though she *didn't* see me – I mean I knew she couldn't really be there. I knew she was dead – *but I saw her*. She was dead and her body was buried in the cemetery in the U.S.A. But all the same she was standing under the fir tree and she was looking at me. No, *not* at me. She was looking as though she expected to see me and there was love in her face. The same love that I had seen one day, one day when she'd been plucking the strings of her guitar. That day when she'd said to me, 'What were you thinking of?' And I said, 'Why do you ask me?' and she said, 'You were looking at me as though you loved me.' I'd said something silly like 'Of course I love you.'

I stopped dead. I stopped dead there in the road. I was shaking. I said out loud:

'Ellie.'

She didn't move, she just stayed there, *looking* . . . Looking straight through me. That's what frightened me because I knew if I thought for a minute I'd know why she didn't see me, and

I didn't want to know. No, I didn't want to know that. I was quite sure that I didn't want to know that. Looking straight at the place where I was – *not seeing me*. I ran then. I ran like a coward, up the rest of the road to where the lights were shining in my house, until I pulled myself out of the silly panic that I was in. This was my triumph. I'd got home. I was the hunter home from the hills, back to my house, back to the things that I'd wanted more than anything in the world, to the wonderful woman whom I belonged to body and soul.

And now we'd get married and we'd live in the House. We'd get all we'd played for! We'd won – Won hands down!

The door wasn't latched. I went in, stamping my feet, and through the open door of the library. And there was Greta standing by the window waiting for me. She was glorious. She was the most glorious and the most lovely thing I'd ever seen. She was like a Brünnhilde, a super Valkyrie with shining golden hair. She smelt and looked and tasted of sex. We'd denied ourselves so long except for occasional brief meetings up in the Folly.

I came straight into her arms, a sailor home from the sea to where he belonged. Yes, it was one of the most wonderful moments of my life.

II

Presently we came down to earth. I sat down and she shoved a small pile of letters towards me. I picked out almost automatically one with an American stamp. It was the air mail letter from Lippincott. I wondered what he'd put in it, why he'd had to write me a letter.

'Well,' said Greta with a deep satisfied sigh, 'we've made it.'

'V-Day all right,' I said.

We both laughed, laughed wildly. There was champagne on the table. I opened it and we drank to each other.

'This place is wonderful,' I said, looking round. 'It's more beautiful than I remember it. Santonix – But I haven't told you. Santonix is dead.'

'Oh dear,' said Greta, 'what a pity. So he really *was* ill?'

'Of course he was ill. I never wanted to think so. I went and saw him when he was dying.'

Greta gave a little shiver.

'I shouldn't like to do that. Did he say anything?'

'Not really. He said I was a damned fool – I ought to have gone the other way.'

'What did he mean – what way?'

'I don't know what he meant,' I said. 'I suppose he was delirious. Didn't know what he was talking about.'

'Well, this house is a fine monument to his memory,' said Greta. 'I think we'll stick to it, don't you?'

I stared at her. 'Of course. Do you think I'm going to live anywhere else?'

'We can't live here all the time,' said Greta. 'Not all the year round. Buried in a hole like this village?'

'But it's where I want to live – it's where I always meant to live.'

'Yes, of course. But after all, Mike, we've got all the money in the world. We can go anywhere! We can go all over the Continent – we'll go on safari in Africa. We'll have adventures. We'll go and look for things – exciting pictures. We'll go to the Angkor Vat. Don't you want to have an adventurous life?'

'Well, I suppose so . . . But we'll always come back here, won't we?'

I had a queer feeling, a queer feeling that something had gone wrong somewhere. That's all I'd ever thought of. My House and Greta. I hadn't wanted anything else. But she did. I saw that. She was just beginning. Beginning to want things. Beginning to know she could have them. I had a sudden cruel foreboding. I began to shiver.

'What's the matter with you, Mike – you're shivering. Have you caught a cold or something?'

'It's not that,' I said.

'What's happened, Mike?'

'I saw Ellie,' I said.

'What do you mean, you saw Ellie?'

'As I was walking up the road I turned the corner and there she was, standing under a fir tree, looking at – I mean looking towards me.'

Greta stared.

'Don't be ridiculous. You – you imagined things.'

'Perhaps one does imagine things. This is Gipsy's Acre after all. Ellie was there all right, looking – looking quite happy. Just like herself as though she'd – she'd always been there and was always going to be there.'

'Mike!' Greta took hold of my shoulder. She shook me. 'Mike, don't say things like that. Had you been drinking before you got here?'

'No, I waited till I got here to you. I knew you'd have champagne waiting for us.'

'Well, let's forget Ellie and drink to ourselves.'

'It *was* Ellie,' I said obstinately.

'Of course it wasn't Ellie! It was just a trick of the light – something like that.'

'It was Ellie, and she was standing there. She was looking – looking for me and at me. But she couldn't see me. Greta, *she couldn't see me.*' My voice rose. 'And I know why. I know *why* she couldn't see me.'

'What do you mean?'

It was then that I whispered for the first time under my breath:

'Because that wasn't me. I wasn't there. There was nothing for her to see but Endless Night.' Then I shouted out in a panic-stricken voice, 'Some are born to Sweet Delight, and some are born to Endless Night. *Me*, Greta, *me*.

'Do you remember, Greta,' I said, 'how she sat on that sofa? She used to play that song on her guitar, singing it in her gentle voice. You must remember.

'"*Every night and every morn*,"' I sang it under my breath, '"*Some to misery are born. Every morn and every night some are born to sweet delight.*" That's Ellie, Greta. She was born to sweet delight. "*Some are born to sweet delight, some are born to endless night.*" That's what Mum knew about me. She knew I was born to endless night. I hadn't got there yet. But she knew. And Santonix knew. He knew I was heading that way. But it mightn't have happened. There was just a moment, just one moment, the time Ellie sang that song. I could have been quite happy, couldn't I, really, married to Ellie? I could have gone on being married to Ellie.'

'No, you couldn't,' said Greta. 'I never thought you were the type of person who lost your nerve, Mike.' She shook me roughly by the shoulder again. 'Wake up.'

I stared at her.

'I'm sorry, Greta. What have I been saying?'

'I suppose they got you down over there in the States. But you did all right, didn't you? I mean, all the investments are all right?'

'Everything's fixed,' I said. 'Everything's fixed for our future. Our glorious, glorious future.'

'You speak very queerly. I'd like to know what Lippincott says in his letter.'

I pulled his letter towards me and opened it. There was nothing inside except a cutting from a paper. Not a new cutting, it was old and rather rubbed. I stared down at it. It was a picture of a street. I recognized the street, with rather a grand building in the background. It was a street in Hamburg with some people coming towards the photographer. Two people in the forefront walking arm in arm. They were Greta and myself. *So Lippincott had known*. He'd known all along that I already knew Greta. Somebody must have sent him this cutting some time, probably with no nefarious intention. Just amused perhaps to recognize Miss Greta Andersen walking along the streets of Hamburg. He had known I knew Greta and I remembered how particularly he had asked me whether I had met or not met Greta Andersen. I had denied it, of course, but he'd known I was lying. It must have begun his suspicion of me.

I was suddenly afraid of Lippincott. He couldn't suspect, of course, that I'd killed Ellie. He suspected something, though. Perhaps he suspected even that.

'Look,' I said to Greta, 'he knew we knew each other. He's known it all along. I've always hated that old fox and he's always hated you,' I said. 'When he knows that we're going to marry, he'll suspect.' But then I knew that Lippincott had certainly suspected Greta and I were going to marry, he suspected that we knew each other, he suspected perhaps that we were lovers.

'Mike, will you stop being a panic-stricken rabbit? Yes, that's what I said. A panic-stricken rabbit. I admired you. I've always admired you. But now you're falling to pieces. You're afraid of everyone.'

'Don't say that to me.'

'Well, it's true.'

'*Endless night.*'

I couldn't think of anything else to say. I was still wondering just what it meant. Endless night. It meant blackness. It meant that I wasn't there to be seen. I could see the dead but the dead couldn't see me although I was living. They couldn't see me because I wasn't really there. The man who loved Ellie wasn't really there. He'd entered of his own accord into endless night. I bent my head lower towards the ground.

'*Endless night*,' I said again.

'Stop saying that,' Greta screamed. 'Stand up! Be a man, Mike. Don't give in to this absurd superstitious fancy.'

'How can I help it?' I said. 'I've sold my soul to Gipsy's Acre, haven't I? Gipsy's Acre's never been safe. It's never been safe for anyone. It wasn't safe for Ellie and it isn't safe for me. Perhaps it isn't safe for you.'

'What do you mean?'

I got up. I went towards her. I loved her. Yes, I loved her still with a last tense sexual desire. But love, hate, desire – aren't they all the same? Three in one and one in three. I could never have hated Ellie, but I hated Greta. I enjoyed hating her. I hated her with all my heart and with a leaping joyous wish – I couldn't wait for the safe ways, I didn't want to wait for them, I came nearer to her.

'You filthy bitch!' I said. 'You hateful, glorious, golden-haired bitch. You're not safe, Greta. You're not safe from *me*. Do you understand? I've learnt to enjoy – to enjoy killing people. I was excited the day that I knew Ellie had gone out with that horse to her death. I enjoyed myself all the morning because of killing, but I've never got near enough to killing until now. This is different. I want more than just knowing that someone's going to die because of a capsule they swallowed at breakfast time. I want more than pushing an old woman over a quarry. I want *to use my hands*.'

Greta was afraid now. She, whom I'd belonged to ever since I met her that day in Hamburg, met her and gone on to pretend illness, to throw up my job, to stay there with her. Yes, I'd belonged to her then, body and soul. I didn't belong to her now. I was myself. I was coming into another kind of kingdom to the one I'd dreamed of.

She was afraid. I loved seeing her afraid and I fastened my

hands round her neck. Yes, even now when I am sitting here writing down all about myself (which, mind you, is a very happy thing to do) – to write all about yourself and what you've been through and what you felt and thought and how you deceived everyone – yes, it's wonderful to do, yes I was wonderfully happy when I killed Greta . . .

CHAPTER 24

There isn't really very much to say after that. I mean, things came to a climax there. One forgets, I suppose, that there can't be anything better to follow – that you've had it all. I just sat there for a long time. I don't know when *They* came. I don't know whether They all came at once . . . They couldn't have been there all along because they wouldn't have let me kill Greta. I noticed that God was there first. I don't mean God, I'm confused, I mean Major Phillpot. I'd liked him always, he'd been nice to me. He was rather like God in some ways, I think. I mean if God had been a human being and not something supernatural – up in the sky somewhere. He was a very fair man, very fair and kind. He looked after things and people. Tried to do his best for people.

I don't know how much he'd known about me. I remembered the curious way he looked at me that morning in the sale room when he said that I was 'fey'. I wonder why he thought I happened to be fey that day.

Then when we were there with that little crumpled heap on the ground that was Ellie in her riding habit . . . I wonder if he knew then or had some idea that I'd had something to do with it.

After Greta's death, as I say I just sat there in my chair, staring down at my champagne glass. It was empty. Everything was very empty, very empty indeed. There was just one light that we'd switched on, Greta and I, but it was in the corner. It didn't give much light and the sun – I think the sun must have set a long time ago. I just sat there and wondered what was going to happen next with a sort of dull wonder.

Then, I suppose, the people began coming. Perhaps a lot of

people came at once. They came very quietly, if so, or else I wasn't hearing or noticing anybody.

Perhaps if Santonix had been there he would have told me what to do. Santonix was dead. He'd gone a different way to my way, so he wouldn't be any help. Nobody really would be any help.

After a bit I noticed Dr Shaw. He was so quiet I hardly knew he was there at first. He was sitting quite near me, just waiting for something. After a while I thought he was waiting for me to speak. I said to him:

'I've come home.'

There were one or two other people moving somewhere behind him. They seemed to be waiting, to be waiting for something that he was going to do.

'Greta's dead,' I said. 'I killed her. I expect you'd better take the body away, hadn't you?'

Somebody somewhere let off a flash bulb. It must have been a police photographer photographing the body. Dr Shaw turned his head and said sharply:

'Not yet.'

He turned his head round back to me again. I leaned towards him and said:

'I saw Ellie tonight.'

'Did you? Where?'

'Outside standing under a fir tree. It was the place I first saw her, you know.' I paused a moment and then said, 'She didn't see me . . . She couldn't see me because I wasn't there.' And after a while I said, 'That upset me. It upset me very much.'

Dr Shaw said, 'It was in the capsule, wasn't it? Cyanide in the capsule? That's what you gave Ellie that morning?'

'It was for her hay fever,' I said, 'she always took a capsule as a preventative against her allergy when she went riding. Greta and I fixed up one or two of the capsules with wasp stuff from the garden shed and joined them together again. We did it up in the Folly. Smart, wasn't it?' And I laughed. It was an odd sort of laugh, I heard it myself. It was more like a queer little giggle. I said, 'You'd examined all the things she took, hadn't you, when you came to see her ankle? Sleeping pills, the allergy capsules, and they were all quite all right, weren't they? No harm in any of them.'

'No harm,' said Dr Shaw. 'They were quite innocent.'

'That was rather clever really, wasn't it?' I said.

'You've been quite clever, yes, but not clever enough.'

'All the same I don't see how you found out.'

'We found out when there was a second death, the death you didn't mean to happen.'

'Claudia Hardcastle?'

'Yes. She died the same way as Ellie. She fell from her horse in the hunting field. Claudia was a healthy girl too, but she just fell from her horse and died. The time wasn't so long there, you see. They picked her up almost at once and there was still the smell of cyanide to go by. If she'd lain in the open air like Ellie for a couple of hours, there'd have been nothing – nothing to smell, nothing to find. I don't see how Claudia got the capsule, though. Unless you'd left one behind in the Folly. Claudia used to go to the Folly sometimes. Her fingerprints were there and she dropped a lighter there.'

'We must have been careless. Filling them was rather tricky.' Then I said:

'You suspected I had something to do with Ellie's death, didn't you? All of you?' I looked round at the shadowy figures. 'Perhaps all of you.'

'Very often one knows. But I wasn't sure whether we'd be able to do anything about it.'

'You ought to caution me,' I said reprovingly.

'I'm not a police officer,' said Dr Shaw.

'What are you then?'

'I'm a doctor.'

'I don't need a doctor,' I said.

'That remains to be seen.'

I looked at Phillpot then, and I said:

'What are *you* doing? Come here to judge me, to preside at my trial?'

'I'm only a Justice of the Peace,' he said. 'I'm here as a friend.'

'A friend of mine?' That startled me.

'A friend of Ellie's,' he said.

I didn't understand. None of it made sense to me but I couldn't help feeling rather important. All of them there! Police and doctor,

Shaw and Phillpot who was a busy man in his way. The whole thing was very complicated. I began to lose count of things. I was very tired, you see. I used to get tired suddenly and go to sleep . . .

And all the coming and going. People came to see me, all sorts of people. Lawyers, a solicitor, I think, and another kind of lawyer with him and doctors. Several doctors. They bothered me and I didn't want to answer them.

One of them kept asking me if there was anything I wanted. I said there was. I said there was only one thing I wanted. I said I wanted a ballpen and a lot of paper. I wanted, you see, to write all about it, how it all came to happen. I wanted to tell them what I'd felt, what I'd thought. The more I thought about myself, the more interesting I thought it would be to everybody. Because I *was* interesting. I was a really interesting person and I'd done interesting things.

The doctors – one doctor, anyway – seemed to think it was a good idea. I said:

'You always let people make a statement, so why can't I write my statement out? Some day, perhaps, everybody can read it.'

They let me do it. I couldn't write very long on end. I used to get tired. Somebody used a phrase like 'diminished responsibility' and somebody else disagreed. All sorts of things you hear. Sometimes they don't think you're even listening. Then I had to appear in court and I wanted them to fetch me my best suit because I had to make a good figure there. It seemed they had had detectives watching me. For some time. Those new servants. I think they'd been engaged or put on my trail by Lippincott. They found out too many things about me and Greta. Funny, after she was dead I never thought of Greta much . . . After I'd killed her she didn't seem to matter any more.

I tried to bring back the splendid triumphant feeling that I'd had when I strangled her. But even that was gone away . . .

They brought my mother to see me quite suddenly one day. There she was looking at me from the doorway. She didn't look as anxious as she used to look. I think all she looked now was sad. She hadn't much to say and nor had I. All she said was:

'I tried, Mike. I tried very hard to keep you safe. I failed. I was always afraid that I should fail.'

I said, 'All right, Mum, it wasn't your fault. I chose to go the way I wanted.'

And I thought suddenly, 'That's what Santonix said. He was afraid for me, too. He hadn't been able to do anything either. Nobody could have done anything – except perhaps I myself . . . I don't know. I'm not sure. But every now and then I remember – I remember that day when Ellie said to me, "What are you thinking of when you look at me like that?" and I said, "Like what?" She said, "As though you loved me." I suppose in a way I did love her. I could have loved her. She was so sweet, Ellie. Sweet delight . . .'

I suppose the trouble with me was that I wanted things too much, always. Wanted them, too, the easy way, the greedy way.

That first time, that first day I came to Gipsy's Acre and met Ellie. As we were going down the road again we met Esther. It put it into my head that day, the warning she gave Ellie, put it in my head to pay her. I knew she was the kind who would do anything for money. I'd pay her. She'd start warning Ellie and frightening her, making her feel that she was in danger. I thought it might make it seem more possible then that Ellie had died from shock. That first day, I know now, I'm sure of it, Esther was really frightened. She was really frightened for Ellie. She warned her, warned her to go away, have nothing to do with Gipsy's Acre. She was warning her, of course, to have nothing to do with *me*. I didn't understand that. Ellie didn't understand either.

Was it *me* Ellie was afraid of? I think it must have been though she didn't know it herself. She knew there was something threatening her, she knew there was danger. Santonix knew the evil in me, too, just like my mother. Perhaps all three of them knew. Ellie knew but she didn't mind, she never minded. It's odd, very odd. I know now. We were very happy together. Yes, very happy. I wish I'd known then that we were happy . . . I had my chance. Perhaps everyone has a chance. I – turned my back on it.

It seems odd, doesn't it, that Greta doesn't matter at all?

And even my beautiful house doesn't matter.

Only Ellie . . . And Ellie can never find me again – Endless Night . . . That's the end of my story –

In my end is the beginning – that's what people are always saying.

But what does it *mean*?

And just where does my story begin? I must try and think . . .

BY THE PRICKING OF MY THUMBS

This book is dedicated to the many readers in this and other countries who write to me asking: 'What has happened to Tommy and Tuppence? What are they doing now?' My best wishes to you all, and I hope you will enjoy meeting Tommy and Tuppence again, years older, but with spirit unquenched!

Agatha Christie

By the pricking of my thumbs
Something wicked this way comes.
Macbeth

BOOK I · SUNNY RIDGE

Mr and Mrs Beresford were sitting at the breakfast table. They were an ordinary couple. Hundreds of elderly couples just like them were having breakfast all over England at that particular moment. It was an ordinary sort of day too, the kind of day that you get five days out of seven. It looked as though it might rain but wasn't quite sure of it.

Mr Beresford had once had red hair. There were traces of the red still, but most of it had gone that sandy-cum-grey colour that red-headed people so often arrive at in middle life. Mrs Beresford had once had black hair, a vigorous curling mop of it. Now the black was adulterated with streaks of grey laid on, apparently at random. It made a rather pleasant effect. Mrs Beresford had once thought of dyeing her hair, but in the end she had decided that she liked herself better as nature had made her. She had decided instead to try a new shade of lipstick so as to cheer herself up.

An elderly couple having breakfast together. A pleasant couple, but nothing remarkable about them. So an onlooker would have said. If the onlooker had been young he or she would have added, 'Oh yes, quite pleasant, but deadly dull, of course, like all old people.'

However, Mr and Mrs Beresford had not yet arrived at the time of life when they thought of themselves as old. And they had no idea that they and many others were automatically pronounced deadly dull solely on that account. Only by the young of course, but then, they would have thought indulgently, young people knew nothing about life. Poor dears, they were always worrying about examinations, or their sex life, or buying some extraordinary clothes, or doing extraordinary things to their hair to make them more noticeable. Mr and Mrs Beresford from their own point of view were just past the prime of life. They liked themselves and liked each other and day succeeded day in a quiet but enjoyable fashion.

There were, of course, moments, everyone has moments. Mr Beresford opened a letter, glanced through it and laid it down, adding it to the small pile by his left hand. He picked up the next letter but forbore to open it. Instead he stayed with it in his hand. He was not looking at the letter, he was looking at the toast-rack. His wife observed him for a few moments before saying,

'What's the matter, Tommy?'

'Matter?' said Tommy vaguely. 'Matter?'

'That's what I said,' said Mrs Beresford.

'Nothing is the matter,' said Mr Beresford. 'What should it be?'

'You've thought of something,' said Tuppence accusingly.

'I don't think I was thinking of anything at all.'

'Oh yes, you were. Has anything happened?'

'No, of course not. What should happen?' He added, 'I got the plumber's bill.'

'Oh,' said Tuppence with the air of one enlightened. 'More than you expected, I suppose.'

'Naturally,' said Tommy, 'it always is.'

'I can't think why we didn't train as plumbers,' said Tuppence. 'If you'd only trained as a plumber, I could have been a plumber's mate and we'd be raking in money day by day.'

'Very short-sighted of us not to see these opportunities.'

'Was that the plumber's bill you were looking at just now?'

'Oh no, that was just an Appeal.'

'Delinquent boys – Racial integration?'

'No. Just another Home they're opening for old people.'

'Well, that's more sensible anyway,' said Tuppence, 'but I don't see why you have to have that worried look about it.'

'Oh, I wasn't thinking of that.'

'Well, what *were* you thinking of?'

'I suppose it put it into my mind,' said Mr Beresford.

'What?' said Tuppence. 'You know you'll tell me in the end.'

'It really wasn't anything important. I just thought that perhaps – well, it was Aunt Ada.'

'Oh, I see,' said Tuppence, with instant comprehension. 'Yes,' she added, softly, meditatively. 'Aunt Ada.'

Their eyes met. It is regrettably true that in these days there is in nearly every family, the problem of what might be called an 'Aunt Ada'. The names are different – Aunt Amelia, Aunt Susan, Aunt Cathy, Aunt Joan. They are varied by grandmothers, aged cousins and even great-aunts. But they exist and present a problem in life which has to be dealt with. Arrangements have to be made. Suitable establishments for looking after the elderly have to be inspected and full questions asked about them. Recommendations are sought from doctors, from friends, who have Aunt Adas of their own who had been 'perfectly happy until she had died' at 'The Laurels, Bexhill', or 'Happy Meadows at Scarborough'.

The days are past when Aunt Elisabeth, Aunt Ada and the rest of them lived on happily in the homes where they had lived for many years previously, looked after by devoted if sometimes somewhat tyrannical old servants. Both sides were thoroughly satisfied with the arrangement. Or there were the innumerable poor relations, indigent nieces, semi-idiotic spinster cousins, all yearning for a good home with three good meals a day and a nice bedroom. Supply and demand complemented each other and all was well. Nowadays, things are different.

For the Aunt Adas of today arrangements have to be made suitable, not merely to an elderly lady who, owing to arthritis or other rheumatic difficulties, is liable to fall downstairs if she is left alone in a house, or who suffers from chronic bronchitis, or who quarrels with her neighbours and insults the tradespeople.

Unfortunately, the Aunt Adas are far more trouble than the opposite end of the age scale. Children can be provided with foster homes, foisted off on relations, or sent to suitable schools where they stay for the holidays, or arrangements can be made for pony treks or camps and on the whole very little objection is made by the children to the arrangements so made for them. The Aunt Adas are very different. Tuppence Beresford's own aunt – Great-aunt Primrose – had been a notable troublemaker. Impossible to satisfy her. No sooner did she enter an establishment guaranteed to provide a good home and all comforts for elderly ladies than after writing a few highly complimentary letters to her niece praising this particular establishment, the next news would be that she had indignantly walked out of it without notice.

'Impossible. I couldn't stay there another minute!'

Within the space of a year Aunt Primrose had been in and out of eleven such establishments, finally writing to say that she had now met a very charming young man. 'Really a very devoted boy. He lost his mother at a young age and he badly needs looking after. I have rented a flat and he is coming to live with me. This arrangement will suit us both perfectly. We are natural affinities. You need have no more anxieties, dear Prudence. My future is settled. I am seeing my lawyer tomorrow as it is necessary that I should make some provision for Mervyn if I should pre-decease him which is, of course, the natural course of events, though I assure you at the moment I feel in the pink of health.'

Tuppence had hurried north (the incident had taken place in Aberdeen). But as it happened, the police had arrived there first and had removed the glamorous Mervyn, for whom they had been seeking for some time, on a charge of obtaining money under false pretences. Aunt Primrose had been highly indignant, and had called it persecution – but after attending the Court proceedings (where twenty-five other cases were taken into account) – had been forced to change her views of her *protégé*.

'I think I ought to go and see Aunt Ada, you know, Tuppence,' said Tommy. 'It's been some time.'

'I suppose so,' said Tuppence, without enthusiasm. 'How long has it been?'

Tommy considered. 'It must be nearly a year,' he said.

'It's more than that,' said Tuppence. 'I think it's over a year.'

'Oh dear,' said Tommy, 'the time does go so fast, doesn't it? I can't believe it's been as long as that. Still, I believe you're right, Tuppence.' He calculated. 'It's awful the way one forgets, isn't it? I really feel very badly about it.'

'I don't think you need,' said Tuppence. 'After all, we send her things and we write letters.'

'Oh yes, I know. You're awfully good about those sort of things, Tuppence. But all the same, one does read things sometimes that are very upsetting.'

'You're thinking of that dreadful book we got from the library,' said Tuppence, 'and how awful it was for the poor old dears. How they suffered.'

'I suppose it was true – taken from life.'

'Oh yes,' said Tuppence, 'there must be places like that. And there are people who are terribly unhappy, who can't help being unhappy. But what else is one to do, Tommy?'

'What can anyone do except be as careful as possible. Be very careful what you choose, find out all about it and make sure she's got a nice doctor looking after her.'

'Nobody could be nicer than Dr Murray, you must admit that.'

'Yes,' said Tommy, the worried look receding from his face. 'Murray's a first-class chap. Kind, patient. If anything was going wrong he'd let us know.'

'So I don't think you need worry about it,' said Tuppence. 'How old is she by now?'

'Eighty-two,' said Tommy. 'No – no. I think it's eighty-three,' he added. 'It must be rather awful when you've outlived everybody.'

'That's only what *we* feel,' said Tuppence. '*They* don't feel it.'

'You can't really tell.'

'Well, your Aunt Ada doesn't. Don't you remember the glee with which she told us the number of her old friends that she'd already outlived? She finished up by saying "and as for Amy Morgan, I've heard she won't last more than another six months. She always used to say I was so delicate and now it's practically a certainty that I shall outlive her. Outlive her by a good many years too." Triumphant, that's what she was at the prospect.'

'All the same –' said Tommy.

'I know,' said Tuppence, 'I know. All the same you feel it's your duty and so you've got to go.'

'Don't you think I'm right?'

'Unfortunately,' said Tuppence, 'I do think you're right. Absolutely right. And I'll come too,' she added, with a slight note of heroism in her voice.

'No,' said Tommy. 'Why should you? She's not your aunt. No, I'll go.'

'Not at all,' said Mrs Beresford. 'I like to suffer too. We'll suffer together. You won't enjoy it and I shan't enjoy it and I don't think for one moment that Aunt Ada will enjoy it. But I quite see it is one of those things that has got to be done.'

'No, I don't want you to go. After all, the last time, remember how frightfully rude she was to you?'

'Oh, I didn't mind that,' said Tuppence. 'It's probably the only bit of the visit that the poor old girl enjoyed. I don't grudge it to her, not for a moment.'

'You've always been nice to her,' said Tommy, 'even though you don't like her very much.'

'Nobody could like Aunt Ada,' said Tuppence. 'If you ask me I don't think anyone ever has.'

'One can't help feeling sorry for people when they get old,' said Tommy.

'I can,' said Tuppence. 'I haven't got as nice a nature as you have.'

'Being a woman you're more ruthless,' said Tommy.

'I suppose that might be it. After all, women haven't really got time to be anything but realistic over things. I mean I'm very sorry for people if they're old or sick or anything, if they're nice people. But if they're not nice people, well, it's different, you must admit. If you're pretty nasty when you're twenty and just as nasty when you're forty and nastier still when you're sixty, and a perfect devil by the time you're eighty – well, really, I don't see why one should be particularly sorry for people, just because they're old. You can't change yourself really. I know some absolute ducks who are seventy and eighty. Old Mrs Beauchamp, and Mary Carr and the baker's grandmother, dear old Mrs Poplett, who used to come in and clean for us. They were all dears and sweet and I'd do anything I could for them.'

'All right, all right,' said Tommy, 'be realistic. But if you really want to be noble and come with me –'

'I want to come with you,' said Tuppence. 'After all, I married you for better or for worse and Aunt Ada is decidedly the worse. So I shall go with you hand in hand. And we'll take her a bunch of flowers and a box of chocolates with soft centres and perhaps a magazine or two. You might write to Miss What's-her-name and say we're coming.'

'One day next week? I could manage Tuesday,' said Tommy, 'if that's all right for you.'

'Tuesday it is,' said Tuppence. 'What's the name of the woman? I can't remember – the matron or the superintendent or whoever she is. Begins with a P.'

'Miss Packard.'

'That's right.'

'Perhaps it'll be different this time,' said Tommy.

'Different? In what way?'

'Oh, I don't know. Something interesting might happen.'

'We might be in a railway accident on the way there,' said Tuppence, brightening up a little.

'Why on earth do you want to be in a railway accident?'

'Well I don't really, of course. It was just –'

'Just what?'

'Well, it would be an adventure of some kind, wouldn't it? Perhaps we could save lives or do something useful. Useful and at the same time exciting.'

'What a hope!' said Mr Beresford.

'I know,' agreed Tuppence. 'It's just that these sort of ideas come to one sometimes.'

CHAPTER 2

WAS IT YOUR POOR CHILD?

How Sunny Ridge had come by its name would be difficult to say. There was nothing prominently ridge-like about it. The grounds were flat, which was eminently more suitable for the elderly occupants. It had an ample, though rather undistinguished garden. It was a fairly large Victorian mansion kept in a good state of repair. There were some pleasant shady trees, a Virginia creeper running up the side of the house, and two monkey puzzles gave an exotic air to the scene. There were several benches in advantageous places to catch the sun, one or two garden chairs and a sheltered veranda on which the old ladies could sit sheltered from the east winds.

Tommy rang the front door bell and he and Tuppence were duly admitted by a rather harassed-looking young woman in a nylon overall. She showed them into a small sitting-room saying rather breathlessly, 'I'll tell Miss Packard. She's expecting you and she'll be down in a minute. You won't mind waiting just a little, will you, but it's old Mrs Carraway. She's been and swallowed her thimble again, you see.'

'How on earth did she do a thing like that?' asked Tuppence, surprised.

'Does it for fun,' explained the household help briefly. 'Always doing it.'

She departed and Tuppence sat down and said thoughtfully, 'I don't think I should like to swallow a thimble. It'd be awfully bobbly as it went down. Don't you think so?'

They had not very long to wait however before the door opened and Miss Packard came in, apologizing as she did so. She was a big, sandy-haired woman of about fifty with the air of calm competence about her which Tommy had always admired.

'I'm sorry if I have kept you waiting, Mr Beresford,' she said. 'How do you do, Mrs Beresford, I'm so glad you've come too.'

'Somebody swallowed something, I hear,' said Tommy.

'Oh, so Marlene told you that? Yes, it was old Mrs Carraway. She's always swallowing things. Very difficult, you know, because one can't watch them all the time. Of course one knows children do it, but it seems a funny thing to be a hobby of an elderly woman, doesn't it? It's grown upon her, you know. She gets worse every year. It doesn't seem to do her any harm, that's the cheeriest thing about it.'

'Perhaps her father was a sword swallower,' suggested Tuppence.

'Now that's a very interesting idea, Mrs Beresford. Perhaps it *would* explain things.' She went on, 'I've told Miss Fanshawe that you were coming, Mr Beresford. I don't know really whether she quite took it in. She doesn't always, you know.'

'How has she been lately?'

'Well, she's failing rather rapidly now, I'm afraid,' said Miss Packard in a comfortable voice. 'One never really knows how much she takes in and how much she doesn't. I told her last night and she said she was sure I must be mistaken because it was term time. She seemed to think that you were still at school. Poor old things, they get very muddled up sometimes, especially over time. However, this morning when I reminded her about your visit, she just said it was quite impossible because you were dead. Oh well,' Miss Packard went on cheerfully, 'I expect she'll recognize you when she sees you.'

'How is she in health? Much the same?'

'Well, perhaps as well as can be expected. Frankly, you know, I don't think she'll be with us very much longer. She doesn't suffer in any way but her heart condition's no better than it was. In fact, it's rather worse. So I think I'd like you to know that it's just as well to be prepared, so that if she did go suddenly it wouldn't be any shock to you.'

'We brought her some flowers,' said Tuppence.

'And a box of chocolates,' said Tommy.

'Oh, that's very kind of you I'm sure. She'll be very pleased. Would you like to come up now?'

Tommy and Tuppence rose and followed Miss Packard from the room. She led them up the broad staircase. As they passed one of the rooms in the passage upstairs, it opened suddenly and a little woman about five foot high trotted out, calling in a loud shrill voice, 'I want my cocoa. I want my cocoa. Where's Nurse Jane? I want my cocoa.'

A woman in a nurse's uniform popped out of the next door and said, 'There, there, dear, it's all right. You've had your cocoa. You had it twenty minutes ago.'

'No I didn't, Nurse. It's not true. I haven't had my cocoa. I'm thirsty.'

'Well, you shall have another cup if you like.'

'I can't have another when I haven't had one.'

They passed on and Miss Packard, after giving a brief rap on a door at the end of the passage, opened it and passed in.

'Here you are, Miss Fanshawe,' she said brightly. 'Here's your nephew come to see you. Isn't that nice?'

In a bed near the window an elderly lady sat up abruptly on her raised pillows. She had iron-grey hair, a thin wrinkled face with a large, high-bridged nose and a general air of disapprobation. Tommy advanced.

'Hullo, Aunt Ada,' he said. 'How are you?'

Aunt Ada paid no attention to him, but addressed Miss Packard angrily.

'I don't know what you mean by showing gentlemen into a

lady's bedroom,' she said. 'Wouldn't have been thought proper at all in my young days! Telling me he's my nephew indeed! Who is he? A plumber or the electrician?'

'Now, now, that's not very nice,' said Miss Packard mildly.

'I'm your nephew, Thomas Beresford,' said Tommy. He advanced the box of chocolates. 'I've brought you a box of chocolates.'

'You can't get round me that way,' said Aunt Ada. 'I know your kind. Say anything, you will. Who's this woman?' She eyed Mrs Beresford with an air of distaste.

'I'm Prudence,' said Mrs Beresford. 'Your niece, Prudence.'

'What a ridiculous name,' said Aunt Ada. 'Sounds like a parlourmaid. My Great-uncle Mathew had a parlourmaid called Comfort and the housemaid was called Rejoice-in-the-Lord. Methodist she was. But my Great-aunt Fanny soon put a stop to that. Told her she was going to be called Rebecca as long as she was in *her* house.'

'I brought you a few roses,' said Tuppence.

'I don't care for flowers in a sick-room. Use up all the oxygen.'

'I'll put them in a vase for you,' said Miss Packard.

'You won't do anything of the kind. You ought to have learnt by now that I know my own mind.'

'You seem in fine form, Aunt Ada,' said Mr Beresford. 'Fighting fit, I should say.'

'I can take your measure all right. What d'you mean by saying that you're my nephew? What did you say your name was? Thomas?'

'Yes. Thomas or Tommy.'

'Never heard of you,' said Aunt Ada. 'I only had one nephew and he was called William. Killed in the last war. Good thing, too. He'd have gone to the bad if he'd lived. I'm tired,' said Aunt Ada, leaning back on her pillows and turning her head towards Miss Packard. 'Take 'em away. You shouldn't let strangers in to see me.'

'I thought a nice little visit might cheer you up,' said Miss Packard unperturbed.

Aunt Ada uttered a deep bass sound of ribald mirth.

'All right,' said Tuppence cheerfully. 'We'll go away again. I'll leave the roses. You might change your mind about them. Come on, Tommy,' said Tuppence. She turned towards the door.

'Well, goodbye, Aunt Ada. I'm sorry you don't remember me.'

Aunt Ada was silent until Tuppence had gone out of the door with Miss Packard and Tommy followed her.

'Come back, *you*,' said Aunt Ada, raising her voice. 'I know you perfectly. You're Thomas. Red-haired you used to be. Carrots, that's the colour your hair was. Come back. I'll talk to you. I don't want the woman. No good her pretending she's your wife. I know better. Shouldn't bring that type of woman in here. Come and sit down here in this chair and tell me about your dear mother. You go away,' added Aunt Ada as a kind of postscript, waving her hand towards Tuppence who was hesitating in the doorway.

Tuppence retired immediately.

'Quite in one of her moods today,' said Miss Packard, unruffled, as they went down the stairs. 'Sometimes, you know,' she added, 'she can be quite pleasant. You would hardly believe it.'

Tommy sat down in the chair indicated to him by Aunt Ada and remarked mildly that he couldn't tell her much about his mother as she had been dead now for nearly forty years. Aunt Ada was unperturbed by this statement.

'Fancy,' she said, 'is it as long as that? Well, time does pass quickly.' She looked him over in a considering manner. 'Why don't you get married?' she said. 'Get some nice capable woman to look after you. You're getting on, you know. Save you taking up with all these loose women and bringing them round and speaking as though they were your wife.'

'I can see,' said Tommy, 'that I shall have to get Tuppence to bring her marriage lines along next time we come to see you.'

'Made an honest woman of her, have you?' said Aunt Ada.

'We've been married over thirty years,' said Tommy, 'and we've got a son and a daughter, and they're both married too.'

'The trouble is,' said Aunt Ada, shifting her ground with dexterity, 'that nobody tells me anything. If you'd kept me properly up to date –'

Tommy did not argue the point. Tuppence had once laid upon him a serious injunction. 'If anybody over the age of sixty-five finds fault with you,' she said, 'never argue. Never try to say you're right. Apologize at once and say it was all your fault and you're very sorry and you'll never do it again.'

It occurred to Tommy at this moment with some force that that would certainly be the line to take with Aunt Ada, and indeed always had been.

'I'm very sorry, Aunt Ada,' he said. 'I'm afraid, you know, one does tend to get forgetful as time goes on. It's not everyone,' he continued unblushingly, 'who has your wonderful memory for the past.'

Aunt Ada smirked. There was no other word for it. 'You have something there,' she said. 'I'm sorry if I received you rather roughly, but I don't care for being imposed upon. You never know in this place. They let in anyone to see you. Anyone at all. If I accepted everyone for what they said they were, they might be intending to rob and murder me in my bed.'

'Oh, I don't think that's very likely,' said Tommy.

'You never know,' said Aunt Ada. 'The things you read in the paper. And the things people come and tell you. Not that I believe everything I'm told. But I keep a sharp look-out. Would you believe it, they brought a strange man in the other day – never seen him before. Called himself Dr Williams. Said Dr Murray was away on his holiday and this was his new partner. New partner! How was I to know he was his new partner? He just said he was, that's all.'

'Was he his new partner?'

'Well, as a matter of fact,' said Aunt Ada, slightly annoyed at losing ground, 'he actually was. But nobody could have known it for sure. There he was, drove up in a car, had that little kind of black box with him, which doctors carry to do blood pressure – and all that sort of thing. It's like the magic box they all used to talk about so much. Who was it, Joanna Southcott's?'

'No,' said Tommy. 'I think that was rather different. A prophecy of some kind.'

'Oh, I see. Well, my point is anyone could come into a place like this and say he was a doctor, and immediately all the nurses would smirk and giggle and say yes, Doctor, of course, Doctor, and more or less stand to attention, silly girls! And if the patient swore she didn't know the man, they'd only say she was forgetful and forgot people. I never forget a face,' said Aunt Ada firmly.

'I never have. How is your Aunt Caroline? I haven't heard from her for some time. Have you seen anything of her?'

Tommy said, rather apologetically, that his Aunt Caroline had been dead for fifteen years. Aunt Ada did not take this demise with any signs of sorrow. Aunt Caroline had after all not been her sister, but merely her first cousin.

'Everyone seems to be dying,' she said, with a certain relish. 'No stamina. That's what's the matter with them. Weak heart, coronary thrombosis, high blood pressure, chronic bronchitis, rheumatoid arthritis – all the rest of it. Feeble folk, all of them. That's how the doctors make their living. Giving them boxes and boxes and bottles and bottles of tablets. Yellow tablets, pink tablets, green tablets, even black tablets, I shouldn't be surprised. Ugh! Brimstone and treacle they used to use in my grandmother's day. I bet that was as good as anything. With the choice of getting well or having brimstone and treacle to drink, you chose getting well every time.' She nodded her head in a satisfied manner. 'Can't really trust doctors, can you? Not when it's a professional matter – some new fad – I'm told there's a lot of poisoning going on here. To get hearts for the surgeons, so I'm told. Don't think it's true, myself. Miss Packard's not the sort of woman who would stand for that.'

Downstairs Miss Packard, her manner slightly apologetic, indicated a room leading off the hall.

'I'm so sorry about this, Mrs Beresford, but I expect you know how it is with elderly people. They take fancies or dislikes and persist in them.'

'It must be very difficult running a place of this kind,' said Tuppence.

'Oh, not really,' said Miss Packard. 'I quite enjoy it, you know. And really, I'm quite fond of them all. One gets fond of people one has to look after, you know. I mean, they have their little ways and their fidgets, but they're quite easy to manage, if you know how.'

Tuppence thought to herself that Miss Packard was one of those people who would know how.

'They're like children, really,' said Miss Packard indulgently. 'Only children are far more logical which makes it difficult sometimes with them. But these people are illogical, they want to be reassured by your telling them what they want to believe. Then they're quite happy again for a bit. I've got a very nice staff here. People with patience, you know, and good temper, and not too brainy, because if you have people who are brainy they are bound to be very impatient. Yes, Miss Donovan, what is it?' She turned her head as a young woman with *pince-nez* came running down the stairs.

'It's Mrs Lockett again, Miss Packard. She says she's dying and she wants the doctor called at once.'

'Oh,' said Miss Packard, unimpressed, 'what's she dying from this time?'

'She says there was mushroom in the stew yesterday and that there must have been fungi in it and that she's poisoned.'

'That's a new one,' said Miss Packard. 'I'd better come up and talk to her. So sorry to leave you, Mrs Beresford. You'll find magazines and papers in that room.'

'Oh, I'll be quite all right,' said Tuppence.

She went into the room that had been indicated to her. It was a pleasant room overlooking the garden with french windows that opened on it. There were easy chairs, bowls of flowers on the tables. One wall had a bookshelf containing a mixture of modern novels and travel books, and also what might be described as old favourites, which possibly many of the inmates might be glad to meet again. There were magazines on a table.

At the moment there was only one occupant in the room. An old lady with white hair combed back off her face who was sitting in a chair, holding a glass of milk in her hand, and looking at it. She had a pretty pink and white face, and she smiled at Tuppence in a friendly manner.

'Good morning,' she said. 'Are you coming to live here or are you visiting?'

'I'm visiting,' said Tuppence. 'I have an aunt here. My husband's with her now. We thought perhaps two people at once was rather too much.'

'That was very thoughtful of you,' said the old lady. She took a sip of milk appreciatively. 'I wonder – no, I think it's quite all right. Wouldn't you like something? Some tea or some coffee perhaps? Let me ring the bell. They're very obliging here.'

'No thank you,' said Tuppence, 'really.'

'Or a glass of milk perhaps. It's not poisoned today.'

'No, no, not even that. We shan't be stopping very much longer.'

'Well, if you're quite sure – but it wouldn't be any trouble, you know. Nobody ever thinks anything is any trouble here. Unless, I mean, you ask for something quite impossible.'

'I daresay the aunt we're visiting sometimes asks for quite impossible things,' said Tuppence. 'She's a Miss Fanshawe,' she added.

'Oh, Miss Fanshawe,' said the old lady. 'Oh yes.'

Something seemed to be restraining her but Tuppence said cheerfully,

'She's rather a tartar, I should imagine. She always has been.'

'Oh, yes indeed she is. I used to have an aunt myself, you know, who was very like that, especially as she grew older. But we're all quite fond of Miss Fanshawe. She can be very, very amusing if she likes. About people, you know.'

'Yes, I daresay she could be,' said Tuppence. She reflected a moment or two, considering Aunt Ada in this new light.

'Very acid,' said the old lady. 'My name is Lancaster, by the way, Mrs Lancaster.'

'My name's Beresford,' said Tuppence.

'I'm afraid, you know, one does enjoy a bit of malice now and then. Her descriptions of some of the other guests here, and the things she says about them. Well, you know, one oughtn't, of course, to find it funny but one does.'

'Have you been living here long?'

'A good while now. Yes, let me see, seven years – eight years. Yes, yes it must be more than eight years.' She sighed. 'One loses touch with things. And people too. Any relations I have left live abroad.'

'That must be rather sad.'

'No, not really. I didn't care for them very much. Indeed, I didn't even know them well. I had a bad illness – a very bad illness – and I was alone in the world, so they thought it was better for me to live in a place like this. I think I'm very lucky to have come here. They are so kind and thoughtful. And the gardens are really beautiful. I know myself that I shouldn't like to be living on my own because I do get very confused sometimes, you know.

Very confused.' She tapped her forehead. 'I get confused here. I mix things up. I don't always remember properly the things that have happened.'

'I'm sorry,' said Tuppence. 'I suppose one always has to have something, doesn't one?'

'Some illnesses are very painful. We have two poor women living here with very bad rheumatoid arthritis. They suffer terribly. So I think perhaps it doesn't matter so much if one gets, well, just a little confused about what happened and where, and who it was, and all that sort of thing, you know. At any rate it's not painful physically.'

'No. I think perhaps you're quite right,' said Tuppence.

The door opened and a girl in a white overall came in with a little tray with a coffee pot on it and a plate with two biscuits, which she set down at Tuppence's side.

'Miss Packard thought you might care for a cup of coffee,' she said.

'Oh. Thank you,' said Tuppence.

The girl went out again and Mrs Lancaster said,

'There, you see. Very thoughtful, aren't they?'

'Yes indeed.'

Tuppence poured out her coffee and began to drink it. The two women sat in silence for some time. Tuppence offered the plate of biscuits but the old lady shook her head.

'No thank you, dear. I just like my milk plain.'

She put down the empty glass and leaned back in her chair, her eyes half closed. Tuppence thought that perhaps this was the moment in the morning when she took a little nap, so she remained silent. Suddenly however, Mrs Lancaster seemed to jerk herself awake again. Her eyes opened, she looked at Tuppence and said,

'I see you're looking at the fireplace.'

'Oh. Was I?' said Tuppence, slightly startled.

'Yes. I wondered –' she leant forward and lowered her voice. '– Excuse me, was it your poor child?'

Tuppence slightly taken aback, hesitated.

'I – no, I don't think so,' she said.

'I wondered. I thought perhaps you'd come for that reason. Someone ought to come some time. Perhaps they will. And looking at the fireplace, the way you did. That's where it is, you know. Behind the fireplace.'

'Oh,' said Tuppence. 'Oh. Is it?'

'Always the same time,' said Mrs Lancaster, in a low voice. 'Always the same time of day.' She looked up at the clock on the mantelpiece. Tuppence looked up also. 'Ten past eleven,' said the old lady. 'Ten past eleven. Yes, it's always the same time every morning.'

She sighed. 'People didn't understand – I told them what I knew – but they wouldn't believe me!'

Tuppence was relieved that at that moment the door opened and Tommy came in. Tuppence rose to her feet.

'Here I am. I'm ready.' She went towards the door turning her head to say, 'Goodbye, Mrs Lancaster.'

'How did you get on?' she asked Tommy, as they emerged into the hall.

'After *you* left,' said Tommy, 'like a house on fire.'

'I seem to have had a bad effect on her, don't I?' said Tuppence. 'Rather cheering, in a way.'

'Why cheering?'

'Well, at my age,' said Tuppence, 'and what with my neat and respectable and slightly boring appearance, it's nice to think that you might be taken for a depraved woman of fatal sexual charm.'

'Idiot,' said Tommy, pinching her arm affectionately. 'Who were you hobnobbing with? She looked a very nice fluffy old lady.'

'She was very nice,' said Tuppence. 'A dear old thing, I think. But unfortunately bats.'

'Bats?'

'Yes. Seemed to think there was a dead child behind the fireplace or something of the kind. She asked me if it was my poor child.'

'Rather unnerving,' said Tommy. 'I suppose there must be some people who are slightly batty here, as well as normal elderly relatives with nothing but age to trouble them. Still, she looked nice.'

'Oh, she was nice,' said Tuppence. 'Nice and very sweet, I think. I wonder what exactly her fancies are and why.'

Miss Packard appeared again suddenly.

'Goodbye, Mrs Beresford. I hope they brought you some coffee?'

'Oh yes, they did, thank you.'

'Well, it's been very kind of you to come, I'm sure,' said Miss Packard. Turning to Tommy, she said, 'And I know Miss Fanshawe has enjoyed your visit very much. I'm sorry she was rude to your wife.'

'I think that gave her a lot of pleasure too,' said Tuppence.

'Yes, you're quite right. She does like being rude to people. She's unfortunately rather good at it.'

'And so she practises the art as often as she can,' said Tommy.

'You're very understanding, both of you,' said Miss Packard.

'The old lady I was talking to,' said Tuppence. 'Mrs Lancaster, I think she said her name was?'

'Oh yes, Mrs Lancaster. We're all very fond of her.'

'She's – is she a little peculiar?'

'Well, she has fancies,' said Miss Packard indulgently. 'We have several people here who have fancies. Quite harmless ones. But – well, there they are. Things that they believe have happened to them. Or to other people. We try not to take any notice, not to encourage them. Just play it down. I think really it's just an exercise in imagination, a sort of phantasy they like to live in. Something exciting or something sad and tragic. It doesn't matter which. But no persecution mania, thank goodness. That would never do.'

'Well, that's over,' said Tommy with a sigh, as he got into the car. 'We shan't need to come again for at least six months.'

But they didn't need to go and see her in six months, for three weeks later Aunt Ada died in her sleep.

CHAPTER 3

A FUNERAL

'Funerals are rather sad, aren't they?' said Tuppence.

They had just returned from attending Aunt Ada's funeral, which had entailed a long and troublesome railway journey since the burial had taken place at the country village in Lincolnshire where most of Aunt Ada's family and forebears had been buried.

'What do you expect a funeral to be?' said Tommy reasonably. 'A scene of mad gaiety?'

'Well, it could be in some places,' said Tuppence. 'I mean the Irish enjoy a wake, don't they? They have a lot of keening and wailing first and then plenty of drink and a sort of mad whoopee. *Drink?*' she added, with a look towards the sideboard.

Tommy went over to it and duly brought back what he considered appropriate. In this case a White Lady.

'Ah, that's more like it,' said Tuppence.

She took off her black hat and threw it across the room and slipped off her long black coat.

'I hate mourning,' she said. 'It always smells of moth balls because it's been laid up somewhere.'

'You don't need to go on wearing mourning. It's only to go to the funeral in,' said Tommy.

'Oh no, I know that. In a minute or two I'm going to go up and put on a scarlet jersey just to cheer things up. You can make me another White Lady.'

'Really, Tuppence, I had no idea that funerals would bring out this party feeling.'

'I said funerals were sad,' said Tuppence when she reappeared a moment or two later, wearing a brilliant cherry-red dress with a ruby and diamond lizard pinned to the shoulder of it, 'because it's funerals like Aunt Ada's that are sad. I mean elderly people and not many flowers. Not a lot of people sobbing and sniffing round. Someone old and lonely who won't be missed much.'

'I should have thought it would be much easier for you to stand that than it would if it were my funeral, for instance.'

'That's where you're entirely wrong,' said Tuppence. 'I don't particularly want to think of your funeral because I'd much prefer to die before you do. But I mean, if I were going to your funeral, at any rate it would be an orgy of grief. I should take a lot of handkerchiefs.'

'With black borders?'

'Well, I hadn't thought of black borders but it's a nice idea. And besides, the Burial service is rather lovely. Makes you feel uplifted. Real grief is real. It makes you feel awful but it *does* something to you. I mean, it works it out like perspiration.'

'Really, Tuppence, I find your remarks about my decease and the effect it will have upon you in exceedingly bad taste. I don't like it. Let's forget about funerals.'

'I agree. Let's forget.'

'The poor old bean's gone,' said Tommy, 'and she went peacefully and without suffering. So, let's leave it at that. I'd better clear up all these, I suppose.'

He went over to the writing table and ruffled through some papers.

'Now where did I put Mr Rockbury's letter?'

'Who's Mr Rockbury? Oh, you mean the lawyer who wrote to you.'

'Yes. About winding up her affairs. I seem to be the only one of the family left by now.'

'Pity she hadn't got a fortune to leave you,' said Tuppence.

'If she had had a fortune she'd have left it to that Cats' Home,' said Tommy. 'The legacy that she's left to them in her will will pretty well eat up all the spare cash. There won't be much left to come to me. Not that I need it or want it anyway.'

'Was she so fond of cats?'

'I don't know. I suppose so. I never heard her mention them. I believe,' said Tommy thoughtfully, 'she used to get rather a lot of fun out of saying to old friends of hers when they came to see her "I've left you a little something in my will, dear" or "This brooch that you're so fond of I've left you in my will." She didn't actually leave anything to anyone except the Cats' Home.'

'I bet she got rather a kick out of that,' said Tuppence. 'I can just see her saying all the things you told me to a lot of her old friends – or so-called old friends because I don't suppose they were people she really liked at all. She just enjoyed leading them up the garden path. I must say she was an old devil, wasn't she, Tommy? Only, in a funny sort of way one likes her for being an old devil. It's something to be able to get some fun out of life when you're old and stuck away in a Home. Shall we have to go to Sunny Ridge?'

'Where's the other letter, the one from Miss Packard? Oh yes, here it is. I put it with Rockbury's. Yes, she says there are certain things there, I gather, which apparently are now my property. She took some furniture with her, you know, when she went to live there. And of course there are her personal effects. Clothes and things like that. I suppose somebody will have to go through them. And letters and things. I'm her executor, so I suppose it's up to me. I don't suppose there's anything we want really, is there? Except there's a small desk there that I always liked. Belonged to old Uncle William, I believe.'

'Well, you might take that as a memento,' said Tuppence. 'Otherwise, I suppose, we just send the things to be auctioned.'

'So you don't really need to go there at all,' said Tommy.

'Oh, I think I'd like to go there,' said Tuppence.

'You'd like to? Why? Won't it be rather a bore to you?'

'What, looking through her things? No, I don't think so. I think I've got a certain amount of curiosity. Old letters and antique jewellery are always interesting and I think one ought to look at them oneself, not just send them to auction or let strangers go through them. No, we'll go and look through the things and see if there's anything we would like to keep and otherwise settle up.'

'Why do you really want to go? You've got some other reason, haven't you?'

'Oh dear,' said Tuppence, 'it is awful being married to someone who knows too much about one.'

'So you *have* got another reason?'

'Not a real one.'

'Come on, Tuppence. You're not really so fond of turning over people's belongings.'

'That, I think, is my duty,' said Tuppence firmly. 'No, the only other reason is –'

'Come on. Cough it up.'

'I'd rather like to see that – that other old pussy again.'

'What, the one who thought there was a dead child behind the fireplace?'

'Yes,' said Tuppence. 'I'd like to talk to her again. I'd like to know what was in her mind when she said all those things. Was it something she remembered or was it something that she'd just imagined? The more I think about it the more extraordinary it seems. Is it a sort of story that she wrote to herself in her mind or is there – was there once something real that happened about a fireplace or about a dead child. What made her think that the dead child might have been *my* dead child? Do I look as though I had a dead child?'

'I don't know how you expect anyone to look who has a dead child,' said Tommy. 'I shouldn't have thought so. Anyway, Tuppence, it is our duty to go and you can enjoy yourself in your *macabre* way on the side. So that's settled. We'll write to Miss Packard and fix a day.'

CHAPTER 4

PICTURE OF A HOUSE

Tuppence drew a deep breath.

'It's just the same,' she said.

She and Tommy were standing on the front doorstep of Sunny Ridge.

'Why shouldn't it be?' asked Tommy.

'I don't know. It's just a feeling I have – something to do with time. Time goes at a different pace in different places. Some places you come back to, and you feel that time has been bustling along at a terrific rate and that all sorts of things will have happened – and changed. But here – Tommy – do you remember Ostend?'

'Ostend? We went there on our honeymoon. Of course I remember.'

'And do you remember the sign written up? TRAMSTILLSTAND – It made us laugh. It seemed so ridiculous.'

'I think it was Knock – not Ostend.'

'Never mind – you remember it. Well, this is like that word – *Tramstillstand* – a portmanteau word. Timestillstand – nothing's happened here. Time has just stood still. Everything's going on here just the same. It's like ghosts, only the other way round.'

'I don't know what you are talking about. Are you going to stand here all day talking about time and not even ring the bell? – Aunt Ada isn't here, for one thing. That's different.' He pressed the bell.

'That's the only thing that will be different. My old lady

will be drinking milk and talking about fireplaces, and Mrs Somebody-or-other will have swallowed a thimble or a teaspoon and a funny little woman will come squeaking out of a room demanding her cocoa, and Miss Packard will come down the stairs, and –'

The door opened. A young woman in a nylon overall said: 'Mr and Mrs Beresford? Miss Packard's expecting you.'

The young woman was just about to show them into the same sitting-room as before when Miss Packard came down the stairs and greeted them. Her manner was suitably not quite as brisk as usual. It was grave, and had a kind of semi-mourning about it – not too much – that might have been embarrassing. She was an expert in the exact amount of condolence which would be acceptable.

Three score years and ten was the Biblical accepted span of life, and the deaths in her establishment seldom occurred below that figure. They were to be expected and they happened.

'So good of you to come. I've got everything laid out tidily for you to look through. I'm glad you could come so soon because as a matter of fact I have already three or four people waiting for a vacancy to come here. You will understand, I'm sure, and not think that I was trying to hurry you in any way.'

'Oh no, of course, we quite understand,' said Tommy.

'It's all still in the room Miss Fanshawe occupied,' Miss Packard explained.

Miss Packard opened the door of the room in which they had last seen Aunt Ada. It had that deserted look a room has when the bed is covered with a dust sheet, with the shapes showing beneath it of folded-up blankets and neatly arranged pillows.

The wardrobe doors stood open and the clothes it had held had been laid on the top of the bed neatly folded.

'What do you usually do – I mean, what do people do mostly with clothes and things like that?' said Tuppence.

Miss Packard, as invariably, was competent and helpful.

'I can give you the name of two or three societies who are only too pleased to have things of that kind. She had quite a good fur stole and a good quality coat but I don't suppose you would have any personal use for them? But perhaps you have charities of your own where you would like to dispose of things.'

Tuppence shook her head.

'She had some jewellery,' said Miss Packard. 'I removed that for safe keeping. You will find it in the right-hand drawer of the dressing-table. I put it there just before you were due to arrive.'

'Thank you very much,' said Tommy, 'for the trouble you have taken.'

Tuppence was staring at a picture over the mantelpiece. It was a small oil painting representing a pale pink house standing adjacent to a canal spanned by a small hump-backed bridge. There was an empty boat drawn up under the bridge against the bank of the canal. In the distance were two poplar trees. It was a very pleasant little scene but nevertheless Tommy wondered why Tuppence was staring at it with such earnestness.

'How funny,' murmured Tuppence.

Tommy looked at her inquiringly. The things that Tuppence thought funny were, he knew by long experience, not really to be described by such an adjective at all.

'What do you mean, Tuppence?'

'It is funny. I never noticed that picture when I was here before. But the odd thing is that I have seen that house somewhere. Or perhaps it's a house just like that that I have seen. I remember it quite well . . . Funny that I can't remember when and where.'

'I expect you noticed it without really noticing you were noticing,' said Tommy, feeling his choice of words was rather clumsy and nearly as painfully repetitive as Tuppence's reiteration of the word 'funny'.

'Did *you* notice it, Tommy, when we were here last time?'

'No, but then I didn't look particularly.'

'Oh, that picture,' said Miss Packard. 'No, I don't think you would have seen it when you were here the last time because I'm almost sure it wasn't hanging over the mantelpiece then. Actually it was a picture belonging to one of our other guests, and she gave it to your aunt. Miss Fanshawe expressed admiration of it once or twice and this other old lady made her a present of it and insisted she should have it.'

'Oh I see,' said Tuppence, 'so of course I couldn't have seen it here before. But I still feel I know the house quite well. Don't you, Tommy?'

'No,' said Tommy.

'Well, I'll leave you now,' said Miss Packard briskly. 'I shall be available at any time that you want me.'

She nodded with a smile, and left the room, closing the door behind her.

'I don't think I really like that woman's teeth,' said Tuppence.

'What's wrong with them?'

'Too many of them. Or too big – "*The better to eat you with, my child*" – Like Red Riding Hood's grandmother.'

'You seem in a very odd sort of mood today, Tuppence.'

'I am rather. I've always thought of Miss Packard as very nice – but today, somehow, she seems to me rather sinister. Have you ever felt that?'

'No, I haven't. Come on, let's get on with what we came here to do – look over poor old Aunt Ada's "effects", as the lawyers call them. That's the desk I told you about – Uncle William's desk. Do you like it?'

'It's lovely. Regency, I should think. It's nice for the old people who come here to be able to bring some of their own things with them. I don't care for the horsehair chairs, but I'd like that little work-table. It's just what we need for that corner by the window where we've got that perfectly hideous whatnot.'

'All right,' said Tommy. 'I'll make a note of those two.'

'And we'll have the picture over the mantelpiece. It's an awfully attractive picture and I'm quite sure that I've seen that house somewhere. Now, let's look at the jewellery.'

They opened the dressing-table drawer. There was a set of cameos and a Florentine bracelet and ear-rings and a ring with different-coloured stones in it.

'I've seen one of these before,' said Tuppence. 'They spell a name usually. Dearest sometimes. Diamond, emerald, amethyst, no, it's not dearest. I don't think it would be really. I can't imagine anyone giving your Aunt Ada a ring that spelt dearest. Ruby, emerald – the difficulty is one never knows where to begin. I'll try again. Ruby, emerald, another ruby, no, I think it's a garnet and an amethyst and another pinky stone, it must be a ruby this time and a small diamond in the middle. Oh, of course, it's *regard*. Rather nice really. So old-fashioned and sentimental.'

She slipped it on to her finger.

'I think Deborah might like to have this,' she said, 'and the Florentine set. She's frightfully keen on Victorian things. A lot of people are nowadays. Now, I suppose we'd better do the clothes. That's always rather *macabre*, I think. Oh, this is the fur stole. Quite valuable, I should think. I wouldn't want it myself. I wonder if there's anyone here – anyone who was especially nice to Aunt Ada – or perhaps some special friend among the other inmates – visitors, I mean. They call them visitors or guests, I notice. It would be nice to offer her the stole if so. It's real sable. We'll ask Miss Packard. The rest of the things can go to the charities. So that's all settled, isn't it? We'll go and find Miss Packard now. Goodbye, Aunt Ada,' she remarked aloud, her eyes turning to the bed. 'I'm glad we came to see you that last time. I'm sorry you didn't like me, but if it was fun to you *not* to like me and say those rude things, I don't begrudge it to you. You had to have *some* fun. And we won't forget you. We'll think of you when we look at Uncle William's desk.'

They went in search of Miss Packard. Tommy explained that they would arrange for the desk and the small work-table to be called for and despatched to their own address and that he would arrange with the local auctioneers to dispose of the rest of the furniture. He would leave the choice of any societies willing to receive clothing to Miss Packard if she wouldn't mind the trouble.

'I don't know if there's anyone here who would like her sable stole,' said Tuppence. 'It's a very nice one. One of her special friends, perhaps? Or perhaps one of the nurses who had done some special waiting on Aunt Ada?'

'That is a very kind thought of yours, Mrs Beresford. I'm afraid Miss Fanshawe hadn't any special friends among our visitors, but Miss O'Keefe, one of the nurses, did do a lot for her and was especially good and tactful, and I think she'd be pleased and honoured to have it.'

'And there's the picture over the mantelpiece,' said Tuppence. 'I'd like to have that – but perhaps the person whom it belonged to, and who gave it to her, would want to have it back. I think we ought to ask her –?'

Miss Packard interrupted. 'Oh, I'm sorry, Mrs Beresford, I'm afraid we can't do that. It was a Mrs Lancaster who gave it to Miss Fanshawe and she isn't with us any longer.'

'Isn't with you?' said Tuppence, surprised. 'A Mrs Lancaster? The one I saw last time I was here – with white hair brushed back from her face. She was drinking milk in the sitting-room downstairs. She's gone away, you say?'

'Yes. It was all rather sudden. One of her relations, a Mrs Johnson, took her away about a week ago. Mrs Johnson had returned from Africa where she's been living for the last four or five years – quite unexpectedly. She is now able to take care of Mrs Lancaster in her own home, since she and her husband are taking a house in England. I don't think,' said Miss Packard, 'that Mrs Lancaster really wanted to leave us. She had become so – set in her ways here, and she got on very well with everyone and was happy. She was very disturbed, quite tearful about it – but what can one do? She hadn't really very much say in the matter, because of course the Johnsons were paying for her stay here. I did suggest that as she had been here so long and settled down so well, it might be advisable to let her remain –'

'How long had Mrs Lancaster been with you?' asked Tuppence.

'Oh, nearly six years, I think. Yes, that's about it. That's why, of course, she'd really come to feel that this was her home.'

'Yes,' said Tuppence. 'Yes, I can understand that.' She frowned and gave a nervous glance at Tommy and then stuck a resolute chin into the air.

'I'm sorry she's left. I had a feeling when I was talking to her that I'd met her before – her face seemed familiar to me. And then afterwards it came back to me that I'd met her with an old friend of mine, a Mrs Blenkinsop. I thought when I came back here again to visit Aunt Ada, that I'd find out from her if that was so. But of course if she's gone back to her own people, that's different.'

'I quite understand, Mrs Beresford. If any of our visitors can get in touch with some of their old friends or someone who knew their relations at one time, it makes a great difference to them. I can't remember a Mrs Blenkinsop ever having been mentioned by her, but then I don't suppose that would be likely to happen in any case.'

'Can you tell me a little more about her, who her relations were, and how she came to come here?'

'There's really very little to tell. As I said, it was about six years ago that we had letters from Mrs Johnson inquiring about the Home, and then Mrs Johnson herself came here and inspected it. She said she'd had mentions of Sunny Ridge from a friend and she inquired the terms and all that and – then she went away. And about a week or a fortnight later we had a letter from a firm of solicitors in London making further inquiries, and finally they wrote saying that they would like us to accept Mrs Lancaster and that Mrs Johnson would bring her here in about a week's time if we had a vacancy. As it happened, we had, and Mrs Johnson brought Mrs Lancaster here and Mrs Lancaster seemed to like the place and liked the room that we proposed to allot her. Mrs Johnson said that Mrs Lancaster would like to bring some of her own things. I quite agreed, because people usually do that and find they're much happier. So it was all arranged very satisfactorily. Mrs Johnson explained that Mrs Lancaster was a relation of her husband's, not a very near one, but that they felt worried about her because they themselves were going out to Africa – to Nigeria I think it was, her husband was taking up an appointment there and it was likely they'd be there for some years before they returned to England, so as they had no home to offer Mrs Lancaster, they wanted to make sure that she was accepted in a place where she would be really happy. They were quite sure from what they'd heard about this place that that was so. So it was all arranged very happily indeed and Mrs Lancaster settled down here very well.'

'I see.'

'Everyone here liked Mrs Lancaster very much. She was a little bit – well, you know what I mean – woolly in the head. I mean, she forgot things, confused things and couldn't remember names and addresses sometimes.'

'Did she get many letters?' said Tuppence. 'I mean letters from abroad and things?'

'Well, I think Mrs Johnson – or Mr Johnson – wrote once or twice from Africa but not after the first year. People, I'm afraid, do forget, you know. Especially when they go to a new country and a different life, and I don't think they'd been very closely in touch with her at any time. I think it was just a distant relation, and a family responsibility, and that was all it meant to them. All the financial arrangements were done through the lawyer,

Mr Eccles, a very nice, reputable firm. Actually we'd had one or two dealings with that firm before so that we knew about them, as they knew about us. But I think most of Mrs Lancaster's friends and relations had passed over and so she didn't hear much from anyone, and I think hardly anyone ever came to visit her. One very nice-looking man came about a year later, I think. I don't think he knew her personally at all well but he was a friend of Mr Johnson's and had also been in the Colonial service overseas. I think he just came to make sure she was well and happy.'

'And after that,' said Tuppence, 'everyone forgot about her.'

'I'm afraid so,' said Miss Packard. 'It's sad, isn't it? But it's the usual rather than the unusual thing to happen. Fortunately, most visitors to us make their own friends here. They get friendly with someone who has their own tastes or certain memories in common, and so things settle down quite happily. I think most of them forget most of their past life.'

'Some of them, I suppose,' said Tommy, 'are a little –' he hesitated for a word '– a little –' his hand went slowly to his forehead, but he drew it away. 'I don't mean –' he said.

'Oh, I know perfectly what you mean,' said Miss Packard. 'We don't take mental patients, you know, but we do take what you might call borderline cases. I mean, people who are rather senile – can't look after themselves properly, or who have certain fancies and imaginations. Sometimes they imagine themselves to be historical personages. Quite in a harmless way. We've had two Marie Antoinettes here, one of them was always talking about something called the *Petit Trianon* and drinking a lot of milk which she seemed to associate with the place. And we had one dear old soul who insisted that she was Madame Curie and that she had discovered radium. She used to read the papers with great interest, especially any news of atomic bombs or scientific discoveries. Then she always explained it was she and her husband who had first started experiments on these lines. Harmless delusions are things that manage to keep you very happy when you're elderly. They don't usually last all the time, you know. You're not Marie Antoinette every day or even Madame Curie. Usually it comes on about once a fortnight. Then I suppose presumably one gets tired of keeping the play-acting up. And of course more often it's just forgetfulness that people suffer from. They can't quite remember who they are. Or they keep saying there's something very important they've forgotten and if they could only remember it. That sort of thing.'

'I see,' said Tuppence. She hesitated, and then said, 'Mrs Lancaster – Was it always things about that particular fireplace in the sitting-room she remembered, or was it any fireplace?'

Miss Packard stared – 'A fireplace? I don't understand what you mean.'

'It was something she said that I didn't understand – Perhaps she'd had some unpleasant association with a fireplace, or read some story that had frightened her.'

'Possibly.'

Tuppence said: 'I'm still rather worried about the picture she gave to Aunt Ada.'

'I really don't think you need worry, Mrs Beresford. I expect she's forgotten all about it by now. I don't think she prized it particularly. She was just pleased that Miss Fanshawe admired it and was glad for her to have it, and I'm sure she'd be glad for you to have it because you admire it. It's a nice picture, I thought so myself. Not that I know much about pictures.'

'I tell you what I'll do. I'll write to Mrs Johnson if you'll give me her address, and just ask if it's all right to keep it.'

'The only address I've got is the hotel in London they were going to – the Cleveland, I think it was called. Yes, the Cleveland Hotel, George Street, W1. She was taking Mrs Lancaster there for about four or five days and after that I think they were going to stay with some relations in Scotland. I expect the Cleveland Hotel will have a forwarding address.'

'Well, thank you – And now, about this fur stole of Aunt Ada's.'

'I'll go and bring Miss O'Keefe to you.'

She went out of the room.

'You and your Mrs Blenkinsops,' said Tommy.

Tuppence looked complacent.

'One of my best creations,' she said. 'I'm glad I was able to make use of her – I was just trying to think of a name and suddenly Mrs Blenkinsop came into my mind. What fun it was, wasn't it?'

'It's a long time ago – No more spies in wartime and counterespionage for us.'

'More's the pity. It *was* fun – living in that guest house – inventing a new personality for myself – I really began to believe I *was* Mrs Blenkinsop.'

'You were lucky you got away safely with it,' said Tommy, 'and in my opinion, as I once told you, you overdid it.'

'I did not. I was perfectly in character. A nice woman, rather silly, and far too much taken up with her three sons.'

'That's what I mean,' said Tommy. 'One son would have been quite enough. Three sons were too much to burden yourself with.'

'They became quite real to me,' said Tuppence. 'Douglas, Andrew and – goodness, I've forgotten the name of the third one now. I know exactly what they looked like and their characters and just where they were stationed, and I talked most indiscreetly about the letters I got from them.'

'Well, that's over,' said Tommy. 'There's nothing to find out in this place – so forget about Mrs Blenkinsop. When I'm dead and buried and you've suitably mourned me and taken up your residence in a home for the aged, I expect you'll be thinking you are Mrs Blenkinsop half of the time.'

'It'll be rather boring to have only one role to play,' said Tuppence.

'Why do you think old people *want* to be Marie Antoinette, and Madame Curie and all the rest of it?' asked Tommy.

'I expect because they get so bored. One does get bored. I'm sure *you* would if you couldn't use your legs and walk about, or perhaps your fingers get too stiff and you can't knit. Desperately you want something to do to amuse yourself so you try on some public character and see what it feels like when you are it. I can understand that perfectly.'

'I'm sure you can,' said Tommy. 'God help the home for the aged that you go to. You'll be Cleopatra most of the time, I expect.'

'I won't be a famous person,' said Tuppence. 'I'll be someone like a kitchenmaid at Anne of Cleves' castle retailing a lot of spicy gossip that I'd heard.'

The door opened, and Miss Packard appeared in company with a tall, freckle-faced young woman in nurse's dress and a mop of red hair.

'This is Miss O'Keefe – Mr and Mrs Beresford. They have something to tell you. Excuse me, will you? One of the patients is asking for me.'

Tuppence duly made the presentation of Aunt Ada's fur stole and Nurse O'Keefe was enraptured.

'Oh! It's lovely. It's too good for me, though. You'll be wanting it yourself –'

'No, I don't really. It's on the big side for me. I'm too small. It's just right for a tall girl like you. Aunt Ada was tall.'

'Ah! she was the grand old lady – she must have been very handsome as a girl.'

'I suppose so,' said Tommy doubtfully. 'She must have been a tartar to look after, though.'

'Oh, she was that, indeed. But she had a grand spirit. Nothing got her down. And she was no fool either. You'd be surprised the way she got to know things. Sharp as a needle, she was.'

'She had a temper, though.'

'Yes, indeed. But it's the whining kind that gets you down – all complaints and moans. Miss Fanshawe was never dull. Grand stories she'd tell you of the old days – Rode a horse once up the staircase of a country house when she was a girl – or so she said – Would that be true now?'

'Well, I wouldn't put it past her,' said Tommy.

'You never know what you can believe here. The tales the old dears come and tell you. Criminals that they've recognized – We must notify the police at once – if not, we're all in danger.'

'Somebody was being poisoned last time we were here, I remember,' said Tuppence.

'Ah! that was only Mrs Lockett. It happens to her every day. But it's not the police she wants, it's a doctor to be called – she's that crazy about doctors.'

'And somebody – a little woman – calling out for cocoa –'

'That would be Mrs Moody. Poor soul, she's gone.'

'You mean left here – gone away?'

'No – it was a thrombosis took her – very sudden. She was one who was very devoted to your Aunt – not that Miss Fanshawe always had time for her – always talking nineteen to the dozen, as she did –'

'Mrs Lancaster has left, I hear.'

'Yes, her folk came for her. She didn't want to go, poor thing.'

'What was the story she told me – about the fireplace in the sitting-room?'

'Ah! she'd lots of stories, that one – about the things that happened to her – and the secrets she knew –'

'There was something about a child – a kidnapped child or a murdered child –'

'It's strange it is, the things they think up. It's the TV as often as not that gives them the ideas –'

'Do you find it a strain, working here with all these old people? It must be tiring.'

'Oh no – I like old people – That's why I took up Geriatric work –'

'You've been here long?'

'A year and a half –' She paused. '– But I'm leaving next month.'

'Oh! why?'

For the first time a certain constraint came into Nurse O'Keefe's manner.

'Well, you see, Mrs Beresford, one needs a change –'

'But you'll be doing the same kind of work?'

'Oh yes –' She picked up the fur stole. 'I'm thanking you again very much – and I'm glad, too, to have something to remember Miss Fanshawe by – She was a grand old lady – You don't find many like her nowadays.'

CHAPTER 5

DISAPPEARANCE OF AN OLD LADY

I

Aunt Ada's things arrived in due course. The desk was installed and admired. The little work-table dispossessed the whatnot – which was relegated to a dark corner of the hall. And the picture of the pale pink house by the canal bridge Tuppence hung over the mantelpiece in her bedroom where she could see it every morning when drinking her early morning tea.

Since her conscience still troubled her a little, Tuppence wrote a letter explaining how the picture had come into their possession but that if Mrs Lancaster would like it returned, she had only got to let them know. This she dispatched to Mrs Lancaster, c/o Mrs Johnson, at the Cleveland Hotel, George Street, London, W1.

To this there was no reply, but a week later the letter was returned with 'Not known at this address' scrawled on it.

'How tiresome,' said Tuppence.

'Perhaps they only stayed for a night or two,' suggested Tommy.

'You'd think they'd have left a forwarding address –'

'Did you put "Please forward" on it?'

'Yes, I did. I know, I'll ring them up and ask – They must have put an address in the hotel register –'

'I'd let it go if I were you,' said Tommy. 'Why make all this fuss? I expect the old pussy has forgotten all about the picture.'

'I might as well try.'

Tuppence sat down at the telephone and was presently connected to the Cleveland Hotel.

She rejoined Tommy in his study a few minutes later.

'It's rather curious, Tommy – they haven't even *been* there. No Mrs Johnson – no Mrs Lancaster – no rooms booked for them – or any trace of their having stayed there before.'

'I expect Miss Packard got the name of the hotel wrong. Wrote it down in a hurry – and then perhaps lost it – or remembered it wrong. Things like that often happen, you know.'

'I shouldn't have thought it would at Sunny Ridge. Miss Packard is so efficient always.'

'Perhaps they didn't book beforehand at the hotel and it was full, so they had to go somewhere else. You know what accommodation in London is like – *Must* you go on fussing?'

Tuppence retired.

Presently she came back.

'I know what I'm going to do. I'll ring up Miss Packard and I'll get the address of the lawyers –'

'What lawyers?'

'Don't you remember she said something about a firm of solicitors who made all the arrangements because the Johnsons were abroad?'

Tommy, who was busy over a speech he was drafting for a

Conference he was shortly to attend, and murmuring under his breath – '*the proper policy if such a contingency should arise*' – said: 'How do you spell contingency, Tuppence?'

'Did you hear what I was saying?'

'Yes, very good idea – splendid – excellent – you do that –'

Tuppence went out – stuck her head in again and said:

'C-o-n-s-i-s-t-e-n-c-y.'

'Can't be – you've got the wrong word.'

'What are you writing about?'

'The Paper I'm reading next at the I.U.A.S. and I do wish you'd let me do it in peace.'

'Sorry.'

Tuppence removed herself. Tommy continued to write sentences and then scratch them out. His face was just brightening, as the pace of his writing increased – when once more the door opened.

'Here it is,' said Tuppence. 'Partingdale, Harris, Lockeridge and Partingdale, 32 Lincoln Terrace, W.C.2. Tel. Holborn 051386. The operative member of the firm is Mr Eccles.' She placed a sheet of paper by Tommy's elbow. 'Now *you* take on.'

'No!' said Tommy firmly.

'Yes! She's *your* Aunt Ada.'

'Where does Aunt Ada come in? Mrs Lancaster is no aunt of mine.'

'But it's *lawyers*,' Tuppence insisted. 'It's a man's job always to deal with lawyers. They just think women are silly and don't pay attention –'

'A very sensible point of view,' said Tommy.

'Oh! Tommy – *do* help. You go and telephone and I'll find the dictionary and look how to spell contingency.'

Tommy gave her a look, but departed.

He returned at last and spoke firmly – 'This matter is now *closed*, Tuppence.'

'You got Mr Eccles?'

'Strictly speaking I got a Mr Wills who is doubtless the dogsbody of the firm of Partingford, Lockjaw and Harrison. But he was fully informed and glib. All letters and communications go via the Southern Counties Bank, Hammersmith branch, who will forward all communications. And there, Tuppence, let me tell you, the trail *stops*. Banks will forward things – but they won't yield any addresses to you or anyone else who asks. They have their code of rules and they'll stick to them – Their lips are sealed like our more pompous Prime Ministers.'

'All right, I'll send a letter care of the Bank.'

'Do that – and for goodness' sake, *leave me alone* – or I shall never get my speech done.'

'Thank you, darling,' said Tuppence. 'I don't know what I'd do without you.' She kissed the top of his head.

'It's the best butter,' said Tommy.

II

It was not until the following Thursday evening that Tommy asked suddenly, 'By the way, did you ever get any answer to the letter you sent care of the Bank to Mrs Johnson –'

'It's nice of you to ask,' said Tuppence sarcastically. 'No, I didn't.' She added meditatively, 'I don't think I shall, either.'

'Why not?'

'You're not really interested,' said Tuppence coldly.

'Look here, Tuppence – I know I've been rather preoccupied – It's all this I.U.A.S. – It's only once a year, thank goodness.'

'It starts on Monday, doesn't it? For five days –'

'Four days.'

'And you all go down to a Hush Hush, top secret house in the country somewhere, and make speeches and read Papers and vet young men for Super Secret assignments in Europe and beyond. I've forgotten what I.U.A.S. stands for. All these initials they have nowadays –'

'International Union of Associated Security.'

'What a mouthful! Quite ridiculous. And I expect the whole place is bugged, and everybody knows everybody else's most secret conversations.'

'Highly likely,' said Tommy with a grin.

'And I suppose you enjoy it?'

'Well, I do in a way. One sees a lot of old friends.'

'All quite ga-ga by now, I expect. Does any of it do any good?'

'Heavens, what a question! Can one ever let oneself believe that you can answer that by a plain Yes or No –'

'And are any of the people any good?'

'I'd answer Yes to that. Some of them are very good indeed.'

'Will old Josh be there?'

'Yes, he'll be there.'

'What is he like nowadays?'

'Extremely deaf, half blind, crippled with rheumatism – and you'd be surprised at the things that *don't* get past him.'

'I see,' said Tuppence. She meditated. 'I wish I were in it, too.'

Tommy looked apologetic.

'I expect you'll find something to do while I'm away.'

'I might at that,' said Tuppence meditatively.

Her husband looked at her with the vague apprehension that Tuppence could always arouse in him.

'Tuppence – what are you up to?'

'Nothing, yet – So far I'm only thinking.'

'What about?'

'Sunny Ridge. And a nice old lady sipping milk and talking in a scatty kind of way about dead children and fireplaces. It intrigued me. I thought then that I'd try and find out more from her next time we came to see Aunt Ada – But there wasn't a next time because Aunt Ada died – And when we were next in Sunny Ridge – Mrs Lancaster had – disappeared!'

'You mean her people had taken her away? That's not a disappearance – it's quite natural.'

'It's a disappearance – no traceable address – no answer to letters – it's a planned disappearance. I'm more and more sure of it.'

'But –'

Tuppence broke in upon his 'But'.

'Listen, Tommy – supposing that sometime or other a crime happened – It seemed all safe and covered up – But then suppose that someone in the family had seen something, or known something – someone elderly and garrulous – someone who chattered to people – someone whom you suddenly realized might be a danger to you – What would you do about it?'

'Arsenic in the soup?' suggested Tommy cheerfully. 'Cosh them on the head – Push them down the staircase –?'

'That's rather extreme – Sudden deaths attract attention. You'd look about for some simpler way – and you'd find one. A nice respectable Home for Elderly Ladies. You'd pay a visit to it, calling yourself Mrs Johnson or Mrs Robinson – or you would get some unsuspecting third party to make arrangements – You'd fix the financial arrangements through a firm of reliable solicitors. You've already hinted, perhaps, that your elderly relative has fancies and mild delusions sometimes – so do a good many of the other old ladies – Nobody will think it odd – if she cackles on about poisoned milk, or dead children behind a fireplace, or a sinister kidnapping; nobody will really listen. They'll just think it's old Mrs So-and-So having her fancies again – nobody will take any *notice at all*.'

'Except Mrs Thomas Beresford,' said Tommy.

'All right, *yes*,' said Tuppence. '*I've* taken notice –'

'But why did you?'

'I don't quite know,' said Tuppence slowly. 'It's like the fairy stories. *By the pricking of my thumbs – Something evil this way comes* – I felt suddenly scared. I'd always thought of Sunny Ridge as such a normal happy place – and suddenly I began to wonder – That's the only way I can put it. I wanted to find out more. And now poor old Mrs Lancaster has disappeared. Somebody's spirited her away.'

'But why should they?'

'I can only think because she was getting worse – worse from their point of view – remembering more, perhaps, talking to people more, or perhaps she recognized someone – or someone recognized her – or told her something that gave her new ideas about something that had once happened. Anyway, for some reason or other she became dangerous to someone.'

'Look here, Tuppence, this whole thing is all somethings and someones. It's just an idea you've thought up. You don't want to go mixing yourself up in things that are no business of yours –'

'There's nothing to be mixed up in according to you,' said Tuppence. 'So you needn't worry at all.'

'You leave Sunny Ridge alone.'

'I don't mean to go back to Sunny Ridge. I think they've told me all they know there. I think that that old lady was quite safe whilst she was there. I want to find out where she is *now* – I want to get to her wherever she is *in time* – before something happens to her.'

'What on earth do you think might happen to her?'

'I don't like to think. But I'm on the trail – I'm going to be Prudence Beresford, Private Investigator. Do you remember when we were Blunts Brilliant Detectives?'

'*I* was,' said Tommy. '*You* were Miss Robinson, my private secretary.'

'Not all the time. Anyway, that's what I'm going to do while you're playing at International Espionage at Hush Hush Manor. It's the "Save Mrs Lancaster" that I'm going to be busy with.'

'You'll probably find her perfectly all right.'

'I hope I shall. Nobody would be better pleased than I should.'

'How do you propose to set about it?'

'As I told you, I've got to think first. Perhaps an advertisement of some kind? No, that would be a mistake.'

'Well, be careful,' said Tommy, rather inadequately.

Tuppence did not deign to reply.

III

On Monday morning, Albert, the domestic mainstay of the Beresfords' life for many long years, ever since he had been roped into anti-criminal activities by them as a carroty-haired lift-boy, deposited the tray of early morning tea on the table between the two beds, pulled back the curtains, announced that it was a fine day, and removed his now portly form from the room.

Tuppence yawned, sat up, rubbed her eyes, poured out a cup of tea, dropped a slice of lemon in it, and remarked that it seemed a nice day, but you never knew.

Tommy turned over and groaned.

'Wake up,' said Tuppence. 'Remember you're going places today.'

'Oh Lord,' said Tommy. 'So I am.'

He, too, sat up and helped himself to tea. He looked with appreciation at the picture over the mantelpiece.

'I must say, Tuppence, your picture looks very nice.'

'It's the way the sun comes in from the window sideways and lights it up.'

'Peaceful,' said Tommy.

'If only I could remember where it was I'd seen it before.'

'I can't see that it matters. You'll remember sometime or other.'

'That's no good. I want to remember *now*.'

'But why?'

'Don't you see? It's the only clue I've got. It was Mrs Lancaster's picture –'

'But the two things don't tie up together anyway,' said Tommy. 'I mean, it's true that the picture once belonged to Mrs Lancaster. But it may have been just a picture she bought at an exhibition or that somebody in her family did. It may have been a picture that somebody gave her as a present. She took it to Sunny Ridge with her because she thought it looked nice. There's no reason it should have anything to do with her *personally*. If it had, she wouldn't have given it to Aunt Ada.'

'It's the only clue I've got,' said Tuppence.

'It's a nice peaceful house,' said Tommy.

'All the same, I think it's an empty house.'

'What do you mean, empty?'

'I don't think,' said Tuppence, 'there's anybody living in it. I don't think anybody's ever going to come out of that house. Nobody's going to walk across that bridge, nobody's going to untie that boat and row away in it.'

'For goodness' sake, Tuppence.' Tommy stared at her. 'What's the matter with you?'

'I thought so the first time I saw it,' said Tuppence. 'I thought "What a nice house that would be to live in." And then I thought "But nobody does live here, I'm sure they don't." That shows you that I have seen it before. Wait a minute. Wait a minute . . . it's coming. It's coming.'

Tommy stared at her.

'Out of a *window*,' said Tuppence breathlessly. 'Out of a car window? No, no, that would be the wrong angle. Running alongside the canal . . . and a little hump-backed bridge and the pink walls of the house, the two poplar trees, more than two. There were *lots* more poplar trees. Oh dear, oh dear, if I could –'

'Oh, come off it, Tuppence.'

'It will come back to me.'

'Good Lord,' Tommy looked at his watch. 'I've got to hurry. You and your *déjà vu* picture.'

He jumped out of bed and hastened to the bathroom. Tuppence lay back on her pillows and closed her eyes, trying to force a recollection that just remained elusively out of reach.

Tommy was pouring out a second cup of coffee in the dining-room when Tuppence appeared flushed with triumph.

'I've got it – I know where I saw that house. It was out of the window of a railway train.'

'Where? When?'

'I don't know. I'll have to think. I remember saying to myself: "Someday I'll go and look at that house" – and I tried to see what the name of the next station was. But you know what railways are nowadays. They've pulled down half the stations – and the next one we went through was all torn down, and grass growing over the platforms, and no name board or anything.'

'Where the hell's my brief-case? Albert!'

A frenzied search took place.

Tommy came back to say a breathless goodbye. Tuppence was sitting looking meditatively at a fried egg.

'Goodbye,' said Tommy. 'And for God's sake, Tuppence, don't go poking into something that's none of your business.'

'I think,' said Tuppence, meditatively, 'that what I shall really do, is to take a few railway journeys.'

Tommy looked slightly relieved.

'Yes,' he said encouragingly, 'you try that. Buy yourself a season ticket. There's some scheme where you can travel a thousand miles all over the British Isles for a very reasonable fixed sum. That ought to suit you down to the ground, Tuppence. You travel by all the trains you can think of in all the likely parts. That ought to keep you happy until I come home again.'

'Give my love to Josh.'

'I will.' He added, looking at his wife in a worried manner, 'I wish you were coming with me. Don't – don't do anything stupid, will you?'

'Of course not,' said Tuppence.

CHAPTER 6

....

TUPPENCE ON THE TRAIL

'Oh dear,' sighed Tuppence, 'oh dear.' She looked round her with gloomy eyes. Never, she said to herself, had she felt more miserable. Naturally she had known she would miss Tommy, but she had no idea how much she was going to miss him.

During the long course of their married life they had hardly ever been separated for any length of time. Starting before their marriage, they had called themselves a pair of 'young adventurers'. They had been through various difficulties and dangers together, they had married, they had had two children and just as the world was seeming rather dull and middle-aged to them, the second war had come about and in what seemed an almost miraculous way they had been tangled up yet again on the outskirts of the British Intelligence. A somewhat unorthodox pair, they had been recruited by a quiet nondescript man who called himself 'Mr Carter', but to whose word everybody seemed to bow. They had had adventures, and once again they had had them together. This, by the way, had not been planned by Mr Carter. Tommy alone had been recruited. But Tuppence displaying all her natural ingenuity, had managed to eavesdrop in such a fashion that when Tommy had arrived at a guest house on the sea coast in the role of a certain Mr Meadows, the first person he had seen there had been a middle-aged lady plying knitting needles, who had looked up at him with innocent eyes and whom he had been forced to greet as Mrs Blenkinsop. Thereafter they had worked as a pair.

'However,' thought Tuppence to herself, 'I can't do it this time.' No amount of eavesdropping, of ingenuity, or anything else would take her to the recesses of Hush Hush Manor or to participation in the intricacies of I.U.A.S. Just an Old Boys Club, she thought resentfully. Without Tommy the flat was empty, the world was lonely, and 'What on earth,' thought Tuppence, 'am I to do with myself?'

The question was really purely rhetorical for Tuppence had already started on the first steps of what she planned to do with herself. There was no question this time of intelligence work, of counter-espionage or anything of that kind. Nothing of an official nature. 'Prudence Beresford, Private Investigator, that's what I am,' said Tuppence to herself.

After a scrappy lunch had been hastily cleared away, the dining-room table was strewn with railway time-tables, guide-books, maps, and a few old diaries which Tuppence had managed to disinter.

Some time in the last three years (not longer, she was sure) she had taken a railway journey, and looking out of the carriage window, had noticed a house. But, what railway journey?

Like most people at the present time, the Beresfords travelled mainly by car. The railway journeys they took were few and far between.

Scotland, of course, when they went to stay with their married daughter Deborah – but that was a night journey.

Penzance – summer holidays – but Tuppence knew that line by heart.

No, this had been a much more casual journey.

With diligence and perseverance, Tuppence had made a meticulous list of all the possible journeys she had taken which might correspond to what she was looking for. One or two race meetings, a visit to Northumberland, two possible places in Wales, a christening, two weddings, a sale they had attended, some puppies she had once delivered for a friend who bred them and who had gone down with influenza. The meeting place had been an arid-looking country junction whose name she couldn't remember.

Tuppence sighed. It seemed as though Tommy's solution was the one she might have to adopt – Buy a kind of circular ticket and actually travel over the most likely stretches of railway line.

In a small notebook she had jotted down any snatches of extra memories – vague flashes – in case they might help.

A hat, for instance – Yes, a hat that she had thrown up on the rack. She had been wearing a hat – so – a wedding or the christening – certainly not puppies.

And – another flash – kicking off her shoes – because her feet hurt. Yes – that was definite – she had been actually looking at the House – and she had kicked off her shoes because her feet hurt.

So, then, it had definitely been a social function she had either been going to, or returning from – Returning from, of course – because of the painfulness of her feet from long standing about in her best shoes. And what kind of a hat? Because that would help – a flowery hat – a summer wedding – or a velvet winter one?

Tuppence was busy jotting down details from the Railway timetables of different lines when Albert came in to ask what she wanted for supper – and what she wanted ordered in from the butcher and the grocer.

'I think I'm going to be away for the next few days,' said Tuppence. 'So you needn't order in anything. I'm going to take some railway journeys.'

'Will you be wanting some sandwiches?'

'I might. Get some ham or something.'

'Egg and cheese do you? Or there's a tin of *pâté* in the larder – it's been there a long while, time it was eaten.' It was a somewhat sinister recommendation, but Tuppence said,

'All right. That'll do.'

'Want letters forwarded?'

'I don't even know where I'm going yet,' said Tuppence.

'I see,' said Albert.

The comfortable thing about Albert was that he always accepted everything. Nothing ever had to be explained to him.

He went away and Tuppence settled down to her planning – what she wanted was: a social engagement involving a hat and party shoes. Unfortunately the ones she had listed involved different railway lines – One wedding on the Southern Railway, the other in East Anglia. The christening north of Bedford.

If she could remember a little more about the scenery . . . She had been sitting on the right-hand side of the train. What had she been looking at *before* the canal – Woods? Trees? Farmland? A distant village?

Straining her brain, she looked up with a frown – Albert had come back. How far she was at that moment from knowing that Albert standing there waiting for attention was neither more nor less than an answer to prayer –

'Well, what is it *now*, Albert?'

'If it's that you're going to be away all day tomorrow –'

'And the day after as well, probably –'

'Would it be all right for me to have the day off?'

'Yes, of course.'

'It's Elizabeth – come out in spots she has. Milly thinks it's measles –'

'Oh dear.' Milly was Albert's wife and Elizabeth was the youngest of his children. 'So Milly wants you at home, of course.'

Albert lived in a small neat house a street or two away.

'It's not that so much – She likes me out of the way when she's got her hands full – she doesn't want me messing things up – But it's the other kids – I could take 'em somewhere out of her way.'

'Of course. You're all in quarantine, I suppose.'

'Oh! well, best for 'em all to get it, and get it over. Charlie's had it, and so has Jean. Anyway, that'll be all right?'

Tuppence assured him that it would be all right.

Something was stirring in the depths of her subconscious – A happy anticipation – a recognition – Measles – Yes, measles. Something to do with measles.

But why should the house by the canal have anything to do with measles . . . ?

Of course! Anthea. Anthea was Tuppence's god-daughter – and Anthea's daughter Jane was at school – her first term – and it was Prize Giving and Anthea had rung up – her two younger children had come out in a measle rash and she had nobody in the house to help and Jane would be terribly disappointed if nobody came – Could Tuppence possibly? –

And Tuppence had said of course – She wasn't doing anything particular – she'd go down to the school and take Jane out and give her lunch and then go back to the sports and all the rest of it. There was a special school train.

Everything came back into her mind with astonishing clarity – even the dress she'd worn – a summer print of cornflowers!

She had seen the house on the return journey.

Going down there she had been absorbed in a magazine she had bought, but coming back she had had nothing to read, and she had looked out of the window until, exhausted by the activities of the day, and the pressure of her shoes, she had dropped off to sleep.

When she had woken up the train had been running beside a canal. It was partially wooded country, an occasional bridge, sometimes a twisting lane or minor road – a distant farm – no villages.

The train began to slow down, for no reason it would seem, except that a signal must be against it. It drew jerkily to a halt by a bridge, a little hump-backed bridge which spanned the canal, a disused canal presumably. On the other side of the canal, close to the water, was the house – a house that Tuppence thought at once was one of the most attractive houses she had ever seen – a quiet, peaceful house, irradiated by the golden light of the late afternoon sun.

There was no human being to be seen – no dogs, or livestock. Yet the green shutters were not fastened. The house must be lived in, but now, at this moment, it was empty.

'I must find out about that house,' Tuppence had thought. 'Someday I must come back here and look at it. It's the kind of house I'd like to live in.'

With a jerk the train lurched slowly forwards.

'I'll look out for the name of the next station – so that I'll know where it is.'

But there had been no appropriate station. It was the time when things were beginning to happen to railways – small stations were closed, even pulled down, grass sprouted on the decayed platforms. For twenty minutes – half an hour – the train ran on, but nothing identifiable was to be seen. Over fields, in the far distance, Tuppence once saw the spire of a church.

Then had come some factory complex – tall chimneys – a line of pre-fab houses, then open country again.

Tuppence had thought to herself – That house was rather like a dream! Perhaps it was a dream – I don't suppose I'll ever go and look for it – too difficult. Besides, rather a pity, perhaps –

Someday, maybe, I'll come across it by accident!

And so – she had forgotten all about it – until a picture hanging on a wall had reawakened a veiled memory.

And now, thanks to one word uttered unwittingly by Albert, the quest was ended.

Or, to speak correctly, a quest was beginning.

Tuppence sorted out three maps, a guide-book, and various other accessories.

Roughly now she knew the area she would have to search. Jane's school she marked with a large cross – the branch railway line, which ran into the main line to London – the time lapse whilst she had slept.

The final area as planned covered a considerable mileage – north of Medchester, south-east of Market Basing which was a small town, but was quite an important railway junction, west probably of Shaleborough.

She'd take the car, and start early tomorrow morning.

She got up and went into the bedroom and studied the picture over the mantelpiece.

Yes, there was no mistake. That was the house she had seen from the train three years ago. The house she had promised to look for someday –

Someday had come – Someday was tomorrow.

BOOK 2 • THE HOUSE ON THE CANAL

CHAPTER 7

....

THE FRIENDLY WITCH

Before leaving the next morning, Tuppence took a last careful look at the picture hanging in her room, not so much to fix its details firmly in her mind, but to memorize its position in the landscape. This time she would be seeing it not from the window of a train but from the road. The angle of approach would be quite different. There might be many hump-backed bridges, many similar disused canals – perhaps other houses looking like this one (but that Tuppence refused to believe).

The picture was signed, but the signature of the artist was illegible – All that could be said was that it began with B.

Turning away from the picture, Tuppence checked her para-phernalia: an A.B.C. and its attached railway map; a selection of ordnance maps; tentative names of places – Medchester, Westleigh – Market Basing – Middlesham – Inchwell – Between them, they enclosed the triangle that she had decided to examine. With her she took a small overnight bag since she would have a three hours' drive before she even arrived at the area of oper-ations, and after that, it meant, she judged, a good deal of slow driving along country roads and lanes looking for likely canals.

After stopping in Medchester for coffee and a snack, she pushed on by a second-class road adjacent to a railway line, and leading through wooded country with plenty of streams.

As in most of the rural districts of England, signposts were plentiful, bearing names that Tuppence had never heard of, and seldom seeming to lead to the place in question. There seemed to be a certain cunning about this part of the road system of England. The road would twist off from the canal, and when you pressed on hopefully to where you thought the canal might have taken itself, you drew a blank. If you had gone in the direction of Great Michelden, the next signpost you came to offered you a choice of two roads, one to Pennington Sparrow and the other to Farlingford. You chose Farlingford and managed actually to get to such a place but almost immediately the next signpost sent you back firmly to Medchester, so that you practically retraced your steps. Actually Tuppence never did find Great Michelden, and for a long time she was quite unable to find the lost canal. If she had had any idea of which village she was looking for, things might have gone more easily. Tracking canals on maps was merely puzzling. Now and again she came to the railway which cheered her up and she would then push on hopefully for Bees Hill, South Winterton and Farrell St Edmund. Farrell St Edmund had once had a station, but it had been abolished some time ago! 'If only,' thought Tuppence, 'there was some well-behaved road that ran alongside a canal, or alongside a railway line, it would make it so much easier.'

The day wore on and Tuppence became more and more baffled. Occasionally she came upon a farm adjacent to a canal but the road having led to the farm insisted on having nothing more to do with the canal and went over a hill and arrived at something called Westpenfold which had a church with a square tower which was no use at all.

From there when disconsolately pursuing a rutted road which seemed the only way out of Westpenfold and which to Tuppence's sense of direction (which was now becoming increasingly unreliable) seemed to lead in the opposite direction to anywhere she could possibly want to go, she came abruptly to a place where two lanes forked right and left. There was the remains of a signpost between them, the arms of which had both broken off.

'Which way?' said Tuppence. 'Who knows? I don't.'

She took the left-hand one.

It meandered on, winding to left and to right. Finally it shot round a bend, widened out and climbed a hill, coming out of woods into open downlike country. Having surmounted the crest it took a steep downward course. Not very far away a plaintive cry sounded –

'Sounds like a *train*,' said Tuppence, with sudden hope.

It *was* a train – Then below her was the railway line and on it a goods train uttering cries of distress as it puffed along. And beyond it was the canal and on the other side of the canal was a house that Tuppence recognized and, leading across the canal was a small hump-backed, pink-bricked bridge. The road dipped under the railway, came up, and made for the bridge. Tuppence drove very gently over the narrow bridge. Beyond it the road went on with the house on the right-hand side of it. Tuppence drove on looking for the way in. There didn't seem to be one. A fairly high wall shielded it from the road.

The house was on her right now. She stopped the car and walked back on to the bridge and looked at what she could see of the house from there.

Most of the tall windows were shuttered with green shutters. The house had a very quiet and empty look. It looked peaceful and kindly in the setting sun. There was nothing to suggest that anyone lived in it. She went back to the car and drove a little farther. The wall, a moderately high one, ran along to her right. The left-hand side of the road was merely a hedge giving on green fields.

Presently she came to a wrought-iron gate in the wall. She parked the car by the side of the road, got out and went over to look through the ironwork of the gate. By standing on tiptoe she could look over it. What she looked into was a garden. The place was certainly not a farm now, though it might have been once. Presumably it gave on fields beyond it. The garden was tended and cultivated. It was not particularly tidy but it looked as though someone was trying rather unsuccessfully to keep it tidy.

From the iron gate a circular path curved through the garden and round to the house. This must be presumably the front door, though it didn't look like a front door. It was inconspicuous though sturdy – a back door. The house looked quite different from this side. To begin with, it was not empty. People lived there. Windows were open, curtains fluttered at them, a garbage pail stood by the door. At the far end of the garden Tuppence could see a large man digging, a big elderly man who dug slowly and with persistence. Certainly looked at from here the house held no enchantment, no artist would have wanted particularly to paint it. It was just a house and somebody lived in it. Tuppence wondered. She hesitated. Should she go on and forget the house altogether? No, she could hardly do that, not after all the trouble she had taken. What time was it? She looked at her watch but her watch had stopped. The sound of a door opening came from inside. She peered through the gate again.

The door of the house had opened and a woman came out. She put down a milk bottle and then, straightening up, glanced towards the gate. She saw Tuppence and hesitated for a moment, and then seeming to make up her mind, she came down the path towards the gate. 'Why,' said Tuppence to herself, 'why, it's a friendly witch!'

It was a woman of about fifty. She had long straggly hair which when caught by the wind, flew out behind her. It reminded Tuppence vaguely of a picture (by Nevinson?) of a young witch on a broomstick. That is perhaps why the term witch had come into her mind. But there was nothing young or beautiful about this woman. She was middle-aged, with a lined face, dressed in a rather slipshod way. She had a kind of steeple hat perched on her head and her nose and her chin came up towards each other. As a description she could have been sinister but she did not look sinister. She seemed to have a beaming and boundless good will. 'Yes,' thought Tuppence, 'you're exactly *like* a witch, but you're a *friendly* witch. I expect you're what they used to call a "white witch".'

The woman came down in a hesitating manner to the gate and spoke. Her voice was pleasant with a faint country burr in it of some kind.

'Were you looking for anything?' she said.

'I'm sorry,' said Tuppence, 'you must think it very rude of me looking into your garden in this way, but – but I wondered about this house.'

'Would you like to come in and look round the garden?' said the friendly witch.

'Well – well – thank you but I don't want to bother you.'

'Oh, it's no bother. I've nothing to do. Lovely afternoon, isn't it?'

'Yes, it is,' said Tuppence.

'I thought perhaps you'd lost your way,' said the friendly witch. 'People do sometimes.'

222 • AGATHA CHRISTIE

'I just thought,' said Tuppence, 'that this was a very attractive-looking house when I came down the hill on the other side of the bridge.'

'That's the prettiest side,' said the woman. 'Artists come and sketch it sometimes – or they used to – once.'

'Yes,' said Tuppence, 'I expect they would. I believe I – I saw a picture – at some exhibition,' she added hurriedly. 'Some house very like this. Perhaps it *was* this.'

'Oh, it may have been. Funny, you know, artists come and do a picture. And then other artists seem to come too. It's just the same when they have the local picture show every year. Artists all seem to choose the same spot. I don't know why. You know, it's either a bit of meadow and brook, or a particular oak tree, or a clump of willows, or it's the same view of the Norman church. Five or six different pictures of the same thing, most of them pretty bad, I should think. But then I don't know anything about art. Come in, do.'

'You're very kind,' said Tuppence. 'You've got a very nice garden,' she added.

'Oh, it's not too bad. We've got a few flowers and vegetables and things. But my husband can't do much work nowadays and I've got no time with one thing and another.'

'I saw this house once from the train,' said Tuppence. 'The train slowed up and I saw this house and I wondered whether I'd ever see it again. Quite some time ago.'

'And now suddenly you come down the hill in your car and there it is,' said the woman. 'Funny, things happen like that, don't they?'

'Thank goodness,' Tuppence thought, 'this woman is extra-ordinarily easy to talk to. One hardly has to imagine anything to explain oneself. One can almost say just what comes into one's head.'

'Like to come inside the house?' said the friendly witch. 'I can see you're interested. It's quite an old house, you know. I mean, late Georgian or something like that, they say, only it's been added on to. Of course, we've only got half the house, you know.'

'Oh I see,' said Tuppence. 'It's divided in two, is that it?'

'This is really the back of it,' said the woman. 'The front's the other side, the side you saw from the bridge. It was a funny way to partition it, I should have thought. I'd have thought it would have been easier to do it the other way. You know, right and left, so to speak. Not back and front. This is all really the back.'

'Have you lived here long?' asked Tuppence.

'Three years. After my husband retired we wanted a little place somewhere in the country where we'd be quiet. Somewhere cheap. This was going cheap because of course it's very lonely. You're not near a village or anything.'

'I saw a church steeple in the distance.'

'Ah, that's Sutton Chancellor. Two and a half miles from here. We're in the parish, of course, but there aren't any houses until you get to the village. It's a very small village too. You'll have a cup of tea?' said the friendly witch. 'I just put the kettle on not two minutes ago when I looked out and saw you.' She raised both hands to her mouth and shouted. 'Amos,' she shouted, 'Amos.'

The big man in the distance turned his head.

'Tea in ten minutes,' she called.

He acknowledged the signal by raising his hand. She turned, opened the door and motioned Tuppence to go in.

'Perry, my name is,' she said in a friendly voice. 'Alice Perry.'

'Mine's Beresford,' said Tuppence. 'Mrs Beresford.'

'Come in, Mrs Beresford, and have a look round.'

Tuppence paused for a second. She thought 'Just for a moment I feel like Hansel and Gretel. The witch asks you into her house. Perhaps it's a gingerbread house . . . It ought to be.'

Then she looked at Alice Perry again and thought that it wasn't the gingerbread house of Hansel and Gretel's witch. This was just a perfectly ordinary woman. No, not quite ordinary. She had a rather strange wild friendliness about her. 'She might be able to do spells,' thought Tuppence, 'but I'm sure they'd be good spells.' She stooped her head a little and stepped over the threshold into the witch's house.

It was rather dark inside. The passages were small. Mrs Perry led her through a kitchen and into a sitting-room beyond it which was evidently the family living-room. There was nothing exciting about the house. It was, Tuppence thought, probably a late Victorian addition to the main part. Horizontally it was narrow. It seemed to consist of a horizontal passage, rather dark, which served a string of rooms. She thought to herself that it certainly was rather an odd way of dividing a house.

'Sit down and I'll bring the tea in,' said Mrs Perry.

'Let me help you.'

'Oh, don't worry, I shan't be a minute. It's all ready on the tray.'

A whistle rose from the kitchen. The kettle had evidently reached the end of its span of tranquillity. Mrs Perry went out and returned in a minute or two with the tea tray, a plate of scones, a jar of jam and three cups and saucers.

'I expect you're disappointed, now you've got inside,' said Mrs Perry.

It was a shrewd remark and very near to the truth.

'Oh no,' said Tuppence.

'Well, I should be if I was you. Because they don't match a bit, do they? I mean the front and the back side of the house don't match. But it is a comfortable house to live in. Not many rooms, not too much light but it makes a great difference in price.'

'Who divided the house and why?'

'Oh, a good many years ago, I believe. I suppose whoever had it thought it was too big or too inconvenient. Only wanted a week-end place or something of that kind. So they kept the good rooms, the dining-room and the drawing-room and made a kitchen out of a small study there was, and a couple of bedrooms and bathroom upstairs, and then walled it up and let the part that was kitchens and old-fashioned sculleries and things, and did it up a bit.'

'Who lives in the other part? Someone who just comes down for weekends?'

'Nobody lives there now,' said Mrs Perry. 'Have another scone, dear.'

'Thank you,' said Tuppence.

'At least nobody's come down here in the last two years. I don't know even who it belongs to now.'

'But when you first came here?'

'There was a young lady used to come down here – an actress they said she was. At least that's what we heard. But we never saw her really. Just caught a glimpse sometimes. She used to come down late on a Saturday night after the show, I suppose. She used to go away on the Sunday evenings.'

BY THE PRICKING OF MY THUMBS · 225

'Quite a mystery woman,' said Tuppence, encouragingly.

'You know that's just the way I used to think of her. I used to make up stories about her in my head. Sometimes I'd think she was like Greta Garbo. You know, the way *she* went about always in dark glasses and pulled-down hats. Goodness now, *I've* got *my* peak hat on.'

She removed the witch's headgear from her head and laughed.

'It's for a play we're having at the parish rooms in Sutton Chancellor,' she said. 'You know – a sort of fairy story play for the children mostly. I'm playing the witch,' she added.

'Oh,' said Tuppence, slightly taken aback, then added quickly, 'What fun.'

'Yes, it is fun, isn't it?' said Mrs Perry. 'Just right for the witch, aren't I?' She laughed and tapped her chin. 'You know. I've got the face for it. Hope it won't put ideas into people's heads. They'll think I've got the evil eye.'

'I don't think they'd think that of you,' said Tuppence. 'I'm sure you'd be a beneficent witch.'

'Well, I'm glad you think so,' said Mrs Perry. 'As I was saying, this actress – I can't remember her name now – Miss Marchment I think it was, but it might have been something else – you wouldn't believe the things I used to make up about her. Really, I suppose, I hardly ever saw or spoke to her. Sometimes I think she was just terribly shy and neurotic. Reporters'd come down after her and things like that, but she never would see them. At other times I used to think – well, you'll say I'm foolish – I used to think quite sinister things about her. You know, that she was afraid of being *recognized*. Perhaps she wasn't an actress at all. Perhaps the police were looking for her. Perhaps she was a criminal of some kind. It's exciting sometimes, making things up in your head. Especially when you don't – well – see many people.'

'Did nobody ever come down here with her?'

'Well, I'm not so sure about that. Of course these partition walls, you know, that they put in when they turned the house into two, well, they're pretty thin and sometimes you'd hear voices and things like that. I think she did bring down someone for weekends occasionally.' She nodded her head. 'A man of some kind. That may have been why they wanted somewhere quiet like this.'

'A married man,' said Tuppence, entering into the spirit of make-believe.

'Yes, it would be a married man, wouldn't it?' said Mrs Perry.

'Perhaps it was her husband who came down with her. He'd taken this place in the country because he wanted to murder her and perhaps he buried her in the garden.'

'My!' said Mrs Perry. 'You do have an imagination, don't you? I never thought of that one.'

'I suppose *someone* must have known all about her,' said Tuppence. 'I mean house agents. People like that.'

'Oh, I suppose so,' said Mrs Perry. 'But I rather liked *not* knowing, if you understand what I mean.'

'Oh yes,' said Tuppence, 'I do understand.'

'It's got an atmosphere, you know, this house. I mean there's a feeling in it, a feeling that anything might have happened.'

'Didn't she have any people come in to clean for her or anything like that?'

'Difficult to get anyone here. There's nobody near at hand.'

The outside door opened. The big man who had been digging in the garden came in. He went to the scullery tap and turned it, obviously washing his hands. Then he came through into the sitting-room.

'This is my husband,' said Mrs Perry. 'Amos. We've got a visitor, Amos. This is Mrs Beresford.'

'How do you do?' said Tuppence.

Amos Perry was a tall, shambling-looking man. He was bigger and more powerful than Tuppence had realized. Although he had a shambling gait and walked slowly, he was a big man of muscular build. He said,

'Pleased to meet you, Mrs Beresford.'

His voice was pleasant and he smiled, but Tuppence wondered for a brief moment whether he was really what she would have called 'all there'. There was a kind of wondering simplicity about the look in his eyes and she wondered, too, whether Mrs Perry had wanted a quiet place to live in because of some mental disability on the part of her husband.

'Ever so fond of the garden, he is,' said Mrs Perry.

At his entrance the conversation dimmed down. Mrs Perry did

most of the talking but her personality seemed to have changed. She talked with rather more nervousness and with particular attention to her husband. Encouraging him, Tuppence thought, rather in a way that a mother might prompt a shy boy to talk, to display the best of himself before a visitor, and to be a little nervous that he might be inadequate. When she'd finished her tea, Tuppence got up. She said,

'I must be going. Thank you, Mrs Perry, very much for your hospitality.'

'You'll see the garden before you go.' Mr Perry rose. 'Come on, *I'll* show you.'

She went with him outdoors and he took her down to the corner beyond where he had been digging.

'Nice, them flowers, aren't they?' he said. 'Got some old-fashioned roses here – See this one, striped red and white.'

'"Commandant Beaurepaire",' said Tuppence.

'Us calls it "York and Lancaster" here,' said Perry. 'Wars of the Roses. Smells sweet, don't it?'

'Smells lovely.'

'Better than them new-fashioned Hybrid Teas.'

In a way the garden was rather pathetic. The weeds were imperfectly controlled, but the flowers themselves were carefully tied up in an amateurish fashion.

'Bright colours,' said Mr Perry. 'I like bright colours. We often get folk to see our garden,' he said. 'Glad you came.'

'Thank you very much,' said Tuppence. 'I think your garden and your house are very nice indeed.'

'You ought to see t'other side of it.'

'Is it to let or to be sold? Your wife says there's nobody living there now.'

'We don't know. We've not seen anyone and there's no board up and nobody's ever come to see over it.'

'It would be a nice house, I think, to live in.'

'You wanting a house?'

'Yes,' said Tuppence, making up her mind quickly. 'Yes, as a matter of fact, we are looking round for some small place in the country, for when my husband retires. That'll be next year probably, but we like to look about in plenty of time.'

'It's quiet here if you like quiet.'

'I suppose,' said Tuppence, 'I could ask the local house agents. Is that how you got your house?'

'Saw an advertisement first we did in the paper. Then we went to the house agents, yes.'

'Where was that – in Sutton Chancellor? That's your village, isn't it?'

'Sutton Chancellor? No. Agents' place is in Market Basing. Russell & Thompson, that's the name. You could go to them and ask.'

'Yes,' said Tuppence, 'so I could. How far is Market Basing from here?'

'It's two miles to Sutton Chancellor and it's seven miles to Market Basing from there. There's a proper road from Sutton Chancellor, but it's all lanes hereabouts.'

'I see,' said Tuppence. 'Well, goodbye, Mr Perry, and thank you very much for showing me your garden.'

'Wait a bit.' He stooped, cut off an enormous paeony and taking Tuppence by the lapel of her coat, he inserted this through the buttonhole in it. 'There,' he said, 'there you are. Looks pretty, it does.'

For a moment Tuppence felt a sudden feeling of panic. This large, shambling, good-natured man suddenly frightened her. He was looking down at her, smiling. Smiling rather wildly, almost leering. 'Pretty it looks on you,' he said again. 'Pretty.'

Tuppence thought 'I'm glad I'm not a young girl . . . I don't think I'd like him putting a flower on me then.' She said goodbye again and hurried away.

The house door was open and Tuppence went in to say goodbye to Mrs Perry. Mrs Perry was in the kitchen, washing up the tea things and Tuppence almost automatically pulled a teacloth off the rack and started drying.

'Thank you so much,' she said, 'both you and your husband. You've been so kind and hospitable to me – *What's that?*'

From the wall of the kitchen, or rather behind the wall where an old-fashioned range had once stood, there came a loud screaming and squawking and a scratching noise too.

'That'll be a jackdaw,' said Mrs Perry, 'dropped down the chimney in the other house. They do this time of the year.

One came down our chimney last week. They make nests in the chimneys, you know.'

'What – in the other house?'

'Yes, there it is again.'

Again the squawking and crying of a distressed bird came to their ears. Mrs Perry said, 'There's no one to bother, you see, in the empty house. The chimneys ought to be swept and all that.'

The squawking scratching noises went on.

'Poor bird,' said Tuppence.

'I know. It won't be able to get up again.'

'You mean it'll just die there?'

'Oh yes. One came down our chimney as I say. Two of them, actually. One was a young bird. It was all right, we put it out and it flew away. The other one was dead.'

The frenzied scuffling and squeaking went on.

'Oh,' said Tuppence, 'I wish we could get at it.'

Mr Perry came in through the door. 'Anything the matter?' he said, looking from one to the other.

'There's a bird, Amos. It must be in the drawing-room chimney next door. Hear it?'

'Eh, it's come down from the jackdaws' nest.'

'I wish we could get in there,' said Mrs Perry.

'Ah, you can't do anything. They'll die from the fright, if nothing else.'

'Then it'll smell,' said Mrs Perry.

'You won't smell anything in here. You're soft-hearted,' he went on, looking from one to the other, 'like all females. We'll get it if you like.'

'Why, is one of the windows open?'

'We can get in through the door.'

'What door?'

'Outside here in the yard. The key's hanging up among those.'

He went outside and along to the end, opening a small door there. It was a kind of potting shed really, but a door from it led into the other house and near the door of the potting shed were six or seven rusty keys hanging on a nail.

'This one fits,' said Mr Perry.

He took down the key and put it in the door, and after exerting a good deal of cajolery and force, the key turned rustily in the lock.

'I went in once before,' he said, 'when I heard water running. Somebody'd forgotten to turn the water off properly.'

He went in and the two women followed him. The door led into a small room which still contained various flower vases on a shelf and a sink with a tap.

'A flower room, I shouldn't wonder,' he said. 'Where people used to do the flowers. See? A lot of the vases left here.'

There was a door out of the flower room. This was not even locked. He opened it and they went through. It was like, Tuppence thought, going through into another world. The passageway outside was covered with a pile carpet. A little way along there was a door half-open and from there the sounds of a bird in distress were coming. Perry pushed the door open and his wife and Tuppence went in.

The windows were shuttered but one side of a shutter was hanging loose and light came in. Although it was dim, there was a faded but beautiful carpet on the floor, a deep sage-green in colour. There was a bookshelf against the wall but no chairs or tables. The furniture had been removed no doubt, the curtains and carpets had been left as fittings to be passed on to the next tenant.

Mrs Perry went towards the fireplace. A bird lay in the grate scuffling and uttering loud squawking sounds of distress. She stooped, picked it up, and said,

'Open the window if you can, Amos.'

Amos went over, pulled the shutter aside, unfastened the other side of it and then pushed at the latch of the window. He raised the lower sash which came gratingly. As soon as it was open Mrs Perry leaned out and released the jackdaw. It flopped on to the lawn, hopped a few paces.

'Better kill it,' said Perry. 'It's damaged.'

'Leave it a bit,' said his wife. 'You never know. They recover very quickly, birds. It's fright that makes them so paralysed looking.'

Sure enough, a few moments later the jackdaw, with a final struggle, a squawk, a flapping of wings flew off.

'I only hope,' said Alice Perry, 'that it doesn't come down that chimney again. Contrary things, birds. Don't know what's good for them. Get into a room, they can never get out of it by themselves. Oh,' she added, 'what a mess.'

She, Tuppence and Mr Perry all stared at the grate. From the chimney had come down a mass of soot, of odd rubble and of broken bricks. Evidently it had been in a bad state of repair for some time.

'Somebody ought to come and live here,' said Mrs Perry, looking round her.

'Somebody ought to look after it,' Tuppence agreed with her. 'Some builder ought to look at it or do something about it or the whole house will come down soon.'

'Probably water has been coming through the roof in the top rooms. Yes, look at the ceiling up there, it's come through there.'

'Oh, what a shame,' said Tuppence, 'to ruin a beautiful house – it really is a beautiful room, isn't it.'

She and Mrs Perry looked together round it appreciatively. Built in 1790 it had all the graciousness of a house of that period. It had had originally a pattern of willow leaves on the discoloured paper.

'It's a ruin now,' said Mr Perry.

Tuppence poked the debris in the grate.

'One ought to sweep it up,' said Mrs Perry.

'Now what do you want to bother yourself with a house that doesn't belong to you?' said her husband. 'Leave it alone, woman. It'll be in just as bad a state tomorrow morning.'

Tuppence stirred the bricks aside with a toe.

'Ooh,' she said with an exclamation of disgust.

There were two dead birds lying in the fireplace. By the look of them they had been dead for some time.

'That's the nest that came down a good few weeks ago. It's a wonder it doesn't smell more than it does,' said Perry.

'What's this thing?' said Tuppence.

She poked with her toe at something lying half hidden in the rubble. Then she bent and picked it up.

'Don't you touch a dead bird,' said Mrs Perry.

'It's not a bird,' said Tuppence. 'Something else must have

come down the chimney. Well I never,' she added, staring at it. 'It's a doll. It's a child's doll.'

They looked down at it. Ragged, torn, its clothes in rags, its head lolling from the shoulders, it had originally been a child's doll. One glass eye dropped out. Tuppence stood holding it.

'I wonder,' she said, 'I wonder how a child's doll ever got up a chimney. Extraordinary.'

CHAPTER 8

SUTTON CHANCELLOR

After leaving the canal house, Tuppence drove slowly on along the narrow winding road which she had been assured would lead her to the village of Sutton Chancellor. It was an isolated road. There were no houses to be seen from it – only field gates from which muddy tracks led inwards. There was little traffic – one tractor came along, and one lorry proudly announcing that it carried Mother's Delight and the picture of an enormous and unnatural-looking loaf. The church steeple she had noticed in the distance seemed to have disappeared entirely – but it finally reappeared quite near at hand after the lane had bent suddenly and sharply round a belt of trees. Tuppence glanced at the speedometer and saw she had come two miles since the canal house.

It was an attractive old church standing in a sizeable churchyard with a lone yew tree standing by the church door.

Tuppence left the car outside the lych-gate, passed through it, and stood for a few moments surveying the church and the churchyard round it. Then she went to the church door with its rounded Norman arch and lifted the heavy handle. It was unlocked and she went inside.

The inside was unattractive. The church was an old one, undoubtedly, but it had had a zealous wash and brush up in Victorian times. Its pitch pine pews and its flaring red and blue glass windows had ruined any antique charm it had once possessed. A middle-aged woman in a tweed coat and skirt was arranging flowers in brass vases round the pulpit – she had already finished the altar. She looked round at Tuppence with a sharply inquiring glance. Tuppence wandered up an aisle looking at memorial tablets on the walls. A family called Warrender seemed to be most fully represented in early years. All of The Priory, Sutton Chancellor. Captain Warrender, Major Warrender, Sarah Elisabeth Warrender, dearly beloved wife of George Warrender. A newer tablet recorded the death of Julia Starke (another beloved wife) of Philip Starke, also of The Priory, Sutton Chancellor – so it would seem the Warrenders had died out. None of them were particularly suggestive or interesting. Tuppence passed out of the church again and walked round it on the outside. The outside, Tuppence thought, was much more attractive than the inside. 'Early Perp. and Dec.,' said Tuppence to herself, having been brought up on familiar terms with ecclesiastical architecture. She was not particularly fond of early Perp. herself.

It was a fair-sized church and she thought that the village of Sutton Chancellor must once have been a rather more important centre of rural life than it was now. She left the car where it was and walked on to the village. It had a village shop and a post office and about a dozen small houses or cottages. One or two of them were thatched but the others were rather plain and unattractive. There were six council houses at the end of the village street looking slightly self-conscious. A brass plate on a door announced 'Arthur Thomas, Chimney Sweep'.

Tuppence wondered if any responsible house agents were likely to engage his services for the house by the canal which certainly needed them. How silly she had been, she thought, not to have asked the name of the house.

She walked back slowly towards the church, and her car, pausing to examine the churchyard more closely. She liked the churchyard. There were very few new burials in it. Most of the stones commemorated Victorian burials, and earlier ones – half defaced by lichen and time. The old stones were attractive. Some of them were upright slabs with cherubs on the tops, with wreaths round them. She wandered about, looking at the inscriptions. Warrenders again. Mary Warrender, aged 47, Alice Warrender, aged 33, Colonel John Warrender killed in Afghanistan. Various infant Warrenders – deeply regretted – and eloquent verses of pious hopes. She wondered if any Warrenders lived here still.

They'd left off being buried here apparently. She couldn't find any tombstones later than 1843. Rounding the big yew tree she came upon an elderly clergyman who was stooping over a row of old tombstones near a wall behind the church. He straightened up and turned round as Tuppence approached.

'Good afternoon,' he said pleasantly.

'Good afternoon,' said Tuppence, and added, 'I've been looking at the church.'

'Ruined by Victorian renovation,' said the clergyman.

He had a pleasant voice and a nice smile. He looked about seventy, but Tuppence presumed he was not quite as far advanced in age as that, though he was certainly rheumatic and rather unsteady on his legs.

'Too much money about in Victorian times,' he said sadly. 'Too many ironmasters. They were pious, but had, unfortunately, no sense of the artistic. No taste. Did you see the east window?' he shuddered.

'Yes,' said Tuppence. 'Dreadful,' she said.

'I couldn't agree with you more. I'm the vicar,' he added, rather unnecessarily.

'I thought you must be,' said Tuppence politely. 'Have you been here long?' she added.

'Ten years, my dear,' he said. 'It's a nice parish. Nice people, what there are of them. I've been very happy here. They don't like my sermons very much,' he added sadly. 'I do the best I can, but of course I can't pretend to be really modern. Sit down,' he added hospitably, waving to a nearby tombstone.

Tuppence sat down gratefully and the vicar took a seat on another one nearby.

'I can't stand very long,' he said, apologetically. He added, 'Can I do anything for you or are you just passing by?'

'Well, I'm really just passing by,' said Tuppence. 'I thought I'd just look at the church. I'd rather lost myself in a car wandering around the lanes.'

'Yes, yes. Very difficult to find one's way about round here. A lot of signposts are broken, you know, and the council don't repair them as they should.' He added, 'I don't know that it matters very much. People who drive down these lanes aren't usually trying to get anywhere in particular. People who *are* keep to the main roads. Dreadful,' he added again. 'Especially the new Motorway. At least, *I* think so. The noise and the speed and the reckless driving. Oh well! pay no attention to me. I'm a crusty old fellow. You'd never guess what I'm doing here,' he went on.

'I saw you were examining some of the gravestones,' said Tuppence. 'Has there been any vandalism? Have teenagers been breaking bits off them?'

'No. One's mind *does* turn that way nowadays what with so many telephone boxes wrecked and all those other things that these young vandals do. Poor children, they don't know any better, I suppose. Can't think of anything more amusing to do than to smash things. Sad, isn't it? Very sad. No,' he said, 'there's been no damage of that kind here. The boys round here are a nice lot on the whole. No, I'm just looking for a child's grave.'

Tuppence stirred on her tombstone. 'A child's grave?' she said.

'Yes. Somebody wrote to me. A Major Waters, he asked if by any possibility a child had been buried here. I looked it up in the parish register, of course, but there was no record of any such name. All the same, I came out here and looked round the stones. I thought, you know, that perhaps whoever wrote might have got hold of some wrong name, or that there had been a mistake.'

'What was the Christian name?' asked Tuppence.

'He didn't know. Perhaps Julia after the mother.'

'How old was the child?'

'Again he wasn't sure – Rather vague, the whole thing. I think myself that the man must have got hold of the wrong village altogether. I never remember a Waters living here or having heard of one.'

'What about the Warrenders?' asked Tuppence, her mind going back to the names in the church. 'The church seems full of tablets to them and their names are on lots of gravestones out here.'

'Ah, that family's died out by now. They had a fine property, an old fourteenth-century Priory. It was burnt down – oh, nearly a hundred years ago now, so I suppose any Warrenders there were left, went away and didn't come back. A new house was built on the site, by a rich Victorian called Starke. A very ugly house but comfortable, they say. Very comfortable. Bathrooms, you know, and all that. I suppose that sort of thing *is* important.'

'It seems a very odd thing,' said Tuppence, 'that someone should write and ask you about a child's grave. Somebody – a relation?'

'The father of the child,' said the vicar. 'One of these war tragedies, I imagine. A marriage that broke up when the husband was on service abroad. The young wife ran away with another man while the husband was serving abroad. There was a child, a child he'd never seen. She'd be grown up by now, I suppose, if she were alive. It must be twenty years ago or more.'

'Isn't it a long time after to be looking for her?'

'Apparently he only heard there *was* a child quite recently. The information came to him by pure chance. Curious story, the whole thing.'

'What made him think that the child had been buried here?'

'I gather somebody who had come across his wife in wartime had told him that his wife had said she was living at Sutton Chancellor. It happens, you know. You meet someone, a friend or acquaintance you haven't seen for years, and they sometimes can give you news from the past that you wouldn't get in any other way. But she's certainly not living here now. Nobody of that name has lived here – not since I've been here. Or in the neighbourhood as far as I know. Of course, the mother *might* have been going by another name. However, I gather the father is employing solicitors and inquiry agents and all that sort of thing, and they will probably be able to get results in the end. It will take time –'

'*Was it your poor child*?' murmured Tuppence.

'I beg your pardon, my dear?'

'Nothing,' said Tuppence. 'Something somebody said to me the other day. "*Was it your poor child*?" It's rather a startling thing to hear suddenly. But I don't really think the old lady who said it knew what she was talking about.'

'I know. I know. I'm often the same. I say things and I don't really know what I mean by them. Most vexing.'

'I expect you know everything about the people who live here *now*?' said Tuppence.

'Well, there certainly aren't very many to know. Yes. Why? Is there someone you wanted to know about?'

'I wondered if there had ever been a Mrs Lancaster living here.'

'Lancaster? No, I don't think I recollect that name.'

'And there's a house – I was driving today rather aimlessly – not minding particularly where I went, just following lanes –'

'I know. Very nice, the lanes round here. And you can find quite rare specimens. Botanical, I mean. In the hedges here. Nobody ever picks flowers in these hedges. We never get any tourists round here or that sort of thing. Yes, I've found some very rare specimens sometimes. Dusty Cranesbell, for instance –'

'There was a house by a canal,' said Tuppence, refusing to be side-tracked into botany. 'Near a little hump-backed bridge. It was about two miles from here. I wondered what its name was.'

'Let me see. Canal – hump-backed bridge. Well . . . there are several houses like that. There's Merricot Farm.'

'It wasn't a farm.'

'Ah, now, I expect it was the Perrys' house – Amos and Alice Perry.'

'That's right,' said Tuppence. 'A Mr and Mrs Perry.'

'She's a striking-looking woman, isn't she? Interesting, I always think. Very interesting. Medieval face, didn't you think so? She's going to play the witch in our play we're getting up. The school children, you know. She looks rather like a witch, doesn't she?'

'Yes,' said Tuppence. 'A friendly witch.'

'As you say, my dear, absolutely rightly. Yes, a friendly witch.'

'But he –'

'Yes, poor fellow,' said the vicar. 'Not completely *compos mentis* – but no harm in him.'

'They were very nice. They asked me in for a cup of tea,' said Tuppence. 'But what I wanted to know was the *name* of the house. I forgot to ask them. They're only living in half of it, aren't they?'

'Yes, yes. In what used to be the old kitchen quarters. *They* call it "Waterside", I think, though I believe the ancient name for it was "Watermead". A pleasanter name, I think.'

'Who does the other part of the house belong to?'

'Well, the whole house used to belong originally to the Bradleys. That was a good many years ago. Yes, thirty or forty at least, I should think. And then it was sold, and then sold again and then it remained empty for a long time. When I came here it was just being used as a kind of weekend place. By some actress – Miss Margrave, I believe. She was not here very much. Just used to come down from time to time. I never knew her. She never came to church. I saw her in the distance sometimes. A beautiful creature. A very beautiful creature.'

'Who does it actually belong to *now*?' Tuppence persisted.

'I've no idea. Possibly it still belongs to her. The part the Perrys live in is only rented to them.'

'I recognized it, you know,' said Tuppence, 'as soon as I saw it, because I've got a picture of it.'

'Oh really? That must have been one of Boscombe's, or was his name Boscobel – I can't remember now. Some name like that. He was a Cornishman, fairly well-known artist, I believe. I rather imagine he's dead now. Yes, he used to come down here fairly often. He used to sketch all round this part of the world. He did some oils here, too. Very attractive landscapes, some of them.'

'This particular picture,' said Tuppence, 'was given to an old aunt of mine who died about a month ago. It was given to her by a Mrs Lancaster. That's why I asked if you knew the name.'

But the vicar shook his head once more.

'Lancaster? Lancaster. No, I don't seem to remember the name. Ah! but here's the person you must ask. Our dear Miss Bligh. Very active, Miss Bligh is. She knows all about the parish. She runs everything. The Women's Institute, the Boy Scouts and the Guides – everything. You ask *her*. She's very active, very active indeed.'

The vicar sighed. The activity of Miss Bligh seemed to worry him. 'Nellie Bligh, they call her in the village. The boys sing it after her sometimes. *Nellie Bligh, Nellie Bligh.* It's not her proper name. That's something more like Gertrude or Geraldine.'

Miss Bligh, who was the tweed-clad woman Tuppence had seen in the church, was approaching them at a rapid trot, still holding a small watering can. She eyed Tuppence with deep curiosity as she approached, increasing her pace and starting a conversation before she reached them.

'Finished my job,' she exclaimed merrily. 'Had a bit of a rush today. Oh yes, had a bit of a rush. Of course, as you know, Vicar, I usually do the church in the morning. But today we had the emergency meeting in the parish rooms and really you wouldn't believe the time it took! So much *argument*, you know. I really think sometimes people object to things just for the fun of doing so. Mrs Partington was particularly irritating. Wanting everything fully discussed, you know, and wondering whether we'd got enough different prices from different firms. I mean, the whole thing is such a small cost anyway, that really a few shillings here or there can't make much difference. And Burkenheads have always been most reliable. I don't think really, Vicar, you know, that you ought to sit on that tombstone.'

'Irreverent, perhaps?' suggested the vicar.

'Oh no, no, of course I didn't mean that *at all*, Vicar. I meant the *stone*, you know, the damp does come through and with your rheumatism –' Her eyes slid sideways to Tuppence questioningly.

'Let me introduce you to Miss Bligh,' said the vicar. 'This is – this is –' he hesitated.

'Mrs Beresford,' said Tuppence.

'Ah yes,' said Miss Bligh. 'I saw you in the church, didn't I, just now, looking round it. I would have come and spoken to you, called your attention to one or two interesting points, but I was in such a hurry to finish my job.'

'I ought to have come and helped you,' said Tuppence, in her sweetest voice. 'But it wouldn't have been much use, would it, because I could see you knew so exactly where every flower ought to go.'

'Well now, it's very nice of you to say so, but it's quite true. I've done the flowers in the church for – oh, I don't know *how* many years it is. We let the school children arrange their own particular pots of wild flowers for festivals, though of course they haven't the least idea, poor little things. I do think a *little* instruction, but Mrs Peake will never have any instruction. She's so particular. She says it spoils their initiative. Are you staying down here?' she asked Tuppence.

'I was going on to Market Basing,' said Tuppence. 'Perhaps you can tell me a nice quiet hotel to stay there?'

'Well, I expect you'll find it a little disappointing. It's just a market town, you know. It doesn't cater at all for the motoring trade. The Blue Dragon is a two-star but really I don't think these stars mean anything *at all* sometimes. I think you'd find The Lamb better. Quieter, you know. Are you staying there for long?'

'Oh no,' said Tuppence, 'just a day or two while I'm looking round the neighbourhood.'

'Not very much to see, I'm afraid. No interesting antiquities or anything like that. We're purely a rural and agricultural district,' said the vicar. 'But peaceful, you know, very peaceful. As I told you, some interesting wild flowers.'

'Ah yes,' said Tuppence, 'I've heard that and I'm anxious to collect a few specimens in the intervals of doing a little mild house hunting,' she added.

'Oh dear, how interesting,' said Miss Bligh. 'Are you thinking of settling in this neighbourhood?'

'Well, my husband and I haven't decided very definitely on any one neighbourhood in particular,' said Tuppence. 'And we're in no hurry. He won't be retiring for another eighteen months. But it's always as well, I think, to look about. Personally, what *I* prefer to do is to stay in one neighbourhood for four or five days, get a list of likely small properties and drive about to see them. Coming down for one day from London to see one particular house is very tiring, I find.'

'Oh yes, you've got your car here, have you?'

'Yes,' said Tuppence. 'I shall have to go to a house agent in Market Basing tomorrow morning. There's nowhere, I suppose, to stay in the village here, is there?'

'Of course, there's Mrs Copleigh,' said Miss Bligh. 'She takes people in the summer, you know. Summer visitors. She's beautifully clean. All her rooms are. Of course, she only does bed and breakfast and perhaps a light meal in the evening. But I don't think she takes anyone in much before August or July at the earliest.'

'Perhaps I could go and see her and find out,' said Tuppence.

'She's a very worthy woman,' said the vicar. 'Her tongue wags a good deal,' he added. 'She never stops talking, not for one single minute.'

'A lot of gossip and chattering is always going on in these small villages,' said Miss Bligh. 'I think it would be a very good idea if I helped Mrs Beresford. I could take her along to Mrs Copleigh and just see what chances there are.'

'That would be very kind of you,' said Tuppence.

'Then we'll be off,' said Miss Bligh briskly. 'Goodbye, Vicar. Still on your quest? A sad task and so unlikely to meet with success. I really think it was a *most* unreasonable request to make.'

Tuppence said goodbye to the vicar and said she would be glad to help him if she could.

'I could easily spend an hour or two looking at the various gravestones. I've got very good eyesight for my age. It's just the name Waters you are looking for?'

'Not really,' said the vicar. 'It's the age that matters, I think. A child of perhaps seven, it would be. A girl. Major Waters thinks that his wife might have changed her name and that probably the child might be known by the name she had taken. And as he doesn't know what that name is, it makes it all very difficult.'

'The whole thing's impossible, so far as I can see,' said Miss Bligh. 'You ought never to have said you would do such a thing, Vicar. It's monstrous, suggesting anything of the kind.'

'The poor fellow seems very upset,' said the vicar. 'A sad history altogether, so far as I can make out. But I mustn't keep you.'

Tuppence thought to herself as she was shepherded by Miss Bligh that no matter what the reputation of Mrs Copleigh for talking, she could hardly talk more than Miss Bligh did. A stream of pronouncements both rapid and dictatorial poured from her lips.

Mrs Copleigh's cottage proved to be a pleasant and roomy one set back from the village street with a neat garden of flowers in front, a whitened doorstep and a brass handle well polished. Mrs Copleigh herself seemed to Tuppence like a character straight out of the pages of Dickens. She was very small and very round, so that she came rolling towards you rather like a rubber ball. She had bright twinkling eyes, blonde hair rolled up in sausage curls on her head and an air of tremendous vigour. After displaying a little doubt to begin with – 'Well, I don't usually, you know. No. My husband and I say "summer visitors, that's different". Everyone does that if they can nowadays. And have to, I'm sure. But not this time of year so much, we don't. Not until July. However, if it's just for a few days and the lady wouldn't mind things being a bit rough, perhaps –'

Tuppence said she didn't mind things being rough and Mrs Copleigh, having surveyed her with close attention, whilst not stopping her flow of conversation, said perhaps the lady would like to come up and see the room, and then things might be arranged.

At that point Miss Bligh tore herself away with some regret because she had not so far been able to extract all the information she wanted from Tuppence, as to where she came from, what her husband did, how old she was, if she had any children and other matters of interest. But it appeared that she had a meeting at her house over which she was going to preside and was terrified at the risk that someone else might seize that coveted post.

'You'll be quite all right with Mrs Copleigh,' she assured Tuppence, 'she'll look after you, I'm sure. Now what about your car?'

'Oh, I'll fetch it presently,' said Tuppence. 'Mrs Copleigh will tell me where I had better put it. I can leave it outside here really because it isn't a very narrow street, is it?'

'Oh, my husband can do better than that for you,' said Mrs Copleigh. 'He'll put it in the field for you. Just round the side lane here, and it'll be quite all right, there. There's a shed he can drive it into.'

Things were arranged amicably on that basis and Miss Bligh hurried away to her appointment. The question of an evening meal was next raised. Tuppence asked if there was a pub in the village.

'Oh, we have nothing as a lady could go to,' said Mrs Copleigh, 'but if you'd be satisfied with a couple of eggs and a slice of ham and maybe some bread and homemade jam –'

Tuppence said that would be splendid. Her room was small but cheerful and pleasant with a rosebud wallpaper and a comfortable-looking bed and a general air of spotless cleanliness.

'Yes, it's a nice wallpaper, miss,' said Mrs Copleigh, who seemed determined to accord Tuppence single status. 'Chose it we did so that any newly married couple should come here on honeymoon. Romantic, if you know what I mean.'

Tuppence agreed that romance was a very desirable thing.

'They haven't got so much to spend nowadays, newly marrieds. Not what they used to. Most of them you see are saving for a house or are making down payments already. Or they've got to buy some furniture on the hire purchase and it doesn't leave anything over for having a posh honeymoon or anything of that kind. They're careful, you know, most of the young folk. They don't go bashing all their money.'

She clattered downstairs again talking briskly as she went. Tuppence lay down on the bed to have half an hour's sleep after a somewhat tiring day. She had, however, great hopes of Mrs Copleigh, and felt that once thoroughly rested herself, she would be able to lead the conversation to the most fruitful subjects possible. She would hear, she was sure, all about the house by the bridge, who had lived there, who had been of evil or good repute in the neighbourhood, what scandals there were and other such likely topics. She was more convinced of this than ever when she had been introduced to Mr Copleigh, a man who barely opened his mouth. His conversation was mostly made up of amiable grunts, usually signifying an affirmative. Sometimes, in more muted tones, a disagreement.

He was content so far as Tuppence could see, to let his wife talk. He himself more or less abstracted his attention, part of the time busy with his plans for the next day which appeared to be market day.

As far as Tuppence was concerned nothing could have turned out better. It could have been distinguished by a slogan – 'You want information, we have it'. Mrs Copleigh was as good as a wireless set or a television. You had only to turn the button and words poured out accompanied by gestures and lots of facial expression. Not only was her figure like a child's rubber ball, her face might also have been made of indiarubber. The various people she was talking about almost came alive in caricature before Tuppence's eyes.

Tuppence ate bacon and eggs and had slices of thick bread and butter and praised the blackberry jelly, home-made, her favourite kind, she truthfully announced, and did her best to absorb the flood of information so that she could write notes down in her notebook later. A whole panorama of the past in this country district seemed to be spread out before her.

There was no chronological sequence which occasionally made things difficult. Mrs Copleigh jumped from fifteen years ago to two years ago to last month, and then back to somewhere in the twenties. All this would want a lot of sorting out. And Tuppence wondered whether in the end she would get anything.

The first button she had pressed had not given her any result. That was a mention of Mrs Lancaster.

'I think she came from hereabouts,' said Tuppence, allowing a good deal of vagueness to appear in her voice. 'She had a picture – a very nice picture done by an artist who I believe was known down here.'

'Who did you say now?'

'A Mrs Lancaster.'

'No, I don't remember any Lancasters in these parts. Lancaster. Lancaster. A gentleman had a car accident, I remember. No, it's the car I'm thinking of. A Lancaster that was. No Mrs Lancaster. It wouldn't be Miss Bolton, would it? She'd be about seventy now I think. She might have married a Mr Lancaster. She went away and travelled abroad and I do hear she married someone.'

'The picture she gave my aunt was by a Mr Boscobel – I think the name was,' said Tuppence. 'What a lovely jelly.'

'I don't put no apple in it either, like most people do. Makes it jell better, they say, but it takes all the flavour out.'

'Yes,' said Tuppence. 'I quite agree with you. It does.'

'Who did you say now? It began with a B but I didn't quite catch it.'

'Boscobel, I think.'

'Oh, I remember Mr Boscowan well. Let's see now. That must have been – fifteen years ago it was at least that he came down here. He came several years running, he did. He liked the place. Actually rented a cottage. One of Farmer Hart's cottages it was, that he kept for his labourer. But they built a new one, they did, the Council. Four new cottages specially for labourers.

'Regular artist, Mr B was,' said Mrs Copleigh. 'Funny kind of coat he used to wear. Sort of velvet or corduroy. It used to have holes in the elbows and he wore green and yellow shirts, he did. Oh, very colourful, he was. I liked his pictures, I did. He had a showing of them one year. Round about Christmas time it was, I think. No, of course not, it must have been in the summer. He wasn't here in the winter. Yes, very nice. Nothing exciting, if you know what I mean. Just a house with a couple of trees or two cows looking over a fence. But all nice and quiet and pretty colours. Not like some of these young chaps nowadays.'

'Do you have a lot of artists down here?'

'Not really. Oh no, not to speak of. One or two ladies comes down in the summer and does sketching sometimes, but I don't think much of them. We had a young fellow a year ago, called himself an artist. Didn't shave properly. I can't say I liked any of his pictures much. Funny colours all swirled round anyhow. Nothing you could recognize a bit. Sold a lot of his pictures, he did at that. And they weren't cheap, mind you.'

'Ought to have been five pounds,' said Mr Copleigh entering the conversation for the first time so suddenly that Tuppence jumped.

'What my husband thinks is,' said Mrs Copleigh, resuming her place as interpreter to him. 'He thinks no picture ought to cost more than five pounds. Paints wouldn't cost as much as that. That's what he says, don't you, George?'

'Ah,' said George.

'Mr Boscowan painted a picture of that house by the bridge and the canal – Waterside or Watermead, isn't it called? I came that way today.'

'Oh, you came along that road, did you? It's not much of a road, is it? Very narrow. Lonely that house is, I always think. *I* wouldn't like to live in that house. Too lonely. Don't you agree, George?'

George made the noise that expressed faint disagreement and possibly contempt at the cowardice of women.

'That's where Alice Perry lives, that is,' said Mrs Copleigh.

Tuppence abandoned her researches on Mr Boscowan to go along with an opinion on the Perrys. It was, she perceived, always better to go along with Mrs Copleigh who was a jumper from subject to subject.

'Queer couple *they* are,' said Mrs Copleigh.

George made his agreeing sound.

'Keep themselves to themselves, they do. Don't mingle much, as you'd say. And she goes about looking like nothing on earth, Alice Perry does.'

'Mad,' said Mr Copleigh.

'Well, I don't know as I'd say *that*. She *looks* mad all right.

All that scatty hair flying about. And she wears men's coats and great rubber boots most of the time. And she says odd things and doesn't sometimes answer you right when you ask her a question. But I wouldn't say she was *mad*. Peculiar, that's all.'

'Do people like her?'

'Nobody knows her hardly, although they've been there several years. There's all sorts of *tales* about her but then, there's always tales.'

'What sort of tales?'

Direct questions were never resented by Mrs Copleigh, who welcomed them as one who was only too eager to answer.

'Calls up spirits, they say, at night. Sitting round a table. And there's stories of lights moving about the house at night. And she reads a lot of clever books, they say. With things drawn in them – circles and stars. If you ask me, it's Amos Perry as is the one that's not quite all right.'

'He's just simple,' said Mr Copleigh indulgently.

'Well, you may be right about that. But there were tales said of him once. Fond of his garden, but doesn't know much.'

'It's only half a house though, isn't it?' said Tuppence. 'Mrs Perry asked me in very kindly.'

'Did she now? Did she really? I don't know as I'd have liked to go into that house,' said Mrs Copleigh.

'Their part of it's all right,' said Mr Copleigh.

'Isn't the other part all right?' said Tuppence. 'The front part that gives on the canal.'

'Well, there used to be a lot of stories about it. Of course, nobody's lived in it for years. They say there's something queer about it. Lot of stories told. But when you come down to it, it's not stories in anybody's memory here. It's all long ago. It was built over a hundred years ago, you know. They say as there was a pretty lady kept there first, built for her, it was, by one of the gentlemen at Court.'

'Queen Victoria's Court?' asked Tuppence with interest.

'I don't think it would be her. *She* was particular, the old Queen was. No, I'd say it was before that. Time of one of them Georges. This gentlemen, he used to come down and see her and the story goes that they had a quarrel and he cut her throat one night.'

'How terrible!' said Tuppence. 'Did they hang him for it?'

'No. Oh no, there was nothing of that sort. The story is, you see, that he had to get rid of the body and he walled her up in the fireplace.'

'Walled her up in the fireplace!'

'Some ways they tell it, they say she was a nun, and she had run away from a convent and that's why she had to be walled up. That's what they do at convents.'

'But it wasn't nuns who walled her up.'

'No, no. He did it. Her lover, what had done her in. And he bricked up all the fireplace, they say, and nailed a big sheet of iron over it. Anyway, she was never seen again, poor soul, walking about in her fine dresses. Some said, of course, she'd gone away with him. Gone away to live in town or back to some other place. People used to hear noises and see lights in the house, and a lot of people don't go near it after dark.'

'But what happened later?' said Tuppence, feeling that to go back beyond the reign of Queen Victoria seemed a little too far into the past for what she was looking for.

'Well, I don't rightly know as there was very much. A farmer called Blodgick took it over when it came up for sale, I believe. He weren't there long either. What they called a gentleman farmer. That's why he liked the house, I suppose, but the farming land wasn't much use to him, and he didn't know how to deal with it. So he sold it again. Changed hands ever so many times it has – Always builders coming along and making alterations – new bathrooms – that sort of thing – A couple had it who were doing chicken farming, I believe, at one time. But it got a name, you know, for being unlucky. But all that's a bit before my time. I believe Mr Boscowan himself thought of buying it at one time. That was when he painted the picture of it.'

'What sort of age was Mr Boscowan when he was down here?'

'Forty, I would say, or maybe a bit more than that. He was a good-looking man in his way. Run into fat a bit, though. Great one for the girls, he was.'

'Ah,' said Mr Copleigh. It was a warning grunt this time.

'Ah well, we all know what artists are like,' said Mrs Copleigh, including Tuppence in this knowledge. 'Go over to France a lot, you know, and get French ways, they do.'

'He wasn't married?'

'Not then he wasn't. Not when he was first down here. Bit keen he was on Mrs Charrington's daughter, but nothing came of it. She was a lovely girl, though, but too young for him. She wasn't more than twenty-five.'

'Who was Mrs Charrington?' Tuppence felt bewildered at this introduction of new characters.

'What the hell am I doing here, anyway?' she thought suddenly as waves of fatigue swept over her – 'I'm just listening to a lot of gossip about people, and imagining things like murder which aren't true at all. *I can see now* – It started when a nice but addle-headed old pussy got a bit mixed up in her head and began reminiscing about stories this Mr Boscowan, or someone like him who may have given the picture to her, told about the house and the legends about it, of someone being walled up alive in a fireplace and she thought it was a child for some reason. And here I am going round investigating mares' nests. Tommy told me I was a fool, and he was quite right – I *am* a fool.'

She waited for a break to occur in Mrs Copleigh's even flow of conversation, so that she could rise, say good night politely and go upstairs to bed.

Mrs Copleigh was still in full and happy spate.

'Mrs Charrington? Oh, she lived in Watermead for a bit,' said Mrs Copleigh. 'Mrs Charrington, and her daughter. She was a nice lady, she was, Mrs Charrington. Widow of an army officer, I believe. Badly off, but the house was being rented cheap. Did a lot of gardening. She was very fond of gardening. Not much good at keeping the house clean, she wasn't. I went and obliged for her, once or twice, but I couldn't keep it up. I had to go on my bicycle, you see, and it's over two miles. Weren't any buses along that road.'

'Did she live there long?'

'Not more than two or three years, I think. Got scared, I expect, after the troubles came. And then she had her own troubles about her daughter, too. Lilian, I think her name was.'

Tuppence took a draught of the strong tea with which the meal was fortified, and resolved to get finished with Mrs Charrington before seeking repose.

'What was the trouble about the daughter? Mr Boscowan?'

'No, it wasn't Mr Boscowan as got her into trouble. I'll never believe that. It was the other one.'

'Who was the other one?' asked Tuppence. 'Someone else who lived down here?'

'I don't think he lived down in these parts. Someone she'd met up in London. She went up there to study ballet dancing, would it be? Or art? Mr Boscowan arranged for her to join some school there. Slate I think its name was.'

'Slade?' suggested Tuppence.

'May have been. That sort of name. Anyway, she used to go up there and that's how she got to know this fellow, whoever he was. Her mother didn't like it. She forbade her to meet him. Fat lot of good that was likely to do. She was a silly woman in some ways. Like a lot of those army officers' wives were, you know. She thought girls would do as they were told. Behind the times, she was. Been out in India and those parts, but when it's a question of a good-looking young fellow and you take your eye off a girl, you won't find she's doing what you told her. Not her. He used to come down here now and then and they used to meet outside.'

'And then she got into trouble, did she?' Tuppence said, using the well-known euphemism, hoping that under that form it would not offend Mr Copleigh's sense of propriety.

'Must have been him, I suppose. Anyway, there it was plain as plain. I saw how it was long before her own mother did. Beautiful creature, she was. Big and tall and handsome. But I don't think, you know, that she was one that could stand up to things. She'd break up, you know. She used to walk about rather wild-like, muttering to herself. If you ask me he treated her bad, that fellow did. Went away and left her when he found out what was happening. Of course, a mother as was a mother would have gone and talked to him and made him see where his duty lay, but Mrs Charrington, she wouldn't have had the spirit to do that. Anyway, her mother got wise, and she took the girl away. Shut up the house, she did and afterwards it was put up for sale. They came back to pack up, I believe, but they never came to the village or said anything to anyone. They never come back here, neither of them. There was some story got around. I never knew if there was any truth in it.'

'Some folk'll make up anything,' said Mr Copleigh unexpectedly.

'Well, you're right there, George. Still they may have been true. Such things happen. And as you say, that girl didn't look quite right in the head to me.'

'What was the story?' demanded Tuppence.

'Well, really, I don't like to say. It's a long time since and I wouldn't like to say anything as I wasn't sure of it. It was Mrs Badcock's Louise who put it about. Awful liar that girl was. The things she'd say. Anything to make up a good story.'

'But what was it?' said Tuppence.

'Said this Charrington girl had killed the baby and after that killed herself. Said her mother went half mad with grief and her relations had to put her in a nursing home.'

Again Tuppence felt confusion mounting in her head. She felt almost as though she was swaying in her chair. Could Mrs Charrington be Mrs Lancaster? Changed her name, gone slightly batty, obsessed about her daughter's fate. Mrs Copleigh's voice was going on remorselessly.

'I never believed a word of that myself. That Badcock girl would say anything. We weren't listening much to hearsay and stories just then – we'd had other things to worry about. Scared stiff we'd been, all over the countryside on account of the things that had been going on – REAL things –'

'Why? What had been happening?' asked Tuppence, marvelling at the things that seemed to happen, and to centre round the peaceful-looking village of Sutton Chancellor.

'I daresay as you'll have read about it all in the papers at the time. Let's see, near as possible it would have been twenty years ago. You'll have read about it for sure. Child murders. Little girl of nine years old first. Didn't come home from school one day. Whole neighbourhood was out searching for her. Dingley Copse she was found in. Strangled, she'd been. It makes me shiver still to think of it. Well, that was the first, then about three weeks later another. The other side of Market Basing, that was. But within the district, as you might say. A man with a car could have done it easy enough.

'And then there were others. Not for a month or two sometimes. And then there'd be another one. Not more than a couple of miles from here, one was; almost in the village, though.'

'Didn't the police – didn't anyone know who'd done it?'

'They tried hard enough,' said Mrs Copleigh. 'Detained a man quite soon, they did. Someone from t'other side of Market Basing. Said he was helping them in their inquiries. You know what that always means. They think they've got him. They pulled in first one and then another but always after twenty-four hours or so they had to let him go again. Found out he couldn't have done it or wasn't in these parts or somebody gave him an alibi.'

'You don't know, Liz,' said Mr Copleigh. 'They may have known quite well who done it. I'd say they *did*. That's often the way of it, or so I've heard. The police know who it is but they can't get the evidence.'

'That's wives, that is,' said Mrs Copleigh, 'wives or mothers or fathers even. Even the police can't do much no matter what they may think. A mother says "my boy was here that night at dinner" or his young lady says she went to the pictures with him that night, and he was with her the whole time, or a father says that he and his son were out in the far field together doing something – well, you can't do anything against it. They may think the father or the mother or his sweetheart's lying, but unless someone else come along and say they saw the boy or the man or whatever it is in some other place, there's not much they can do. It was a terrible time. Right het up we all were round here. When we heard another child was missing we'd make parties up.'

'Aye, that's right,' said Mr Copleigh.

'When they'd got together they'd go out and they'd search. Sometimes they found her at once and sometimes they wouldn't find her for weeks. Sometimes she was quite near her home in a place you'd have thought we must have looked at already. Maniac, I suppose it must have been. It's awful,' said Mrs Copleigh in a righteous tone, 'it's awful, that there should be men like that. They ought to be shot. They ought to be strangled themselves. And I'd do it to them for one, if anyone would let me. Any man who kills children and assaults them. What's the good putting them in loony bins and treating them with all the home comforts and living soft. And then sooner or later they let 'em out again, say they're cured and send them home. That happened somewhere in Norfolk. My sister lives there and she told me about it. He went back home and two days later he'd done in someone else. Crazy they are, these doctors, some of them, saying these men are cured when they are not.'

'And you've no idea down here who it might have been?' said Tuppence. 'Do you think really it was a stranger?'

'Might have been a stranger to us. But it must have been someone living within – oh! I'd say a range of twenty miles around. It mightn't have been here in this village.'

'You always thought it was, Liz.'

'You get het up,' said Mrs Copleigh. 'You think it's sure to be here in your own neighbourhood because you're afraid, I suppose. I used to look at people. So did you, George. You'd say to yourself I wonder if it could be *that* chap, he's seemed a bit queer lately. That sort of thing.'

'I don't suppose really he looked queer at all,' said Tuppence. 'He probably looked just like everyone else.'

'Yes, it could be you've got something there. I've heard it said that you wouldn't know, and whoever it was had never seemed mad at all, but other people say there's always a terrible glare in their eyes.'

'Jeffreys, he was the sergeant of police here then,' said Mr Copleigh, 'he always used to say he had a good idea but there was nothing doing.'

'They never caught the man?'

'No. Over six months it was, nearly a year. Then the whole thing stopped. And there's never been anything of that kind round here since. No, I think he must have gone away. Gone away altogether. That's what makes people think they might know who it was.'

'You mean because of people who *did* leave the district?'

'Well, of course it made people talk, you know. They'd say it might be so-and-so.'

Tuppence hesitated to ask the next question, but she felt that with Mrs Copleigh's passion for talking it wouldn't matter if she did.

'Who did *you* think it was?' she asked.

'Well, it's that long ago I'd hardly like to say. But there *was* names mentioned. Talked of, you know, and looked at. Some as thought it might be Mr Boscowan.'

'Did they?'

'Yes, being an artist and all, artists are queer. They say that. But I didn't think it was him!'

'There was more as said it was Amos Perry,' said Mr Copleigh.

'Mrs Perry's husband?'

'Yes. He's a bit queer, you know, simple-minded. He's the sort of chap that might have done it.'

'Were the Perrys living here then?'

'Yes. Not at Watermead. They had a cottage about four or five miles away. Police had an eye on him, I'm sure of that.'

'Couldn't get anything on him, though,' said Mrs Copleigh. 'His wife spoke for him always. Stayed at home with her in the evenings, he did. Always, she said. Just went along sometimes to the pub on a Saturday night, but none of these murders took place on a Saturday night, so there wasn't anything in that. Besides, Alice Perry was the kind you'd believe when she gave evidence. She'd never let up or back down. You couldn't frighten her out of it. Anyway, *he's* not the one. I never thought so. I know I've nothing to go on but I've a sort of feeling if I'd had to put my finger on anyone I'd have put it on Sir Philip.'

'Sir Philip?' Again Tuppence's head reeled. Yet another character was being introduced. Sir Philip. 'Who's Sir Philip?' she asked.

'Sir Philip Starke – Lives up in the Warrender House. Used to be called the Old Priory when the Warrenders lived in it – before it burnt down. You can see the Warrender graves in the churchyard and tablets in the church, too. Always been Warrenders here practically since the time of King James.'

'Was Sir Philip a relation of the Warrenders?'

'No. Made his money in a big way, I believe, or his father did. Steelworks or something of that kind. Odd sort of man was Sir Philip. The works were somewhere up north, but he lived here. Kept to himself he did. What they call a rec – rec – rec-something.'

'Recluse,' suggested Tuppence.

'That's the word I'm looking for. Pale he was, you know, and thin and bony and fond of flowers. He was a botanist. Used to collect all sorts of silly little wild flowers, the kind you wouldn't look at twice. He even wrote a book on them, I believe. Oh yes, he was clever, very clever. His wife was a nice lady, and very handsome, but sad looking, I always thought.'

Mr Copleigh uttered one of his grunts. 'You're daft,' he said. 'Thinking it might have been Sir Philip. He was fond of children, Sir Philip was. He was always giving parties for them.'

'Yes I know. Always giving fêtes, having lovely prizes for the children. Egg and spoon races – all those strawberry and cream teas he'd give. He'd no children of his own, you see. Often he'd stop children in a lane and give them a sweet or give them a sixpence to buy sweets. But I don't know. *I* think he overdid it. He was an odd man. I thought there was something wrong when his wife suddenly up and left him.'

'When did his wife leave him?'

'It'd be about six months after all this trouble began. Three children had been killed by then. Lady Starke went away suddenly to the south of France and she never came back. She wasn't the kind, you'd say, to do that. She was a quiet lady, respectable. It's not as though she left him for any other man. No, she wasn't the kind to do that. So *why* did she go and leave him? I always say it's because she knew something – found out about something –'

'Is he still living here?'

'Not regular, he isn't. He comes down once or twice a year but the house is kept shut up most of the time with a caretaker there. Miss Bligh in the village – she used to be his secretary – she sees to things for him.'

'And his wife?'

'She's dead, poor lady. Died soon after she went abroad. There's a tablet put up to her in the church. Awful for her it would be. Perhaps she wasn't sure at first, then perhaps she began to suspect her husband, and then perhaps she got to be quite sure. She couldn't bear it and she went away.'

'The things you women imagine,' said Mr Copleigh.

'All I say is there was *something* that wasn't right about Sir Philip. He was too fond of children, I think, and it wasn't in a natural kind of way.'

'Women's fancies,' said Mr Copleigh.

Mrs Copleigh got up and started to move things off the table.

'About time,' said her husband. 'You'll give this lady here bad dreams if you go on about things as were over years ago and have nothing to do with anyone here any more.'

'It's been very interesting hearing,' said Tuppence. 'But I am very sleepy. I think I'd better go to bed now.'

'Well, we usually goes early to bed,' said Mrs Copleigh, 'and you'll be tired after the long day you've had.'

'I am. I'm frightfully sleepy.' Tuppence gave a large yawn. 'Well, good night and thank you very much.'

'Would you like a call and a cup of tea in the morning? Eight o'clock too early for you?'

'No, that would be fine,' said Tuppence. 'But don't bother if it's a lot of trouble.'

'No trouble at all,' said Mrs Copleigh.

Tuppence pulled herself wearily up to bed. She opened her suitcase, took out the few things she needed, undressed, washed and dropped into bed. It was true what she had told Mrs Copleigh. She was dead tired. The things she had heard passed through her head in a kind of kaleidoscope of moving figures and of all sorts of horrific imaginings. Dead children – too many dead children. Tuppence wanted just one dead child behind a fireplace. The fireplace had to do perhaps with Waterside. The child's doll. A child that had been killed by a demented young girl driven off her rather weak brains by the fact that her lover had deserted her. Oh dear me, what melodramatic language I'm using, thought Tuppence. All such a muddle – the chronology all mixed up – one can't be sure what happened when.

She went to sleep and dreamt. There was a kind of Lady of Shalott looking out of the window of the house. There was a scratching noise coming from the chimney. Blows were coming from behind a great iron plate nailed up there. The clanging sounds of the hammer. Clang, clang, clang. Tuppence woke up. It was Mrs Copleigh knocking on the door. She came in brightly, put the tea down by Tuppence's bed, pulled the curtains, hoped Tuppence had slept well. No one had ever, Tuppence thought, looked more cheerful than Mrs Copleigh did. *She* had had no bad dreams!

CHAPTER 9

A MORNING IN MARKET BASING

'Ah well,' said Mrs Copleigh, as she bustled out of the room. 'Another day. That's what I always say when I wake up.'

'Another day?' thought Tuppence, sipping strong black tea. 'I wonder if I'm making an idiot of myself . . . ? Could be . . . Wish I had Tommy here to talk to. Last night muddled me.'

Before she left her room, Tuppence made entries in her notebook on the various facts and names that she had heard the night before, which she had been far too tired to do when she went up to bed. Melodramatic stories, of the past, containing perhaps grains of truth here and there but mostly hearsay, malice, gossip, romantic imagination.

'Really,' thought Tuppence. 'I'm beginning to know the love lives of a quantity of people right back to the eighteenth century, I think. But what does it all amount to? And what am I looking for? I don't even *know* any longer. The awful thing is that I've got involved and I can't leave off.'

Having a shrewd suspicion that the first thing she might be getting involved with was Miss Bligh, whom Tuppence recognized as the overall menace of Sutton Chancellor, she circumvented all kind offers of help by driving off to Market Basing post haste, only pausing, when the car was accosted by Miss Bligh with shrill cries, to explain to that lady that she had an urgent appointment . . . When would she be back? Tuppence was vague – Would she care to lunch? – Very kind of Miss Bligh, but Tuppence was afraid –

'Tea, then. Four-thirty I'll expect you.' It was almost a Royal Command. Tuppence smiled, nodded, let in the clutch and drove on.

Possibly, Tuppence thought – if she got anything interesting out of the house agents in Market Basing – Nellie Bligh might provide additional useful information. She was the kind of woman who prided herself on knowing all about everyone. The snag was that she would be determined to know all about Tuppence. Possibly by this afternoon Tuppence would have recovered sufficiently to be once more her own inventive self!

'Remember, Mrs Blenkinsop,' said Tuppence, edging round a sharp corner and squeezing into a hedge to avoid being annihilated by a frolicsome tractor of immense bulk.

Arrived in Market Basing she put the car in a parking lot in the main square, and went into the post office and entered a vacant telephone box.

The voice of Albert answered – using his usual response – a single 'Hallo' uttered in a suspicious voice.

'Listen, Albert – I'll be home tomorrow. In time for dinner, anyway – perhaps earlier. Mr Beresford will be back, too, unless he rings up. Get us something – chicken, I think.'

'Right, Madam. Where are you –'

But Tuppence had rung off.

The life of Market Basing seemed centred in its important main square – Tuppence had consulted a classified directory before leaving the post office and three out of the four house and estate agents were situated in the square – the fourth in something called George Street.

Tuppence scribbled down the names and went out to look for them.

She started with Messrs Lovebody & Slicker which appeared to be the most imposing.

A girl with spots received her.

'I want to make some inquiries about a house.'

The girl received this news without interest. Tuppence might have been inquiring about some rare animal.

'I don't know, I'm sure,' said the girl, looking round to ascertain if there was one of her colleagues to whom she could pass Tuppence on –

'A *house*,' said Tuppence. 'You *are* house agents, aren't you?'

'House agents and auctioneers. The Cranberry Court auction's on Wednesday if it's that you're interested in, catalogues two shillings.'

'I'm not interested in auctions. I want to ask about a house.'

'Furnished?'

'Unfurnished – To buy – or rent.'

Spots brightened a little.

'I think you'd better see Mr Slicker.'

Tuppence was all for seeing Mr Slicker and was presently

seated in a small office opposite a tweed-suited young man in horsy checks, who began turning over a large number of particulars of desirable residences – murmuring comments to himself . . . '8 Mandeville Road – architect built, three bed, American kitchen – Oh, no, that's gone – Amabel Lodge – picturesque residence, four acres – reduced price for quick sale –'

Tuppence interrupted him forcefully: 'I have seen a house I like the look of – In Sutton Chancellor – or rather, near Sutton Chancellor – by a canal –'

'Sutton Chancellor,' Mr Slicker looked doubtful – 'I don't think we have any property there on our books at present. What name?'

'It doesn't seem to have any written up – Possibly Waterside. Rivermead – once called Bridge House. I gather,' said Tuppence, 'the house is in two parts. One half is let but the tenant there could not tell me anything about the other half, which fronts on the canal and which is the one in which I am interested. It appears to be unoccupied.'

Mr Slicker said distantly that he was afraid he couldn't help her, but condescended to supply the information that perhaps Messrs Blodget & Burgess might do so. By the tone in his voice the clerk seemed to imply this Messrs Blodget & Burgess were a very inferior firm.

Tuppence transferred herself to Messrs Blodget & Burgess who were on the opposite side of the square – and whose premises closely resembled those of Messrs Lovebody & Slicker – the same kind of sale bills and forthcoming auctions in their rather grimy windows. Their front door had recently been repainted a rather bilious shade of green, if that was accounted to be a merit.

The reception arrangements were equally discouraging, and Tuppence was given over to a Mr Sprig, an elderly man of apparently despondent disposition. Once more Tuppence retailed her wants and requirements.

Mr Sprig admitted to being aware of the existence of the residence in question, but was not helpful, or as far as it seemed, much interested.

'It's not in the market, I'm afraid. The owner doesn't want to sell.'

'Who is the owner?'

'Really I doubt if I know. It has changed hands rather frequently – there was a rumour at one moment of a compulsory purchase order.'

'What did any local government want it for?'

'Really, Mrs – er – (he glanced down at Tuppence's name jotted down on his blotter) – Mrs Beresford, if you could tell me the answer to that question you would be wiser than most victims are these days. The ways of local councils and planning societies are always shrouded in mystery. The rear portion of the house had a few necessary repairs done to it and was let at an exceedingly low rent to a – er – ah yes, a Mr and Mrs Perry. As to the actual owners of the property, the gentleman in question lives abroad and seems to have lost interest in the place. I imagine there was some question of a minor inheriting, and it was administered by executors. Some small legal difficulties arose – the law tends to be expensive, Mrs Beresford – I fancy the owner is quite content for the house to fall down – no repairs are done except to the portion the Perrys inhabit. The actual land, of course, might always prove valuable in the future – the repair of derelict houses is seldom profitable. If you are interested in a property of that kind, I am sure we could offer you something far more worth your while. What, if I may ask, is there which especially appealed to you in this property?'

'I liked the look of it,' said Tuppence. 'It's a very *pretty* house – I saw it first from the train –'

'Oh, I see –' Mr Sprig masked as best he could an expression of 'the foolishness of women is incredible' – and said soothingly, 'I should really forget all about it if I were you.'

'I suppose you could write and ask the owners if they would be prepared to sell – or if you would give me their – or his address –'

'We will get into communication with the owners' solicitors if you insist – but I can't hold out much hope.'

'I suppose one always has to go through solicitors for everything nowadays.' Tuppence sounded both foolish and fretful . . . 'And lawyers are always so *slow* over everything.'

'Ah yes – the law is prolific of delays –'

'And so are *banks* – just as bad!'

'Banks –' Mr Sprig sounded a little startled.

'So many people give you a *bank* as an address. That's tiresome too.'

'Yes – yes – as you say – But people are so restless these days and move about so much – living abroad and all that.' He opened a desk drawer. 'Now I have a property here, Crossgates – two miles from Market Basing – very good condition – nice garden –'

Tuppence rose to her feet.

'No thank you.'

She bade Mr Sprig a firm goodbye and went out into the square.

She paid a brief visit to the third establishment which seemed to be mainly preoccupied with sales of cattle, chicken farms and general farms in a derelict condition.

She paid a final visit to Messrs Roberts & Wiley in George Street – which seemed to be a small but pushing business, anxious to oblige – but generally uninterested and ignorant of Sutton Chancellor and anxious to sell residences as yet only half built at what seemed ridiculously exorbitant sums – an illustration of one made Tuppence shudder. The eager young man seeing his possible client firm in departure, admitted unwillingly that such a place as Sutton Chancellor did exist.

'Sutton Chancellor you mentioned. Better try Blodget & Burgess in the square. They handle some property thereabouts – but it's all in very poor condition – run down –'

'There's a pretty house near there, by a canal bridge – I saw it from the train. Why does nobody want to live there?'

'Oh! I know the place, this – Riverbank – You wouldn't get anyone to live in it – Got a reputation as haunted.'

'You mean – ghosts?'

'So they say – Lots of tales about it. Noises at nights. And groans. If you ask me, it's death-watch beetle.'

'Oh dear,' said Tuppence. 'It looked to me so nice and isolated.'

'Much too isolated most people would say. Floods in winter – think of that.'

'I see that there's a lot to think about,' said Tuppence bitterly.

She murmured to herself as she sent her steps towards The

Lamb and Flag at which she proposed to fortify herself with lunch.

'A lot to think about – floods, death-watch beetle, ghosts, clanking chains, absentee owners and landlords, solicitors, banks – a house that nobody wants or loves – except perhaps *me* . . . Oh well, what I want now is FOOD.'

The food at The Lamb and Flag was good and plentiful – hearty food for farmers rather than phony French menus for tourists passing through – Thick savoury soup, leg of pork and apple sauce, Stilton cheese – or plums and custard if you preferred it – which Tuppence didn't –

After a desultory stroll round, Tuppence retrieved her car and started back to Sutton Chancellor – unable to feel that her morning had been fruitful.

As she turned the last corner and Sutton Chancellor church came into view, Tuppence saw the vicar emerging from the churchyard. He walked rather wearily. Tuppence drew up by him.

'Are you still looking for that grave?' she asked.

The vicar had one hand at the small of his back.

'Oh dear,' he said, 'my eyesight is not very good. So many of the inscriptions are nearly erased. My back troubles me, too. So many of these stones lie flat on the ground. Really, when I bend over sometimes I fear that I shall never get up again.'

'I shouldn't do it any more,' said Tuppence. 'If you've looked in the parish register and all that, you've done all you can.'

'I know, but the poor fellow seemed so keen, so earnest. I'm quite sure that it's all wasted labour. However, I really felt it was my duty. I have still got a short stretch I haven't done, over there from beyond the yew tree to the far wall – although most of the stones are eighteenth century. But I should like to feel I had finished my task properly. Then I could not reproach myself. However, I shall leave it till tomorrow.'

'Quite right,' said Tuppence. 'You mustn't do too much in one day. I tell you what,' she added. 'After I've had a cup of tea with Miss Bligh, I'll go and have a look myself. From the yew tree to the wall, do you say?'

'Oh, but I couldn't possibly ask you –'

'That's all right. I shall quite like to do it. I think it's very interesting prowling round in a churchyard. You know, the older inscriptions give you a sort of picture of the people who lived here and all that sort of thing. I shall quite enjoy it, I shall really. Do go back home and rest.'

'Well, of course, I really have to do something about my sermon this evening, it's quite true. You are a very kind friend, I'm sure. A *very* kind friend.'

He beamed at her and departed into the vicarage. Tuppence glanced at her watch. She stopped at Miss Bligh's house. 'Might as well get it over,' thought Tuppence. The front door was open and Miss Bligh was just carrying a plate of fresh-baked scones across the hall into the sitting-room.

'Oh! so there you are, dear Mrs Beresford. I'm *so* pleased to see you. Tea's quite ready. The kettle is on. I've only got to fill up the teapot. I hope you did all the shopping you wanted,' she added, looking in a rather marked manner at the painfully evident empty shopping bag hanging on Tuppence's arm.

'Well, I didn't have much luck really,' said Tuppence, putting as good a face on it as she could. 'You know how it is sometimes – just one of those days when people just haven't got the particular colour or the particular kind of thing you want. But I always enjoy looking round a new place even if it isn't a very interesting one.'

A whistling kettle let forth a strident shriek for attention and Miss Bligh shot back into the kitchen to attend to it, scattering a batch of letters waiting for the post on the hall table.

Tuppence stooped and retrieved them, noticing as she put them back on the table that the topmost one was addressed to a Mrs Yorke, Rosetrellis Court for Elderly Ladies – at an address in Cumberland.

'Really,' thought Tuppence. 'I am beginning to feel as if the whole of the country is full of nothing but Homes for the Elderly! I suppose in next to no time Tommy and I will be living in one!'

Only the other day, some would-be kind and helpful friend had written to recommend a very nice address in Devon – married couples – mostly retired Service people. Quite good cooking – You brought your own furniture and personal belongings.

Miss Bligh reappeared with the teapot and the two ladies sat down to tea.

Miss Bligh's conversation was of a less melodramatic and juicy nature than that of Mrs Copleigh, and was concerned more with the procuring of information, than of giving it.

Tuppence murmured vaguely of past years of Service abroad – the domestic difficulties of life in England, gave details of a married son and a married daughter both with children and gently steered the conversation to the activities of Miss Bligh in Sutton Chancellor which were numerous – The Women's Institute, Guides, Scouts, the Conservative Ladies Union, Lectures, Greek Art, Jam Making, Flower Arrangement, the Sketching Club, the Friends of Archaeology – The vicar's health, the necessity of making him take care of himself, his absentmindedness – Unfortunate differences of opinion between churchwardens –

Tuppence praised the scones, thanked her hostess for her hospitality and rose to go.

'You are so wonderfully energetic, Miss Bligh,' she said. 'How you manage to do all you do, I cannot imagine. I must confess that after a day's excursion and shopping, I like just a nice little rest on my bed – just half an hour or so of shut-eye – A very comfortable bed, too. I must thank you very much for recommending me to Mrs Copleigh –'

'A most reliable woman, though of course she talks too much –'

'Oh! I found all her local tales most entertaining.'

'Half the time she doesn't know what she's talking about! Are you staying here for long?'

'Oh no – I'm going home tomorrow. I'm disappointed at not having heard of any suitable little property – I had hopes of that very picturesque house by the canal –'

'You're well out of that. It's in a very poor state of repair – Absentee landlords – it's a disgrace –'

'I couldn't even find out who it belongs to. I expect *you* know. You seem to know everything here –'

'I've never taken much interest in that house. It's always changing hands – One can't keep pace. The Perrys live in half of it – and the other half just goes to rack and ruin.'

Tuppence said goodbye again and drove back to Mrs Copleigh's. The house was quiet and apparently empty. Tuppence went up to her bedroom, deposited her empty shopping bag, washed her face and powdered her nose, tiptoed out of the house again, looking up and down the street, then leaving her car where it was, she walked swiftly round the corner, and took a footpath through the field behind the village which eventually led to a stile into the churchyard.

Tuppence went over the stile into the churchyard, peaceful in the evening sun, and began to examine the tombstones as she had promised. She had not really had any ulterior motive in doing so. There was nothing here she hoped to discover. It was really just kindliness on her part. The elderly vicar was rather a dear, and she would like him to feel that his conscience was entirely satisfied. She had brought a notebook and pencil with her in case there was anything of interest to note down for him. She presumed she was merely to look for a gravestone that might have been put up commemorating the death of some child of the required age. Most of the graves here were of an older date. They were not very interesting, not old enough to be quaint or to have touching or tender inscriptions. They were mostly of fairly elderly people. Yet she lingered a little as she went along, making mental pictures in her mind. Jane Elwood, departed this life January the 6th, aged 45. William Marl, departed this life January the 5th, deeply regretted. Mary Treves, five years old. March 14th 1835. That was too far back. 'In thy presence is the fulness of joy.' Lucky little Mary Treves.

She had almost reached the far wall now. The graves here were neglected and overgrown, nobody seemed to care about this bit of the cemetery. Many of the stones were no longer upright but lay about on the ground. The wall here was damaged and crumbling. In places it had been broken down.

Being right behind the church, it could not be seen from the road – and no doubt children came here to do what damage they could. Tuppence bent over one of the stone slabs – The original lettering was worn away and unreadable – But heaving it up sideways, Tuppence saw some coarsely scrawled letters and words, also by now partly overgrown.

She stopped to trace them with a forefinger, and got a word here and there –

Whoever . . . offend . . . one of these little ones . . .

Millstone . . . Millstone . . . Millstone . . . and below – in uneven cutting by an amateur hand:

Here lies Lily Waters.

Tuppence drew a deep breath – She was conscious of a shadow behind her, but before she could turn her head – something hit her on the back of her head and she fell forwards on to the tombstone into pain and darkness.

BOOK 3 • MISSING – A WIFE

CHAPTER 10

A CONFERENCE – AND AFTER

I

'Well, Beresford,' said Major-General Sir Josiah Penn, K.M.G., C.B., D.S.O., speaking with the weight appropriate to the impressive stream of letters after his name. 'Well, what do you think of all that yackety-yack?'

Tommy gathered by that remark that Old Josh, as he was irreverently spoken of behind his back, was not impressed with the result of the course of the conferences in which they had been taking part.

'Softly, softly catchee monkey,' said Sir Josiah, going on with his remarks. 'A lot of talk and nothing said. If anybody does say anything sensible now and then, about four beanstalks immediately get up and howl it down. *I* don't know why we come to these things. At least, I *do* know. I know why I do. Nothing else to do. If I didn't come to these shows, I'd have to stay at home. Do you know what happens to me there? I get bullied, Beresford. Bullied by my housekeeper, bullied by my gardener. He's an elderly Scot and he won't so much as let me touch my own peaches. So I come along here, throw my weight about and pretend to myself that I'm performing a useful function, ensuring the security of this country! Stuff and nonsense.

'What about you? You're a relatively young man. What do you come and waste your time for? Nobody'll listen to you, even if you do say something worth hearing.'

Tommy, faintly amused that despite his own, as he considered, advanced age, he could be regarded as a youngster by Major-General Sir Josiah Penn, shook his head. The General must be, Tommy thought, considerably past eighty, he was rather deaf, heavily bronchial, but he was nobody's fool.

'Nothing would ever get done at all if you weren't here, sir,' said Tommy.

'I like to think so,' said the General. 'I'm a toothless bulldog – but I can still bark. How's Mrs Tommy? Haven't seen her for a long time.'

Tommy replied that Tuppence was well and active.

'She was always active. Used to make me think of a dragonfly sometimes. Always darting off after some apparently absurd idea of her own and then we'd find it wasn't absurd. Good fun!' said the General, with approval. 'Don't like these earnest middle-aged women you meet nowadays, all got a Cause with a capital C. And as for the girls nowadays –' he shook his head. 'Not what they used to be when I was a young man. Pretty as a picture, they used to be then. Their muslin frocks! *Cloche* hats, they used to wear at one time. Do you remember? No, I suppose you'd have been at school. Had to look right down underneath the brim before you could see the girl's face. Tantalizing it was, *and* they knew it! I remember now – let me see – she was a relative of yours – an aunt wasn't she? – Ada. Ada Fanshawe –'

'Aunt Ada?'

'Prettiest girl I ever knew.'

Tommy managed to contain the surprise he felt. That his Aunt Ada could ever have been considered pretty seemed beyond belief. Old Josh was dithering on.

'Yes, pretty as a picture. Sprightly, too! Gay! Regular tease. Ah, I remember last time I saw her. I was a subaltern just off to India. We were at a moonlight picnic on the beach . . . She and I wandered away together and sat on a rock looking at the sea.'

Tommy looked at him with great interest. At his double chins, his bald head, his bushy eyebrows and his enormous paunch. He thought of Aunt Ada, of her incipient moustache, her grim smile, her iron-grey hair, her malicious glance. Time, he thought. What Time does to one! He tried to visualize a handsome young subaltern and a pretty girl in the moonlight. He failed.

'Romantic,' said Sir Josiah Penn with a deep sigh. 'Ah yes, romantic. I would have liked to propose to her that night, but you couldn't propose if you were a subaltern. Not on your pay. We'd have had to wait five years before we could be married. That was too long an engagement to ask any girl to agree to.

Ah well! you know how things happen. I went out to India and it was a long time before I came home on leave. We wrote to one another for a bit, then things slacked off. As it usually happens. I never saw her again. And yet, you know, I never quite forgot her. Often thought of her. I remember I nearly wrote to her once, years later. I'd heard she was in the neighbourhood where I was staying with some people. I thought I'd go and see her, ask if I could call. Then I thought to myself "Don't be a damn' fool. She probably looks quite different by now."

'I heard a chap mention her some years later. Said she was one of the ugliest women he'd ever seen. I could hardly believe it when I heard him say that, but I think now perhaps I was lucky I never *did* see her again. What's she doing now? Alive still?'

'No. She died about two or three weeks ago, as a matter of fact,' said Tommy.

'Did she really, did she really? Yes, I suppose she'd be – what now, she'd be seventy-five or seventy-six? Bit older than that perhaps.'

'She was eighty,' said Tommy.

'Fancy now. Dark-haired lively Ada. Where did she die? Was she in a nursing home or did she live with a companion or – she never married, did she?'

'No,' said Tommy, 'she never married. She was in an old ladies' home. Rather a nice one, as a matter of fact. Sunny Ridge, it's called.'

'Yes, I've heard of that. Sunny Ridge. Someone my sister knew was there, I believe. A Mrs – now what was the name – a Mrs Carstairs? D'you ever come across her?'

'No. I didn't come across anyone much there. One just used to go and visit one's own particular relative.'

'Difficult business, too, I think. I mean, one never knows what to say to them.'

'Aunt Ada was particularly difficult,' said Tommy. 'She was a tartar, you know.'

'She would be.' The General chuckled. 'She could be a regular little devil when she liked when she was a girl.'

He sighed.

'Devilish business, getting old. One of my sister's friends

used to get fancies, poor old thing. Used to say she'd killed somebody.'

'Good Lord,' said Tommy. 'Had she?'

'Oh, I don't suppose so. Nobody seems to think she had. I suppose,' said the General, considering the idea thoughtfully, 'I suppose she *might* have, you know. If you go about saying things like that quite cheerfully, nobody *would* believe you, would they? Entertaining thought that, isn't it?'

'Who did she think she'd killed?'

'Blessed if I know. Husband perhaps? Don't know who he was or what he was like. She was a widow when we first came to know her. Well,' he added with a sigh, 'sorry to hear about Ada. Didn't see it in the paper. If I had I'd have sent flowers or something. Bunch of rosebuds or something of that kind. That's what girls used to wear on their evening dresses. A bunch of rosebuds on the shoulder of an evening dress. Very pretty it was. I remember Ada had an evening dress – sort of hydrangea colour, mauvy. Mauvy-blue and she had pink rosebuds on it. She gave me one once. They weren't real, of course. Artificial. I kept it for a long time – years. I know,' he added, catching Tommy's eye, 'makes you laugh to think of it, doesn't it. I tell you, my boy, when you get really old and *gaga* like I am, you get sentimental again. Well, I suppose I'd better toddle off and go back to the last act of this ridiculous show. Best regards to Mrs T. when you get home.'

In the train the next day, Tommy thought back over this conversation, smiling to himself and trying again to picture his redoubtable aunt and the fierce Major-General in their young days.

'I must tell Tuppence this. It'll make her laugh,' said Tommy. 'I wonder what Tuppence has been doing while I've been away?'

He smiled to himself.

II

The faithful Albert opened the front door with a beaming smile of welcome.

'Glad to see you back, sir.'

'I'm glad to be back –' Tommy surrendered his suitcase – 'Where's Mrs Beresford?'

'Not back yet, sir.'

'Do you mean she's away?'

'Been away three or four days. But she'll be back for dinner. She rang up yesterday and said so.'

'What's she up to, Albert?'

'I couldn't say, sir. She took the car, but she took a lot of railway guides as well. She might be anywhere, as you might say.'

'You might indeed,' said Tommy with feeling. 'John o' Groat's – or Land's End – and probably missed the connection at Little Dither on the Marsh on the way back. God bless British Railways. She rang up yesterday, you say. Did she say where she was ringing from?'

'She didn't say.'

'What time yesterday was this?'

'Yesterday morning. Before lunch. Just said everything was all right. She wasn't quite sure of what time she'd get home, but she thought she'd be back well before dinner and suggested a chicken. That do you all right, sir?'

'Yes,' said Tommy, regarding his watch, 'but she'll have to make it pretty quickly now.'

'I'll hold the chicken back,' said Albert.

Tommy grinned. 'That's right,' he said. 'Catch it by the tail. How've you been, Albert? All well at home?'

'Had a scare of measles – But it's all right. Doctor says it's only strawberry rash.'

'Good,' said Tommy. He went upstairs, whistling a tune to himself. He went into the bathroom, shaved and washed, strode from there into the bedroom and looked around him. It had that curious look of disoccupancy some bedrooms put on when their owner is away. Its atmosphere was cold and unfriendly. Everything was scrupulously tidy and scrupulously clean. Tommy had the depressed feeling that a faithful dog might have had. Looking round him, he thought it was as though Tuppence had never been. No spilled powder, no book cast down open with its back splayed out.

'Sir.'

It was Albert, standing in the doorway.

'Well?'

'I'm getting worried about the chicken.'

'Oh damn the chicken,' said Tommy. 'You seem to have that chicken on your nerves.'

'Well, I took it as you and she wouldn't be later than eight. Not later than eight, sitting down, I mean.'

'I should have thought so, too,' said Tommy, glancing at his wrist watch. 'Good Lord, is it nearly five and twenty to nine?'

'Yes it is, sir. And the chicken –'

'Oh, come on,' said Tommy, 'you get that chicken out of the oven and you and I'll eat it between us. Serve Tuppence right. Getting back well before dinner indeed!'

'Of course some people do eat dinner late,' said Albert. 'I went to Spain once and believe me, you couldn't get a meal before ten o'clock. Ten p.m. I ask you! Heathens!'

'All right,' said Tommy, absentmindedly. 'By the way, have you no idea where she has been all this time?'

'You mean the missus? I dunno, sir. Rushing around, I'd say. Her first idea was going to places by train, as far as I can make out. She was always looking in A.B.C.s and timetables and things.'

'Well,' said Tommy, 'we all have our ways of amusing ourselves, I suppose. Hers seems to have been railway travel. I wonder where she is all the same. Sitting in the Ladies' Waiting Room at Little Dither on the Marsh, as likely as not.'

'She knew as you was coming home today though, didn't she, sir?' said Albert. 'She'll get here somehow. Sure to.'

Tommy perceived that he was being offered loyal allegiance. He and Albert were linked together in expressing disapprobation of a Tuppence who in the course of her flirtations with British Railways was neglecting to come home in time to give a returning husband his proper welcome.

Albert went away to release the chicken from its possible fate of cremation in the oven.

Tommy, who had been about to follow him, stopped and looked towards the mantelpiece. He walked slowly to it and looked at the picture that hung there. Funny, her being so sure that she had seen that particular house before. Tommy felt quite certain that *he* hadn't seen it. Anyway, it was quite an ordinary house. There must be plenty of houses like that.

He stretched up as far as he could towards it and then, still not able to get a good view, unhooked it and took it close to the electric lamp. A quiet, gentle house. There was the artist's signature. The name began with a B though he couldn't make out exactly what the name was. Bosworth – Bouchier – He'd get a magnifying glass and look at it more closely. A merry chime of cowbells came from the hall. Albert had highly approved of the Swiss cowbells that Tommy and Tuppence had brought back some time or other from Grindelwald. He was something of a virtuoso on them. Dinner was served. Tommy went to the dining-room. It was odd, he thought, that Tuppence hadn't turned up by now. Even if she had had a puncture, which seemed probable, he rather wondered that she hadn't rung up to explain or excuse her delay.

'She might know that I'd worry,' said Tommy to himself. Not, of course, that he ever *did* worry – not about Tuppence. Tuppence was always all right. Albert contradicted this mood.

'Hope she hasn't had an accident,' he remarked, presenting Tommy with a dish of cabbage, and shaking his head gloomily.

'Take that away. You know I hate cabbage,' said Tommy. 'Why should she have had an accident? It's only half past nine now.'

'Being on the road is plain murder nowadays,' said Albert. 'Anyone might have an accident.'

The telephone bell rang. 'That's her,' said Albert. Hastily reposing the dish of cabbage on the sideboard, he hurried out of the room. Tommy rose, abandoning his plate of chicken, and followed Albert. He was just saying 'Here, I'll take it,' when Albert spoke.

'Yes, sir? Yes, Mr Beresford is at home. Here he is now.' He turned his head to Tommy. 'It's a Dr Murray for you, sir.'

'Dr Murray?' Tommy thought for a moment. The name seemed familiar but for the moment he couldn't remember who Dr Murray was. If Tuppence had had an accident – and then with a sigh of relief he remembered that Dr Murray had been the doctor who attended the old ladies at Sunny Ridge. Something, perhaps, to do with Aunt Ada's funeral forms. True child of his time, Tommy immediately assumed that it must be a question of some form or other – something he ought to have signed, or Dr Murray ought to have signed.

'Hullo,' he said, 'Beresford here.'

'Oh, I'm glad to catch you. You remember me, I hope. I attended your aunt, Miss Fanshawe.'

'Yes, of course I remember. What can I do?'

'I really wanted to have a word or two with you sometime. I don't know if we can arrange a meeting, perhaps in town one day?'

'Oh I expect so, yes. Quite easily. But – er – is it something you can't say over the phone?'

'I'd rather not say it over the telephone. There's no immediate hurry. I won't pretend there is but – but I should like to have a chat with you.'

'Nothing wrong?' said Tommy, and wondered why he put it that way. Why should there be anything wrong?

'Not really. I may be making a mountain out of a molehill. Probably am. But there have been some rather curious developments at Sunny Ridge.'

'Nothing to do with Mrs Lancaster, is it?' asked Tommy.

'Mrs Lancaster?' The doctor seemed surprised. 'Oh no. She left some time ago. In fact – before your aunt died. This is something quite different.'

'I've been away – only just got back. May I ring you up tomorrow morning – we could fix something then.'

'Right. I'll give you my telephone number. I shall be at my surgery until ten a.m.'

'Bad news?' asked Albert as Tommy returned to the dining-room.

'For God's sake, don't croak, Albert,' said Tommy irritably. 'No – of course it isn't bad news.'

'I thought perhaps the missus –'

'She's all right,' said Tommy. 'She always is. Probably gone haring off after some wild-cat clue or other – You know what she's like. I'm not going to worry any more. Take away this plate of chicken – You've been keeping it hot in the oven and it's inedible. Bring me some coffee. And then I'm going to bed.

'There will probably be a letter tomorrow. Delayed in the post – you know what our posts are like – or there will be a wire from her – or she'll ring up.'

But there was no letter next day – no telephone call – no wire.

Albert eyed Tommy, opened his mouth and shut it again several times, judging quite rightly that gloomy predictions on his part would not be welcomed.

At last Tommy had pity on him. He swallowed a last mouthful of toast and marmalade, washed it down with coffee, and spoke –

'All right, Albert, I'll say it first – *Where is she?* What's happened to her? And what are we going to do about it?'

'Get on to the police, sir?'

'I'm not sure. You see –' Tommy paused.

'If she's had an accident –'

'She's got her driving licence on her – and plenty of identifying papers – Hospitals are very prompt at reporting these things – and getting in touch with relatives – all that. I don't want to be precipitate – she – she mightn't want it. You've no idea – no idea at all, Albert, where she was going – Nothing she said? No particular place – or county. Not a mention of some name?'

Albert shook his head.

'What was she feeling like? Pleased? – Excited? Unhappy? Worried?'

Albert's response was immediate.

'Pleased as Punch – Bursting with it.'

'Like a terrier off on the trail,' said Tommy.

'That's right, sir – you know how she gets –'

'On to something – Now I wonder –' Tommy paused in consideration.

Something had turned up, and, as he had just said to Albert, Tuppence had rushed off like a terrier on the scent. The day before yesterday she had rung up to announce her return. Why, then, hadn't she returned? Perhaps, at this moment, thought Tommy, she's sitting somewhere telling lies to people so hard that she can't think of anything else!

If she were engrossed in pursuit, she would be extremely annoyed if he, Tommy, were to rush off to the police bleating like a sheep that his wife had disappeared – He could hear Tuppence saying 'How you could be so fatuous as to do such a thing! I can look after myself *perfectly*. You ought to know that by this time!' (But could she look after herself?)

One was never quite sure where Tuppence's imagination could take her.

Into *danger*? There hadn't, so far, been any evidence of danger in this business – Except, as aforesaid, in Tuppence's imagination.

If he were to go to the police, saying his wife had not returned home as she announced she was going to do – The police would sit there, looking tactful though possibly grinning inwardly, and would then presumably, still in a tactful way, ask what men friends his wife had got!

'I'll find her myself,' declared Tommy. 'She's *somewhere*. Whether it's north, south, east or west I've no idea – and she was a silly cuckoo not to leave word when she rang up, where she was.'

'A gang's got her, perhaps –' said Albert.

'Oh! be your age, Albert, you've outgrown that sort of stuff years ago!'

'What are you going to do, sir?'

'I'm going to London,' said Tommy, glancing at the clock. 'First I'm going to have lunch at my club with Dr Murray who rang me up last night, and who's got something to say to me about my late deceased aunt's affairs – I might possibly get a useful hint from him – After all, this business started at Sunny Ridge. I am also taking that picture that's hanging over our bedroom mantelpiece up with me –'

'You mean you're taking it to Scotland Yard?'

'No,' said Tommy. 'I'm taking it to Bond Street.'

CHAPTER 11

BOND STREET AND DR MURRAY

I

Tommy jumped out of a taxi, paid the driver and leaned back into the cab to take out a rather clumsily done up parcel which was clearly a picture. Tucking as much of it as he could under his arm, he entered the New Athenian Galleries, one of the longest established and most important picture galleries in London.

Tommy was not a great patron of the arts but he had come to the New Athenian because he had a friend who officiated there.

'Officiated' was the only word to use because the air of sympathetic interest, the hushed voice, the pleasurable smile, all seemed highly ecclesiastical.

A fair-haired young man detached himself and came forward, his face lighting up with a smile of recognition.

'Hullo, Tommy,' he said. 'Haven't seen you for a long time. What's that you've got under your arm? Don't tell me you've been taking to painting pictures in your old age? A lot of people do – results usually deplorable.'

'I doubt if creative art was ever my long suit,' said Tommy. 'Though I must admit I found myself strongly attracted the other day by a small book telling in the simplest terms how a child of five can learn to paint in water colours.'

'God help us if you're going to take to that. Grandma Moses in reverse.'

'To tell you the truth, Robert, I merely want to appeal to your expert knowledge of pictures. I want your opinion on this.'

Deftly Robert took the picture from Tommy and skilfully removed its clumsy wrappings with the expertise of a man accustomed to handle the parcelling up and deparcelling of all different-sized works of art. He took the picture and set it on a chair, peered into it to look at it, and then withdrew five or six steps away. He turned his gaze towards Tommy.

'Well,' he said, 'what about it? What do you want to know? Do you want to sell it, is that it?'

'No,' said Tommy, 'I don't want to sell it, Robert. I want to know about it. To begin with, I want to know who painted it.'

'Actually,' said Robert, 'if you *had* wanted to sell it, it would be quite saleable nowadays. It wouldn't have been, ten years ago. But Boscowan's just coming into fashion again.'

'Boscowan?' Tommy looked at him inquiringly. 'Is that the name of the artist? I saw it was signed with something beginning with B but I couldn't read the name.'

'Oh, it's Boscowan all right. Very popular painter about twenty-five years ago. Sold well, had plenty of shows. People bought him all right. Technically a very good painter. Then, in the usual cycle of events, he went out of fashion. Finally, hardly any demand at all for his works but lately he's had a revival. He, Stitchwort, and Fondella. They're all coming up.'

'Boscowan,' repeated Tommy.

'B-o-s-c-o-w-a-n,' said Robert obligingly.

'Is he still painting?'

'No. He's dead. Died some years ago. Quite an old chap by then. Sixty-five, I think, when he died. Quite a prolific painter, you know. A lot of his canvases about. Actually we're thinking of having a show of him here in about four or five months' time. We ought to do well over it, I think. Why are you so interested in him?'

'It'd be too long a story to tell you,' said Tommy. 'One of these days I'll ask you out to lunch and give you the doings from the beginning. It's a long, complicated and really rather an idiotic story. All I wanted to know is all about this Boscowan and if you happen to know by any chance where this house is that's represented here.'

'I couldn't tell you the last for a moment. It's the sort of thing he did paint, you know. Small country houses in rather isolated spots usually, sometimes a farmhouse, sometimes just a cow or two around. Sometimes a farm cart, but if so, in the far distance. Quiet rural scenes. Nothing sketchy or messy. Sometimes the surface looks almost like enamel. It was a peculiar technique and people liked it. A good many of the things he painted were in France, Normandy mostly. Churches. I've got one picture of his here now. Wait a minute and I'll get it for you.'

He went to the head of the staircase and shouted down to someone below. Presently he came back holding a small canvas which he propped on another chair.

'There you are,' he said. 'Church in Normandy.'

'Yes,' said Tommy, 'I see. The same sort of thing. My wife says nobody ever lived in that house – the one I brought in. I see now what she meant. I don't see that anybody was attending service in that church or ever will.'

'Well, perhaps your wife's got something. Quiet, peaceful dwellings with no human occupancy. He didn't often paint people, you know. Sometimes there's a figure or two in the landscape, but more often not. In a way I think that gives them their special charm. A sort of isolationist feeling. It was as though he removed all the human beings, and the peace of the countryside was all the better without them. Come to think of it, that's maybe why the general taste has swung round to him. Too many people nowadays, too many cars, too many noises on the road, too much noise and bustle. Peace, perfect peace. Leave it all to Nature.'

'Yes, I shouldn't wonder. What sort of a man was he?'

'I didn't know him personally. Before my time. Pleased with himself by all accounts. Thought he was a better painter than he was, probably. Put on a bit of side. Kindly, quite likeable. Eye for the girls.'

'And you've no idea where this particular piece of countryside exists? It *is* England, I suppose.'

'I should think so, yes. Do you want me to find out for you?'

'Could you?'

'Probably the best thing to do would be to ask his wife, his widow rather. He married Emma Wing, the sculptor. Well known. Not very productive. Does quite powerful work. You could go and ask her. She lives in Hampstead. I can give you the address. We've been corresponding with her a good deal lately over the question of this show of her husband's work we're doing. We're having a few of her smaller pieces of sculpture as well. I'll get the address for you.'

He went to the desk, turned over a ledger, scrawled something on a card and brought it back.

'There you are, Tommy,' he said. 'I don't know what the deep dark mystery is. Always been a man of mystery, haven't you? It's a nice representation of Boscowan's work you've got there. We might like to use it for the show. I'll send you a line to remind you nearer the time.'

'You don't know a Mrs Lancaster, do you?'

'Well, I can't think of one off-hand. Is she an artist or something of the kind?'

'No, I don't think so. She's just an old lady living for the last few years in an old ladies' home. She comes into it because this picture belonged to her until she gave it away to an aunt of mine.'

'Well I can't say the name means anything to me. Better go and talk to Mrs Boscowan.'

'What's she like?'

'She was a good bit younger than he was, I should say. Quite a personality.' He nodded his head once or twice. 'Yes, quite a personality. You'll find that out I expect.'

He took the picture, handed it down the staircase with instructions to someone below to do it up again.

'Nice for you having so many myrmidons at your beck and call,' said Tommy.

He looked round him, noticing his surroundings for the first time.

'What's this you've got here now?' he said with distaste.

'Paul Jaggerowski – Interesting young Slav. Said to produce all his works under the influence of drugs – Don't you like him?'

Tommy concentrated his gaze on a big string bag which seemed to have enmeshed itself in a metallic green field full of distorted cows.

'Frankly, no.'

'Philistine,' said Robert. 'Come out and have a bite of lunch.'

'Can't. I've got a meeting with a doctor at my club.'

'Not ill, are you?'

'I'm in the best of health. My blood pressure is so good that it disappoints every doctor to whom I submit it.'

'Then what do you want to see a doctor for?'

'Oh,' said Tommy cheerfully – 'I've just got to see a doctor about a body. Thanks for your help. Goodbye.'

II

Tommy greeted Dr Murray with some curiosity – He presumed it was some formal matter to do with Aunt Ada's decease, but why on earth Dr Murray would not at least mention the subject of his visit over the telephone, Tommy couldn't imagine.

'I'm afraid I'm a little late,' said Dr Murray, shaking hands, 'but the traffic was pretty bad and I wasn't exactly sure of the locality. I don't know this part of London very well.'

'Well, too bad you had to come all the way here,' said Tommy. 'I could have met you somewhere more convenient, you know.'

'You've time on your hands then just now?'

'Just at the moment, yes. I've been away for the last week.'

'Yes, I believe someone told me so when I rang up.'

Tommy indicated a chair, suggested refreshment, placed cigarettes and matches by Dr Murray's side. When the two men had established themselves comfortably Dr Murray opened the conversation.

'I'm sure I've aroused your curiosity,' he said, 'but as a matter of fact we're in a spot of trouble at Sunny Ridge. It's a difficult and perplexing matter and in one way it's nothing to do with you. I've no earthly right to trouble you with it but there's just an off chance that you might know something which would help me.'

'Well, of course, I'll do anything I can. Something to do with my aunt, Miss Fanshawe?'

'Not directly, no. But in a way she does come into it. I can speak to you in confidence, can't I, Mr Beresford?'

'Yes, certainly.'

'As a matter of fact I was talking the other day to a mutual friend of ours. He was telling me a few things about you. I gather that in the last war you had rather a delicate assignment.'

'Oh, I wouldn't put it quite as seriously as that,' said Tommy, in his most non-committal manner.

'Oh no, I quite realize that it's not a thing to be talked about.'

'I don't really think that matters nowadays. It's a good long time since the war. My wife and I were younger then.'

'Anyway, it's nothing to do with that, that I want to talk to you about, but at least I feel that I can speak frankly to you, that I can trust you not to repeat what I am now saying, though it's possible that it all may have to come out later.'

'A spot of trouble at Sunny Ridge, you say?'

'Yes. Not very long ago one of our patients died. A Mrs Moody. I don't know if you ever met her or if your aunt ever talked about her.'

'Mrs Moody?' Tommy reflected. 'No, I don't think so. Anyway, not so far as I remember.'

'She was not one of our older patients. She was still on the right side of seventy and she was not seriously ill in any way. It was just a case of a woman with no near relatives and no one to look after her in the domestic line. She fell into the category of what I often call to myself a flutterer. Women who more and more resemble hens as they grow older. They cluck. They forget things. They run themselves into difficulties and they worry. They get themselves wrought up about nothing at all. There is very little the matter with them. They are not strictly speaking mentally disturbed.'

'But they just cluck,' Tommy suggested.

'As you say. Mrs Moody clucked. She caused the nurses a fair amount of trouble although they were quite fond of her. She had a habit of forgetting when she'd had her meals, making a fuss because no dinner had been served to her when as a matter of fact she had actually just eaten a very good dinner.'

'Oh,' said Tommy, enlightened, 'Mrs Cocoa.'

'I beg your pardon?'

'I'm sorry,' said Tommy, 'it's a name my wife and I had for her. She was yelling for Nurse Jane one day when we passed along the passage and saying she hadn't had her cocoa. Rather a nice-looking scatty little woman. But it made us both laugh, and we fell into the habit of calling her Mrs Cocoa. And so she's died.'

'I wasn't particularly surprised when the death happened,' said Dr Murray. 'To be able to prophesy with any exactitude when elderly women will die is practically impossible. Women whose health is seriously affected, who, one feels as a result of physical examination, will hardly last the year out, sometimes are good for another ten years. They have a tenacious hold on life which mere physical disability will not quench. There are other people whose health is reasonably good and who may, one thinks, make old bones. They on the other hand, catch bronchitis, or 'flu, seem unable to have the stamina to recuperate from it, and die with surprising ease. So, as I say, as a medical attendant to an elderly ladies' home, I am not surprised when what might be called a fairly unexpected death occurs. This case of Mrs Moody, however, was somewhat different. She died in her sleep without having exhibited any sign of illness and I could not help feeling that in my opinion her death was unexpected. I will use the phrase that has always intrigued me in Shakespeare's play, *Macbeth*. I have always wondered what Macbeth meant when he said of his wife, "She should have died hereafter."'

'Yes, I remember wondering once myself what Shakespeare was getting at,' said Tommy. 'I forget whose production it was and who was playing Macbeth, but there was a strong suggestion in that particular production, and Macbeth certainly played it in a way to suggest that he was hinting to the medical attendant that Lady Macbeth would be better out of the way. Presumably the medical attendant took the hint. It was then that Macbeth, feeling safe after his wife's death, feeling that she could no longer damage him by her indiscretions or her rapidly failing mind, expresses his genuine affection and grief for her. "She should have died hereafter."'

'Exactly,' said Dr Murray. 'It is what I felt about Mrs Moody. I felt that she should have died hereafter. Not just three weeks ago of no apparent cause –'

Tommy did not reply. He merely looked at the doctor inquiringly.

'Medical men have certain problems. If you are puzzled over the cause of a patient's death there is only one sure way to tell. By a post mortem. Post mortems are not appreciated by relatives of the deceased, but if a doctor demands a post mortem and the result is, as it perfectly well may be, a case of natural causes, or some disease or malady which does not always give outward signs or symptoms, then the doctor's career can be quite seriously affected by his having made a questionable diagnosis –'

'I can see that it must have been difficult.'

'The relatives in question are distant cousins. So I took it upon myself to get their consent as it was a matter of medical interest to know the cause of death. When a patient dies in her sleep it is advisable to add to one's medical knowledge. I wrapped it up a good bit, mind you, didn't make it too formal. Luckily they couldn't care less. I felt very relieved in mind. Once the autopsy had been performed and if all was well, I could give a death certificate without a qualm. Anyone can die of what is amateurishly called heart failure, from one of several different causes. Actually Mrs Moody's heart was in really very good shape for her age. She suffered from arthritis and rheumatism and occasional trouble with her liver, but none of these things seemed to accord with her passing away in her sleep.'

Dr Murray came to a stop. Tommy opened his lips and then shut them again. The doctor nodded.

'Yes, Mr Beresford. You can see where I am tending. Death has resulted from an overdose of morphine.'

'Good Lord!' Tommy stared and the ejaculation escaped him.

'Yes. It seemed quite incredible, but there was no getting away from the analysis. The question was: How was that morphia administered? She was not on morphia. She was not a patient who suffered pain. There were three possibilities, of course. She might have taken it by accident. Unlikely. She might have got hold of some other patient's medicine by mistake but that again is not particularly likely. Patients are not entrusted with supplies of morphia, and we do not accept drug addicts who might have a supply of such things in their possession. It could have been deliberate suicide but I should be very slow to accept that. Mrs Moody, though a worrier, was of a perfectly cheerful disposition and I am quite sure had never thought of ending her life. The third possibility is that a fatal overdose was deliberately administered to her. But by whom, and why? Naturally, there are supplies of morphia and other drugs which Miss Packard as a registered hospital nurse and matron, is perfectly entitled to have in her possession and which she keeps in a locked cupboard. In such cases as sciatica or rheumatoid arthritis there can be such severe and desperate pain that morphia is occasionally administered. We have hoped that we may come across some circumstance in which Mrs Moody had a dangerous amount of morphia administered to her by mistake or which she herself took under the delusion that it was a cure for indigestion or insomnia. We have not been able to find any such circumstances possible. The next thing we have done, at Miss Packard's suggestion and I agreed with her, is to look carefully into the records of such deaths as have taken place at Sunny Ridge in the last two years. There have not been many of them, I am glad to say. I think seven in all, which is a pretty fair average for people of that age group. Two deaths of bronchitis, perfectly straightforward, two of 'flu, always a possible killer during the winter months owing to the slight resistance offered by frail, elderly women. And three others.'

He paused and said, 'Mr Beresford, I am not satisfied about those three others, certainly not about two of them. They were perfectly probable, they were not unexpected, but I will go as far as saying that they were *unlikely*. They are not cases that on reflection and research I am entirely satisfied about. One has to accept the possibility that, unlikely as it seems, there is someone at Sunny Ridge who is, possibly for mental reasons, a killer. An entirely unsuspected killer.'

There was silence for some moments. Tommy gave a sigh.

'I don't doubt what you've told me,' he said, 'but all the same, frankly, it seems unbelievable. These things – surely, they can't happen.'

'Oh yes,' said Dr Murray grimly, 'they happen all right. You go over some of the pathological cases. A woman who took on domestic service. She worked as a cook in various households. She was a nice, kind, pleasant-seeming woman, gave her employers faithful service, cooked well, enjoyed being with them. Yet, sooner or later, things happened. Usually a plate of sandwiches. Sometimes picnic food. For no apparent motive arsenic was added. Two or three poisoned sandwiches among the rest. Apparently sheer chance dictated who took and ate them. There seemed no personal venom. Sometimes no tragedy happened. The same woman was three or four months in a situation and there was no trace of illness. Nothing. Then she left to go to another job, and in that next job, within three weeks, two of the family died after eating bacon for breakfast. The fact that all these things happened in different parts of England and at irregular intervals made it some time before the police got on her track. She used a different name, of course, each time. But there are so many pleasant, capable, middle-aged women who can cook, it was hard to find out which particular woman it was.'

'Why did she do it?'

'I don't think anybody has ever really known. There have been several different theories, especially of course by psychologists. She was a somewhat religious woman and it seems possible that some form of religious insanity made her feel that she had a divine command to rid the world of certain people, but it does not seem that she herself had borne them any personal animus.

'Then there was the French woman, Jeanne Gebron, who was called The Angel of Mercy. She was so upset when her neighbours had ill children, she hurried to nurse those children. Sat devotedly at their bedside. There again it was some time before people discovered that the children she nursed *never recovered. Instead they all died.* And *why*? It is true that when she was young her own child died. She appeared to be prostrated with grief. Perhaps that was the cause of her career of crime. If *her* child died so should the children of other women. Or it may be, as some thought, that her own child was also one of the victims.'

'You're giving me chills down my spine,' said Tommy.

'I'm taking the most melodramatic examples,' said the doctor. 'It may be something much simpler than that. You remember in the case of Armstrong, anyone who had in any way offended him or insulted him, or indeed, if he even thought anyone had insulted him, that person was quickly asked to tea and given arsenic sandwiches. A sort of intensified touchiness. His first crimes were obviously mere crimes for personal advantage. Inheriting of money. The removal of a wife so that he could marry another woman.

'Then there was Nurse Warriner who kept a Home for elderly people. They made over what means they had to her, and were guaranteed a comfortable old age until death came – But death did not delay very long. There, too, it was morphia that was administered – a very kindly woman, but with no scruples – she regarded herself, I believe, as a benefactor.'

'You've no idea, if your surmise about these deaths is true, who it could be?'

'No. There seems no pointer of any kind. Taking the view that the killer is probably insane, insanity is a very difficult thing to recognize in some of its manifestations. Is it somebody, shall we say, who dislikes elderly people, who had been injured or has had her life ruined or so she thinks, by somebody elderly? Or is it possibly someone who has her own ideas of mercy killing and thinks that everyone over sixty years of age should be kindly exterminated. It could be anyone, of course. A patient? Or a member of the staff – a nurse or a domestic worker?

'I have discussed this at great length with Millicent Packard who runs the place. She is a highly competent woman, shrewd, businesslike, with keen supervision both of the guests there and of her own staff. She insists that she has no suspicion and no clue whatever and I am sure that is perfectly true.'

'But why come to me? What can I do?'

'Your aunt, Miss Fanshawe, was a resident there for some years – she was a woman of very considerable mental capacity, though she often pretended otherwise. She had unconventional ways of amusing herself by putting on an appearance of senility. But she was actually very much all there – What I want you to try and do, Mr Beresford, is to think hard – you and your wife, too – Is there anything you can remember that Miss Fanshawe ever said or hinted, that might give us a clue – Something she had seen or noticed, something that someone had told her, something that she herself had thought peculiar. Old ladies see and notice a lot, and a really shrewd one like Miss Fanshawe would know a surprising amount of what went on in a place like Sunny Ridge. These old ladies are not busy, you see, they have all the time in the world to look around them and make deductions – and even jump to conclusions – that may seem fantastic, but are sometimes, surprisingly, entirely correct.'

Tommy shook his head.

'I know what you mean – But I can't remember anything of that kind.'

'Your wife's away from home, I gather. You don't think she might remember something that hadn't struck you?'

'I'll ask her – but I doubt it.' He hesitated, then made up his mind. 'Look here, there was something that worried my wife – about one of the old ladies, a Mrs Lancaster.'

'Mrs Lancaster? Yes?'

'My wife's got it into her head that Mrs Lancaster has been taken away by some so-called relations very suddenly. As a matter of fact, Mrs Lancaster gave a picture to my aunt as a present, and my wife felt that she ought to offer to return the picture to Mrs Lancaster, so she tried to get in touch with her to know if Mrs Lancaster would like the picture returned to her.'

'Well, that was very thoughtful of Mrs Beresford, I'm sure.'

'Only she found it very hard to get in touch with her. She got the address of the hotel where they were supposed to be staying – Mrs Lancaster and her relations – but nobody of that name had been staying there or had booked rooms there.'

'Oh? That was rather odd.'

'Yes. Tuppence thought it was rather odd, too. They had left no other forwarding address at Sunny Ridge. In fact, we have made several attempts to get in touch with Mrs Lancaster, or with this Mrs – Johnson I think the name was – but have been quite unable to get in touch with them. There was a solicitor who I believe paid all the bills – and made all the arrangements with Miss Packard and we got into communication with him. But he could only give me the address of a bank. Banks,' said Tommy drily, 'don't give you any information.'

'Not if they've been told not to by their clients, I agree.'

'My wife wrote to Mrs Lancaster care of the bank, and also to Mrs Johnson, but she's never had any reply.'

'That seems a little unusual. Still, people don't always answer letters. They may have gone abroad.'

'Quite so – it didn't worry me. But it has worried my wife. She seems convinced that something has happened to Mrs Lancaster. In fact, during the time I was away from home, she said she was going to investigate further – I don't know what exactly she meant to do, perhaps see the hotel personally, or the bank, or try the solicitor. Anyway, she was going to try and get a little more information.'

Dr Murray looked at him politely, but with a trace of patient boredom in his manner.

'What did she think exactly –?'

'She thinks that Mrs Lancaster is in danger of some kind – even that something may have happened to her.'

The doctor raised his eyebrows.

'Oh! really, I should hardly think –'

'This may seem quite idiotic to you,' said Tommy, 'but you see, my wife rang up saying she would be back yesterday evening – and – *she didn't arrive.*'

'She said definitely that she *was* coming back?'

'Yes. She knew I was coming home, you see, from this conference business. So she rang up to let our man, Albert, know that she'd be back to dinner.'

'And that seems to you an unlikely thing for her to do?' said Murray. He was now looking at Tommy with some interest.

'Yes,' said Tommy. 'It's *very* unlike Tuppence. If she'd been delayed or changed her plans she would have rung up again or sent a telegram.'

'And you're worried about her?'

'Yes, I am,' said Tommy.

'H'm! Have you consulted the police?'

'No,' said Tommy. 'What'd the police think? It's not as though I had any reason to believe that she is in trouble or danger or anything of that kind. I mean, if she'd had an accident or was in a hospital, anything like that, somebody would communicate with me soon enough, wouldn't they?'

'I should say so – yes – if she had some means of identification on her.'

'She'd have her driving licence on her. Probably letters and various other things.'

Dr Murray frowned.

Tommy went on in a rush:

'And now you come along – And bring up all this business of Sunny Ridge – People who've died when they oughtn't to have died. Supposing this old bean got on to something – saw something, or suspected something – and began chattering about it – She'd have to be silenced in some way, so she was whisked out of it quickly, and taken off to some place or other where she wouldn't be traced. I can't help feeling that the whole thing ties up somehow –'

'It's odd – it's certainly odd – What do you propose to do next?'

'I'm going to do a bit of searching myself – Try these solicitors first – They may be quite all right, but I'd like to have a look at them, and draw my own conclusions.'

CHAPTER 12

TOMMY MEETS AN OLD FRIEND

I

From the opposite side of the road, Tommy surveyed the premises of Messrs. Partingdale, Harris, Lockeridge and Partingdale.

They looked eminently respectable and old-fashioned. The brass plate was well worn but nicely polished. He crossed the street and passed through swing doors to be greeted by the muted note of typewriters at full speed.

He addressed himself to an open mahogany window on his right which bore the legend INQUIRIES –

Inside was a small room where three women were typing

and two male clerks were bending over desks copying documents.

There was a faint, musty atmosphere with a decidedly legal flavour.

A woman of thirty-five odd, with a severe air, faded blonde hair, and *pince-nez* rose from her typewriter and came to the window.

'Can I help you?'

'I would like to see Mr Eccles.'

The woman's air of severity redoubled.

'Have you an appointment?'

'I'm afraid not. I'm just passing through London today.'

'I'm afraid Mr Eccles is rather busy this morning. Perhaps another member of the firm –'

'It was Mr Eccles I particularly wanted to see. I have already had some correspondence with him.'

'Oh I see. Perhaps you'll give me your name.'

Tommy gave his name and address and the blonde woman retired to confer with the telephone on her desk. After a murmured conversation she returned.

'The clerk will show you into the waiting-room. Mr Eccles will be able to see you in about ten minutes' time.'

Tommy was ushered into a waiting-room which had a bookcase of rather ancient and ponderous-looking law tomes and a round table covered with various financial papers. Tommy sat there and went over in his own mind his planned methods of approach. He wondered what Mr Eccles would be like. When he was shown in at last and Mr Eccles rose from a desk to receive him, he decided for no particular reason that he could name to himself that he did not like Mr Eccles. He also wondered why he did not like Mr Eccles. There seemed no valid reason for dislike. Mr Eccles was a man of between forty and fifty with greyish hair thinning a little at the temples. He had a long rather sad-looking face with a particularly wooden expression, shrewd eyes, and quite a pleasant smile which from time to time rather unexpectedly broke up the natural melancholy of his countenance.

'Mr Beresford?'

'Yes. It is really rather a trifling matter, but my wife has been worried about it. She wrote to you, I believe, or possibly she may have rung you up, to know if you could give her the address of a Mrs Lancaster.'

'Mrs Lancaster,' said Mr Eccles, retaining a perfect poker face. It was not even a question. He just left the name hanging in the air.

'A cautious man,' thought Tommy, 'but then it's second nature for lawyers to be cautious. In fact, if they were one's own lawyers one would prefer them to be cautious.'

He went on:

'Until lately living at a place called Sunny Ridge, an establishment – and a very good one – for elderly ladies. In fact, an aunt of my own was there and was extremely happy and comfortable.'

'Oh yes, of course, of course. I remember now. Mrs Lancaster. She is, I think, no longer living there? That is right, is it not?'

'Yes,' said Tommy.

'At the moment I do not exactly recall –' he stretched out a hand towards the telephone – 'I will just refresh my memory –'

'I can tell you quite simply,' said Tommy. 'My wife wanted Mrs Lancaster's address because she happens to be in possession of a piece of property which originally belonged to Mrs Lancaster. A picture, in fact. It was given by Mrs Lancaster as a present to my aunt, Miss Fanshawe. My aunt died recently, and her few possessions have come into our keeping. This included the picture which was given her by Mrs Lancaster. My wife likes it very much but she feels rather guilty about it. She thinks that it may be a picture Mrs Lancaster values and in that case she feels she ought to offer to return it to Mrs Lancaster.'

'Ah, I see,' said Mr Eccles. 'It is very conscientious of your wife, I am sure.'

'One never knows,' said Tommy, smiling pleasantly, 'what elderly people may feel about their possessions. She may have been glad for my aunt to have it since my aunt admired it, but as my aunt died very soon after having received this gift, it seems, perhaps, a little unfair that it should pass into the possession of strangers. There is no particular title on the picture. It represents a house somewhere in the country. For all I know it may be some family house associated with Mrs Lancaster.'

'Quite, quite,' said Mr Eccles, 'but I don't think –'

There was a knock and the door opened and a clerk entered and produced a sheet of paper which he placed before Mr Eccles. Mr Eccles looked down.

'Ah yes, ah yes, I remember now. Yes, I believe Mrs –' he glanced down at Tommy's card lying on his desk – 'Beresford rang up and had a few words with me. I advised her to get into touch with the Southern Counties Bank, Hammersmith branch. This is the only address I myself know. Letters addressed to the bank's address, care of Mrs Richard Johnson would be forwarded. Mrs Johnson is, I believe, a niece or distant cousin of Mrs Lancaster's and it was Mrs Johnson who made all the arrangements with me for Mrs Lancaster's reception at Sunny Ridge. She asked me to make full inquiries about the establishment, since she had only heard about it casually from a friend. We did so, I can assure you, most carefully. It was said to be an excellent establishment and I believe Mrs Johnson's relative, Mrs Lancaster, spent several years there quite happily.'

'She left there, though, rather suddenly,' Tommy suggested.

'Yes. Yes, I believe she did. Mrs Johnson, it seems, returned rather unexpectedly recently from East Africa – so many people have done so! She and her husband had, I believe, resided in Kenya for many years. They were making various new arrangements and felt able to assume personal care of their elderly relative. I am afraid I have no knowledge of Mrs Johnson's present whereabouts. I had a letter from her thanking me and settling accounts she owed, and directing that if there was any necessity for communicating with her I should address my letters care of the bank as she was undecided as yet where she and her husband would actually be residing. I am afraid, Mr Beresford, that that is all I know.'

His manner was gentle but firm. It displayed no embarrassment of any kind nor disturbance. But the finality of his voice was very definite. Then he unbent and his manner softened a little.

'I shouldn't really worry, you know, Mr Beresford,' he said reassuringly. 'Or rather, I shouldn't let your wife worry. Mrs Lancaster, I believe, is quite an old lady and inclined to be forgetful. She's probably forgotten all about this picture that she gave away. She is, I believe, seventy-five or seventy-six years of age. One forgets very easily at that age, you know.'

'Did you know her personally?'

'No, I never actually met her.'

'But you knew Mrs Johnson?'

'I met her when she came here occasionally to consult me as to arrangements. She seemed a pleasant, businesslike woman. Quite competent in the arrangements she was making.' He rose and said, 'I am so sorry I can't help you, Mr Beresford.'

It was a gentle but firm dismissal.

Tommy came out on to the Bloomsbury street and looked about him for a taxi. The parcel he was carrying, though not heavy, was of a fairly awkward size. He looked up for a moment at the building he had just left. Eminently respectable, long established. Nothing you could fault there, nothing apparently wrong with Messrs Partingdale, Harris, Lockeridge and Partingdale, nothing wrong with Mr Eccles, no signs of alarm or despondency, no shiftiness or uneasiness. In books, Tommy thought gloomily, a mention of Mrs Lancaster or Mrs Johnson should have brought a guilty start or a shifty glance. Something to show that the names registered, that all was not well. Things didn't seem to happen like that in real life. All Mr Eccles had looked like was a man who was too polite to resent having his time wasted by such an inquiry as Tommy had just made.

But all the same, thought Tommy to himself, *I don't like Mr Eccles*. He recalled to himself vague memories of the past, of other people that he had for some reason not liked. Very often those hunches – for hunches is all they were – had been right. But perhaps it was simpler than that. If you had had a good many dealings in your time with personalities, you had a sort of feeling about them, just as an expert antique dealer knows instinctively the taste and look and feel of a forgery before getting down to expert tests and examinations. The thing just is *wrong*. The same with pictures. The same presumably with a cashier in a bank who is offered a first-class spurious banknote.

'He sounds all right,' thought Tommy. 'He looks all right, he speaks all right, but all the same –' He waved frantically at a taxi which gave him a direct and cold look, increased its speed and drove on. 'Swine,' thought Tommy.

His eyes roved up and down the street, seeking for a more obliging vehicle. A fair amount of people were walking on the pavement. A few hurrying, some strolling, one man gazing at a brass plate just across the road from him. After a close scrutiny, he turned round and Tommy's eyes opened a little wider. He knew that face. He watched the man walk to the end of the street, pause, turn and walk back again. Somebody came out of the building behind Tommy and at that moment the man opposite increased his pace a little, still walking on the other side of the road but keeping pace with the man who had come out of the door. The man who had come out of Messrs Partingdale, Harris, Lockeridge and Partingdale's doorway was, Tommy thought, looking after his retreating figure, almost certainly Mr Eccles. At the same moment a taxi lingering in a pleasant tempting manner, came along. Tommy raised his hand, the taxi drew up, he opened the door and got in.

'Where to?'

Tommy hesitated for a moment, looking at his parcel. About to give an address he changed his mind and said, '14 Lyon Street.'

A quarter of an hour later he had reached his destination. He rang the bell after paying off the taxi and asked for Mr Ivor Smith. When he entered a second-floor room, a man sitting at a table facing the window, swung round and said with faint surprise,

'Hullo, Tommy, fancy seeing you. It's a long time. What are you doing here? Just tooling round looking up your old friends?'

'Not quite as good as that, Ivor.'

'I suppose you're on your way home after the Conference?'

'Yes.'

'All a lot of the usual talky-talky, I suppose? No conclusions drawn and nothing helpful said.'

'Quite right. All a sheer waste of time.'

'Mostly listening to old Bogie Waddock shooting his mouth off, I expect. Crashing bore. Gets worse every year.'

'Oh! well –'

Tommy sat down in the chair that was pushed towards him, accepted a cigarette, and said,

'I just wondered – it's a very long shot – whether you know anything of a derogatory nature about one Eccles, solicitor, of the firm of Messrs Partingdale, Harris, Lockeridge and Partingdale.'

'Well, well, well,' said the man called Ivor Smith. He raised his eyebrows. They were very convenient eyebrows for raising. The end of them near the nose went up and the opposite end of the cheek went down for an almost astonishing extent. They made him on very little provocation look like a man who had had a severe shock, but actually it was quite a common gesture with him. 'Run up against Eccles somewhere have you?'

'The trouble is,' said Tommy, 'that I know nothing about him.'

'And you want to know something about him?'

'Yes.'

'Hm. What made you come to see me?'

'I saw Anderson outside. It was a long time since I'd seen him but I recognized him. He was keeping someone or other under observation. Whoever it was, it was someone in the building from which I had just emerged. Two firms of lawyers practise there and one firm of chartered accountants. Of course it may be any one of them or any member of any one of them. But a man walking away down the street looked to me like Eccles. And I just wondered if by a lucky chance it could have been my Mr Eccles that Anderson was giving his attention to?'

'Hm,' said Ivor Smith. 'Well, Tommy, you always were a pretty good guesser.'

'Who *is* Eccles?'

'Don't you know? Haven't you any idea?'

'I've no idea whatever,' said Tommy. 'Without going into a long history, I went to him for some information about an old lady who has recently left an old ladies' home. The solicitor employed to make arrangements for her was Mr Eccles. He appears to have done it with perfect decorum and efficiency. I wanted her present address. He says he hasn't got it. Quite possibly he hasn't . . . but I wondered. He's the only clue to her whereabouts I've got.'

'And you want to find her?'

'Yes.'

'I don't think it sounds as though I'm going to be much good to you. Eccles is a very respectable, sound solicitor who makes a large income, has a good many highly respectable clients, works for the landed gentry, professional classes and retired soldiers and sailors, generals and admirals and all that sort of thing. He's the acme of respectability. I should imagine from what you're talking about, that he was strictly within his lawful activities.'

'But you're – interested in him,' suggested Tommy.

'Yes, we're very interested in Mr James Eccles.' He sighed. 'We've been interested in him for at least six years. We haven't progressed very far.'

'Very interesting,' said Tommy. 'I'll ask you again. Who exactly *is* Mr Eccles?'

'You mean what do we suspect Eccles of? Well, to put it in a sentence, we suspect him of being one of the best organizing brains in criminal activity in this country.'

'Criminal activity?' Tommy looked surprised.

'Oh yes, yes. No cloak and dagger. No espionage, no counter-espionage. No, plain criminal activity. He is a man who has so far as we can discover never performed a criminal act in his life. He has never stolen anything, he's never forged anything, he's never converted funds, we can't get any kind of evidence against him. But all the same whenever there's a big planned organized robbery, there we find, somewhere in the background, Mr Eccles leading a blameless life.'

'Six years,' said Tommy thoughtfully.

'Possibly even longer than that. It took a little time, to get on to the pattern of things. Bank holdups, robberies of private jewels, all sorts of things where the big money was. They're all jobs that followed a certain pattern. You couldn't help feeling that the same mind had planned them. The people who directed them and who carried them out never had to do any planning at all. They went where they were told, they did what they were ordered, they never had to think. Somebody else was doing the thinking.'

'And what made you hit on Eccles?'

Ivor Smith shook his head thoughtfully. 'It would take too long to tell you. He's a man who has a lot of acquaintances, a lot of friends. There are people he plays golf with, there are people who service his car, there are firms of stockbrokers who act for him. There are companies doing a blameless business in which he is interested. The plan is getting clearer but his part in it hasn't got much clearer, except that he is very conspicuously absent on certain occasions. A big bank robbery cleverly planned (and no expense spared, mind you), consolidating the get-away and all the rest of it, and where's Mr Eccles when it happens? Monte Carlo or Zurich or possibly even fishing for salmon in Norway. You can be quite sure Mr Eccles is never within a hundred miles of where criminal activities are happening.'

'Yet you suspect him?'

'Oh yes. I'm quite sure in my own mind. But whether we'll ever catch him I don't know. The man who tunnelled through the floor of a bank, the man who knocked out the night watchman, the cashier who was in it from the beginning, the bank manager who supplied the information, none of them know Eccles, probably they've never even seen him. There's a long chain leading away – and no one seems to know more than just one link beyond themselves.'

'The good old plan of the cell?'

'More or less, yes, but there's some original thinking. Some day we'll get a chance. Somebody who oughtn't to know *anything*, will know *something*. Something silly and trivial, perhaps, but something that strangely enough may be evidence at last.'

'Is he married – got a family?'

'No, he has never taken risks like that. He lives alone with a housekeeper and a gardener and a butler-valet. He entertains in a mild and pleasant way, and I dare swear that every single person who's entered his house as his guest is beyond suspicion.'

'And nobody's getting rich?'

'That's a good point you've put your finger on, Thomas. Somebody *ought* to be getting rich. Somebody ought to be *seen* to be getting rich. But that part of it's very cleverly arranged. Big wins on race courses, investments in stocks and shares, all things which are natural, just chancy enough to make big money at, and all apparently genuine transactions. There's a lot of money stacked up abroad in different countries and different places. It's a great big, vast, money-making concern – and the money's always on the move – going from place to place.'

'Well,' said Tommy, 'good luck to you. I hope you get your man.'

'I think I shall, you know, some day. There might be a hope if one could jolt him out of his routine.'

'Jolt him with what?'

'Danger,' said Ivor. 'Make him feel he's in danger. Make him feel someone's on to him. Get him uneasy. If you once get a man uneasy, he may do something foolish. He may make a mistake. That's the way you get chaps, you know. Take the cleverest man there is, who can plan brilliantly and never put a foot wrong. Let some little thing rattle him and he'll make a mistake. So I'm hoping. Now let's hear your story. You might know something that would be useful.'

'Nothing to do with crime, I'm afraid – very small beer.'

'Well, let's hear about it.'

Tommy told his story without undue apologies for the triviality of it. Ivor, he knew, was not a man to despise triviality. Ivor, indeed, went straight to the point which had brought Tommy on his errand.

'And your wife's disappeared, you say?'

'It's not like her.'

'That's serious.'

'Serious to me all right.'

'So I can imagine. I only met your missus once. She's sharp.'

'If she goes after things she's like a terrier on a trail,' said Thomas.

'You've not been to the police?'

'No.'

'Why not?'

'Well, first because I can't believe that she's anything but all right. Tuppence is always all right. She just goes all out after any hare that shows itself. She mayn't have had time to communicate.'

'Mmm. I don't like it very much. She's looking for a house, you say? That just *might* be interesting because among various odds and ends that we followed, which incidentally have not led to much, are a kind of trail of house agents.'

'House agents?' Tommy looked surprised.

'Yes. Nice, ordinary, rather mediocre house agents in small provincial towns in different parts of England, but none of them so very far from London. Mr Eccles's firm does a lot of business with and for house agents. Sometimes he's the solicitor for the buyers and sometimes for the sellers, and he employs various house agencies, on behalf of clients. Sometimes we rather wondered why. None of it seems very profitable, you see –'

'But you think it might mean something or lead to something?'

'Well, if you remember the big London Southern Bank robbery some years ago, there was a house in the country – a lonely house. That was the thieves' rendezvous. They weren't very noticeable there, but that's where the stuff was brought and cached away. People in the neighbourhood began to have a few stories about them, and wonder who these people were who came and went at rather unusual hours. Different kinds of cars arriving in the middle of the night and going away again. People are curious about their neighbours in the country. Sure enough, the police raided the place, they got some of the loot, and they got three men, including one who was recognized and identified.'

'Well, didn't that lead you somewhere?'

'Not really. The men wouldn't talk, they were well defended and represented, they got long sentences in gaol and within a year and a half they were all out of the jug again. Very clever rescues.'

'I seem to remember reading about it. One man disappeared from a criminal court where he was brought up by two warders.'

'That's right. All very cleverly arranged and an enormous amount of money spent on the escape.

'But we think that whoever was responsible for the staff work realized he made a mistake in having one house for too long a time, so that the local people got interested. Somebody, perhaps, thought it would be a better idea to get subsidiaries living in, say, as many as *thirty* houses in *different places*. People come and take a house, mother and daughter, say, a widow, or a retired army man and his wife. Nice quiet people. They have a few repairs done to the house, get a local builder in and improve the plumbing, and perhaps some other firm down from London to decorate, and then after a year or a year and a half circumstances arise, and the occupiers sell the house and go off abroad to live. Something like that. All very natural and pleasant. During their tenancy that house has been used perhaps for rather unusual purposes! But no one suspects such a thing. Friends come to see them, not very often. Just occasionally. One night, perhaps, a kind of anniversary party for a middle-aged, or elderly couple; or a coming of age party. A lot of cars coming and going. Say there are five major robberies done within six months but each time the loot passes through, or is cached in, not just one of these houses, but five different houses in five different parts of the countryside. It's only a supposition as yet, my dear Tommy, but we're working on it. Let's say your old lady lets a picture of a certain house go out of her possession and supposing that's a *significant* house. And supposing that that's the house that your missus has recognized somewhere, and has gone dashing off to investigate. And supposing someone doesn't want that particular house investigated – It might tie up, you know.'

'It's very far-fetched.'

'Oh yes – I agree. But these times we live in are far-fetched times – In our particular world incredible things happen.'

II

Somewhat wearily Tommy alighted from his fourth taxi of the day and looked appraisingly at his surroundings. The taxi had deposited him in a small *cul-de-sac* which tucked itself coyly under one of the protuberances of Hampstead Heath. The *cul-de-sac* seemed to have been some artistic 'development'. Each house was wildly different from the house next to it. This particular one seemed to consist of a large studio with skylights in it, and attached to it (rather like a gumboil), on one side was what seemed to be a little cluster of three rooms. A ladder staircase painted bright green ran up the outside of the house. Tommy opened the small gate, went up a path and not seeing a bell applied himself to the knocker. Getting no response, he paused for a few moments and then started again with the knocker, a little louder this time.

The door opened so suddenly that he nearly fell backwards. A woman stood on the doorstep. At first sight Tommy's first impression was that this was one of the plainest women he had ever seen. She had a large expanse of flat, pancake-like face, two enormous eyes which seemed of impossibly different colours, one green and one brown, a noble forehead with a quantity of wild hair rising up from it in a kind of thicket. She wore a purple overall with blotches of clay on it, and Tommy noticed that the hand that held the door open was one of exceeding beauty of structure.

'Oh,' she said. Her voice was deep and rather attractive. 'What is it? I'm busy.'

'Mrs Boscowan?'

'Yes. What do you want?'

'My name's Beresford. I wondered if I might speak to you for a few moments.'

'I don't know. Really, must you? What is it – something about a picture?' Her eye had gone to what he held under his arm.

'Yes. It's something to do with one of your husband's pictures.'

'Do you want to sell it? I've got plenty of his pictures. I don't want to buy any more of them. Take it to one of these galleries or something. They're beginning to buy him now. You don't look as though you needed to sell pictures.'

'Oh no, I don't want to sell anything.'

Tommy felt extraordinary difficulty in talking to this particular woman. Her eyes, unmatching though they were, were very fine eyes and they were looking now over his shoulder down the street with an air of some peculiar interest at something in the far distance.

'Please,' said Tommy. 'I wish you would let me come in. It's so difficult to explain.'

'If you're a painter I don't want to talk to you,' said Mrs Boscowan. 'I find painters very boring always.'

'I'm not a painter.'

'Well, you don't look like one, certainly.' Her eyes raked him up and down. 'You look more like a civil servant,' she said disapprovingly.

'Can I come in, Mrs Boscowan?'

'I'm not sure. Wait.'

She shut the door rather abruptly. Tommy waited. After about four minutes had passed the door opened again.

'All right,' she said. 'You can come in.'

She led him through the doorway, up a narrow staircase and into the large studio. In a corner of it there was a figure and various implements standing by it. Hammers and chisels. There was also a clay head. The whole place looked as though it had recently been savaged by a gang of hooligans.

'There's never any room to sit up here,' said Mrs Boscowan.

She threw various things off a wooden stool and pushed it towards him.

'There. Sit down here and speak to me.'

'It's very kind of you to let me come in.'

'It is rather, but you looked so worried. You are worried, aren't you, about something?'

'Yes I am.'

'I thought so. What are you worried about?'

'My wife,' said Tommy, surprising himself by his answer.

'Oh, worried about your wife? Well, there's nothing unusual in that. Men are always worrying about their wives. What's the matter – has she gone off with someone or playing up?'

'No. Nothing like that.'

'Dying? Cancer?'

'No,' said Tommy. 'It's just that I don't know where she is.'

'And you think I might? Well, you'd better tell me her name and something about her if you think I can find her for you. I'm not sure, mind you,' said Mrs Boscowan, 'that I shall want to. I'm warning you.'

'Thank God,' said Tommy, 'you're more easy to talk to than I thought you were going to be.'

'What's the picture got to do with it? It is a picture, isn't it – must be, that shape.'

Tommy undid the wrappings.

'It's a picture signed by your husband,' said Tommy. 'I want you to tell me what you can about it.'

'I see. What exactly do you want to know?'

'When it was painted and where it is.'

Mrs Boscowan looked at him and for the first time there was a slight look of interest in her eyes.

'Well, that's not difficult,' she said. 'Yes, I can tell you all about it. It was painted about fifteen years ago – no, a good deal longer than that I should think. It's one of his fairly early ones. Twenty years ago, I should say.'

'You know where it is – the place I mean?'

'Oh yes, I can remember quite well. Nice picture. I always

liked it. That's the little hump-backed bridge and the house and the name of the place is Sutton Chancellor. About seven or eight miles from Market Basing. The house itself is about a couple of miles from Sutton Chancellor. Pretty place. Secluded.'

She came up to the picture, bent down and peered at it closely.

'That's funny,' she said. 'Yes, that's very odd. I wonder now.'

Tommy did not pay much attention.

'What's the name of the house?' he asked.

'I can't really remember. It got renamed, you know. Several times. I don't know what there was about it. A couple of rather tragic things happened there, I think, then the next people who came along renamed it. Called the Canal House once, or Canal Side. Once it was called Bridge House then Meadowside – or Riverside was another name.'

'Who lived there – or who lives there now? Do you know?'

'Nobody I know. Man and a girl lived there when first I saw it. Used to come down for weekends. Not married, I think. The girl was a dancer. May have been an actress – no, I think she was a dancer. Ballet dancer. Rather beautiful but dumb. Simple, almost wanting. William was quite soft about her, I remember.'

'Did he paint her?'

'No. He didn't often paint people. He used to say sometimes he wanted to do a sketch of them, but he never did much about it. He was always silly over girls.'

'They were the people who were there when your husband was painting the house?'

'Yes, I think so. Part of the time anyway. They only came down weekends. Then there was some kind of a bust up. They had a row, I think, or he went away and left her or she went away and left him. I wasn't down there myself. I was working in Coventry then doing a group. After that I think there was just a governess in the house and the child. I don't know who the child was or where she came from but I suppose the governess was looking after her. Then I think something happened to the child. Either the governess took her away somewhere or perhaps she died. What do you want to know about the people who lived in the house twenty years ago? Seems to me idiotic.'

'I want to hear anything I can about that house,' said Tommy.

'You see, my wife went away to look for that house. She said she'd seen it out of a train somewhere.'

'Quite right,' said Mrs Boscowan, 'the railway line runs just the other side of the bridge. You can see the house very well from it, I expect.' Then she said, 'Why did she want to find that house?'

Tommy gave a much abridged explanation – she looked at him doubtfully.

'You haven't come out of a mental home or anything, have you?' said Mrs Boscowan. 'On parole or something, whatever they call it.'

'I suppose I must sound a little like that,' said Tommy, 'but it's quite simple really. My wife wanted to find out about this house and so she tried to take various train journeys to find out where it was she'd seen it. Well, I think she did find out. I think she went there to this place – something Chancellor?'

'Sutton Chancellor, yes. Very one-horse place it used to be. Of course it may be a big development or even one of these new dormitory towns by now.'

'It might be anything, I expect,' said Tommy. 'She telephoned she was coming back but she didn't come back. And I want to know what's happened to her. I think she went and started investigating that house and perhaps – perhaps she ran into danger.'

'What's dangerous about it?'

'I don't know,' said Tommy. 'Neither of us knew. I didn't even think there could be any danger about it, but my wife did.'

'E.S.P.?'

'Possibly. She's a little like that. She has hunches. You never heard of or knew a Mrs Lancaster twenty years ago or any time up to a month ago?'

'Mrs Lancaster? No, I don't think so. Sort of name one might remember, mightn't it be. No. What about Mrs Lancaster?'

'She was the woman who owned this picture. She gave it as a friendly gesture to an aunt of mine. Then she left an old people's home rather suddenly. Her relatives took her away. I've tried to trace her but it isn't easy.'

'Who's the one who's got the imagination, you or your wife?

You seem to have thought up a lot of things and to be rather in a state, if I may say so.'

'Oh yes, you can say so,' said Tommy. 'Rather in a state and all about nothing at all. That's what you mean, isn't it? I suppose you're right too.'

'No,' said Mrs Boscowan. Her voice had altered slightly. 'I wouldn't say about nothing at all.'

Tommy looked at her inquiringly.

'There's one thing that's odd about that picture,' said Mrs Boscowan. 'Very odd. I remember it quite well, you know. I remember most of William's pictures although he painted such a lot of them.'

'Do you remember who it was sold to, if it was sold?'

'No, I don't remember that. Yes, I think it was sold. There was a whole batch of his paintings sold from one of his exhibitions. They ran back for about three or four years before this and a couple of years later than this. Quite a lot of them were sold. Nearly all of them. But I can't remember by now who it was sold to. That's asking too much.'

'I'm very grateful to you for all you have remembered.'

'You haven't asked me yet why I said there was something odd about the picture. This picture that you brought here.'

'You mean it isn't your husband's – somebody else painted it?'

'Oh no. That's the picture that William painted. "House by a Canal", I think he called it in the catalogue. But it isn't as it was. You see, there's something wrong with it.'

'What's wrong with it?'

Mrs Boscowan stretched out a clay-smeared finger and jabbed at a spot just below the bridge spanning the canal.

'There,' she said. 'You see? There's a boat tied up under the bridge, isn't there?'

'Yes,' said Tommy puzzled.

'Well, that boat wasn't there, not when I saw it last. William never painted that boat. When it was exhibited *there was no boat of any kind.*'

'You mean that somebody not your husband painted the boat in here afterwards?'

'Yes. Odd, isn't it? I wonder why. First of all I was surprised to see the boat there, a place where there wasn't any boat, then I can see quite well that it wasn't painted by William. *He* didn't put it in at any time. Somebody else did. I wonder who?'

She looked at Tommy.

'And I wonder why?'

Tommy had no solution to offer. He looked at Mrs Boscowan. His Aunt Ada would have called her a scatty woman but Tommy did not think of her in that light. She was vague, with an abrupt way of jumping from one subject to another. The things she said seemed to have very little relation to the last thing she had said a minute before. She was the sort of person, Tommy thought, who might know a great deal more than she chose to reveal. Had she loved her husband or been jealous of her husband or despised her husband? There was really no clue whatever in her manner, or indeed her words. But he had the feeling that that small painted boat tied up under the bridge had caused her uneasiness. She hadn't liked the boat being there. Suddenly he wondered if the statement she had made was true. Could she really remember from long years back whether Boscowan had painted a boat at the bridge or had not? It seemed really a very small and insignificant item. If it had been only a year ago when she had seen the picture last – but apparently it was a much longer time than that. And it had made Mrs Boscowan uneasy. He looked at her again and saw that she was looking at him. Her curious eyes resting on him not defiantly, but only thoughtfully. Very, very thoughtfully.

'What are you going to do now?' she said.

That at least was easy. Tommy had no difficulty in knowing what he was going to do now.

'I shall go home tonight – see if there is any news of my wife – any word from her. If not, tomorrow I shall go to this place,' he said. 'Sutton Chancellor. I hope that I may find my wife there.'

'It would depend,' said Mrs Boscowan.

'Depend on what?' said Tommy sharply.

Mrs Boscowan frowned. Then she murmured, seemingly to herself, 'I wonder where she is?'

'You wonder where who is?'

Mrs Boscowan had turned her glance away from him. Now her eyes swept back.

'Oh,' she said. 'I meant your wife.' Then she said, 'I hope she is all right.'

'Why shouldn't she be all right? Tell me, Mrs Boscowan, is there something wrong with that place – with Sutton Chancellor?'

'With Sutton Chancellor? With the place?' She reflected. 'No, I don't think so. Not with the *place*.'

'I suppose I meant the house,' said Tommy. 'This house by the canal. Not Sutton Chancellor village.'

'Oh, the house,' said Mrs Boscowan. 'It was a good house really. Meant for lovers, you know.'

'Did lovers live there?'

'Sometimes. Not often enough really. If a house is built for lovers, it ought to be lived in by lovers.'

'Not put to some other use by someone.'

'You're pretty quick,' said Mrs Boscowan. 'You saw what I meant, didn't you? You mustn't put a house that was meant for one thing to the wrong use. It won't like it if you do.'

'Do you know anything about the people who have lived there of late years?'

She shook her head. 'No. No. I don't know anything about the house at all. It was never important to me, you see.'

'But you're thinking of something – no, someone?'

'Yes,' said Mrs Boscowan. 'I suppose you're right about that. I was thinking of – someone.'

'Can't you tell me about the person you were thinking of?'

'There's really nothing to say,' said Mrs Boscowan. 'Sometimes, you know, one just wonders where a person is. What's happened to them or how they might have – developed. There's a sort of feeling –' She waved her hands – 'Would you like a kipper?' she said unexpectedly.

'A kipper?' Tommy was startled.

'Well, I happen to have two or three kippers here. I thought perhaps you ought to have something to eat before you catch a train. Waterloo is the station,' she said. 'For Sutton Chancellor, I mean. You used to have to change at Market Basing. I expect you still do.'

It was a dismissal. He accepted it.

CHAPTER 13

ALBERT ON CLUES

I

Tuppence blinked her eyes. Vision seemed rather dim. She tried to lift her head from the pillow but winced as a sharp pain ran through it, and let it drop again on to the pillow. She closed her eyes. Presently she opened them again and blinked once more.

With a feeling of achievement she recognized her surroundings. 'I'm in a hospital ward,' thought Tuppence. Satisfied with her mental progress so far, she attempted no more brainy deduction. She was in a hospital ward and her head ached. Why it ached, why she was in a hospital ward, she was not quite sure. 'Accident?' thought Tuppence.

There were nurses moving around beds. That seemed natural enough. She closed her eyes and tried a little cautious thought. A faint vision of an elderly figure in clerical dress, passed across a mental screen. 'Father?' said Tuppence doubtfully. 'Is it Father?' She couldn't really remember. She supposed so.

'But what am I doing being ill in a hospital?' thought Tuppence. 'I mean, I nurse in a hospital, so I ought to be in uniform. V.A.D. uniform. Oh dear,' said Tuppence.

Presently a nurse materialized near her bed.

'Feeling better now, dear?' said the nurse with a kind of false cheerfulness. 'That's nice, isn't it?'

Tuppence wasn't quite sure whether it *was* nice. The nurse said something about a nice cup of tea.

'I seem to be a patient,' said Tuppence rather disapprovingly to herself. She lay still, resurrecting in her own mind various detached thoughts and words.

'Soldiers,' said Tuppence. 'V.A.D.s. That's it, of course. I'm a V.A.D.'

The nurse brought her some tea in a kind of feeding cup and supported her whilst she sipped it. The pain went through her head again. 'A V.A.D., that's what I am,' said Tuppence aloud.

The nurse looked at her in an uncomprehending fashion.

'My head hurts,' said Tuppence, adding a statement of fact.

'It'll be better soon,' said the nurse.

She removed the feeding cup, reporting to a sister as she passed along. 'Number 14's awake. She's a bit wonky, though, I think.'

'Did she say anything?'

'Said she was a V.I.P.,' said the nurse.

The ward sister gave a small snort indicating that that was how she felt towards unimportant patients who reported themselves to be V.I.P.s.

'We shall see about that,' said the sister. 'Hurry up, Nurse, don't be all day with that feeding cup.'

Tuppence remained half drowsy on her pillows. She had not yet got beyond the stage of allowing thoughts to flit through her mind in a rather disorganized procession.

There was somebody who ought to be here, she felt, somebody she knew quite well. There was something very strange about this hospital. It wasn't the hospital she remembered. It wasn't the one she had nursed in. 'All soldiers, that was,' said Tuppence to herself. 'The surgical ward, I was on A and B rows.' She opened her eyelids and took another look round. She decided it was a hospital she had never seen before and that it had nothing to do with the nursing of surgical cases, military or otherwise.

'I wonder where this is,' said Tuppence. 'What place?' She tried to think of the name of some place. The only places she could think of were London and Southampton.

The ward sister now made her appearance at the bedside.

'Feeling a little better, I hope,' she said.

'I'm all right,' said Tuppence. 'What's the matter with me?'

'You hurt your head. I expect you find it rather painful, don't you?'

'It aches,' said Tuppence. 'Where am I?'

'Market Basing Royal Hospital.'

Tuppence considered this information. It meant nothing to her at all.

'An old clergyman,' she said.

'I beg your pardon?'

'Nothing particular. I –'

'We haven't been able to write your name on your diet sheet yet,' said the ward sister.

She held her Biro pen at the ready and looked inquiringly at Tuppence.

'My name?'

'Yes,' said the sister. 'For the records,' she added helpfully.

Tuppence was silent, considering. Her name. What was her name? 'How silly,' said Tuppence to herself, 'I seem to have forgotten it. And yet I must have a name.' Suddenly a faint feeling of relief came to her. The elderly clergyman's face flashed suddenly across her mind and she said with decision,

'Of course. Prudence.'

'P-r-u-d-e-n-c-e?'

'That's right,' said Tuppence.

'That's your Christian name. The surname?'

'Cowley. C-o-w-l-e-y.'

'Glad to get that straight,' said the sister, and moved away again with the air of one whose records were no longer worrying her.

Tuppence felt faintly pleased with herself. Prudence Cowley. Prudence Cowley in the V.A.D. and her father was a clergyman at – at something vicarage and it was wartime and . . . 'Funny,' said Tuppence to herself, 'I seem to be getting this all wrong. It seems to me it all happened a long time ago.' She murmured to herself, 'Was it your poor child?' She wondered. Was it she who had just said that or was it somebody else said it to her?

The sister was back again.

'Your address,' she said, 'Miss – Miss Cowley, or is it Mrs Cowley? Did you ask about a child?'

'Was it your poor child? Did somebody say that to me or am I saying it to them?'

'I think I should sleep a little if I were you now, dear,' said the sister.

She went away and took the information she had obtained to the proper place.

'She seems to have come to herself, Doctor,' she remarked, 'and she says her name is Prudence Cowley. But she doesn't seem to remember her address. She said something about a child.'

'Oh well,' said the doctor, with his usual casual air, 'we'll give her another twenty-four hours or so. She's coming round from the concussion quite nicely.'

II

Tommy fumbled with his latchkey. Before he could use it the door came open and Albert stood in the open aperture.

'Well,' said Tommy, 'is she back?'

Albert slowly shook his head.

'No word from her, no telephone message, no letters waiting – no telegrams?'

'Nothing I tell you, sir. Nothing whatever. And nothing from anyone else either. They're lying low – but they've got her. That's what I think. They've got her.'

'What the devil do you mean – they've got her?' said Tommy. 'The things you read. Who've got her?'

'Well, you know what I mean. The gang.'

'What gang?'

'One of those gangs with flick knives maybe. Or an international one.'

'Stop talking rubbish,' said Tommy. 'D'you know what I think?'

Albert looked inquiringly at him.

'I think it's extremely inconsiderate of her not to send us word of some kind,' said Tommy.

'Oh,' said Albert, 'well, I see what you mean. I suppose you *could* put it that way. If it makes you happier,' he added rather unfortunately. He removed the parcel from Tommy's arms. 'I see you brought that picture back,' he said.

'Yes, I've brought the bloody picture back,' said Tommy. 'A fat lot of use it's been.'

'You haven't learnt anything from it?'

'That's not quite true,' said Tommy. 'I *have* learnt something from it but whether what I've learnt is going to be any use to me I don't know.' He added, 'Dr Murray didn't ring up, I suppose, or Miss Packard from Sunny Ridge Nursing Home? Nothing like that?'

'Nobody's rung up except the greengrocer to say he's got some nice aubergines. He knows the missus is fond of aubergines. He always lets her know. But I told him she wasn't available just now.' He added, 'I've got a chicken for your dinner.'

'It's extraordinary that you can never think of anything but chickens,' said Tommy, unkindly.

'It's what they call a *poussin* this time,' said Albert. 'Skinny,' he added.

'It'll do,' said Tommy.

The telephone rang. Tommy was out of his seat and had rushed to it in a moment.

'Hallo . . . hallo?'

A faint and far-away voice spoke. 'Mr Thomas Beresford? Can you accept a personal call from Invergashly?'

'Yes.'

'Hold the line, please.'

Tommy waited. His excitement was calming down. He had to wait some time. Then a voice he knew, crisp and capable, sounded. The voice of his daughter.

'Hallo, is that you, Pop?'

'Deborah!'

'Yes. Why are you sounding so breathless, have you been running?'

Daughters, Tommy thought, were always critical.

'I wheeze a bit in my old age,' he said. 'How are you, Deborah?'

'Oh, I'm all right. Look here, Dad, I saw something in the paper. Perhaps you've seen it too. I wondered about it. Something about someone who had had an accident and was in hospital.'

'Well? I don't think I saw anything of that kind. I mean, not to notice it in any way. Why?'

'Well it – it didn't sound too bad. I supposed it was a car accident or something like that. It mentioned that the woman, whoever it was – an elderly woman – gave her name as Prudence Cowley but they were unable to find her address.'

'Prudence Cowley? You mean –'

'Well yes. I only – well – I only wondered. That *is* Mother's name, isn't it? I mean it was her name.'

'Of course.'

'I always forget about the Prudence. I mean we've never thought of her as Prudence, you and I, or Derek either.'

'No,' said Tommy. 'No. It's not the kind of Christian name one would associate much with your mother.'

'No, I know it isn't. I just thought it was – rather odd. You don't think it might be some relation of hers?'

'I suppose it might be. Where was this?'

'Hospital at Market Basing, I think it said. They wanted to know more about her, I gather. I just wondered – well, I know it's awfully silly, there must be quantities of people called Cowley and quantities of people called Prudence. But I thought I'd just ring up and find out. Make sure, I mean, that Mother was at home and all right and all that.'

'I see,' said Tommy. 'Yes, I see.'

'Well, go on, Pop, is she at home?'

'No,' said Tommy, 'she isn't at home and I don't know either whether she is all right or not.'

'What do you mean?' said Deborah. 'What's Mother been doing? I suppose you've been up in London with that hush-hush utterly secret idiotic survival from past days, jawing with all the old boys.'

'You're quite right,' said Tommy. 'I got back from that yesterday evening.'

'And you found Mother away – or did you know she was away? Come on, Pop, tell me about it. You're worried. I know when you're worried well enough. What's Mother been doing? She's been up to something, hasn't she? I wish at her age she'd learn to sit quiet and not do things.'

'She's been worried,' said Tommy. 'Worried about something that happened in connection with your Great-aunt Ada's death.'

'What sort of thing?'

'Well, something that one of the patients at the nursing home said to her. She got worried about this old lady. She started talking a good deal and your mother was worried about some of the things she said. And so, when we went to look through Aunt Ada's things we suggested talking to this old lady and it seems she'd left rather suddenly.'

'Well, that seems quite natural, doesn't it?'

'Some of her relatives came and fetched her away.'

'It still seems quite natural,' said Deborah. 'Why did Mother get the wind up?'

'She got it into her head,' said Tommy, 'that something might have happened to this old lady.'

'I see.'

'Not to put too fine a point on it, as the saying goes, she seems to have disappeared. All in quite a natural way. I mean, vouched for by lawyers and banks and all that. Only – we haven't been able to find out where she is.'

'You mean Mother's gone off to look for her somewhere?'

'Yes. And she didn't come back when she said she was coming back, two days ago.'

'And haven't you heard from her?'

'No.'

'I wish to goodness you could look after Mother properly,' said Deborah, severely.

'None of us have ever been able to look after her properly,' said Tommy. 'Not you either, Deborah, if it comes to that. It's the same way she went off in the war and did a lot of things that she'd no business to be doing.'

'But it's different now. I mean, she's quite *old*. She ought to sit at home and take care of herself. I suppose she's been getting bored. That's at the bottom of it all.'

'Market Basing Hospital, did you say?' said Tommy.

'Melfordshire. It's about an hour or an hour and a half from London, I think, by train.'

'That's it,' said Tommy. 'And there's a village near Market Basing called Sutton Chancellor.'

'What's that got to do with it?' said Deborah.

'It's too long to go into now,' said Tommy. 'It has to do with a picture painted of a house near a bridge by a canal.'

'I don't think I can hear you very well,' said Deborah. 'What are you talking about?'

'Never mind,' said Tommy. 'I'm going to ring up Market Basing Hospital and find out a few things. I've a feeling that it's your mother, all right. People, if they've had concussion, you know, often remember things first that happened when they were a child, and only get slowly to the present. She's gone back to her maiden name. She may have been in a car accident, but I shouldn't be surprised if somebody hadn't given her a conk on the head. It's the sort of thing that happens to your mother. She gets into things. I'll let you know what I find out.'

Forty minutes later, Tommy Beresford glanced at his wrist

watch and breathed a sigh of utter weariness, as he replaced the receiver with a final clang on the telephone rest. Albert made an appearance.

'What about your dinner, sir?' he demanded. 'You haven't eaten a thing, and I'm sorry to say I forgot about that chicken – Burnt to a cinder.'

'I don't want anything to eat,' said Tommy. 'What I want is a drink. Bring me a double whisky.'

'Coming, sir,' said Albert.

A few moments later he brought the required refreshment to where Tommy had slumped down in the worn but comfortable chair reserved for his special use.

'And now, I suppose,' said Tommy, 'you want to hear everything.'

'Matter of fact, sir,' said Albert in a slightly apologetic tone, 'I know most of it. You see, seeing as it was a question of the missus and all that, I took the liberty of lifting up the extension in the bedroom. I didn't think you'd mind, sir, not as it was the missus.'

'I don't blame you,' said Tommy. 'Actually, I'm grateful to you. If I had to start explaining –'

'Got on to everyone, didn't you? The hospital and the doctor and the matron.'

'No need to go over it all again,' said Tommy.

'Market Basing Hospital,' said Albert. 'Never breathed a word of that, she didn't. Never left it behind as an address or anything like that.'

'She didn't intend it to be her address,' said Tommy. 'As far as I can make out she was probably coshed on the head in an out of the way spot somewhere. Someone took her along in a car and dumped her at the side of the road somewhere, to be picked up as an ordinary hit and run.' He added, 'Call me at six-thirty tomorrow morning. I want to get an early start.'

'I'm sorry about your chicken getting burnt up again in the oven. I only put it in to keep warm and forgot about it.'

'Never mind chickens,' said Tommy. 'I've always thought they were very silly birds, running under cars and clucking about. Bury the corpse tomorrow morning and give it a good funeral.'

'She's not at death's door or anything, is she, sir?' asked Albert.

'Subdue your melodramatic fancies,' said Tommy. 'If you'd done any proper listening you'd have heard that she's come nicely to herself again, knows who she is or was and where she is and they've sworn to keep her there waiting for me until I arrive to take charge of her again. On no account is she to be allowed to slip out by herself and go off again doing some more tomfool detective work.'

'Talking of detective work,' said Albert, and hesitated with a slight cough.

'I don't particularly want to talk about it,' said Tommy. 'Forget it, Albert. Teach yourself book-keeping or window-box gardening or something.'

'Well, I was just thinking – I mean, as a matter of clues –'

'Well, what about clues?'

'I've been thinking.'

'That's where all the trouble in life comes from. Thinking.'

'Clues,' said Albert again. 'That picture, for instance. That's a clue, isn't it?'

Tommy observed that Albert had hung the picture of the house by the canal up on the wall.

'If that picture's a clue to something, what do you think it's a clue to?' He blushed slightly at the inelegancy of the phrase he had just coined. 'I mean – what's it all about? It ought to mean something. What I was thinking of,' said Albert, 'if you'll excuse me mentioning it –'

'Go ahead, Albert.'

'What I was thinking of was that desk.'

'Desk?'

'Yes. The one that came by the furniture removers with the little table and the two chairs and the other things. Family property, it was, you said?'

'It belonged to my Aunt Ada,' said Tommy.

'Well, that's what I meant, sir. That's the sort of place where you find clues. In old desks. Antiques.'

'Possibly,' said Tommy.

'It wasn't my business, I know, and I suppose I really oughtn't to have gone messing about with it, but while you were away, sir, I couldn't help it. I had to go and have a look.'

'What – a look into the desk?'

'Yes, just to see if there might be a clue there. You see, desks like that, they have secret drawers.'

'Possibly,' said Tommy.

'Well, there you are. There might be a clue there, hidden. Shut up in the secret drawer.'

'It's an agreeable idea,' said Tommy. 'But there's no reason as far as I know for my Aunt Ada to hide things away in secret drawers.'

'You never know with old ladies. They like tucking things away. Like jackdaws, they are, or magpies. I forget which it is. There might be a secret will in it or something written in invisible ink or a treasure. Where you'd find some hidden treasure.'

'I'm sorry, Albert, but I think I'm going to have to disappoint you. I'm pretty sure there's nothing of that kind in that nice old family desk which once belonged to my Uncle William. Another man who turned crusty in his old age besides being stone deaf and having a very bad temper.'

'What I thought is,' said Albert, 'it wouldn't do any harm to look, would it?' He added virtuously, 'It needed cleaning out anyway. You know how old things are with old ladies. They don't turn them out much – not when they're rheumatic and find it hard to get about.'

Tommy paused for a moment or two. He remembered that Tuppence and he had looked quickly through the drawers of the desk, had put their contents such as they were in two large envelopes and removed a few skeins of wool, two cardigans, a black velvet stole and three fine pillow-cases from the lower drawers which they had placed with other clothing and odds and ends for disposal. They had also looked through such papers as there had been in the envelopes after their return home with them. There had been nothing there of particular interest.

'We looked through the contents, Albert,' he said. 'Spent a couple of evenings really. One or two quite interesting old letters, some recipes for boiling ham, some other recipes for preserving fruit, some ration books and coupons and things dating back to the war. There was nothing of any interest.'

'Oh, that,' said Albert, 'but that's just papers and things, as you might say. Just ordinary go and come what everybody gets holed up in desks and drawers and things. I mean real secret stuff. When I was a boy, you know, I did six months with an antique dealer – helping him fake up things as often as not. But I got to know about secret drawers that way. They usually run to the same pattern. Three or four well-known kinds and they vary it now and then. Don't you think, sir, you ought to have a look? I mean, I didn't like to go it meself with you not here. I would have been presuming.' He looked at Tommy with the air of a pleading dog.

'Come on, Albert,' said Tommy, giving in. 'Let's go and presume.'

'A very nice piece of furniture,' thought Tommy, as he stood by Albert's side, surveying this specimen of his inheritance from Aunt Ada. 'Nicely kept, beautiful old polish on it, showing the good workmanship and craftsmanship of days gone by.'

'Well, Albert,' he said, 'go ahead. This is your bit of fun. But don't go and strain it.'

'Oh, I was ever so careful. I didn't crack it, or slip knives into it or anything like that. First of all we let down the front and put it on these two slab things that pull out. That's right, you see, the flap comes down this way and that's where the old lady used to sit. Nice little mother-of-pearl blotting case your Aunt Ada had. It was in the left-hand drawer.'

'There are these two things,' said Tommy.

He drew out two delicate pilastered shallow vertical drawers.

'Oh, them, sir. You can push papers in them, but there's nothing really secret about them. The most usual place is to open the little middle cupboard – and then at the bottom of it usually there's a little depression and you slide the bottom out and there's a space. But there's other ways and places. This desk is the kind that has a kind of well underneath.'

'That's not very secret either, is it? You just slide back a panel –'

'The point is, it looks as though you'd found all there was to find. You push back the panel, there's the cavity and you can put a good many things in there that you want to keep a bit from being pawed over and all that. But that's not all, as you might say. Because you see, here there's a little piece of wood in front, like a little ledge. And you can pull that up, you see.'

'Yes,' said Tommy, 'yes, I can see that. You pull that up.'

'And you've got a secret cavity here, just behind the middle lock.'

'But there's nothing in it.'

'No,' said Albert, 'it looks disappointing. But if you slip your hand into that cavity and you wiggle it along either to the left or the right, there are two little thin drawers, one each side. There's a little semi-circle cut out of the top, and you can hook your finger over that – and pull gently towards you –' During these remarks Albert seemed to be getting his wrist in what was almost a contortionist position. 'Sometimes they stick a little. Wait – wait – here she comes.'

Albert's hooked forefinger drew something towards him from inside. He clawed it gently forward until the narrow small drawer showed in the opening. He hooked it out and laid it before Tommy, with the air of a dog bringing his bone to his master.

'Now wait a minute, sir. There's something in here, something wrapped up in a long thin envelope. Now we'll do the other side.'

He changed hands and resumed his contortionist clawings. Presently a second drawer was brought to light and was laid beside the first one.

'There's something in here, too,' said Albert. 'Another sealed-up envelope that someone's hidden here one time or another. I've not tried to open either of them – I wouldn't do such a thing.' His voice was virtuous in the extreme. 'I left that to you – But what I say is – they may be *clues* –'

Together he and Tommy extracted the contents of the dusty drawers. Tommy took out first a sealed envelope rolled up lengthways with an elastic band round it. The elastic band parted as soon as it was touched.

'Looks valuable,' said Albert.

Tommy glanced at the envelope. It bore the superscription 'Confidential'.

'There you are,' said Albert. '"Confidential". It's a clue.'

Tommy extracted the contents of the envelope. In a faded handwriting, and very scratchy handwriting at that, there was a half-sheet of notepaper. Tommy turned it this way and that and Albert leaned over his shoulder, breathing heavily.

'Mrs MacDonald's recipe for Salmon Cream,' Tommy read.

'Given to me as a special favour. Take 2 pounds of middle cut of salmon, 1 pint of Jersey cream, a wineglass of brandy and a fresh cucumber.' He broke off. 'I'm sorry, Albert, it's a clue which will lead us to good cookery, no doubt.'

Albert uttered sounds indicative of disgust and disappointment.

'Never mind,' said Tommy. 'Here's another one to try.'

The next sealed envelope did not appear to be one of quite such antiquity. It had two pale grey wax seals affixed to it, each bearing a representation of a wild rose.

'Pretty,' said Tommy, 'rather fanciful for Aunt Ada. How to cook a beef steak pie, I expect.'

Tommy ripped open the envelope. He raised his eyebrows. Ten carefully folded five-pound notes fell out.

'Nice thin ones,' said Tommy. 'They're the old ones. You know, the kind we used to have in the war. Decent paper. Probably aren't legal tender nowadays.'

'Money!' said Albert. 'What she want all that money for?'

'Oh, that's an old lady's nest egg,' said Tommy. 'Aunt Ada always had a nest egg. Years ago she told me that every woman should always have fifty pounds in five-pound notes with her in case of what she called emergencies.'

'Well, I suppose it'll still come in handy,' said Albert.

'I don't suppose they're absolutely obsolete. I think you can make some arrangement to change them at a bank.'

'There's another one still,' said Albert. 'The one from the other drawer –'

The next was bulkier. There seemed to be more inside it and it had three large important-looking red seals. On the outside was written in the same spiky hand 'In the event of my death, this envelope should be sent unopened to my solicitor, Mr Rockbury of Rockbury & Tomkins, or to my nephew Thomas Beresford. Not to be opened by any unauthorized person.'

There were several sheets of closely written paper. The handwriting was bad, very spiky and here and there somewhat illegible. Tommy read it aloud with some difficulty.

'I, Ada Maria Fanshawe, am writing down here certain matters which have come to my knowledge and which have been told me

*by people who are residing in this nursing home called Sunny Ridge.
I cannot vouch for any of this information being correct but there
seems to be some reason to believe that suspicious – possibly criminal
– activities are taking place here or have taken place here. Elizabeth
Moody, a foolish woman, but not I think untruthful, declares that
she has recognized here a well-known criminal. There may be a
poisoner at work among us. I myself prefer to keep an open mind,
but I shall remain watchful. I propose to write down here any facts
that come to my knowledge. The whole thing may be a mare's nest.
Either my solicitor or my nephew Thomas Beresford, is asked to
make full investigation.'*

'There,' said Albert triumphantly – 'Told you so! It's a CLUE!'

BOOK 4 •
HERE IS A CHURCH AND HERE IS THE STEEPLE
OPEN THE DOORS AND THERE ARE THE PEOPLE

CHAPTER 14

EXERCISE IN THINKING

'I suppose what we ought to do is think,' said Tuppence.

After a glad reunion in the hospital, Tuppence had eventually been honourably discharged. The faithful pair were now comparing notes together in the sitting-room of the best suite in The Lamb and Flag at Market Basing.

'You leave thinking alone,' said Tommy. 'You know what that doctor told you before he let you go. No worries, no mental exertion, very little physical activity – take everything easy.'

'What else am I doing now?' demanded Tuppence. 'I've got my feet up, haven't I, and my head on two cushions? And as for thinking, thinking isn't necessarily mental exertion. I'm not doing mathematics, or studying economics, or adding up the household accounts. Thinking is just resting comfortably, and leaving one's mind open in case something interesting or important should just come floating in. Anyway, wouldn't you rather I did a little thinking with my feet up and my head on cushions, rather than go in for action again?'

'I certainly don't want you going in for action again,' said Tommy. 'That's *out*. You understand? Physically, Tuppence, you will remain quiescent. If possible, I shan't let you out of my sight because I don't trust you.'

'All right,' said Tuppence. 'Lecture ends. Now let's think. Think together. Pay no attention to what doctors have said to you. If you knew as much as I do about doctors –'

'Never mind about the doctors,' said Tommy, 'you do as *I* tell you.'

'All right. I've no wish at present for physical activity, I assure you. The point is that we've got to compare notes. We've got hold of a lot of things. It's as bad as a village jumble sale.'

'What do you mean by things?'

'Well, facts. All sorts of facts. Far too many facts. And not only facts – Hearsay, suggestions, legends, gossip. The whole thing is like a bran tub with different kinds of parcels wrapped up and shoved down in the sawdust.'

'Sawdust is right,' said Tommy.

'I don't quite know whether you're being insulting or modest,' said Tuppence. 'Anyway, you do agree with me, don't you? We've got far too *much* of everything. There are wrong things and right things, and important things and unimportant things and they're all mixed up together. We don't know where to start.'

'I do,' said Tommy.

'All right,' said Tuppence. 'Where are you starting?'

'I'm starting with your being coshed on the head,' said Tommy.

Tuppence considered a moment. 'I don't see really that that's a starting point. I mean, it's the last thing that happened, not the first.'

'It's the first in my mind,' said Tommy. 'I won't have people coshing my wife. And it's a *real* point to start from. It's not imagination. It's a *real* thing that *really* happened.'

'I couldn't agree with you more,' said Tuppence. 'It really happened and it happened to me, and I'm not forgetting it. I've been thinking about it – Since I regained the power of thought, that is.'

'Have you any idea as to who did it?'

'Unfortunately, no. I was bending down over a gravestone and whoosh!'

'Who could it have been?'

'I suppose it must have been somebody in Sutton Chancellor. And yet that seems so unlikely. I've hardly spoken to anyone.'

'The vicar?'

'It couldn't have been the vicar,' said Tuppence. 'First because he's a nice old boy. And secondly because he wouldn't have been nearly strong enough. And thirdly because he's got very asthmatic breathing. He couldn't possibly have crept up behind me without my hearing him.'

'Then if you count the vicar out –'

'Don't you?'

'Well,' said Tommy, 'yes, I do. As you know, I've been to see him and talked to him. He's been a vicar here for years and everyone knows him. I suppose a fiend incarnate *could* put on a show of being a kindly vicar, but not for more than about a week or so at the outside, I'd say. Not for about ten or twelve years.'

'Well, then,' said Tuppence, 'the next suspect would be Miss Bligh. Nellie Bligh. Though heaven knows why. She can't have thought I was trying to steal a tombstone.'

'Do you feel it might have been her?'

'Well, I don't really. Of course, she's *competent*. If she wanted to follow me and see what I was doing, and conk me, she'd make a success of it. And like the vicar, she was there – on the spot – She was in Sutton Chancellor, popping in and out of her house to do this and that, and she could have caught sight of me in the churchyard, come up behind me on tiptoe out of curiosity, seen me examining a grave, objected to my doing so for some particular reason, and hit me with one of the church metal flower vases or anything else handy. But don't ask me *why*. There seems no possible reason.'

'Who next, Tuppence? Mrs Cockerell, if that's her name?'

'Mrs Copleigh,' said Tuppence. 'No, it wouldn't be Mrs Copleigh.'

'Now why are you so sure of that? She lives in Sutton Chancellor, she could have seen you go out of the house and she could have followed you.'

'Oh yes, yes, but she talks too much,' said Tuppence.

'I don't see where talking too much comes into it.'

'If you'd listened to her a whole evening as I did,' said Tuppence, 'you'd realize that anyone who talks as much as she does, non-stop in a constant flow, could not possibly be a woman of action as well! She couldn't have come up anywhere near me without talking at the top of her voice as she came.'

Tommy considered this.

'All right,' he said. 'You have good judgement in that kind of thing, Tuppence. Wash out Mrs Copleigh. Who else is there?'

'Amos Perry,' said Tuppence. 'That's the man who lives at

the Canal House. (I have to call it the Canal House because it's got so many other odd names. And it was called that originally.) The husband of the friendly witch. There's something a bit queer about him. He's a bit simple minded and he's a big powerful man, and he could cosh anyone on the head if he wanted to, and I even think it's possible in certain circumstances he might want to – though I don't exactly know why he should want to cosh *me*. He's a better possibility really than Miss Bligh who seems to me just one of those tiresome, efficient women who go about running parishes and poking their noses into things. Not at all the type who would get up to the point of physical attack, except for some wildly emotional reason.' She added, with a slight shiver, 'You know, I felt frightened of Amos Perry the first time I saw him. He was showing me his garden. I felt suddenly that I – well, that I wouldn't like to get on the wrong side of him – or meet him in a dark road at night. I felt he was a man that wouldn't often want to be violent but who could be violent if something took him that way.'

'All right,' said Tommy. 'Amos Perry. Number one.'

'And there's his wife,' said Tuppence slowly. 'The friendly witch. She was nice and I liked her – I don't want it to be her – I don't think it *was* her, but she's mixed up in things, I think . . . Things that have to do with that house. That's another point, you see, Tommy – We don't know what the important thing is in all this – I've begun to wonder whether everything doesn't circulate round that *house* – whether the *house* isn't the central point. The picture – That picture does mean something, doesn't it, Tommy? It must, I think.'

'Yes,' said Tommy, 'I think it must.'

'I came here trying to find Mrs Lancaster – but nobody here seems to have heard of her. I've been wondering whether I got things the wrong way round – that Mrs Lancaster was in danger (because I'm still sure of that) *because she owned that picture*. I don't think *she* was ever in Sutton Chancellor – but she was either given, or she bought, a picture of a house here. And that picture *means* something – is in some way a menace to someone.'

'Mrs Cocoa – Mrs Moody – told Aunt Ada that she recognized someone at Sunny Ridge – someone connected with 'criminal activities'. I think the criminal activities are connected with the picture and with the house by the canal, and a child who perhaps was killed there.'

'Aunt Ada admired Mrs Lancaster's picture – and Mrs Lancaster gave it to her – and perhaps she talked about it – where she got it, or who had given it to her, and where the house was –'

'Mrs Moody was bumped off because she definitely recognized someone who had been "connected with criminal activities".'

'Tell me again about your conversation with Dr Murray,' said Tuppence. 'After telling you about Mrs Cocoa, he went on to talk about certain types of killers, giving examples of real life cases. One was a woman who ran a nursing home for elderly patients – I remember reading about it vaguely, though I can't remember the woman's name. But the idea was that they made over what money they had to her, and then they lived there until they died, well fed and looked after, and without any money worries. And they *were* very happy – only they usually died well within a year – quite peacefully in their sleep. And at last people began to notice. She was tried and convicted of murder – But had no conscience pangs and protested that what she had done was really a kindness to the old dears.'

'Yes. That's right,' said Tommy. 'I can't remember the name of the woman now.'

'Well, never mind about that,' said Tuppence. 'And then he cited another case. A case of a woman, a domestic worker or a cook or a housekeeper. She used to go into service into different families. Sometimes nothing happened, I believe, and sometimes it was a kind of mass poisoning. Food poisoning, it was supposed to be. All with quite reasonable symptoms. Some people recovering.'

'She used to prepare sandwiches,' said Tommy, 'and make them up into packets and send them out for picnics with them. She was very nice and very devoted and she used to get, if it was a mass poisoning, some of the symptoms and signs herself. Probably exaggerating their effect. Then she'd go away after that and she'd take another place, in quite a different part of England. It went on for some years.'

'That's right, yes. Nobody, I believe, has ever been able to understand *why* she did it. Did she get a sort of addiction for it – a sort of habit of it? Was it fun for her? Nobody really ever knew. She never seems to have had any personal malice for any of the people whose deaths she seems to have caused. Bit wrong in the top storey?'

'Yes. I think she must have been, though I suppose one of the trick cyclists would probably do a great deal of analysis and find out it had all something to do with a canary of a family she'd known years and years ago as a child who had given her a shock or upset her or something. But anyway, that's the sort of thing it was.

'The third one was queerer still,' said Tommy. 'A French woman. A woman who'd suffered terribly from the loss of her husband and her child. She was brokenhearted and she was an angel of mercy.'

'That's right,' said Tuppence, 'I remember. They called her the angel of whatever the village was. *Givon* or something like that. She went to all the neighbours and nursed them when they were ill. Particularly she used to go to children when they were ill. She nursed them devotedly. But sooner or later, after apparently a slight recovery, they grew much worse and died. She spent hours crying and went to the funeral crying and everybody said they wouldn't know what they'd have done without the angel who'd nursed their darlings and done everything she could.'

'Why do you want to go over all this again, Tuppence?'

'Because I wondered if Dr Murray had a reason for mentioning them.'

'You mean he connected –'

'I think he connected up three classical cases that are well known, and tried them on, as it were, like a glove, to see if they fitted anyone at Sunny Ridge. I think in a way any of them might have fitted. Miss Packard would fit in with the first one. The efficient matron of a Home.'

'You really have got your knife into that woman. I always liked her.'

'I daresay people *have* liked murderers,' said Tuppence very reasonably. 'It's like swindlers and confidence tricksmen who always look so honest and seem so honest. I daresay murderers all seem very nice and particularly soft-hearted. That sort of thing. Anyway, Miss Packard *is* very efficient and she has all the means to hand whereby she could produce a nice natural death without suspicion. And only someone like Mrs Cocoa would be likely to suspect her. Mrs Cocoa might suspect her because she's a bit batty herself and can understand batty people, or she might have come across her somewhere before.'

'I don't think Miss Packard would profit financially by any of her elderly inmates' deaths.'

'You don't know,' said Tuppence. 'It would be a cleverer way to do it, *not* to benefit from all of them. Just get one or two of them, perhaps, rich ones, to leave you a lot of money, but to always have some deaths that were quite natural as well, and where you didn't get anything. So you see I think that Dr Murray might, just *might*, have cast a glance at Miss Packard and said to himself, "Nonsense, I'm imagining things." But all the same the thought stuck in his mind. The second case he mentioned would fit with a domestic worker, or cook, or even some kind of hospital nurse. Somebody employed in the place, a middle-aged reliable woman, but who was batty in that particular way. Perhaps used to have little grudges, dislikes for some of the patients there. We can't go guessing at that because I don't think we know anyone well enough –'

'And the third one?'

'The third one's more difficult,' Tuppence admitted. 'Someone devoted. Dedicated.'

'Perhaps he just added that for good measure,' said Tommy. He added, 'I wonder about that Irish nurse.'

'The nice one we gave the fur stole to?'

'Yes, the nice one Aunt Ada liked. The very sympathetic one. She seemed so fond of everyone, so sorry if they died. She was very worried when she spoke to us, wasn't she? You said so – she was leaving, and she didn't really tell us why.'

'I suppose she might have been a rather neurotic type. Nurses aren't supposed to be too sympathetic. It's bad for patients. They are told to be cool and efficient and inspire confidence.'

'Nurse Beresford speaking,' said Tommy, and grinned.

'But to come back to the picture,' said Tuppence. 'If we just concentrate on the picture. Because I think it's very interesting what you told me about Mrs Boscowan, when you went to see her. She sounds – she sounds *interesting*.'

'She was interesting,' said Tommy. 'Quite the most interesting person I think we've come across in this unusual business. The sort of person who seems to *know* things, but not by thinking about them. It was as though she knew something about this place that I didn't, and that perhaps you don't. But she knows *something.*'

'It was odd what she said about the boat,' said Tuppence. 'That the picture hadn't had a boat originally. Why do you think it's got a boat now?'

'Oh,' said Tommy, 'I don't know.'

'Was there any name painted on the boat? I don't remember seeing one – but then I never looked at it very closely.'

'It's got *Waterlily* on it.'

'A very appropriate name for a boat – what does that remind me of?'

'I've no idea.'

'And she was quite positive that her husband didn't paint that boat – He could have put it in afterwards.'

'She says *not* – she was very definite.'

'Of course,' said Tuppence, 'there's another possibility we haven't gone into. About my coshing, I mean – the outsider – somebody perhaps who followed me here from Market Basing that day to see what I was up to. Because I'd been there asking all those questions. Going into all those house agents. Blodget & Burgess and all the rest of them. They put me off about the house. They were evasive. More evasive than would be natural. It was the same sort of evasion as we had when we were trying to find out where Mrs Lancaster had gone. Lawyers and banks, an owner who can't be communicated with because he's abroad. The same sort of *pattern.* They send someone to follow my car, they want to see what I am doing, and in due course I am coshed. Which brings us,' said Tuppence, 'to the gravestone in the churchyard. Why didn't anyone want me to look at old gravestones? They were all pulled about anyway – a group of boys, I should say, who'd got bored with wrecking telephone boxes, and went into the churchyard to have some fun and sacrilege behind the church.'

'You say there were painted words – or roughly carved words?'

'Yes – done with a chisel, I should think. Someone who gave it up as a bad job.

'The name – Lily Waters – and the age – seven years old. That was done properly – and then the other bits of words – It looked like "Whosoever . . ." and then "offend least of these" – and – "Millstone" –'

'Sounds familiar.'

'It should do. It's definitely biblical – but done by someone who wasn't quite sure what the words he wanted to remember were –'

'Very odd – the whole thing.'

'And why anyone should object – I was only trying to help the vicar – and the poor man who was trying to find his lost child – There we are – back to the lost child motif again – Mrs Lancaster talked about a poor child walled up behind a fireplace, and Mrs Copleigh chattered about walled-up nuns and murdered children, and a mother who killed a baby, and a lover, and an illegitimate baby, and a suicide – It's all old tales and gossip and hearsay and legends, mixed up in the most glorious kind of hasty pudding! All the same, Tommy, there was one actual *fact* – not just hearsay or legend –'

'You mean?'

'I mean that in the chimney of this Canal House, this old rag doll fell out – A child's doll. It had been there a very, very long time, all covered with soot and rubble –'

'Pity we haven't got it,' said Tommy.

'I *have*,' said Tuppence. She spoke triumphantly.

'You brought it away with you?'

'Yes. It startled me, you know. I thought I'd like to take it and examine it. Nobody wanted it or anything. I should imagine the Perrys would just have thrown it into the ashcan straight away. I've got it here.'

She rose from her sofa, went to her suitcase, rummaged a little and then brought out something wrapped in newspaper.

'Here you are, Tommy, have a look.'

With some curiosity Tommy unwrapped the newspaper. He took out carefully the wreck of a child's doll. It's limp arms and legs hung down, faint festoons of clothing dropped off as he touched them. The body seemed made of a very thin suède leather sewn up over a body that had once been plump with sawdust and now was sagging because here and there the sawdust had escaped. As Tommy handled it, and he was quite gentle in his touch, the body suddenly disintegrated, flapping over in a great wound from which there poured out a cupful of sawdust and with it small pebbles that ran to and fro about the floor. Tommy went round picking them up carefully.

'Good Lord,' he said to himself, 'Good Lord!'

'How odd,' Tuppence said, 'it's full of pebbles. Is that a bit of the chimney disintegrating, do you think? The plaster or something crumbling away?'

'No,' said Tommy. 'These pebbles were *inside* the body.'

He had gathered them up now carefully, he poked his finger into the carcase of the doll and a few more pebbles fell out. He took them over to the window and turned them over in his hand. Tuppence watched him with uncomprehending eyes.

'It's a funny idea, stuffing a doll with pebbles,' she said.

'Well, they're not exactly the usual kind of pebbles,' said Tommy. 'There was a very good reason for it, I should imagine.'

'What do you mean?'

'Have a look at them. Handle a few.'

She took some wonderingly from his hand.

'They're nothing but pebbles,' she said. 'Some are rather large and some small. Why are you so excited?'

'Because, Tuppence, I'm beginning to understand things. Those aren't pebbles, my dear girl, they're *diamonds*.'

CHAPTER 15
....
EVENING AT THE VICARAGE

I

'Diamonds!' Tuppence gasped.

Looking from him to the pebbles she still held in her hand, she said:

'These dusty-looking things, *diamonds*?'

Tommy nodded.

'It's beginning to make sense now, you see, Tuppence. It ties up. The Canal House. The picture. You wait until Ivor Smith hears about that doll. He's got a bouquet waiting for you already, Tuppence –'

'What for?'

'For helping to round up a big criminal gang!'

'You and your Ivor Smith! I suppose that's where you've been all this last week, abandoning me in my last days of convalescence in that dreary hospital – just when I wanted brilliant conversation and a lot of cheering up.'

'I came in visiting hours practically every evening.'

'You didn't tell me much.'

'I was warned by that dragon of a sister not to excite you. But Ivor himself is coming here the day after tomorrow, and we've got a little social evening laid on at the vicarage.'

'Who's coming?'

'Mrs Boscowan, one of the big local landowners, your friend Miss Nellie Bligh, the vicar, of course, you and I –'

'And Mr Ivor Smith – what's his real name?'

'As far as I know, it's Ivor Smith.'

'You are always so cautious –' Tuppence laughed suddenly.

'What's amusing you?'

'I was just thinking that I'd like to have seen you and Albert discovering secret drawers in Aunt Ada's desk.'

'All the credit goes to Albert. He positively delivered a lecture on the subject. He learnt all about it in his youth from an antique dealer.'

'Fancy your Aunt Ada really leaving a secret document like that, all done up with seals all over. She didn't actually know anything, but she was ready to believe there was somebody in Sunny Ridge who was dangerous. I wonder if she knew it was Miss Packard.'

'That's only your idea.'

'It's a very good idea if it's a criminal gang we're looking for. They'd need a place like Sunny Ridge, respectable and well run, with a competent criminal to run it. Someone properly qualified to have access to drugs whenever she needed them. And by accepting any deaths that occurred as quite natural, it would influence a doctor to think they were quite all right.'

'You've got it all taped out, but actually the real reason you started to suspect Miss Packard was because you didn't like her teeth –'

'The better to eat you with,' said Tuppence meditatively. 'I'll tell you something else, Tommy – Supposing this picture – the picture of the Canal House – *never belonged to Mrs Lancaster at all –*'

'But we know it did.' Tommy stared at her.

'No, we don't. We only know that Miss Packard said so – It was Miss Packard who said that Mrs Lancaster gave it to Aunt Ada.'

'But why should –' Tommy stopped –

'Perhaps that's why Mrs Lancaster was taken away – so that she shouldn't tell us that the picture didn't belong to her, and that she didn't give it to Aunt Ada.'

'I think that's a very far-fetched idea.'

'Perhaps – But the picture was painted in Sutton Chancellor – The house in the picture is a house in Sutton Chancellor – We've reason to believe that that house is – or was – used as one of their hidey-holes by a criminal association – Mr Eccles is believed to be the man behind this gang. Mr Eccles was the man responsible for sending Mrs Johnson to remove Mrs Lancaster. I don't believe Mrs Lancaster was ever in Sutton Chancellor, or was ever in the Canal House, or had a picture of it – though I think she heard someone at Sunny Ridge talk about it – Mrs Cocoa perhaps? So she started chattering, and that was dangerous, so she had to be removed. And one day I shall find her! Mark my words, Tommy.'

'The Quest of Mrs Thomas Beresford.'

II

'You look remarkably well, if I may say so, Mrs Tommy,' said Mr Ivor Smith.

'I'm feeling perfectly well again,' said Tuppence. 'Silly of me to let myself get knocked out, I suppose.'

'You deserve a medal – Especially for this doll business. How you get on to these things, I don't know!'

'She's the perfect terrier,' said Tommy. 'Puts her nose down on the trail and off she goes.'

'You're not keeping me out of this party tonight,' said Tuppence suspiciously.

'Certainly not. A certain amount of things, you know, have been cleared up. I can't tell you how grateful I am to you two.

We were getting *somewhere*, mind you, with this remarkably clever association of criminals who have been responsible for a stupendous amount of robberies over the last five or six years. As I told Tommy when he came to ask me if I knew anything about our clever legal gentleman, Mr Eccles, we've had our suspicions of him for a long time but he's not the man you'll easily get evidence against. Too careful by far. He practises as a solicitor – an ordinary genuine business with perfectly genuine clients.

'As I told Tommy, one of the important points has been this chain of houses. Genuine respectable houses with quite genuine respectable people living in them, living there for a short time – then leaving.

'Now, thanks to you, Mrs Tommy, and your investigation of chimneys and dead birds, we've found quite certainly one of those houses. The house where a particular amount of the spoil was concealed. It's been quite a clever system, you know, getting jewels or various things of that kind changed into packets of rough diamonds, hiding them, and then when the time comes they are flown abroad, or taken abroad in fishing boats, when all the hue and cry about one particular robbery has died down.'

'What about the Perrys? Are they – I hope they're not – mixed up in it?'

'One can't be sure,' said Mr Smith. 'No, one can't be sure. It seems likely to me that Mrs Perry, at least, knows something, or certainly knew something once.'

'Do you mean she really is one of the criminals?'

'It mightn't be that. It might be, you know, that they had a hold on her.'

'What sort of hold?'

'Well, you'll keep this confidential, I know you can hold your tongue in these things, but the local police have always had the idea that the husband, Amos Perry, might just possibly have been the man who was responsible for a wave of child murders a good many years ago. He is not fully competent mentally. The medical opinion was that he *might* quite easily have had a compulsion to do away with children. There was never any direct evidence, but his wife was perhaps over-anxious to provide him always with adequate alibis. If so, you see, that might give a gang of unscrupulous people a hold on her and they may have put her in as tenant of part of a house where they knew she'd keep her mouth shut. They may really have had some form of damaging evidence against her husband. You met them – what do you feel about them both, Mrs Tommy?'

'I liked *her*,' said Tuppence. 'I think she was – well, as I say I summed her up as a friendly witch, given to white magic but not black.'

'What about him?'

'I was frightened of him,' said Tuppence. 'Not all the time. Just once or twice. He seemed suddenly to go big and terrifying. Just for a minute or two. I couldn't think what I was frightened of, but I was frightened. I suppose, as you say, I felt that he wasn't quite right in his head.'

'A lot of people are like that,' said Mr Smith. 'And very often they're not dangerous at all. But you can't tell, and you can't be sure.'

'What are we going to do at the vicarage tonight?'

'Ask some questions. See a few people. Find out things that may give us a little more of the information we need.'

'Will Major Waters be there? The man who wrote to the vicar about his child?'

'There doesn't seem to be any such person! There was a coffin buried where the old gravestone had been removed – a child's coffin, lead lined – And it was full of loot. Jewels and gold objects from a burglary near St Albans. The letter to the vicar was with the object of finding out what had happened to the grave. The local lads' sabotage had messed things up.'

III

'I am so deeply sorry, my dear,' said the vicar, coming to meet Tuppence with both hands outstretched. 'Yes, indeed, my dear, I have been so terribly upset that this should happen to you when you have been so kind. When you were doing this to help me. I really felt – yes, indeed I have, that it was all my fault. I shouldn't have let you go poking among gravestones, though really we had no reason to believe – no reason at all – that some band of young hooligans –'

'Now don't disturb yourself, Vicar,' said Miss Bligh, suddenly appearing at his elbow. 'Mrs Beresford knows, I'm sure, that it was nothing to do with *you*. It was indeed extremely kind of her to offer to help, but it's all over now, and she's quite well again. Aren't you, Mrs Beresford?'

'Certainly,' said Tuppence, faintly annoyed, however, that Miss Bligh should answer for her health so confidently.

'Come and sit down here and have a cushion behind your back,' said Miss Bligh.

'I don't need a cushion,' said Tuppence, refusing to accept the chair that Miss Bligh was officiously pulling forward. Instead, she sat down in an upright and exceedingly uncomfortable chair on the other side of the fireplace.

There was a sharp rap on the front door and everyone in the room jumped. Miss Bligh hurried out.

'Don't worry, Vicar,' she said. 'I'll go.'

'Please, if you will be so kind.'

There were low voices outside in the hall, then Miss Bligh came back shepherding a big woman in a brocade shift, and behind her a very tall thin man, a man of cadaverous appearance. Tuppence stared at him. A black cloak was round his shoulders, and his thin gaunt face was like the face from another century. He might have come, Tuppence thought, straight out of an El Greco canvas.

'I'm very pleased to see you,' said the vicar, and turned. 'May I introduce Sir Philip Starke, Mr and Mrs Beresford. Mr Ivor Smith. Ah! Mrs Boscowan. I've not seen you for many, many years – Mr and Mrs Beresford.'

'I've met Mr Beresford,' said Mrs Boscowan. She looked at Tuppence. 'How do you do,' she said. 'I'm glad to meet you. I heard you'd had an accident.'

'Yes. I'm all right again now.'

The introductions completed, Tuppence sat back in her chair. Tiredness swept over her as it seemed to do rather more frequently than formerly, which she said to herself was possibly a result of concussion. Sitting quietly, her eyes half closed, she was nevertheless scrutinizing everyone in the room with close attention. She was not listening to the conversation, she was only looking. She had a feeling that a few of the characters in the drama – the drama in which she had unwittingly involved herself – were assembled here as they might be in a dramatic scene. Things were drawing together, forming themselves into a compact nucleus. With the coming of Sir Philip Starke and Mrs Boscowan it was as though two hitherto unrevealed characters were suddenly presenting themselves. They had been there all along, as it were, outside the circle, but now they had come inside. They were somehow concerned, implicated. They had come here this evening – why, she wondered? Had someone summoned them? Ivor Smith? Had he commanded their presence, or only gently demanded it? Or were they perhaps as strange to him as they were to her? She thought to herself: 'It all began in Sunny Ridge, but Sunny Ridge isn't the real heart of the matter. That was, had always been, here, in Sutton Chancellor. Things had happened here. Not very lately, almost certainly not lately. Long ago. Things which had nothing to do with Mrs Lancaster – but Mrs Lancaster had become unknowingly involved. So where was Mrs Lancaster now?'

A little cold shiver passed over Tuppence.

'I think,' thought Tuppence, 'I think perhaps she's *dead* . . .'

If so, Tuppence felt, she herself had failed. She had set out on her quest worried about Mrs Lancaster, feeling that Mrs Lancaster was threatened with some danger and she had resolved to find Mrs Lancaster, protect her.

'And if she isn't dead,' thought Tuppence, 'I'll still do it!'

Sutton Chancellor . . . That was where the beginning of something meaningful and dangerous had happened. The house with the canal was part of it. Perhaps it was the centre of it all, or was it Sutton Chancellor itself? A place where people had lived, had come to, had left, had run away, had vanished, had disappeared and reappeared. Like Sir Philip Starke.

Without turning her head Tuppence's eyes went to Sir Philip Starke. She knew nothing about him except what Mrs Copleigh had poured out in the course of her monologue on the general inhabitants. A quiet man, a learned man, a botanist, an industrialist, or at least one who owned a big stake in industry. Therefore a rich man – and a man who loved children. There she was, back at it. Children again. The house by the canal and the bird in the chimney, and out of the chimney had fallen a child's doll, shoved up there by someone. A child's doll that held within its skin a handful of diamonds – the proceeds of crime. This was one of the headquarters of a big criminal undertaking. But there had been crimes more sinister than robberies. Mrs Copleigh had said 'I always fancied myself as *he* might have done it.'

Sir Philip Starke. A murderer? Behind her half-closed eyelids, Tuppence studied him with the knowledge clearly in her mind that she was studying him to find out if he fitted in any way with her conception of a murderer – and a child murderer at that.

How old was he, she wondered. Seventy at least, perhaps older. A worn ascetic face. Yes, definitely ascetic. Very definitely a tortured face. Those large dark eyes. El Greco eyes. The emaciated body.

He had come here this evening, why, she wondered? Her eyes went on to Miss Bligh. Sitting a little restlessly in her chair, occasionally moving to push a table nearer someone, to offer a cushion, to move the position of the cigarette box or matches. Restless, ill at ease. She was looking at Philip Starke. Every time she relaxed, her eyes went to him.

'Doglike devotion,' thought Tuppence. 'I think she must have been in love with him once. I think in a way perhaps she still is. You don't stop being in love with anyone because you get old. People like Derek and Deborah think you do. They can't imagine anyone who isn't young being in love. But I think she – I think she is still in love with him, hopelessly, devotedly in love. Didn't someone say – was it Mrs Copleigh or the vicar who had said, that Miss Bligh had been his secretary as a young woman, that she still looked after his affairs here?

'Well,' thought Tuppence, 'it's natural enough. Secretaries often fall in love with their bosses. So say Gertrude Bligh had loved Philip Starke. Was that a useful fact at all? Had Miss Bligh known or suspected that behind Philip Starke's calm ascetic personality there ran a horrifying thread of madness? *So fond of children always.*'

'Too fond of children, I thought,' Mrs Copleigh had said.

Things did take you like that. Perhaps that was a reason for his looking so tortured.

'Unless one is a pathologist or a psychiatrist or something, one doesn't know anything about mad murderers,' thought Tuppence. '*Why* do they want to kill children? What gives them that urge? Are they sorry about it afterwards? Are they disgusted, are they desperately unhappy, are they terrified?'

At that moment she noticed that his gaze had fallen on her. His eyes met hers and seemed to leave some message.

'You are thinking about me,' those eyes said. 'Yes, it's true what you are thinking. I am a haunted man.'

Yes, that described him exactly – He was a haunted man.

She wrenched her eyes away. Her gaze went to the vicar. She liked the vicar. He was a dear. Did he know anything? He might, Tuppence thought, or he might be living in the middle of some evil tangle that he never even suspected. Things happened all round him, perhaps, but he wouldn't know about them, because he had that rather disturbing quality of innocence.

Mrs Boscowan? But Mrs Boscowan was difficult to know anything about. A middle-aged woman, a personality, as Tommy had said, but that didn't express enough. As though Tuppence had summoned her, Mrs Boscowan rose suddenly to her feet.

'Do you mind if I go upstairs and have a wash?' she said.

'Oh! of course.' Miss Bligh jumped to her feet. 'I'll take you up, shall I, Vicar?'

'I know my way perfectly,' said Mrs Boscowan. 'Don't bother – Mrs Beresford?'

Tuppence jumped slightly.

'I'll show you,' said Mrs Boscowan, 'where things are. Come with me.'

Tuppence got up as obediently as a child. She did not describe it so to herself. But she knew that she had been summoned and when Mrs Boscowan summoned, you obeyed.

By then Mrs Boscowan was through the door to the hall and Tuppence had followed her. Mrs Boscowan started up the stairs – Tuppence came up behind her.

'The spare room is at the top of the stairs,' said Mrs Boscowan. 'It's always kept ready. It has a bathroom leading out of it.'

She opened the door at the top of the stairs, went through, switched on the light and Tuppence followed her in.

'I'm very glad to have found you here,' said Mrs Boscowan. 'I hoped I should. I was worried about you. Did your husband tell you?'

'I gathered you'd said something,' said Tuppence.

'Yes, I was worried.' She closed the door behind them, shutting them, as it were, into a private place of private consultation. 'Have you felt at all,' said Emma Boscowan, 'that Sutton Chancellor is a dangerous place?'

'It's been dangerous for me,' said Tuppence.

'Yes, I know. It's lucky it wasn't worse, but then – yes, I think I can understand that.'

'You know something,' said Tuppence. 'You know something about all this, don't you?'

'In a way,' said Emma Boscowan, 'in a way I do, and in a way I don't. One has instincts, feelings, you know. When they turn out to be right, it's worrying. This whole criminal gang business, it seems so extraordinary. It doesn't seem to have anything to do with –' She stopped abruptly.

'I mean, it's just one of those things that are going on – that have always gone on really. But they're very well organized now, like businesses. There's nothing really dangerous, you know, not about the criminal part of it. It's the *other*. It's knowing just where the danger is and how to guard against it. You must be careful, Mrs Beresford, you really must. You're one of those people who rush into things and it wouldn't be safe to do that. Not here.'

Tuppence said slowly, 'My old aunt – or rather Tommy's old aunt, she wasn't mine – someone told her in the nursing home where she died – that there was a killer.'

Emma nodded her head slowly.

'There were two deaths in that nursing home,' said Tuppence, 'and the doctor isn't satisfied about them.'

'Is that what started you off?'

'No,' said Tuppence, 'it was before that.'

'If you have time,' said Emma Boscowan, 'will you tell me very quickly – as quickly as you can because someone may interrupt us – just what happened at that nursing home or old ladies' home or whatever it was, to start you off?'

'Yes, I can tell you very quickly,' said Tuppence. She proceeded to do so.

'I see,' said Emma Boscowan. 'And you don't know where this old lady, this Mrs Lancaster, is now?'

'No, I don't.'

'Do you think she's dead?'

'I think she – might be.'

'Because she knew something?'

'Yes. She knew about something. Some murder. Some child perhaps who was killed.'

'I think you've gone wrong there,' said Mrs Boscowan. 'I think the child got mixed up in it and perhaps she got it mixed up. Your old lady, I mean. She got the child mixed up with something else, some other kind of killing.'

'I suppose it's possible. Old people do get mixed up. But there *was* a child murderer loose here, wasn't there? Or so the woman I lodged with here said.'

'There were several child murders in this part of the country, yes. But that was a good long time ago, you know. I'm not sure. The vicar wouldn't know. He wasn't here then. But Miss Bligh was. Yes, yes, she must have been here. She must have been a fairly young girl then.'

'I suppose so.'

Tuppence said, 'Has she always been in love with Sir Philip Starke?'

'You saw that, did you? Yes, I think so. Completely devoted beyond idolatry. We noticed it when we first came here, William and I.'

'What made you come here? Did you live in the Canal House?'

'No, we never lived there. He liked to paint it. He painted it several times. What's happened to the picture your husband showed me?'

'He brought it home again,' said Tuppence. 'He told me what you said about the boat – that your husband didn't paint it – the boat called *Waterlily* –'

'Yes. It wasn't painted by my husband. When I last saw the picture there was no boat there. Somebody painted it in.'

'And called it *Waterlily* – And a man who didn't exist, Major *Waters* – wrote about a child's grave – a child called Lilian – but there was no child buried in that grave, only a child's coffin, full of the proceeds of a big robbery. The painting of the boat must have been a message – a message to say where the loot was hidden – It all seems to tie up with crime . . .'

'It seems to, yes – But one can't be sure what –'

Emma Boscowan broke off abruptly. She said quickly, 'She's coming up to find us. Go into the bathroom –'

'Who?'

'Nellie Bligh. Pop into the bathroom – bolt the door.'

'She's just a busybody,' said Tuppence, disappearing into the bathroom.

'Something a little more than that,' said Mrs Boscowan.

Miss Bligh opened the door and came in, brisk and helpful.

'Oh, I hope you found everything you wanted?' she said. 'There were fresh towels and soap, I hope? Mrs Copleigh comes in to look after the vicar, but I really have to see she does things properly.'

Mrs Boscowan and Miss Bligh went downstairs together. Tuppence joined them just as they reached the drawing-room door. Sir Philip Starke rose as she came into the room, rearranged her chair and sat down beside her.

'Is that the way you like it, Mrs Beresford?'

'Yes, thank you,' said Tuppence. 'It's very comfortable.'

'I'm sorry to hear –' his voice had a vague charm to it, though it had some elements of a ghostlike voice, far-away, lacking in resonance, yet with a curious depth – 'about your accident,' he said. 'It's so sad nowadays – all the accidents there are.'

His eyes were wandering over her face and she thought to herself, 'He's making just as much a study of me as I made of him.' She gave a sharp half-glance at Tommy, but Tommy was talking to Emma Boscowan.

'What made you come to Sutton Chancellor in the first place, Mrs Beresford?'

'Oh, we're looking for a house in the country in a vague sort of way,' said Tuppence. 'My husband was away from home attending some congress or other and I thought I'd have a tour round a likely part of the countryside – just to see what there was going, and the kind of price one would have to pay, you know.'

'I hear you went and looked at the house by the canal bridge?'

'Yes, I did. I believe I'd once noticed it from the train. It's a very attractive-looking house – from the outside.'

'Yes. I should imagine, though, that even the outside needs a great deal doing to it, to the roof and things like that. Not so attractive on the wrong side, is it?'

'No, it seems to me a curious way to divide up a house.'

'Oh well,' said Philip Starke, 'people have different ideas, don't they?'

'You never lived in it, did you?' asked Tuppence.

'No, no, indeed. My house was burnt down many years ago. There's part of it left still. I expect you've seen it or had it pointed out to you. It's above this vicarage, you know, a bit up the hill. At least what they call a hill in this part of the world. It was never much to boast of. My father built it way back in 1890 or so. A proud mansion. Gothic overlays, a touch of Balmoral. Our architects nowadays rather admire that kind of thing again, though actually forty years ago it was shuddered at. It had everything a so-called gentleman's house ought to have.' His voice was gently ironic. 'A billiard room, a morning room, ladies' parlour, colossal dining-room, a ballroom, about fourteen bedrooms, and once had – or so I should imagine – a staff of fourteen servants to look after it.'

'You sound as though you never liked it much yourself.'

'I never did. I was a disappointment to my father. He was a very successful industrialist. He hoped I would follow in his footsteps. I didn't. He treated me very well. He gave me a large income, or allowance – as it used to be called – and let me go my own way.'

'I heard you were a botanist.'

'Well, that was one of my great relaxations. I used to go looking for wild flowers, especially in the Balkans. Have you ever been to the Balkans looking for wild flowers? It's a wonderful place for them.'

'It sounds very attractive. Then you used to come back and live here?'

'I haven't lived here for a great many years now. In fact, I've never been back to live here since my wife died.'

'Oh,' said Tuppence, slightly embarrassed. 'Oh, I'm – I'm sorry.'

'It's quite a long time ago now. She died before the war. In 1938. She was a very beautiful woman,' he said.

'Do you have pictures of her in your house here still?'

'Oh no, the house is empty. All the furniture, pictures and things were sent away to be stored. There's just a bedroom and an office and a sitting-room where my agent comes, or I come if I have to come down here and see to any estate business.'

'It's never been sold?'

'No. There's some talk of having a development of the land there. I don't know. Not that I have any feeling for it. My father hoped that he was starting a kind of feudal domain. I was to succeed him and my children were to succeed me and so on and so on and so on.' He paused a minute and said then, 'But Julia and I never had any children.'

'Oh,' said Tuppence softly, 'I see.'

'So there's nothing to come here for. In fact I hardly ever do. Anything that needs to be done here Nellie Bligh does for me.' He smiled over at her. 'She's been the most wonderful secretary. She still attends to my business affairs or anything of that kind.'

'You never come here and yet you don't want to sell it?' said Tuppence.

'There's a very good reason why not,' said Philip Starke.

A faint smile passed over the austere features.

'Perhaps after all I do inherit some of my father's business sense. The land, you know, is improving enormously in value. It's a better investment than money would be, if I sold it. Appreciates every day. Some day, who knows, we'll have a grand new dormitory town built on that land.'

'Then you'll be rich?'

'Then I'll be an even richer man than I am at present,' said Sir Philip. 'And I'm quite rich enough.'

'What do you do most of the time?'

'I travel, and I have interests in London. I have a picture gallery there. I'm by way of being an art dealer. All those things are interesting. They occupy one's time – till the moment when the hand is laid on your shoulder which says "Depart".'

'Don't,' said Tuppence. 'That sounds – it gives me the shivers.'

'It needn't give you the shivers. I think you're going to have a long life, Mrs Beresford, and a very happy one.'

'Well, I'm very happy at present,' said Tuppence. 'I suppose I shall get all the aches and pains and troubles that old people do get. Deaf and blind and arthritis and a few other things.'

'You probably won't mind them as much as you think you will. If I may say so, without being rude, you and your husband seem to have a very happy life together.'

'Oh, we have,' said Tuppence. 'I suppose really,' she said, 'there's nothing in life like being happily married, is there?'

A moment later she wished she had not uttered these words. When she looked at the man opposite her, who she felt had grieved for so many years and indeed might still be grieving for the loss of a very much loved wife, she felt even more angry with herself.

CHAPTER 16

THE MORNING AFTER

I

It was the morning after the party.

Ivor Smith and Tommy paused in their conversation and looked at each other, then they looked at Tuppence. Tuppence was staring into the grate. Her mind looked far away.

'Where have we got to?' said Tommy.

With a sigh Tuppence came back from where her thoughts had been wandering, and looked at the two men.

'It seems all tied up still to me,' she said. 'The party last night? What was it for? What did it all mean?' She looked at Ivor Smith. 'I suppose it meant something to you two. You know where we are?'

'I wouldn't go as far as that,' said Ivor. 'We're not all after the same thing, are we?'

'Not quite,' said Tuppence.

The men both looked at her inquiringly.

'All right,' said Tuppence. 'I'm a woman with an obsession. *I want to find Mrs Lancaster*. I want to be sure that she's all right.'

'You want to find Mrs Johnson first,' said Tommy. 'You'll never find Mrs Lancaster till you find Mrs Johnson.'

'Mrs Johnson,' said Tuppence. 'Yes, I wonder – But I suppose none of that part of it interests you,' she said to Ivor Smith.

'Oh it does, Mrs Tommy, it does very much.'

'What about Mr Eccles?'

Ivor smiled. 'I think,' he said, 'that retribution might be over-taking Mr Eccles shortly. Still, I wouldn't bank on it. He's a man who covers his tracks with incredible ingenuity. So much so, that one imagines that there aren't really any tracks at all.' He added thoughtfully under his breath, 'A great administrator. A great planner.'

'Last night –' began Tuppence, and hesitated – 'Can I ask questions?'

'You can ask them,' Tommy told her. 'But don't bank on getting any satisfactory answers from old Ivor here.'

'Sir Philip Starke,' said Tuppence – 'Where does he come in? He doesn't seem to fit as a likely criminal – unless he was the kind that –'

She stopped, hastily biting off a reference to Mrs Copleigh's wilder suppositions as to child murderers –

'Sir Philip Starke comes in as a very valuable source of information,' said Ivor Smith. 'He's the biggest landowner in these parts – and in other parts of England as well.'

'In Cumberland?'

Ivor Smith looked at Tuppence sharply. 'Cumberland? Why do you mention Cumberland? What do you know about Cumberland, Mrs Tommy?'

'Nothing,' said Tuppence. 'For some reason or other it just came into my head.' She frowned and looked perplexed. 'And a red and white striped rose on the side of a house – one of those old-fashioned roses.'

She shook her head.

'Does Sir Philip Starke own the Canal House?'

'He owns the land – He owns most of the land hereabouts.'

'Yes, he said so last night.'

'Through him, we've learned a good deal about leases and tenancies that have been cleverly obscured through legal complexities –'

'Those house agents I went to see in the Market Square – Is there something phony about them, or did I imagine it?'

'You didn't imagine it. We're going to pay them a visit this morning. We are going to ask some rather awkward questions.'

'Good,' said Tuppence.

'We're doing quite nicely. We've cleared up the big post office robbery of 1965, and the Albury Cross robberies, and the Irish Mail train business. We've found some of the loot. Clever places they manufactured in these houses. A new bath installed in one, a service flat made in another – a couple of its rooms a little smaller than they ought to have been thereby providing for an interesting recess. Oh yes, we've found out a great deal.'

'But what about the *people*?' said Tuppence. 'I mean the people who thought of it, or ran it – apart from Mr Eccles, I mean. There must have been others who knew something.'

'Oh yes. There were a couple of men – one who ran a night club, conveniently just off the M1. Happy Hamish they used to call him. Slippery as an eel. And a woman they called Killer Kate – but that was a long time ago – one of our more interesting criminals. A beautiful girl, but her mental balance was doubtful. They eased her out – she might have become a danger to them. They were a strictly business concern – in it for loot – not for murder.'

'And was the Canal House one of their hideaway places?'

'At one time, Ladymead, they called it then. It's had a lot of different names in its time.'

'Just to make things more difficult, I suppose,' said Tuppence. 'Ladymead. I wonder if that ties up with some particular thing.'

'What should it tie up with?'

'Well, it doesn't really,' said Tuppence. 'It just started off another hare in my mind, if you know what I mean. The trouble is,' she added, 'I don't really know what I mean myself now. The picture, too. Boscowan painted the picture and then somebody else painted a boat into it, with a name on the boat –'

'*Tiger Lily.*'

'No, *Waterlily*. And his wife says that he didn't paint the boat.'

'Would she know?'

'I expect she would. If you were married to a painter, and especially if you were an artist yourself, I think you'd know if it was a different style of painting. She's rather frightening, I think,' said Tuppence.

'Who – Mrs Boscowan?'

'Yes. If you know what I mean, powerful. Rather over-whelming.'

'Possibly. Yes.'

'She knows things,' said Tuppence, 'but I'm not sure that she knows them because she knows them, if you know what I mean.'

'I don't,' said Tommy firmly.

'Well, I mean, there's one way of knowing things. The other way is that you sort of feel them.'

'That's rather the way you go in for, Tuppence.'

'You can say what you like,' said Tuppence, apparently following her own track of thought, 'the whole thing ties up round Sutton Chancellor. Round Ladymead, or Canal House or whatever you like to call it. And all the people who lived there, now and in past times. Some things I think might go back a long way.'

'You're thinking of Mrs Copleigh.'

'On the whole,' said Tuppence, 'I think Mrs Copleigh just put in a lot of things which have made everything more difficult. I think she's got all her times and dates mixed up too.'

'People do,' said Tommy, 'in the country.'

'I know that,' said Tuppence, 'I was brought up in a country vicarage, after all. They date things by events, they don't date them by years. They don't say "that happened in 1930" or "that happened in 1925" or things like that. They say "that happened the year after the old mill burned down" or "that happened after the lightning struck the big oak and killed Farmer James" or "that was the year we had the polio epidemic". So naturally, of course, the things they do remember don't go in any particular sequence. Everything's very difficult,' she added. 'There are just bits poking up here and there, if you know what I mean. Of course the point is,' said Tuppence with the air of someone who suddenly makes an important discovery, 'the trouble is that I'm old myself.'

'You are eternally young,' said Ivor gallantly.

'Don't be daft,' said Tuppence, scathingly. 'I'm old because I remember things that same way. I've gone back to being primitive in my aids to memory.'

She got up and walked round the room.

'This is an annoying kind of hotel,' she said.

She went through the door into her bedroom and came back again shaking her head.

'No Bible,' she said.

'Bible?'

'Yes. You know, in old-fashioned hotels, they've always got a Gideon Bible by your bed. I suppose so that you can get saved any moment of the day or night. Well, they don't have that here.'

'Do you want a Bible?'

'Well, I do rather. I was brought up properly and I used to know my Bible quite well, as any good clergyman's daughter should. But now, you see, one rather forgets. Especially as they don't read the lessons properly any more in churches. They give you some new version where all the wording, I suppose, is technically right and a proper translation, but sounds nothing like it used to. While you two go to the house agents, I shall drive into Sutton Chancellor,' she added.

'What for? I forbid you,' said Tommy.

'Nonsense – I'm not going to sleuth. I shall just go into the church and look at the Bible. If it's some modern version, I shall go and ask the vicar, he'll have a Bible, won't he? The proper kind, I mean. Authorized Version.'

'What do you want the Authorized Version for?'

'I just want to refresh my memory over those words that were scratched on the child's tombstone . . . They interested me.'

'It's all very well – but I don't trust you, Tuppence – don't trust you not to get into trouble once you're out of my sight.'

'I give you my word I'm not going to prowl about in graveyards any more. The church on a sunny morning and the vicar's study – that's all – what could be more harmless?'

Tommy looked at his wife doubtfully and gave in.

II

Having left her car by the lych-gate at Sutton Chancellor, Tuppence looked round her carefully before entering the church precincts. She had the natural distrust of one who has suffered grievous bodily harm in a certain geographical spot. There did not on this occasion seem to be any possible assailants lurking behind the tombstones.

She went into the church, where an elderly woman was on her knees polishing some brasses. Tuppence tiptoed up to the lectern and made a tentative examination of the volume that rested there. The woman cleaning the brasses looked up with a disapproving glance.

'I'm not going to steal it,' said Tuppence reassuringly, and carefully closing it again, she tiptoed out of the church.

She would have liked to examine the spot where the recent

excavations had taken place, but that she had undertaken on no account to do.

'*Whosoever shall offend*,' she murmured to herself. 'It might mean that, but if so it would have to be someone –'

She drove the car the short distance to the vicarage, got out and went up the path to the front door. She rang but could hear no tinkle from inside. 'Bell's broken, I expect,' said Tuppence, knowing the habits of vicarage bells. She pushed the door and it responded to her touch.

She stood inside in the hall. On the hall table a large envelope with a foreign stamp took up a good deal of space. It bore the printed legend of a Missionary Society in Africa.

'I'm glad I'm not a missionary,' thought Tuppence.

Behind that vague thought, there lay something else, something connected with some hall table somewhere, something that she ought to remember . . . Flowers? Leaves? Some letter or parcel?

At that moment the vicar came out from the door on the left.

'Oh,' he said. 'Do you want me? I – oh, it's Mrs Beresford, isn't it?'

'Quite right,' said Tuppence. 'What I really came to ask you was whether by any chance you had a Bible.'

'Bible,' said the vicar, looking rather unexpectedly doubtful. 'A Bible.'

'I thought it likely that you might have,' said Tuppence.

'Of course, of course,' said the vicar. 'As a matter of fact, I suppose I've got several. I've got a Greek Testament,' he said hopefully. 'That's not what you want, I suppose?'

'No,' said Tuppence. 'I want,' she said firmly, 'the Authorized Version.'

'Oh dear,' said the vicar. 'Of course, there must be several in the house. Yes, several. We don't use that version in the church now, I'm sorry to say. One has to fall in with the bishop's ideas, you know, and the bishop is very keen on modernization, for young people and all that. A pity, I think. I have so many books in my library here that some of them, you know, get pushed behind the others. But I *think* I can find you what you want. I *think* so. If not, we'll ask Miss Bligh. She's here somewhere looking out the vases for the children who arrange their wild flowers for the Children's Corner in the church.' He left Tuppence in the hall and went back into the room where he had come from.

Tuppence did not follow him. She remained in the hall, frowning and thinking. She looked up suddenly as the door at the end of the hall opened and Miss Bligh came through it. She was holding up a very heavy metal vase.

Several things clicked together in Tuppence's head.

'Of course,' said Tuppence, '*of course.*'

'Oh, can I help – I – oh, it's Mrs Beresford.'

'Yes,' said Tuppence, and added, 'And *it's Mrs Johnson, isn't it?*'

The heavy vase fell to the floor. Tuppence stooped and picked it up. She stood weighing it in her hand. 'Quite a handy weapon,' she said. She put it down. 'Just the thing to cosh anyone with from behind,' she said – 'That's what you did to me, didn't you, *Mrs Johnson.*'

'I – I – what did you say? I – I – I never –'

But Tuppence had no need to stay longer. She had seen the effect of her words. At the second mention of Mrs Johnson, Miss Bligh had given herself away in an unmistakable fashion. She was shaking and panic-stricken.

'There was a letter on your hall table the other day,' said Tuppence, 'addressed to a Mrs Yorke at an address in Cumberland. That's where you took her, isn't it, Mrs Johnson, when you took her away from Sunny Ridge? That's where she is now. Mrs Yorke or Mrs Lancaster – you used either name – York and Lancaster like the striped red and white rose in the Perrys' garden –'

She turned swiftly and went out of the house leaving Miss Bligh in the hall, still supporting herself on the stair rail, her mouth open, staring after her. Tuppence ran down the path to the gate, jumped into her car and drove away. She looked back towards the front door, but no one emerged. Tuppence drove past the church and back towards Market Basing, but suddenly changed her mind. She turned the car, drove back the way she had come, and took the left-hand road leading to the Canal House bridge. She abandoned the car, looked over the gate to see if either of the Perrys were in the garden, but there was no sign of them. She went through the gate and up the path to the back door.

That was closed too and the windows were shut.

Tuppence felt annoyed. Perhaps Alice Perry had gone to Market Basing to shop. She particularly wanted to see Alice Perry. Tuppence knocked at the door, rapping first gently then loudly. Nobody answered. She turned the handle but the door did not give. It was locked. She stood there, undecided.

There were some questions she wanted badly to ask Alice Perry. Possibly Mrs Perry might be in Sutton Chancellor. She might go back there. The difficulty of Canal House was that there never seemed to be anyone in sight and hardly any traffic came over the bridge. There was no one to ask where the Perrys might be this morning.

CHAPTER 17

MRS LANCASTER

I

Tuppence stood there frowning, and then, suddenly, quite unexpectedly, the door opened. Tuppence drew back a step and gasped. The person confronting her was the last person in the world she expected to see. In the doorway, dressed exactly the same as she had been at Sunny Ridge, and smiling the same way with that air of vague amiability, was Mrs Lancaster in person.

'Oh,' said Tuppence.

'Good morning. Were you wanting Mrs Perry?' said Mrs Lancaster. 'It's market day, you know. So lucky I was able to let you in. I couldn't find the key for some time. I think it must be a duplicate anyway, don't you? But do come in. Perhaps you'd like a cup of tea or something.'

Like one in a dream, Tuppence crossed the threshold. Mrs Lancaster, still retaining the gracious air of a hostess, led Tuppence along into the sitting-room.

'Do sit down,' she said. 'I'm afraid I don't know where all the cups and things are. I've only been here a day or two. Now – let me see . . . But – surely – I've met you before, haven't I?'

'Yes,' said Tuppence, 'when you were at Sunny Ridge.'

'Sunny Ridge, now, Sunny Ridge. That seems to remind me

of something. Oh, of course, dear Miss Packard. Yes, a very nice place.'

'You left it in rather a hurry, didn't you?' said Tuppence.

'People are so very bossy,' said Mrs Lancaster. 'They hurry you so. They don't give you time to *arrange* things or *pack* properly or *anything*. Kindly meant, I'm sure. Of course, I'm very fond of dear Nellie Bligh, but she's a very masterful kind of woman. I sometimes think,' Mrs Lancaster added, bending forward to Tuppence, 'I sometimes think, you know, that she is not quite –' she tapped her forehead significantly. 'Of course it *does* happen. Especially to spinsters. Unmarried women, you know. Very given to good works and all that but they take very odd fancies sometimes. Curates suffer a great deal. They seem to think sometimes, these women, that the curate has made them an offer of marriage but really he never thought of doing anything of the kind. Oh yes, poor Nellie. So sensible in some ways. She's been wonderful in the parish here. And she was always a first-class secretary, I believe. But all the same she has some very curious ideas at times. Like taking me away at a moment's notice from dear Sunny Ridge, and then up to Cumberland – a very bleak house, and, again quite suddenly, bringing me here –'

'Are you living here?' said Tuppence.

'Well, if you can *call* it that. It's a very peculiar arrangement altogether. I've only been here two days.'

'Before that, you were at Rosetrellis Court, in Cumberland –'

'Yes, I believe that was the name of it. Not such a pretty name as Sunny Ridge, do you think? In fact I never really settled down, if you know what I mean. And it wasn't nearly as well run. The service wasn't as good and they had a very inferior brand of coffee. Still, I was getting used to things and I had found one or two interesting acquaintances there. One of them who knew an aunt of mine quite well years ago in India. It's so nice, you know, when you find *connections*.'

'It must be,' said Tuppence.

Mrs Lancaster continued cheerfully.

'Now let me see, you came to Sunny Ridge, but not to stay, I think. I think you came to see one of the guests there.'

'My husband's aunt,' said Tuppence, 'Miss Fanshawe.'

'Oh yes. Yes of course. I remember now. And wasn't there something about a child of yours behind the chimney piece?'

'No,' said Tuppence, 'no, it wasn't my child.'

'But that's why you've come here, isn't it? They've had trouble with a chimney here. A bird got into it, I understand. This place wants repairing. I don't like being here at *all*. No, not at all and I shall tell Nellie so as soon as I see her.'

'You're lodging with Mrs Perry?'

'Well, in a way I am, and in a way I'm not. I think I could trust you with a secret, couldn't I?'

'Oh yes,' said Tuppence, 'you can trust me.'

'Well, I'm not really here at all. I mean not in this part of the house. This is the Perrys' part of the house.' She leaned forward. 'There's another one, you know, if you go upstairs. Come with me. I'll take you.'

Tuppence rose. She felt that she was in rather a crazy kind of dream.

'I'll just lock the door first, it's safer,' said Mrs Lancaster.

She led Tuppence up a rather narrow staircase to the first floor. She took her through a double bedroom with signs of occupation – presumably the Perrys' room – and through a door leading out of that into another room next door. It contained a washstand and a tall wardrobe of maple wood. Nothing else. Mrs Lancaster went to the maple wardrobe, fumbled at the back of it, then with sudden ease pushed it aside. There seemed to be castors on the wardrobe and it rolled out from the wall easily enough. Behind the wardrobe there was, rather strangely, Tuppence thought, a grate. Over the mantelpiece there was a mirror with a small shelf under the mirror on which were china figures of birds.

To Tuppence's astonishment Mrs Lancaster seized the bird in the middle of the mantelshelf and gave it a sharp pull. Apparently the bird was stuck to the mantelpiece. In fact, by a swift touch Tuppence perceived that all the birds were firmly fastened down. But as a result of Mrs Lancaster's action there was a click and the whole mantelpiece came away from the wall and swung forward.

'Clever, isn't it?' said Mrs Lancaster. 'It was done a long time ago, you know, when they altered the house. The priest's hole, you know, they used to call this room but I don't think it was really a priest's hole. No, nothing to do with priests. I've never thought so. Come through. This is where I live now.'

She gave another push. The wall in front of her also swung back and a minute or two later they were in a large attractive-looking room with windows that gave out on the canal and the hill opposite.

'A lovely room, isn't it?' said Mrs Lancaster. 'Such a lovely view. I always liked it. I lived here for a time as a girl, you know.'

'Oh, I see.'

'Not a lucky house,' said Mrs Lancaster. 'No, they always said it wasn't a lucky house. I think, you know,' she added, 'I think I'll shut up this again. One can't be too careful, can one?'

She stretched out a hand and pushed the door they had come through back again. There was a sharp click as the mechanism swung into place.

'I suppose,' said Tuppence, 'that this was one of the alterations they made to the house when they wanted to use it as a hiding place.'

'They did a lot of alterations,' said Mrs Lancaster. 'Sit down, do. Do you like a high chair or a low one? I like a high one myself. I'm rather rheumatic, you know. I suppose you thought there might have been a child's body there,' added Mrs Lancaster. 'An absurd idea really, don't you think so?'

'Yes, perhaps.'

'Cops and robbers,' said Mrs Lancaster, with an indulgent air. 'One is so foolish when one is young, you know. All that sort of thing. Gangs – big robberies – it has such an appeal for one when one is young. One thinks being a gunman's moll would be the most wonderful thing in the world. I thought so once. Believe me –' she leaned forward and tapped Tuppence on the knee '– believe me, *it's not true*. It isn't really. I thought so once, but one wants more than that, you know. There's no thrill really in just stealing things and getting away with it. It needs good organization, of course.'

'You mean Mrs Johnson or Miss Bligh – whichever you call her –'

'Well, of course, she's always Nellie Bligh to me. But for some reason or other – to facilitate things, she says – she calls herself

Mrs Johnson now and then. But she's never been married, you know. Oh no. She's a regular spinster.'

A sound of knocking came to them from below.

'Dear me,' said Mrs Lancaster, 'that must be the Perrys back again. I'd no idea they were going to be back so soon.'

The knocking went on.

'Perhaps we ought to let them in,' suggested Tuppence.

'No, dear, we won't do that,' said Mrs Lancaster. 'I can't stand people always interfering. We're having such a nice little talk up here, aren't we? I think we'll just stay up here – oh dear, now they're calling under the window. Just look out and see who it is.'

Tuppence went to the window.

'It's Mr Perry,' she said.

From below, Mr Perry shouted,

'Julia! Julia!'

'Impertinence,' said Mrs Lancaster. 'I don't allow people like Amos Perry to call me by my Christian name. No, indeed. Don't worry, dear,' she added, 'we're quite safe here. And we can have a nice little talk. I'll tell you all about myself – I've really had a very interesting life – Eventful – Sometimes I think I ought to write it down. I was mixed up, you see. I was a wild girl, and I was mixed up with – well, really just a common gang of criminals. No other word for it. Some of them *very* undesirable people. Mind you, there *were* nice people among them. Quite good class.'

'Miss Bligh?'

'No, no, Miss Bligh never had anything to do with crime. Not Nellie Bligh. Oh no, she's very churchy, you know. Religious: All that. But there are different ways of religion. Perhaps you know that, do you?'

'I suppose there are a lot of different sects,' Tuppence suggested.

'Yes, there have to be, for ordinary people. But there are others besides ordinary people. There are some special ones, under special commands. There are special legions. Do you understand what I mean, my dear?'

'I don't think I do,' said Tuppence. 'Don't you think we ought to let the Perrys into their own house? They're getting rather upset –'

'No, we're not going to let the Perrys in. Not till – well, not till I've told you all about it. You mustn't be frightened, my dear. It's all quite – quite natural, quite harmless. There's no pain of any kind. It'll be just like going to sleep. Nothing worse.'

Tuppence stared at her, then she jumped up and went towards the door in the wall.

'You can't get out that way,' said Mrs Lancaster. 'You don't know where the catch is. It's not where you think it is at all. Only I know that. I know all the secrets of this place. I lived here with the criminals when I was a girl until I went away from them all and got salvation. Special salvation. That's what was given to me – to expiate my sin – The child, you know – I killed it. I was a dancer – I didn't want a child – Over there, on the wall – that's my picture – as a dancer –'

Tuppence followed the pointing finger. On the wall hung an oil painting, full length, of a girl in a costume of white satin leaves with the legend 'Waterlily'.

'Waterlily was one of my best roles. Everyone said so.'

Tuppence came back slowly and sat down. She stared at Mrs Lancaster. As she did so words repeated in her head. Words heard at Sunny Ridge. '*Was it your poor child?*' She had been frightened then, frightened. She was frightened now. She was as yet not quite sure what she was frightened of, but the same fear was there. Looking at that benignant face, that kindly smile.

'I had to obey the commands given me – There have to be agents of destruction. I was appointed to that. I accepted my appointment. They go free of sin, you see. I mean, the children went free of sin. They were not old enough to sin. So I sent them to Glory as I was appointed to do. Still innocent. Still not knowing evil. You can see what a great honour it was to be chosen. To be one of the specially chosen. I always loved children. I had none of my own. That was very cruel, wasn't it, or it seemed cruel. But it was retribution really for what I'd done. You know perhaps what I'd done.'

'No,' said Tuppence.

'Oh, you seem to know so much. I thought perhaps you'd know that too. There was a doctor. I went to him. I was only seventeen then and I was frightened. He said it would be all right to have the child taken away so that nobody would ever know. But it wasn't all right, you see. I began to have dreams. I had dreams that the child was always there, asking me why it had never had life. The child told me it wanted companions. It was a girl, you know. Yes, I'm sure it was a girl. She came and she wanted other children. Then I got the command. *I* couldn't have any children. I'd married and I thought I'd have children, then my husband wanted children passionately but the children never came, because I was cursed, you see. You understand that, don't you? But there was a way, a way to atone. To atone for what I'd done. What I'd done was murder, wasn't it, and you could only atone for murder with other murders, because the other murders wouldn't be really murders, they would be *sacrifices*. They would be offered up. You do see the difference, don't you? The children went to keep my child company. Children of different ages but young. The command would come and then –' she leaned forward and touched Tuppence '– it was such a happy thing to do. You understand that, don't you? It was so happy to release them so that they'd never know sin like I knew sin. I couldn't tell anyone, of course, nobody was ever to know. That was the thing I had to be sure about. But there were people sometimes who got to know or to suspect. Then of course – well, I mean it had to be death for them too, so that *I* should be safe. So I've always been quite safe. You understand, don't you?'

'Not – not quite.'

'But you do *know*. That's why you came here, isn't it? You knew. You knew the day I asked you at Sunny Ridge. I saw by your face. I said "Was it your poor child?" I thought you'd come, perhaps because you were a mother. One of those whose children I'd killed. I hoped you'd come back another time and then we'd have a glass of milk together. It was usually milk. Sometimes cocoa. Anyone who knew about me.'

She moved slowly across the room and opened a cupboard in a corner of the room.

'Mrs Moody –' said Tuppence, 'was she one?'

'Oh, you know about her – she wasn't a mother – she'd been a dresser at the theatre. She recognized me so she had to go.' Turning suddenly she came towards Tuppence holding a glass of milk and smiling persuasively.

'Drink it up,' she said. 'Just drink it up.'

Tuppence sat silent for a moment, then she leapt to her feet and rushed to the window. Catching up a chair, she crashed the glass. She leaned her head out and screamed:

'Help! Help!'

Mrs Lancaster laughed. She put the glass of milk down on a table and leant back in her chair and laughed.

'How stupid you are. Who do you think will come? Who do you think *can* come? They'd have to break down doors, they'd have to get through that wall and by that time – there are other things, you know. It needn't be milk. Milk is the easy way. Milk and cocoa and even tea. For little Mrs Moody I put it in cocoa – she loved cocoa.'

'The morphia? How did you get it?'

'Oh, that was easy. A man I lived with years ago – he had cancer – the doctor gave me supplies for him – to keep in my charge – other drugs too – I said later that they'd all been thrown away – but I kept them, and other drugs and sedatives too – I thought they might come in useful some day – and they did – I've still got a supply – I never take anything of the kind myself – I don't believe in it.' She pushed the glass of milk towards Tuppence – 'Drink it up, it's much the easiest way. The other way – the trouble is, I can't be sure just where I put it.'

She got up from her chair and began walking round the room.

'Where *did* I put it? Where did I? I forget everything now I'm getting old.'

Tuppence yelled again. 'Help!' but the canal bank was empty still. Mrs Lancaster was still wandering round the room.

'I thought – I certainly thought – oh, of course, in my knitting bag.'

Tuppence turned from the window. Mrs Lancaster was coming towards her.

'What a silly woman you are,' said Mrs Lancaster, 'to want it this way.'

Her left arm shot out and she caught Tuppence's shoulder. Her right hand came from behind her back. In it was a long thin stiletto blade. Tuppence struggled. She thought, 'I can stop her easily. Easily. She's an old woman. Feeble. She can't –'

Suddenly in a cold tide of fear she thought, 'But *I'm* an old woman too. I'm not as strong as I think myself. I'm not as strong as she is. Her hands, her grasp, her fingers. I suppose because she's mad and mad people, I've always heard, are strong.'

The gleaming blade was approaching near her. Tuppence screamed. Down below she heard shouts and blows. Blows now on the doors as though someone were trying to force the doors or windows. 'But they'll never get through,' thought Tuppence. 'They'll never get through this trick doorway here. Not unless they know the mechanism.'

She struggled fiercely. She was still managing to hold Mrs Lancaster away from her. But the other was the bigger woman. A big strong woman. Her face was still smiling but it no longer had the benignant look. It had the look now of someone enjoying herself.

'Killer Kate,' said Tuppence.

'You know my nickname? Yes, but I've sublimated that. I've become a killer of the Lord. It's the Lord's will that I should kill you. So that makes it all right. You do see that, don't you? You see, it makes it all right.'

Tuppence was pressed now against the side of a big chair. With one arm Mrs Lancaster held her against the chair, and the pressure increased – no further recoil was possible. In Mrs Lancaster's right hand the sharp steel of the stiletto approached.

Tuppence thought, 'I mustn't panic – I mustn't panic –' But following that came with sharp insistence, '*But what can I do?*' To struggle was unavailing.

Fear came then – the same sharp fear of which she had the first indication in Sunny Ridge –

'*Is it your poor child?*'

That had been the first warning – but she had misunderstood it – she had not known it was a warning.

Her eyes watched the approaching steel but strangely enough it was not the gleaming metal and its menace that frightened her into a state of paralysis; it was the face above it – it was the smiling benignant face of Mrs Lancaster – smiling happily, contentedly – a woman pursuing her appointed task, with gentle reasonableness.

'She doesn't *look* mad,' thought Tuppence – 'That's what's so awful – Of course she doesn't because in her own mind she's sane. She's a perfectly normal, reasonable human being – that's what she *thinks* – Oh Tommy, Tommy, what have I got myself into this time?'

Dizziness and limpness submerged her. Her muscles relaxed – somewhere there was a great crash of broken glass. It swept her away, into darkness and unconsciousness.

II

'That's better – you're coming round – drink this, Mrs Beresford.'

A glass pressed against her lips – she resisted fiercely – Poisoned milk – who had said that once – something about 'poisoned milk'? She wouldn't drink poisoned milk . . . No, not milk – quite a different smell –

She relaxed, her lips opened – she sipped –

'Brandy,' said Tuppence with recognition.

'Quite right! Go on – drink some more –'

Tuppence sipped again. She leaned back against cushions, surveyed her surroundings. The top of a ladder showed through the window. In front of the window there was a mass of broken glass on the floor.

'I heard the glass break.'

She pushed away the brandy glass and her eyes followed up the hand and arm to the face of the man who had been holding it.

'El Greco,' said Tuppence.

'I beg your pardon.'

'It doesn't matter.'

She looked round the room.

'Where is she – Mrs Lancaster, I mean?'

'She's – resting – in the next room –'

'I see.' But she wasn't sure that she did see. She would see better presently. Just now only one idea would come at a time –

'Sir Philip Starke.' She said it slowly and doubtfully. 'That's right?'

'Yes – Why did you say El Greco?'

'Suffering.'

'I beg your pardon.'

'The picture – In Toledo – Or in the Prado – I thought so a long time ago – no, not very long ago –' She thought about it – made a discovery – 'Last night. A party – At the vicarage –'

'You're doing fine,' he said encouragingly.

It seemed very natural, somehow, to be sitting here, in this room with broken glass on the floor, talking to this man – with the dark agonized face –

'I made a mistake – at Sunny Ridge. I was all wrong about her – I was afraid, then – a – wave of fear – But I got it wrong – I wasn't afraid of *her* – I was afraid *for* her – I thought something was going to happen to her – I wanted to protect her – to save her – I –' She looked doubtfully at him. 'Do you understand? Or does it sound silly?'

'Nobody understands better than I do – nobody in this world.'

Tuppence stared at him – frowning.

'Who – who was she? I mean Mrs Lancaster – Mrs Yorke – that's not real – that's just taken from a rose tree – who was she – herself?'

Philip Starke said harshly:

'*Who was she? Herself? The real one, the true one*
Who was she – with God's Sign upon her brow?

'Did you ever read Peer Gynt, Mrs Beresford?'

He went to the window. He stood there a moment, looking out – Then he turned abruptly.

'She was my wife, God help me.'

'Your wife – But she died – the tablet in the church –'

'She died abroad – that was the story I circulated – And I put up a tablet to her memory in the church. People don't like to ask too many questions of a bereaved widower. I didn't go on living here.'

'Some people said she had left you.'

'That made an acceptable story, too.'

'You took her away when you found out – about the children –'

'So you know about the children?'

'She told me – It seemed – unbelievable.'

'Most of the time she was quite normal – no one would have guessed. But the police were beginning to suspect – I had to act – I had to save her – to protect her – You understand – can you understand – in the very least?'

'Yes,' said Tuppence, 'I can understand quite well.'

'She was – so lovely once –' His voice broke a little. 'You see her – there,' he pointed to the painting on the wall. 'Waterlily

– She was a wild girl – always. Her mother was the last of the Warrenders – an old family – inbred – Helen Warrender – ran away from home. She took up with a bad lot – a gaolbird – her daughter went on the stage – she trained as a dancer – Waterlily was her most popular role – then she took up with a criminal gang – for excitement – purely to get a kick out of it – She was always being disappointed –

'When she married me, she had finished with all that – she wanted to settle down – to live quietly – a family life – with children. I was rich – I could give her all the things she wanted. But we had no children. It was a sorrow to both of us. She began to have obsessions of guilt – Perhaps she had always been slightly unbalanced – I don't know – What do causes matter? – She was –'

He made a despairing gesture.

'I loved her – I always loved her – no matter what she was – what she did – I wanted her safe – to keep her safe – not shut up – a prisoner for life, eating her heart out. And we did keep her safe – for many many years.'

'We?'

'Nellie – my dear faithful Nellie Bligh. My dear Nellie Bligh. She was wonderful – planned and arranged it all. The Homes for the Elderly – every comfort and luxury. And no temptations – *no children* – keep children out of her way – It seemed to work – these homes were in faraway places – Cumberland – North Wales – no one was likely to recognize her – or so we thought. It was on Mr Eccles's advice – a very shrewd lawyer – his charges were high – but I relied on him.'

'Blackmail?' suggested Tuppence.

'I never thought of it like that. He was a friend, and an adviser –'

'Who painted the boat in the picture – the boat called *Waterlily*?'

'I did. It pleased her. She remembered her triumph on the stage. It was one of Boscowan's pictures. She liked his pictures. Then, one day, she wrote a name in black pigment on the bridge – the name of a dead child – So I painted a boat to hide it and labelled the boat *Waterlily* –'

The door in the wall swung open – The friendly witch came through it.

She looked at Tuppence and from Tuppence to Philip Starke.

'All right again?' she said in a matter-of-fact way.

'Yes,' said Tuppence. The nice thing about the friendly witch, she saw, was that there wasn't going to be any fuss.

'Your husband's down below, waiting in the car. I said I'd bring you down to him – if that's the way you want it?'

'That's the way I want it,' said Tuppence.

'I thought you would.' She looked towards the door into the bedroom. 'Is she – in there?'

'Yes,' said Philip Starke.

Mrs Perry went to the bedroom. She came out again –

'I see –' She looked at him inquiringly.

'She offered Mrs Beresford a glass of milk – Mrs Beresford didn't want it.'

'And so, I suppose, she drank it herself?'

He hesitated.

'Yes.'

'Dr Mortimer will be along later,' said Mrs Perry.

She came to help Tuppence to her feet, but Tuppence rose unaided.

'I'm not hurt,' she said. 'It was just shock – I'm quite all right now.'

She stood facing Philip Starke – neither of them seemed to have anything to say. Mrs Perry stood by the door in the wall.

Tuppence spoke at last.

'There is nothing I can do, is there?' she said, but it was hardly a question.

'Only one thing – It was Nellie Bligh who struck you down in the churchyard that day.'

Tuppence nodded.

'I've realized it must have been.'

'She lost her head. She thought you were on the track of her, of our, secret. She – I'm bitterly remorseful for the terrible strain I've subjected her to all these long years. It's been more than any woman ought to be asked to bear –'

'She loved you very much, I suppose,' said Tuppence. 'But I don't think we'll go on looking for any Mrs Johnson, if that is what you want to ask *us* not to do.'

'Thank you – I'm very grateful.'

There was another silence. Mrs Perry waited patiently. Tuppence looked round her. She went to the broken window and looked at the peaceful canal down below.

'I don't suppose I shall ever see this house again. I'm looking at it very hard, so that I shall be able to remember it.'

'Do you want to remember it?'

'Yes, I do. Someone said to me that it was a house that had been put to the wrong use. I know what they meant now.'

He looked at her questioningly, but did not speak.

'Who sent you here to find me?' asked Tuppence.

'Emma Boscowan.'

'I thought so.'

She joined the friendly witch and they went through the secret door and on down.

A house for lovers, Emma Boscowan had said to Tuppence. Well, that was how she was leaving it – in the possession of two lovers – one dead and one who suffered and lived –

She went out through the door to where Tommy and the car were waiting.

She said goodbye to the friendly witch. She got into the car.

'Tuppence,' said Tommy.

'I know,' said Tuppence.

'Don't do it again,' said Tommy. 'Don't ever do it again.'

'I won't.'

'That's what you say now, but you will.'

'No, I shan't. I'm too old.'

Tommy pressed the starter. They drove off.

'Poor Nellie Bligh,' said Tuppence.

'Why do you say that?'

'So terribly in love with Philip Starke. Doing all those things for him all those years – such a lot of wasted doglike devotion.'

'Nonsense!' said Tommy. 'I expect she's enjoyed every minute of it. Some women do.'

'Heartless brute,' said Tuppence.

'Where do you want to go – The Lamb and Flag at Market Basing?'

'No,' said Tuppence. 'I want to go home. HOME, Thomas. And stay there.'

'Amen to that,' said Mr Beresford. '*And if Albert welcomes us with a charred chicken, I'll kill him!*'

PASSENGER TO FRANKFURT

To Margaret Guillaume

'Leadership, besides being a great creative force, can be diabolical . . .'

Jan Smuts

INTRODUCTION

The Author speaks:

The first question put to an author, personally, or through the post, is:

'Where do you get your ideas from?'

The temptation is great to reply: 'I always go to Harrods,' or 'I get them mostly at the Army & Navy Stores,' or, snappily, 'Try Marks and Spencer.'

The universal opinion seems firmly established that there is a magic source of ideas which authors have discovered how to tap.

One can hardly send one's questioners back to Elizabethan times, with Shakespeare's:

Tell me, where is fancy bred,
Or in the heart or in the head?
How begot, how nourished?
Reply, reply.

You merely say firmly: 'My own head.'

That, of course, is no help to anybody. If you like the look of your questioner you relent and go a little further.

'If one idea in particular seems attractive, and you feel you could do something with it, then you toss it around, play tricks with it, work it up, tone it down, and gradually get it into shape. Then, of course, you have to start writing it. That's not nearly such fun – it becomes hard work. Alternatively, you can tuck it carefully away, in storage, for perhaps using in a year or two years' time.'

A second question – or rather a statement – is then likely to be:

'I suppose you take most of your characters from real life?'

An indignant denial to that monstrous suggestion.

'No, I don't. I invent them. They are *mine*. They've got to be *my* characters – doing what I want them to do, being what I want them to be – coming alive for me, having their own ideas sometimes, but only because I've made them become *real*.'

So the author has produced the ideas, and the characters – but now comes the third necessity – the setting. The first two come from inside sources, but the third is outside – it must be there – waiting – in existence already. You don't invent that – it's there – it's real.

You have been perhaps for a cruise on the Nile – you remember it all – just the setting you want for this particular story. You have had a meal at a Chelsea café. A quarrel was going on – one girl pulled out a handful of another girl's hair. An excellent start for the book you are going to write next. You travel on the Orient Express. What fun to make it the scene for a plot you are considering. You go to tea with a friend. As you arrive her brother closes a book he is reading – throws it aside, says: 'Not bad, but why on earth didn't they ask Evans?'

So you decide immediately a book of yours shortly to be written will bear the title, *Why Didn't They Ask Evans?*

You don't know yet who Evans is going to be. Never mind. Evans will come in due course – the title is fixed.

So, in a sense, you don't invent your settings. They are outside you, all around you, in existence – you have only to stretch out your hand and pick and choose. A railway train, a hospital, a London hotel, a Caribbean beach, a country village, a cocktail party, a girls' school.

But one thing only applies – they must be there – in existence. Real people, real places. A definite place in time and space. If here and now – how shall you get full information – apart from the evidence of your own eyes and ears? The answer is frighteningly simple.

It is what the Press brings to you every day, served up in your morning paper under the general heading of News. Collect it from the front page. What is going on in the world today? What is everyone saying, thinking, doing? Hold up a mirror to 1970 in England.

Look at that front page every day for a month, make notes, consider and classify.

Every day there is a killing.

A girl strangled.

Elderly woman attacked and robbed of her meagre savings.

Young men or boys – attacking or attacked.

Buildings and telephone kiosks smashed and gutted.

Drug smuggling.

Robbery and assault.

Children missing and children's murdered bodies found not far from their homes.

Can this be England? Is England *really* like this? One feels – no – not yet, *but it could be.*

Fear is awakening – fear of what may be. Not so much because of actual happenings but because of the possible causes behind them. Some known, some unknown, but *felt*. And not only in our own country. There are smaller paragraphs on other pages – giving news from Europe – from Asia – from the Americas – Worldwide News.

Hi-jacking of planes.

Kidnapping.

Violence.

Riots.

Hate.

Anarchy – all growing stronger.

All seeming to lead to worship of destruction, pleasure in cruelty.

What does it all mean? An Elizabethan phrase echoes from the past, speaking of Life:

> . . . *it is a tale*
> *Told by an idiot, full of sound and fury,*
> *Signifying nothing.*

And yet one knows – of one's own knowledge – how much goodness there is in this world of ours – the kindnesses done, the goodness of heart, the acts of compassion, the kindness of neighbour to neighbour, the helpful actions of girls and boys.

Then why this fantastic atmosphere of daily news – of things that happen – that are actual *facts*?

To write a story in this year of Our Lord 1970 – you must come to terms with your background. If the background is fantastic, then the story must accept its background. It, too, must be a fantasy – an extravaganza. The setting must include the fantastic facts of daily life.

Can one envisage a fantastic cause? A secret Campaign for Power? Can a maniacal desire for destruction create a new world? Can one go a step further and suggest deliverance by fantastic and impossible-sounding means?

Nothing is impossible, science has taught us that.

This story is in essence a fantasy. It pretends to be nothing more.

But most of the things that happen in it are happening, or giving promise of happening in the world of today.

It is not an impossible story – it is only a fantastic one.

BOOK I • INTERRUPTED JOURNEY

....
PASSENGER TO FRANKFURT

I

'Fasten your seat-belts, please.' The diverse passengers in the
plane were slow to obey. There was a general feeling that they
couldn't possibly be arriving at Geneva yet. The drowsy groaned
and yawned. The more than drowsy had to be gently roused by
an authoritative stewardess.

'Your seat-belts, please.'

The dry voice came authoritatively over the Tannoy. It explained
in German, in French, and in English that a short period of rough
weather would shortly be experienced. Sir Stafford Nye opened
his mouth to its full extent, yawned and pulled himself upright
in his seat. He had been dreaming very happily of fishing an
English river.

He was a man of forty-five, of medium height, with a smooth,
olive, clean-shaven face. In dress he rather liked to affect the
bizarre. A man of excellent family, he felt fully at ease indulging
any such sartorial whims. If it made the more conventionally
dressed of his colleagues wince occasionally, that was merely a
source of malicious pleasure to him. There was something about
him of the eighteenth-century buck. He liked to be noticed.

His particular kind of affectation when travelling was a kind
of bandit's cloak which he had once purchased in Corsica. It
was of a very dark purply-blue, had a scarlet lining and had a
kind of burnous hanging down behind which he could draw up
over his head when he wished to, so as to obviate draughts.

Sir Stafford Nye had been a disappointment in diplomatic
circles. Marked out in early youth by his gifts for great things,
he had singularly failed to fulfil his early promise. A peculiar and
diabolical sense of humour was wont to afflict him in what should

have been his most serious moments. When it came to the point, he found that he always preferred to indulge his delicate Puckish malice to boring himself. He was a well-known figure in public life without ever having reached eminence. It was felt that Stafford Nye, though definitely brilliant, was not – and presumably never would be – a safe man. In these days of tangled politics and tangled foreign relations, safety, especially if one were to reach ambassadorial rank, was preferable to brilliance. Sir Stafford Nye was relegated to the shelf, though he was occasionally entrusted with such missions as needed the art of intrigue, but were not of too important or public a nature. Journalists sometimes referred to him as the dark horse of diplomacy.

Whether Sir Stafford himself was disappointed with his own career, nobody ever knew. Probably not even Sir Stafford himself. He was a man of a certain vanity, but he was also a man who very much enjoyed indulging his own proclivities for mischief.

He was returning now from a commission of inquiry in Malaya. He had found it singularly lacking in interest. His colleagues had, in his opinion, made up their minds beforehand what their findings were going to be. They saw and they listened, but their preconceived views were not affected. Sir Stafford had thrown a few spanners into the works, more for the hell of it than from any pronounced convictions. At all events, he thought, it had livened things up. He wished there were more possibilities of doing that sort of thing. His fellow members of the commission had been sound, dependable fellows, and remarkably dull. Even the well-known Mrs Nathaniel Edge, the only woman member, well known as having bees in her bonnet, was no fool when it came down to plain facts. She saw, she listened and she played safe.

He had met her before on the occasion of a problem to be solved in one of the Balkan capitals. It was there that Sir Stafford Nye had not been able to refrain from embarking on a few interesting suggestions. In that scandal-loving periodical *Inside News* it was insinuated that Sir Stafford Nye's presence in that Balkan capital was intimately connected with Balkan problems, and that his mission was a secret one of the greatest delicacy. A kind of friend had sent Sir Stafford a copy of this with the relevant passage marked. Sir Stafford was not taken aback. He read it with a delighted grin. It amused him very much to reflect how ludicrously far from the truth the journalists were on this occasion. His presence in Sofiagrad had been due entirely to a blameless interest in the rarer wild flowers and to the urgencies of an elderly friend of his, Lady Lucy Cleghorn, who was indefatigable in her quest for these shy floral rarities, and who at any moment would scale a rock cliff or leap joyously into a bog at the sight of some flowerlet, the length of whose Latin name was in inverse proportion to its size.

A small band of enthusiasts had been pursuing this botanical search on the slopes of mountains for about ten days when it occurred to Sir Stafford that it was a pity the paragraph was not true. He was a little – just a little – tired of wild flowers and, fond as he was of dear Lucy, her ability despite her sixty-odd years to race up hills at top speed, easily outpacing him, sometimes annoyed him. Always just in front of him he saw the seat of those bright royal blue trousers and Lucy, though scraggy enough elsewhere, goodness knows, was decidedly too broad in the beam to wear royal blue corduroy trousers. A nice little international pie, he had thought, in which to dip his fingers, in which to play about . . .

In the aeroplane the metallic Tannoy voice spoke again. It told the passengers that owing to heavy fog at Geneva, the plane would be diverted to Frankfurt airport and proceed from there to London. Passengers to Geneva would be re-routed from Frankfurt as soon as possible. It made no difference to Sir Stafford Nye. If there was fog in London, he supposed they would re-route the plane to Prestwick. He hoped that would not happen. He had been to Prestwick once or twice too often. Life, he thought, and journeys by air, were really excessively boring. If only – he didn't know – if only – *what*?

II

It was warm in the Transit Passenger Lounge at Frankfurt, so Sir Stafford Nye slipped back his cloak, allowing its crimson lining to drape itself spectacularly round his shoulders. He was drinking a glass of beer and listening with half an ear to the various announcements as they were made.

'Flight 4387. Flying to Moscow. Flight 2381 bound for Egypt and Calcutta.'

Journeys all over the globe. How romantic it ought to be.

But there was something about the atmosphere of a Passengers' Lounge in an airport that chilled romance. It was too full of people, too full of things to buy, too full of similarly coloured seats, too full of plastic, too full of human beings, too full of crying children. He tried to remember who had said:

> I wish I loved the Human Race;
> I wish I loved its silly face.

Chesterton perhaps? It was undoubtedly true. Put enough people together and they looked so painfully alike that one could hardly bear it. An interesting face now, thought Sir Stafford. What a difference it would make. He looked disparagingly at two young women, splendidly made up, dressed in the national uniform of their country – England he presumed – of shorter and shorter miniskirts, and another young woman, even better made up – in fact quite good-looking – who was wearing what he believed to be called a culotte suit. She had gone a little further along the road of fashion.

He wasn't very interested in nice-looking girls who looked like all the other nice-looking girls. He would like someone to be different. Someone sat down beside him on the plastic-covered artificial leather settee on which he was sitting. Her face attracted his attention at once. Not precisely because it was different, in fact he almost seemed to recognize it as a face he knew. Here was someone he had seen before. He couldn't remember where or when but it was certainly familiar. Twenty-five or six, he thought, possibly, as to age. A delicate high-bridged aquiline nose, a black heavy bush of hair reaching to her shoulders. She had a magazine in front of her but she was not paying attention to it. She was, in fact, looking with something that was almost eagerness at him. Quite suddenly she spoke. It was a deep contralto voice, almost as deep as a man's. It had a very faint foreign accent. She said,

'Can I speak to you?'

He studied her for a moment before replying. No – not what one might have thought – this wasn't a pick-up. This was something else.

'I see no reason,' he said, 'why you should not do so. We have time to waste here, it seems.'

'Fog,' said the woman, 'fog in Geneva, fog in London, perhaps. Fog everywhere. I don't know what to do.'

'Oh, you mustn't worry,' he said reassuringly, 'they'll land you somewhere all right. They're quite efficient, you know. Where are you going?'

'I was going to Geneva.'

'Well, I expect you'll get there in the end.'

'I have to get there *now*. If I can get to Geneva, it will be all right. There is someone who will meet me there. I can be safe.'

'Safe?' He smiled a little.

She said, 'Safe is a four-letter word but not the kind of four-letter word that people are interested in nowadays. And yet it can mean a lot. It means a lot to me.' Then she said, 'You see, if I can't get to Geneva, if I have to leave this plane here, or go on in this plane to London with no arrangements made, I shall be killed.' She looked at him sharply. 'I suppose you don't believe that.'

'I'm afraid I don't.'

'It's quite true. People can be. They are, every day.'

'Who wants to kill you?'

'Does it matter?'

'Not to me.'

'You can believe me if you wish to believe me. I am speaking the truth. I want help. Help to get to London safely.'

'And why should you select me to help you?'

'Because I think that you know something about death. You have known of death, perhaps seen death happen.'

He looked sharply at her and then away again.

'Any other reason?' he said.

'Yes. This.' She stretched out her narrow olive-skinned hand and touched the folds of the voluminous cloak. 'This,' she said.

For the first time his interest was aroused.

'Now what do you mean by that?'

'It's unusual – characteristic. It's not what everyone wears.'

'True enough. It's one of my affectations, shall we say?'

'It's an affectation that could be useful to me.'

'What do you mean?'

'I am asking you something. Probably you will refuse but you might not refuse because I think you are a man who is ready to take risks. Just as I am a woman who takes risks.'

'I'll listen to your project,' he said, with a faint smile.

'I want your cloak to wear. I want your passport. I want your boarding ticket for the plane. Presently, in twenty minutes or so, say, the flight for London will be called. I shall have your passport, I shall wear your cloak. And so I shall travel to London and arrive safely.'

'You mean you'll pass yourself off as me? My dear girl.'

She opened a handbag. From it she took a small square mirror.

'Look there,' she said. 'Look at me and then look at your own face.'

He saw then, saw what had been vaguely nagging at his mind. His sister, Pamela, who had died about twenty years ago. They had always been very alike, he and Pamela. A strong family resemblance. She had had a slightly masculine type of face. His face, perhaps, had been, certainly in early life, of a slightly effeminate type. They had both had the high-bridged nose, the tilt of eyebrows, the slightly sideways smile of the lips. Pamela had been tall, five foot eight, he himself five foot ten. He looked at the woman who had tendered him the mirror.

'There is a facial likeness between us, that's what you mean, isn't it? But my dear girl, it wouldn't deceive anyone who knew me or knew you.'

'Of course it wouldn't. Don't you understand? It doesn't need to. I am travelling wearing slacks. You have been travelling with the hood of your cloak drawn up round your face. All I have to do is to cut off my hair, wrap it up in a twist of newspaper, throw it in one of the litter-baskets here. Then I put on your burnous, I have your boarding card, ticket, and passport. Unless there is someone who knows you well on this plane, and I presume there is not or they would have spoken to you already, then I can safely travel as you. Showing your passport when it's necessary, keeping the burnous and cloak drawn up so that my nose and eyes and mouth are about all that are seen. I can walk out safely when the plane reaches its destination because no one will know I have travelled by it. Walk out safely and disappear into the crowds of the city of London.'

'And what do I do?' asked Sir Stafford, with a slight smile.

'I can make a suggestion if you have the nerve to face it.'

'Suggest,' he said. 'I always like to hear suggestions.'

'You get up from here, you go away and buy a magazine or a newspaper, or a gift at the gift counter. You leave your cloak hanging here on the seat. When you come back with whatever it is, you sit down somewhere else – say at the end of that bench opposite here. There will be a glass in front of you, this glass still. In it there will be something that will send you to sleep. Sleep in a quiet corner.'

'What happens next?'

'You will have been presumably the victim of a robbery,' she said. 'Somebody will have added a few knock-out drops to your drink, and will have stolen your wallet from you. Something of that kind. You declare your identity, say that your passport and things are stolen. You can easily establish your identity.'

'You know who I am? My name, I mean?'

'Not yet,' she said. 'I haven't seen your passport yet. I've no idea who you are.'

'And yet you say I can establish my identity easily.'

'I am a good judge of people. I know who is important or who isn't. You are an important person.'

'And why should I do all this?'

'Perhaps to save the life of a fellow human being.'

'Isn't that rather a highly coloured story?'

'Oh yes. Quite easily not believed. Do you believe it?'

He looked at her thoughtfully. 'You know what you're talking like? A beautiful spy in a thriller.'

'Yes, perhaps. But I am not beautiful.'

'And you're not a spy?'

'I might be so described, perhaps. I have certain information. Information I want to preserve. You will have to take my word for it, it is information that would be valuable to your country.'

'Don't you think you're being rather absurd?'

'Yes I do. If this was written down it would look absurd. But so many absurd things are true, aren't they?'

He looked at her again. She was very like Pamela. Her voice, although foreign in intonation, was like Pamela's. What she proposed was ridiculous, absurd, quite impossible, and probably dangerous. Dangerous to him. Unfortunately, though, that was what attracted him. To have the nerve to suggest such a thing to him! What would come of it all? It would be interesting, certainly, to find out.

'What do I get out of it?' he said. 'That's what I'd like to know.'

She looked at him consideringly. 'Diversion,' she said. 'Something out of the everyday happenings? An antidote to boredom, perhaps. We've not got very long. It's up to you.'

'And what happens to *your* passport? Do I have to buy myself a wig, if they sell such a thing, at the counter? Do I have to impersonate a female?'

'No. There's no question of exchanging places. You have been robbed and drugged but you remain yourself. Make up your mind. There isn't long. Time is passing very quickly. I have to do my own transformation.'

'You win,' he said. 'One mustn't refuse the unusual, if it is offered to one.'

'I hoped you might feel that way, but it was a toss-up.'

From his pocket Stafford Nye took out his passport. He slipped it into the outer pocket of the cloak he had been wearing. He rose to his feet, yawned, looked round him, looked at his watch, and strolled over to the counter where various goods were displayed for sale. He did not even look back. He bought a paperback book and fingered some small woolly animals, a suitable gift for some child. Finally he chose a panda. He looked round the lounge, came back to where he had been sitting. The cloak was gone and so had the girl. A half glass of beer was on the table still. Here, he thought, is where I take the risk. He picked up the glass, moved away a little, and drank it. Not quickly. Quite slowly. It tasted much the same as it had tasted before.

'Now I wonder,' said Sir Stafford. 'Now I wonder.'

He walked across the lounge to a far corner. There was a somewhat noisy family sitting there, laughing and talking together. He sat down near them, yawned, let his head fall back on the edge of the cushion. A flight was announced leaving for Teheran. A large number of passengers got up and went to queue by the requisite numbered gate. The lounge still remained half full. He opened his paperback book. He yawned again. He was really sleepy now, yes, he was very sleepy . . . He must just think out where it was best for him to go off to sleep. Somewhere he could remain . . .

Trans-European Airways announced the departure of their plane, Flight 309 for London.

III

Quite a good sprinkling of passengers rose to their feet to obey the summons. By this time though, more passengers had entered the transit lounge waiting for other planes. Announcements followed as to fog at Geneva and other disabilities of travel. A slim man of middle height wearing a dark blue cloak with its red lining showing and with a hood drawn up over a close-cropped head, not noticeably more untidy than many of the heads of young men nowadays, walked across the floor to take his place in the queue for the plane. Showing a boarding ticket, he passed out through gate No. 9.

More announcements followed. Swissair flying to Zürich. BEA to Athens and Cyprus – and then a different type of announcement.

'Will Miss Daphne Theodofanous, passenger to Geneva, kindly come to the flight desk. Plane to Geneva is delayed owing to fog. Passengers will travel by way of Athens. The aeroplane is now ready to leave.'

Other announcements followed dealing with passengers to Japan, to Egypt, to South Africa, air lines spanning the world. Mr Sidney Cook, passenger to South Africa, was urged to come to the flight desk where there was a message for him. Daphne Theodofanous was called for again.

'This is the last call before the departure of Flight 309.'

In a corner of the lounge a little girl was looking up at a man in a dark suit who was fast asleep, his head resting against the cushion of the red settee. In his hand he held a small woolly panda.

The little girl's hand stretched out towards the panda. Her mother said:

'Now, Joan, don't touch that. The poor gentleman's asleep.'

'Where is he going?'

'Perhaps he's going to Australia too,' said her mother, 'like we are.'

'Has he got a little girl like me?'

'I think he must have,' said her mother.

The little girl sighed and looked at the panda again. Sir Stafford Nye continued to sleep. He was dreaming that he was trying to shoot a leopard. A very dangerous animal, he was saying to the safari guide who was accompanying him. 'A very dangerous animal, so I've always heard. You can't trust a leopard.'

The dream switched at that moment, as dreams have a habit of doing, and he was having tea with his Great-Aunt Matilda, and trying to make her hear. She was deafer than ever! He had not heard any of the announcements except the first one for Miss Daphne Theodofanous. The little girl's mother said:

'I've always wondered, you know, about a passenger that's missing. Nearly always, whenever you go anywhere by air, you hear it. Somebody they can't find. Somebody who hasn't heard the call or isn't on the plane or something like that. I always wonder who it is and what they're doing, and *why* they haven't come. I suppose this Miss What's-a-name or whatever it is will just have missed her plane. What will they do with her then?'

Nobody was able to answer her question because nobody had the proper information.

CHAPTER 2
LONDON

Sir Stafford Nye's flat was a very pleasant one. It looked out upon Green Park. He switched on the coffee percolator and went to see what the post had left him this morning. It did not appear to have left him anything very interesting. He sorted through the letters, a bill or two, a receipt and letters with rather uninteresting postmarks. He shuffled them together and placed them on the table where some mail was already lying, accumulating from the last two days. He'd have to get down to things soon, he supposed. His secretary would be coming in some time or other this afternoon.

He went back to the kitchen, poured coffee into a cup and brought it to the table. He picked up the two or three letters that he had opened late last night when he arrived. One of them he referred to, and smiled a little as he read it.

'Eleven-thirty,' he said. 'Quite a suitable time. I wonder now. I expect I'd better just think things over, and get prepared for Chetwynd.'

Somebody pushed something through the letter-box. He went out into the hall and got the morning paper. There was very little news in the paper. A political crisis, an item of foreign news which might have been disquieting, but he didn't think it was. It was merely a journalist letting off steam and trying to make things rather more important than they were. Must give the people something to read. A girl had been strangled in the park. Girls were always being strangled. One a day, he thought callously. No child had been kidnapped or raped this morning. That was a nice surprise. He made himself a piece of toast and drank his coffee.

Later, he went out of the building, down into the street, and walked through the park in the direction of Whitehall. He was smiling to himself. Life, he felt, was rather good this morning. He began to think about Chetwynd. Chetwynd was a silly fool if there ever was one. A good façade, important-seeming, and a nicely suspicious mind. He'd rather enjoy talking to Chetwynd.

He reached Whitehall a comfortable seven minutes late. That was only due to his own importance compared with that of Chetwynd, he thought. He walked into the room. Chetwynd was sitting behind his desk and had a lot of papers on it and a secretary there. He was looking properly important, as he always did when he could make it.

'Hullo, Nye,' said Chetwynd, smiling all over his impressively handsome face. 'Glad to be back? How was Malaya?'

'Hot,' said Stafford Nye.

'Yes. Well, I suppose it always is. You meant atmospherically, I suppose, not politically?'

'Oh, purely atmospherically,' said Stafford Nye.

He accepted a cigarette and sat down.

'Get any results to speak of?'

'Oh, hardly. Not what you'd call results. I've sent in my report. All a lot of talky-talky as usual. How's Lazenby?'

'Oh, a nuisance as he always is. He'll never change,' said Chetwynd.

'No, that would seem too much to hope for. I haven't served

on anything with Bascombe before. He can be quite fun when he likes.'

'Can he? I don't know him very well. Yes. I suppose he can.'

'Well, well, well. No other news, I suppose?'

'No, nothing. Nothing I think that would interest you.'

'You didn't mention in your letter quite why you wanted to see me.'

'Oh, just to go over a few things, that's all. You know, in case you'd brought any special dope home with you. Anything we ought to be prepared for, you know. Questions in the House. Anything like that.'

'Yes, of course.'

'Came home by air, didn't you? Had a bit of trouble, I gather.'

Stafford Nye put on the face he had been determined to put on beforehand. It was slightly rueful, with a faint tinge of annoyance.

'Oh, so you heard about that, did you?' he said. 'Silly business.'

'Yes. Yes, must have been.'

'Extraordinary,' said Stafford Nye, 'how things always get into the press. There was a paragraph in the stop press this morning.'

'You'd rather they wouldn't have, I suppose?'

'Well, makes me look a bit of an ass, doesn't it?' said Stafford Nye. 'Got to admit it. At my age too!'

'What happened exactly? I wondered if the report in the paper had been exaggerating.'

'Well, I suppose they made the most of it, that's all. You know what these journeys are. Damn boring. There was fog at Geneva so they had to re-route the plane. Then there was two hours' delay at Frankfurt.'

'Is that when it happened?'

'Yes. One's bored stiff in these airports. Planes coming, planes going. Tannoy going full steam ahead. Flight 302 leaving for Hong Kong, Flight 109 going to Ireland. This, that and the other. People getting up, people leaving. And you just sit there yawning.'

'What happened exactly?' said Chetwynd.

'Well, I'd got a drink in front of me, Pilsner as a matter of fact, then I thought I'd got to get something else to read. I'd read everything I'd got with me so I went over to the counter and bought some wretched paperback or other. Detective story, I think it was, and I bought a woolly animal for one of my nieces. Then I came back, finished my drink, opened my paperback and then I went to sleep.'

'Yes, I see. You went to sleep.'

'Well, a very natural thing to do, isn't it? I suppose they called my flight but if they did I didn't hear it. I didn't hear it apparently for the best of reasons. I'm capable of going to sleep in an airport any time but I'm also capable of hearing an announcement that concerns me. This time I didn't. When I woke up, or came to, however you like to put it, I was having a bit of medical attention. Somebody apparently had dropped a Mickey Finn or something or other in my drink. Must have done it when I was away getting the paperback.'

'Rather an extraordinary thing to happen, wasn't it?' said Chetwynd.

'Well, it's never happened to me before,' said Stafford Nye. 'I hope it never will again. It makes you feel an awful fool, you know. Besides having a hangover. There was a doctor and some nurse creature, or something. Anyway, there was no great harm done apparently. My wallet had been pinched with some money in it and my passport. It was awkward of course. Fortunately, I hadn't got much money. My travellers' cheques were in an inner pocket. There always has to be a bit of red tape and all that if you lose your passport. Anyway, I had letters and things and identification was not difficult. And in due course things were squared up and I resumed my flight.'

'Still, very annoying for you,' said Chetwynd. 'A person of your status, I mean.' His tone was disapproving.

'Yes,' said Stafford Nye. 'It doesn't show me in a very good light, does it? I mean, not as bright as a fellow of my – er – status ought to be.' The idea seemed to amuse him.

'Does this often happen, did you find out?'

'I don't think it's a matter of general occurrence. It could be. I suppose any person with a pick-pocket trend could notice a fellow asleep and slip a hand into a pocket, and if he's accomplished in his profession, get hold of a wallet or a pocket-book or something like that, and hope for some luck.'

'Pretty awkward to lose a passport.'

'Yes, I shall have to put in for another one now. Make a lot of explanations, I suppose. As I say, the whole thing's a damn silly business. And let's face it, Chetwynd, it doesn't show me in a very favourable light, does it?'

'Oh, not your fault, my dear boy, not your fault. It could happen to anybody, anybody at all.'

'Very nice of you to say so,' said Stafford Nye, smiling at him agreeably. 'Teach me a sharp lesson, won't it?'

'You don't think anyone wanted *your* passport specially?'

'I shouldn't think so,' said Stafford Nye. 'Why should they want my passport. Unless it was a matter of someone who wished to annoy me and that hardly seems likely. Or somebody who took a fancy to my passport photo – and that seems even less likely!'

'Did you see anyone you knew at this – where did you say you were – Frankfurt?'

'No, no. Nobody at all.'

'Talk to anyone?'

'Not particularly. Said something to a nice fat woman who'd got a small child she was trying to amuse. Came from Wigan, I think. Going to Australia. Don't remember anybody else.'

'You're sure?'

'There was some woman or other who wanted to know what she did if she wanted to study archaeology in Egypt. Said I didn't know anything about that. I told her she'd better go and ask the British Museum. And I had a word or two with a man who I think was an anti-vivisectionist. Very passionate about it.'

'One always feels,' said Chetwynd, 'that there might be something *behind* things like this.'

'Things like what?'

'Well, things like what happened to you.'

'I don't see what can be behind this,' said Sir Stafford. 'I daresay journalists could make up some story, they're so clever at that sort of thing. Still, it's a silly business. For goodness' sake, let's forget it. I suppose now it's been mentioned in the press, all my friends will start asking me about it. How's old Leyland? What's he up to nowadays? I heard one or two things about him out there. Leyland always talks a bit too much.'

The two men talked amiable shop for ten minutes or so, then Sir Stafford got up and went out.

'I've got a lot of things to do this morning,' he said. 'Presents to buy for my relations. The trouble is that if one goes to Malaya, all one's relations expect you to bring exotic presents to them. I'll go round to Liberty's, I think. They have a nice stock of Eastern goods there.'

He went out cheerfully, nodding to a couple of men he knew in the corridor outside. After he had gone, Chetwynd spoke through the telephone to his secretary.

'Ask Colonel Munro if he can come to me.'

Colonel Munro came in, bringing another tall middle-aged man with him.

'Don't know whether you know Horsham,' he said, 'in Security.'

'Think I've met you,' said Chetwynd.

'Nye's just left you, hasn't he?' said Colonel Munro. 'Anything in this story about Frankfurt? Anything, I mean, that we ought to take any notice of?'

'Doesn't seem so,' said Chetwynd. 'He's a bit put out about it. Thinks it makes him look a silly ass. Which it does, of course.'

The man called Horsham nodded his head. 'That's the way he takes it, is it?'

'Well, he tried to put a good face upon it,' said Chetwynd.

'All the same, you know,' said Horsham, 'he's not really a silly ass, is he?'

Chetwynd shrugged his shoulders. 'These things happen,' he said.

'I know,' said Colonel Munro, 'yes, yes, I know. All the same, well, I've always felt in some ways that Nye is a bit unpredictable. That in some ways, you know, he mightn't be really *sound* in his views.'

The man called Horsham spoke. 'Nothing against him,' he said. 'Nothing at all as far as *we* know.'

'Oh, I didn't mean there was. I didn't mean that at all,' said Chetwynd. 'It's just – how shall I put it? – he's not always very serious about things.'

Mr Horsham had a moustache. He found it useful to have a moustache. It concealed moments when he found it difficult to avoid smiling.

'He's not a stupid man,' said Munro. 'Got brains, you know. You don't think that – well, I mean you don't think there could be anything at all doubtful about this?'

'On his part? It doesn't seem so.'

'You've been into it all, Horsham?'

'Well, we haven't had very much time yet. But as far as it goes it's all right. But his passport *was* used.'

'Used? In what way?'

'It passed through Heathrow.'

'You mean someone represented himself as Sir Stafford Nye?'

'No, no,' said Horsham, 'not in so many words. We could hardly hope for that. It went through with other passports. There was no alarm out, you know. He hadn't even woken up, I gather, at that time, from the dope or whatever it was he was given. He was still at Frankfurt.'

'But someone could have stolen that passport and come on the plane and so got into England?'

'Yes,' said Munro, 'that's the presumption. Either someone took a wallet which had money in it and a passport, or else someone wanted a passport and settled on Sir Stafford Nye as a convenient person to take it from. A drink was waiting on a table, put a pinch in that, wait till the man went off to sleep, take the passport and chance it.'

'But after all, they look at a passport. Must have seen it wasn't the right man,' said Chetwynd.

'Well, there must have been a certain resemblance, certainly,' said Horsham. 'But it isn't as though there was any notice of his being missing, any special attention drawn to that particular passport in any way. A large crowd comes through on a plane that's overdue. A man looks reasonably like the photograph in his passport. That's all. Brief glance, handed back, pass it on. Anyway what they're looking for usually is the *foreigners* that are coming in, not the British lot. Dark hair, dark blue eyes, clean shaven, five foot ten or whatever it is. That's about all you want to see. Not on a list of undesirable aliens or anything like that.'

'I know, I know. Still, you'd say if anybody wanted merely to pinch a wallet or some money or that, they wouldn't use the passport, would they. Too much risk.'

'Yes,' said Horsham. 'Yes, that is the interesting part of it. Of course,' he said, 'we're making investigations, asking a few questions here and there.'

'And what's your own opinion?'

'I wouldn't like to say yet,' said Horsham. 'It takes a little time, you know. One can't hurry things.'

'They're all the same,' said Colonel Munro, when Horsham had left the room. 'They never will tell you anything, those damned security people. If they think they're on the trail of anything, they won't admit it.'

'Well, that's natural,' said Chetwynd, 'because they might be wrong.'

It seemed a typically political view.

'Horsham's a pretty good man,' said Munro. 'They think very highly of him at headquarters. He's not likely to be wrong.'

CHAPTER 3

THE MAN FROM THE CLEANERS

Sir Stafford Nye returned to his flat. A large woman bounced out of the small kitchen with welcoming words.

'See you got back all right, sir. Those nasty planes. You never know, do you?'

'Quite true, Mrs Worrit,' said Sir Stafford Nye. 'Two hours late, the plane was.'

'Same as cars, aren't they,' said Mrs Worrit. 'I mean, you never know, do you, what's going to go wrong with *them*. Only it's more worrying, so to speak, being up in the air, isn't it? Can't just draw up to the kerb, not the same way, can you? I mean, there you are. I wouldn't go by one myself, not if it was ever so.' She went on, 'I've ordered in a few things. I hope that's all right. Eggs, butter, coffee, tea –' She ran off the words with the loquacity of a Near Eastern guide showing a Pharaoh's palace. 'There,' said Mrs Worrit, pausing to take breath, 'I think that's all as you're likely to want. I've ordered the French mustard.'

'Not Dijon, is it? They always try and give you Dijon.'

'I don't know who *he* was, but it's Esther Dragon, the one you like, isn't it?'

'Quite right,' said Sir Stafford, 'you're a wonder.'

Mrs Worrit looked pleased. She retired into the kitchen again, as Sir Stafford Nye put his hand on his bedroom door handle preparatory to going into the bedroom.

'All right to give your clothes to the gentleman what called for them, I suppose, sir? You hadn't said or left word or anything like that.'

'What clothes?' said Sir Stafford Nye, pausing.

'Two suits, it was, the gentleman said as called for them. Twiss and Bonywork it was, think that's the same name as called before. We'd had a bit of a dispute with the White Swan laundry if I remember rightly.'

'Two suits?' said Sir Stafford Nye. 'Which suits?'

'Well, there was the one you travelled home in, sir. I made out that would be one of them. I wasn't quite so sure about the other, but there was the blue pinstripe that you didn't leave no orders about when you went away. It could do with cleaning, and there was a repair wanted doing to the right-hand cuff, but I didn't like to take it on myself while you were away. I never likes to do that,' said Mrs Worrit with an air of palpable virtue.

'So the chap, whoever he was, took those suits away?'

'I hope I didn't do wrong, sir.' Mrs Worrit became worried.

'I don't mind the blue pinstripe. I daresay it's all for the best. The suit I came home in, well –'

'It's a bit thin, that suit, sir, for this time of year, you know, sir. All right for those parts as you've been in where it's hot. And it could do with a clean. He said as you'd rung up about them. That's what the gentleman said as called for them.'

'Did he go into my room and pick them out himself?'

'Yes, sir. I thought that was best.'

'Very interesting,' said Sir Stafford. 'Yes, very interesting.'

He went into his bedroom and looked round it. It was neat and tidy. The bed was made, the hand of Mrs Worrit was apparent, his electric razor was on charge, the things on the dressing-table were neatly arranged.

He went to the wardrobe and looked inside. He looked in the drawers of the tallboy that stood against the wall near the window.

It was all quite tidy. It was tidier indeed than it should have been. He had done a little unpacking last night and what little he had done had been of a cursory nature. He had thrown underclothing and various odds and ends in the appropriate drawer but he had not arranged them neatly. He would have done that himself either today or tomorrow. He would not have expected Mrs Worrit to do it for him. He expected her merely to keep things as she found them. Then, when he came back from abroad, there would be a time for rearrangements and readjustments because of climate and other matters. So someone had looked round here, someone had taken out drawers, looked through them quickly, hurriedly, had replaced things, partly because of his hurry, more tidily and neatly than he should have done. A quick careful job and he had gone away with two suits and a plausible explanation. One suit obviously worn by Sir Stafford when travelling and a suit of thin material which might have been one taken abroad and brought home. So why?

'Because,' said Sir Stafford thoughtfully, to himself, 'because somebody was looking for something. But what? And who? And also perhaps why?' Yes, it was interesting.

He sat down in a chair and thought about it. Presently his eyes strayed to the table by the bed on which sat, rather pertly, a small furry panda. It started a train of thought. He went to the telephone and rang a number.

'That you, Aunt Matilda?' he said. 'Stafford here.'

'Ah, my dear boy, so you're back. I'm so glad. I read in the paper they'd got cholera in Malaya yesterday, at least I think it was Malaya. I always get so mixed up with those places. I hope you're coming to see me soon? Don't pretend you're busy. You can't be busy all the time. One really only accepts that sort of thing from tycoons, people in industry, you know, in the middle of mergers and takeovers. I never know what it all really means. It used to mean doing your work properly but now it means things all tied up with atom bombs and factories in concrete,' said Aunt Matilda, rather wildly. 'And those terrible computers that get all one's figures wrong, to say nothing of making them the wrong shape. Really, they have made life so difficult for us nowadays. You wouldn't believe the things they've done to my bank account. And to my postal address too. Well, I suppose I've lived too long.'

392 • AGATHA CHRISTIE

'Don't you believe it! All right if I come down next week?'

'Come down tomorrow if you like. I've got the vicar coming to dinner, but I can easily put him off.'

'Oh, look here, no need to do that.'

'Yes there is, every need. He's a most irritating man and he wants a new organ too. This one does quite well as it is. I mean the trouble is with the organist, really, not the organ. An absolutely abominable musician. The vicar's sorry for him because he lost his mother whom he was very fond of. But really, being fond of your mother doesn't make you play the organ any better, does it? I mean, one has to look at things as they are.'

'Quite right. It will have to be next week – I've got a few things to see to. How's Sybil?'

'Dear child! Very naughty but such fun.'

'I brought her home a woolly panda,' said Sir Stafford Nye.

'Well, that was very nice of you, dear.'

'I hope she'll like it,' said Sir Stafford, catching the panda's eye and feeling slightly nervous.

'Well, at any rate, she's got very good manners,' said Aunt Matilda, which seemed a somewhat doubtful answer, the meaning of which Sir Stafford did not quite appreciate.

Aunt Matilda suggested likely trains for next week with the warning that they very often did not run, or changed their plans, and also commanded that he should bring her down a Camembert cheese and half a Stilton.

'Impossible to get anything down here now. Our own grocer – such a nice man, so thoughtful and such good taste in what we all liked – turned suddenly into a supermarket, six times the size, all rebuilt, baskets and wire trays to carry round and try to fill up with things you don't want and mothers always losing their babies, and crying and having hysterics. Most exhausting. Well, I'll be expecting you, dear boy.' She rang off.

The telephone rang again at once.

'Hullo? Stafford? Eric Pugh here. Heard you were back from Malaya – what about dining tonight?'

'Like to very much.'

'Good – Limpits Club – eight-fifteen?'

Mrs Worrit panted into the room as Sir Stafford replaced the receiver.

'A gentleman downstairs wanting to see you, sir,' she said. 'At least I mean, I suppose he's that. Anyway he said he was sure you wouldn't mind.'

'What's his name?'

'Horsham, sir, like the place on the way to Brighton.'

'Horsham.' Sir Stafford Nye was a little surprised.

He went out of his bedroom, down a half flight of stairs that led to the big sitting-room on the lower floor. Mrs Worrit had made no mistake. Horsham it was, looking as he had looked half an hour ago, stalwart, trustworthy, cleft chin, rubicund cheeks, bushy grey moustache and a general air of imperturbability.

'Hope you don't mind,' he said agreeably, rising to his feet.

'Hope I don't mind what?' said Sir Stafford Nye.

'Seeing me again so soon. We met in the passage outside Mr Gordon Chetwynd's door – if you remember?'

'No objections at all,' said Sir Stafford Nye.

He pushed a cigarette-box along the table.

'Sit down. Something forgotten, something left unsaid?'

'Very nice man, Mr Chetwynd,' said Horsham. 'We've got him quietened down, I think. He and Colonel Munro. They're a bit upset about it all, you know. About you, I mean.'

'Really?'

Sir Stafford Nye sat down too. He smiled, he smoked, and he looked thoughtfully at Henry Horsham. 'And where do we go from here?' he asked.

'I was just wondering if I might ask, without undue curiosity, where you're going from here?'

'Delighted to tell you,' said Sir Stafford Nye. 'I'm going to stay with an aunt of mine, Lady Matilda Cleckheaton. I'll give you the address if you like.'

'I know it,' said Henry Horsham. 'Well, I expect that's a very good idea. She'll be glad to see you've come home safely all right. Might have been a near thing, mightn't it?'

'Is that what Colonel Munro thinks and Mr Chetwynd?'

'Well, you know what it is, sir,' said Horsham. 'You know well enough. They're always in a state, gentlemen in that department. They're not sure whether they trust you or not.'

'Trust me?' said Sir Stafford Nye in an offended voice. 'What do you mean by that, Mr Horsham?'

Mr Horsham was not taken aback. He merely grinned.

'You see,' he said, 'you've got a reputation for not taking things seriously.'

'Oh. I thought you meant I was a fellow traveller or a convert to the wrong side. Something of that kind.'

'Oh no, sir, they just don't think you're serious. They think you like having a bit of a joke now and again.'

'One cannot go entirely through life taking oneself and other people seriously,' said Sir Stafford Nye, disapprovingly.

'No. But you took a pretty good risk, as I've said before, didn't you?'

'I wonder if I know in the least what you are talking about.'

'I'll tell you. Things go wrong, sir, sometimes, and they don't always go wrong because people have made them go wrong. What you might call the Almighty takes a hand, or the other gentleman – the one with the tail, I mean.'

Sir Stafford Nye was slightly diverted.

'Are you referring to fog at Geneva?' he said.

'Exactly, sir. There was fog at Geneva and that upset people's plans. Somebody was in a nasty hole.'

'Tell me all about it,' said Sir Stafford Nye. 'I really would like to know.'

'Well, a passenger was missing when that plane of yours left Frankfurt yesterday. You'd drunk your beer and you were sitting in a corner snoring nicely and comfortably by yourself. One passenger didn't report and they called her and they called her again. In the end, presumably, the plane left without her.'

'Ah. And what had happened to her?'

'It would be interesting to know. In any case, your passport arrived at Heathrow even if you didn't.'

'And where is it now? Am I supposed to have got it?'

'No. I don't think so. That would be rather too quick work. Good reliable stuff, that dope. Just right, if I may say so. It put you out and it didn't produce any particularly bad effects.'

'It gave me a very nasty hangover,' said Sir Stafford.

'Ah well, you can't avoid that. Not in the circumstances.'

'What would have happened,' Sir Stafford asked, 'since you seem to know all about everything, if I had refused to accept the proposition that may – I will only say may – have been put up to me?'

'It's quite possible that it would have been curtains for Mary Ann.'

'Mary Ann? Who's Mary Ann?'

'Miss Daphne Theodofanous.'

'That's the name I do seem to have heard – being summoned as a missing traveller?'

'Yes, that's the name she was travelling under. We call her Mary Ann.'

'Who is she – just as a matter of interest?'

'In her own line she's more or less the tops.'

'And what is her line? Is she ours or is she theirs, if you know who "theirs" is? I must say I find a little difficulty myself when making my mind up about that.'

'Yes, it's not so easy, is it? What with the Chinese and the Russkies and the rather queer crowd that's behind all the student troubles and the New Mafia and the rather odd lot in South America. And the nice little nest of financiers who seem to have got something funny up their sleeves. Yes, it's not easy to say.'

'Mary Ann,' said Sir Stafford Nye thoughtfully. 'It seems a curious name to have for her if her real one is Daphne Theodofanous.'

'Well, her mother's Greek, her father was an Englishman, and her grandfather was an Austrian subject.'

'What would have happened if I hadn't made her a – loan of a certain garment?'

'She might have been killed.'

'Come, come. Not really?'

'We're worried about the airport at Heathrow. Things have happened there lately, things that need a bit of explaining. If the plane had gone via Geneva as planned, it would have been all right. She'd have had full protection all arranged. But this other way – there wouldn't have been time to arrange anything and you don't know who's who always, nowadays. Everyone's playing a double game or a treble or a quadruple one.'

'You alarm me,' said Sir Stafford Nye. 'But she's all right, is she? Is that what you're telling me?'

'I hope she's all right. We haven't heard anything to the contrary.'

'If it's any help to you,' said Sir Stafford Nye, 'somebody called here this morning while I was out talking to my little pals in Whitehall. He represented that I telephoned a firm of cleaners and he removed the suit that I wore yesterday, and also another suit. Of course it may have been merely that he took a fancy to the other suit, or he may have made a practice of collecting various gentlemen's suitings who have recently returned from abroad. Or – well, perhaps you've got an "or" to add?'

'He might have been looking for something.'

'Yes, I think he was. Somebody's been looking for something. All very nice and tidily arranged again. Not the way I left it. All right, he was looking for something. What was he looking for?'

'I'm not sure myself,' said Horsham, slowly. 'I wish I was. There's something going on – somewhere. There are bits of it sticking out, you know, like a badly done up parcel. You get a peep here and a peep there. One moment you think it's going on at the Bayreuth Festival and the next minute you think it's tucking out of a South American estancia and then you get a bit of a lead in the USA. There's a lot of nasty business going on in different places, working up to something. Maybe politics, maybe something quite different from politics. It's probably money.' He added: 'You know Mr Robinson, don't you? Or rather Mr Robinson knows you, I think he said.'

'Robinson?' Sir Stafford Nye considered. 'Robinson. Nice English name.' He looked across to Horsham. 'Large, yellow face?' he said. 'Fat? Finger in financial pies generally?' He asked: 'Is he, too, on the side of the angels – is that what you're telling me?'

'I don't know about angels,' said Henry Horsham. 'He's pulled us out of a hole in this country more than once. People like Mr Chetwynd don't go for him much. Think he's too expensive, I suppose. Inclined to be a mean man, Mr Chetwynd. A great one for making enemies in the wrong place.'

'One used to say "Poor but honest",' said Sir Stafford Nye thoughtfully. 'I take it that you would put it differently. You would describe our Mr Robinson as expensive but honest. Or shall we put it, honest but expensive.' He sighed. 'I wish you could tell me what all this is about,' he said plaintively. 'Here I seem to be mixed up in something and no idea what it is.' He looked at Henry Horsham hopefully, but Horsham shook his head.

'None of us knows. Not exactly,' he said.

'What am I supposed to have got hidden here that someone comes fiddling and looking for?'

'Frankly, I haven't the least idea, Sir Stafford.'

'Well, that's a pity because I haven't either.'

'As far as *you* know you haven't got anything. Nobody gave you anything to keep, to take anywhere, to look after?'

'Nothing whatsoever. If you mean Mary Ann, she said she wanted her life saved, that's all.'

'And unless there's a paragraph in the evening papers, you *have* saved her life.'

'It seems rather the end of the chapter, doesn't it? A pity. My curiosity is rising. I find I want to know very much what's going to happen next. All you people seem very pessimistic.'

'Frankly, we are. Things are going badly in this country. Can you wonder?'

'I know what you mean. I sometimes wonder myself –'

CHAPTER 4

DINNER WITH ERIC

I

'Do you mind if I tell you something, old man?' said Eric Pugh.

Sir Stafford Nye looked at him. He had known Eric Pugh for a good many years. They had not been close friends. Old Eric, or so Sir Stafford thought, was rather a boring friend. He was, on the other hand, faithful. And he was the type of man who, though not amusing, had a knack of knowing things. People said things to him and he remembered what they said and stored them up. Sometimes he could push out a useful bit of information.

'Come back from that Malay Conference, haven't you?'

'Yes,' said Sir Stafford.

'Anything particular turn up there?'

'Just the usual,' said Sir Stafford.

'Oh. I wondered if something had – well, you know what I mean. Anything had occurred to put the cat among the pigeons.'

'What, at the Conference? No, just painfully predictable. Everyone said just what you thought they'd say only they said it unfortunately at rather greater length than you could have imagined possible. I don't know why I go on these things.'

Eric Pugh made a rather tedious remark or two as to what the Chinese were really up to.

'I don't think they're really up to anything,' said Sir Stafford. 'All the usual rumours, you know, about the diseases poor old Mao has got and who's intriguing against him and why.'

'And what about the Arab-Israeli business?'

'That's proceeding according to plan also. Their plan, that is to say. And anyway, what's that got to do with Malaya?'

'Well, I didn't really mean so much Malaya.'

'You're looking rather like the Mock Turtle,' said Sir Stafford Nye. '"Soup of the evening, beautiful soup." Wherefore this gloom?'

'Well, I just wondered if you'd – you'll forgive me, won't you? – I mean you haven't done anything to blot your copybook, have you, in any way?'

'Me?' said Sir Stafford, looking highly surprised.

'Well, you know what you're like, Staff. You like giving people a jolt sometimes, don't you?'

'I have behaved impeccably of late,' said Sir Stafford. 'What have you been hearing about me?'

'I hear there was some trouble about something that happened in a plane on your way home.'

'Oh? Who did you hear that from?'

'Well, you know, I saw old Cartison.'

'Terrible old bore. Always imagining things that haven't happened.'

'Yes, I know. I know he is like that. But he was just saying that somebody or other – Winterton, at least – seemed to think you'd been up to something.'

'Up to something? I wish I had,' said Sir Stafford Nye.

'There's some espionage racket going on somewhere and he got a bit worried about certain people.'

'What do they think I am – another Philby, something of that kind?'

'You know you're very unwise sometimes in the things you say, the things you make jokes about.'

'It's very hard to resist sometimes,' his friend told him. 'All these politicians and diplomats and the rest of them. They're so bloody solemn. You'd like to give them a bit of a stir up now and again.'

'Your sense of fun is very distorted, my boy. It really is. I worry about you sometimes. They wanted to ask you some questions about something that happened on the flight back and they seem to think that you didn't, well – that perhaps you didn't exactly speak the truth about it all.'

'Ah, that's what they think, is it? Interesting. I think I must work that up a bit.'

'Now don't do anything rash.'

'I must have my moments of fun sometimes.'

'Look here, old fellow, you don't want to go and ruin your career just by indulging your sense of humour.'

'I am quickly coming to the conclusion that there is nothing so boring as having a career.'

'I know, I know. You are always inclined to take that point of view, and you haven't got on as far as you ought to have, you know. You were in the running for Vienna at one time. I don't like to see you muck up things.'

'I am behaving with the utmost sobriety and virtue, I assure you,' said Sir Stafford Nye. He added, 'Cheer up, Eric. You're a good friend, but really, I'm not guilty of fun and games.'

Eric shook his head doubtfully.

It was a fine evening. Sir Stafford walked home across Green Park. As he crossed the road in Birdcage Walk, a car leaping down the street missed him by a few inches. Sir Stafford was an athletic man. His leap took him safely on to the pavement. The car disappeared down the street. He wondered. Just for a moment he could have sworn that that car had deliberately tried to run him down. An interesting thought. First his flat had been searched, and now he himself might have been marked down. Probably a mere coincidence. And yet, in the course of his life, some of which had been spent in wild neighbourhoods and places, Sir Stafford Nye had come in contact with danger. He knew, as it were, the touch and feel and smell of danger. He felt it now. Someone, somewhere was gunning for him. But why? For what reason? As far as he knew, he had not stuck his neck out in any way. He wondered.

He let himself into his flat and picked up the mail that lay on the floor inside. Nothing much. A couple of bills and copy of *Lifeboat* periodical. He threw the bills on to his desk and put a finger through the wrapper of *Lifeboat*. It was a cause to which he occasionally contributed. He turned the pages without much attention because he was still absorbed in what he was thinking. Then he stopped the action of his fingers abruptly. Something was taped between two of the pages. Taped with adhesive tape. He looked at it closely. It was his passport returned to him unexpectedly in this fashion. He tore it free and looked at it. The last stamp on it was the arrival stamp at Heathrow the day before. She had used his passport, getting back here safely, and had chosen this way to return it to him. Where was she now? He would like to know.

He wondered if he would ever see her again. Who was she? Where had she gone, and why? It was like waiting for the second act of a play. Indeed, he felt the first act had hardly been played yet. What had he seen? An old-fashioned curtain-raiser, perhaps. A girl who had ridiculously wanted to dress herself up and pass herself off as of the male sex, who had passed the passport control of Heathrow without attracting suspicion of any kind to herself and who had now disappeared through that gateway into London. No, he would probably never see her again. It annoyed him. But why, he thought, why do I want to? She wasn't particularly attractive, she wasn't anything. No, that wasn't quite true. She was something, or someone, or she could not have induced him, with no particular persuasion, with no overt sex stimulation, nothing except a plain demand for help, to do what she wanted. A demand from one human being to another human being because, or so she had intimated, not precisely in words, but nevertheless it was what she *had* intimated, she knew people and she recognized in him a man who was willing to take a risk to help another human being. And he had taken a risk, too, thought Sir Stafford Nye. She could have put anything in that beer glass of his. He could have been found, if she had so willed it, found as a dead body in a seat tucked away in the corner of a departure lounge in an airport. And if she had, as no doubt she must have had, a knowledgeable recourse to drugs, his death might have been passed off as an attack of heart trouble due to altitude or difficult pressurizing – something or other like that. Oh well, why think about it? He wasn't likely to see her again and he was annoyed.

Yes, he was annoyed, and he didn't like being annoyed. He considered the matter for some minutes. Then he wrote out an advertisement, to be repeated three times. '*Passenger to Frankfurt. November 3rd. Please communicate with fellow traveller to London.*' No more than that. Either she would or she wouldn't. If it ever came to her eyes she would know by whom that advertisement had been inserted. She had had his passport, she knew his name. She could look him up. He might hear from her. He might not. Probably not. If not, the curtain-raiser would remain a curtain-raiser, a silly little play that received late-comers to the theatre and diverted them until the real business of the evening began. Very useful in pre-war times. In all probability, though, he would not hear from her again and one of the reasons might be that she might have accomplished whatever it was she had come to do in London, and have now left the country once more, flying abroad to Geneva, or the Middle East, or to Russia or to China or to South America, or to the United States. And why, thought Sir Stafford, do I include South America? There must be a reason. She had not mentioned South America. Nobody had mentioned South America. Except Horsham, that was true. And even Horsham had only mentioned South America among a lot of other mentions.

On the following morning as he walked slowly homeward, after handing in his advertisement, along the pathway across St James's Park his eye picked out, half unseeing, the autumn flowers. The chrysanthemums looking by now stiff and leggy with their button tops of gold and bronze. Their smell came to him faintly, a rather goatlike smell, he had always thought, a smell that reminded him of hillsides in Greece. He must remember to keep his eye on the Personal Column. Not yet. Two or three days at least would have to pass before his own advertisement was put in and before there had been time for anyone to put in one in answer. He must not miss it if there was an answer because, after all, it was irritating not to know – not to have any idea what all this was about.

He tried to recall not the girl at the airport but his sister Pamela's face. A long time since her death. He remembered her. Of course he remembered her, but he could not somehow picture her face. It irritated him not to be able to do so. He had paused just when he was about to cross one of the roads. There was no traffic except for a car jigging slowly along with the solemn demeanour of a bored dowager. An elderly car, he thought. An old-fashioned Daimler limousine. He shook his shoulders. Why stand here in this idiotic way, lost in thought?

He took an abrupt step to cross the road and suddenly with surprising vigour the dowager limousine, as he had thought of it in his mind, accelerated. Accelerated with a sudden astonishing speed. It bore down on him with such swiftness that he only just had time to leap across on to the opposite pavement. It disappeared with a flash, turning round the curve of the road further on.

'I wonder,' said Sir Stafford to himself. 'Now I wonder. Could it be that there *is* someone that doesn't like me? Someone following me, perhaps, watching me take my way home, waiting for an opportunity?'

II

Colonel Pikeaway, his bulk sprawled out in his chair in the small room in Bloomsbury where he sat from ten to five with a short interval for lunch, was surrounded as usual by an atmosphere of thick cigar smoke; with his eyes closed, only an occasional blink showed that he was awake and not asleep. He seldom raised his head. Somebody had said that he looked like a cross between an ancient Buddha and a large blue frog, with perhaps, as some impudent youngster had added, just a touch of a bar sinister from a hippopotamus in his ancestry.

The gentle buzz of the intercom on his desk roused him. He blinked three times and opened his eyes. He stretched forth a rather weary-looking hand and picked up the receiver.

'Well?' he said.

His secretary's voice spoke.

'The Minister is here waiting to see you.'

'Is he now?' said Colonel Pikeaway. 'And what Minister is that? The Baptist minister from the church round the corner?'

'Oh no, Colonel Pikeaway, it's Sir George Packham.'

'Pity,' said Colonel Pikeaway, breathing asthmatically. 'Great pity. The Reverend McGill is far more amusing. There's a splendid touch of hell fire about him.'

'Shall I bring him in, Colonel Pikeaway?'

'I suppose he will expect to be brought in at once. Under Secretaries are far more touchy than Secretaries of State,' said Colonel Pikeaway gloomily. 'All these Ministers insist on coming in and having kittens all over the place.'

Sir George Packham was shown in. He coughed and wheezed. Most people did. The windows of the small room were tightly closed. Colonel Pikeaway reclined in his chair, completely smothered in cigar ash. The atmosphere was almost unbearable and the room was known in official circles as the 'small cat-house'.

'Ah, my dear fellow,' said Sir George, speaking briskly and cheerfully in a way that did not match his ascetic and sad appearance. 'Quite a long time since we've met, I think.'

'Sit down, sit down do,' said Pikeaway. 'Have a cigar?'

Sir George shuddered slightly.

'No, thank you,' he said, 'no, thanks very much.'

He looked hard at the windows. Colonel Pikeaway did not take the hint. Sir George cleared his throat and coughed again before saying:

'Er – I believe Horsham has been to see you.'

'Yes, Horsham's been and said his piece,' said Colonel Pikeaway, slowly allowing his eyes to close again.

'I thought it was the best way. I mean, that he should call upon you here. It's most important that things shouldn't get round anywhere.'

'Ah,' said Colonel Pikeaway, 'but they will, won't they?'

'I beg your pardon?'

'They will,' said Colonel Pikeaway.

'I don't know how much you – er – well, know about this last business.'

'We know everything here,' said Colonel Pikeaway. 'That's what we're for.'

'Oh – oh yes, yes certainly. About Sir S.N. – you know who I mean?'

'Recently a passenger from Frankfurt,' said Colonel Pikeaway.

'Most extraordinary business. Most extraordinary. One wonders – one really does not know, one can't begin to imagine . . .'

Colonel Pikeaway listened kindly.

'What is one to think?' pursued Sir George. 'Do you know him personally?'

'I've come across him once or twice,' said Colonel Pikeaway.

'One really cannot help wondering –'

Colonel Pikeaway subdued a yawn with some difficulty. He was rather tired of Sir George's thinking, wondering, and imagining. He had a poor opinion anyway of Sir George's process of thought. A cautious man, a man who could be relied upon to run his department in a cautious manner. Not a man of scintillating intellect. Perhaps, thought Colonel Pikeaway, all the better for that. At any rate, those who think and wonder and are not quite sure are reasonably safe in the place where God and the electors have put them.

'One cannot quite forget,' continued Sir George, 'the disillusionment we have suffered in the past.'

Colonel Pikeaway smiled kindly.

'Charleston, Conway and Courtfold,' he said. 'Fully trusted, vetted and approved of. All beginning with C, all crooked as sin.'

'Sometimes I wonder if we can trust anyone,' said Sir George unhappily.

'That's easy,' said Colonel Pikeaway, 'you can't.'

'Now take Stafford Nye,' said Sir George. 'Good family, excellent family, knew his father, his grandfather.'

'Often a slip-up in the third generation,' said Colonel Pikeaway. The remark did not help Sir George.

'I cannot help doubting – I mean, sometimes he doesn't really seem serious.'

'Took my two nieces to see the châteaux of the Loire when I was a young man,' said Colonel Pikeaway unexpectedly. 'Man fishing on the bank. I had my fishing-rod with me, too. He said to me, "*Vous n'êtes pas un pêcheur sérieux. Vous avez des femmes avec vous.*"'

'You mean you think Sir Stafford –?'

'No, no, never been mixed up with women much. Irony's his trouble. Likes surprising people. He can't help liking to score off people.'

'Well, that's not very satisfactory, is it?'

'Why not?' said Colonel Pikeaway. 'Liking a private joke is much better than having some deal with a defector.'

'If one could feel that he was really sound. What would you say – your personal opinion?'

'Sound as a bell,' said Colonel Pikeaway. 'If a bell is sound. It makes a sound, but that's different, isn't it?' He smiled kindly. 'Shouldn't worry, if I were you,' he said.

III

Sir Stafford Nye pushed aside his cup of coffee. He picked up the newspaper, glancing over the headlines, then he turned it carefully to the page which gave Personal advertisements. He'd looked down that particular column for seven days now. It was disappointing but not surprising. Why on earth should he expect to find an answer? His eye went slowly down miscellaneous peculiarities which had always made that particular page rather fascinating in his eyes. They were not so strictly personal. Half of them or even more than half were disguised advertisements or offers of things for sale or wanted for sale. They should perhaps have been put under a different heading but they had found their way here considering that they were more likely to catch the eye that way. They included one or two of the hopeful variety.

'Young man who objects to hard work and who would like an easy life would be glad to undertake a job that would suit him.'

'Girl wants to travel to Cambodia. Refuses to look after children.'

'Firearm used at Waterloo. What offers.'

'Glorious fun-fur coat. Must be sold immediately. Owner going abroad.'

'Do you know Jenny Capstan? Her cakes are superb. Come to 14 Lizzard Street, S.W.3.'

For a moment Stafford Nye's finger came to a stop. Jenny Capstan. He liked the name. Was there any Lizzard Street? He supposed so. He had never heard of it. With a sigh, the finger went down the column and almost at once was arrested once more.

'Passenger from Frankfurt, Thursday Nov. 11, Hungerford Bridge 7.20.'

Thursday, November 11th. That was – yes, that was today. Sir Stafford Nye leaned back in his chair and drank more coffee. He was excited, stimulated. Hungerford. Hungerford Bridge. He got up and went into the kitchenette. Mrs Worrit was cutting potatoes into strips and throwing them into a large bowl of water. She looked up with some slight surprise.

'Anything you want, sir?'

'Yes,' said Sir Stafford Nye. 'If anyone said Hungerford Bridge to you, where would you go?'

'Where should I go?' Mrs Worrit considered. 'You mean if I wanted to go, do you?'

'We can proceed on that assumption.'

'Well, then, I suppose I'd go to Hungerford Bridge, wouldn't I?'

'You mean you would go to Hungerford in Berkshire?'

'Where is that?' said Mrs Worrit.

'Eight miles beyond Newbury.'

'I've heard of Newbury. My old man backed a horse there last year. Did well, too.'

'So you'd go to Hungerford near Newbury?'

'No, of course I wouldn't,' said Mrs Worrit. 'Go all that way – what for? I'd go to Hungerford Bridge, of course.'

'You mean –?'

'Well, it's near Charing Cross. You know where it is. Over the Thames.'

'Yes,' said Sir Stafford Nye. 'Yes, I do know where it is quite well. Thank you, Mrs Worrit.'

It had been, he felt, rather like tossing a penny heads or tails. An advertisement in a morning paper in London meant Hungerford Railway Bridge in London. Presumably therefore that is what the advertiser meant, although about this particular advertiser Sir Stafford Nye was not at all sure. Her ideas, from the brief experience he had had of her, were original ideas. They were not the normal responses to be expected. But still, what else could one do. Besides, there were probably other Hungerfords, and possibly they would also have bridges, in various parts of England. But today, well, today he would see.

IV

It was a cold windy evening with occasional bursts of thin misty rain. Sir Stafford Nye turned up the collar of his mackintosh and plodded on. It was not the first time he had gone across Hungerford Bridge, but it had never seemed to him a walk to take for pleasure. Beneath him was the river and crossing the bridge were large quantities of hurrying figures like himself. Their mackintoshes pulled round them, their hats pulled down and on the part of one and all of them an earnest desire to get home and out of the wind and rain as soon as possible. It would be, thought Sir Stafford Nye, very difficult to recognize anybody in this scurrying crowd. 7.20. Not a good moment to choose for a rendezvous of any kind. Perhaps it was Hungerford Bridge in Berkshire. Anyway, it seemed very odd.

He plodded on. He kept an even pace, not overtaking those ahead of him, pushing past those coming the opposite way. He went fast enough not to be overtaken by the others behind him, though it would be possible for them to do so if they wanted to. A joke, perhaps, thought Stafford Nye. Not quite his kind of joke, but someone else's.

And yet – not her brand of humour either, he would have thought. Hurrying figures passed him again, pushing him slightly aside. A woman in a mackintosh was coming along, walking heavily. She collided with him, slipped, dropped to her knees. He assisted her up.

'All right?'

'Yes, thanks.'

She hurried on, but as she passed him, her wet hand, by which he had held her as he pulled her to her feet, slipped something into the palm of his hand, closing the fingers over it. Then she was gone, vanishing behind him, mingling with the crowd. Stafford Nye went on. He couldn't overtake her. She did not wish to be overtaken, either. He hurried on and his hand held something firmly. And so, at long last it seemed, he came to the end of the bridge on the Surrey side.

A few minutes later he had turned into a small café and sat

there behind a table, ordering coffee. Then he looked at what was in his hand. It was a very thin oilskin envelope. Inside it was a cheap quality white envelope. That too he opened. What was inside surprised him. It was a ticket.

A ticket for the Festival Hall for the following evening.

CHAPTER 5

WAGNERIAN MOTIF

Sir Stafford Nye adjusted himself more comfortably in his seat and listened to the persistent hammering of the Nibelungen, with which the programme began.

Though he enjoyed Wagnerian opera, *Siegfried* was by no means his favourite of the operas composing the Ring. *Rheingold* and *Götterdämmerung* were his two preferences. The music of the young Siegfried, listening to the songs of the birds, had always for some strange reason irritated him instead of filling him with melodic satisfaction. It might have been because he went to a performance in Munich in his young days which had displayed a magnificent tenor of unfortunately over-magnificent proportions, and he had been too young to divorce the joy of music from the visual joy of seeing a young Siegfried that looked even passably young. The fact of an outsized tenor rolling about on the ground in an access of boyishness had revolted him. He was also not particularly fond of birds and forest murmurs. No, give him the Rhine Maidens every time, although in Munich even the Rhine Maidens in those days had been of fairly solid proportions. But that mattered less. Carried away by the melodic flow of water and the joyous impersonal song, he had not allowed visual appreciation to matter.

From time to time he looked about him casually. He had taken his seat fairly early. It was a full house, as it usually was. The intermission came. Sir Stafford rose and looked about him. The seat beside his had remained empty. Someone who was supposed to have arrived had not arrived. Was that the answer, or was it merely a case of being excluded because someone had arrived late, which practice still held on the occasions when Wagnerian music was listened to.

He went out, strolled about, drank a cup of coffee, smoked a cigarette, and returned when the summons came. This time, as he drew near, he saw that the seat next to his was filled. Immediately his excitement returned. He regained his seat and sat down. Yes, it was the woman of the Frankfurt Air Lounge. She did not look at him, she was looking straight ahead. Her face in profile was as clean-cut and pure as he remembered it. Her head turned slightly, and her eyes passed over him but without recognition. So intent was that non-recognition that it was as good as a word spoken. This was a meeting that was not to be acknowledged. Not now, at any event. The lights began to dim. The woman beside him turned.

'Excuse me, could I look at your programme? I have dropped mine, I'm afraid, coming to my seat.'

'Of course,' he said.

He handed over the programme and she took it from him. She opened it, studied the items. The lights went lower. The second half of the programme began. It started with the overture to *Lohengrin*. At the end of it she handed back the programme to him with a few words of thanks.

'Thank you so much. It was very kind of you.'

The next item was the Siegfried forest murmur music. He consulted the programme she had returned to him. It was then that he noticed something faintly pencilled at the foot of a page. He did not attempt to read it now. Indeed, the light would have not been sufficient. He merely closed the programme and held it. He had not, he was quite sure, written anything there himself. Not, that is, in his own programme. She had, he thought, had her own programme ready, folded perhaps in her handbag and had already written some message ready to pass to him. Altogether, it seemed to him, there was still that atmosphere of secrecy, of danger. The meeting on Hungerford Bridge and the envelope with the ticket forced into his hand. And now the silent woman who sat beside him. He glanced at her once or twice with the quick, careless glance that one gives to a stranger sitting next to one. She lolled back in her seat; her high-necked dress was of dull black crêpe, an antique torque of gold encircled her neck. Her dark hair was cropped closely and shaped to her head. She did not glance at him or return any look. He wondered. Was

there someone in the seats of the Festival Hall watching her
– or watching him? Noting whether they looked or spoke to
each other? Presumably there must be, or there must be at least
the possibility of such a thing. She had answered his appeal in
the newspaper advertisement. Let that be enough for him. His
curiosity was unimpaired, but he did at least know now that
Daphne Theodofanous – alias Mary Ann – was here in London.
There were possibilities in the future of his learning more of what
was afoot. But the plan of campaign must be left to her. He must
follow her lead. As he had obeyed her in the airport, so he would
obey her now and – let him admit it – life had become suddenly
more interesting. This was better than the boring conferences of
his political life. Had a car really tried to run him down the other
night? He thought it had. Two attempts – not only one. It was
easy enough to imagine that one was the target of assault, people
drove so recklessly nowadays that you could easily fancy malice
aforethought when it was not so. He folded his programme, did
not look at it again. The music came to its end. The woman next
to him spoke. She did not turn her head or appear to speak to
him, but she spoke aloud, with a little sigh between the words
as though she was communing with herself or possibly to her
neighbour on the other side.

'The young Siegfried,' she said, and sighed again.

The programme ended with the March from *Die Meistersinger*.
After enthusiastic applause, people began to leave their seats. He
waited to see if she would give him any lead, but she did not. She
gathered up her wrap, moved out of the row of chairs, and with
a slightly accelerated step, moved along with other people and
disappeared in the crowd.

Stafford Nye regained his car and drove home. Arrived there,
he spread out the Festival Hall programme on his desk and
examined it carefully, after putting the coffee to percolate.

The programme was disappointing to say the least of it. There
did not appear to be any message inside. Only on one page
above the list of the items, were the pencil marks that he had
vaguely observed. But they were not words or letters or even
figures. They appeared to be merely a musical notation. It was as
though someone had scribbled a phrase of music with a somewhat
inadequate pencil. For a moment it occurred to Stafford Nye

there might perhaps be a secret message he could bring out by applying heat. Rather gingerly, and in a way rather ashamed of his melodramatic fancy, he held it towards the bar of the electric fire but nothing resulted. With a sigh he tossed the programme back on to the table. But he felt justifiably annoyed. All this rigmarole, a rendezvous on a windy and rainy bridge overlooking the river! Sitting through a concert by the side of a woman of whom he yearned to ask at least a dozen questions – and at the end of it? Nothing! No further on. Still, she *had* met him. But why? If she didn't want to speak to him, to make further arrangements with him, why had she come at all?

His eyes passed idly across the room to his bookcase which he reserved for various thrillers, works of detective fiction and an occasional volume of science fiction; he shook his head. Fiction, he thought, was infinitely superior to real life. Dead bodies, mysterious telephone calls, beautiful foreign spies in profusion! However, this particular elusive lady might not have done with him yet. Next time, he thought, he would make some arrangements of his own. Two could play at the game that she was playing.

He pushed aside the programme and drank another cup of coffee and went to the window. He had the programme still in his hand. As he looked out towards the street below his eyes fell back again on the open programme in his hand and he hummed to himself, almost unconsciously. He had a good ear for music and he could hum the notes that were scrawled there quite easily. Vaguely they sounded familiar as he hummed them. He increased his voice a little. What was it now? Tum, tum, tum tum ti-tum. Tum. Yes, definitely familiar.

He started opening his letters.

They were mostly uninteresting. A couple of invitations, one from the American Embassy, one from Lady Athelhampton, a Charity Variety performance which Royalty would attend and for which it was suggested five guineas would not be an exorbitant fee to obtain a seat. He threw them aside lightly. He doubted very much whether he wished to accept any of them. He decided that instead of remaining in London he would without more ado go and see his Aunt Matilda, as he had promised. He was fond of his Aunt Matilda though he did not visit her very often. She lived in a rehabilitated apartment consisting of a series of rooms in one wing of a large Georgian manor house in the country which she had inherited from his grandfather. She had a large, beautifully proportioned sitting-room, a small oval dining-room, a new kitchen made from the old housekeeper's room, two bedrooms for guests, a large comfortable bedroom for herself with an adjoining bathroom, and adequate quarters for a patient companion who shared her daily life. The remains of a faithful domestic staff were well provided for and housed. The rest of the house remained under dust sheets with periodical cleaning. Stafford Nye was fond of the place, having spent holidays there as a boy. It had been a gay house then. His eldest uncle had lived there with his wife and their two children. Yes, it had been pleasant there then. There had been money and a sufficient staff to run it. He had not specially noticed in those days the portraits and pictures. There had been large-sized examples of Victorian art occupying pride of place – overcrowding the walls, but there had been other masters of an older age. Yes, there had been some good portraits there. A Raeburn, two Lawrences, a Gainsborough, a Lely, two rather dubious Vandykes. A couple of Turners, too. Some of them had had to be sold to provide the family with money. He still enjoyed when visiting there strolling about and studying the family pictures.

His Aunt Matilda was a great chatterbox but she always enjoyed his visits. He was fond of her in a desultory way, but he was not quite sure why it was that he had suddenly wanted to visit her now. And what it was that had brought family portraits into his mind? Could it have been because there was a portrait of his sister Pamela by one of the leading artists of the day twenty years ago. He would like to see that portrait of Pamela and look at it more closely. See how close the resemblance had been between the stranger who had disrupted his life in this really outrageous fashion and his sister.

He picked up the Festival Hall programme again with some irritation and began to hum the pencilled notes. Tum, tum, ti tum – Then it came to him and he knew what it was. It was the Siegfried motif. Siegfried's Horn. The Young Siegfried motif. That was what the woman had said last night. Not apparently to him, not apparently to anybody. But it had been the message, a message that would have meant nothing to anyone around since it would have seemed to refer to the music that had just been played. And the motif had been written on his programme also in musical terms. The Young Siegfried. It must have meant something. Well, perhaps further enlightenment would come. The Young Siegfried. What the hell *did* that mean? Why and how and when and what? Ridiculous! All those questioning words.

He rang the telephone and obtained Aunt Matilda's number.

'But of course, Staffy dear, it will be lovely to have you. Take the four-thirty train. It still runs, you know, but it gets here an hour and a half later. And it leaves Paddington later – five-fifteen. That's what they mean by improving the railways, I suppose. Stops at several most absurd stations on the way. All right. Horace will meet you at King's Marston.'

'He's still there then?'

'Of course he's still there.'

'I suppose he is,' said Sir Stafford Nye.

Horace, once a groom, then a coachman, had survived as a chauffeur, and apparently was still surviving. 'He must be at least eighty,' said Sir Stafford. He smiled to himself.

CHAPTER 6

PORTRAIT OF A LADY

I

'You look very nice and brown, dear,' said Aunt Matilda, surveying him appreciatively. 'That's Malaya, I suppose. If it *was* Malaya you went to? Or was it Siam or Thailand? They change the names of all these places and really it makes it very difficult. Anyway, it wasn't Vietnam, was it? You know, I don't like the sound of Vietnam *at all*. It's all very confusing, North Vietnam and South Vietnam and the Viet-Cong and the Viet – whatever the other thing is and all wanting to fight each other and nobody wanting to stop. They won't go to Paris or wherever it is and sit round tables and talk sensibly. Don't you think really, dear – I've been thinking it over and I thought it would be a very nice solution – couldn't you make a lot of football fields and then they could all go and fight each other there, but with less lethal weapons. Not that nasty palm burning stuff. You know. Just hit each other and punch each other and all that. They'd enjoy it, everyone would enjoy it and you could charge admission for people to go and see them do it. I do think really that we don't understand giving people the things they really want.'

'I think it's a very fine idea of yours, Aunt Matilda,' said Sir Stafford Nye as he kissed a pleasantly perfumed, pale pink wrinkled cheek. 'And how are you, my dear?'

'Well, I'm old,' said Lady Matilda Cleckheaton. 'Yes, I'm old. Of course you don't know what it is to be old. If it isn't one thing it's another. Rheumatism or arthritis or a nasty bit of asthma or a sore throat or an ankle you've turned. Always *something*, you know. Nothing very important. But there it is. Why have you come to see me, dear?'

Sir Stafford was slightly taken aback by the directness of the query.

'I usually come and see you when I return from a trip abroad.'

'You'll have to come one chair nearer,' said Aunt Matilda. 'I'm just that bit deafer since you saw me last. You look different . . . Why do you look different?'

'Because I'm more sunburnt. You said so.'

'Nonsense, that's not what I mean at all. Don't tell me it's a girl at last.'

'A girl?'

'Well, I've always felt it might be one some day. The trouble is you've got too much sense of humour.'

'Now why should you think that?'

'Well, it's what people do think about you. Oh yes, they do. Your sense of humour is in the way of your career, too. You know, you're all mixed up with all these people. Diplomatic and political. What they call younger statesmen and elder statesmen and middle statesmen too. And all those different Parties. Really I think it's too silly to have too many Parties. First of all those awful, awful Labour people.' She raised her Conservative nose into the air. 'Why, when I was a girl there wasn't such a thing as a *Labour* Party. Nobody would have known what you meant by it. They'd have said "nonsense". Pity it wasn't nonsense, too. And then there's the Liberals, of course, but they're terribly wet.

And then there are the Tories, or the Conservatives as they call themselves again now.'

'And what's the matter with them?' asked Stafford Nye, smiling slightly.

'Too many earnest women. Makes them lack gaiety, you know.'

'Oh well, no political party goes in for gaiety much nowadays.'

'Just so,' said Aunt Matilda. 'And then of course that's where you go wrong. You want to cheer things up. You want to have a little gaiety and so you make a little gentle fun at people and of course they don't like it. They say "*Ce n'est pas un garçon sérieux*," like that man in the fishing.'

Sir Stafford Nye laughed. His eyes were wandering round the room.

'What are you looking at?' said Lady Matilda.

'Your pictures.'

'You don't want me to sell them, do you? Everyone seems to be selling their pictures nowadays. Old Lord Grampion, you know. He sold his Turners and he sold some of his ancestors as well. And Geoffrey Gouldman. All those lovely horses of his. By Stubbs, weren't they? Something like that. Really, the prices one gets!

'But I don't want to sell my pictures. I like them. Most of them in this room have a real interest because they're ancestors. I know nobody wants ancestors nowadays but then I'm old-fashioned. I like ancestors. My own ancestors, I mean. What are you looking at? Pamela?'

'Yes, I was. I was thinking about her the other day.'

'Astonishing how alike you two are. I mean, it's not even as though you were twins, though they say that different sex twins, even if they are twins, can't be identical, if you know what I mean.'

'So Shakespeare must have made rather a mistake over Viola and Sebastian.'

'Well, ordinary brothers and sisters can be alike, can't they? You and Pamela were always very alike – to look at, I mean.'

'Not in any other way? Don't you think we were alike in character?'

'No, not in the least. That's the funny part of it. But of course you and Pamela have what I call the family face. Not a Nye face. I mean the Baldwen-White face.'

Sir Stafford Nye had never quite been able to compete when it came down to talking on a question of genealogy with his great-aunt.

'I've always thought that you and Pamela both took after Alexa,' she went on.

'Which was Alexa?'

'Your great-great – I think one more great – grandmother. Hungarian. A Hungarian countess or baroness or something. Your great-great-grandfather fell in love with her when he was at Vienna in the Embassy. Yes. Hungarian. That's what she was. Very sporting too. They are sporting, you know, Hungarians. She rode to hounds, rode magnificently.'

'Is she in the picture gallery?'

'She's on the first landing. Just over the head of the stairs, a little to the right.'

'I must go and look at her when I go to bed.'

'Why don't you go and look at her now and then you can come back and talk about her.'

'I will if you like.' He smiled at her.

He ran out of the room and up the staircase. Yes, she had a sharp eye, old Matilda. That was the face. That was the face that he had seen and remembered. Remembered not for its likeness to himself, not even for its likeness to Pamela, but for a closer resemblance still to this picture here. A handsome girl brought home by his Ambassador great-great-great-grandfather if that was enough greats. Aunt Matilda was never satisfied with only a few. About twenty she had been. She had come here and been high-spirited and rode a horse magnificently and danced divinely and men had fallen in love with her. But she had been faithful, so it was always said, to great-great-great-grandfather, a very steady and sober member of the Diplomatic Service. She had gone with him to foreign Embassies and returned here and had had children – three or four children, he believed. Through one of those children the inheritance of her face, her nose, the turn of her neck had been passed down to him and to his sister, Pamela. He wondered if the young woman who had doped his beer and

forced him to lend her his cloak and who had depicted herself as
being in danger of death unless he did what she asked, had been
possibly related as a fifth or sixth cousin removed, a descendant of
the woman pictured on the wall at which he looked. Well, it could
be. They had been of the same nationality, perhaps. Anyway their
faces had resembled each other a good deal. How upright she'd
sat at the opera, how straight that profile, the thin, slightly arched
aquiline nose. And the atmosphere that hung about her.

II

'Find it?' asked Lady Matilda, when her nephew returned to
the white drawing-room, as her sitting-room was usually called.
'Interesting face, isn't it?'

'Yes, quite handsome, too.'

'It's much better to be interesting than handsome. But you
haven't been in Hungary or Austria, have you? You wouldn't
meet anyone like her out in Malaya? She wouldn't be sitting
around a table there making little notes or correcting speeches
or things like that. She was a wild creature, by all accounts.
Lovely manners and all the rest of it. But wild. Wild as a wild
bird. She didn't know what danger was.'

'How do you know so much about her?'

'Oh, I agree I wasn't a contemporary of hers, I wasn't born
until several years after she was dead. All the same, I've always
been interested in her. She was adventurous, you know. Very
adventurous. Very queer stories were told about her, about things
she was mixed up in.'

'And how did my great-great-great-grandfather react to that?'

'I expect it worried him to death,' said Lady Matilda. 'They
say he was devoted to her, though. By the way, Staffy, did you
ever read The Prisoner of Zenda?'

'Prisoner of Zenda? Sounds very familiar.'

'Well, of course it's familiar, it's a book.'

'Yes, yes, I realize it's a book.'

'You wouldn't know about it, I expect. After your time. But
when I was a girl – that's about the first taste of romance we got.
Not pop singers or Beatles. Just a romantic novel. We weren't
allowed to read novels when I was young. Not in the morning
anyway. You could read them in the afternoon.'

'What extraordinary rules,' said Sir Stafford. 'Why is it wrong to read novels in the morning and not in the afternoon?'

'Well, in the mornings, you see, girls were supposed to be doing something useful. You know, doing the flowers or cleaning the silver photograph frames. All the things we girls did. Doing a bit of studying with the governess – all that sort of thing. In the afternoon we were allowed to sit down and read a story book and *The Prisoner of Zenda* was usually one of the first ones that came our way.'

'A very nice, respectable story, was it? I seem to remember something about it. Perhaps I did read it. All very pure, I suppose. Not too sexy?'

'Certainly not. We didn't have sexy books. We had romance. *The Prisoner of Zenda* was very romantic. One fell in love, usually, with the hero, Rudolf Rassendyll.'

'I seem to remember that name too. Bit florid, isn't it?'

'Well, I still think it was rather a romantic name. Twelve years old, I must have been. It made me think of it, you know, your going up and looking at that portrait. Princess Flavia,' she added.

Stafford Nye was smiling at her.

'You look young and pink and very sentimental,' he said.

'Well, that's just what I'm feeling. Girls can't feel like that nowadays. They're swooning with love, or they're fainting when somebody plays the guitar or sings in a very loud voice, but they're not sentimental. But I wasn't in love with Rudolf Rassendyll. I was in love with the other one – his double.'

'Did he have a double?'

'Oh yes, a king. The King of Ruritania.'

'Ah, of course, now I know. That's where the word Ruritania comes from: one is always throwing it about. Yes, I think I did read it, you know. The King of Ruritania, and Rudolf Rassendyll was stand-in for the King and fell in love with Princess Flavia to whom the King was officially betrothed.'

Lady Matilda gave some more deep sighs.

'Yes. Rudolf Rassendyll had inherited his red hair from an ancestress, and somewhere in the book he bows to the portrait and says something about the – I can't remember the name now – the Countess Amelia or something like that from whom he inherited his looks and all the rest of it. So I looked at you and thought of you as Rudolf Rassendyll and you went out and looked at a picture of someone who might have been an ancestress of yours and saw whether she reminded you of someone. So you're mixed up in a romance of some kind, are you?'

'What on earth makes you say that?'

'Well, there aren't so many patterns in life, you know. One recognizes patterns as they come up. It's like a book on knitting. About sixty-five different fancy stitches. Well, you know a particular stitch when you see it. Your stitch, at the moment, I should say, is the romantic adventure.' She sighed. 'But you won't tell me about it, I suppose.'

'There's nothing to tell,' said Sir Stafford.

'You always were quite an accomplished liar. Well, never mind. You bring her to see me some time. That's all I'd like, before the doctors succeed in killing me with yet another type of antibiotic that they've just discovered. The different coloured pills I've had to take by this time! You wouldn't believe it.'

'I don't know why you say "she" and "her" –'

'Don't you? Oh, well, I know a she when I come across a she. There's a she somewhere dodging about in your life. What beats me is how you found her. In Malaya, at the conference table? Ambassador's daughter or minister's daughter? Good-looking secretary from the Embassy pool? No, none of it seems to fit. Ship coming home? No, you don't use ships nowadays. Plane, perhaps.'

'You are getting slightly nearer,' Sir Stafford Nye could not help saying.

'Ah!' She pounced. 'Air hostess?'

He shook his head.

'Ah well. Keep your secret. I shall find out, mind you. I've always had a good nose for things going on where you're concerned. Things generally as well. Of course I'm out of everything nowadays, but I meet my old cronies from time to time and it's quite easy, you know, to get a hint or two from them. People are worried. Everywhere – they're worried.'

'You mean there's a general kind of discontent – upset?'

'No, I didn't mean that at all. I mean the highups are worried. Our awful governments are worried. The dear old sleepy Foreign

Office is worried. There are things going on, things that shouldn't be. Unrest.'

'Student unrest?'

'Oh, student unrest is just one flower on the tree. It's blossoming everywhere and in every country, or so it seems. I've got a nice girl who comes, you know, and reads the papers to me in the mornings. I can't read them properly myself. She's got a nice voice. Takes down my letters and she reads things from the papers and she's a good kind girl. She reads the things I want to know, not the things that she thinks are right for me to know. Yes, everyone's worried, as far as I can make out and this, mind you, came more or less from a very old friend of mine.'

'One of your old military cronies?'

'He's a major-general, if that's what you mean, retired a good many years ago but still in the know. Youth is what you might call the spearhead of it all. But that's not really what's so worrying. They – whoever *they* are – work through youth. Youth in every country. Youth urged on. Youth chanting slogans, slogans that sound exciting, though they don't always know what they mean. So easy to start a revolution. That's natural to youth. All youth has always rebelled. You rebel, you pull down, you want the world to be different from what it is. But you're blind, too. There are bandages over the eyes of youth. They can't see where things are taking them. What's going to come next? What's in front of them? And who it is behind them, urging them on? That's what's frightening about it. You know, someone holding out the carrot to get the donkey to come along and at the same time there is someone behind the donkey urging it on with a stick.'

'You've got some extraordinary fancies.'

'They're not only fancies, my dear boy. That's what people said about Hitler. Hitler and the Hitler Youth. But it was a long careful preparation. It was a war that was worked out in detail. It was a fifth column being planted in different countries all ready for the supermen. The supermen were to be the flower of the German nation. That's what they thought and believed in passionately. Somebody else is perhaps believing something like that now. It's a creed that they'll be willing to accept – if it's offered cleverly enough.'

'Who are you talking about? Do you mean the Chinese or the Russians? What do you mean?'

'I don't know. I haven't the faintest idea. But there's something somewhere, and it's running on the same lines. Pattern again, you see. Pattern! The Russians? Bogged down by Communism, I should think they're considered old-fashioned. The Chinese? I think they've lost their way. Too much Chairman Mao, perhaps. I don't know who these people are who are doing the planning. As I said before, it's why and where and when and *who*.'

'Very interesting.'

'It's so frightening, this same idea that always recurs. History repeating itself. The young hero, the golden superman that all must follow.' She paused, then said, 'Same idea, you know. The young Siegfried.'

CHAPTER 7

ADVICE FROM GREAT-AUNT MATILDA

Great-Aunt Matilda looked at him. She had a very sharp and shrewd eye. Stafford Nye had noticed that before. He noticed it particularly at this moment.

'So you've heard that term before,' she said. 'I see.'

'What does it mean?'

'You don't know?' She raised her eyebrows.

'Cross my heart and wish to die,' said Sir Stafford, in nursery language.

'Yes, we always used to say that, didn't we,' said Lady Matilda. 'Do you really mean what you're saying?'

'I don't know anything about it.'

'But you'd heard the term before.'

'Yes. Someone said it to me.'

'Anyone important?'

'It could be. I suppose it could be. What do you mean by "anyone important"?'

'Well, you've been involved in various Government missions lately, haven't you? You've represented this poor, miserable country as best you could, which I shouldn't wonder wasn't rather better than many others could do, sitting round a table and talking. I don't know whether anything's come of all that.'

'Probably not,' said Stafford Nye. 'After all, one isn't optimistic when one goes into these things.'

'One does one's best,' said Lady Matilda correctively.

'A very Christian principle. Nowadays if one does one's worst one often seems to get on a good deal better. What does all this mean, Aunt Matilda?'

'I don't suppose *I* know,' said his aunt.

'Well, you very often do know things.'

'Not exactly. I just pick up things here and there.'

'Yes?'

'I've got a few old friends left, you know. Friends who are in the know. Of course most of them are either practically stone deaf or half blind or a little bit gone in the top storey or unable to walk straight. But something still functions. Something, shall we say, up here.' She hit the top of her neatly arranged white head. 'There's a good deal of alarm and despondency about. More than usual. That's one of the things I've picked up.'

'Isn't there always?'

'Yes, yes, but this is a bit more than that. Active instead of passive, as you might say. For a long time, as I have noticed from the outside, and you, no doubt, from the inside, we have felt that things are in a mess. A rather bad mess. But now we've got to a point where we feel that perhaps something might have been done about the mess. There's an element of danger in it. Something is going on – something is brewing. Not just in one country. In quite a lot of countries. They've recruited a service of their own and the danger about that is that it's a service of young people. And the kind of people who will go anywhere, do anything, unfortunately believe anything, and so long as they are promised a certain amount of pulling down, wrecking, throwing spanners in the works, then they think the cause must be a good one and that the world will be a different place. They're not creative, that's the trouble – only destructive. The creative young write poems, write books, probably compose music, paint pictures just as they always have done. They'll be all right – But once people learn to love destruction for its own sake, evil leadership gets its chance.'

'You say "they" or "them". Who do you mean?'

'Wish I knew,' said Lady Matilda. 'Yes, I wish I knew. Very much indeed. If I hear anything useful, I'll tell you. Then you can do something about it.'

'Unfortunately, *I* haven't got anyone to tell, I mean to pass it on to.'

'Yes, don't pass it on to just anyone. You can't trust people. Don't pass it on to any one of those idiots in the Government, or connected with government or hoping to be participating in government after this lot runs out. Politicians don't have time to look at the world they're living in. They see the country they're living in and they see it as one vast electoral platform. That's quite enough to put on their plates for the time being. They do things which they honestly believe will make things better and then they're surprised when they don't make things better because they're not the things that people want to have. And one can't help coming to the conclusion that politicians have a feeling that they have a kind of divine right to tell lies in a good cause. It's not really so very long ago since Mr Baldwin made his famous remark – 'If I had spoken the truth, I should have lost the election.' Prime Ministers still feel like that. Now and again we have a great man, thank God. But it's rare.'

'Well, what do you suggest ought to be done?'

'Are you asking my advice? Mine? Do you know how old I am?'

'Getting on for ninety,' suggested her nephew.

'Not quite as old as that,' said Lady Matilda, slightly affronted. 'Do I look it, my dear boy?'

'No, darling. You look a nice, comfortable sixty-six.'

'That's better,' said Lady Matilda. 'Quite untrue. But better. If I get a tip of any kind from one of my dear old admirals or an old general or even possibly an air marshal – they do hear things, you know – they've got cronies still and the old boys get together and talk. And so it gets around. There's always been the grapevine and there still is a grapevine, no matter how elderly the people are. The young Siegfried. We want a clue to just what that means – I don't know if he's a person or a password or the name of a Club or a new Messiah or a Pop singer. But that term covers *something*. There's the musical motif too. I've rather forgotten my Wagnerian days.' Her aged voice croaked out a partially recognizable melody. 'Siegfried's horn call, isn't that it? Get a recorder, why don't you? Do I mean a recorder. I don't mean a record that you put on a gramophone – I mean the things that schoolchildren play. They have classes for them. Went to a talk the other day. Our vicar got it up. Quite interesting. You know, tracing the history of the recorder and the kind of recorders there were from the Elizabethan age onwards. Some big, some small, all different notes and sounds. Very interesting. Interesting hearing in two senses. The recorders themselves. Some of them give out lovely noises. And the history. Yes. Well, what was I saying?'

'You told me to get one of these instruments, I gather.'

'Yes. Get a recorder and learn to blow Siegfried's horn call on that. You're musical, you always were. You can manage that, I hope?'

'Well, it seems a very small part to play in the salvation of the world, but I dare say I could manage that.'

'And have the thing ready. Because, you see –' she tapped on the table with her spectacle case – 'you might want it to impress the wrong people some time. Might come in useful. They'd welcome you with open arms and then you might learn a bit.'

'You certainly have ideas,' said Sir Stafford admiringly.

'What else can you have when you're my age?' said his great-aunt. 'You can't get about. You can't meddle with people much, you can't do any gardening. All you *can* do is sit in your chair and have ideas. Remember that when you're forty years older.'

'One remark you made interested me.'

'Only one?' said Lady Matilda. 'That's rather poor measure considering how much I've been talking. What was it?'

'You suggested that I might be capable of impressing the wrong people with my recorder – did you mean that?'

'Well, it's one way, isn't it? The right people don't matter. But the wrong people – well, you've got to find out things, haven't you? You've got to permeate things. Rather like a death-watch beetle,' she said thoughtfully.

'So I should make significant noises in the night?'

'Well, that sort of thing, yes. We had death-watch beetle in the east wing here once. Very expensive it was to put it right. I dare say it will be just as expensive to put the world right.'

'In fact a good deal more expensive,' said Stafford Nye.

'That won't matter,' said Lady Matilda. 'People never mind spending a great deal of money. It impresses them. It's when you want to do things economically, they won't play. We're the same people, you know. In this country, I mean. We're the same people we always were.'

'What do you mean by that?'

'We're capable of doing big things. We were good at running an empire. We weren't good at *keeping* an empire running, but then you see we didn't need an empire any more And we recognized that. Too difficult to keep up. Robbie made me see that,' she added.

'Robbie?' It was faintly familiar.

'Robbie Shoreham. Robert Shoreham. He's a very old friend of mine. Paralysed down the left side. But he can talk still and he's got a moderately good hearing-aid.'

'Besides being one of the most famous physicists in the world,' said Stafford Nye. 'So he's another of your old cronies, is he?'

'Known him since he was a boy,' said Lady Matilda. 'I suppose it surprises you that we should be friends, have a lot in common and enjoy talking together?'

'Well, I shouldn't have thought that –'

'That we had much to talk about? It's true I could never do mathematics. Fortunately, when I was a girl one didn't even try. Mathematics came easily to Robbie when he was about four years old, I believe. They say nowadays that that's quite natural. He's got plenty to talk about. He liked me always because I was frivolous and made him laugh. And I'm a good listener, too. And really, he says some very interesting things sometimes.'

'So I suppose,' said Stafford Nye drily.

'Now don't be superior. Molière married his housemaid, didn't he, and made a great success of it – if it *is* Molière I mean. If a man's frantic with brains he doesn't really want a woman who's also frantic with brains to talk to. It would be exhausting. He'd much prefer a lovely nitwit who can make him laugh. I wasn't bad-looking when I was young,' said Lady Matilda complacently. 'I know I have no academic distinctions. I'm not in the least intellectual. But Robert has always said that I've got a great deal of common sense, of intelligence.'

'You're a lovely person,' said Sir Stafford Nye. 'I enjoy coming to see you and I shall go away remembering all the things you've said to me. There are a good many more things, I expect, that you could tell me but you're obviously not going to.'

'Not until the right moment comes,' said Lady Matilda, 'but I've got your interests at heart. Let me know what you're doing from time to time. You're dining at the American Embassy, aren't you, next week?'

'How did you know that? I've been asked.'

'And you've accepted, I understand.'

'Well, it's all in the course of duty.' He looked at her curiously. 'How do you manage to be so well informed?'

'Oh, Milly told me.'

'Milly?'

'Milly Jean Cortman. The American Ambassador's wife. A most attractive creature, you know. Small and rather perfect-looking.'

'Oh, you mean Mildred Cortman.'

'She was christened Mildred but she preferred Milly Jean. I was talking to her on the telephone about some Charity Matinée or other – she's what we used to call a pocket Venus.'

'A most attractive term to use,' said Stafford Nye.

CHAPTER 8

AN EMBASSY DINNER

I

As Mrs Cortman came to meet him with outstretched hand, Stafford Nye recalled the term his great-aunt had used. Milly Jean Cortman was a woman of between thirty-five and forty. She had delicate features, big blue-grey eyes, a very perfectly shaped head with bluish-grey hair tinted to a particularly attractive shade which fitted her with a perfection of grooming. She was very popular in London. Her husband, Sam Cortman, was a big, heavy man, slightly ponderous. He was very proud of his wife. He himself was one of those slow, rather over-emphatic talkers. People found their attention occasionally straying when he was elucidating at some length a point which hardly needed making.

'Back from Malaya, aren't you, Sir Stafford? It must have been quite interesting to go out there, though it's not the time of year I'd have chosen. But I'm sure we're all glad to see you back. Let me see now. You know Lady Aldborough and Sir John, and Herr von Roken, Frau von Roken. Mr and Mrs Staggenham.'

They were all people known to Stafford Nye in more or less degree. There was a Dutchman and his wife whom he had not met before, since they had only just taken up their appointment. The Staggenhams were the Minister of Social Security and his wife. A particularly uninteresting couple, he had always thought.

'And the Countess Renata Zerkowski. I think she said she'd met you before.'

'It must be about a year ago. When I was last in England,' said the Countess.

And there she was, the passenger from Frankfurt again. Self-possessed, at ease, beautifully turned out in faint grey-blue with a touch of chinchilla. Her hair dressed high (a wig?) and a ruby cross of antique design round her neck.

'Signor Gasparo, Count Reitner, Mr and Mrs Arbuthnot.'

About twenty-six in all. At dinner Stafford Nye sat between the dreary Mrs Staggenham and Signora Gasparo on the other side of him. Renata Zerkowski sat exactly opposite him.

An Embassy dinner. A dinner such as he so often attended, holding much of the same type of guests. Various members of the Diplomatic Corps, junior ministers, one or two industrialists, a sprinkling of socialites usually included because they were good conversationalists, natural, pleasant people to meet, though one or two, thought Stafford Nye, one or two were maybe different. Even while he was busy sustaining his conversation with Signora Gasparo, a charming person to talk to, a chatterbox, slightly flirtatious; his mind was roving in the same way that his eye also roved, though the latter was not very noticeable. As it roved round the dinner table, you would not have said that he was summing up conclusions in his own mind. He had been asked here. Why? For any reason or for no reason in particular. Because his name had come up automatically on the list that the secretaries produced from time to time with checks against such members as were due for their turn. Or as the extra man or the extra woman required for the balancing of the table. He had always been in request when an extra was needed.

'Oh yes,' a diplomatic hostess would say, 'Stafford Nye will do beautifully. You will put him next to Madame So-and-so, or Lady Somebody else.'

He had been asked perhaps to fill in for no further reason than that. And yet, he wondered. He knew by experience that there were certain other reasons. And so his eye with its swift social amiability, its air of not looking really at anything in particular, was busy.

Amongst these guests there was someone perhaps who for some reason mattered, was important. Someone who had been asked – not to fill in – on the contrary – someone who had had a selection of other guests invited to fit in round him – or her. Someone who mattered. He wondered – he wondered which of them it might be.

Cortman knew, of course. Milly Jean, perhaps. One never really knew with wives. Some of them were better diplomats than their husbands. Some of them could be relied upon merely for their charm, for their adaptability, their readiness to please, their lack of curiosity. Some again, he thought ruefully to himself, were, as far as their husbands were concerned, disasters. Hostesses who, though they may have brought prestige or money to a diplomatic marriage, were yet capable at any moment of saying or doing the wrong thing, and creating an unfortunate situation. If that was to be guarded against, it would need one of the guests, or two or even three of the guests, to be what one might call professional smoothers-over.

Did this dinner party this evening mean anything but a social event? His quick and noticing eye had by now been round the dinner table picking out one or two people whom so far he had not entirely taken in. An American business man. Pleasant, not socially brilliant. A professor from one of the universities of the Middle West. A married couple, the husband German, the wife predominantly, almost aggressively American. A very beautiful woman, too. Sexually, highly attractive, Sir Stafford thought. Was one of them important? Initials floated through his mind.

FBI. CIA. The business man perhaps a CIA man, there for a purpose. Things were like that nowadays. Not as they used to be. How had the formula gone? Big Brother is watching you. Yes, well it went further than that now. Transatlantic Cousin is watching you. High Finance for Middle Europe is watching you. A diplomatic difficulty has been asked here for *you* to watch *him*. Oh yes. There was often a lot behind things nowadays. But was that just another formula, just another fashion? Could it really mean more than that, something vital, something real? How did one talk of events in Europe nowadays? The Common Market. Well, that was fair enough, that dealt with trade, with economics, with the inter-relationships of countries.

That was the stage to set. But behind the stage. Back-stage. Waiting for the cue. Ready to prompt if prompting were needed. What was going on? Going on in the big world and behind the big world. He wondered.

Some things he knew, some things he guessed at, some things, he thought to himself, I know nothing about and nobody wants me to know anything about them.

His eyes rested for a moment on his vis-à-vis, her chin tilted upward, her mouth just gently curved in a polite smile, and their eyes met. Those eyes told him nothing, the smile told him nothing. What was she doing here? She was in her element, she fitted in, she knew this world. Yes, she was at home here. He could find out, he thought, without much difficulty where she figured in the diplomatic world, but would that tell him where she really had her place?

The young woman in the slacks who had spoken to him suddenly at Frankfurt had had an eager intelligent face. Was that the real woman, or was this casual social acquaintance the real woman? Was one of those personalities a part being played? And if so, which one? And there might be more than just those two personalities. He wondered. He wanted to find out.

Or had the fact that he had been asked to meet her been pure coincidence? Milly Jean was rising to her feet. The other ladies rose with her. Then suddenly an unexpected clamour arose. A clamour from outside the house. Shouts. Yells. The crash of breaking glass in a window. Shouts. Sounds – surely pistol shots. Signora Gasparo spoke, clutching Stafford Nye's arm.

'What again!' she exclaimed. '*Dio*! – again it is those terrible students. It is the same in our country. Why do they attack Embassies? They fight, resist the police – go marching, shouting idiotic things, lie down in the streets. *Si, si*. We have them in Rome – in Milan – We have them like a pest everywhere in Europe. Why are they never happy, these young ones? What do they want?'

Stafford Nye sipped his brandy and listened to the heavy accents of Mr Charles Staggenham, who was being pontifical and taking his time about it. The commotion had subsided. It would seem that the police had marched off some of the hotheads. It was one of those occurrences which once would have been thought extraordinary and even alarming but which were now taken as a matter of course.

'A larger police force. That's what we need. A larger police force. It's more than these chaps can deal with. It's the same everywhere, they say. I was talking to Herr Lurwitz the other day. They have their troubles, so have the French. Not quite so much of it in the Scandinavian countries. What do they all want – just trouble? I tell you if I had my way –'

Stafford Nye removed his mind to another subject while keeping up a flattering pretence as Charles Staggenham explained just what his way would be, which in any case was easily to be anticipated beforehand.

'Shouting about Vietnam and all that. What do any of them know about Vietnam. None of them have ever been there, have they?'

'One would think it very unlikely,' said Sir Stafford Nye.

'Man was telling me earlier this evening, they've had a lot of trouble in California. In the universities – If we had a sensible policy . . .'

Presently the men joined the ladies in the drawing-room. Stafford Nye, moving with that leisurely grace, that air of complete lack of purpose he found so useful, sat down by a golden-haired, talkative woman whom he knew moderately well, and who could be guaranteed seldom to say anything worth listening to as regards ideas or wit, but who was excessively knowledgeable about all her fellow creatures within the bounds of her acquaintance. Stafford Nye asked no direct questions but presently, without the lady being even aware of the means by which he had guided the subject of conversation, he was hearing a few remarks about the Countess Renata Zerkowski.

'Still very good-looking isn't she? She doesn't come over here very often nowadays. Mostly New York, you know, or that wonderful island place. You know the one I mean. Not Minorca. One of the other ones in the Mediterranean. Her sister's married to that soap king, at least I think it's a soap king. Not the Greek one. He's Swedish, I think. Rolling in money. And then of course, she spends a lot of time in some castle place in the Dolomites – or near Munich – very musical, she always has been. She said you'd met before, didn't she?'

'Yes. A year or two years ago, I think.'

'Oh yes, I suppose when she was over in England before. They say she was mixed up in the Czechoslovakian business. Or do I mean the Polish trouble? Oh dear, it's so difficult, isn't it. All the names, I mean. They have so many z's and k's. Most peculiar, and so hard to spell. She's very literary. You know, gets up petitions for people to sign. To give writers asylum here, or whatever it is. Not that anyone really pays much attention. I mean, what else can one think of nowadays except how one can possibly pay one's own taxes. The travel allowance makes things a little better but not much. I mean, you've got to get the money, haven't you, before you can take it abroad. I don't know how anyone manages to have money now, but there's a lot of it about. Oh yes, there's a lot of it about.'

She looked down in a complacent fashion at her left hand, on which were two solitaire rings, one a diamond and one an emerald, which seemed to prove conclusively that a considerable amount of money had been spent upon her at least.

The evening drew on to its close. He knew very little more about his passenger from Frankfurt than he had known before. He knew that she had a façade, a façade it seemed to him, very highly faceted, if you could use those two alliterative words together. She was interested in music. Well, he had met her at the Festival Hall, had he not? Fond of outdoor sports. Rich relations who owned Mediterranean islands. Given to supporting literary charities. Somebody in fact who had good connections, was well related, had entries to the social field. Not apparently highly political and yet, quietly perhaps, affiliated to some group. Someone who moved about from place to place and country to country. Moving among the rich, amongst the talented, about the literary world.

He thought of espionage for a moment or two. That seemed the most likely answer. And yet he was not wholly satisfied with it.

The evening drew on. It came at last to be his turn to be collected by his hostess. Milly Jean was very good at her job.

'I've been longing to talk to you for ages. I wanted to hear about Malaya. I'm so stupid about all these places in Asia, you know, I mix them up. Tell me, what happened out there? Anything interesting or was everything terribly boring?'

'I'm sure you can guess the answer to that one.'

'Well, I should guess it was very boring. But perhaps you're not allowed to say so.'

'Oh yes, I can think it, and I can say it. It wasn't really my cup of tea, you know.'

'Why did you go then?'

'Oh well, I'm always fond of travelling, I like seeing countries.'

'You're such an intriguing person in many ways. Really, of course, all diplomatic life is very boring, isn't it? *I* oughtn't to say so. I only say it to you.'

Very blue eyes. Blue like bluebells in a wood. They opened a little wider and the black brows above them came down gently at the outside corners while the inside corners went up a little. It made her face look like a rather beautiful Persian cat. He wondered what Milly Jean was really like. Her soft voice was that of a southerner. The beautifully shaped little head, her profile with the perfection of a coin – what was she really like? No fool, he thought. One who could use social weapons when needed, who could charm when she wished to, who could withdraw into being enigmatic. If she wanted anything from anyone she would be adroit in getting it. He noticed the intensity of the glance she was giving him now. Did she want something of him? He didn't know. He didn't think it could be likely. She said, 'Have you met Mr Staggenham?'

'Ah yes. I was talking to him at the dinner table. I hadn't met him before.'

'He is said to be very important,' said Milly Jean. 'He's the President of PBF as you know.'

'One should know all those things,' said Sir Stafford Nye. 'PBF and DCV. LYH. And all the world of initials.'

'Hateful,' said Milly Jean. 'Hateful. All these initials, no personalities, no *people* any more. Just initials. What a hateful world! That's what I sometimes think. What a hateful world. I want it to be different, quite, quite different –'

Did she mean that? He thought for one moment that perhaps she did. Interesting . . .

II

Grosvenor Square was quietness itself. There were traces of broken glass still on the pavements. There were even eggs, squashed tomatoes and fragments of gleaming metal. But above, the stars were peaceful. Car after car drove up to the Embassy door to collect the home-going guests. The police were there in the corners of the square but without ostentation. Everything was under control. One of the political guests leaving spoke to one of the police officers. He came back and murmured, 'Not too many arrests. Eight. They'll be up at Bow Street in the morning. More or less the usual lot. Petronella was here, of course, and Stephen and his crowd. Ah well. One would think they'd get tired of it one of these days.'

'You live not very far from here, don't you?' said a voice in Sir Stafford Nye's ear. A deep contralto voice. 'I can drop you on my way.'

'No, no. I can walk perfectly. It's only ten minutes or so.'

'It will be no trouble to me, I assure you,' said the Countess Zerkowski. She added, 'I'm staying at the St James's Tower.'

The St James's Tower was one of the newer hotels.

'You are very kind.'

It was a big, expensive-looking hire car that waited. The chauffeur opened the door, the Countess Renata got in and Sir Stafford Nye followed her. It was she who gave Sir Stafford Nye's address to the chauffeur. The car drove off.

'So you know where I live?' he said.

'Why not?'

He wondered just what that answer meant: Why not?

'Why not indeed,' he said. 'You know so much, don't you?' He added, 'It was kind of you to return my passport.'

'I thought it might save certain inconveniences. It might be simpler if you burnt it. You've been issued with a new one, I presume –'

'You presume correctly.'

'Your bandit's cloak you will find in the bottom drawer of your tallboy. It was put there tonight. I believed that perhaps to purchase another one would not satisfy you, and indeed that to find one similar might not be possible.'

'It will mean more to me now that it has been through certain – adventures,' said Stafford Nye. He added, 'It has served its purpose.'

The car purred through the night.

The Countess Zerkowski said:

'Yes. It has served its purpose since I am here – alive . . .'

Sir Stafford Nye said nothing. He was assuming, rightly or not, that she wanted him to ask questions, to press her, to know more of what she had been doing, of what fate she had escaped. She wanted him to display curiosity, but Sir Stafford Nye was not going to display curiosity. He rather enjoyed not doing so. He heard her laugh very gently. Yet he fancied, rather surprisingly, that it was a pleased laugh, a laugh of satisfaction, not of stalemate.

'Did you enjoy your evening?' she said.

'A good party, I think, but Milly Jean always gives good parties.'

'You know her well then?'

'I knew her when she was a girl in New York before she married. A pocket Venus.'

She looked at him in faint surprise.

'Is that your term for her?'

'Actually, no. It was said to me by an elderly relative of mine.'

'Yes, it isn't a description that one hears given often of a woman nowadays. It fits her, I think, very well. Only –'

'Only what?'

'Venus is seductive, is she not? Is she also ambitious?'

'You think Milly Jean Cortman is ambitious?'

'Oh yes. That above all.'

'And you think to be the wife of the Ambassador to St James's is insufficient to satisfy ambition?'

'Oh no,' said the Countess. 'That is only the beginning.'

He did not answer. He was looking out through the car window. He began to speak, then stopped himself. He noted her quick glance at him, but she too was silent. It was not till they were going over a bridge with the Thames below them that he said:

'So you are not giving me a lift home and you are not going back to the St James's Tower. We are crossing the Thames. We met there once before, crossing a bridge. Where are you taking me?'

'Do you mind?'

'I think I do.'

'Yes, I can see you might.'

'Well of course you are quite in the mode. Hi-jacking is the fashion nowadays, isn't it? You have hi-jacked me. Why?'

'Because, like once before, I have need of you.' She added, 'And others have need of you.'

'Indeed.'

'And that does not please you.'

'It would please me better to be asked.'

'If I had asked, would you have come?'

'Perhaps yes, perhaps no.'

'I am sorry.'

'I wonder.'

They drove on through the night in silence. It was not a drive through lonely country, they were on a main road. Now and then the lights picked up a name or a signpost so that Stafford Nye saw quite clearly where their route lay. Through Surrey and through the first residential portions of Sussex. Occasionally he thought they took a detour or a side road which was not the most direct route, but even of this he could not be sure. He almost asked his companion whether this was being done because they might possibly have been followed from London. But he had determined rather firmly on his policy of silence. It was for her to speak, for her to give information. He found her, even with the additional information he had been able to get, an enigmatic character.

They were driving to the country after a dinner party in London. They were, he was pretty sure, in one of the more expensive types of hire car. This was something planned beforehand. Reasonable, nothing doubtful or unexpected about it.

Soon, he imagined, he would find out where it was they were going. Unless, that is, they were going to drive as far as the coast. That also was possible, he thought. Haslemere, he saw on a signpost. Now they were skirting Godalming. All very plain and above board. The rich countryside of moneyed suburbia. Agreeable woods, handsome residences. They took a few side turns and then as the car finally slowed, they seemed to be arriving at their destination. Gates. A small white lodge by the gates. Up a drive, well-kept rhododendrons on either side of it. They turned round a bend and drew up before a house. 'Stockbroker Tudor,' murmured Sir Stafford Nye, under his breath. His companion turned her head inquiringly.

'Just a comment,' said Stafford Nye. 'Pay no attention. I take it we are now arriving at the destination of your choice?'

'And you don't admire the look of it very much.'

'The grounds seem well-kept up,' said Sir Stafford, following the beam of the headlights as the car rounded the bend. 'Takes money to keep these places up and in good order. I should say this was a comfortable house to live in.'

'Comfortable but not beautiful. The man who lives in it prefers comfort to beauty, I should say.'

'Perhaps wisely,' said Sir Stafford. 'And yet in some ways he is very appreciative of beauty, of some kinds of beauty.'

They drew up before the well-lighted porch. Sir Stafford got out and tendered an arm to help his companion. The chauffeur had mounted the steps and pressed the bell. He looked inquiringly at the woman as she ascended the steps.

'You won't be requiring me again tonight, m'lady?'

'No. That's all for now. We'll telephone down in the morning.'

'Good night. Good night, sir.'

There were footsteps inside and the door was flung open. Sir Stafford had expected some kind of butler, but instead there was a tall grenadier of a parlour-maid. Grey-haired, tight-lipped, eminently reliable and competent, he thought. An invaluable asset and hard to find nowadays. Trustworthy, capable of being fierce.

'I am afraid we are a little late,' said Renata.

'The master is in the library. He asked that you and the gentleman should come to him there when you arrived.'

CHAPTER 9

THE HOUSE NEAR GODALMING

She led the way up the broad staircase and the two of them followed her. Yes, thought Stafford Nye, a very comfortable house. Jacobean paper, a most unsightly carved oak staircase but pleasantly shallow treads. Pictures nicely chosen but of no particular artistic interest. A rich man's house, he thought. A man, not of bad taste, a man of conventional tastes. Good thick pile carpet of an agreeable plum-coloured texture.

On the first floor, the grenadier-like parlour-maid went to the first door along it. She opened it and stood back to let them go in but she made no announcement of names. The Countess went in first and Sir Stafford Nye followed her. He heard the door shut quietly behind him.

There were four people in the room. Sitting behind a large desk which was well covered with papers, documents, an open map or two and presumably other papers which were in the course of discussion, was a large, fat man with a very yellow face. It was a face Sir Stafford Nye had seen before, though he could not for the moment attach the proper name to it. It was a man whom he had met only in a casual fashion, and yet the occasion had been an important one. He should know, yes, definitely he should know. But why – why wouldn't the name come?

With a slight struggle, the figure sitting at the desk rose to his feet. He took the Countess Renata's outstretched hand.

'You've arrived,' he said, 'splendid.'

'Yes. Let me introduce you, though I think you already know him. Sir Stafford Nye, Mr Robinson.'

Of course. In Sir Stafford Nye's brain something clicked like a camera. That fitted in, too, with another name. Pikeaway. To say that he knew all about Mr Robinson was not true. He knew about Mr Robinson all that Mr Robinson permitted to be known. His name, as far as anyone knew, *was* Robinson, though it might have been any name of foreign origin. No one had ever suggested anything of that kind. Recognition came also of his personal appearance. The high forehead, the melancholy dark eyes, the large generous mouth, and the impressive white teeth

– false teeth, presumably, but at any rate teeth of which it might have been said, like in Red Riding Hood, 'the better to eat you with, child!'

He knew, too, what Mr Robinson stood for. Just one simple word described it. Mr Robinson represented Money with a capital M. Money in its every aspect. International money, world-wide money, private home finances, banking, money not in the way that the average person looked at it. You never thought of him as a very rich man. Undoubtedly he was a very rich man but that wasn't the important thing. He was one of the arrangers of money, the great clan of bankers. His personal tastes might even have been simple, but Sir Stafford Nye doubted if they were. A reasonable standard of comfort, even luxury, would be Mr Robinson's way of life. But not more than that. So behind all this mysterious business there was the power of money.

'I heard of you just a day or two ago,' said Mr Robinson, as he shook hands, 'from our friend Pikeaway, you know.'

That fitted in, thought Stafford Nye, because now he remembered that on the solitary occasion before that he had met Mr Robinson, Colonel Pikeaway had been present. Horsham, he remembered, had spoken of Mr Robinson. So now there was Mary Ann (or the Countess Zerkowski?) and Colonel Pikeaway sitting in his own smoke-filled room with his eyes half closed either going to sleep or just waking up, and there was Mr Robinson with his large, yellow face, and so there was money at stake somewhere, and his glance shifted to the three other people in the room because he wanted to see if he knew who they were and what they represented, or if he could guess.

In two cases at least he didn't need to guess. The man who sat in the tall porter's chair by the fireplace, an elderly figure framed by the chair as a picture frame might have framed him, was a face that had been well known all over England. Indeed, it still *was* well known, although it was very seldom seen nowadays. A sick man, an invalid, a man who made very brief appearances, and then it was said, at physical cost to himself in pain and difficulty. Lord Altamount. A thin emaciated face, outstanding nose, grey hair which receded just a little from the forehead, and then flowed back in a thick grey mane; somewhat prominent ears that cartoonists had used in their time, and a deep piercing glance that not so much observed as probed. Probed deeply into what it was looking at. At the moment it was looking at Sir Stafford Nye. He stretched out a hand as Stafford Nye went towards him.

'I don't get up,' said Lord Altamount. His voice was faint, an old man's voice, a far-away voice. 'My back doesn't allow me. Just come back from Malaya, haven't you, Stafford Nye?'

'Yes.'

'Was it worth your going? I expect you think it wasn't. You're probably right, too. Still, we have to have these excrescences in life, these ornamental trimmings to adorn the better kind of diplomatic lies. I'm glad you could come here or were brought here tonight. Mary Ann's doing, I suppose?'

So that's what he calls her and thinks of her as, thought Stafford Nye to himself. It was what Horsham had called her. She was in with them then, without a doubt. As for Altamount, he stood for – what did he stand for nowadays? Stafford Nye thought to himself. He stands for England. He still stands for England until he's buried in Westminster Abbey or a country mausoleum, whatever he chooses. He has *been* England, and he knows England, and I should say he knows the value of every politician and government official in England pretty well, even if he's never spoken to them.

Lord Altamount said:

'This is our colleague, Sir James Kleek.'

Stafford Nye didn't know Kleek. He didn't think he'd even heard of him. A restless, fidgety type. Sharp, suspicious glances that never rested anywhere for long. He had the contained eagerness of a sporting dog awaiting the word of command. Ready to start off at a glance from his master's eye.

But who was his master? Altamount or Robinson?

Stafford's eye went round to the fourth man. He had risen to his feet from the chair where he had been sitting close to the door. Bushy moustache, raised eyebrows, watchful, withdrawn, managing in some way to remain familiar yet almost unrecognizable.

'So it's you,' said Sir Stafford Nye, 'how are you, Horsham?'

'Very pleased to see you here, Sir Stafford.'

Quite a representative gathering, Stafford Nye thought, with a swift glance round.

They had set a chair for Renata not far from the fire and

Lord Altamount. She had stretched out a hand – her left hand, he noticed – and he had taken it between his two hands, holding it for a minute, then dropping it. He said:

'You took risks, child, you take too many risks.'

Looking at him, she said, 'It was you who taught me that, and it's the only way of life.'

Lord Altamount turned his head towards Sir Stafford Nye.

'It wasn't I who taught you to choose your man. You've got a natural genius for that.' Looking at Stafford Nye, he said, 'I know your great-aunt, or your great-great-aunt, is she?'

'Great-Aunt Matilda,' said Stafford Nye immediately.

'Yes. That's the one. One of the Victorian *tours-de-force* of the 'nineties. She must be nearly ninety herself now.'

He went on:

'I don't see her very often. Once or twice a year perhaps. But it strikes me every time – that sheer vitality of hers that outlives her bodily strength. They have the secret of that, those indomitable Victorians and some of the Edwardians as well.'

Sir James Kleek said, 'Let me get you a drink, Nye? What will you have?'

'Gin and tonic, if I may.'

The Countess refused with a small shake of the head.

James Kleek brought Nye his drink and set it on the table near Mr Robinson. Stafford Nye was not going to speak first. The dark eyes behind the desk lost their melancholy for a moment. They had quite suddenly a twinkle in them.

'Any questions?' he said.

'Too many,' said Sir Stafford Nye. 'Wouldn't it be better to have explanations first, questions later?'

'Is that what you'd like?'

'It might simplify matters.'

'Well, we start with a few plain statements of facts. You may or you may not have been asked to come here. If not, that fact may rankle slightly.'

'He prefers to be asked always,' said the Countess. 'He said as much to me.'

'Naturally,' said Mr Robinson.

'I was hi-jacked,' said Stafford Nye. 'Very fashionable, I know. One of our more modern methods.'

He kept his tone one of light amusement.

'Which invites, surely, a question from you,' said Mr Robinson. 'Just one small word of three letters. Why?'

'Quite so. Why? I admire your economy of speech. This is a private committee – a committee of inquiry. An inquiry of world-wide significance.'

'Sounds interesting,' said Sir Stafford Nye.

'It is more than interesting. It is poignant and immediate. Four different ways of life are represented in this room tonight,' said Lord Altamount. 'We represent different branches. I have retired from active participation in the affairs of this country, but I am still a consulting authority. I have been consulted and asked to preside over this particular inquiry as to what is going on in the world in this particular year of our Lord, because something *is* going on. James, here, has his own special task. He is my right-hand man. He is also our spokesman. Explain the general set-out, if you will, Jamie, to Sir Stafford here.'

It seemed to Stafford Nye that the gun dog quivered. At last! At last I can speak and get on with it! He leaned forward a little in his chair.

'If things happen in the world, you have to look for a cause for them. The outward signs are always easy to see but they're not, or so the Chairman –' he bowed to Lord Altamount – 'and Mr Robinson and Mr Horsham believe, important. It's always been the same way. You take a natural force, a great fall of water that will give you turbine power. You take the discovery of uranium from pitchblende, and that will give you in due course nuclear power that had not been dreamt of or known. When you found coal and minerals, they gave you transport, power, energy. There are forces at work always that give you certain things. But behind each of them there is *someone who controls it*. You've got to find who's controlling the powers that are slowly gaining ascendancy in practically every country in Europe, further afield still in parts of Asia. Less, possibly, in Africa, but again in the American continents both north and south. You've got to get behind the things that are happening and find out the motive force that's making them happen. One thing that makes things happen is *money*.'

He nodded towards Mr Robinson.

'Mr Robinson, there, knows as much about money as anybody in the world, I suppose.'

'It's quite simple,' said Mr Robinson. 'There are big movements afoot. There has to be money behind them. We've got to find out where that money's coming from. Who's operating with it? Where do they get it from? Where are they sending it to? Why? It's quite true what James says: I know a lot about money! As much as any man alive knows today. Then there are what you might call trends. It's a word we use a good deal nowadays! Trends or tendencies – there are innumerable words one uses. They mean not quite the same thing, but they're in relationship with each other. A tendency, shall we say, to rebellion shows up. Look back through history. You'll find it coming again and again, repeating itself like a periodic table, repeating a pattern. A desire for rebellion, the means of rebellion, the form the rebellion takes. It's not a thing particular to any particular country. If it arises in one country, it will arise in other countries in less or more degrees. That's what you mean, sir, isn't it?' He half turned towards Lord Altamount. 'That's the way you more or less put it to me.'

'Yes, you're expressing things very well, James.'

'It's a pattern, a pattern that arises and seems inevitable. You can recognize it where you find it. There was a period when a yearning towards crusades swept countries. All over Europe people embarked in ships, they went off to deliver the Holy Land. All quite clear, a perfectly good pattern of determined behaviour. But *why* did they go? That's the interest of history, you know. Seeing why these desires and patterns arise. It's not always a materialistic answer either. All sorts of things can cause rebellion, a desire for freedom, freedom of speech, freedom of religious worship, again a series of closely related patterns. It led people to embrace emigration to other countries, to formation of new religions very often as full of tyranny as the forms of religion they had left behind. But in all this, if you look hard enough, if you make enough investigations, you can see what started the onset of these and many other – I'll use the same word – patterns. In some ways it's like a virus disease. The virus can be carried – round the world, across seas, up mountains. It can go and infect. It goes apparently without being set in motion. But one can't be sure, even now, that that was always really true.

There could have been causes. Causes that made things happen. One can go a few steps further. There are *people*. One person – ten persons – a few hundred persons who are capable of being and setting in motion a cause. So it is not the *end process* that one has to look at. It is the first people who set the cause in motion. You have your crusaders, you have your religious enthusiasts, you have your desires for liberty, you have all the other patterns but you've got to go further back still. Further back to a hinterland. Visions, dreams. The prophet Joel knew it when he wrote "Your old men shall dream dreams, your young men shall see visions." And of those two, which are the more powerful? Dreams are not destructive. But visions can open new worlds to you – and visions can also destroy the worlds that already exist . . .'

James Kleek turned suddenly towards Lord Altamount. 'I don't know if it connects up, sir,' he said, 'but you told me a story once of somebody in the Embassy at Berlin. A woman.'

'Oh that? Yes, I found it interesting at the time. Yes, it has a bearing on what we are talking about now. One of the Embassy wives, clever, intelligent woman, well educated. She was very anxious to go personally and hear the Führer speak. I am talking, of course, of a time immediately preceding the 1939 war. She was curious to know what oratory could do. Why was everyone so impressed? And so she went. She came back and said, "It's extraordinary. I wouldn't have believed it. Of course I don't understand German very well but I was carried away, too. And I see now why everyone is. I mean, his ideas were wonderful . . . They inflamed you. The things he said. I mean, you just felt there *was* no other way of thinking, that a whole new world would happen if only one followed him. Oh, I can't explain properly. I'm going to write down as much as I can remember, and then if I bring it to you to see, you'll see better than my just trying to tell you the effect it had."

'I told her that was a very good idea. She came to me the next day and she said, "I don't know if you'll believe this. I started to write down the things I'd heard, the things Hitler had said. What they'd *meant* – but – it was frightening – *there wasn't anything to write down at all, I didn't seem able to remember a single stimulating or exciting sentence.* I have some of the words, but it doesn't seem to mean the same things as when I wrote them down. They are just – oh, they are just *meaningless*. I don't understand.'

'That shows you one of the great dangers one doesn't always remember, *but it exists*. There are people capable of communicating to others a wild enthusiasm, a kind of vision of life and of happening. They can do that though it is not really by what they *say*, it is not the *words you hear*, it is not even the idea described. It's something else. It's the magnetic power that a very few men have of starting something, of producing and creating a vision. By their personal magnetism perhaps, a tone of voice, perhaps some emanation that comes forth straight from the *flesh*. I don't know, *but it exists*.

'Such people have power. The great religious teachers had this power, and so has an evil spirit power also. Belief can be created in a certain movement, in certain things to be done, things that will result in a new heaven and a new earth, and people will believe it and work for it and fight for it and even die for it.'

He lowered his voice as he said: 'Jan Smuts puts it in a phrase. He said Leadership, besides being a great creative force, can be *diabolical*.'

Stafford Nye moved in his chair.

'I understand what you mean. It is interesting what you say. I can see perhaps that it might be true.'

'But you think it's exaggerated, of course.'

'I don't know that I do,' said Stafford Nye. 'Things that sound exaggerated are very often not exaggerated at all. They are only things that you haven't heard said before or thought about before. And therefore they come to you as so unfamiliar that you can hardly do anything about them except accept them. By the way, may I ask a simple question? What *does* one do about them?'

'If you come across the suspicion that this sort of thing is going on, you must find out about them,' said Lord Altamount. 'You've got to go like Kipling's mongoose: Go and find out. Find out where the money comes from and where the ideas are coming from, and where, if I may say so, the *machinery* comes from. Who is directing the machinery? There's a chief of staff, you know, as well as a commander-in-chief. That's what we're trying to do. We'd like you to come and help us.'

It was one of the rare occasions in his life when Sir Stafford

Nye was taken aback. Whatever he may have felt on some former occasions, he had always managed to conceal the fact. But this time it was different. He looked from one to the other of the men in the room. At Mr Robinson, impassively yellow-faced with his mouthful of teeth displayed; to Sir James Kleek, a somewhat brash talker, Sir Stafford Nye had considered him, but nevertheless he had obviously his uses; Master's dog, he called him in his own mind. He looked at Lord Altamount, the hood of the porter's chair framed round his head. The lighting was not strong in the room. It gave him the look of a saint in a niche in a cathedral somewhere. Ascetic. Fourteenth-century. A great man. Yes, Altamount had been one of the great men of the past. Stafford Nye had no doubt of that, but he was now a very old man. Hence, he supposed, the necessity for Sir James Kleek, and Lord Altamount's reliance on him. He looked past them to the enigmatic, cool creature who had brought him here, the Countess Renata Zerkowski alias Mary Ann, alias Daphne Theodofanous. Her face told him nothing. She was not even looking at him. His eyes came round last to Mr Henry Horsham of Security.

With faint surprise he observed that Henry Horsham was grinning at him.

'But look here,' said Stafford Nye, dropping all formal language, and speaking rather like the schoolboy of eighteen he had once been. 'Where on earth do I come in? What do *I* know? Quite frankly, I'm not distinguished in any way in my own profession, you know. They don't think very much of me at the FO. Never have.'

'We know that,' said Lord Altamount.

It was Sir James Kleek's turn to grin and he did so.

'All the better perhaps,' he remarked, and added apologetically as Lord Altamount frowned at him, 'Sorry, sir.'

'This is a committee of investigation,' said Mr Robinson. 'It is not a question of what you have done in the past, of what other people's opinion of you may be. What we are doing is to recruit a committee to investigate. There are not very many of us at the moment forming this committee. We ask you to join it because we think that you have certain qualities which may help in an investigation.'

Stafford Nye turned his head towards the Security man. 'What about it, Horsham?' he said. 'I can't believe you'd agree with that?'

'Why not?' said Henry Horsham.

'Indeed? What are my "qualities", as you call them? I can't, quite frankly, believe in them myself.'

'You're not a hero-worshipper,' said Horsham. 'That's why. You're the kind who sees through humbug. You don't take anyone at their own or the world's valuation. You take them at your own valuation.'

Ce n'est pas un garçon sérieux. The words floated through Sir Stafford Nye's mind. A curious reason for which to be chosen for a difficult and exacting job.

'I've got to warn you,' he said, 'that my principal fault, and one that's been frequently noticed about me and which has cost me several good jobs is, I think, fairly well known. I'm not, I should say, a sufficiently serious sort of chap for an important job like this.'

'Believe it or not,' said Mr Horsham, 'that's one of the reasons why they want you. I'm right, my lord, aren't I?' He looked towards Lord Altamount.

'Public service!' said Lord Altamount. 'Let me tell you that very often one of the most serious disadvantages in public life is when people in a public position take themselves too seriously. We feel that you won't. Anyway,' he said, 'Mary Ann thinks so.'

Sir Stafford Nye turned his head. So here she was, no longer a countess. She had become Mary Ann again.

'You don't mind my asking,' he said, 'but who are you really? I mean, are you a real countess.'

'Absolutely. *Geboren*, as the Germans say. My father was a man of pedigree, a good sportsman, a splendid shot, and had a very romantic but somewhat dilapidated castle in Bavaria. It's still there, the castle. As far as that goes, I have connections with that large portion of the European world which is still heavily snobbish as far as birth is concerned. A poor and shabby countess sits down first at the table whilst a rich American with a fabulous fortune in dollars in the bank is kept waiting.'

'What about Daphne Theodofanous? Where does she come in?'

'A useful name for a passport. My mother was Greek.'

'And Mary Ann?'

It was almost the first smile Stafford Nye had seen on her face. Her eyes went to Lord Altamount and from him to Mr Robinson.

'Perhaps,' she said, 'because I'm a kind of maid-of-all-work, going places, looking for things, taking things from one country to another, sweeping under the mat, do anything, go anywhere, clear up the mess.' She looked towards Lord Altamount again. 'Am I right, Uncle Ned?'

'Quite right, my dear. Mary Ann you are and always will be to us.'

'Were you taking something on that plane? I mean taking something important from one country to another?'

'Yes. It was known I was carrying it. If you hadn't come to my rescue, if you hadn't drunk possibly poisoned beer and handed over your bandit cloak of bright colours as a disguise, well, accidents happen sometimes. I shouldn't have got here.'

'What were you carrying – or mustn't I ask? Are there things I shall never know?'

'There are a lot of things you will never know. There are a lot of things you won't be allowed to ask. I think that question of yours I shall answer. A bare answer of fact. If I am allowed to do so.'

Again she looked at Lord Altamount.

'I trust your judgment,' said Lord Altamount. 'Go ahead.'

'Give him the dope,' said the irreverent James Kleek.

Mr Horsham said, 'I suppose you've got to know. *I* wouldn't tell you, but then I'm Security. Go ahead, Mary Ann.'

'One sentence. *I was bringing a birth certificate. That's all.* I don't tell you any more and it won't be any use your asking any more questions.'

Stafford Nye looked round the assembly.

'All right. I'll join. I'm flattered at your asking me. Where do we go from here?'

'You and I,' said Renata, 'leave here tomorrow. We go to the Continent. You may have read, or know, that there's a Musical Festival taking place in Bavaria. It is something quite new which has only come into being in the last two years. It has a rather formidable German name meaning "The Company of Youthful Singers" and is supported by the Governments of several different countries. It is in opposition to the traditional festivals and productions of Bayreuth. Much of the music given is modern – new young composers are given the chance of their compositions being heard. Whilst thought of highly by some, it is utterly repudiated and held in contempt by others.'

'Yes,' said Sir Stafford, 'I have read about it. Are we going to attend it?'

'We have seats booked for two of the performances.'

'Has this festival any special significance in our investigation?'

'No,' said Renata. 'It is more in the nature of what you might call an exit and entry convenience. We go there for an ostensible and true reason, and we leave it for our next step in due course.'

He looked round. 'Instructions? Do I get any marching orders? Am I to be briefed?'

'Not in your meaning of those terms. You are going on a voyage of exploration. You will learn things as you go along. You will go as yourself, knowing only what you know at present. You go as a lover of music, as a slightly disappointed diplomat who had perhaps hoped for some post in his own country which he has not been given. Otherwise, you will know nothing. It is safer so.'

'But that is the sum of activities at present? Germany, Bavaria, Austria, the Tyrol – that part of the world?'

'It is one of the centres of interest.'

'It is not the only one?'

'Indeed, not even the principal one. There are other spots on the globe, all of varying importance and interest. How much importance each one holds is what we have to find out.'

'And I don't know, or am not to be told, anything about these other centres?'

'Only in cursory fashion. One of them, we think the most important one, has its headquarters in South America, there are two with headquarters in the United States of America, one in California, the other in Baltimore. There is one in Sweden, there is one in Italy. Things have become very active in the latter in the last six months. Portugal and Spain also have smaller centres.

Paris, of course. There are further interesting spots just "coming into production", you might say. As yet not fully developed.'

'You mean Malaya, or Vietnam?'

'No. No, all that lies rather in the past. It was a good rallying cry for violence and student indignation and for many other things.

'What is being promoted, you must understand, is the growing organization of youth everywhere against their mode of government; against their parental customs, against very often the religions in which they have been brought up. There is the insidious cult of permissiveness, there is the increasing cult of violence. Violence not as a means of gaining money, but violence for the love of violence. That particularly is stressed, and the reasons for it are to the people concerned one of the most important things and of the utmost significance.'

'Permissiveness, is that important?'

'It is a way of life, no more. It lends itself to certain abuses but not unduly.'

'What about drugs?'

'The cult of drugs has been deliberately advanced and fomented. Vast sums of money have been made that way, but it is not, or so we think, entirely activated for the money motive.'

All of them looked at Mr Robinson, who slowly shook his head.

'No,' he said, 'it *looks* that way. There are people who are being apprehended and brought to justice. Pushers of drugs will be followed up. But there is more than just the drug racket behind all this. The drug racket is a means, and an evil means, of making money. But there is more to it than that.'

'But who –' Stafford Nye stopped.

'Who and what and why and where? The four W's. That is your mission, Sir Stafford,' said Mr Robinson. 'That's what you've got to find out. You and Mary Ann. It won't be easy, and one of the hardest things in the world, remember, is to keep one's secrets.'

Stafford Nye looked with interest at the fat yellow face of Mr Robinson. Perhaps the secret of Mr Robinson's domination in the financial world was just that. His secret was that he kept his secret. Mr Robinson's mouth showed its smile again. The large teeth gleamed.

'If you know a thing,' he said, 'it is always a great temptation to show that you know it; to talk about it, in other words. It is not that you want to give information, it is not that you have been offered payment to give information. It is that you want to show how important you are. Yes, it's just as simple as that. In fact,' said Mr Robinson, and he half closed his eyes, 'everything in this world is so very, *very* simple. That's what people don't understand.'

The Countess got to her feet and Stafford Nye followed her example.

'I hope you will sleep well and be comfortable,' said Mr Robinson. 'This house is, I think, moderately comfortable.'

Stafford Nye murmured that he was quite sure of that, and on that point he was shortly to be proved to have been quite right. He laid his head on the pillow and went to sleep immediately.

BOOK 2 • JOURNEY TO SIEGFRIED

CHAPTER 10

THE WOMAN IN THE SCHLOSS

I

They came out of the Festival Youth Theatre to the refreshing night air. Below them in a sweep of the ground, was a lighted restaurant. On the side of the hill was another, smaller one. The restaurants varied slightly in price though neither of them was inexpensive. Renata was in evening dress of black velvet, Sir Stafford Nye was in white tie and full evening dress.

'A very distinguished audience,' murmured Stafford Nye to his companion. 'Plenty of money there. A young audience on the whole. You wouldn't think they could afford it.'

'Oh! that can be seen to – it *is* seen to.'

'A subsidy for the élite of youth? That kind of thing?'

'Yes.'

They walked towards the restaurant on the high side of the hill.

'They give you an hour for the meal. Is that right?'

'Technically an hour. Actually an hour and a quarter.'

'That audience,' said Sir Stafford Nye, 'most of them, nearly all of them, I should say, are real lovers of music.'

'Most of them, yes. It's important, you know.'

'What do you mean – important?'

'That the enthusiasm should be genuine. At both ends of the scale,' she added.

'What did you mean, exactly, by that?'

'Those who practise and organize violence must love violence, must want it, must yearn for it. The seal of ecstasy in every movement, of slashing, hurting, destroying. And the same thing with the music. The ears must appreciate every moment of the harmonies and beauties. There can be no pretending in this game.'

'Can you double the rôles – do you mean you can combine violence *and* a love of music or a love of art?'

'It is not always easy, I think, but yes. There are many who can. It is safer really, if they don't have to combine rôles.'

'It's better to keep it simple, as our fat friend Mr Robinson would say? Let the lovers of music love music, let the violent practitioners love violence. Is that what you mean?'

'I think so.'

'I am enjoying this very much. The two days that we have stayed here, the two nights of music that we have enjoyed. I have not enjoyed all the music because I am not perhaps sufficiently modern in my taste. I find the clothes very interesting.'

'Are you talking of the stage production?'

'No, no, I was talking of the audience, really. You and I, the squares, the old-fashioned. You, Countess, in your society gown, I in my white tie and tails. Not a comfortable get-up, it never has been. And then the others, the silks and the velvets, the ruffled shirts of the men, real lace, I noticed, several times – and the plush and the hair and the luxury of *avant garde*, the luxury of the eighteen-hundreds or you might almost say of the Elizabethan age or of Van Dyck pictures.'

'Yes, you are right.'

'I'm no nearer, though, to what it all *means*. I haven't *learnt* anything. I haven't found out anything.'

'You mustn't be impatient. This is a rich show, supported, asked for, demanded perhaps by youth and provided by –'

'By whom?'

'We don't know yet. We shall know.'

'I'm so glad you are sure of it.'

They went into the restaurant and sat down. The food was good though not in any way ornate or luxurious. Once or twice they were spoken to by an acquaintance or a friend. Two people who recognized Sir Stafford Nye expressed pleasure and surprise at seeing him. Renata had a bigger circle of acquaintances since she knew more foreigners – well-dressed women, a man or two, mostly German or Austrian, Stafford Nye thought, one or two Americans. Just a few desultory words. Where people had come from or were going to, criticism or appreciation of the musical fare. Nobody wasted much time since the interval for eating had not been very long.

They returned to their seats for the two final musical offerings. A Symphonic Poem, 'Disintegration in Joy', by a new young composer, Solukonov, and then the solemn grandeur of the March of the Meistersingers.

They came out again into the night. The car which was at their disposal every day was waiting there to take them back to the small but exclusive hotel in the village street. Stafford Nye said good-night to Renata. She spoke to him in a lowered voice.

'Four a.m.,' she said. 'Be ready.'

She went straight into her room and shut the door and he went to his.

The faint scrape of fingers on his door came precisely at three minutes to four the next morning. He opened the door and stood ready.

'The car is waiting,' she said. 'Come.'

II

They lunched at a small mountain inn. The weather was good, the mountains beautiful. Occasionally Stafford Nye wondered what on earth he was doing here. He understood less and less of his travelling companion. She spoke little. He found himself watching her profile. Where was she taking him? What was her real reason? At last, as the sun was almost setting, he said:

'Where are we going? Can I ask?'

'You can ask, yes.'

'But you do not reply?'

'I could reply. I could tell you things, but would they mean anything? It seems to me that if you come to where we are going without my preparing you with explanations (which cannot in the nature of things mean anything), your first impressions will have more force and significance.'

He looked at her again thoughtfully. She was wearing a tweed coat trimmed with fur, smart travelling clothes, foreign in make and cut.

'Mary Ann,' he said thoughtfully.

There was a faint question in it.

'No,' she said, 'not at the moment.'

'Ah. You are still the Countess Zerkowski.'

'At the moment I am still the Countess Zerkowski.'

'Are you in your own part of the world?'

'More or less. I grew up as a child in this part of the world. For a good portion of each year we used to come here in the autumn to a Schloss not very many miles from here.'

He smiled and said thoughtfully, 'What a nice word it is. A Schloss. So solid-sounding.'

'Schlösser are not standing very solidly nowadays. They are mostly disintegrated.'

'This is Hitler's country, isn't it? We're not far, are we, from Berchtesgaden?'

'It lies over there to the north-east.'

'Did your relations, your friends – did they accept Hitler, believe in him? Perhaps I ought not to ask things like that.'

'They disliked him and all he stood for. But they said "Heil Hitler". They acquiesced in what had happened to their country. What else could they do? What else could anybody do at that date?'

'We are going towards the Dolomites, are we not?'

'Does it matter where we are, or which way we are going?'

'Well, this is a voyage of exploration, is it not?'

'Yes, but the exploration is not geographical. We are going to see a personality.'

'You make me feel –' Stafford Nye looked up at the landscape of swelling mountains reaching up to the sky – 'as though we were going to visit the famous Old Man of the Mountain.'

'The Master of the Assassins, you mean, who kept his followers under drugs so that they died for him wholeheartedly, so that they killed, knowing that they themselves would also be killed, but believing, too, that that would transfer them immediately to the Moslem Paradise – beautiful women, hashish and erotic dreams – perfect and unending happiness.'

She paused a minute and then said:

'Spell-binders! I suppose they've always been there throughout the ages. People who make you believe in them so that you are ready to die for them. Not only Assassins. The Christians died also.'

'The holy Martyrs? Lord Altamount?'

'Why do you say Lord Altamount?'

'I saw him that way – suddenly – that evening. Carved in stone – in a thirteenth-century cathedral, perhaps.'

'One of us may have to die. Perhaps more.'

She stopped what he was about to say.

'There is another thing I think of sometimes. A verse in the New Testament – Luke, I think. Christ at the Last Supper saying to his followers: "You are my companions and my friends, *yet one of you is a devil.*" So in all probability one of *us* is a devil.'

'You think it possible?'

'Almost certain. Someone we trust and know, but who goes to sleep at night, not dreaming of martyrdom but of thirty pieces of silver, and who wakes with the feel of them in the palm of his hand.'

'The love of money?'

'Ambition covers it better. How does one recognize a devil? How would one *know*? A devil would stand out in a crowd, would be exciting – would advertise himself – would exercise leadership.'

She was silent a moment and then said in a thoughtful voice:

'I had a friend once in the Diplomatic Service who told me how she had said to a German woman how moved she herself had been at the performance of the Passion Play at Oberammergau. But the German woman said scornfully: "You do not understand. *We* Germans have no need of a Jesus Christ! We have our Adolf Hitler here with us. He is greater than any Jesus that ever lived." She was quite a nice ordinary woman. But that is how she felt. Masses of people felt it. Hitler was a spell-binder. He spoke and they listened – and accepted the sadism, the gas chambers, the tortures of the Gestapo.'

She shrugged her shoulders and then said in her normal voice, 'All the same, it's odd that you should have said what you did just now.'

'What was that?'

'About the Old Man of the Mountain. The head of the Assassins.'

'Are you telling me there *is* an Old Man of the Mountain here?'

'No. Not an Old Man of the Mountain, but there might be an Old Woman of the Mountain.'

'An Old Woman of the Mountain. What's she like?'

'You'll see this evening.'

'What are we doing this evening?'

'Going into society,' said Renata.

'It seems a long time since you've been Mary Ann.'

'You'll have to wait till we're doing some air travel again.'

'I suppose it's very bad for one's morale,' Stafford Nye said thoughtfully, 'living high up in the world.'

'Are you talking socially?'

'No. Geographically. If you live in a castle on a mountain peak overlooking the world below you, well, it makes you despise the ordinary folk, doesn't it? You're the top one, you're the grand one. That's what Hitler felt in Berchtesgaden, that's what many people feel perhaps who climb mountains and look down on their fellow creatures in valleys below.'

'You must be careful tonight,' Renata warned him. 'It's going to be ticklish.'

'Any instructions?'

'You're a disgruntled man. You're one that's against the Establishment, against the conventional world. You're a rebel, but a secret rebel. Can you do it?'

'I can try.'

The scenery had grown wilder. The big car twisted and turned up the roads, passing through mountain villages, sometimes looking down on a bewilderingly distant view where lights shone on a river, where the steeples of churches showed in the distance.

'Where are we going, Mary Ann?'

'To an Eagle's nest.'

The road took a final turn. It wound through a forest. Stafford Nye thought he caught glimpses now and again of deer or of animals of some kind. Occasionally, too, there were leather-jacketed men with guns. Keepers, he thought. And then they came finally to a view of an enormous Schloss standing on a crag. Some of it, he thought, was partially ruined, though most of it had been restored and rebuilt. It was both massive and magnificent but there was nothing new about it or in the message it held. It was representative of past power, power held through bygone ages.

'This was originally the Grand Duchy of Liechtenstolz. The Schloss was built by the Grand Duke Ludwig in 1790,' said Renata.

'Who lives there now? The present Grand Duke?'

'No. They're all gone and done with. Swept away.'

'And who lives here now then?'

'Someone who has present-day power,' said Renata.

'Money?'

'Yes. Very much so.'

'Shall we meet Mr Robinson, flown on ahead by air to greet us?'

'The last person you'll meet here will be Mr Robinson, I can assure you.'

'A pity,' said Stafford Nye. 'I like Mr Robinson. He's quite something, isn't he? Who is he really – what nationality is he?'

'I don't think anybody has ever known. Everyone tells one something different. Some people say he's a Turk, some that he's an Armenian, some that he's Dutch, some that he's just plain English. Some say that his mother was a Circassian slave, a Russian Grand-Duchess, an Indian Begum and so on. Nobody knows. One person told me that his mother was a Miss McLellan from Scotland. I think that's as likely as anything.'

They had drawn up beneath a large portico. Two men-servants in livery came down the steps. Their bows were ostentatious as they welcomed the guests. The luggage was removed; they had a good deal of luggage with them. Stafford Nye had wondered to begin with why he had been told to bring so much, but he was beginning to understand now that from time to time there was need for it. There would, he thought, be need for it this evening. A few questioning remarks and his companion told him that this was so.

They met before dinner, summoned by the sound of a great resounding gong. As he paused in the hall, he waited for her to join him coming down the stairs. She was in full elaborate evening dress tonight, wearing a dark red velvet gown, rubies round her neck and a ruby tiara on her head. A manservant stepped forward and conducted them. Flinging open the door, he announced:

'The Gräfin Zerkowski, Sir Stafford Nye.'

'Here we come, and I hope we look the part,' said Sir Stafford Nye to himself.

He looked down in a satisfied manner at the sapphire and diamond studs in the front of his shirt. A moment later he had drawn his breath in an astonished gasp. Whatever he had expected to see it had not been this. It was an enormous room, rococo in style, chairs and sofas and hangings of the finest brocades and velvets. On the walls there were pictures that he could not recognize all at once, but where he noted almost immediately – for he was fond of pictures – what was certainly a Cézanne, a Matisse, possibly a Renoir. Pictures of inestimable value.

Sitting on a vast chair, throne-like in its suggestion, was an enormous woman. A whale of a woman, Stafford Nye thought, there really was no other word to describe her. A great, big, cheesy-looking woman, wallowing in fat. Double, treble, almost quadruple chins. She wore a dress of stiff orange satin. On her head was an elaborate crown-like tiara of precious stones. Her hands, which rested on the brocaded arms of her seat, were also enormous. Great, big, fat hands with great, big, fat, shapeless fingers. On each finger, he noticed, was a solitaire ring. And in each ring, he thought, was a genuine solitaire stone. A ruby, an emerald, a sapphire, a diamond, a pale green stone which he did not know, a chrysoprase, perhaps, a yellow stone which, if not a topaz, was a yellow diamond. She was horrible, he thought. She wallowed in her fat. A great, white, creased, slobbering mass of fat was her face. And set in it, rather like currants in a vast currant bun, were two small black eyes. Very shrewd eyes, looking on the world, appraising it, appraising him, not appraising Renata, he thought. Renata she knew. Renata was here by command, by appointment. However you liked to put it. Renata had been told to bring *him* here. He wondered why. He couldn't really think why, but he was quite sure of it. It was at him she was looking. She was appraising *him*, summing *him* up. Was he what she wanted? Was he, yes, he'd rather put it this way, was he what the customer had ordered?

I'll have to make quite sure that I know what it is she does want, he thought. I'll have to do my best, otherwise . . . Otherwise he could quite imagine that she might raise a fat ringed hand and say to one of the tall, muscular footmen: 'Take him and throw him over the battlements.' It's ridiculous, thought Stafford Nye. Such things can't happen nowadays. Where am I? What kind of a parade, a masquerade or a theatrical performance am I taking part in?

'You have come very punctual to time, child.'

It was a hoarse, asthmatic voice which had once had an undertone, he thought, of strength, possibly even of beauty. That was over now. Renata came forward, made a slight curtsy. She picked up the fat hand and dropped a courtesy kiss upon it.

'Let me present to you Sir Stafford Nye. The Gräfin Charlotte von Waldsausen.'

The fat hand was extended towards him. He bent over it in the foreign style. Then she said something that surprised him.

'I know your great-aunt,' she said.

He looked astounded, and he saw immediately that she was amused by that, but he saw too, that she had expected him to be surprised by it. She laughed, a rather queer, grating laugh. Not attractive.

'Shall we say, I used to know her. It is many, many years since I have seen her. We were in Switzerland together, at Lausanne, as girls. Matilda. Lady Matilda Baldwen-White.'

'What a wonderful piece of news to take home with me,' said Stafford Nye.

'She is older than I am. She is in good health?'

'For her age, in very good health. She lives in the country quietly. She has arthritis, rheumatism.'

'Ah yes, all the ills of old age. She should have injections of procaine. That is what the doctors do here in this altitude. It is very satisfactory. Does she know that you are visiting me?'

'I imagine that she has not the least idea of it,' said Sir Stafford Nye. 'She knew only that I was going to this festival of modern music.'

'Which you enjoyed, I hope?'

'Oh, enormously. It is a fine Festival Opera Hall, is it not?'

'One of the finest. Pah! It makes the old Bayreuth Festival Hall look like a comprehensive school! Do you know what it cost to build, that Opera House?'

She mentioned a sum in millions of marks. It quite took Stafford Nye's breath away, but he was under no necessity to conceal that. She was pleased with the effect it made upon him.

'With money,' she said, 'if one knows, if one has the ability, if one has the discrimination, what is there that money cannot do? It can give one the best.'

She said the last two words with a rich enjoyment, a kind of smacking of the lips which he found both unpleasant and at the same time slightly sinister.

'I see that here,' he said, as he looked round the walls.

'You are fond of art? Yes, I see you are. There, on the east wall is the finest Cézanne in the world today. Some say that the – ah, I forget the name of it at the moment, the one in the Metropolitan in New York – is finer. That is not true. The best Matisse, the best Cézanne, the best of all that great school of art are here. Here in my mountain eyrie.'

'It is wonderful,' said Sir Stafford. 'Quite wonderful.'

Drinks were being handed round. The Old Woman of the Mountain, Sir Stafford Nye noticed, did not drink anything. It was possible, he thought, that she feared to take any risks over her blood pressure with that vast weight.

'And where did you meet this child?' asked the mountainous Dragon.

Was it a trap? He did not know, but he made his decision.

'At the American Embassy, in London.'

'Ah yes, so I heard. And how is – ah, I forget her name now – ah yes, Milly Jean, our southern heiress? Attractive, did you think?'

'Most charming. She has a great success in London.'

'And poor dull Sam Cortman, the United States Ambassador?'

'A very sound man, I'm sure,' said Stafford Nye politely.

She chuckled.

'Aha, you're tactful, are you not? Ah well, he does well enough. He does what he is told as a good politician should. And it is enjoyable to be Ambassador in London. She could do that for him, Milly Jean. Ah, she could get him an Embassy anywhere in the world, with that well-stuffed purse of hers. Her father owns half the oil in Texas, he owns land, goldfields, everything. A coarse, singularly ugly man – But what does she look like? A gentle little aristocrat. Not blatant, not rich. That is very clever of her, is it not?'

'Sometimes it presents no difficulties,' said Sir Stafford Nye.

'And you? You are not rich?'

'I wish I was.'

'The Foreign Office nowadays, it is not, shall we say, very rewarding?'

'Oh well, I would not put it like that . . . After all, one goes places, one meets amusing people, one sees the world, one sees something of what goes on.'

'Something, yes. But not everything.'

'That would be very difficult.'

'Have you ever wished to see what – how shall I put it – what goes on behind the scenes in life?'

'One has an idea sometimes.' He made his voice non-committal.

'I have heard it said that that is true of you, that you have sometimes ideas about things. Not perhaps the conventional ideas?'

'There have been times when I've been made to feel the bad boy of the family,' said Stafford Nye and laughed.

Old Charlotte chuckled.

'You don't mind admitting things now and again, do you?'

'Why pretend? People always know what you're concealing.'

She looked at him.

'What do you want out of life, young man?'

He shrugged his shoulders. Here again, he had to play things by ear.

'Nothing,' he said.

'Come now, come now, am I to believe that?'

'Yes, you can believe it. I am not ambitious. Do I look ambitious?'

'No, I will admit that.'

'I ask only to be amused, to live comfortably, to eat, to drink in moderation, to have friends who amuse me.'

The old woman leant forward. Her eyes snapped open and shut three or four times. Then she spoke in a rather different voice. It was like a whistling note.

'Can you hate? Are you capable of hating?'

'To hate is a waste of time.'

'I see. I see. There are no lines of discontent in your face.

That is true enough. All the same, I think you are ready to take a certain path which will lead you to a certain place, and you will go along it smiling, as though you did not care, but all the same, in the end, if you find the right advisers, the right helpers, you might attain what you want, if you are capable of wanting.'

'As to that,' said Stafford Nye, 'who isn't?' He shook his head at her very gently. 'You see too much,' he said. 'Much too much.'

Footmen threw open a door.

'Dinner is served.'

The proceedings were properly formal. They had indeed almost a royal tinge about them. The big doors at the far end of the room were flung open, showing through to a brightly lighted ceremonial dining-room, with a painted ceiling and three enormous chandeliers. Two middle-aged women approached the Gräfin, one on either side. They wore evening dress, their grey hair was carefully piled on their heads, each wore a diamond brooch. To Sir Stafford Nye, all the same, they brought a faint flavour of wardresses. They were, he thought, not so much security guards as perhaps high-class nursing attendants in charge of the health, the toilet and other intimate details of the Gräfin Charlotte's existence. After respectful bows, each one of them slipped an arm below the shoulder and elbow of the sitting woman. With the ease of long practice aided by the effort which was obviously as much as she could make, they raised her to her feet in a dignified fashion.

'We will go in to dinner now,' said Charlotte.

With her two female attendants, she led the way. On her feet she looked even more a mass of wobbling jelly, yet she was still formidable. You could not dispose of her in your mind as just a fat old woman. She was somebody, knew she was somebody, intended to be somebody. Behind the three of them he and Renata followed.

As they entered through the portals of the dining-room, he felt it was almost more a banquet hall than a dining-room. There was a bodyguard here. Tall, fair-haired, handsome young men. They wore some kind of uniform. As Charlotte entered there was a clash as one and all drew their swords. They crossed them overhead to make a passageway, and Charlotte, steadying herself, passed along that passageway, released by her attendants and making her progress solo to a vast carved chair with gold fittings and upholstered in golden brocade at the head of the long table. It was rather like a wedding procession, Stafford Nye thought. A naval or military one. In this case surely, military, strictly military – but lacking a bridegroom.

They were all young men of super physique. None of them, he thought, was older than thirty. They had good looks, their health was evident. They did not smile, they were entirely serious, they were – he thought of a word for it – yes, dedicated. Perhaps not so much a military procession as a religious one. The servitors appeared, old-fashioned servitors belonging, he thought, to the Schloss's past, to a time before the 1939 war. It was like a super production of a period historic play. And queening over it, sitting in the chair or the throne or whatever you liked to call it, at the head of the table, was not a queen or an empress but an old woman noticeable mainly for her avoirdupois weight and her extraordinary and intense ugliness. Who was she? What was she doing here? Why?

Why all this masquerade, why this bodyguard, a security body-guard perhaps? Other diners came to the table. They bowed to the monstrosity on the presiding throne and took their places. They wore ordinary evening dress. No introductions were made.

Stafford Nye, after long years of sizing up people, assessed them. Different types. A great many different types. Lawyers, he was certain. Several lawyers. Possibly accountants or financiers; one or two army officers in plain clothes. They were of the Household, he thought, but they were also in the old-fashioned feudal sense of the term those who 'sat below the salt'.

Food came. A vast boar's head pickled in aspic, venison, a cool refreshing lemon sorbet, a magnificent edifice of pastry – a super millefeuille that seemed of unbelievable confectionary richness.

The vast woman ate, ate greedily, hungrily, enjoying her food. From outside came a new sound. The sound of the powerful engine of a super sports car. It passed the windows in a white flash. There came a cry inside the room from the bodyguard. A great cry of 'Heil! Heil! Heil Franz!'

The bodyguard of young men moved with the ease of a military manoeuvre known by heart. Everyone had risen to their feet. Only the old woman sat without moving, her head lifted high, on her dais. And, so Stafford Nye thought, a new excitement now permeated the room.

The other guests, or the other members of the household, whatever they were, disappeared in a way that somehow reminded Stafford of lizards disappearing into the cracks of a wall. The golden-haired boys formed a new figure, their swords flew out, they saluted their patroness, she bowed her head in acknowledgment, their swords were sheathed and they turned, permission given, to march out through the door of the room. Her eyes followed them, then went first to Renata, and then to Stafford Nye.

'What do you think of them?' she said. 'My boys, my youth corps, my children. Yes, my children. Have you a word that can describe them?'

'I think so,' said Stafford Nye. 'Magnificent.' He spoke to her as to Royalty. 'Magnificent, ma'am.'

'Ah!' She bowed her head. She smiled, the wrinkles multiplying all over her face. It made her look exactly like a crocodile.

A terrible woman, he thought, a terrible woman, impossible, dramatic. Was any of this happening? He couldn't believe it was. What could this be but yet another festival hall in which a production was being given.

The doors clashed open again. The yellow-haired band of the young supermen marched as before through it. This time they did not wield swords, instead they sang. Sang with unusual beauty of tone and voice.

After a good many years of pop music Stafford Nye felt an incredulous pleasure. Trained voices, these. Not raucous shouting. Trained by masters of the singing art. Not allowed to strain their vocal cords, to be off key. They might be the new Heroes of a New World, but what they sang was not new music. It was music he had heard before. An arrangement of the Preislied, there must be a concealed orchestra somewhere, he thought, in a gallery round the top of the room. It was an arrangement or adaptation of various Wagnerian themes. It passed from the Preislied to the distant echoes of the Rhine music.

The Elite Corps made once more a double lane where somebody was expected to make an entrance. It was not the old Empress this time. She sat on her dais awaiting whoever was coming.

And at last he came. The music changed as he came. It gave out that motif which by now Stafford Nye had got by heart. The melody of the Young Siegfried. Siegfried's horn call, rising up in its youth and its triumph, its mastery of a new world which the young Siegfried came to conquer.

Through the doorway, marching up between the lines of what were clearly his followers, came one of the handsomest young men Stafford Nye had ever seen. Golden-haired, blue-eyed, perfectly proportioned, conjured up as it were by the wave of a magician's wand, he came forth out of the world of myth. Myth, heroes, resurrection, rebirth, it was all there. His beauty, his strength, his incredible assurance and arrogance.

He strode through the double lines of his bodyguard, until he stood before the hideous mountain of womanhood that sat there on her throne; he knelt on one knee, raised her hand to his lips, and then rising to his feet, he threw up one arm in salutation and uttered the cry that Stafford Nye had heard from the others. 'Heil!' His German was not very clear, but Stafford Nye thought he distinguished the syllables 'Heil to the great mother!'

Then the handsome young hero looked from one side to the other. There was some faint recognition, though an uninterested one, of Renata, but when his gaze turned to Stafford Nye, there was definite interest and appraisal. Caution, thought Stafford Nye. Caution! He must play his part right now. Play the part that was expected of him. Only – what the hell was that part? What was he doing here? What were he or the girl supposed to be doing here? Why had they come?

The hero spoke.

'So,' he said, 'we have guests!' And he added, smiling with the arrogance of a young man who knows that he is vastly superior to any other person in the world. 'Welcome, guests, welcome to you both.'

Somewhere in the depths of the Schloss a great bell began tolling. It had no funereal sound about it, but it had a disciplinary air. The feeling of a monastery summoned to some holy office.

'We must sleep now,' said old Charlotte. 'Sleep. We will meet again tomorrow morning at eleven o'clock.'

She looked towards Renata and Sir Stafford Nye.

'You will be shown to your rooms. I hope you will sleep well.'

It was the Royal dismissal.

Stafford Nye saw Renata's arm fly up in the Fascist salute, but it was addressed not to Charlotte, but to the golden-haired boy. He thought she said: 'Heil Franz Joseph.' He copied her gesture and he, too, said 'Heil!'

Charlotte spoke to them.

'Would it please you tomorrow morning to start the day with a ride through the forest?'

'I should like it of all things,' said Stafford Nye.

'And you, child?'

'Yes, I too.'

'Very good then. It shall be arranged. Good night to you both. I am glad to welcome you here. Franz Joseph – give me your arm. We will go into the Chinese Boudoir. We have much to discuss, and you will have to leave in good time tomorrow morning.'

The menservants escorted Renata and Stafford Nye to their apartments. Nye hesitated for a moment on the threshold. Would it be possible for them to have a word or two now? He decided against it. As long as the castle walls surrounded them it was well to be careful. One never knew – each room might be wired with microphones.

Sooner or later, though, he *had* to ask questions. Certain things aroused a new and sinister apprehension in his mind. He was being persuaded, inveigled into something. But what? And whose doing was it?

The bedrooms were handsome, yet oppressive. The rich hangings of satin and velvets, some of them antique, gave out a faint perfume of decay, tempered by spices. He wondered how often Renata had stayed here before.

CHAPTER 11

THE YOUNG AND THE LOVELY

After breakfasting on the following morning in a small breakfast-room downstairs, he found Renata waiting for him. The horses were at the door.

Both of them had brought riding clothes with them. Everything they could possibly require seemed to have been intelligently anticipated.

They mounted and rode away down the castle drive. Renata spoke with the groom at some length.

'He asked if we would like him to accompany us but I said no. I know the tracks round here fairly well.'

'I see. You have been here before?'

'Not very often of late years. Early in my life I knew this place very well.'

He gave her a sharp look. She did not return it. As she rode beside him, he watched her profile – the thin, aquiline nose, the head carried so proudly on the slender neck. She rode a horse well, he saw that.

All the same, there was a sense of ill ease in his mind this morning. He wasn't sure why . . .

His mind went back to the Airport Lounge. The woman who had come to stand beside him. The glass of Pilsner on the table . . . Nothing in it that there shouldn't have been – neither then, nor later. A risk he had accepted. Why, when all that was long over, should it rouse uneasiness in him now?

They had a brief canter following a ride through the trees. A beautiful property, beautiful woods. In the distance he saw horned animals. A paradise for a sportsman, a paradise for the old way of living, a paradise that contained – what? A serpent? As it was in the beginning – with Paradise went a serpent. He drew rein and the horses fell to a walk. He and Renata were alone – no microphones, no listening walls – The time had come for his questions.

'Who is she?' he said urgently. 'What is she?'

'It's easy to answer. So easy that it's hardly believable.'

'Well?' he said.

'She's oil. Copper. Goldmines in South Africa. Armaments in Sweden. Uranium deposits in the north. Nuclear development, vast stretches of cobalt. She's all those things.'

'And yet, I hadn't heard about her, I didn't know her name, I didn't know –'

'She has not wanted people to know.'

'Can one keep such things quiet?'

'Easily, if you have enough copper and oil and nuclear deposits and armaments and all the rest of it. Money can advertise, or money can keep secrets, can hush things up.'

'But who *actually* is she?'

'Her grandfather was American. He was mainly railways, I think. Possibly Chicago hogs in those times. It's like going back into history, finding out. He married a German woman. You've heard of her, I expect. Big Belinda, they used to christen her. Armaments, shipping, the whole industrial wealth of Europe. She was her father's heiress.'

'Between those two, unbelievable wealth,' said Sir Stafford Nye. 'And so – power. Is that what you're telling me?'

'Yes. She didn't just inherit things, you know. She made money as well. She'd inherited brains, she was a big financier in her own right. Everything she touched multiplied itself. Turned to incredible sums of money, and she invested them. Taking advice, taking other people's judgment, but in the end always using her own. And always prospering. Always adding to her wealth so that it was too fabulous to be believed. Money creates money.'

'Yes, I can understand that. Wealth *has* to increase if there's a superfluity of it. But – what did *she* want? What has *she* got?'

'You said it just now. Power.'

'And she lives here? Or does she –?'

'She visits America and Sweden. Oh yes, she visits places, but not often. This is where she prefers to be, in the centre of a web like a vast spider controlling all the threads. The threads of finance. Other threads too.'

'When you say, other threads –'

'The arts. Music, pictures, writers. Human beings – young human beings.'

'Yes. One might know that. Those pictures, a wonderful collection.'

'There are galleries of them upstairs in the Schloss. There are Rembrandts and Giottos and Raphaels and there are cases of jewels – some of the most wonderful jewels in the world.'

'All belonging to one ugly, gross old woman. Is she satisfied?'

'Not yet, but well on the way to being.'

'Where is she going, what does she want?'

'She loves youth. That is her mode of power. To control youth. The world is full of rebellious youth at this moment.

That's been helped on. Modern philosophy, modern thought, writers and others whom she finances and controls.'

'But how can –?' He stopped.

'I can't tell you because I don't know. It's an enormous ramification. She's behind it in one sense, supports rather curious charities, earnest philanthropists and idealists, raises innumerable grants for students and artists and writers.'

'And yet you say it's not –'

'No, it's not yet complete. It's a great upheaval that's being planned. It's believed in, it's the new heaven and the new earth. That's what's been promised by leaders for thousands of years. Promised by religions, promised by those who support Messiahs, promised by those who come back to teach the law, like the Buddha. Promised by politicians. The crude heaven of an easy attainment such as the Assassins believed in, and the Old Man of the Assassins promised his followers and, from their point of view, gave to them.'

'Is she behind drugs as well?'

'Yes. Without conviction, of course. Only a means of having people bent to her will. It's one way, too, of destroying people. The weak ones. The ones she thinks are no good, although they had once shown promise. She'd never take drugs herself – she's strong. But drugs destroy weak people more easily and naturally than anything else.'

'And force? What about force? You can't do everything by propaganda.'

'No, of course not. Propaganda is the first stage and behind it there are vast armaments piling up. Arms that go to deprived countries and then on elsewhere. Tanks and guns and nuclear weapons that go to Africa and the South Seas and South America. In South America there's a lot building up. Forces of young men and women drilling and training. Enormous arms dumps – means of chemical warfare –'

'It's a nightmare! How do you know all this, Renata?'

'Partly because I've been told it; from information received, partly because I have been instrumental in proving some of it.'

'But *you*. You and *she*?'

'There's always something idiotic behind all great and vast projects.' She laughed suddenly. 'Once, you see, she was in love with my grandfather. A foolish story. He lived in this part of the world. He had a castle a mile or two from here.'

'Was he a man of genius?'

'Not at all. He was just a very good sportsman. Handsome, dissolute and attractive to women. And so, because of that, she is in a sense my protectress. And I am one of her converts or slaves! I work for her. I find people for her. I carry out her commands in different parts of the world.'

'Do you?'

'What do you mean by that?'

'I wondered,' said Sir Stafford Nye.

He did wonder. He looked at Renata and he thought again of the airport. He was working *for* Renata, he was working *with* Renata. She had brought him to this Schloss. Who had told her to bring him here? Big, gross Charlotte in the middle of her spider's web? He had had a reputation, a reputation of being unsound in certain diplomatic quarters. He could be useful to these people perhaps, but useful in a small and rather humiliating way. And he thought suddenly, in a kind of fog of question marks: Renata??? I took a risk with her at Frankfurt airport. But I was right. It came off. Nothing happened to me. But all the same, he thought, who is she? *What* is she? I don't know. I can't be *sure*. One can't in the world today be sure of *anyone*. Anyone at all. She was told perhaps to get me. To get me into the hollow of her hand, so that business at Frankfurt might have been cleverly thought out. It fitted in with my sense of risk, and it would make me sure of her. It would make me trust her.

'Let's canter again,' she said. 'We've walked the horses too long.'

'I haven't asked you what *you* are in all this?'

'I take orders.'

'From whom?'

'There's an opposition. There's always an opposition. There are people who have a suspicion of what's going on, of how the world is going to be made to change, of how with money, wealth, armaments, idealism, great trumpeting words of power that's going to happen. There are people who say it shall *not* happen.'

'And you are with them?'

'I say so.'

'What do you mean by that, Renata?'

She said, '*I say so.*'

He said: 'That young man last night –'

'Franz Joseph?'

'Is that his name?'

'It is the name he is known by.'

'But he has another name, hasn't he?'

'Do you think so?'

'He is, isn't he, the young Siegfried?'

'You saw him like that? You realized that's what he was, what he stands for?'

'I think so. Youth. Heroic youth. Aryan youth, it has to be Aryan youth in this part of the world. There is still that point of view. A super race, the supermen. They must be of Aryan descent.'

'Oh yes, it's lasted on from the time of Hitler. It doesn't always come out into the open much and, in other places all over the world, it isn't stressed so much. South America, as I say, is one of the strongholds. And Peru and South Africa also.'

'What does the young Siegfried do? What does he do besides look handsome and kiss the hand of his protectress?'

'Oh, he's quite an orator. He speaks and his following would follow him to death.'

'Is that true?'

'He believes it.'

'And you?'

'I think I might believe it.' She added: 'Oratory is very frightening, you know. What a voice can do, what words can do, and not particularly convincing words at that. The *way* they are said. His voice rings like a bell, and women cry and scream and faint away when he addresses them – you'll see that for yourself.

'You saw Charlotte's Bodyguard last night all dressed up – people do love dressing up nowadays. You'll see them all over the world in their own chosen get-up, different in different places, some with their long hair and their beards, and girls in their streaming white nightgowns, talking of peace and beauty, and the wonderful world that is the world of the young which is to be theirs when they've destroyed enough of the old world. The original Country of the Young was west of the Irish Sea, wasn't it? A very simple place, a different Country of the Young from what we're planning now – It was silver sands, and sunshine and singing in the waves . . .

'But now we want Anarchy, and breaking down and destroying. Only Anarchy can benefit those who march behind it. It's frightening, it's also wonderful – because of its violence, because it's bought with pain and suffering –'

'So that is how you see the world today?'

'Sometimes.'

'And what am *I* to do next?'

'Come with your guide. I'm your guide. Like Virgil with Dante, I'll take you down into hell, I'll show you the sadistic films partly copied from the old SS, show you cruelty and pain and violence worshipped. And I'll show you the great dreams of paradise in peace and beauty. You won't know which is which and what is what. But you'll have to make up your mind.'

'Do I trust you, Renata?'

'That will be your choice. You can run away from me if you like, or you can stay with me and see the new world. The new world that's in the making.'

'Pasteboard,' said Sir Stafford Nye violently.

She looked at him inquiringly.

'Like Alice in Wonderland. The cards, the pasteboard cards all rising up in the air. Flying about. Kings and Queens and Knaves. All sorts of things.'

'You mean – what do you mean exactly?'

'I mean it isn't real. It's make-believe. The whole damn thing is make-believe.'

'In one sense, yes.'

'All dressed up playing parts, putting on a show. I'm getting nearer, aren't I, to the meaning of things?'

'In a way, yes, and in a way, no –'

'There's one thing I'd like to ask you because it puzzles me. Big Charlotte ordered you to bring me to see her – why? What did she know about me? What use did she think she could make of me?'

'I don't quite know – possibly a kind of *Eminence Grise* – working behind a façade. That would suit you rather well.'

'But she knows nothing whatever about me!'

'Oh, *that*!' Suddenly Renata went into peals of laughter. 'It's so ridiculous, really – the same old nonsense all over again.'

'I don't understand you, Renata.'

'No – because it's so simple. Mr Robinson would understand.'

'Would you kindly explain what you are talking about?'

'It's the same old business – "*It's not what you are. It's who you know*". Your Great-Aunt Matilda and Big Charlotte were at school together –'

'You actually mean –'

'Girls together.'

He stared at her. Then he threw his head back and roared with laughter.

CHAPTER 12
COURT JESTER

They left the Schloss at midday, saying goodbye to their hostess. Then they had driven down the winding road, leaving the Schloss high above them and they had come at last, after many hours of driving, to a stronghold in the Dolomites – an amphitheatre in the mountains where meetings, concerts and reunions of the various Youth Groups were held.

Renata had brought him there, his guide, and from his seat on the bare rock he had watched what went on and had listened. He understood a little more what she had been talking about earlier that day. This great mass gathering, animated as all mass gatherings can be whether they are called by an evangelistic religious leader in Madison Square, New York, or in the shadow of a Welsh church or in a football crowd or in the super demonstrations which marched to attack embassies and police and universities and all the rest of it.

She had brought him there to show him the meaning of that one phrase: 'The Young Siegfried'.

Franz Joseph, if that was really his name, had addressed the crowd. His voice, rising, falling, with its curious exciting quality, its emotional appeal, had held sway over that groaning, almost

474 · AGATHA CHRISTIE

moaning crowd of young women and young men. Every word that he had uttered had seemed pregnant with meaning, had held incredible appeal. The crowd had responded like an orchestra. His voice had been the baton of the conductor. And yet, what had the boy said? What had been the young Siegfried's message? There were no words that he could remember when it came to an end, but he knew that he had been moved, promised things, roused to enthusiasm. And now it was over. The crowd had surged round the rocky platform, calling, crying out. Some of the girls had been screaming with enthusiasm. Some of them had fainted. What a world it was nowadays, he thought. Everything used the whole time to arouse emotion. Discipline? Restraint? None of those things counted for anything any more. Nothing mattered but to *feel*.

What sort of a world, thought Stafford Nye, could that make?

His guide had touched him on the arm and they had disentangled themselves from the crowd. They had found their car and the driver had taken them by roads with which he was evidently well acquainted, to a town and an inn on a mountain side where rooms had been reserved for them.

They walked out of the inn presently and up the side of a mountain by a well-trodden path until they came to a seat. They sat there for some moments in silence. It was then that Stafford Nye had said again, 'Pasteboard.'

For some five minutes or so they sat looking down the valley, then Renata said, 'Well?'

'What are you asking me?'

'What you think so far of what I have shown you?'

'I'm not convinced,' said Stafford Nye.

She gave a sigh, a deep, unexpected sigh.

'That's what I hoped you would say.'

'It's none of it true, is it? It's a gigantic show. A show put on by a producer – a complete group of producers, perhaps.

'That monstrous woman pays the producer, hires the producer. We've not seen the producer. What we've seen today is the star performer.'

'What do you think of him?'

'He's not real either,' said Stafford Nye. 'He's just an actor. A first-class actor, superbly produced.'

A sound surprised him. It was Renata laughing. She got up from her seat. She looked suddenly excited, happy, and at the same time faintly ironical.

'I knew it,' she said. 'I knew you'd see. I knew you'd have your feet on the ground. You've always known, haven't you, about everything you've met in life? You've known humbug, you've known everything and everyone for what they really are.

'No need to go to Stratford and see Shakespearean plays to know what part you are cast for – The Kings and the great men have to have a Jester – The King's Jester who tells the King the truth, and talks common sense, and makes fun of all the things that are taking in other people.'

'So that's what I am, is it? A Court Jester?'

'Can't you feel it yourself? That's what we want – That's what we need. "Pasteboard," you said. "Cardboard". A vast, well-produced, splendid *show*! And how right you are. But people are taken in. They think something's wonderful, or they think something's devilish, or they think it's something terribly important. Of course it isn't – only – only one's got to find out just how to *show* people – that the whole thing, all of it, is just *silly*. Just damn *silly*. That's what you and I are going to do.'

'Is it your idea that in the end we debunk all this?'

'It seems wildly unlikely, I agree. But you know once people are shown that something isn't real, that it's just one enormous leg-pull, well –'

'Are you proposing to preach a gospel of common sense?'

'Of course not,' said Renata. 'Nobody'd listen to that, would they?'

'Not just at present.'

'No. We'll have to give them evidence – facts – truth –'

'Have we got such things?'

'Yes. What I brought back with me via Frankfurt – what you helped to bring safely into England –'

'I don't understand –'

'Not yet – You will know later. For now we've got a part to play. We're ready and willing, fairly panting to be indoctrinated. We worship youth. We're followers and believers in the young Siegfried.'

'*You* can put that over, no doubt. I'm not so sure about myself.

I've never been very successful as a worshipper of anything. The King's Jester isn't. He's the great debunker. Nobody's going to appreciate that very much just now, are they?'

'Of course they're not. No. You don't let that side of yourself show. Except, of course, when talking about your masters and betters, politicians and diplomats, Foreign Office, the Establishment, all the other things. Then you can be embittered, malicious, witty, slightly cruel.'

'I still don't see my rôle in the world crusade.'

'That's a very ancient one, the one that everybody understands and appreciates. Something in it for you. That's your line. You haven't been appreciated in the past, but the young Siegfried and all he stands for will hold out the hope of reward to you. Because you give him all the inside dope he wants about your own country, he will promise you places of power in that country in the good times to come.'

'You insinuate that this is a world movement. Is that true?'

'Of course it is. Rather like one of those hurricanes, you know, that have names. Flora or Little Annie. They come up out of the south or the north or the east or the west, but they come up from nowhere and destroy everything. That's what everyone wants. In Europe and Asia and America. Perhaps Africa, though there won't be so much enthusiasm there. They're fairly new to power and graft and things. Oh yes, it's a world movement all right. Run by youth and all the intense vitality of youth. They haven't got knowledge and they haven't got experience, but they've got vision and vitality, and they're backed by money. Rivers and rivers of money pouring in. There's been too much materialism, so we've asked for something else, and we've got it. But as it's based on hate, it can't get anywhere. It can't move off the ground. Don't you remember in 1919 everyone going about with a rapt face saying Communism was the answer to everything. That Marxist doctrine would produce a new heaven brought down to a new earth. So many noble ideas flowing about. But then, you see, whom have you got to work out the ideas with? After all, only the same human beings you've always had. You can create a third world now, or so everyone thinks, but the third world will have the same people in it as the first world or the second world or whatever names you like to call things. And when you have the same human beings running things, they'll run them the same way. You've only got to look at history.'

'Does anybody care to look at history nowadays?'

'No. They'd much rather look forward to an unforeseeable future. Science was once going to be the answer to everything. Freudian beliefs and unrepressed sex would be the next answer to human misery. There'd be no more people with mental troubles. If anyone had said that mental homes would be even fuller as the result of shutting out repressions nobody would have believed him.'

Stafford Nye interrupted her:

'I want to know something,' said Sir Stafford Nye.

'What is it?'

'Where are we going next?'

'South America. Possibly Pakistan or India on the way. And we must certainly go to the USA. There's a lot going on there that's very interesting indeed. Especially in California –'

'Universities?' Sir Stafford sighed. 'One gets very tired of universities. They repeat themselves so much.'

They sat silent for some minutes. The light was failing, but a mountain peak showed softly red.

Stafford Nye said in a nostalgic tone:

'If we had some more music *now* – this moment – do you know what I'd order?'

'More Wagner? Or have you torn yourself free from Wagner?'

'No – you're quite right – more Wagner. I'd have Hans Sachs sitting under his elder tree, saying of the world: "Mad, mad, all mad" –'

'Yes – that expresses it. It's lovely music, too. But *we're* not mad. We're sane.'

'Eminently sane,' said Stafford Nye. 'That is going to be the difficulty. There's one more thing I want to know.'

'Well?'

'Perhaps you won't tell me. But I've *got* to know. Is there going to be any fun to be got out of this mad business that we're attempting?'

'Of course there is. Why not?'

'Mad, mad, all mad – but we'll enjoy it all very much. Will our lives be long, Mary Ann?'

'Probably not,' said Renata.

'That's the spirit. I'm with you, my comrade, and my guide. Shall we get a better world as a result of our efforts?'

'I shouldn't think so, but it might be a kinder one. It's full of beliefs without kindness at present.'

'Good enough,' said Stafford Nye. 'Onward!'

BOOK 3 • AT HOME AND ABROAD

CHAPTER 13

CONFERENCE IN PARIS

In a room in Paris five men were sitting. It was a room that had seen historic meetings before. Quite a number of them. This meeting was in many ways a meeting of a different kind yet it promised to be no less historic.

Monsieur Grosjean was presiding. He was a worried man doing his best to slide over things with facility and a charm of manner that had often helped him in the past. He did not feel it was helping him so much today. Signor Vitelli had arrived from Italy by air an hour before. His gestures were feverish, his manner unbalanced.

'It is beyond anything,' he was saying, 'it is beyond anything one could have imagined.'

'These students,' said Monsieur Grosjean, 'do we not all suffer?'

'This is more than students. It is beyond students. What can one compare this to? A swarm of bees. A disaster of nature intensified. Intensified beyond anything one could have imagined. They march. They have machine-guns. Somewhere they have acquired planes. They propose to take over the whole of North Italy. But it is madness, that! They are children – nothing more. And yet they have bombs, explosives. In the city of Milan alone they outnumber the police. What can we do, I ask you? The military? The army too – it is in revolt. They say they are with *les jeunes*. They say there is no hope for the world except in anarchy. They talk of something they call the Third World, but this cannot just happen.'

Monsieur Grosjean sighed. 'It is very popular among the young,' he said, 'the anarchy. A belief in anarchy. We know that from the days of Algeria, from all the troubles from which our country and our colonial empire has suffered. And what can we do? The military? In the end they back the students.'

'The students, ah, the students,' said Monsieur Poissonier.

He was a member of the French government to whom the word 'student' was anathema. If he had been asked he would have admitted to a preference for Asian 'flu or even an outbreak of bubonic plague. Either was preferable in his mind to the activities of students. A world with no students in it! That was what Monsieur Poissonier sometimes dreamt about. They were good dreams, those. They did not occur often enough.

'As for magistrates,' said Monsieur Grosjean, 'what has happened to our judicial authorities? The police – yes, they are loyal still, but the judiciary, they will not impose sentences, not on young men who are brought before them, young men who have destroyed property, government property, private property – every kind of property. And why not, one would like to know? I have been making inquiries lately. The Préfecture have suggested certain things to me. An increase is needed, they say, in the standard of living among judiciary authorities, especially in the provincial areas.'

'Come, come,' said Monsieur Poissonier, 'you must be careful what you suggest.'

'*Ma foi*, why should I be careful? Things need bringing into the open. We have had frauds before, gigantic frauds and there is money now circulating around. Money, and we do not know where it comes from, but the Préfecture have said to me – and I believe it – that they begin to get an idea of where it is *going*. Do we contemplate, can we contemplate a corrupt state subsidized from some outside source?'

'In Italy too,' said Signor Vitelli, 'in Italy, ah, I could tell you things. Yes, I could tell you of what we suspect. But who, who is corrupting our world? A group of industrialists, a group of tycoons? How could such a thing be so.'

'This business has got to stop,' said Monsieur Grosjean. 'Action must be taken. Military action. Action from the Air Force. These anarchists, these marauders, they come from every class. It must be put down.'

'Control by tear gas has been fairly successful,' said Poissonier dubiously.

'Tear gas is not enough,' said Monsieur Grosjean. 'The same result could be got by setting students to peel bunches of onions. Tears would flow from their eyes. It needs more than that.'

Monsieur Poissonier said in a shocked voice:

'You are not suggesting the use of nuclear weapons?'

'Nuclear weapons? *Quelle blague*! What can we do with nuclear weapons. What would become of the soil of France, of the air of France if we use nuclear weapons? We can destroy Russia, we know that. We also know that Russia can destroy us.'

'You're not suggesting that groups of marching and demonstrating students could destroy our authoritarian forces?'

'That is exactly what I am suggesting. I have had a warning of such things. Of stock-piling of arms, and various forms of chemical warfare and of other things. I have had reports from some of our eminent scientists. Secrets are known. Stores – held in secret – weapons of warfare have been stolen. What is to happen next, I ask you. What is to happen next?'

The question was answered unexpectedly and with more rapidity than Monsieur Grosjean could possibly have calculated. The door opened and his principal secretary approached his master, his face showing urgent concern. Monsieur Grosjean looked at him with displeasure.

'Did I not say I wanted no interruptions?'

'Yes indeed, Monsieur le Président, but this is somewhat unusual –' He bent towards his master's ear. 'The Marshal is here. He demands entrance.'

'The Marshal? You mean –'

The secretary nodded his head vigorously several times to show that he did mean. Monsieur Poissonier looked at his colleague in perplexity.

'He demands admission. He will not take refusal.'

The two other men in the room looked first at Grosjean and then at the agitated Italian.

'Would it not be better,' said Monsieur Coin, the Minister for Home Affairs, 'if –'

He paused at the 'if' as the door was once more flung open and a man strode in. A very well-known man. A man whose word had been not only law, but above law in the country of

France for many past years. To see him at this moment was an unwelcome surprise for those sitting there.

'Ah, I welcome you, dear colleagues,' said the Marshal. 'I come to help you. Our country is in danger. Action must be taken, immediate action! I come to put myself at your service. I take over all responsibility for acting in this crisis. There may be danger. I know there is, but honour is above danger. The salvation of France is above danger. They march this way now. A vast herd of students, of criminals who have been released from jails, some of them who have committed the crime of homicide. Men who have committed incendiarism. They shout names. They sing songs. They call on the names of their teachers, of their philosophers, of those who have led them on this path of insurrection. Those who will bring about the doom of France unless something is done. You sit here, you talk, you deplore things. More than that must be done. I have sent for two regiments. I have alerted the air force, special coded wires have gone out to our neighbouring ally, to my friends in Germany, for she is our ally now in this crisis!

'Riot must be put down. Rebellion! Insurrection! The danger to men, women and children, to property. I go forth now to quell the insurrection, to speak to them as their father, their leader. These students, these criminals even, they are my children. They are the youth of France. I go to speak to them of that. They shall listen to me, governments will be revised, their studies can be resumed under their own auspices. Their grants have been insufficient, their lives have been deprived of beauty, of leadership. I come to promise all this. I speak in my own name. I shall speak also in your name, the name of the Government, you have done your best, you have acted as well as you know how. But it needs higher leadership. It needs *my* leadership. I go now. I have lists of further coded wires to be sent. Such nuclear deterrents as can be used in unfrequented spots can be put into action in such a modified form that though they may bring terror to the mob, we ourselves shall know that there is no real danger in them. I have thought out everything. My plan will go. Come, my loyal friends, accompany me.'

'Marshal, we cannot allow – you cannot imperil yourself. We must . . .'

'I listen to nothing you say. I embrace my doom, my destiny.'

The Marshal strode to the door.

'My staff is outside. My chosen bodyguard. I go now to speak to these young rebels, this young flower of beauty and terror, to tell them where their duty lies.'

He disappeared through the door with the grandeur of a leading actor playing his favourite part.

'*Bon Dieu*, he means it!' said Monsieur Poissonier.

'He will risk his life,' said Signor Vitelli. 'Who knows? It is brave, he is a brave man. It is gallant, yes, but what will happen to him? In the mood *les jeunes* are in now, they might kill him.'

A pleasurable sigh fell from Monsieur Poissonier's lips. It might be true, he thought. Yes, it might be true.

'It is possible,' he said. 'Yes, they might kill him.'

'One cannot wish that, of course,' said Monsieur Grosjean carefully.

Monsieur Grosjean did wish it. He hoped for it, though a natural pessimism led him to have the second thought that things seldom fell out in the way you wanted them to. Indeed, a much more awful prospect confronted him. It was quite possible, it was within the traditions of the Marshal's past, that somehow or other he might induce a large pack of exhilarated and bloodthirsty students to listen to what he said, trust in his promises, and insist on restoring him to the power that he had once held. It was the sort of thing that had happened once or twice in the career of the Marshal. His personal magnetism was such that politicians had before now met their defeat when they least expected it.

'We must restrain him,' he cried.

'Yes, yes,' said Signor Vitelli, 'he cannot be lost to the world.'

'One fears,' said Monsieur Poissonier. 'He has too many friends in Germany, too many contacts, and you know they move very quickly in military matters in Germany. They might leap at the opportunity.'

'*Bon Dieu, Bon Dieu*,' said Monsieur Grosjean, wiping his brow. 'What shall we do? What can we do? What is that noise? I hear rifles, do I not?'

'No, no,' said Monsieur Poissonier consolingly. 'It is the canteen coffee trays you hear.'

'There is a quotation I could use,' said Monsieur Grosjean,

who was a great lover of the drama, 'if I could only remember it. A quotation from Shakespeare. "Will nobody rid me of this –"'

'"turbulent priest,"' said Monsieur Poissonier. 'From the play, Becket.'

'A madman like the Marshal is worse than a priest. A priest should at least be harmless, though indeed even His Holiness the Pope received a delegation of students only yesterday. He *blessed* them. He called them his children.'

'A Christian gesture, though,' said Monsieur Coin dubiously.

'One can go too far even with Christian gestures,' said Monsieur Grosjean.

CHAPTER 14

CONFERENCE IN LONDON

In the Cabinet Room at 10 Downing Street, Mr Cedric Lazenby, the Prime Minister, sat at the head of the table and looked at his assembled Cabinet without any noticeable pleasure. The expression on his face was definitely gloomy, which in a way afforded him a certain relief. He was beginning to think that it was only in the privacy of his Cabinet Meetings that he could relax his face into an unhappy expression, and could abandon that look which he presented usually to the world, of a wise and contented optimism which had served him so well in the various crises of political life.

He looked round at Gordon Chetwynd, who was frowning, at Sir George Packham who was obviously worrying, thinking, and wondering as usual, at the military imperturbability of Colonel Munro, at Air Marshal Kenwood, a tight-lipped man who did not trouble to conceal his profound distrust of politicians. There was also Admiral Blunt, a large formidable man, who tapped his fingers on the table and bided his time until his moment should come.

'It is not too good,' the Air Marshal was saying. 'One has to admit it. Four of our planes hi-jacked within the last week. Flew 'em to Milan. Turned the passengers out, and flew them on somewhere else. Actually Africa. Had pilots waiting there. Black men.'

'Black Power,' said Colonel Munro thoughtfully.

'Or Red Power?' suggested Lazenby. 'I feel, you know, that all our difficulties might stem from Russian indoctrination. If one could get into touch with the Russians – I really think a personal visit at top level –'

'You stick where you are, Prime Minister,' said Admiral Blunt. 'Don't you start arseing around with the Russkies again. All *they* want at present is to keep out of all this mess. They haven't had as much trouble there with their students as most of us have. All they mind about is keeping an eye on the Chinese to see what they'll be up to next.'

'I do think that personal influence –'

'You stay here and look after your own country,' said Admiral Blunt. True to his name, and as was his wont, he said it bluntly.

'Hadn't we better hear – have a proper report of what's actually been happening?' Gordon Chetwynd looked towards Colonel Munro.

'Want facts? Quite right. They're all pretty unpalatable. I presume you want, not particulars of what's been happening here so much, as the general world situation?'

'Quite so.'

'Well, in France the Marshal's in hospital still. Two bullets in his arm. Hell's going on in political circles. Large tracts of the country are held by what they call the Youth Power troops.'

'You mean they've got arms?' said Gordon Chetwynd in a horrified voice.

'They've got a hell of a lot,' said the Colonel. 'I don't know really where they've got them from. There are certain ideas as to that. A large consignment was sent from Sweden to West Africa.'

'What's that got to do with it?' said Mr Lazenby. 'Who cares? Let them have all the arms they want in West Africa. They can go on shooting each other.'

'Well, there's something a little curious about it as far as our Intelligence reports go. Here is a list of the armaments that were sent to West Africa. The interesting thing is they were sent there, but they were sent out again. They were accepted, delivery was acknowledged, payment may or may not have been made, but they were sent out of the country again before five days had passed. They were sent out, re-routed elsewhere.'

'But what's the idea of that?'

'The idea seems to be,' said Munro, 'that they were never really intended for West Africa. Payments were made and they were sent on somewhere else. It seems possible that they went on from Africa to the Near East. To the Persian Gulf, to Greece and to Turkey. Also, a consignment of planes was sent to Egypt. From Egypt they were sent to India, from India they were sent to Russia.'

'I thought they were sent *from* Russia.'

'– And from Russia they went to Prague. The whole thing's mad.'

'I don't understand,' said Sir George, 'one wonders –'

'Somewhere there seems to be some central organization which is directing the supplies of various things. Planes, armaments, bombs, both explosive and those that are used in germ warfare. All these consignments are moving in unexpected directions. They are delivered by various cross-country routes to trouble-spots, and used by leaders and regiments – if you like to call them that – of the Youth Power. They mostly go to the leaders of young guerrilla movements, professed anarchists who preach anarchy, and accept – though one doubts if they ever pay for – some of the latest most up-to-date models.'

'Do you mean to say we're facing something like war on a world scale?' Cedric Lazenby was shocked.

The mild man with the Asiatic face who sat lower down at the table, and had not yet spoken, lifted up his face with the Mongolian smile, and said:

'That is what one is now forced to believe. Our observations tell us –'

Lazenby interrupted.

'You'll have to stop observing. UNO will have to take arms itself and put all this down.'

The quiet face remained unmoved.

'That would be against our principles,' he said.

Colonel Munro raised his voice and went on with his summing up.

'There's fighting in some parts of every country. South-East Asia claimed Independence long ago and there are four, five different divisions of power in South America, Cuba, Peru,

Guatemala and so on. As for the United States, you know Washington was practically burned out – the West is overrun with Youth Power Armed Forces – Chicago is under Martial Law. You know about Sam Cortman? Shot last night on the steps of the American Embassy here.'

'He was to attend here today,' said Lazenby. 'He was going to have given us his views of the situation.'

'I don't suppose that would have helped much,' said Colonel Munro. 'Quite a nice chap – but hardly a live wire.'

'But who's *behind* all this?' Lazenby's voice rose fretfully.

'It could be the Russians, of course –' He looked hopeful. He still envisaged himself flying to Moscow.

Colonel Munro shook his head. 'Doubt it,' he said.

'A personal appeal,' said Lazenby. His face brightened with hope. 'An entirely new sphere of influence. The Chinese . . . ?'

'Nor the Chinese,' said Colonel Munro. 'But you know there's been a big revival in Neo-Fascism in Germany.'

'You don't really think the Germans could possibly . . .'

'I don't think they're behind all this necessarily, but when you say possibly – yes, I think possibly they easily could. They've done it before, you know. Prepared things years before, planned them, everything ready, waiting for the word GO. Good planners, very good planners. Staff work excellent. I admire them, you know. Can't help it.'

'But Germany seemed to be so peaceful and well run.'

'Yes, of course it is up to a point. But do you realize, South America is practically alive with Germans, with young Neo-Fascists, and they've got a big Youth Federation there. Call themselves the Super-Aryans, or something of that kind. You know, a bit of the old stuff still, swastikas and salutes, and someone who's running it, called the Young Wotan or the Young Siegfried or something like that. Lot of Aryan nonsense.'

There was a knock on the door and the secretary entered.

'Professor Eckstein is here, sir.'

'We'd better have him in,' said Cedric Lazenby. 'After all, if anyone can tell us what our latest research weapons are, he's the man. We may have something up our sleeve that can soon put an end to all this nonsense.' Besides being a professional traveller to foreign parts in the rôle of peacemaker,

Mr Lazenby had an incurable fund of optimism seldom justified by results.

'We could do with a good secret weapon,' said the Air Marshal hopefully.

Professor Eckstein, considered by many to be Britain's top scientist, when you first looked at him seemed supremely unimportant. He was a small man with old-fashioned mutton-chop whiskers and an asthmatic cough. He had the manner of one anxious to apologize for his existence. He made noises like 'ah', 'hrrumph', 'mrrh', blew his nose, coughed asthmatically again and shook hands in a shy manner, as he was introduced to those present. A good many of them he already knew and these he greeted with nervous nods of the head. He sat down on the chair indicated and looked round him vaguely. He raised a hand to his mouth and began to bite his nails.

'The heads of the Services are here,' said Sir George Packham. 'We are very anxious to have your opinion as to what can be done.'

'Oh,' said Professor Eckstein, 'done? Yes, yes, done?'

There was a silence.

'The world is fast passing into a state of anarchy,' said Sir George.

'Seems so, doesn't it? At least, from what I read in the paper. Not that I trust to that. Really, the things journalists think up. Never any accuracy in their statements.'

'I understand you've made some most important discoveries lately, Professor,' said Cedric Lazenby encouragingly.

'Ah yes, so we have. So we have.' Professor Eckstein cheered up a little. 'Got a lot of very nasty chemical warfare fixed up. If we ever wanted it. Germ warfare, you know, biological stuff, gas laid on through normal gas outlets, air pollution and poisoning of water supplies. Yes, if you wanted it, I suppose we could kill half the population of England given about three days to do it in.' He rubbed his hands. 'That what you want?'

'No, no indeed. Oh dear, of course not.' Mr Lazenby looked horrified.

'Well, that's what I mean, you know. It's not a question of not having enough lethal weapons. We've got too much. Everything we've got is *too* lethal. The difficulty would be in keeping anybody alive, even ourselves. Eh? All the people at the top, you know. Well – *us*, for instance.' He gave a wheezy, happy little chuckle.

'But that isn't what we *want*,' Mr Lazenby insisted.

'It's not a question of what you *want*, it's a question of what we've *got*. Everything we've got is terrifically lethal. If you want everybody under thirty wiped off the map, I expect you could do it. Mind you, you'd have to take a lot of the older ones as well. It's difficult to segregate one lot from the other, you know. Personally, I should be against that. We've got some very good young Research fellows. Bloody-minded, but clever.'

'What's gone wrong with the world?' asked Kenwood suddenly.

'That's the point,' said Professor Eckstein. 'We don't know. We don't know up at our place in spite of all we *do* know about this, that and the other. We know a bit more about the moon nowadays, we know a lot about biology, we can transplant hearts and livers; brains, too, soon, I expect, though I don't know how *that'll* work out. But we don't know who is doing *this*. Somebody is, you know. It's a sort of high-powered background stuff. Oh yes, we've got it cropping up in different ways. You know, crime rings, drug rings, all that sort of thing. A high-powered lot, directed by a few good, shrewd brains behind the scenes. We've had it going on in this country or that country, occasionally on a European scale. But it's going a bit further now, other side of the globe – Southern Hemisphere. Down to the Antarctic Circle before we've finished, I expect.' He appeared to be pleased with his diagnosis.

'People of ill-will –'

'Well, you could put it like that. Ill-will for ill-will's sake or ill-will for the sake of money or power. Difficult, you know, to get at the *point* of it all. The poor dogsbodies themselves don't know. They want violence and they like violence. They don't like the world, they don't like our materialistic attitude. They don't like a lot of our nasty ways of making money, they don't like a lot of the fiddles we do. They don't like seeing poverty. They want a better world. Well, you *could* make a better world, perhaps, if you thought about it long enough. But the trouble is, if you insist on taking away something first, you've got to put something back in its place. Nature won't have a vacuum – an old saying, but true. Dash it all, it's like a heart transplant. You take one heart away but you've got to put another one there. One that works. And you've got to arrange about the heart you're going to put there *before* you take away the faulty heart that somebody's got at present. Matter of fact, I think a lot of those things are better left alone altogether, but nobody would listen to me, I suppose. And anyway it's not my subject.'

'A gas?' suggested Colonel Munro.

Professor Eckstein brightened.

'Oh, we've got all sorts of *gases* in stock. Mind you, some of them are reasonably harmless. Mild deterrents, shall we say. We've got all *those*.' He beamed like a complacent hardware dealer.

'Nuclear weapons?' suggested Mr Lazenby.

'Don't you monkey with *that*! You don't want a radio-active England, do you, or a radio-active continent, for that matter?'

'So you can't help us,' said Colonel Munro.

'Not until somebody's found out a bit more about all this,' said Professor Eckstein. 'Well, I'm sorry. But I must impress upon you that most of the things we're working on nowadays are *dangerous*.' He stressed the word. '*Really* dangerous.'

He looked at them anxiously, as a nervous uncle might look at a group of children left with a box of matches to play with, and who might quite easily set the house on fire.

'Well, thank you, Professor Eckstein,' said Mr Lazenby. He did not sound particularly thankful.

The Professor gathering correctly that he was released, smiled all round and trotted out of the room.

Mr Lazenby hardly waited for the door to close before venting his feelings.

'All alike, these scientists,' he said bitterly. 'Never any practical good. Never come up with anything sensible. All they can do is split the atom – and then tell *us* not to mess about with it!'

'Just as well if we never had,' said Admiral Blunt, again bluntly. 'What *we* want is something homely and domestic like a kind of selective weedkiller which would –' He paused abruptly. 'Now what the devil –?'

'Yes, Admiral?' said the Prime Minister politely.

'Nothing – just reminded me of something. Can't remember what –'

The Prime Minister sighed.

'Any more scientific experts waiting on the mat?' asked Gordon Chetwynd, glancing hopefully at his wristwatch.

'Old Pikeaway is here, I believe,' said Lazenby. 'Got a picture – or a drawing – or a map or something or other he wants us to look at –'

'What's it all about?'

'I don't know. It seems to be all bubbles,' said Mr Lazenby vaguely.

'Bubbles? Why bubbles?'

'I've no idea. Well,' he sighed, 'we'd better have a look at it.'

'Horsham's here, too –'

'He may have something new to tell us,' said Chetwynd.

Colonel Pikeaway stumped in. He was supporting a rolled-up burden which with Horsham's aid was unrolled and which with some difficulty was propped up so that those sitting round the table could look at it.

'Not exactly drawn to scale yet, but it gives you a rough idea,' said Colonel Pikeaway.

'What does it mean, if anything?'

'Bubbles?' murmured Sir George. An idea came to him. 'Is it a gas? A new gas?'

'You'd better deliver the lecture, Horsham,' said Pikeaway. 'You know the general idea.'

'I only know what I've been told. It's a rough diagram of an association of world control.'

'By whom?'

'By groups who own or control the sources of power – the raw materials of power.'

'And the letters of the alphabet?'

'Stand for a person or a code name for a special group. They are intersecting circles that by now cover the globe.

'That circle marked "A" stands for armaments. Someone, or some group is in control of armaments. All types of armaments. Explosives, guns, rifles. All over the world armaments are being produced according to plan, dispatched ostensibly to under-developed nations, backward nations, nations at war. But they don't remain where they are sent. They are re-routed almost immediately elsewhere. To guerrilla warfare in the South American Continent – to rioting and fighting in the USA – to Depots of Black Power – to various countries in Europe.

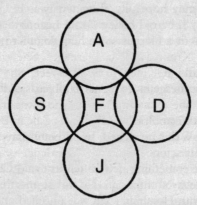

'"D" represents drugs – a network of suppliers run them from various depots and stockpiles. All kinds of drugs, from the more harmless varieties up to the true killers. The headquarters seem likely to be situated in the Levant, and to pass out through Turkey, Pakistan, India and Central Asia.'

'They make money out of it?'

'Enormous sums of money. But it's more than just an association of Pushers. It has a more sinister side to it. It's being used to finish off the weaklings amongst the young, shall we say, to make them complete slaves. Slaves so that they cannot live and exist or do jobs for their employers without a supply of drugs.'

Kenwood whistled.

'That's a bad show, isn't it? Don't you know at all who those Drug Pushers are?'

'Some of them, yes. But only the lesser fry. Not the real controllers. Drug headquarters are, so far as we can judge, in Central Asia and the Levant. They get delivered from there in the tyres of cars, in cement, in concrete, in all kinds of machinery and industrial goods. They're delivered all over the world and passed on as ordinary trade goods to where they are meant to go.

'"F" stands for finance. Money! A money spider's web in the centre of it all. You'll have to go to Mr Robinson to tell you about money. According to a memo here, money is coming very largely from America and there's also a headquarters in Bavaria. There's a vast reserve in South Africa, based on gold and diamonds. Most of the money is going to South America. One of the principal controllers, if I may so put it, of money, is a very powerful and talented woman. She's old now: must be near to death. But she is still strong and active. Her name was Charlotte Krapp. Her father owned the vast Krapp yards in Germany. She was a financial genius herself and operated in Wall Street. She accumulated fortune after fortune by investments in all parts of the world. She owns transport, she owns machinery, she owns industrial concerns. All these things. She lives in a vast castle in Bavaria – from there she directs a flow of money to different parts of the globe.

'"S" represents science – the new knowledge of chemical and biological warfare – Various young scientists have defected – There is a nucleus of them in the US, we believe, vowed and dedicated to the cause of anarchy.'

'Fighting for anarchy? A contradiction in terms. Can there be such a thing?'

'You believe in anarchy if you are young. You want a new world, and to begin with you must pull down the old one – just as you pull down a house before you build a new one to replace it. But if you don't know where you are going, if you don't know where you are being lured to go, or even pushed to go, what will the new world be like, and where will the believers be when they get it? Some of them slaves, some of them blinded by hate, some by violence and sadism, both preached and practised. Some of them – and God help those – still idealistic, still believing as people did in France at the time of the French Revolution that that revolution would bring prosperity, peace, happiness, contentment to its people.'

'And what are *we* doing about all this? What are we proposing to do about it?' It was Admiral Blunt who spoke.

'What are we doing about it? All that we can. I assure you, all you who are here, we are doing all that we can. We have people working for us in every country. We have agents, inquirers, those who gather information, and bring it back here –'

THE RING

F	Big Charlotte	— Bavaria
A	Eric Olafsson	— Sweden, Industrialist, Armaments
D	Said to go by the name of Demetrios	— Smyrna, Drugs
S	Dr Sarolensky	— Colorado, USA, Physicist-Chemist. Suspicion only
J		— A woman. Goes by Code name of Juanita. Said to be dangerous. No knowledge of her real name.

'Which is very necessary,' said Colonel Pikeaway. 'First we've got to *know* – know who's who, who's with us and who's against us. And after that we've got to see what, if anything, can be done.'

'Our name for this diagram is The Ring. Here's a list of what we know about the Ring leaders. Those with a query mean that we know only the name they go by – or alternatively we only suspect that they are the ones we want.'

CHAPTER 15

AUNT MATILDA TAKES A CURE

I

'A cure of some kind, I thought?' Lady Matilda hazarded.

'A cure?' said Dr Donaldson. He looked faintly puzzled for a moment, losing his air of medical omniscience, which, of course, so Lady Matilda reflected, was one of the slight disadvantages attached to having a younger doctor attending one rather than the older specimen to whom one has been accustomed for several years.

'That's what we used to call them,' Lady Matilda explained. 'In my young days, you know, you went for the Cure. Marienbad, Carlsbad, Baden-Baden, all the rest of it. Just the other day I read about this new place in the paper. Quite new and up to date. Said to be all new ideas and things like that. Not that I'm really sold on new ideas, but I wouldn't really be afraid of them. I mean, they would probably be all the same things all over again. Water tasting of bad eggs and the latest sort of diet and walking to take the Cure, or the Waters, or whatever they call them now, at a rather inconvenient hour in the morning. And I expect they give you massage or something. It used to be seaweed. But this place is somewhere in the mountains. Bavaria or Austria or somewhere like that. So I don't suppose it would be seaweed. Shaggy moss, perhaps – sounds like a dog. And perhaps quite a nice mineral water as well as the eggy sulphury one, I mean. Superb buildings, I understand. The only thing one is nervous about nowadays is that they never seem to put banisters in any up-to-date modern buildings. Flights of marble steps and all that, but nothing to hang on to.'

'I think I know the place you mean,' said Dr Donaldson. 'It's been publicized a good deal, in the press.'

'Well, you know what one is at my age,' said Lady Matilda. 'One likes trying new things. Really, I think it is just to amuse one. It doesn't really make one feel one's health would be any better. Still, you don't think it would be a bad idea, do you, Dr Donaldson?'

Dr Donaldson looked at her. He was not so young as Lady Matilda labelled him in her mind. He was just approaching forty and he was a tactful and kindly man and willing to indulge his elderly patients as far as he considered it desirable, without any actual danger of their attempting something obviously unsuitable.

'I'm sure it wouldn't do you any harm at all,' he said. 'Might be quite a good idea. Of course travel's a bit tiring though one flies to places very quickly and easily nowadays.'

'Quickly, yes. Easily, no,' said Lady Matilda. 'Ramps and moving staircases and in and out of buses from the airport to the plane, and the plane to another airport and from the airport to another bus. All that, you know. But I understand one can have wheelchairs in the airports.'

'Of course you can. Excellent idea. If you promise to do that and not think you can walk everywhere . . .'

'I know, I know,' said his patient, interrupting him. 'You do understand. You're really a very understanding man. One has one's pride, you know, and while you can still hobble around with a stick or a little support, you don't really want to look absolutely a crock or bedridden or something. It'd be easier if I was a man,' she mused. 'I mean, one could tie up one's leg with one of those enormous bandages and padded things as though one had the gout. I mean, gout is all right for the male sex. Nobody thinks anything the worse of them. Some of their older friends think they've been tucking in to the port too much because that used to be the old idea, though I believe that is not really true at all. Port wine does *not* give you gout. Yes, a wheelchair, and I could fly to Munich or somewhere like that. One could arrange for a car or something at the other end.'

'You will take Miss Leatheran with you, of course.'

'Amy? Oh, of course. I couldn't do without her. Anyway, you think no harm would be done?'

'I think it might do you a world of good.'

'You really *are* a nice man.'

Lady Matilda gave him the twinkle from her eyes with which now he was becoming familiar.

'You think it'll amuse me and cheer me up to go somewhere new and see some new faces, and of course you're quite right. But I like to think that I'm taking a Cure, though really there's nothing for me to be cured of. Not really, is there? I mean, except old age. Unfortunately old age doesn't get cured, it only gets more so, doesn't it?'

'The point is really, will you enjoy yourself? Well, I think you will. When you get tired, by the way, when doing anything, stop doing it.'

'I shall still drink glasses of water if the water tastes of rotten eggs. Not because I like them or because frankly I think they do me any good. But it has a sort of mortifying feeling. It's like old women in our village always used to be. They always wanted a nice, strong medicine either coloured black or purple or deep pink, heavily flavoured with peppermint. They thought that did much more good than a nice little pill or a bottle that only appeared to be full of ordinary water without any exotic colouring.'

'You know too much about human nature,' said Dr Donaldson.

'You're very nice to me,' said Lady Matilda. 'I appreciate it. Amy!'

'Yes, Lady Matilda?'

'Get me an atlas, will you. I've lost track of Bavaria and the countries round it.'

'Let me see now. An atlas. There'll be one in the library, I suppose. There must be some old atlases about, dating back to about 1920 or thereabouts, I suppose.'

'I wondered if we had anything a little more modern.'

'Atlas,' said Amy, deep in reflection.

'If not, you can buy one and bring it along tomorrow morning. It's going to be very difficult because all the names are different, the countries are different, and I shan't know where I am. But you'll have to help me with that. Find a big magnifying glass, will you? I have an idea I was reading in bed with one the other day and it probably slipped down between the bed and the wall.'

Her requirements took a little time to satisfy but the atlas, the magnifying glass and an older atlas by which to check, were finally produced and Amy, nice woman that she was, Lady Matilda thought, was extremely helpful.

'Yes, here it is. It still seems to be called Monbrügge or something like that. It's either in the Tyrol or Bavaria. Everything seems to have changed places and got different names –'

II

Lady Matilda looked around her bedroom in the Gasthaus. It was well appointed. It was very expensive. It combined comfort with an appearance of such austerity as might lead the inhabitant to identify herself with an ascetic course of exercises, diet and possibly painful courses of massage. Its furnishings, she thought, were interesting. They provided for all tastes. There was a large framed Gothic script on the wall. Lady Matilda's German was not as good as it had been in her girlhood, but it dealt, she thought, with the golden and enchanting idea of a return to youth. Not only did youth hold the future in its hands but the old were being nicely indoctrinated to feel that they themselves might know such a second golden flowering.

Here there were gentle aids so as to enable one to pursue the doctrine of any of the many paths in life which attracted different classes of people. (Always presuming that they had enough money to pay for it.) Beside the bed was a Gideon Bible such as Lady Matilda when travelling in the United States had often found by her bedside. She picked it up approvingly, opened it at random and dropped a finger on one particular verse. She read it, nodding her head contentedly and made a brief note of it on a note pad that was lying on her bed table. She had often done that in the course of her life – it was her way of obtaining divine guidance at short notice.

> *I have been young and now am old, yet have I not seen the righteous forsaken.*

She made further researches of the room. Handily placed but not too apparent was an *Almanach de Gotha*, modestly situated on a lower shelf on the bedside table. A most invaluable book for those who wished to familiarize themselves with the higher strata of society reaching back for several hundred years and which were still being observed and noted and checked by those of aristocratic lineage or interested in the same. It will come in handy, she thought, I can read up a good deal on that.

Near the desk, by the stove of period porcelain, were paperback editions of certain preachings and tenets by the modern prophets of the world. Those who were now or had recently been crying in the wilderness were here to be studied and approved by young followers with haloes of hair, strange raiment, and earnest hearts. Marcuse, Guevara, Lévi-Strauss, Fanon.

In case she was going to hold any conversations with golden youth she had better read up a little on that also.

At that moment there was a timid tap on the door. It opened slightly and the face of the faithful Amy came round the corner. Amy, Lady Matilda thought suddenly, would look exactly like a sheep when she was ten years older. A nice, faithful, kindly sheep. At the moment, Lady Matilda was glad to think, she looked still like a very agreeable plump lamb with nice curls of hair, thoughtful and kindly eyes, and able to give kindly baa's rather than to bleat.

'I do hope you slept well.'

'Yes, my dear, I did, excellently. Have you got that thing?'

Amy always knew what she meant. She handed it to her employer.

'Ah, my diet sheet. I see.' Lady Matilda perused it, then said, 'How incredibly unattractive! What's this water like one's supposed to drink?'

'It doesn't taste very nice.'

'No, I don't suppose it would. Come back in half an hour. I've got a letter I want you to post.'

Moving aside her breakfast tray, she moved over to the desk. She thought for a few minutes and then wrote her letter. 'It ought to do the trick,' she murmured.

'I beg your pardon, Lady Matilda, what did you say?'

'I was writing to the old friend I mentioned to you.'

'The one you said you haven't seen for about fifty or sixty years?'

Lady Matilda nodded.

'I do hope –' Amy was apologetic. 'I mean – I – it's such a long time. People have short memories nowadays. I do hope that she'll remember all about you and everything.'

'Of course she will,' said Lady Matilda. 'The people you don't forget are the people you knew when you were about ten to twenty. They stick in your mind for ever. You remember what hats they wore, and the way they laughed, and you remember their faults and their good qualities and everything about them. Now anyone I met twenty years ago, shall we say, I simply can't remember who they are. Not if they're mentioned to me, and not if I saw them even. Oh yes, she'll remember about *me*. And all about Lausanne. You get that letter posted. I've got to do a little homework.'

She picked up the *Almanach de Gotha* and returned to bed, where she made a serious study of such items as might come in useful. Some family relationships and various other kinships of the useful kind. Who had married whom, who had lived where, what misfortunes had overtaken others. Not that the person whom she had in mind was herself likely to be found in the *Almanach de Gotha*. But she lived in a part of the world, had come there deliberately to live in a Schloss belonging to originally noble ancestors, and she had absorbed the local respect and adulation for those above all of good breeding. To good birth, even impaired with poverty, she herself, as Lady Matilda well knew, had no claim whatever. She had had to make do with money. Oceans of money. Incredible amounts of money.

Lady Matilda Cleckheaton had no doubt at all that she herself, the daughter of an eighth Duke, would be bidden to some kind of festivity. Coffee, perhaps, and delicious creamy cakes.

III

Lady Matilda Cleckheaton made her entrance into one of the grand reception rooms of the Schloss. It had been a fifteen-mile drive. She had dressed herself with some care, though somewhat to the disapproval of Amy. Amy seldom offered advice, but she was so anxious for her principal to succeed in whatever she was undertaking that she had ventured this time on a moderate remonstrance.

'You don't think your red dress is really a little *worn*, if you know what I mean. I mean just beneath the arms, and, well, there are two or three very shiny patches –'

'I know, my dear, I know. It is a shabby dress but it is nevertheless a Patou model. It is old but it was enormously expensive. I am not trying to look rich or extravagant. I am an impoverished member of an aristocratic family. Anyone of under fifty, no doubt, would despise me. But my hostess is living and has lived for some years in a part of the world where the rich will be kept waiting for their meal while the hostess will be willing to wait for a shabby, elderly woman of impeccable descent. Family traditions are things that one does not lose easily. One absorbs them, even, when one goes to a new neighbourhood. In my trunk, by the way, you will find a feather boa.'

'Are you going to put on a feather boa?'

'Yes, I am. An ostrich feather one.'

'Oh dear, that must be years old.'

'It is, but I've kept it very carefully. You'll see, Charlotte will recognize what it is. She will think one of the best families in England was reduced to wearing her old clothes that she had kept carefully for years. And I'll wear my sealskin coat, too. That's a little worn, but such a magnificent coat in its time.'

Thus arrayed, she set forth. Amy went with her as a well-dressed though only quietly smart attendant.

Matilda Cleckheaton had been prepared for what she saw. A whale, as Stafford had told her. A wallowing whale, a hideous old woman sitting in a room surrounded with pictures worth a fortune. Rising with some difficulty from a throne-like chair which could have figured on a stage representing the palace of some magnificent prince from any age from the Middle Ages down.

'Matilda!'

'Charlotte!'

'Ah! After all these years. How strange it seems!'

They exchanged words of greeting and pleasure, talking partly in German and partly in English. Lady Matilda's German was slightly faulty. Charlotte spoke excellent German, excellent English though with a strong guttural accent, and occasionally English with an American accent. She was really, Lady Matilda thought, quite splendidly hideous. For a moment she felt a fondness almost dating back to the past although, she reflected the next moment, Charlotte had been a most detestable girl. Nobody had really liked her and she herself had certainly not done so. But there is a great bond, say what we will, in the memories of old schooldays. Whether Charlotte had liked her or not she did not know. But Charlotte, she remembered, had certainly – what used to be called in those days – sucked up to her. She had had visions, possibly, of staying in a ducal castle in England. Lady Matilda's father, though of most praiseworthy lineage, had been one of the most impecunious of English dukes. His estate had only been held together by the rich wife he had married whom he had treated with the utmost courtesy, and who had enjoyed bullying him whenever able to do so. Lady Matilda had been fortunate enough to be his daughter by a second marriage. Her own mother had been extremely agreeable and also a very successful actress, able to play the part of looking a duchess far more than any real duchess could do.

They exchanged reminiscences of past days, the tortures they had inflicted on some of their instructors, the fortunate and unfortunate marriages that had occurred to some of their schoolmates. Matilda made a few mentions of certain alliances and families culled from the pages of the *Almanach de Gotha* – 'but of course that must have been a terrible marriage for Elsa. One of the

Bourbons de Parme, was it not? Yes, yes, well, one knows what that leads to. Most unfortunate.'

Coffee was brought, delicious coffee, plates of millefeuille pastry and delicious cream cakes.

'I should not touch any of this,' cried Lady Matilda. 'No indeed! My doctor, he is most severe. He said that I must adhere strictly to the Cure while I was here. But after all this is a day of holiday, is it not? Of renewal of youth. That is what interests me so much. My great-nephew who visited you not long ago – I forget who brought him here, the Countess – ah, it began with a Z, I cannot remember her name.'

'The Countess Renata Zerkowski –'

'Ah, that was the name, yes. A very charming young woman, I believe. And she brought him to visit you. It was most kind of her. He was so impressed. Impressed, too, with all your beautiful possessions. Your way of living, and indeed, the wonderful things which he had heard about you. How you have a whole movement of – oh, I do not know how to give the proper term. A Galaxy of Youth. Golden, beautiful youth. They flock round you. They worship you. What a wonderful life you must live. Not that I could support such a life. I have to live very quietly. Rheumatoid arthritis. And also the financial difficulties. Difficulty in keeping up the family house. Ah well, you know what it is for us in England – our taxation troubles.'

'I remember that nephew of yours, yes. He was agreeable, a very agreeable man. The Diplomatic Service, I understand?'

'Ah yes. But it is – well, you know, I cannot feel that his talents are being properly recognized. He does not say much. He does not complain, but he feels that he is – well, he feels that he has not been appreciated as he should. The powers that be, those who hold office at present, what are they?'

'*Canaille!*' said Big Charlotte.

'Intellectuals with no *savoir faire* in life. Fifty years ago it would have been different,' said Lady Matilda, 'but nowadays his promotion has been not advanced as it should. I will even tell you, in confidence, of course, that he has been distrusted. They suspect him, you know, of being in with – what shall I call it? – rebellious, revolutionary tendencies. And yet one must realize what the future could hold for a man who could embrace more advanced views.'

'You mean he is not, then, how do you say it in England, in sympathy with the Establishment, as they call it?'

'Hush, hush, we must not say these things. At least *I* must not,' said Lady Matilda.

'You interest me,' said Charlotte.

Matilda Cleckheaton sighed.

'Put it down, if you like, to the fondness of an elderly relative. Staffy has always been a favourite of mine. He has charm and wit. I think also he has ideas. He envisages the future, a future that should differ a good deal from what we have at present. Our country, alas, is politically in a very bad state. Stafford seems to be very much impressed by things you said to him or showed to him. You've done so much for music, I understand. What we need I cannot but feel is the ideal of the super race.'

'There should and could be a super race. Adolf Hitler had the right idea,' said Charlotte. 'A man of no importance in himself, but he had artistic elements in his character. And undoubtedly he had the power of leadership.'

'Ah yes. Leadership, that is what we need.'

'You had the wrong allies in the last war, my dear. If England and Germany now had arrayed themselves side by side, if they had had the same ideals, of youth, strength, two Aryan nations with the right ideals. Think where your country and mine might have arrived today? Yet perhaps even that is too narrow a view to take. In some ways the communists and the others have taught us a lesson. Workers of the world unite? But that is to set one's sights too low. Workers are only our material. It is "Leaders of the world unite!" Young men with the gift of leadership, of good blood. And we must start, not with the middle-aged men set in their ways, repeating themselves like a gramophone record that has stuck. We must seek among the student population, the young men with brave hearts, with great ideas, willing to march, willing to be killed but willing also to kill. To kill without any compunction – because it is certain that without aggressiveness, without violence, without attack – there can be no victory. I must show you something –'

With somewhat of a struggle she succeeded in rising to her

feet. Lady Matilda followed suit, underlining a little her difficulty, which was not quite as much as she was making out.

'It was in May 1940,' said Charlotte, 'when Hitler Youth went on to its second stage. When Himmler obtained from Hitler a charter. The charter of the famous SS. It was formed for the destruction of the eastern peoples, the slaves, the appointed slaves of the world. It would make room for the German master race. The SS executive instrument came into being.' Her voice dropped a little. It held for a moment a kind of religious awe.

Lady Matilda nearly crossed herself by mistake.

'The Order of the Death's Head,' said Big Charlotte.

She walked slowly and painfully down the room and pointed to where on the wall hung, framed in gilt and surmounted with a skull, the Order of the Death's Head.

'See, it is my most cherished possession. It hangs here on my wall. My golden youth band, when they come here, salute it. And in our archives in the castle here are folios of its chronicles. Some of them are only reading for strong stomachs, but one must learn to accept these things. The deaths in gas chambers, the torture cells, the trials at Nuremberg speak venomously of all those things. But it was a great tradition. Strength through pain. They were trained young, the boys, so that they should not falter or turn back or suffer from any kind of softness. Even Lenin, preaching his Marxist doctrine, declared "Away with softness!" It was one of his first rules for creating a perfect State. But we were too narrow. We wished to confine our great dream only to the German master race. But there are other races. They too can attain masterhood through suffering and violence and through the considered practice of anarchy. We must pull down, pull down all the soft institutions. Pull down the more humiliating forms of religion. There is a religion of strength, the old religion of the Viking people. And we have a leader, young as yet, gaining in power every day. What did some great man say? Give me the tools and I will do the job. Something like that. Our leader has already the tools. He will have more tools. He will have the planes, the bombs, the means of chemical warfare. He will have the men to fight. He will have the transport. He will have shipping and oil. He will have what one might call the Aladdin's creation of genie. You rub the lamp and the genie appears. It is all in your hands. The means of production, the means of wealth and our young leader, a leader by birth as well as by character. He has all this.'

She wheezed and coughed.

'Let me help you.'

Lady Matilda supported her back to her seat. Charlotte gasped a little as she sat down.

'It's sad to be old, but I shall last long enough. Long enough to see the triumph of a new world, a new creation. That is what you want for your nephew. I will see to it. Power in his own country, that is what he wants, is it not? You would be ready to encourage the spearhead there?'

'I had influence once. But now –' Lady Matilda shook her head sadly. 'All that is gone.'

'It will come again, dear,' said her friend. 'You were right to come to me. I have a certain influence.'

'It is a great cause,' said Lady Matilda. She sighed and murmured, 'The Young Siegfried.'

IV

'I hope you enjoyed meeting your old friend,' said Amy as they drove back to the Gasthaus.

'If you could have heard all the nonsense I talked, you wouldn't believe it,' said Lady Matilda Cleckheaton.

CHAPTER 16
PIKEAWAY TALKS

'The news from France is very bad,' said Colonel Pikeaway, brushing a cloud of cigar ash off his coat. 'I heard Winston Churchill say that in the last war. There was a man who could speak in plain words and no more than needed. It was very impressive. It told us what we needed to know. Well, it's a long time since then, but I say it again today. The news from France is very bad.'

He coughed, wheezed and brushed a little more ash off himself.

'The news from Italy is very bad,' he said. 'The news from

Russia, I imagine, could be very bad if they let much out about it. They've got trouble there too. Marching bands of students in the street, shop windows smashed, Embassies attacked. News from Egypt is very bad. News from Jerusalem is very bad. News from Syria is very bad. That's all more or less normal, so we needn't worry too much. News from Argentine is what I'd call peculiar. Very peculiar indeed. Argentine, Brazil, Cuba, they've all got together. Call themselves the Golden Youth Federated States, or something like that. It's got an army, too. Properly drilled, properly armed, properly commanded. They've got planes, they've got bombs, they've got God-knows-what. And most of them seem to know what to do with them, which makes it worse. There's a singing crowd as well, apparently. Pop songs, old local folk songs, and bygone battle hymns. They go along rather like the Salvation Army used to do – no blasphemy intended – I'm not crabbing the Salvation Army. Jolly good work they did always. And the girls – pretty as Punch in their bonnets.'

He went on:

'I've heard that something's going on in that line in the civilized countries, starting with *us*. Some of us can be called civilized still, I suppose? One of our politicians the other day, I remember, said we were a splendid nation, chiefly because we were permissive, we had demonstrations, we smashed things, we beat up anyone if we hadn't anything better to do, we got rid of our high spirits by showing violence, and our moral purity by taking most of our clothes off. I don't know what he thought he was talking about – politicians seldom do – but they can make it sound all right. That's why they are politicians.'

He paused and looked across at the man he was talking to.

'Distressing – sadly distressing,' said Sir George Packham. 'One can hardly believe – one worries – if one could only – Is that all the news you've got?' he asked plaintively.

'Isn't it enough? You're hard to satisfy. World anarchy well on its way – that's what we've got. A bit wobbly still – not fully established yet, but very near to it – very near indeed.'

'But action can surely be taken against all this?'

'Not so easy as you think. Tear gas puts a stop to rioting for a while and gives the police a break. And naturally we've got plenty of germ warfare and nuclear bombs and all the other pretty bags of tricks – What do you think would happen if we started using those? Mass massacre of all the marching girls and boys, and the housewife's shopping circle, and the old age pensioners at home, and a good quota of our pompous politicians as they tell us we've never had it so good, and in addition you and me – Ha, ha!

'And anyway,' added Colonel Pikeaway, 'if it's only news you're after, I understand you've got some hot news of your own arriving today. Top secret from Germany, Herr Heinrich Spiess himself.'

'How on earth did you hear that? It's supposed to be strictly –'

'We know everything here,' said Colonel Pikeaway, using his pet phrase – that's what we're for.

'Bringing some tame doctor, too, I understand –' he added.

'Yes, a Dr Reichardt, a top scientist, I presume –'

'No. Medical doctor – Loony-bins –'

'Oh dear – a psychologist?'

'Probably. The ones that run loony-bins are mostly that. With any luck he'll have been brought over so that he can examine the heads of some of our young firebrands. Stuffed full they are of German philosophy, Black Power philosophy, dead French writers' philosophy, and so on and so forth. Possibly they'll let him examine some of the heads of our legal lights who preside over our judicial courts here saying we must be very careful not to do anything to damage a young man's ego because he *might* have to earn his living. We'd be a lot safer if they sent them all round to get plenty of National Assistance to live on and then they could go back to their rooms, not do any work, and enjoy themselves reading more philosophy. However, I'm out of date. I know that. You needn't tell me so.'

'One has to take into account the new modes of thought,' said Sir George Packham. 'One feels, I mean one hopes – well, it's difficult to say –'

'Must be very worrying for you,' said Colonel Pikeaway. 'Finding things so difficult to say.'

His telephone rang. He listened, then handed it to Sir George.

'Yes?' said Sir George. 'Yes? Oh yes. Yes. I agree. I suppose – No – no – not the Home Office. No. Privately, you mean. Well,

508 • AGATHA CHRISTIE

I suppose we'd better use – er –' Sir George looked round him cautiously.

'This place isn't bugged,' said Colonel Pikeaway amiably.

'Code word Blue Danube,' said Sir George Packham in a loud, hoarse whisper. 'Yes, yes. I'll bring Pikeaway along with me. Oh yes, of course. Yes, yes. Get on to him. Yes, say you particularly want him to come, but to remember our meeting has got to be strictly private.'

'We can't take my car then,' said Pikeaway. 'It's too well known.'

'Henry Horsham's coming to fetch us in the Volkswagen.'

'Fine,' said Colonel Pikeaway. 'Interesting, you know, all this.'

'You don't think –' said Sir George and hesitated.

'I don't think what?'

'I mean just really – well, I – mean, if you wouldn't mind my suggesting – a clothes brush?'

'Oh, this.' Colonel Pikeaway hit himself lightly on the shoulder and a cloud of cigar ash flew up and made Sir George choke.

'Nanny,' Colonel Pikeaway shouted. He banged a buzzer on his desk.

A middle-aged woman came in with a clothes brush, appearing with the suddenness of a genie summoned by Aladdin's lamp.

'Hold your breath, please, Sir George,' she said. 'This may be a little pungent.'

She held the door open for him and he retired outside while she brushed Colonel Pikeaway, who coughed and complained:

'Damned nuisance these people are. Always wanting you to get fixed up like a barber's dummy.'

'I should not describe your appearance as quite like that, Colonel Pikeaway. You ought to be used to my cleaning you up nowadays. And you know the Home Secretary suffers from asthma.'

'Well, that's his fault. Not taking proper care to have pollution removed from the streets of London.

'Come on, Sir George, let's hear what our German friend has come over to say. Sounds as though it's a matter of some urgency.'

CHAPTER 17
....
HERR HEINRICH SPIESS

Herr Heinrich Spiess was a worried man. He did not seek to conceal the fact. He acknowledged, indeed, without concealment, that the situation which these five men had come together to discuss was a serious situation. At the same time, he brought with him that sense of reassurance which had been his principal asset in dealing with the recently difficult political life in Germany. He was a solid man, a thoughtful man, a man who could bring common sense to any assemblies he attended. He gave no sense of being a brilliant man, and that in itself was reassuring. Brilliant politicians had been responsible for about two-thirds of the national states of crisis in more countries than one. The other third of trouble had been caused by those politicians who were unable to conceal the fact that although duly elected by democratic governments, they had been unable to conceal their remarkably poor powers of judgment, common sense and, in fact, any noticeable brainy qualities.

'This is not in any sense an official visit, you understand,' said the Chancellor.

'Oh quite, quite.'

'A certain piece of knowledge has come to me which I thought is essential we should share. It throws a rather interesting light on certain happenings which have puzzled as well as distressed us. This is Dr Reichardt.'

Introductions were made. Dr Reichardt was a large and comfortable-looking man with the habit of saying 'Ach, so' from time to time.

'Dr Reichardt is in charge of a large establishment in the neighbourhood of Karlsruhe. He treats there mental patients. I think I am correct in saying that you treat there between five and six hundred patients, am I not right?'

'Ach, so,' said Dr Reichardt.

'I take it that you have several different forms of mental illness?'

'Ach, so. I have different forms of mental illness, but nevertheless, I have a special interest in, and treat almost exclusively one particular type of mental trouble.' He branched off into German and Herr Spiess presently rendered a brief translation in case some of his English colleagues should not understand. This was both necessary and tactful. Two of them did in part, one of them definitely did not, and the two others were truly puzzled.

'Dr Reichardt has had,' explained Herr Spiess, 'the greatest success in his treatment of what as a layman I describe as megalomania. The belief that you are someone other than you are. Ideas of being more important than you are. Ideas that if you have persecution mania –'

'Ach, no!' said Dr Reichardt. 'Persecution mania, *no*, that I do not treat. There is no persecution mania in my clinic. Not among the group with whom I am specially interested. On the contrary, they hold the delusions that they do because they wish to be happy. And they are happy, and I can keep them happy. But if I cure them, see you, they will not be happy. So I have to find a cure that will restore sanity to them, and yet they will be happy just the same. We call this particular state of mind –'

He uttered a long and ferociously sounding German word of at least eight syllables.

'For the purposes of our English friends, I shall still use my term of megalomania, though I know,' continued Herr Spiess, rather quickly, 'that that is not the term you use nowadays, Dr Reichardt. So, as I say, you have in your clinic six hundred patients.'

'And at one time, the time to which I am about to refer, I had eight hundred.'

'Eight hundred!'

'It was interesting – most interesting.'

'You have such persons – to start at the beginning –'

'We have God Almighty,' explained Dr Reichardt. 'You comprehend?'

Mr Lazenby looked slightly taken aback.

'Oh – er – yes – er – yes. Very interesting, I am sure.'

'There are one or two young men, of course, who think they are Jesus Christ. But that is not so popular as the Almighty. And then there are the others. I had at the time I am about to mention twenty-four Adolf Hitlers. This you must understand was at the time when Hitler was alive. Yes, twenty-four or twenty-five

Adolf Hitlers –' he consulted a small notebook which he took from his pocket – 'I have made some notes here, yes. Fifteen Napoleons. Napoleon, he is always popular, ten Mussolinis, five reincarnations of Julius Caesar, and many other cases, very curious and very interesting. But that I will not weary you with at this moment. Not being specially qualified in the medical sense, it would not be of any interest to you. We will come to the incident that matters.'

Dr Reichardt spoke again at rather shorter length, and Herr Spiess continued to translate.

'There came to him one day a government official. Highly thought of at that time – this was during the war, mind you – by the ruling government. I will call him for the moment Martin B. You will know who I mean. He brought with him his chief. In fact he brought with him – well, we will not beat about the bush – he brought the Führer himself.'

'Ach, so,' said Dr Reichardt.

'It was a great honour, you understand, that he should come to inspect,' went on the doctor. 'He was gracious, mein Führer. He told me that he had heard very good reports of my successes. He said that there had been trouble lately. Cases from the army. There, more than once there had been men believing they were Napoleon, sometimes believing they were some of Napoleon's Marshals and sometimes, you comprehend, behaving accordingly, giving out military orders and causing therefore military difficulties. I would have been happy to have given him any professional knowledge that might be useful to him, but Martin B. who accompanied him said that that would not be necessary. Our great Führer, however,' said Dr Reichardt, looking at Herr Spiess slightly uneasily, 'did not want to be bothered with such details. He said that no doubt it would be better if medically qualified men with some experience as neurologists should come and have a consultation. What he wanted was to – ach, well, he wanted to see round, and I soon found what he was really interested to see. It should not have surprised me. Oh no, because you see, it was a symptom that one recognizes. The strain of his life was already beginning to tell on the Führer.'

'I suppose he was beginning to think he was God Almighty

himself at that time,' said Colonel Pikeaway unexpectedly, and he chuckled.

Dr Reichardt looked shocked.

'He asked me to let him know certain things. He said that Martin B. had told him that I actually had a large number of patients thinking, not to put too fine a point on it, that they were themselves Adolf Hitler. I explained to him that this was not uncommon, that naturally with the respect, the worship they paid to Hitler, it was only natural that the great wish to be like him should end eventually by them identifying themselves with him. I was a little anxious when I mentioned this but I was delighted to find that he expressed great signs of satisfaction. He took it, I am thankful to say, as a compliment, this passionate wish to find identity with himself. He next asked if he could meet a representative number of these patients with this particular affliction. We had a little consultation. Martin B. seemed doubtful, but he took me aside and assured me that Herr Hitler actually wished to have this experience. What he himself was anxious to ensure was that Herr Hitler did not meet – well, in short, that Herr Hitler was not to be allowed to run any risks. If any of these so-called Hitlers, believing passionately in themselves as such, were inclined to be a little violent or dangerous . . . I assured him that he need have no worry. I suggested that I should collect a group of the most amiable of our Führers and assemble them for him to meet. Herr B. insisted that the Führer was very anxious to interview and mingle with them without my accompanying him. The patients, he said, would not behave naturally if they saw the chief of the establishment there, and if there was no danger . . . I assured him again that there was no danger. I said, however, that I should be glad if Herr B. would wait upon him. There was no difficulty about that. It was arranged. Messages were sent to the Führers to assemble in a room for a very distinguished visitor who was anxious to compare notes with them.

'Ach, so. Martin B. and the Führer were introduced into the assembly. I retired, closing the door, and chatted with the two ADC's who had accompanied them. The Führer, I said, was looking in a particularly anxious state. He had no doubt had many troubles of late. This I may say was very shortly before the end of the war when things, quite frankly, were going badly.

The Führer himself, they told me, had been greatly distressed of late but was convinced that he could bring the war to a successful close if the ideas which he was continually presenting to his general staff were acted upon, and accepted promptly.'

'The Führer, I presume,' said Sir George Packham, 'was at that time – I mean to say – no doubt he was in a state that –'

'We need not stress these points,' said Herr Spiess. 'He was completely beyond himself. Authority had to be taken for him on several points. But all that you will know well enough from the researches you have made in my country.'

'One remembers that at the Nuremberg trials –'

'There's no need to refer to the Nuremberg trials, I'm sure,' said Mr Lazenby decisively. 'All that is far behind us. We look forward to a great future in the Common Market with your Government's help, with the Government of Monsieur Grosjean and your other European colleagues. The past is the past.'

'Quite so,' said Herr Spiess, 'and it is of the past that we now talk. Martin B. and Herr Hitler remained for a very short time in the assembly room. They came out again after seven minutes. Herr B. expressed himself to Dr Reichardt as very well satisfied with their experience. Their car was waiting and he and Herr Hitler must proceed immediately to where they had another appointment. They left very hurriedly.'

There was a silence.

'And then?' asked Colonel Pikeaway. 'Something happened? Or had already happened?'

'The behaviour of one of our Hitler patients was unusual,' said Dr Reichardt. 'He was a man who had a particularly close resemblance to Herr Hitler, which had given him always a special confidence in his own portrayal. He insisted now more fiercely than ever that he *was* the Führer, that he must go immediately to Berlin, that he must preside over a Council of the General Staff. In fact, he behaved with no signs of the former slight amelioration which he had shown in his condition. He seemed so unlike himself that I really could not understand this change taking place so suddenly. I was relieved, indeed, when two days later, his relations called to take him home for future private treatment there.'

'And you let him go,' said Herr Spiess.

514 · AGATHA CHRISTIE

'Naturally I let him go. They had a responsible doctor with them, he was a voluntary patient, not certified, and therefore he was within his rights. So he left.'

'I don't see –' began Sir George Packham.

'Herr Spiess has a theory –'

'It's not a theory,' said Spiess. 'What I am telling you is fact. The Russians concealed it, we've concealed it. Plenty of evidence and proof has come in. Hitler, our Führer, *remained in the asylum by his own consent* that day and a man with the nearest resemblance to the real Hitler departed with Martin B. It was that patient's body which was subsequently found in the bunker. I will not beat about the bush. We need not go into unnecessary details.'

'We all have to know the truth,' said Lazenby.

'The real Führer was smuggled by a pre-arranged underground route to the Argentine and lived there for some years. He had a son there by a beautiful Aryan girl of good family. Some say she was an English girl. Hitler's mental condition worsened, and he died insane, believing himself to be commanding his armies in the field. It was the only plan possibly by which he could ever have escaped from Germany. He accepted it.'

'And you mean that for all these years nothing has leaked out about this, nothing has been known?'

'There have been rumours, there are always rumours. If you remember, one of the Czar's daughters in Russia was said to have escaped the general massacre of her family.'

'But that was –' George Packham stopped. 'False – quite false.'

'It was proved false by one set of people. It was accepted by another set of people, both of whom had known her. That Anastasia was indeed Anastasia, or that Anastasia, Grand Duchess of Russia, was really only a peasant girl. Which story was true? Rumours! The longer they go on, the less people believe them, except for those who have romantic minds, who go on believing them. It has often been rumoured that Hitler was alive, not dead. There is no one who has ever said with certainty that they have examined his dead body. The Russians declared so. They brought no proofs, though.'

'Do you really mean to say – Dr Reichardt, do *you* support this extraordinary story?'

'Ach,' said Dr Reichardt. 'You ask me, but I have told you my part. It was certainly Martin B. who came to my sanatorium. It was Martin B. who brought with him the Führer. It was Martin B. who treated him as the Führer, who spoke to him with the deference with which one speaks to the Führer. As for me, I lived already with some hundreds of Führers, of Napoleons, of Julius Caesars. You must understand that the Hitlers who lived in my sanatorium, they looked alike, they could have been, nearly all of them *could* have been, Adolf Hitler. They themselves could never have believed in themselves with the passion, the vehemence with which they knew that they were Hitler, unless they had had a basic resemblance, with make-up, clothing, continual acting, and playing of the part. I had had no personal meeting with Herr Adolf Hitler at any previous time. One saw pictures of him in the papers, one knew roughly what our great genius looked like, but one knew only the pictures that he wished shown. So he came, he was the Führer, Martin B., the man best to be believed on that subject, said he was the Führer. No, I had no doubts. I obeyed orders. Herr Hitler wished to go alone into a room to meet a selection of his – what shall one say? – his plaster copies. He went in. He came out. An exchange of clothing could have been made, not very different clothing in any case. Was it he himself or one of the self-appointed Hitlers who came out? Rushed out quickly by Martin B. and driven away while the real man could have stayed behind, could have enjoyed playing his part, could have known that in this way and in this way only could he manage to escape from the country which at any moment might surrender. He was already disturbed in mind, mentally affected by rage and anger that the orders he gave, the wild fantastic messages sent to his staff, what they were to do, what they were to say, the impossible things they were to attempt, were not, as of old, immediately obeyed. He could feel already that he was no longer in supreme command. But he had a small faithful two or three and they had a plan for him, to get him out of this country, out of Europe, to a place where he could rally round him in a different continent his Nazi followers, the young ones who believed so passionately in him. The swastika would rise again there. He played his part. No doubt, he enjoyed it. Yes, that would be in keeping with a man whose reason was already tottering. He would show these others that he could play the part of Adolf Hitler better than they did. He laughed to himself occasionally, and my doctors, my nurses, they would look in, they would see some slight change. One patient who seemed unusually mentally disturbed, perhaps. Pah, there was nothing in that. It was always happening. With the Napoleons, with the Julius Caesars, with all of them. Some days, as one would say if one was a layman, they are madder than usual. That is the only way I can put it. So now it is for Herr Spiess to speak.'

'Fantastic!' said the Home Secretary.

'Yes, fantastic,' said Herr Spiess patiently, 'but fantastic things can happen, you know. In history, in real life, no matter how fantastic.'

'And nobody suspected, nobody knew?'

'It was very well planned. It was well planned, well thought out. The escape route was ready, the exact details of it are not clearly known, but one can make a pretty good recapitulation of them. Some of the people who were concerned, who passed a certain personage on from place to place under different disguises, under different names, some of those people, on our looking back and making inquiries, we find did not live as long as they might have done.'

'You mean in case they should give the secret away or should talk too much?'

'The SS saw to that. Rich rewards, praise, promises of high positions in the future and then – death is a much easier answer. And the SS were used to death. They knew the different ways of it, they knew means of disposing of bodies – Oh yes, I will tell you that, this has been inquired into for some time now. The knowledge has come little by little to us, and we have made inquiries, documents have been acquired and the truth has come out. Adolf Hitler certainly reached South America. It is said that a marriage ceremony was performed – that a child was born. The child was branded in the foot with the mark of the swastika. Branded as a baby. I have seen trusted agents whom I can believe. They have seen that branded foot in South America. There that child was brought up, carefully guarded, shielded, prepared – prepared as the Dalai Lama might have been prepared for his great destiny. For that was the idea behind the fanatical young, the idea was greater than the idea that they had started out with. This was not merely a revival of the new Nazis, the new German super race. It was that, yes, but it was many more things besides. It was the young of many other nations, the super race of the young men of nearly every country in Europe, to join together, to join the ranks of anarchy, to destroy the old world, that materialistic world, to usher in a great new band of killing, murdering, violent brothers. Bent first on destruction and then on rising to power. And they had now their leader. A leader with the right blood in his veins and a leader who, though he grew up with no great likeness to his dead father, was – no, *is* – a golden-haired fair Nordic boy, taking presumably after the looks of his mother. A golden boy. A boy whom the whole world could accept. The Germans and the Austrians first because it was the great article of their faith, of their music, the young Siegfried. So he grew up as the young Siegfried who would command them all, who would lead them into the promised land. Not the promised land of the Jews, whom they despised, where Moses led his followers. The Jews were dead under the ground, killed or murdered in the gas chambers. This was to be a land of their own, a land gained by their own prowess. The countries of Europe were to be banded together with the countries of South America. There already they had their spearhead, their anarchists, their prophets, their Guevaras, the Castros, the Guerrillas, their followers, a long arduous training in cruelty and torture and violence and death and after it, glorious life. Freedom! As Rulers of the New World State. The appointed conquerors.'

'Absurd nonsense,' said Mr Lazenby. 'Once all this is put a stop to – the whole thing will collapse. This is all quite ridiculous. What *can* they do?' Cedric Lazenby sounded merely querulous.

Herr Spiess shook his heavy, wise head.

'You may ask. I tell you the answer, which is – *they do not know*. They don't know where they're going. They don't know what is going to be done with them.'

'You mean they're not the real leaders?'

'They are the young marching Heroes, treading their path to glory, on the stepping-stones of violence, of pain, of hatred. They have now their following not only in South America and Europe. The cult has travelled north. In the United States, there too the young men riot, they march, they follow the banner of the Young Siegfried. They are taught his ways, they are taught to kill, to enjoy pain, they are taught the rules of the Death's Head, the rules of Himmler. They are being trained, you see. They are being secretly indoctrinated. They do not know what they're being trained for. But we do, some of us at least. And you? In this country?'

'Four or five of us, perhaps,' said Colonel Pikeaway.

'In Russia they know, in America they have begun to know. They know that there are the followers of the Young Hero, Siegfried, based on the Norse Legends, and that a young Siegfried is the leader. That that is their new religion. The religion of the glorious boy, the golden triumph of youth. In him the old Nordic Gods have risen again.

'But that, of course,' said Herr Spiess, dropping his voice to a commonplace tone, 'that of course is not the simple prosaic truth. There are some powerful personalities behind this. Evil men with first-class brains. A first-class financier, a great industrialist, someone who controls mines, oil, stores of uranium, who owns scientists of the top class, and those are the ones, a committee of men, who themselves do not look particularly interesting or extraordinary, but nevertheless have got control. They control the sources of power, and control through certain means of their own the young men who kill and the young men who are slaves. By control of drugs they acquire slaves. Slaves in every country who little by little progress from soft drugs to hard drugs and who are then completely subservient, completely dependent on men whom they do not even know but who secretly own them body and soul. Their craving need for a particular drug makes them slaves, and in due course, these slaves prove to be no good, because of their dependence on drugs, they will only be capable of sitting in apathy dreaming sweet dreams, and so they will be left to die, or even helped to die. They will not inherit that kingdom in which they believe. Strange religions are being deliberately introduced to them. The gods of the old days disguised.'

'And permissive sex also plays its part, I suppose?'

'Sex can destroy itself. In old Roman times the men who steeped themselves in vice, who were oversexed, who ran sex to death until they were bored and weary of sex, sometimes fled from it and went out into the desert and became Anchorites like St Simeon Stylites. Sex will exhaust itself. It does its work for the time being, but it cannot rule you as drugs rule you. Drugs and sadism and the love of power and hatred. A desire for pain for its own sake. The pleasures of inflicting it. They are teaching themselves the pleasures of evil. Once the pleasures of evil get a hold on you, you cannot draw back.'

'My dear Chancellor – I really can't believe you – I mean, well – I mean if there are these tendencies, they must be put down by adopting strong measures. I mean, really, one – one can't go on pandering to this sort of thing. One must take a firm stand – a firm stand.'

'Shut up, George.' Mr Lazenby pulled out his pipe, looked at it, put it back in his pocket again. 'The best plan, I think,' he said, his *idée fixe* reasserting itself, 'would be for me to fly to Russia. I understand that – well, that these facts are known to the Russians.'

'They know sufficient,' said Herr Spiess. 'How much they will admit they know –' he shrugged his shoulders – 'that is difficult to say. It is never easy to get the Russians to come out in the open. They have their own troubles on the Chinese border. They believe perhaps less in the far advanced stage, into which the movement has got, than we do.'

'I should make mine a special mission, I should.'

'I should stay here if I were you, Cedric.'

Lord Altamount's quiet voice spoke from where he leaned rather wearily back in his chair. 'We need you here, Cedric,' he said. There was gentle authority in his voice. 'You are the head of our Government – you must remain here. We have our trained agents – our own emissaries who are qualified for foreign missions.'

'Agents?' Sir George Packham dubiously demanded. 'What can agents do at this stage? We must have a report from – Ah, Horsham, there you are – I did not notice you before. Tell us – what agents have we got? And what can they possibly do?'

'We've got some very good agents,' said Henry Horsham quietly. 'Agents bring you information. Herr Spiess also has brought you information. Information which *his* agents have obtained for *him*. The trouble is – always has been – (you've only got to read about the last war) *nobody wishes to believe the news the agents bring.*'

'Surely – Intelligence –'

'Nobody wants to accept that the agents *are* intelligent! But they are, you know. They are highly trained and their reports, nine times out of ten, are *true*. What happens then? The High-Ups refuse to believe it, don't want to believe it, go further and refuse to act upon it in any way.'

'Really, my dear Horsham – I can't –'

Horsham turned to the German.

'Even in your country, sir, didn't that happen? True reports were brought in, but they weren't always acted upon. *People don't want to know – if truth is unpalatable.*'

'I have to agree – that can and does happen – not often, of that I assure you – But yes – sometimes –'

Mr Lazenby was fidgeting again with his pipe.

'Let us not argue about information. It is a question of dealing – of acting upon the information we have got. This is not merely a national crisis – it is an international crisis. Decisions must be taken at top level – we must act. Munro, the police must be reinforced by the Army – military measures must be set in motion. Herr Spiess, you have always been a great military nation – rebellions must be put down by armed forces before they get out of hand. You would agree with that policy, I am sure –'

'The policy, yes. But these insurrections are already what you term "out of hand". They have tools, rifles, machine-guns, explosives, grenades, bombs, chemical and other gases –'

'But with our nuclear weapons – a mere threat of nuclear warfare – and –'

'These are not just disaffected schoolboys. With this Army of Youth there are scientists – young biologists, chemists, physicists. To start – or to engage in nuclear warfare in Europe –' Herr Spiess shook his head. 'Already we have had an attempt to poison the water supply at Cologne – Typhoid.'

'The whole position is incredible –' Cedric Lazenby looked round him hopefully – 'Chetwynd – Munro – Blunt?'

Admiral Blunt was, somewhat to Lazenby's surprise, the only one to respond.

'I don't know where the Admiralty comes in – not quite our pigeon. I'd advise you, Cedric, if you want to do the best thing for yourself, to take your pipe, and a big supply of tobacco, and get as far out of range of any nuclear warfare you are thinking of starting as you can. Go and camp in the Antarctic, or somewhere where radio-activity will take a long time catching up with you. Professor Eckstein warned us, you know, and he knows what he's talking about.'

CHAPTER 18
PIKEAWAY'S POSTSCRIPT

The meeting broke up at this point. It split into a definite rearrangement.

The German Chancellor with the Prime Minister, Sir George Packham, Gordon Chetwynd and Dr Reichardt departed for lunch at Downing Street.

Admiral Blunt, Colonel Munro, Colonel Pikeaway and Henry Horsham remained to make their comments with more freedom of speech than they would have permitted themselves if the VIP's had remained.

The first remarks made were somewhat disjointed.

'Thank goodness they took George Packham with them,' said Colonel Pikeaway. 'Worry, fidget, wonder, surmise – gets me down sometimes.'

'You ought to have gone with them, Admiral,' said Colonel Munro. 'Can't see Gordon Chetwynd or George Packham being able to stop our Cedric from going off for a top-level consultation with the Russians, the Chinese, the Ethiopians, the Argentinians or anywhere else the fancy takes him.'

'I've got other kites to fly,' said the Admiral gruffly. 'Going to the country to see an old friend of mine.' He looked with some curiosity at Colonel Pikeaway.

'Was the Hitler business really a surprise to you, Pikeaway?'

Colonel Pikeaway shook his head.

'Not really. We've known all about the rumours of our Adolf turning up in South America and keeping the swastika flying for years. Fifty-to-fifty chance of its being true. Whoever the chap was, madman, play-acting impostor, or the real thing, he passed in his checks quite soon. Nasty stories about that, too – he wasn't an asset to his supporters.'

'*Whose body was it in the Bunker?* is still a good talking point,' said Blunt. 'Never been any definite identification. Russians saw to that.'

He got up, nodded to the others and went towards the door.

Munro said thoughtfully, 'I suppose Dr Reichardt knows the truth – though he played it cagey.'

'What about the Chancellor?' said Horsham.

'Sensible man,' grunted the Admiral, turning his head back from the doorway. 'He was getting his country the way he wanted it, when this youth business started playing fun and games with the civilized world – Pity!' He looked shrewdly at Colonel Munro.

'What about the Golden-Haired Wonder? Hitler's son? Know all about him?'

'No need to worry,' said Colonel Pikeaway unexpectedly.

The Admiral let go of the door-handle and came back and sat down.

'All my eye and Betty Martin,' said Colonel Pikeaway. 'Hitler never had a son.'

'You can't be sure of that.'

'We *are* sure – Franz Joseph, the Young Siegfried, the idolized Leader, is a common or garden fraud, a rank impostor. He's the son of an Argentinian carpenter and a good-looking blonde, a small-part German opera singer – inherited his looks and his singing voice from his mother. He was carefully chosen for the part he was to play, groomed for stardom. In his early youth he was a professional actor – he was branded in the foot with a swastika – a story made up for him full of romantic details. He was treated like a dedicated Dalai Lama.'

'And you've proof of this?'

'Full documentation,' Colonel Pikeaway grinned. 'One of my best agents got it. Affidavits, photostats, signed declaration, including one from the mother, and medical evidence as to the date of the scar, copy of the original birth certificate of Karl Aguileros – and signed evidence of his identity with the so-called Franz Joseph. The whole bag of tricks. My agent got away with it just in time. They were after her – might have got her if she hadn't had a bit of luck at Frankfurt.'

'And where are these documents now?'

'In a safe place. Waiting for the right moment for a spectacular debunking of a first-class impostor –'

'Do the Government know this? – the Prime Minister?'

'I never tell all I know to politicians – not until I can't avoid it, or until I'm quite sure they'll do the right thing.'

'You *are* an old devil, Pikeaway,' said Colonel Munro.

'Somebody has to be,' said Colonel Pikeaway, sadly.

CHAPTER 19

SIR STAFFORD NYE HAS VISITORS

Sir Stafford Nye was entertaining guests. They were guests with whom he had previously been unacquainted except for one of them whom he knew fairly well by sight. They were good-looking young men, serious-minded and intelligent, or so he should judge. Their hair was controlled and stylish, their clothes were well cut though not unduly old-fashioned. Looking at them, Stafford Nye was unable to deny that he liked the look of them. At the same time he wondered what they wanted with him. One of them he knew was the son of an oil king. Another of them, since leaving the university, had interested himself in politics. He had an uncle who owned a chain of restaurants. The third one was a young man with beetle brows who frowned and to whom perpetual suspicion seemed to be second nature.

'It's very good of you to let us come and call upon you, Sir Stafford,' said the one who seemed to be the blond leader of the three.

His voice was very agreeable. His name was Clifford Bent.

'This is Roderick Ketelly and this is Jim Brewster. We're all anxious about the future. Shall I put it like that?'

'I suppose the answer to that is, aren't we all?' said Sir Stafford Nye.

'We don't like things the way they're going,' said Clifford Bent. 'Rebellion, anarchy, all that. Well, it's all right as a philosophy. Frankly I think we may say that we all seem to go through a phase of it but one does come out the other side. We want people to be able to pursue academic careers without their being interrupted. We want a good sufficiency of demonstrations but not demonstrations of hooliganism and violence. We want intelligent demonstrations. And what we want, quite frankly, or so I think, is a new political party. Jim Brewster here has been paying serious attention to entirely new ideas and plans concerning trade union matters. They've tried to shout him down and talk him out, but he's gone on talking, haven't you, Jim?'

'Muddle-headed old fools, most of them,' said Jim Brewster.

'We want a sensible and serious policy for youth, a more economical method of government. We want different ideas to obtain in education but nothing fantastic or high-falutin'. And we shall want, if we win seats, and if we are able finally to form a government – and I don't see why we shouldn't – to put these ideas into action. There are a lot of people in our movement. We stand for youth, you know, just as well as the violent ones do. We stand for moderation and we mean to have a sensible government, with a reduction in the number of MP's, and we're noting down, looking for the men already in politics no matter what their particular persuasion is, if we think they're men of sense. We've come here to see if we can interest you in our aims. At the moment they are still in a state of flux but we have got as far as knowing the men we want. I may say that we don't want the ones we've got at present and we don't want the ones who might be put in instead. As for the third party, it seems to have died out of the running, though there are one or two good people there who suffer now for being in a minority, but I think they would come over to our way of thinking. We want to interest you. We want, one of these days, perhaps not so far distant as you might think – we want someone who'd understand and put out a proper, successful foreign policy. The rest of the world's in a worse mess than we are now. Washington's razed to the ground, Europe has continual military actions, demonstrations, wrecking of airports. Oh well, I don't need to write you a news letter of the past six months, but our aim is not so much to put the world on its legs again as to put England on its legs again. To have the right men to do it. We want young men, a great many young men and we've got a great many young men who aren't revolutionary, who aren't anarchistic, who will be willing to try and make a country run profitably. And we want some of the older men – I don't mean men of sixty-odd, I mean men of forty or fifty – and we've come to you because, well, we've heard things about you. We know about you and you're the sort of man we want.'

'Do you think you are wise?' said Sir Stafford.

'Well, *we*, think we are.'

The second young man laughed slightly.

'We hope you'll agree with us there.'

'I'm not sure that I do. You're talking in this room very freely.'

'It's your sitting-room.'

'Yes, yes, it's my flat and it's my sitting-room. But what you are saying, and in fact what you might be going to say, might be unwise. That means both for you as well as me.'

'Oh! I think I see what you're driving at.'

'You are offering me something. A way of life, a new career and you are suggesting a breaking of certain ties. You are suggesting a form of disloyalty.'

'We're not suggesting your becoming a defector to any other country, if that's what you mean.'

'No, no, this is not an invitation to Russia or an invitation to China or an invitation to other places mentioned in the past, but I think it is an invitation connected with some foreign interests.' He went on: 'I've recently come back from abroad. A very interesting journey. I have spent the last three weeks in South America. There is something I would like to tell you. I have been conscious since I returned to England that I have been followed.'

'Followed? You don't think you imagined it?'

'No, I don't think I've imagined it. Those are the sort of things I have learned to notice in the course of my career. I have been in some fairly far distant and – shall we say? – interesting parts of the world. You chose to call upon me to sound me as to a proposition. It might have been safer, though, if we had met elsewhere.'

He got up, opened the door into the bathroom and turned the tap.

'From the films I used to see some years ago,' he said, 'if you wished to disguise your conversation when a room was bugged, you turned on taps. I have no doubt that I am somewhat old-fashioned and that there are better methods of dealing with these things now. But at any rate perhaps we could speak a little more clearly now, though even then I still think we should be careful. South America,' he went on, 'is a very interesting part of the world. The Federation of South American countries (Spanish Gold has been one name for it), comprising by now Cuba, the Argentine, Brazil, Peru, one or two others not quite settled and fixed but coming into being. Yes. Very interesting.'

'And what are your views on the subject,' the suspicious-looking Jim Brewster asked. 'What have you got to say about things?'

'I shall continue to be careful,' said Sir Stafford. 'You will have more dependence on me if I do not talk unadvisedly. But I think that can be done quite well after I turn off the bath water.'

'Turn it off, Jim,' said Cliff Bent.

Jim grinned suddenly and obeyed.

Stafford Nye opened a drawer at the table and took out a recorder.

'Not a very practised player yet,' he said.

He put it to his lips and started a tune. Jim Brewster came back, scowling.

'What's this? A bloody concert we're going to put on?'

'Shut up,' said Cliff Bent. 'You ignoramus, you don't know anything about music.'

Stafford Nye smiled.

'You share my pleasure in Wagnerian music, I see,' he said. 'I was at the Youth Festival this year and enjoyed the concerts there very much.'

Again he repeated the tune.

'Not any tune I know,' said Jim Brewster. 'It might be the Internationale or the Red Flag or God Save the King or Yankee Doodle or the Star-Spangled Banner. What the devil is it?'

'It's a motif from an opera,' said Ketelly. 'And shut your mouth. We know all we want to know.'

'The horn call of a young Hero,' said Stafford Nye.

He brought his hand up in a quick gesture, the gesture from the past meaning 'Heil Hitler'. He murmured very gently,

'The new Siegfried.'

All three rose.

'You're quite right,' said Clifford Bent. 'We must all, I think, be very careful.'

He shook hands.

'We are glad to know that you will be with us. One of the things this country will need in its future – its great future, I hope – will be a first-class Foreign Minister.'

They went out of the room. Stafford Nye watched them through the slightly open door go into the lift and descend.

He gave a curious smile, shut the door, glanced up at the clock on the wall and sat down in an easy chair – to wait . . .

His mind went back to the day, a week ago now, when he and Mary Ann had gone their separate ways from Kennedy Airport. They had stood there, both of them finding it difficult to speak. Stafford Nye had broken the silence first.

'Do you think we'll ever meet again? I wonder . . .'

'Is there any reason why we shouldn't?'

'Every reason, I should think.'

She looked at him, then quickly away again.

'These partings have to happen. It's – part of the job.'

'The job! It's always the job with you, isn't it?'

'It has to be.'

'You're a professional. I'm only an amateur. You're a –' he broke off. 'What are you? Who are you? I don't really know, do I?'

'No.'

He looked at her then. He saw sadness, he thought, in her face. Something that was almost pain.

'So I have to – wonder . . . You think I ought to trust you, I suppose?'

'No, not that. That is one of the things that I have learnt, that life has taught me. There is nobody that one can trust. Remember that – always.'

'So that is your world? A world of distrust, of fear, of danger.'

'I wish to stay alive. I am alive.'

'I know.'

'And I want *you* to stay alive.'

'*I* trusted you – in Frankfurt . . .'

'You took a risk.'

'It was a risk well worth taking. You know that as well as I do.'

'You mean because –?'

'Because we have been together. And now – That is my flight being called. Is this companionship of ours which started in an airport, to end here in another airport? You are going where? To do what?'

'To do what I have to do. To Baltimore, to Washington, to Texas. To do what I have been told to do.'

'And I? I have been told nothing. I am to go back to London – and do what there?'

'Wait.'

'Wait for what?'

'For the advances that almost certainly will be made to you.'

'And what am I to do then?'

She smiled at him, with the sudden gay smile that he knew so well.

'Then you play it by ear. You'll know how to do it, none better. You'll like the people who approach you. They'll be well chosen. It's important, very important, that we should know who they are.'

'I must go. Goodbye, Mary Ann.'

'*Auf Wiedersehen.*'

In the London flat, the telephone rang. At a singularly apposite moment, Stafford Nye thought, bringing him back from his past memories just at that moment of their farewell. '*Auf Wiedersehen,*' he murmured, as he rose to his feet, crossed to take the receiver off, 'let it be so.'

A voice spoke whose wheezy accents were quite unmistakable.

'Stafford Nye?'

He gave the requisite answer: 'No smoke without fire.'

'My doctor says I should give up smoking. Poor fellow,' said Colonel Pikeaway, 'he might as well give up hope of that. Any news?'

'Oh yes. Thirty pieces of silver. Promised, that is to say.'

'Damned swine!'

'Yes, yes, keep calm.'

'And what did you say?'

'I played them a tune. Siegfried's Horn motif. I was following an elderly aunt's advice. It went down very well.'

'Sounds crazy to me!'

'Do you know a song called Juanita? I must learn that too, in case I need it.'

'Do you know who Juanita is?'

'I think so.'

'H'm, I wonder – heard of in Baltimore last.'

'What about your Greek girl, Daphne Theodofanous? Where is she now, I wonder?'

'Sitting in an airport somewhere in Europe waiting for you, probably,' said Colonel Pikeaway.

'Most of the European airports seem to be closed down because they've been blown up or more or less damaged. High explosive, hi-jackers, high jinks.

> *'The boys and girls come out to play*
> *The moon doth shine as bright as day –*
> *Leave your supper and leave your sleep*
> *And shoot your playfellow in the street.'*

'The Children's Crusade *à la mode*.'

'Not that I really know much about it. I only know the one that Richard Coeur de Lion went to. But in a way this whole business is rather like the Children's Crusade. Starting with idealism, starting with ideas of the Christian world delivering the holy city from pagans, and ending with death, death and again, death. Nearly all the children died. Or were sold into slavery. This will end the same way unless we can find some means of getting them out of it . . .'

CHAPTER 20

THE ADMIRAL VISITS AN OLD FRIEND

'Thought you must all be dead here,' said Admiral Blunt with a snort.

His remark was addressed not to the kind of butler which

he would have liked to see opening this front door, but to the young woman whose surname he could never remember but whose Christian name was Amy.

'Rung you up at least four times in the last week. Gone abroad, that's what they said.'

'We have been abroad. We've only just come back.'

'Matilda oughtn't to go rampaging about abroad. Not at her time of life. She'll die of blood pressure or heart failure or something in one of these modern airplanes. Cavorting about, full of explosives put in them by the Arabs or the Israelis or somebody or other. Not safe at all any longer.'

'Her doctor recommended it to her.'

'Oh well, we all know what doctors are.'

'And she has really come back in very good spirits.'

'Where's she been, then?'

'Oh, taking a Cure. In Germany or – I never can quite remember whether it's Germany or Austria. That new place, you know, the Golden Gasthaus.'

'Ah yes, I know the place you mean. Costs the earth, doesn't it?'

'Well, it's said to produce very remarkable results.'

'Probably only a different way of killing you quicker,' said Admiral Blunt. 'How did *you* enjoy it?'

'Well, not really very much. The scenery was very nice, but –'

An imperious voice sounded from the floor above.

'Amy. Amy! What are you doing, talking in the hall all this time? Bring Admiral Blunt up here. I'm waiting for him.'

'Gallivanting about,' said Admiral Blunt, after he had greeted his old friend. 'That's how you'll kill yourself one of these days. You mark my words –'

'No, I shan't. There's no difficulty at all in travelling nowadays.'

'Running about all those airports, ramps, stairs, buses.'

'Not at all. I had a wheelchair.'

'A year or two ago when I saw you, you said you wouldn't hear of such a thing. You said you had too much pride to admit you needed one.'

'Well, I've had to give up some of my pride, nowadays, Philip. Come and sit down here and tell me why you wanted to come and see me so much all of a sudden. You've neglected me a great deal for the last year.'

'Well, I've not been so well myself. Besides, I've been looking into a few things. You know the sort of thing. Where they ask your advice but don't mean in the least to take it. They can't leave the Navy alone. Keep on wanting to fiddle about with it, drat them.'

'You look quite well to me,' said Lady Matilda.

'You don't look so bad yourself, my dear. You've got a nice sparkle in your eye.'

'I'm deafer than when you saw me last. You'll have to speak up more.'

'All right. I'll speak up.'

'What do you want, gin and tonic or whisky or rum?'

'You seem ready to dispense strong liquor of any kind. If it's all the same to you, I'll have a gin and tonic.'

Amy rose and left the room.

'And when she brings it,' said the Admiral, 'get rid of her again, will you? I want to talk to you. Talk to you particularly is what I mean.'

Refreshment brought, Lady Matilda made a dismissive wave of the hand and Amy departed with the air of one who is pleasing herself, not her employer. She was a tactful young woman.

'Nice girl,' said the Admiral, 'very nice.'

'Is that why you asked me to get rid of her and see she shut the door? So that she mightn't overhear you saying something nice about her?'

'No. I wanted to consult you.'

'What about? Your health or where to get some new servants or what to grow in the garden?'

'I want to consult you very seriously. I thought perhaps you might be able to remember something for me.'

'Dear Philip, how touching that you should think I can remember *anything*. Every year my memory gets worse. I've come to the conclusion one only remembers what's called the "friends of one's youth". Even horrid girls one was at school with one remembers, though one doesn't want to. That's where I've been now, as a matter of fact.'

'Where've you been now? Visiting schools?'

'No, no, no, I went to see an old school friend whom I haven't seen for thirty – forty – fifty – that sort of time.'

'What was she like?'

'Enormously fat and even nastier and horrider than I remembered her.'

'You've got very queer tastes, I must say, Matilda.'

'Well, go on, tell me. Tell me what it is you want me to remember?'

'I wondered if you remembered another friend of yours. Robert Shoreham.'

'Robbie Shoreham? Of course I do.'

'The scientist feller. Top scientist.'

'Of course. He wasn't the sort of man one would ever forget. I wonder what put him into your head.'

'Public need.'

'Funny you should say that,' said Lady Matilda. 'I thought the same myself the other day.'

'You thought what?'

'That he was needed. Or someone like him – if there is anyone like him.'

'There isn't. Now listen, Matilda. People talk to you a bit. They tell you things. I've told you things myself.'

'I've always wondered why, because you can't believe that I'll understand them or be able to describe them. And that was even more the case with Robbie than with you.'

'I don't tell you naval secrets.'

'Well, he didn't tell me scientific secrets. I mean, only in a very general way.'

'Yes, but he used to talk to you about them, didn't he?'

'Well, he liked saying things that would astonish me sometimes.'

'All right, then, here it comes. I want to know if he ever talked to you, in the days when he could talk properly, poor devil, about something called Project B.'

'Project B.' Matilda Cleckheaton considered thoughtfully. 'Sounds vaguely familiar,' she said. 'He used to talk about Project this or that sometimes, or Operation that or this. But you must realize that none of it ever made any kind of *sense* to me, and he knew it didn't. But he used to like – oh, how shall I put it? – astonishing me rather, you know. Sort of describing it the way that a conjuror might describe how he takes three rabbits out of a hat without your knowing how he did it. Project B? Yes, that was a good long time ago . . . He was wildly excited for a bit. I used to say to him sometimes "How's Project B going on?"'

'I know, I know, you've always been a tactful woman. You can always remember what people were doing or interested in. And even if you don't know the first thing about it you'd show an interest. I described a new kind of naval gun to you once and you must have been bored stiff. But you listened as brightly as though it was the thing you'd been waiting to hear about all your life.'

'As you tell me, I've been a tactful woman and a good listener, even if I've never had much in the way of brains.'

'Well, I want to hear a little more what Robbie said about Project B.'

'He said – well, it's very difficult to remember now. He mentioned it after talking about some operation that they used to do on people's brains. You know, the people who were terribly melancholic and who were thinking of suicide and who were so worried and neurasthenic that they had awful anxiety complexes. Stuff like that, the sort of thing people used to talk of in connection with Freud. And he said that the side effects were impossible. I mean, the people were quite happy and meek and docile and didn't worry any more, or want to kill themselves, but they – well I mean they didn't worry *enough* and therefore they used to get run over and all sorts of things like that because they weren't thinking of any danger and didn't notice it. I'm putting it badly but you do understand what I mean. And anyway, he said, that was going to be the trouble, he thought, with Project B.'

'Did he describe it at all more closely than that?'

'He said I'd put it into his head,' said Matilda Cleckheaton unexpectedly.

'What? Do you mean to say a scientist – a top-flight scientist like Robbie actually said to you that you had put something into his scientific brain? You don't know the first thing about science.'

'Of course not. But I used to try and put a little common sense into people's brains. The cleverer they are, the less common sense they have. I mean, really, the people who matter are the people who thought of simple things like perforations on postage stamps, or like somebody Adam, or whatever his name was – No – MacAdam in America who put black stuff on roads so that farmers could get all their crops from farms to the coast and make a better profit. I mean, they do much more good than all the high-powered scientists do. Scientists can only think of things for destroying you. Well, that's the sort of thing I said to Robbie. Quite nicely, of course, as a kind of joke. He'd been just telling me that some splendid things had been done in the scientific world about germ warfare and experiments with biology and what you can do to unborn babies if you get at them early enough. And also some peculiarly nasty and very unpleasant gases and saying how silly people were to protest against nuclear bombs because they were really a kindness compared to some of the other things that had been invented since then. And so I said it'd be much more to the point if Robbie, or someone clever like Robbie, could think of something really sensible. And he looked at me with that, you know, little twinkle he has in his eye sometimes and said, "Well what would you consider sensible?" And I said, "Well, instead of inventing all these germ warfares and these nasty gases, and all the rest of it, why don't you just invent something that makes people feel happy?" I said it oughtn't to be any more difficult to do. I said, "You've talked about this operation where, I think you said, they took out a bit of the front of your brain or maybe the back of your brain. But anyway it made a great difference in people's dispositions. They'd become quite different. They hadn't worried any more or they hadn't wanted to commit suicide. But," I said, "well, if you can change people like that just by taking a little bit of bone or muscle or nerve or tinkering up a gland or taking out a gland or putting in more of a gland," I said, "if you can make all that difference in people's dispositions, why can't you invent something that will make people pleasant or just sleepy perhaps? Supposing you had something, not a sleeping draught, but just something that people sat down in a chair and had a nice dream. Twenty-four hours or so and just woke up to be fed now and again." I said it would be a much better idea.'

'And is that what Project B was?'

'Well, of course he never told me what it was exactly. But he was excited with an idea and he said I'd put it into his head, so it must have been something rather pleasant I'd put into his head, mustn't it? I mean, I hadn't suggested any ideas to him of any nastier ways for killing people and I didn't want people even – you know – to cry, like tear gas or anything like that. Perhaps laughing – yes, I believe I mentioned laughing gas. I said well if you have your teeth out, they give you three sniffs of it and you laugh, well, surely, surely you could invent something that's as useful as that but would last a little longer. Because I believe laughing gas only lasts about fifty seconds, doesn't it? I know my brother had some teeth out once. The dentist's chair was very near the window and my brother was laughing so much, when he was unconscious, I mean, that he stretched his leg right out and put it through the dentist's window and all the glass fell in the street, and the dentist was very cross about it.'

'Your stories always have such strange side-kicks,' said the Admiral. 'Anyway, this is what Robbie Shoreham had chosen to get on with, from your advice.'

'Well, I don't know what it was exactly. I mean, I don't think it was sleeping or laughing. At any rate, it was *something*. It wasn't really Project B. It had another name.'

'What sort of a name?'

'Well, he did mention it once I think, or twice. The name he'd given it. Rather like Benger's Food,' said Aunt Matilda, considering thoughtfully.

'Some soothing agent for the digestion?'

'I don't think it had anything to do with the digestion. I rather think it was something you sniffed or something, perhaps it was a gland. You know we talked of so many things that you never quite knew what he was talking about at the moment. Benger's Food. Ben – Ben – it did begin with Ben. And there was a pleasant word associated with it.'

'Is that all you can remember about it?'

'I think so. I mean, this was just a talk we had once and then, quite a long time afterwards, he told me I'd put something into his head for Project Ben something. And after that, occasionally, if I remembered, I'd ask him if he was still working on Project Ben and then sometimes he'd be very exasperated and say no, he'd come up against a snag and he was putting it all aside now because it was in – in – well, I mean the next eight words were pure jargon and I couldn't remember them and you wouldn't understand them if I said them to you. But in the end, I think – oh dear, oh dear, this is all about eight or nine years ago – in the end he came one day and he said, "Do you remember Project Ben?" I said, "Of course I remember it. Are you still working on it?" And he said no, he was determined to lay it all aside. I said I was sorry. Sorry if he'd given it up and he said, "Well, it's not only that I can't get what I was trying for. I know now that it *could* be got. I know where I went wrong. I know just what the snag was, I know just how to put that snag right again. I've got Lisa working on it with me. Yes, it could work. It'd require experimenting on certain things but it could work." "Well," I said to him, "what are you worrying about?" And he said, "Because I don't know what it would really do to people." I said something about his being afraid it would kill people or maim them for life or something. "No," he said, "it's not like that." He said, it's a – oh, of course, now I remember. He called it Project Benvo. Yes. And that's because it had to do with *benevolence*.'

'Benevolence!' said the Admiral, highly surprised. 'Benevolence? Do you mean charity?'

'No, no, no. I think he meant simply that you could make people benevolent. *Feel* benevolent.'

'Peace and good will towards men?'

'Well, he didn't put it like that.'

'No, that's reserved for religious leaders. They preach that to you and if you did what they preach it'd be a very happy world. But Robbie, I gather, was not preaching. He proposed to do something in his laboratory to bring about this result by purely physical means.'

'That's the sort of thing. And he said you can never tell when things *are* beneficial to people or when they're not. They are in one way, they're not in another. And he said things about – oh, penicillin and sulphonamides and heart transplants and things like pills for women, though we hadn't got "The Pill" then. But you know, things that seem all right and they're wonder-drugs or wonder-gases or wonder-something or other, and then there's something about them that makes them go wrong as well as right, and then you wish they weren't there and had never been thought of. Well, that's the sort of thing that he seemed to be trying to get over to me. It was all rather difficult to understand. I said, "Do you mean you don't like to take the risk?" and he said, "You're quite right. I don't like to take the risk. That's the trouble because, you see, I don't know in the least what the risk will be. That's what happens to us poor devils of scientists. We take the risks and the risks are not in what we've discovered, it's the risks of what the people we'll have to tell about it will do with what we've discovered." I said, "Now you're talking about nuclear weapons again and atom bombs," and he said, "Oh, to Hell with nuclear weapons and atomic bombs. We've gone far beyond that."

'"But if you're going to make people nice-tempered and benevolent," I said, "what have you got to worry about?" And he said, "You don't *understand*, Matilda. You'll never understand. My fellow scientists in all probability would not understand either. And no politicians would ever understand. And so, you see, it's too big a risk to be taken. At any rate one would have to think for a long time."

'"But," I said, "you could bring people out of it again, just like laughing gas, couldn't you? I mean, you could make people benevolent just for a short time, and then they'd get all right again – or all wrong again – it depends which way you look at it, I should have thought." And he said, "No. This will be, you see, permanent. Quite permanent because it affects the –" and then he went into jargon again. You know, long words and numbers. Formulas, or molecular changes – something like that. I expect really it must be something like what they do to cretins. You know, to make them stop being cretins, like giving them thyroid or taking it away from them. I forget which it is. Something like that. Well, I expect there's some nice little gland somewhere and if you take it away or smoke it out, or do something drastic to it – but then, the people are permanently –'

'Permanently *benevolent*? You're sure that's the right word? Benevolence?'

'Yes, because that's why he nicknamed it *Benvo*.'

'But what did his colleagues think, I wonder, about his backing out?'

'I don't think he had many who knew. Lisa what's-her-name, the Austrian girl; she'd worked on it with him. And there was one young man called Leadenthal or some name like that, but he died of tuberculosis. And he rather spoke as though the other people who worked with him were merely assistants who didn't know exactly what he was doing or trying for. I see what you're getting at,' said Matilda suddenly. 'I don't think he ever told anybody, really. I mean, I think he destroyed his formulas or notes or whatever they were and gave up the whole idea. And then he had his stroke and got ill, and now, poor dear, he can't speak very well. He's paralysed one side. He can hear fairly well. He listens to music. That's his whole life now.'

'His life's work's ended, you think?'

'He doesn't even see friends. I think it's painful to him to see them. He always makes some excuse.'

'But he's alive,' said Admiral Blunt. 'He's alive still. Got his address?'

'It's in my address book somewhere. He's still in the same place. North Scotland somewhere. But – oh, do understand – he was such a wonderful man once. He isn't now. He's just almost dead. For all intents and purposes.'

'There's always hope,' said Admiral Blunt. 'And belief,' he added. 'Faith.'

'And benevolence, I suppose,' said Lady Matilda.

CHAPTER 21

PROJECT BENVO

Professor John Gottlieb sat in his chair looking very steadfastly at the handsome young woman sitting opposite him. He scratched his ear with a rather monkey-like gesture which was characteristic of him. He looked rather like a monkey anyway. A prognathous jaw, a high mathematical head which made a slight contrast in terms, and a small wizened frame.

'It's not every day,' said Professor Gottlieb, 'that a young lady brings me a letter from the President of the United States. However,' he said cheerfully, 'Presidents don't always know exactly what they're doing. What's this all about? I gather you're vouched for on the highest authority.'

'I've come to ask you what you know or what you can tell me about something called Project Benvo.'

'Are you really Countess Renata Zerkowski?'

'Technically, possibly, I am. I'm more often known as Mary Ann.'

'Yes, that's what they wrote me under separate cover. And you want to know about Project Benvo. Well, there was such a thing. Now it's dead and buried and the man who thought of it also, I expect.'

'You mean Professor Shoreham.'

'That's right. Robert Shoreham. One of the greatest geniuses of our age. Einstein, Niels Bohr and some others. But Robert Shoreham didn't last as long as he should. A great loss to science – what is it Shakespeare says of Lady Macbeth: "*She should have died hereafter.*"'

'He's not dead,' said Mary Ann.

'Oh. Sure of that? Nothing's been heard of him for a long time.'

'He's an invalid. He lives in the north of Scotland. He is paralysed, can't speak very well, can't walk very well. He sits most of the time listening to music.'

'Yes, I can imagine that. Well, I'm glad about that. If he can do that he won't be too unhappy. Otherwise it's a pretty fair hell for a brilliant man who isn't brilliant any more. Who's, as it were, dead in an invalid chair.'

'There *was* such a thing as Project Benvo?'

'Yes, he was very keen about it.'

'He talked to you about it?'

'He talked to some of us about it in the early days. You're not a scientist yourself, young woman, I suppose?'

'No, I'm –'

'You're just an agent, I suppose. I hope you're on the right side. We still have to hope for miracles these days, but I don't think you'll get anything out of Project Benvo.'

'Why not? You said he worked on it. It would have been a very great invention, wouldn't it? Or discovery, or whatever you call these things?'

'Yes, it would have been one of the greatest discoveries of the age. I don't know just what went wrong. It's happened before now. A thing goes along all right but in the last stages somehow, it doesn't click. Breaks down. Doesn't do what's expected of it and you give up in despair. Or else you do what Shoreham did.'

'What was that?'

'He destroyed it. Every damn bit of it. He told me so himself. Burnt all the formulas, all the papers concerning it, all the data. Three weeks later he had his stroke. I'm sorry. You see, I can't help you. I never knew any details about it, nothing but its main idea. I don't even remember that now, except for one thing. Benvo stood for Benevolence.'

CHAPTER 22
JUANITA

Lord Altamount was dictating.

The voice that had once been ringing and dominant was now reduced to a gentleness that had still an unexpectedly special appeal. It seemed to come gently out of the shadows of the past, but to be emotionally moving in a way that a more dominant tone would not have been.

James Kleek was taking down the words as they came, pausing every now and then when a moment of hesitation came, allowing for it and waiting gently himself.

'Idealism,' said Lord Altamount, 'can arise and indeed usually does so when moved by a natural antagonism to injustice. That is a natural revulsion from crass materialism. The natural idealism of youth is fed more and more by a desire to destroy those two phases of modern life, injustice and crass materialism. That desire to destroy what is evil, sometimes leads to a love of destruction for its own sake. It can lead to a pleasure in violence and in the infliction of pain. All this can be fostered and strengthened from outside by those who are gifted by a natural power of leadership. This original idealism arises in a non-adult stage. It should and could lead on to a desire for a new world. It should lead also towards a love of all human beings, and of goodwill towards them. But those who have once learnt to love violence for its own sake will never become adult. They will be fixed in their own retarded development and will so remain for their lifetime.'

The buzzer went. Lord Altamount gestured and James Kleek lifted it up and listened.

'Mr Robinson is here.'

'Ah yes. Bring him in. We can go on with this later.'

James Kleek rose, laying aside his notebook and pencil.

Mr Robinson came in. James Kleek set a chair for him, one sufficiently widely proportioned to receive his form without discomfort. Mr Robinson smiled his thanks and arranged himself by Lord Altamount's side.

'Well,' said Lord Altamount. 'Got anything new for us? Diagrams? Circles? Bubbles?'

He seemed faintly amused.

'Not exactly,' said Mr Robinson imperturbably, 'it's more like plotting the course of a river –'

'River?' said Lord Altamount. 'What sort of a river?'

'A river of money,' said Mr Robinson, in the slightly apologetic voice he was wont to use when referring to his speciality. 'It's really just like a river, money is – coming from somewhere and definitely going to somewhere. Really very interesting – that is, if you are interested in these things – It tells its own story, you see –'

James Kleek looked as though he didn't see, but Altamount said, 'I understand. Go on.'

'It's flowing from Scandinavia – from Bavaria – from the USA – from South-east Asia – fed by lesser tributaries on the way –'

'And going – where?'

'Mainly to South America – meeting the demands of the now securely established Headquarters of Militant Youth –'

'And representing four of the five intertwined Circles you showed us – Armaments, Drugs, Scientific and Chemical Warfare Missiles as well as Finance?'

'Yes – we think we know now fairly accurately who controls these various groups –'

'What about Circle J – Juanita?' asked James Kleek.

'As yet we cannot be sure.'

'James has certain ideas as to that,' said Lord Altamount. 'I hope he may be wrong – yes, I hope so. The initial J is interesting. What does it stand for – Justice? Judgment?'

'A dedicated killer,' said James Kleek. 'The female of the species is more deadly than the male.'

'There are historical precedents,' admitted Altamount. 'Jael setting butter in a lordly dish before Sisera – and afterwards driving the nail through his head. Judith executing Holofernes, and applauded for it by her countrymen. Yes, you may have something there.'

'So you think you know who Juanita is, do you?' said Mr Robinson. 'That's interesting.'

'Well, perhaps I'm wrong, sir, but there have been things that made me think –'

'Yes,' said Mr Robinson, 'we have all had to think, haven't we? Better say who you think it is, James.'

'The Countess Renata Zerkowski.'

'What makes you pitch upon her?'

'The places she's been, the people she's been in contact with. There's been too much coincidence about the way she has been turning up in different places, and all that. She's been in Bavaria. She's been visiting Big Charlotte there. What's more, she took Stafford Nye with her. I think that's significant –'

'You think they're in this together?' asked Altamount.

'I wouldn't like to say that. I don't know enough about him, but . . .' He paused.

'Yes,' said Lord Altamount, 'there have been doubts about him. He was suspected from the beginning.'

'By Henry Horsham?'

'Henry Horsham for one, perhaps. Colonel Pikeaway isn't sure, I imagine. He's been under observation. Probably knows it too. He's not a fool.'

'Another of them,' said James Kleek savagely. 'Extraordinary, how we can breed them, how we trust them, tell 'em our secrets, let them know what we're doing, go on saying: "If there's one person I'm absolutely sure of it's – oh, McLean, or Burgess, or Philby, or any of the lot." And now – Stafford Nye.'

'Stafford Nye, indoctrinated by Renata alias Juanita,' said Mr Robinson.

'There was that curious business at Frankfurt airport,' said Kleek, 'and there was the visit to Charlotte. Stafford Nye, I gather, has since been in South America with her. As for she herself – do we know where she is now?'

'I dare say Mr Robinson does,' said Lord Altamount. 'Do you, Mr Robinson?'

'She's in the United States. I've heard that after staying with friends in Washington or near it, she was in Chicago, then in California and that she went from Austin to visit a top-flight scientist. That's the last I've heard.'

'What's she doing there?'

'One would presume,' said Mr Robinson, in his calm voice, 'that she is trying to obtain information.'

'What information?'

Mr Robinson sighed.

'That is what one wishes one knew. One presumes that it is the same information that *we* are anxious to obtain and that she is doing it on our behalf. But one never knows – it may be for the other side.'

He turned to look at Lord Altamount.

'Tonight, I understand, you are travelling to Scotland. Is that right?'

'Quite right.'

'I don't think he ought to, sir,' said James Kleek. He turned an anxious face to his employer. 'You've not been so well lately, sir. It'll be a very tiring journey whichever way you go. Air or train. Can't you leave it to Munro and Horsham?'

'At my age it's a waste of time to take care,' said Lord Altamount. 'If I can be useful I would like to die in harness, as the saying goes.'

He smiled at Mr Robinson.

'You'd better come with us, Robinson.'

CHAPTER 23

JOURNEY TO SCOTLAND

I

The Squadron Leader wondered a little what it was all about. He was accustomed to being left only partly in the picture. That was Security's doing, he supposed. Taking no chances. He'd done this sort of thing before more than once. Flying a plane of people out to an unlikely spot, with unlikely passengers, being careful to ask no questions except such as were of an entirely factual nature. He knew some of his passengers on this flight but not all of them. Lord Altamount he recognized. An ill man, a very sick man, he thought, a man who, he judged, kept himself alive by sheer willpower. The keen hawk-faced man with him was his special guard dog, presumably. Seeing not so much to his safety as to his welfare. A faithful dog who never left his side. He would have with him restoratives, stimulants, all the medical box of tricks. The Squadron Leader wondered why there wasn't a doctor also in attendance. It would have been an extra precaution. Like a death's head, the old man looked. A noble death's head. Something made of marble in a museum. Henry Horsham the Squadron Leader knew quite well. He knew several of the Security lot. And Colonel Munro, looking slightly less fierce than usual, rather more worried. Not very happy on the whole. There was also a large, yellow-faced man. Foreigner, he might be. Asiatic? What was he doing, flying in a plane to the North of Scotland? The Squadron Leader said deferentially to Colonel Munro:

'Everything laid on, sir? The car is here waiting.'

'How far exactly is the distance?'

'Seventeen miles, sir, roughish road but not too bad. There are extra rugs in the car.'

'You have your orders? Repeat, please, if you will, Squadron Leader Andrews.'

The Squadron Leader repeated and the Colonel nodded satisfaction. As the car finally drove off, the Squadron Leader looked after it, wondering to himself why on earth those particular people were here on this drive over the lonely moor to a venerable old castle where a sick man lived as a recluse without friends or visitors in the general run of things. Horsham knew, he supposed. Horsham must know a lot of strange things. Oh well, Horsham wasn't likely to tell him anything.

The car was well and carefully driven. It drew up at last over a gravel driveway and came to a stop before the porch. It was a turreted building of heavy stone. Lights hung at either side of the big door. The door itself opened before there was any need to ring a bell or demand admittance.

An old Scottish woman of sixty-odd with a stern, dour face, stood in the doorway. The chauffeur helped the occupants out.

James Kleek and Horsham helped Lord Altamount to alight and supported him up the steps. The old Scottish woman stood aside and dropped a respectful curtsy to him. She said:

'Good evening, y'r lordship. The master's waiting for you. He knows you're arriving, we've got rooms prepared and fires for you in all of them.'

Another figure had arrived in the hall now. A tall lean woman between fifty and sixty, a woman who was still handsome. Her black hair was parted in the middle, she had a high forehead, an aquiline nose and a tanned skin.

'Here's Miss Neumann to look after you,' said the Scottish woman.

'Thank you, Janet,' said Miss Neumann. 'Be sure the fires are kept up in the bedrooms.'

'I will that.'

Lord Altamount shook hands with her.

'Good evening, Miss Neumann.'

'Good evening, Lord Altamount. I hope you are not too tired by your journey.'

'We had a very good flight. This is Colonel Munro, Miss Neumann. This is Mr Robinson, Sir James Kleek and Mr Horsham, of the Security Department.'

'I remember Mr Horsham from some years ago, I think.'

'I hadn't forgotten,' said Henry Horsham. 'It was at the Leveson Foundation. You were already, I think, Professor Shoreham's secretary at that time?'

'I was first his assistant in the laboratory, and afterwards his secretary. I am still, as far as he needs one, his secretary. He also has to have a hospital nurse living here more or less permanently. There have to be changes from time to time – Miss Ellis who is here now took over from Miss Bude only two days ago. I have suggested that she should stay near at hand to the room in which we ourselves shall be. I thought you would prefer privacy, but that she ought not to be out of call in case she was needed.'

'Is he in very bad health?' asked Colonel Munro.

'He doesn't actually suffer,' said Miss Neumann, 'but you must prepare yourself, if you have not seen him, that is, for a long time. He is only what is left of a man.'

'Just one moment before you take us to him. His mental processes are not too badly depleted? He can understand what one says to him?'

'Oh, yes, he can understand perfectly, but as he is semi-paralysed, he is unable to speak with much clarity, though that varies, and is unable to walk without help. His brain, in my opinion, is as good as ever it was. The only difference is that he tires very easily now. Now, would you like some refreshment first?'

'No,' said Lord Altamount. 'No, I don't want to wait. This is a rather urgent matter on which we have come, so if you will take us to him now – he expects us, I understand?'

'He expects you, yes,' said Lisa Neumann.

She led the way up some stairs, along a corridor and opened a room of medium size. It had tapestries on the wall, the heads of stags looked down on them, the place had been a one-time shooting-box. It had been little changed in its furnishing or arrangements. There was a big record-player on one side of the room.

The tall man sat in a chair by the fire. His head trembled a little, so did his left hand. The skin of his face was pulled down one side. Without beating about the bush, one could only describe him one way, as a wreck of a man. A man who had once been tall, sturdy, strong. He had a fine forehead, deep-set eyes, and a rugged, determined-looking chin. The eyes, below the heavy eyebrows, were intelligent. He said something. His voice was not weak, it made fairly clear sounds but not always recognizable ones. The faculty of speech had only partly gone from him, he was still understandable.

Lisa Neumann went to stand by him, watching his lips, so that she could interpret what he said if necessary.

'Professor Shoreham welcomes you. He is very pleased to see you here, Lord Altamount, Colonel Munro, Sir James Kleek, Mr Robinson and Mr Horsham. He would like me to tell you that his hearing is reasonably good. Anything you say to him he will be able to hear. If there is any difficulty I can assist. What he wants to say to you he will be able to transmit through me. If he gets too tired to articulate, I can lip-read and we also converse in a perfected sign language if there is any difficulty.'

'I shall try,' said Colonel Munro, 'not to waste your time and to tire you as little as possible, Professor Shoreham.'

The man in the chair bent his head in recognition of the words.

'Some questions I can ask of Miss Neumann.'

Shoreham's hand went out in a faint gesture towards the woman standing by his side. Sounds came from his lips, again not quite recognizable to them, but she translated quickly.

'He says he can depend on me to transcribe anything you wish to say to him or I to you.'

'You have, I think, already received a letter from me,' said Colonel Munro.

'That is so,' said Miss Neumann. 'Professor Shoreham received your letter and knows its contents.'

A hospital nurse opened the door just a crack – but she did not come in. She spoke in a low whisper:

'Is there anything I can get or do, Miss Neumann? For any of the guests or for Professor Shoreham?'

'I don't think there is anything, thank you, Miss Ellis. I should be glad, though, if you could stay in your sitting-room just along the passage, in case we should need anything.'

'Certainly – I quite understand.' She went away, closing the door softly.

'We don't want to lose time,' said Colonel Munro. 'No doubt Professor Shoreham is in tune with current affairs.'

'Entirely so,' said Miss Neumann, 'as far as he is interested.'

'Does he keep in touch with scientific advancements and such things?'

Robert Shoreham's head shook slightly from side to side. He himself answered.

'I have finished with all that.'

'But you know roughly the state the world is in? The success of what is called the Revolution of Youth. The seizing of power by youthful fully-equipped forces.'

Miss Neumann said, 'He is in touch entirely with everything that is going on – in a political sense, that is.'

'The world is now given over to violence, pain, revolutionary tenets, a strange and incredible philosophy of rule by an anarchic minority.'

A faint look of impatience went across the gaunt face.

'He knows all that,' said Mr Robinson, speaking unexpectedly. 'No need to go over a lot of things again. He's a man who knows everything.'

He said:

'Do you remember Admiral Blunt?'

Again the head bowed. Something like a smile showed on the twisted lips.

'Admiral Blunt remembers some scientific work you had done on a certain project – I think project is what you call these things? Project Benvo.'

They saw the alert look which came into the eyes.

'Project Benvo,' said Miss Neumann. 'You are going back quite a long time, Mr Robinson, to recall that.'

'It was *your* project, wasn't it?' said Mr Robinson.

'Yes, it was his project.' Miss Neumann now spoke more easily for him, as a matter of course.

'We cannot use nuclear weapons, we cannot use explosives or gas or chemistry, but *your* project, Project Benvo, we *could* use.'

There was silence and nobody spoke. And then again the queer distorted sounds came from Professor Shoreham's lips.

'He says, of course,' said Miss Neumann, 'Benvo *could* be used successfully in the circumstances in which we find ourselves –'

The man in the chair had turned to her and was saying something to her.

'He wants me to explain it to you,' said Miss Neumann. 'Project B, later called Project Benvo, was something that he worked upon for many years but which at last he laid aside for reasons of his own.'

'Because he had failed to make his project materialize?'

'No, he had not failed,' said Lisa Neumann. 'We had not failed. I worked with him on this project. He laid it aside for certain reasons, but he did not fail. He succeeded. He was on the right track, he developed it, he tested it in various laboratory experiments, and it worked.' She turned to Professor Shoreham again, made a few gestures with her hand, touching her lips, ear, mouth in a strange kind of code signal.

'I am asking if he wants me to explain just what Benvo does.'

'We do want you to explain.'

'And he wants to know how you learnt about it.'

'We learnt about it,' said Colonel Munro, 'through an old friend of yours, Professor Shoreham. Not Admiral Blunt, he could not remember very much, but the other person to whom you had once spoken about it, Lady Matilda Cleckheaton.'

Again Miss Neumann turned to him and watched his lips. She smiled faintly.

'He says he thought Matilda was dead years ago.'

'She is very much alive. It is she who wanted us to know about this discovery of Professor Shoreham's.'

'Professor Shoreham will tell you the main points of what you want to know, though he has to warn you that this knowledge will be quite useless to you. Papers, formulae, accounts and proofs of this discovery were all destroyed. But since the only way to satisfy your questions is for you to learn the main outline of Project Benvo, I can tell you fairly clearly of what it consists. You know the uses and purpose of tear gas as used by the police in controlling riot crowds; violent demonstrations and so on. It induces a fit of weeping, painful tears and sinus inflammation.'

'And this is something of the same kind?'

'No, it is not in the least of the same kind but it can have the same purpose. It came into the heads of scientists that one can change not only men's principal reactions and feeling, but also mental characteristics. You can change a man's character. The qualities of an aphrodisiac are well known. They lead to a condition of sexual desire, there are various drugs or gases or glandular operations – any of these things can lead to a change in your mental vigour, increased energy as by alterations to the thyroid gland, and Professor Shoreham wishes to tell you that there is a certain process – he will not tell you now whether it is glandular, or a gas that can be manufactured, but there is something that can change a man in his outlook on life – his reaction to people and to life generally. He may be in a state of homicidal fury, he may be pathologically violent, and yet, by the influence of Project Benvo, he turns into something, or rather *someone*, quite different. He becomes – there is only one word for it, I believe, which is embodied in its name – he becomes *benevolent*. He wishes to benefit others. He exudes kindness. He has a horror of causing pain or inflicting violence. Benvo can be released over a big area, it can affect hundreds, thousands of people if manufactured in big enough quantities, and if distributed successfully.'

'How long does it last?' said Colonel Munro. 'Twenty-four hours? Longer?'

'You don't understand,' said Miss Neumann. 'It is *permanent*.'

'Permanent? You've changed a man's nature, you've altered a component, a physical component, of course, of his being which has produced the effect of a permanent change in his nature. And you cannot go back on that? You cannot put him back to where he was again. It has to be accepted as a permanent change?'

'Yes. It was, perhaps, a discovery more of medical interest at first, but Professor Shoreham had conceived of it as a deterrent to be used in war, in mass risings, riotings, revolutions, anarchy. He didn't think of it as merely medical. It does not produce happiness in the subject, only a great wish for others to be happy. That is an effect, he says, that everyone feels in their life at one time or another. They have a great wish to make someone, one person or many people – to make them comfortable, happy, in good health, all these things. And since people can and do feel these things, there is, we both believed, a component that controls that desire in their bodies, and if you once put that component in operation it can go on in perpetuity.'

'Wonderful,' said Mr Robinson.

He spoke thoughtfully rather than enthusiastically.

'Wonderful. What a thing to have discovered. What a thing to be able to put into action if – but why?'

The head resting towards the back of the chair turned slowly towards Mr Robinson. Miss Neumann said:

'He says you understand better than the others.'

'But it's the answer,' said James Kleek. 'It's the *exact* answer! It's wonderful.' His face was enthusiastically excited.

Miss Neumann was shaking her head.

'Project Benvo,' she said, 'is not for sale and not for a gift. It has been relinquished.'

'Are you telling us the answer is no?' said Colonel Munro incredulously.

'Yes. Professor Shoreham says the answer is no. He decided that it was against –' she paused a minute and turned to look at the man in the chair. He made quaint gestures with his head, with one hand, and a few guttural sounds came from his mouth. She waited and then she said, 'He will tell you himself, he was afraid. Afraid of what science has done in its time of triumph. The things it has found out and known, the things it has discovered and given to the world. The wonder drugs that have not always been wonder drugs, the penicillin that has saved lives and the penicillin that has taken lives, the heart transplants that have brought disillusion and the disappointment of a death not expected. He has lived in the period of nuclear fission; new weapons that have slain. The tragedies of radio-activity; the pollutions that new industrial discoveries have brought about. He has been afraid of what science could do, used indiscriminately.'

'But this is a benefit. A benefit to everyone,' cried Munro.

'So have many things been. Always greeted as great benefits to humanity, as great wonders. And then come the side effects, and worse than that, the fact that they have sometimes brought not benefit but disaster. And so he decided that he would give up. He says' – she read from a paper she held, whilst beside her he nodded agreement from his chair –

> '"I am satisfied that I have done what I set out to do, that I made my discovery. But I decided not to put it into circulation. It must be destroyed. And so it has been destroyed. And so the answer to you is no. There is no benevolence on tap. There could have been once, but now all the formulae, all the know-how, my notes and my account of the necessary procedure are gone – burnt to ashes – I have destroyed my brain child."'

II

Robert Shoreham struggled into raucous difficult speech.

'I have destroyed my brain child and nobody in the world knows how I arrived at it. One man helped me but he is dead. He died of tuberculosis a year after we had come to success. You must go away again. I cannot help you.'

'But this knowledge of yours means you could save the world!'

The man in the chair made a curious noise. It was laughter. Laughter of a crippled man.

'Save the world. Save the world! What a phrase! That's what your young people are doing, they think! They're going ahead in violence and hatred to save the world. But they don't know how! They will have to do it *themselves*, out of their own hearts, out of their own minds. We can't give them an artificial way of doing it. No. An artificial goodness? An artificial kindness? None of that. It wouldn't be *real*. It wouldn't *mean* anything. It would be against Nature.' He said slowly: '*Against God*.'

The last two words came out unexpectedly, clearly enunciated.

He looked round at his listeners. It was as though he pleaded with them for understanding, yet at the same time had no real hope of it.

'I had a right to destroy what I had created –'

'I doubt it very much,' said Mr Robinson, 'knowledge is knowledge. What you have given birth to – what you have made come to life, you should not destroy.'

'You have a right to your opinion – but the fact you will have to accept.'

'No,' Mr Robinson brought the word out with force.

Lisa Neumann turned on him angrily.

'What do you mean by "No"?'

Her eyes were flashing. A handsome woman, Mr Robinson thought. A woman who had been in love with Robert Shoreham all her life probably. Had loved him, worked with him, and now lived beside him, ministering to him with her intellect, giving him devotion in its purest form without pity.

'There are things one gets to know in the course of one's lifetime,' said Mr Robinson. 'I don't suppose mine will be a long life. I carry too much weight to begin with.' He sighed as he looked down at his bulk. 'But I do know some things. I'm right, you know, Shoreham. You'll have to admit I'm right, too. You're an honest man. You wouldn't have destroyed your work. You couldn't have brought yourself to do it. You've got it somewhere still, locked away, hidden away, not in this house, probably. I'd guess, and I'm only making a guess, that you've got it somewhere in a safe deposit or a bank. She knows you've got it there, too. You trust her. She's the only person in the world you do trust.'

Shoreham said, and this time his voice was almost distinct:

'Who are *you*? Who the devil are you?'

'I'm just a man who knows about money,' said Mr Robinson, 'and the things that branch off from money, you know. People and their idiosyncrasies and their practices in life. If you liked to, you could lay your hand on the work that you've put away. I'm not saying that you could do the same work now, but I think it's all there somewhere. You've told us your views, and I wouldn't say they were all wrong,' said Mr Robinson.

'Possibly you're right. Benefits to humanity are tricky things to deal with. Poor old Beveridge, freedom from want, freedom from fear, freedom from whatever it was, he thought he was making a heaven on earth by saying that and planning for it and getting it done. But it hasn't made heaven on earth and I don't suppose your benvo or whatever you call it (sounds like a patent food) will bring heaven on earth either. Benevolence has its dangers just like everything else. What it will do is save a lot of suffering, pain, anarchy, violence, slavery to drugs. Yes, it'll save quite a lot of bad things from happening, and it *might* save something that was important. It might – just *might* – make a difference to people. Young people. This Benvoleo of yours – now I've made it sound like a patent cleaner – is going to make people benevolent and I'll admit perhaps that it's going to make them condescending, smug and pleased with themselves, but there's just a chance, too, that if you change people's natures by force and they have to go on using that particular kind of nature until they die, one or two of them – not many – might discover that they had a natural vocation, in humility, not pride, for what they were being forced to do. *Really* change themselves, I mean, before they died. Not be able to get out of a new habit they'd learnt.'

Colonel Munro said, 'I don't understand what the hell you're all talking about.'

Miss Neumann said, 'He's talking nonsense. You have to take Professor Shoreham's answer. He will do what he likes with his own discoveries. You can't coerce him.'

'No,' said Lord Altamount. 'We're not going to coerce you or torture you, Robert, or force you to reveal your hiding-places. You'll do what you think right. That's agreed.'

'Edward?' said Robert Shoreham. His speech failed him slightly again, his hands moved in gesture, and Miss Neumann translated quickly.

'Edward? He says you are Edward Altamount?'

Shoreham spoke again and she took the words from him.

'He asks you, Lord Altamount, if you are definitely, with your whole heart and mind, asking him to put Project Benvo in your jurisdiction. He says –' she paused, watching, listening – 'he says you are the only man in public life that he ever trusted. If it is *your* wish –'

James Kleek was suddenly on his feet. Anxious, quick to move like lightning, he stood by Lord Altamount's chair.

'Let me help you up, sir. You're ill. You're not well. Please stand back a little, Miss Neumann. I – I must get to him. I – I have his remedies here. I know what to do –'

His hand went into his pocket and came out again with a hypodermic syringe.

'Unless he gets this at once it'll be too late–' He had caught up Lord Altamount's arm, rolling up his sleeve, pinching the flesh between his fingers, he held the hypodermic ready.

But someone else moved. Horsham was across the room, pushing Colonel Munro aside: his hand closed over James Kleek's as he wrenched the hypodermic away. Kleek struggled but Horsham was too strong for him. And Munro was now there, too.

'So it's been *you*, James Kleek,' he said. 'You who've been the traitor, a faithful disciple who wasn't a faithful disciple.'

Miss Neumann had gone to the door – had flung it open and was calling.

'Nurse! Come quickly. Come.'

The nurse appeared. She gave one quick glance to Professor Shoreham, but he waved her away and pointed across the room to where Horsham and Munro still held a struggling Kleek. Her hand went into the pocket of her uniform.

Shoreham stammered out, 'It's Altamount. A heart attack.'

'Heart attack, my foot,' roared Munro. 'It's attempted murder.' He stopped.

'Hold the chap,' he said to Horsham, and leapt across the room.

'Mrs Cortman? Since when have you entered the nursing profession? We'd rather lost sight of you since you gave us the slip in Baltimore.'

Milly Jean was still wrestling with her pocket. Now her hand came out with the small automatic in it. She glanced towards Shoreham but Munro blocked her, and Lisa Neumann was standing in front of Shoreham's chair.

James Kleek yelled, 'Get Altamount, Juanita – quick – get Altamount.'

Her arm flashed up and she fired.

James Kleek said,

'Damned good shot!'

Lord Altamount had had a classical education. He murmured faintly, looking at James Kleek,

'Jamie? *Et tu Brute?*' and collapsed against the back of his chair.

III

Dr McCulloch looked round him, a little uncertain of what he was going to do or say next. The evening had been a somewhat unusual experience for him.

Lisa Neumann came to him and set a glass by his side.

'A hot toddy,' she said.

'I always knew you were a woman in a thousand, Lisa.' He sipped appreciatively.

'I must say I'd like to know what all this has been about – but I gather it's the sort of thing that's so hush-hush that nobody's going to tell me anything.'

'The Professor – he's all right, isn't he?'

'The Professor?' He looked at her anxious face, kindly. 'He's fine. If you ask me, it's done him a world of good.'

'I thought perhaps the shock –'

'I'm quite all right,' said Shoreham. 'Shock treatment is what I needed. I feel – how shall I put it – *alive* again.' He looked surprised.

McCulloch said to Lisa, 'Notice how much stronger his voice is? It's apathy really that's the enemy in these cases – what *he* wants is to work again – the stimulation of some brain work. Music is all very well – it's kept him soothed and able to enjoy life in a mild way. But he's really a man of great intellectual power – and he misses the mental activity that was the essence of life to him. Get him started on it again if you can.'

He nodded encouragingly at her as she looked doubtfully at him.

'I think, Dr McCulloch,' said Colonel Munro, 'that we owe you a few explanations of what happened this evening, even though, as you surmise, the powers-that-be will demand a hush-hush policy. Lord Altamount's death –' He hesitated.

'The bullet didn't actually kill him,' said the doctor, 'death was due to shock. That hypodermic would have done the trick – strychnine. The young man –'

'I only just got it away from him in time,' said Horsham.

'Been the fly in the ointment all along?' asked the doctor.

'Yes – regarded with trust and affection for over seven years. The son of one of Lord Altamount's oldest friends –'

'It happens. And the lady – in it together, do I understand?'

'Yes. She got the post here by false credentials. She is also wanted by the police for murder.'

'Murder?'

'Yes. Murder of her husband, Sam Cortman, the American Ambassador. She shot him on the steps of the Embassy – and told a fine tale of young men, masked, attacking him.'

'Why did she have it in for him? Political or personal?'

'He found out about some of her activities, we think.'

'I'd say he suspected infidelity,' said Horsham. 'instead he discovered a hornets' nest of espionage and conspiracy, and his wife running the show. He didn't know quite how to deal with it. Nice chap, but slow-thinking – and she had the sense to act quickly. Wonderful how she registered grief at the Memorial Service.'

'Memorial –' said Professor Shoreham.

Everyone, slightly startled, turned round to look at him.

'Difficult word to say, memorial – but I mean it. Lisa, you and I are going to have to start work again.'

'But, Robert –'

'I'm alive again. Ask the doctor if I ought to take things easy.'

Lisa turned her eyes inquiringly on McCulloch.

'If you do, you'll shorten your life and sink back into apathy –'

'There you are,' said Shoreham. 'Fash-fashion – medical fashion today. Make everyone, even if they're – at – death's door – go on working –'

Dr McCulloch laughed and got up.

'Not far wrong. I'll send you some pills along to help.'

'I shan't take them.'

'You'll do.'

At the door the doctor paused. 'Just want to know – how did you get the police along so quickly?'

'Squadron Leader Andrews,' said Munro, 'had it all in hand. Arrived on the dot. We knew the woman was around somewhere, but had no idea she was in the house already.'

'Well – I'll be off. Is all you've told me true? Feel I shall wake up any minute, having dropped off to sleep half way through the latest thriller. Spies, murders, traitors, espionage, scientists –'

He went out.

There was a silence.

Professor Shoreham said slowly and carefully:

'Back to work –'

Lisa said as women have always said:

'You must be *careful*, Robert –'

'Not – not careful. Time might be short.'

He said again:

'Memorial –'

'What *do* you mean? You said it before.'

'Memorial? Yes. To Edward. His Memorial! Always used to think he had the face of a martyr.'

Shoreham seemed lost in thought.

'I'd like to get hold of Gottlieb. May be dead. Good man to work with. With him and with you, Lisa – get the stuff out of the bank –'

'Professor Gottlieb is alive – in the Baker Foundation, Austin, Texas,' said Mr Robinson.

'What are you talking of doing?' said Lisa.

'Benvo, of course! Memorial to Edward Altamount. He died for it, didn't he? Nobody should die in vain.'

EPILOGUE
··

Sir Stafford Nye wrote out a telegraph message for the third time.

ZP 354XB 91 DEP S.Y.

HAVE ARRANGED FOR MARRIAGE CEREMONY TO BE PERFORMED ON THURSDAY OF NEXT WEEK AT ST CHRISTOPHERS IN THE VALE LOWER STAUNTON 2.30 PM STOP ORDINARY CHURCH OF ENGLAND SERVICE IF R.C. OR GREEK ORTHODOX DESIRED PLEASE WIRE INSTRUCTIONS STOP WHERE ARE YOU AND WHAT NAME DO YOU WISH TO USE FOR MARRIAGE CEREMONY STOP NAUGHTY NIECE OF MINE FIVE YEARS OLD AND HIGHLY DISOBEDIENT WISHES TO ATTEND AS BRIDESMAID RATHER SWEET REALLY NAME OF SYBIL STOP LOCAL HONEYMOON AS I THINK WE HAVE TRAVELLED ENOUGH LATELY STOP SIGNED PASSENGER TO FRANKFURT.

TO STAFFORD NYE BXY42698

ACCEPT SYBIL AS BRIDESMAID SUGGEST GREAT AUNT MATILDA AS MATRON OF HONOUR STOP ALSO ACCEPT PROPOSAL OF MARRIAGE THOUGH NOT OFFICIALLY MADE STOP C OF E QUITE SATISFACTORY ALSO HONEYMOON ARRANGEMENTS STOP INSIST PANDA SHOULD ALSO BE PRESENT STOP NO GOOD SAYING WHERE I AM AS I SHANT BE WHEN THIS REACHES YOU STOP SIGNED MARY ANN

'Do I look all right?' asked Stafford Nye nervously, twisting his head to look in the glass.

He was having a dress rehearsal of his wedding clothes.

'No worse than any other bridegroom,' said Lady Matilda. 'They're always nervous. Not like brides who are usually quite blatantly exultant.'

'Suppose she doesn't come?'

'She'll come.'

'I feel – I feel – rather queer inside.'

'That's because you would have a second helping of pâté de foie gras. You've just got bridegroom's nerves. Don't fuss so much, Staffy. You'll be all right on the night – I mean you'll be all right when you get to the church –'

'That reminds me –'

'You haven't forgotten to buy the ring?'

'No, no, it's just I forgot to tell you that I've got a present for you, Aunt Matilda.'

'That's very nice of you, dear boy.'

'You said the organist had gone –'

'Yes, thank goodness.'

'I've brought you a new organist.'

'Really, Staffy, what an extraordinary idea! Where did you get him?'

'Bavaria – he sings like an angel –'

'We don't need him to sing. He'll have to play the organ.'

'He can do that too – he's a very talented musician.'

'Why does he want to leave Bavaria and come to England?'

'His mother died.'

'Oh dear, that's what happened to our organist. Organists' mothers seem to be very delicate. Will he require mothering? I'm not very good at it.'

'I dare say some grandmothering or great-grandmothering would do.'

The door was suddenly flung open and an angelic-looking child in pink pyjamas, powdered with rosebuds, made a dramatic entrance – and said in dulcet tones as of one expecting a rapturous welcome –

'It's me.'

'Sybil, why aren't you in bed?'

'Things aren't very pleasant in the nursery –'

'That means you've been a naughty girl, and Nannie isn't pleased with you. What did you do?'

Sybil looked at the ceiling and began to giggle.

'It was a caterpillar – a furry one. I put it on her and it went down *here*.'

Sybil's finger indicated a spot in the middle of her chest which in dressmaking parlance is referred to as 'the cleavage'.

'I don't wonder Nannie was cross – ugh,' said Lady Matilda.

Nannie entered at this moment, said that Miss Sybil was over-excited, wouldn't say her prayers, and wouldn't go to bed.

Sybil crept to Lady Matilda's side.

'I want to say my prayers with you, Tilda –'

'Very well – but then you go straight to bed.'

'Oh yes, Tilda.'

Sybil dropped on her knees, clasped her hands, and uttered various peculiar noises which seemed to be a necessary preliminary to approaching the Almighty in prayer. She sighed, groaned, grunted, gave a final catarrhal snort, and launched herself:

'Please God bless Daddy and Mummy in Singapore, and Aunt Tilda, and Uncle Staffy, and Amy and Cook and Ellen, and Thomas, and all the dogs, and my Pony Grizzle, and Margaret and Diana my best friends, and Joan, the last of my friends, and make me a good girl for Jesus' sake, Amen. And please God make Nannie nice.'

Sybil rose to her feet, exchanged glances with Nannie with the assurance of having won a victory, said goodnight and disappeared.

'Someone must have told her about Benvo,' said Lady Matilda. 'By the way, Staffy, who's going to be your best man?'

'Forgot all about it – Have I got to have one?'

'It's usual.'

Sir Stafford Nye picked up a small furry animal.

'Panda shall be my best man – please Sybil – please Mary Ann – And why not? Panda's been in it from the beginning – ever since Frankfurt . . .'

POSTERN OF FATE

For Hannibal and his master

Four great gates has the city of Damascus . . .
Postern of Fate, the Desert Gate, Disaster's Cavern, Fort of
    Fear . . .
Pass not beneath, O Caravan, or pass not singing. Have
    you heard
That silence where the birds are dead, yet something pipeth
    like a bird?
from *Gates of Damascus* by James Elroy Flecker

BOOK I

....
MAINLY CONCERNING BOOKS

'Books!' said Tuppence.

She produced the word rather with the effect of a bad-tempered explosion.

'What did you say?' said Tommy.

Tuppence looked across the room at him.

'I said "books",' she said.

'I see what you mean,' said Thomas Beresford.

In front of Tuppence were three large packing cases. From each of them various books had been extracted. The larger part of them were still filled with books.

'It's incredible,' said Tuppence.

'You mean the room they take up?'

'Yes.'

'Are you trying to put them all on the shelves?'

'I don't know what I'm trying to do,' said Tuppence. 'That's the awkward part of it. One doesn't know ever, exactly, what one wants to do. Oh dear,' she sighed.

'Really,' said her husband, 'I should have thought that that was not at all characteristic of you. The trouble with you has always been that you knew much too well what you *do* want to do.'

'What I mean is,' said Tuppence, 'that here we are, getting older, getting a bit – well, let's face it – definitely rheumatic, especially when one is stretching; you know, stretching putting in books or lifting things down from shelves or kneeling down to look at the bottom shelves for something, then finding it a bit difficult to get up again.'

'Yes, yes,' said Tommy, 'that's an account of our general disabilities. Is that what you started to say?'

'No, it isn't what I started to say. What I started to say was, it was lovely to be able to buy a new home and find just the place we wanted to go and live in, and just the house there we'd always dreamt of having – with a little alteration, of course.'

'Knocking one or two rooms into each other,' said Tommy, 'and adding to it what you call a veranda and your builder calls a lodger, though I prefer to call it a loggia.'

'And it's going to be very nice,' said Tuppence firmly.

'When you've done it I shan't know it! Is that the answer?' said Tommy.

'Not at all. All I said was that when you see it finished you're going to be delighted and say what an ingenious and clever and artistic wife you have.'

'All right,' said Tommy. 'I'll remember the right thing to say.'

'You won't need to remember,' said Tuppence. 'It will burst upon you.'

'What's that got to do with books?' said Tommy.

'Well, we brought two or three cases of books with us. I mean, we sold off the books we didn't much care about. We brought the ones we really couldn't bear to part with, and then, of course, the what-you-call-'ems – I can't remember their name now, but the people who were selling us this house – they didn't want to take a lot of their own things with them, and they said if we'd like to make an offer they would leave things including books, and we came and looked at things –'

'And we made some offers,' said Tommy.

'Yes. Not as many as they hoped we would make, I expect. Some of the furniture and ornaments were too horrible. Well, fortunately we didn't have to take those, but when I came and saw the various books – there were some nursery ones, you know, some down in the sitting-room – and there are one or two old favourites. I mean, there still are. There are one or two of my own special favourites. And so I thought it'd be such fun to have them. You know, the story of Androcles and the Lion,' she said. 'I remember reading that when I was eight years old. Andrew Lang.'

'Tell me, Tuppence, were you clever enough to read at eight years old?'

'Yes,' said Tuppence, 'I read at five years old. Everybody

could, when I was young. I didn't know one even had to sort of learn. I mean, somebody would read stories aloud, and you liked them very much and you remembered where the book went back on the shelf and you were always allowed to take it out and have a look at it yourself, and so you found you were reading it too, without bothering to learn to spell or anything like that. It wasn't so good later,' she said, 'because I've never been able to spell very well. And if somebody had taught me to spell when I was about four years old I can see it would have been very good indeed. My father did teach me to do addition and subtraction and multiplication, of course, because he said the multiplication table was the most useful thing you could learn in life, and I learnt long division too.'

'What a clever man he must have been!'

'I don't think he was specially clever,' said Tuppence, 'but he was just very, very nice.'

'Aren't we getting away from the point?'

'Yes, we are,' said Tuppence. 'Well, as I said, when I thought of reading Androcles and the Lion again – it came in a book of stories about animals, I think, by Andrew Lang – oh, I loved that. And there was a story about "a day in my life at Eton" by an Eton schoolboy. I can't think why I wanted to read that, but I did. It was one of my favourite books. And there were some stories from the classics, and there was Mrs Molesworth, *The Cuckoo Clock, Four Winds Farm* –'

'Well, that's all right,' said Tommy. 'No need to give me a whole account of your literary triumphs in early youth.'

'What I mean is,' said Tuppence, 'that you can't get them nowadays. I mean, sometimes you get reprints of them, but they've usually been altered and have different pictures in them. Really, the other day I couldn't recognize *Alice in Wonderland* when I saw it. Everything looks so peculiar in it. There are the books I really could get still. Mrs Molesworth, one or two of the old fairy books – Pink, Blue and Yellow – and then, of course, lots of later ones which I'd enjoyed. Lots of Stanley Weymans and things like that. There are quite a lot here, left behind.'

'All right,' said Tommy. 'You were tempted. You felt it was a good buy.'

'Yes. At least – what d'you mean a "goodbye"?'

'I mean b-u-y,' said Tommy.

'Oh. I thought you were going to leave the room and were saying goodbye to me.'

'Not at all,' said Tommy, 'I was deeply interested. Anyway, it *was* a good b-u-y.'

'And I got them very cheap, as I tell you. And – and here they all are among our own books and others. Only, we've got such a terrible lot now of books, and the shelves we had made I don't think are going to be nearly enough. What about your special sanctum? Is there room there for more books?'

'No, there isn't,' said Tommy. 'There's not going to be enough for my own.'

'Oh dear, oh dear,' said Tuppence, 'that's so like us. Do you think we might have to build on an extra room?'

'No,' said Tommy, 'we're going to economize. We said so the day before yesterday. Do you remember?'

'That was the day before yesterday,' said Tuppence. 'Time alters. What I am going to do now is put in these shelves all the books I really can't bear to part with. And then – and then we can look at the others and – well, there might be a children's hospital somewhere and there might, anyway, be places which would like books.'

'Or we could sell them,' said Tommy.

'I don't suppose they're the sort of books people would want to buy very much. I don't think there are any books of rare value or anything like that.'

'You never know your luck,' said Tommy. 'Let's hope something out of print will fulfil some bookseller's long-felt want.'

'In the meantime,' said Tuppence, 'we have to put them into the shelves, and look inside them, of course, each time to see whether it's a book I do really want and I can really remember. I'm trying to get them roughly – well, you know what I mean, sort of sorted. I mean, adventure stories, fairy stories, children's stories and those stories about schools, where the children were always very rich – L. T. Meade, I think. And some of the books we used to read to Deborah when she was small, too. How we all used to love *Winnie the Pooh*. And there was *The Little Grey Hen* too, but I didn't care very much for that.'

'I think you're tiring yourself,' said Tommy. 'I think I should leave off what you're doing now.'

'Well, perhaps I will,' said Tuppence, 'but I think if I could just finish this side of the room, just get the books in here . . .'

'Well, I'll help you,' said Tommy.

He came over, tilted the case so that the books fell out, gathered up armfuls of them and went to the shelves and shoved them in.

'I'm putting the same sized ones together, it looks neater,' he said.

'Oh, I don't call that sorting,' said Tuppence.

'Sorting enough to get on with. We can do more of that later. You know, make everything really nice. We'll sort it on some wet day when we can't think of anything else to do.'

'The trouble is we always can think of something else to do.'

'Well now, there's another seven in there. Now then, there's only this top corner. Just bring me that wooden chair over there, will you? Are its legs strong enough for me to stand on it? Then I can put some on the top shelf.'

With some care he climbed on the chair. Tuppence lifted up to him an armful of books. He insinuated them with some care on to the top shelf. Disaster only happened with the last three which cascaded to the floor, narrowly missing Tuppence.

'Oh,' said Tuppence, 'that was painful.'

'Well, I can't help it. You handed me up too many at once.'

'Oh well, that does look wonderful,' said Tuppence, standing back a little. 'Now then, if you'll just put these in the second shelf from the bottom, there's a gap there, that will finish up this particular caseful anyway. It's a good thing too. These ones I'm doing this morning aren't really ours, they're the ones we bought. We may find treasures.'

'We may,' said Tommy.

'I think we shall find treasures. I think I really shall find something. Something that's worth a lot of money, perhaps.'

'What do we do then? Sell it?'

'I expect we'll have to sell it, yes,' said Tuppence. 'Of course we might just keep it and show it to people. You know, not exactly boasting, but just say, you know: "Oh yes, we've got really one or two interesting finds." I think we shall make an interesting find, too.'

'What – one old favourite you've forgotten about?'

'Not exactly that. I meant something startling, surprising. Something that'll make all the difference to our lives.'

'Oh Tuppence,' said Tommy, 'what a wonderful mind you've got. Much more likely to find something that's an absolute disaster.'

'Nonsense,' said Tuppence. 'One must have hope. It's the great thing you have to have in life. Hope. Remember? I'm always full of hope.'

'I know you are,' said Tommy. He sighed. 'I've often regretted it.'

CHAPTER 2

THE BLACK ARROW

Mrs Thomas Beresford replaced *The Cuckoo Clock*, by Mrs Molesworth, choosing a vacant place on the third shelf from the bottom. The Mrs Molesworths were congregated here together. Tuppence drew out *The Tapestry Room* and held it thoughtfully in her fingers. Or she might read *Four Winds Farm*. She couldn't remember *Four Winds Farm* as well as she could remember *The Cuckoo Clock* and *The Tapestry Room*. Her fingers wandered . . . Tommy would be back soon.

She was getting on. Yes, surely she was getting on. If only she didn't stop and pull out old favourites and read them. Very agreeable but it took a lot of time. And when Tommy asked her in the evening when he came home how things were going and she said, 'Oh very well now,' she had to employ a great deal of tact and finesse to prevent him from going upstairs and having a real look at how the bookshelves were progressing. It all took a long time. Getting into a house always took a long time, much longer than one thought. And so many irritating people. Electricians, for instance, who came and appeared to be displeased with what they had done the last time they came and took up more large areas in the floor and, with cheerful faces, produced more pitfalls for the unwary housewife to walk along and put a foot wrong and be rescued just in time by the unseen electrician who was groping beneath the floor.

'Sometimes,' said Tuppence, 'I really wish we hadn't left Bartons Acre.'

'Remember the dining-room,' Tommy had said, 'and remember those attics, and remember what happened to the garage. Nearly wrecked the car, you know it did.'

'I suppose we could have had it patched up,' said Tuppence.

'No,' said Tommy, 'we'd have had to practically replace the damaged building, or else we had to move. This is going to be a very nice house some day. I'm quite sure of that. Anyway, there's going to be room in it for all the things we want to do.'

'When you say the things we want to do,' Tuppence had said, 'you mean the things we want to find places for and to keep.'

'I know,' said Tommy. 'One keeps far too much. I couldn't agree with you more.'

At that moment Tuppence considered something – whether they ever were going to do anything with this house, that is to say, beyond getting into it. It sounded simple but had turned out complex. Partly, of course, all these books.

'If I'd been a nice ordinary child of nowadays,' said Tuppence, 'I wouldn't have learned to read so easily when I was young. Children nowadays who are four, or five, or six, don't seem to be able to read when they get to ten or eleven. I can't think why it was so easy for all of us. We could all read. Me and Martin next door and Jennifer down the road and Cyril and Winifred. All of us. I don't mean we could all spell very well but we could read anything we wanted to. I don't know how we learnt. Asking people, I suppose. Things about posters and Carter's Little Liver Pills. We used to read all about them in the fields when trains got near London. It was very exciting. I always wondered what they were. Oh dear, I must think of what I'm doing.'

She removed some more books. Three-quarters of an hour passed with her absorbed first in *Alice Through the Looking-Glass*, then with Charlotte Yonge's *Unknown to History*. Her hands lingered over the fat shabbiness of *The Daisy Chain*.

'Oh, I must read that again,' said Tuppence. 'To think of the years and years and years it is since I did read it. Oh dear, how exciting it was, wondering, you know, whether Norman was going

to be allowed to be confirmed or not. And Ethel and – what was
the name of the place? Coxwell or something like – and Flora
who was worldly. I wonder why everyone was "worldly" in those
days, and how poorly it was thought of, being worldly. I wonder
what we are now. Do you think we're all worldly or not?'

'I beg yer pardon, ma'am?'

'Oh nothing,' said Tuppence, looking round at her devoted
henchman, Albert, who had just appeared in the doorway.

'I thought you called for something, madam. And you rang
the bell, didn't you?'

'Not really,' said Tuppence. 'I just leant on it getting up on a
chair to take a book out.'

'Is there anything I can take down for you?'

'Well, I wish you would,' said Tuppence. 'I'm falling off those
chairs. Some of their legs are very wobbly, some of them rather
slippery.'

'Any book in particular?'

'Well, I haven't got on very far with the third shelf up. Two
shelves down from the top, you know. I don't know what books
are there.'

Albert mounted on a chair and banging each book in turn to
dislodge such dust as it had managed to gather on it, handed
things down. Tuppence received them with a good deal of
rapture.

'Oh, fancy! All these. I really have forgotten a lot of these.
Oh, here's *The Amulet* and here's *The Psamayad*. Here's *The
New Treasure Seekers*. Oh, I love all those. No, don't put them
in shelves yet, Albert. I think I'll have to have read them first. Well,
I mean, one or two of them first, perhaps. Now, what's this
one? Let me see. *The Red Cockade*. Oh yes, that was one of
the historical ones. That was very exciting. And there's *Under
the Red Robe*, too. Lots of Stanley Weyman. Lots and lots. Of
course I used to read those when I was about ten or eleven. I
shouldn't be surprised if I don't come across *The Prisoner of
Zenda*.' She sighed with enormous pleasure at the remembrance.
'*The Prisoner of Zenda*. One's first introduction, really, to the
romantic novel. The romance of Princess Flavia. The King of
Ruritania. Rudolph Rassendyll, some name like that, whom one
dreamt of at night.'

Albert handed down another selection.

'Oh yes,' said Tuppence, 'That's better, really. That's earlier again. I must put the early ones all together. Now, let me see. What have we got here? *Treasure Island*. Well, that's nice but of course I have read *Treasure Island* again, and I've seen, I think, two films of it. I don't like seeing it on films, it never seems right. Oh – and here's *Kidnapped*. Yes, I always liked that.'

Albert stretched up, overdid his armful, and *Catriona* fell more or less on Tuppence's head.

'Oh, sorry, madam. Very sorry.'

'It's quite all right,' said Tuppence, 'it doesn't matter. *Catriona*. Yes. Any more Stevensons up there?'

Albert handed the books down now more gingerly. Tuppence uttered a cry of excessive delight.

'*The Black Arrow* I declare! *The Black Arrow*! Now that's one of the first books really I ever got hold of and read. Yes. I don't suppose you ever did, Albert. I mean, you wouldn't have been born, would you? Now let me think. Let me think. *The Black Arrow*. Yes, of course, it was that picture on the wall with eyes – real eyes – looking through the eyes of the picture. It was splendid. So frightening, just that. Oh yes. *The Black Arrow*. What was it? It was all about – oh yes, the cat, the dog? No. *The cat, the rat, and Lovell, the dog, Rule all England under the hog*. That's it. The hog was Richard the Third, of course. Though nowadays they all write books saying he was really wonderful. Not a villain at all. But I don't believe that. Shakespeare didn't either. After all, he started his play by making Richard say: "I am determined so to prove a villain." Ah yes. *The Black Arrow*.'

'Some more, madam?'

'No, thank you, Albert. I think I'm rather too tired to go on now.'

'That's all right. By the way, the master rang and said he'd be half an hour late.'

'Never mind,' said Tuppence.

She sat down in the chair, took *The Black Arrow*, opened the pages and engrossed herself.

'Oh dear,' she said, 'how wonderful this is. I've really forgotten it quite enough to enjoy reading it all over again. It was so exciting.'

Silence fell. Albert returned to the kitchen. Tuppence leaned back in the chair. Time passed. Curled up in the rather shabby armchair, Mrs Thomas Beresford sought the joys of the past by applying herself to the perusal of Robert Louis Stevenson's *The Black Arrow*.

In the kitchen time also passed. Albert applied himself to the various manoeuvres with the stove. A car drove up. Albert went to the side door.

'Shall I put it in the garage, sir?'

'No,' said Tommy, 'I'll do that. I expect you're busy with dinner. Am I very late?'

'Not really, sir, just about when you said. A little early, in fact.'

'Oh.' Tommy disposed of the car and then came into the kitchen, rubbing his hands. 'Cold out. Where's Tuppence?'

'Oh, missus, she's upstairs with the books.'

'What, still those miserable books?'

'Yes. She's done a good many more today and she's spent most of the time reading.'

'Oh dear,' said Tommy. 'All right, Albert. What are we having?'

'Fillets of lemon sole, sir. It won't take long to do.'

'All right. Well, make it about quarter of an hour or so anyway. I want to wash first.'

Upstairs, on the top floor Tuppence was still sitting in the somewhat shabby armchair, engrossed in *The Black Arrow*. Her forehead was slightly wrinkled. She had come across what seemed to her a somewhat curious phenomenon. There seemed to be what she could only call a kind of interference. The particular page she had got to – she gave it a brief glance, 64 or was it 65? She couldn't see – anyway, apparently somebody had underlined some of the words on the page. Tuppence had spent the last quarter of an hour studying this phenomenon. She didn't see why the words had been underlined. They were not in sequence, they were not a quotation, therefore, in the book. They seemed to be words that had been singled out and had then been underlined in red ink. She read under her breath: 'Matcham could not restrain a little cry. Dick started with surprise and dropped the windac from his fingers. They were all afoot, loosing sword and dagger in the sheath. Ellis held up his hand. The white of his eyes shone. Let, large –' Tuppence shook her head. It didn't make sense. None of it did.

She went over to the table where she kept her writing things, picked out a few sheets recently sent by a firm of note-paper printers for the Beresfords to make a choice of the paper to be stamped with their new address: The Laurels.

'Silly name,' said Tuppence, 'but if you go changing names all the time, then all your letters go astray.'

She copied things down. Now she realized something she hadn't realized before.

'That makes all the difference,' said Tuppence.

She traced letters on the page.

'So there you are,' said Tommy's voice, suddenly. 'Dinner's practically in. How are the books going?'

'This lot's terribly puzzling,' said Tuppence. 'Dreadfully puzzling.'

'What's puzzling?'

'Well, this is *The Black Arrow* of Stevenson's and I wanted to read it again and I began. It was all right, and then suddenly – all the pages were rather queer because I mean a lot of the words had been underlined in red ink.'

'Oh well, one does that,' said Tommy. 'I don't mean solely in red ink, but I mean one does underline things. You know, something you want to remember, or a quotation of something. Well, you know what I mean.'

'I know what you mean,' said Tuppence, 'but it doesn't go like that. And it's letters, you see.'

'What do you mean by letters?'

'Come here,' said Tuppence.

Tommy came and sat on the arm of the chair. Tommy read: '"Matcham could not restrain a little cry and even died starter started with surprise and dropped the window from his fingers the two big fellows on the – something I can't read – shell was an expected signal. They were all afoot together tightening loosing sword and dagger." It's mad,' he said.

'Yes,' said Tuppence, 'that's what I thought at first. It was mad. But it isn't mad, Tommy.'

Some cowbells rang from downstairs.

'That's supper in.'

'Never mind,' said Tuppence, 'I've got to tell you this first. We can get down to things about it later but it's really so extraordinary. I've got to tell you this straight away.'

'Oh, all right. Have you got one of your mare's nests?'

'No, I haven't. It's just that I took out the letters, you see. Well – on this page, you see, well – the M of "Matcham" which is the first word, the M is underlined and the A and after that there are three more, three or four more words. They don't come in sequence in the book. They've just been picked out, I think, and they've been underlined – the letters in them – because they wanted the right letters and the next one, you see, is the R from "restrain" underlined and the Y of "cry", and then there's J from "Jack", O from "shot", R from "ruin", D from "death" and A from "death" again, N from "murrain" –'

'For goodness' sake,' said Tommy, 'do stop.'

'Wait,' said Tuppence. 'I've got to find out. Now you see because I've written out these, do you see what this is? I mean if you take those letters out and write them in order on this piece of paper, do you see what you get with the ones I've done first? M-A-R-Y. Those four were underlined.'

'What does that make?'

'It makes Mary.'

'All right,' said Tommy, 'it makes Mary. Somebody called Mary. A child with an inventive nature, I expect, who is trying to point out that this was her book. People are always writing their names in books and things like that.'

'All right. Mary,' said Tuppence. 'And the next thing that comes underlined makes the word J-o-r-d-a-n.'

'You see? Mary Jordan,' said Tommy. 'It's quite natural. Now you know her whole name. Her name was Mary Jordan.'

'Well, this book didn't belong to her. In the beginning it says in a rather silly, childish-looking writing, it says "Alexander", Alexander Parkinson, I think.'

'Oh well. Does it really matter?'

'Of course it matters,' said Tuppence.

'Come on, I'm hungry,' said Tommy.

'Restrain yourself,' said Tuppence, 'I'm only going to read you the next bit until the writing stops – or at any rate stops in the next four pages. The letters are picked from odd places on various pages. They don't run in sequence – there can't be anything in the words that matters – it's just the letters. Now then. We've got M-a-r-y J-o-r-d-a-n. That's right. Now do you know what the next four words are? D-i-d n-o-t, not, d-i-e n-a-t-u-r-a-l-y. That's meant to be "naturally", but they didn't know it had two "*l*s". Now then, what's that? *Mary Jordan did not die naturally.* There you are,' said Tuppence. 'Now the next sentence made is: *It was one of us. I think I know which one.* That's all. Can't find anything else. But it is rather exciting, isn't it?'

'Look here, Tuppence,' said Tommy, 'you're not going to get a thing about this, are you?'

'What do you mean, a thing, about this?'

'Well, I mean working up a sort of mystery.'

'Well, it's a mystery to me,' said Tuppence. '*Mary Jordan did not die naturally. It was one of us. I think I know which.* Oh, Tommy, you must say that it is very intriguing.'

CHAPTER 3

VISIT TO THE CEMETERY

'Tuppence!' Tommy called, as he came into the house.

There was no answer. With some annoyance, he ran up the stairs and along the passage on the first floor. As he hastened along it, he nearly put his foot through a gaping hole, and swore promptly.

'Some other bloody careless electrician,' he said.

Some days before he had had the same kind of trouble. Electricians arriving in a kindly tangle of optimism and efficiency had started work. 'Coming along fine now, not much more to do,' they said. 'We'll be back this afternoon.' But they hadn't been back that afternoon; Tommy was not precisely surprised. He was used, now, to the general pattern of labour in the building trade, electrical trade, gas employees and others. They came, they showed efficiency, they made optimistic remarks, they went away to fetch something. They didn't come back. One rang up numbers on the telephone but they always seemed to be the wrong numbers. If they were the right numbers, the right man was not working at this particular branch of the trade, whatever it was. All one had to do was to be careful to not rick an ankle, fall through a hole, damage yourself in some way or another. He was far more afraid of Tuppence damaging herself than he was of doing the damage to himself. He had had more experience than Tuppence. Tuppence, he thought, was more at risk from scalding herself from kettles or disasters with the heat of the stove. But where was Tuppence now? He called again.

'Tuppence! Tuppence!'

He worried about Tuppence. Tuppence was one of those people you had to worry about. If you left the house, you gave her last words of wisdom and she gave you last promises of doing exactly what you counselled her to do: No she would not be going out except just to buy half a pound of butter, and after all you couldn't call that dangerous, could you?

'It could be dangerous if *you* went out to buy half a pound of butter,' said Tommy.

'Oh,' said Tuppence, 'don't be an idiot.'

'I'm not being an idiot,' Tommy had said. 'I am just being a wise and careful husband, looking after something which is one of my favourite possessions. I don't know why it is –'

'Because,' said Tuppence, 'I am so charming, so good-looking, such a good companion and because I take so much care of you.'

'That also, maybe,' said Tommy, 'but I could give you another list.'

'I don't feel I should like that,' said Tuppence. 'No, I don't think so. I think you have several saved-up grievances. But don't worry. Everything will be quite all right. You've only got to come back and call me when you get in.'

But now where was Tuppence?

'The little devil,' said Tommy. 'She's gone out somewhere.'

He went on into the room upstairs where he had found her before. Looking at another child's book, he supposed. Getting excited again about some silly words that a silly child had underlined in red ink. On the trail of Mary Jordan, whoever she was. Mary Jordan, who hadn't died a natural death. He couldn't help wondering. A long time ago, presumably, the people who'd had the house and sold it to them had been named Jones. They hadn't been there very long, only three or four years. No, this child of the

Robert Louis Stevenson book dated from further back than that. Anyway, Tuppence wasn't here in this room. There seemed to be no loose books lying about with signs of having had interest shown in them.

'Ah, where the hell can she be?' said Thomas.

He went downstairs again, shouting once or twice. There was no answer. He examined one of the pegs in the hall. No signs of Tuppence's mackintosh. Then she'd gone out. Where had she gone? And where was Hannibal? Tommy varied the use of his vocal cords and called out for Hannibal.

'Hannibal – Hannibal – Hanny-boy. Come on, Hannibal.'

No Hannibal.

Well, at any rate, she's got Hannibal with her, thought Tommy.

He didn't know if it was worse or better that Tuppence should have Hannibal. Hannibal would certainly allow no harm to come to Tuppence. The question was, might Hannibal do some damage to other people? He was friendly when taken visiting people, but people who wished to visit Hannibal, to enter any house in which he lived, were always definitely suspect in Hannibal's mind. He was ready at all risks to both bark and bite if he considered it necessary. Anyway, where was everybody?

He walked a little way along the street, could see no signs of any small black dog with a medium-sized woman in a bright red mackintosh walking in the distance. Finally, rather angrily, he came back to the house.

Rather an appetizing smell met him. He went quickly to the kitchen, where Tuppence turned from the stove and gave him a smile of welcome.

'You're ever so late,' she said. 'This is a casserole. Smells rather good, don't you think? I put some rather unusual things in it this time. There were some herbs in the garden, at least I hope they were herbs.'

'If they weren't herbs,' said Tommy, 'I suppose they were Deadly Nightshade, or Digitalis leaves pretending to be something else but really foxglove. Where on earth have you been?'

'I took Hannibal for a walk.'

Hannibal, at this moment, made his own presence felt. He rushed at Tommy and gave him such a rapturous welcome as nearly to fell him to the ground. Hannibal was a small black dog, very glossy, with interesting tan patches on his behind and each side of his cheeks. He was a Manchester terrier of very pure pedigree and he considered himself to be on a much higher level of sophistication and aristocracy than any other dog he met.

'Oh, good gracious. I took a look round. Where've you been? It wasn't very nice weather.'

'No, it wasn't. It was very sort of foggy and misty. Ah – I'm quite tired, too.'

'Where did you go? Just down the street for the shops?'

'No, it's early closing day for the shops. No . . . Oh no, I went to the cemetery.'

'Sounds gloomy,' said Tommy. 'What did you want to go to the cemetery for?'

'I went to look at some of the graves.'

'It still sounds rather gloomy,' said Tommy. 'Did Hannibal enjoy himself?'

'Well, I had to put Hannibal on the lead. There was something that looked like a verger who kept coming out of the church and I thought he wouldn't like Hannibal because – well, you never know, Hannibal mightn't like him and I didn't want to prejudice people against us the moment we'd arrived.'

'What did you want to look in the cemetery for?'

'Oh, to see what sort of people were buried there. Lots of people, I mean it's very, very full up. It goes back a long way. It goes back well in the eighteen hundreds and I think one or two older than that, only the stone's so rubbed away you can't really see.'

'I still don't see why you wanted to go to the cemetery.'

'I was making my investigations,' said Tuppence.

'Investigations about what?'

'I wanted to see if there were any Jordans buried there.'

'Good gracious,' said Tommy. 'Are you still on that? Were you looking for –'

'Well, Mary Jordan died. We know she died. We know because we had a book that said she didn't die a natural death, but she'd still have to be buried somewhere, wouldn't she?'

'Undeniably,' said Tommy, 'unless she was buried in this garden.'

'I don't think that's very likely,' said Tuppence, 'because I think that it was only this boy or girl – it must have been a boy, I think – of course it was a boy, his name was Alexander – and he obviously thought he'd been rather clever in knowing that she'd not died a natural death. But if he was the only person who'd made up his mind about that or who'd discovered it – well, I mean, nobody else had, I suppose. I mean, she just died and was buried and nobody said . . .'

'Nobody said there had been foul play,' suggested Tommy.

'That sort of thing, yes. Poisoned or knocked on the head or pushed off a cliff or run over by a car or – oh, lots of ways I can think of.'

'I'm sure you can,' said Tommy. 'Only good thing about you, Tuppence, is that at least you have a kindly heart. You wouldn't put them into execution just for fun.'

'But there wasn't any Mary Jordan in the cemetery. There weren't any Jordans.'

'Disappointing for you,' said Tommy. 'Is that thing you're cooking ready yet, because I'm pretty hungry. It smells rather good.'

'It's absolutely done *à point*,' said Tuppence. 'So, as soon as you've washed, we eat.'

CHAPTER 4
LOTS OF PARKINSONS

'Lots of Parkinsons,' said Tuppence as they ate. 'A long way back but an amazing lot of them. Old ones, young ones and married ones. Bursting with Parkinsons. And Capes, and Griffins and Underwoods and Overwoods. Curious to have both of them, isn't it?'

'I had a friend called George Underwood,' said Tommy.

'Yes, I've known Underwoods, too. But not Overwoods.'

'Male or female?' said Thomas, with slight interest.

'A girl, I think it was. Rose Overwood.'

'Rose Overwood,' said Tommy, listening to the sound of it. 'I don't think somehow it goes awfully well together.' He added, 'I must ring up those electricians after lunch. Be very careful, Tuppence, or you'll put your foot through the landing upstairs.'

'Then I shall be a natural death, or an unnatural death, one of the two.'

'A curiosity death,' said Tommy. 'Curiosity killed the cat.'

'Aren't you at all curious?' asked Tuppence.

'I can't see any earthly reason for being curious. What have we got for pudding?'

'Treacle tart.'

'Well, I must say, Tuppence, it was a delicious meal.'

'I'm very glad you liked it,' said Tuppence.

'What is that parcel outside the back door? Is it that wine we ordered?'

'No,' said Tuppence, 'it's bulbs.'

'Oh,' said Tommy, 'bulbs.'

'Tulips,' said Tuppence. 'I'll go and talk to old Isaac about them.'

'Where are you going to put them?'

'I think along the centre path in the garden.'

'Poor old fellow, he looks as if he might drop dead any minute,' said Tommy.

'Not at all,' said Tuppence. 'He's enormously tough, is Isaac. I've discovered, you know, that gardeners are like that. If they're very good gardeners they seem to come to their prime when they're over eighty, but if you get a strong, hefty-looking young man about thirty-five who says, "I've always wanted to work in a garden," you may be quite sure that he's probably no good at all. They're just prepared to brush up a few leaves now and again and anything you want them to do they always say it's the wrong time of year, and as one never knows oneself when the right time of year is, at least I don't, well then, you see, they always get the better of you. But Isaac's wonderful. He knows about everything.' Tuppence added, 'There ought to be some crocuses as well. I wonder if they're in the parcel, too. Well, I'll go out and see. It's his day for coming and he'll tell me all about it.'

'All right,' said Tommy, 'I'll come out and join you presently.'

Tuppence and Isaac had a pleasant reunion. The bulbs were unpacked, discussions were held as to where things would show to best advantage. First the early tulips, which were expected to rejoice the heart at the end of February, then a consideration of the handsome fringed parrot tulips, and some tulips called, as far as Tuppence could make out, *viridiflora*, which would be exceptionally beautiful with long stems in the month of May and early June. As these were of an interesting green pastel colour, they agreed to plant them as a collection in a quiet part of the garden where they could be picked and arranged in interesting floral arrangements in the drawing-room, or by the short approach to the house through the front gate where they would arouse envy and jealousy among callers. They must even rejoice the artistic feelings of tradesmen delivering joints of meat and crates of grocery.

At four o'clock Tuppence produced a brown teapot full of good strong tea in the kitchen, placed a sugar basin full of lumps of sugar and a milk jug by it, and called Isaac in to refresh himself before departing. She went in search of Tommy.

I suppose he's asleep somewhere, thought Tuppence to herself as she looked from one room into another. She was glad to see a head sticking up on the landing out of the sinister pit in the floor.

'It's all right now, ma'am,' said the electrician, 'no need to be careful any more. It's all fixed.' He added that he was starting work on a different portion of the house on the following morning.

'I do hope,' said Tuppence, 'that you will really come.' She added, 'Have you seen Mr Beresford anywhere?'

'Aye, your husband, you mean? Yes, he's up on an upper floor, I think. Dropping things, he was. Yes, rather heavy things, too. Must have been some books, I think.'

'Books!' said Tuppence. 'Well I never!'

The electrician retreated down into his own personal under-world in the passage and Tuppence went up to the attic converted to the extra book library at present devoted to children's books.

Tommy was sitting on the top of a pair of steps. Several books were around him on the floor and there were noticeable gaps in the shelves.

'So there you are,' said Tuppence, 'after pretending you weren't interested or anything. You've been looking at lots of books, haven't you? You've disarranged a lot of the things that I put away so neatly.'

'Well, I'm sorry about that,' said Tommy, 'but, well I thought I'd perhaps just have a look round.'

'Did you find any other books that have got any underlined things in them in red ink?'

'No. Nothing else.'

'How annoying,' said Tuppence.

'I think it must have been Alexander's work, Master Alexander Parkinson,' said Tommy.

'That's right,' said Tuppence. 'One of the Parkinsons, the numerous Parkinsons.'

'Well, I think he must have been rather a lazy boy, although of course, it must have been rather a bother doing that underlining and all. But there's no more information re Jordan,' said Tommy.

'I asked old Isaac. He knows a lot of people round here. He says he doesn't remember any Jordans.'

'What are you doing with that brass lamp you've got by the front door?' asked Tommy, as he came downstairs.

'I'm taking it to the White Elephant Sale,' said Tuppence.

'Why?'

'Oh, because it's always been a thorough nuisance. We bought it somewhere abroad, didn't we?'

'Yes, I think we must have been mad. You never liked it. You said you hated it. Well, I agree. And it's awfully heavy too, very heavy.'

'But Miss Sanderson was terribly pleased when I said that they could have it. She offered to fetch it but I said I'd run it down to them in the car. It's today we take the thing.'

'I'll run down with it if you like.'

'No, I'd rather like to go.'

'All right,' said Tommy. 'Perhaps I'd better come with you and just carry it in for you.'

'Oh, I think I'll find someone who'll carry it in for me,' said Tuppence.

'Well, you might or you might not. Don't go and strain yourself.'

'All right,' said Tuppence.

'You've got some other reason for wanting to go, haven't you?'

'Well, I just thought I'd like to chat a bit with people,' said Tuppence.

'I never know what you're up to, Tuppence, but I know the look in your eye when you *are* up to something.'

'You take Hannibal for a walk,' said Tuppence. 'I can't take him to the White Elephant Sale. I don't want to get into a dog-fight.'

'All right. Want to go for a walk, Hannibal?'

Hannibal, as was his habit, immediately replied in the affirmative. His affirmatives and his negatives were always quite impossible to miss. He wriggled his body, wagged his tail, raised one paw, put it down again and came and rubbed his head hard against Tommy's leg.

'That's right,' he obviously said, 'that's what you exist for, my dear slave. We're going out for a lovely walk down the street. Lots of smells, I hope.'

'Come on,' said Tommy. 'I'll take the lead with me, and don't run into the road as you did the last time. One of those awful great "long vehicles" was nearly the end of you.'

Hannibal looked at him with the expression of 'I'm always a very good dog who'll do exactly what I am told.' False as the statement was, it often succeeded in deceiving even those people who were in closest contact with Hannibal.

Tommy put the brass lamp into the car, murmuring it was rather heavy. Tuppence drove off in the car. Having seen her turn the corner, Tommy attached the lead to Hannibal's collar and took him down the street. Then he turned up the lane towards the church, and removed Hannibal's lead since very little traffic came up this particular road. Hannibal acknowledged the privilege by grunting and sniffing in various tufts of grass with which the pavement next to the wall was adorned. If he could have used human language it was clear that what he would have said was: 'Delicious! Very rich. Big dog here. Believe it's that beastly Alsatian.' Low growl. 'I don't like Alsatians. If I see the one again that bit me once I'll bite him. Ah! Delicious, delicious. Very nice little bitch here. Yes – yes – I'd like to meet her. I wonder if she lives far away. Expect she comes out of this house. I wonder now.'

'Come out of that gate, now,' said Tommy. 'Don't go into a house that isn't yours.'

Hannibal pretended not to hear.

'Hannibal!'

Hannibal redoubled his speed and turned a corner which led towards the kitchen.

'Hannibal!' shouted Tommy. 'Do you hear me?'

'Hear you, Master?' said Hannibal. 'Were you calling me? Oh yes, of course.'

A sharp bark from inside the kitchen caught his ear. He scampered out to join Tommy. Hannibal walked a few inches behind Tommy's heel.

'Good boy,' said Tommy.

'I am a good boy, aren't I?' said Hannibal. 'Any moment you need me to defend you, here I am less than a foot away.'

They had arrived at a side gate which led into the church-yard. Hannibal, who in some way had an extraordinary knack of altering his size when he wanted to, instead of appearing somewhat broad-shouldered, possibly a somewhat too plump dog, he could at any moment make himself like a thin black thread. He now squeezed himself through the bars of the gate with no difficulty at all.

'Come back, Hannibal,' called Tommy. 'You can't go into the churchyard.'

Hannibal's answer to that, if there had been any, would have been, 'I am in the churchyard already, Master.' He was scampering gaily round the churchyard with the air of a dog who has been let out in a singularly pleasant garden.

'You awful dog!' said Tommy.

He unlatched the gate, walked in and chased Hannibal, lead in hand. Hannibal was now at the far corner of the churchyard, and seemed to have every intention of trying to gain access through the door of the church, which was slightly ajar. Tommy, however, reached him in time and attached the lead. Hannibal looked up with the air of one who had intended this to happen all along. 'Putting me on the lead, are you?' he said. 'Yes, of course, I know it's a kind of prestige. It shows that I am a very valuable dog.' He wagged his tail. Since there seemed nobody to oppose Hannibal walking in the churchyard with his master, suitably secured as he was by a stalwart lead, Tommy wandered round, checking perhaps Tuppence's researches of a former day.

He looked first at a worn stone monument more or less behind a little side door into the church. It was, he thought, probably one of the oldest. There were several of them there, most of them bearing dates in the eighteen-hundreds. There was one, however, that Tommy looked at longest.

'Odd,' he said, 'damned odd.'

Hannibal looked up at him. He did not understand this piece of Master's conversation. He saw nothing about the gravestone to interest a dog. He sat down, looked up at his master enquiringly.

············· CHAPTER 5 ·············

THE WHITE ELEPHANT SALE

I

Tuppence was pleasurably surprised to find the brass lamp which she and Tommy now regarded with such repulsion welcomed with the utmost warmth.

'How very good of you, Mrs Beresford, to bring us something as nice as that. Most interesting, most interesting. I suppose it must have come from abroad on your travels once.'

'Yes. We bought it in Egypt,' said Tuppence.

She was quite doubtful by this time, a period of eight to ten years having passed, as to where she had bought it. It might have been Damascus, she thought, and it might equally well have been Baghdad or possibly Tehran. But Egypt, she thought, since Egypt was doubtless in the news at this moment, would be far more interesting. Besides, it looked rather Egyptian. Clearly, if she had got it from any other country, it dated from some period when they had been copying Egyptian work.

'Really,' she said, 'it's rather big for our house, so I thought –'

'Oh, I think really we ought to raffle it,' said Miss Little.

Miss Little was more or less in charge of things. Her local nickname was 'The Parish Pump', mainly because she was so well informed about all things that happened in the parish. Her surname was misleading. She was a large woman of ample proportions. Her Christian name was Dorothy, but she was always called Dotty.

'I hope you're coming to the sale, Mrs Beresford?'

Tuppence assured her that she was coming.

'I can hardly wait to buy,' she said chattily.

'Oh, I'm so glad you feel like that.'

'I think it's a very good thing,' said Tuppence. 'I mean, the White Elephant idea, because it's – well, it is so true, isn't it? I mean, what's one person's white elephant is somebody else's pearl beyond price.'

'Ah, really we *must* tell that to the vicar,' said Miss Price-Ridley, an angular lady with a lot of teeth. 'Oh yes, I'm sure he would be very much amused.'

'That papier-mâché basin, for instance,' said Tuppence, raising this particular trophy up.

'Oh really, do you think anyone will buy that?'

'I shall buy it myself if it's for sale when I come here tomorrow,' said Tuppence.

'But nowadays, they have such pretty plastic washing-up bowls.'

'I'm not very fond of plastic,' said Tuppence. 'That's a really good papier-mâché bowl that you've got there. I mean if you put things down in that, lots of china together, they wouldn't break. And there's an old-fashioned tin-opener too. The kind with a bull's head that one never sees nowadays.'

'Oh, but it's such hard work, that. Don't you think the ones that you put on an electric thing are much better?'

Conversation on these lines went on for a short time and then Tuppence asked if there were any services that she could render.

'Ah, dear Mrs Beresford, perhaps you would arrange the curio stall. I'm sure you're very artistic.'

'Not really artistic at all,' said Tuppence, 'but I would love to arrange the stall for you. You must tell me if I'm doing it wrong,' she added.

'Oh, it's so nice to have some extra help. We are so pleased to meet you, too. I suppose you're nearly settled into your house by now?'

'I thought we should be settled by now,' said Tuppence, 'but it seems as though there's a long time to go still. It's so very hard with electricians and then carpenters and people. They're always coming back.'

A slight dispute arose with people near her supporting the claims of electricians and the Gas Board.

'Gas people are the worst,' said Miss Little, with firmness, 'because, you see, they come all the way over from Lower Stamford. The electricity people only have to come from Wellbank.'

The arrival of the vicar to say a few words of encouragement and good cheer to the helpers changed the subject. He also expressed himself very pleased to meet his new parishioner, Mrs Beresford.

'We know all about you,' he said. 'Oh yes indeed. And your husband. A most interesting talk I had the other day about you both. What an interesting life you must have had. I dare say it's not supposed to be spoken of, so I won't. I mean, in the last war. A wonderful performance on your and your husband's part.'

'Oh, do tell us, Vicar,' said one of the ladies, detaching herself from the stall where she was setting up jars of jam.

'I was told in strict confidence,' said the vicar. 'I think I saw you walking round the churchyard yesterday, Mrs Beresford.'

'Yes,' said Tuppence. 'I looked into the church first. I see you have one or two very attractive windows.'

'Yes, yes, they date back to the fourteenth century. That is, the one in the north aisle does. But of course most of them are Victorian.'

'Walking round the churchyard,' said Tuppence, 'it seemed to me there were a great many Parkinsons buried there.'

'Yes, yes, indeed. There've always been big contingents of Parkinsons in this part of the world, though of course I don't remember any of them myself, but you do, I think, Mrs Lupton.'

Mrs Lupton, an elderly lady who was supporting herself on two sticks, looked pleased.

'Yes, yes,' she said. 'I remember when Mrs Parkinson was alive – you know, old Mrs Parkinson, *the* Mrs Parkinson who lived in the Manor House, wonderful old lady she was. Quite wonderful.'

'And there were some Somers I saw, and the Chattertons.'

'Ah, I see you're getting up well with our local geography of the past.'

'I think I heard something about a Jordan – Annie or Mary Jordan, was it?'

Tuppence looked round her in an enquiring fashion. The name of Jordan seemed to cause no particular interest.

'Somebody had a cook called Jordan. I think, Mrs Blackwell. Susan Jordan I think it was. She only stayed six months, I think. Quite unsatisfactory in many ways.'

'Was that a long time ago?'

'Oh no. Just about eight or ten years ago I think. Not more than that.'

'Are there any Parkinsons living here now?'

'Oh no. They're all gone long ago. One of them married a first cousin and went to live in Kenya, I believe.'

'I wonder,' said Tuppence, managing to attach herself to Mrs Lupton, who she knew had something to do with the local children's hospital, 'I wonder if you want any extra children's books. They're all old ones, I mean. I got them in an odd lot when we were bidding for some of the furniture that was for sale in our house.'

'Well, that's very kind of you, I'm sure, Mrs Beresford. Of course we do have some very good ones, given to us you know. Special editions for children nowadays. One does feel it's a pity they should have to read all those old-fashioned books.'

'Oh, do you think so?' said Tuppence. 'I loved the books that I had as a child. Some of them,' she said, 'had been my grandmother's when she was a child. I believe I liked those best of all. I shall never forget reading *Treasure Island*, Mrs Molesworth's *Four Winds Farm* and some of Stanley Weyman's.'

She looked round her enquiringly – then, resigning herself, she looked at her wrist-watch, exclaimed at finding how late it was and took her leave.

II

Tuppence, having got home, put the car away in the garage and walked round the house to the front door. The door was open, so she walked in. Albert then came from the back premises and bowed to greet her.

'Like some tea, madam? You must be very tired.'

'I don't think so,' said Tuppence. 'I've had tea. They gave me tea down at the Institute. Quite good cake, but very nasty buns.'

'Buns is difficult. Buns is nearly as difficult as doughnuts. Ah,' he sighed. 'Lovely doughnuts Amy used to make.'

'I know. Nobody's were like them,' said Tuppence.

Amy had been Albert's wife, now some years deceased. In Tuppence's opinion, Amy had made wonderful treacle tart but had never been very good with doughnuts.

'I think doughnuts are dreadfully difficult,' said Tuppence, 'I've never been able to do them myself.'

'Well, it's a knack.'

'Where's Mr Beresford? Is he out?'

'Oh no, he's upstairs. In that room. You know. The book-room or whatever you like to call it. I can't get out of the way of calling it the attic still, myself.'

'What's he doing up there?' said Tuppence, slightly surprised.

'Well, he's still looking at the books, I think. I suppose he's still arranging them, getting them finished as you might say.'

'Still seems to me very surprising,' said Tuppence. 'He's really been very rude to us about those books.'

'Ah well,' said Albert, 'gentlemen are like that, aren't they? They likes big books mostly, you know, don't they? Something scientific that they can get their teeth into.'

'I shall go up and rout him out,' said Tuppence. 'Where's Hannibal?'

'I think he's up there with the master.'

But at that moment Hannibal made his appearance. Having barked with the ferocious fury he considered necessary for a good guard dog, he had correctly assumed that it was his beloved mistress who had returned and not someone who had come to steal the teaspoons or to assault his master and mistress. He came wriggling down the stairs, his pink tongue hanging out, his tail wagging.

'Ah,' said Tuppence, 'pleased to see your mother?'

Hannibal said he was very pleased to see his mother. He leapt upon her with such force that he nearly knocked her to the ground.

'Gently,' said Tuppence, 'gently. You don't want to kill me, do you?'

Hannibal made it clear that the only thing he wanted to do was to eat her because he loved her so much.

590 • AGATHA CHRISTIE

'Where's Master? Where's Father? Is he upstairs?'

Hannibal understood. He ran up a flight, turned his head over his shoulder and waited for Tuppence to join him.

'Well, I never,' said Tuppence as, slightly out of breath, she entered the book-room to see Tommy astride a pair of steps, taking books in and out. 'Whatever are you doing? I thought you were going to take Hannibal for a walk.'

'We have been for a walk,' said Tommy. 'We went to the churchyard.'

'Why on earth did you take Hannibal into the churchyard? I'm sure they wouldn't like dogs there.'

'He was on the lead,' said Tommy, 'and anyway I didn't take him. He took me. He seemed to like the churchyard.'

'I hope he hasn't got a thing about it,' said Tuppence. 'You know what Hannibal is like. He likes arranging a routine always. If he's going to have a routine of going to the churchyard every day, it will really be very difficult for us.'

'He's really been very intelligent about the whole thing,' said Tommy.

'When you say intelligent, you just mean he's selfwilled,' said Tuppence.

Hannibal turned his head and came and rubbed his nose against the calf of her leg.

'He's telling you,' said Tommy, 'that he is a very clever dog. Cleverer than you or I have been so far.'

'And what do you mean by that?' asked Tuppence.

'Have you been enjoying yourself?' asked Tommy, changing the subject.

'Well, I wouldn't go as far as that,' said Tuppence. 'People were very kind to me and nice to me and I think soon I shan't get them mixed up so much as I do at present. It's awfully difficult at first, you know, because people look rather alike and wear the same sort of clothes and you don't know at first which is which. I mean, unless somebody is very beautiful or very ugly. And that doesn't seem to happen so noticeably in the country, does it?'

'I'm telling you,' said Tommy, 'that Hannibal and I have been extremely clever.'

'I thought you said it was Hannibal?'

Tommy reached out his hand and took a book from the shelf in front of him.

'*Kidnapped*,' he remarked. 'Oh yes, another Robert Louis Stevenson. Somebody must have been very fond of Robert Louis Stevenson. *The Black Arrow*, *Kidnapped*, *Catriona* and two others, I think. All given to Alexander Parkinson by a fond grandmother and one from a generous aunt.'

'Well,' said Tuppence, 'what about it?'

'And I've found his grave,' said Tommy.

'Found what?'

'Well, Hannibal did. It's right in the corner against one of the small doors into the church. I suppose it's the other door to the vestry, something like that. It's very rubbed and not well kept up, but that's it. He was fourteen when he died. Alexander Richard Parkinson. Hannibal was nosing about there. I got him away from it and managed to make out the inscription, in spite of its being so rubbed.'

'Fourteen,' said Tuppence. 'Poor little boy.'

'Yes,' said Tommy, 'it's sad and –'

'You've got something in your head,' said Tuppence. 'I don't understand.'

'Well, I wondered. I suppose, Tuppence, you've infected me. That's the worst of you. When you get keen on something, you don't go on with it by yourself, you get somebody else to take an interest in it too.'

'I don't quite know what you mean,' said Tuppence.

'I wondered if it was a case of cause and effect.'

'What do you mean, Tommy?'

'I was wondering about Alexander Parkinson who took a lot of trouble, though no doubt he enjoyed himself doing it, making a kind of code, a secret message in a book. "*Mary Jordan did not die naturally.*" Supposing that was true? Supposing Mary Jordan, whoever she was, didn't die naturally? Well then, don't you see, perhaps the next thing that happened was that Alexander Parkinson died.'

'You don't mean – you don't think –'

'Well, one wonders,' said Tommy. 'It started me wondering – fourteen years old. There was no mention of what he died of. I suppose there wouldn't be on a gravestone. There was just a text: *In thy presence is the fullness of joy*. Something like that. But – it might have been because he knew something that was dangerous to somebody else. And so – and so he died.'

'You mean he was killed? You're just imagining things,' said Tuppence.

'Well you started it. Imagining things, or wondering. It's much the same thing, isn't it?'

'We shall go on wondering, I suppose,' said Tuppence, 'and we shan't be able to find out anything because it was all such years and years and years ago.'

They looked at each other.

'Round about the time we were trying to investigate the Jane Finn business,' said Tommy.

They looked at each other again; their minds going back to the past.

CHAPTER 6

PROBLEMS

I

Moving house is often thought of beforehand as an agreeable exercise which the movers are going to enjoy, but it does not always turn out as expected.

Relations have to be reopened or adjusted with electricians, with builders, with carpenters, with painters, with wall-paperers, with providers of refrigerators, gas stoves, electric appliances, with upholsterers, makers of curtains, hangers-up of curtains, those who lay linoleum, those who supply carpets. Every day has not only its appointed task but usually something between four and twelve extra callers, either long expected or those whose coming was quite forgotten.

But there were moments when Tuppence with sighs of relief announced various finalities in different fields.

'I really think our kitchen is almost perfect by now,' she said. 'Only I can't find the proper kind of flour bin yet.'

'Oh,' said Tommy, 'does it matter very much?'

'Well, it does rather. I mean, you buy flour very often in three-pound bags and it won't go into these kinds of containers.

They're all so dainty. You know, one has a pretty rose on it and the other's got a sunflower and they'll not take more than a pound. It's all so silly.'

At intervals, Tuppence made other suggestions.

'The Laurels,' she said. 'Silly name for a house, I think. I don't see why it's called The Laurels. It hasn't got any laurels. They could have called it The Plane Trees much better. Plane trees are very nice,' said Tuppence.

'Before The Laurels it was called Long Scofield, so they told me,' said Tommy.

'That name doesn't seem to mean anything either,' said Tuppence.

'What is a Scofield, and who lived in it then?'

'I think it was the Waddingtons.'

'One gets so mixed,' said Tuppence. 'Waddingtons and then the Joneses, the people who sold it to us. And before that the Blackmores? And once, I suppose the Parkinsons. Lots of Parkinsons. I'm always running into more Parkinsons.'

'What way do you mean?'

'Well, I suppose it's that I'm always asking,' said Tuppence. 'I mean, if I could find out something about the Parkinsons, we could get on with our – well, with our problem.'

'That's what one always seems to call everything nowadays. The problem of Mary Jordan, is that it?'

'Well, it's not just that. There's the problem of the Parkinsons and the problem of Mary Jordan and there must be a lot of other problems too. Mary Jordan didn't die naturally, then the next thing the message said was, "It was one of us." Now did that mean one of the Parkinson family or did it mean just someone who lived in the house? Say there were two or three Parkinsons, and some older Parkinsons, and people with different names but who were aunts to the Parkinsons or nephews and nieces to the Parkinsons, and I suppose something like a housemaid and a parlour maid and a cook and perhaps a governess and perhaps – well, not an *au pair* girl, it would be too long ago for an *au pair* girl – but "one of us" must mean a householdful. Households were fuller then than they are now. Well, Mary Jordan could have been a housemaid or a parlour maid or even the cook. And why should someone want her to die, and not die naturally? I mean, somebody must have wanted her to die or else her death would have been natural, wouldn't it? – I'm going to another coffee morning the day after tomorrow,' said Tuppence.

'You seem to be always going to coffee mornings.'

'Well, it's a very good way of getting to know one's neighbours and all the people who live in the same village. After all, it's not very big, this village. And people are always talking about their old aunts or people they knew. I shall try and start on Mrs Griffin, who was evidently a great character in the neighbourhood. I should say she ruled everyone with a rod of iron. You know. She bullied the vicar and she bullied the doctor and I think she bullied the district nurse and all the rest of it.'

'Wouldn't the district nurse be helpful?'

'I don't think so. She's dead. I mean, the one who would have been here in the Parkinsons' time is dead, and the one who is here now hasn't been here very long. No sort of interest in the place. I don't think she even knew a Parkinson.'

'I wish,' said Tommy desperately, 'oh, how I wish that we could forget *all* the Parkinsons.'

'You mean, then we shouldn't have a problem?'

'Oh dear,' said Tommy. 'Problems again.'

'It's Beatrice,' said Tuppence.

'What's Beatrice?'

'Who introduced problems. Really, it's Elizabeth. The cleaning help we had before Beatrice. She was always coming to me and saying, "Oh madam, could I speak to you a minute? You see, I've got a problem," and then Beatrice began coming on Thursdays and she must have caught it, I suppose. So she had problems too. It's just a way of saying something – but you always call it a problem.'

'All right,' said Tommy. 'We'll admit that's so. You've got a problem – I've got a problem – We've both got problems.'

He sighed, and departed.

Tuppence came down the stairs slowly, shaking her head. Hannibal came up to her hopefully, wagging his tail and wriggling in hopes of favours to come.

'No, Hannibal,' said Tuppence. 'You've had a walk. You've had your morning walk.'

Hannibal intimated that she was quite mistaken, he hadn't had a walk.

'You are one of the worst liars among dogs I have ever known,' said Tuppence. 'You've been for a walk with Father.'

Hannibal made his second attempt, which was to endeavour to show by various attitudes that any dog would have a second walk if only he had an owner who could see things in that light. Disappointed in this effort, he went down the stairs and proceeded to bark loudly and make every pretence of being about to make a sharp snap bite at a tousled-haired girl who was wielding a Hoover. He did not like the Hoover, and he objected to Tuppence having a lengthy conversation with Beatrice.

'Oh, don't let him bite me,' said Beatrice.

'He won't bite you,' said Tuppence. 'He only pretends he's going to.'

'Well, I think he'll really do it one day,' said Beatrice. 'By the way, madam, I wonder if I could speak to you for a moment.'

'Oh,' said Tuppence. 'You mean –'

'Well, you see, madam, I've got a problem.'

'I thought that was it,' said Tuppence. 'What sort of problem is it? And, by the way, do you know any family here or anyone who lived here at one time called Jordan?'

'Jordan now. Well, I can't really say. There was the Johnsons, of course, and there was – ah yes, one of the constables was a Johnson. And so was one of the postmen. George Johnson. He was a friend of mine.' She giggled.

'You never heard of a Mary Jordan who died?'

Beatrice merely looked bewildered – and she shook her head and went back to the assault.

'About this problem, madam?'

'Oh yes, your problem.'

'I hope you don't mind my asking you, madam, but it's put me in a queer position, you see, and I don't like –'

'Well, if you can tell me quickly,' said Tuppence. 'I've got to go out to a coffee morning.'

'Oh yes. At Mrs Barber's isn't it?'

'That's right,' said Tuppence. 'Now what's the problem?'

'Well, it's a coat. Ever such a nice coat it was. At Simmonds it was, and I went in and tried it on and it seemed to me very nice, it did. Well, there was one little spot on the skirt, you know, just round near the hem but that didn't seem to me would matter much. Anyway, well, it – er –'

'Yes,' said Tuppence, 'it what?'

'It made me see why it was so inexpensive, you see. So I got it. And so that was all right. But when I got home I found there was a label on it and instead of saying £3.70 it was labelled £6. Well, ma'am, I didn't like to do that, so I didn't know what to do. I went back to the shop and I took the coat with me – I thought I'd better take it back and explain, you see, that I hadn't meant to take it away like that and then you see the girl who sold it to me – very nice girl she is, her name is Gladys, yes, I don't know what her other name is – but anyway she was ever so upset, she was, and I said, "Well, that's all right, I'll pay extra," and she said, "No, you can't do that because it's all entered up." You see – you do see what I mean?'

'Yes, I think I see what you mean,' said Tuppence.

'And so she said, "Oh you can't do that, it will get *me* into trouble."'

'Why should it get her into trouble?'

'Well, that's what I felt. I mean to say, well, I mean it'd been sold to me for less and I'd brought it back and I didn't see why it could put *her* in trouble. She said if there was any carelessness like that and they hadn't noticed the right ticket and they'd charged me the wrong price, as likely as not she'd get the sack for it.'

'Oh, I shouldn't think that would happen,' said Tuppence. 'I think you were quite right. I don't see what else you could do.'

'Well, but there it is, you see. She made such a fuss and she was beginning to cry and everything, so I took the coat away again and now I don't know whether I've cheated the shop or whether – I don't really know what to do.'

'Well,' said Tuppence, 'I really think I'm too old to know what one ought to do nowadays because everything is so odd in shops. The prices are odd and everything is difficult. But if I were you and you want to pay something extra, well perhaps you'd better give the money to what's-her-name – Gladys something. She can put the money in the till or somewhere.'

'Oh well, I don't know as I'd like to do that because she might keep it, you see. I mean, if she kept the money, oh well, I mean it wouldn't be difficult would it, because I suppose I've stolen the money and I wouldn't have stolen it really. I mean then it would have been Gladys who stole it, wouldn't it, and I don't know that I trust her all that much. Oh dear.'

'Yes,' said Tuppence, 'life is very difficult, isn't it? I'm terribly sorry, Beatrice, but I really think you've got to make up your own mind about this. If you can't trust your friend –'

'Oh, she's not exactly a friend. I only buy things there. And she's ever so nice to talk to. But I mean, well, she's not exactly a friend, you know. I think she had a little trouble once before the last place she was in. You know, they said she kept back money on something she'd sold.'

'Well in that case,' said Tuppence, in slight desperation, 'I shouldn't do anything.'

The firmness of her tone was such that Hannibal came into the consultation. He barked loudly at Beatrice and took a running leap at the Hoover which he considered one of his principal enemies. 'I don't trust that Hoover,' said Hannibal. 'I'd like to bite it up.'

'Oh, be quiet, Hannibal. Stop barking. Don't bite anything or anyone,' said Tuppence. 'I'm going to be awfully late.'

She rushed out of the house.

II

'Problems,' said Tuppence, as she went down the hill and along Orchard Road. Going along there, she wondered as she'd done before if there'd ever been an orchard attached to any of the houses. It seemed unlikely nowadays.

Mrs Barber received her with great pleasure. She brought forward some very delicious-looking éclairs.

'What lovely things,' said Tuppence. 'Did you get them at Betterby's?'

Betterby's was the local confectionery shop.

'Oh no, my aunt made them. She's wonderful, you know. She does wonderful things.'

'Éclairs are very difficult things to make,' said Tuppence. 'I could never succeed with them.'

'Well, you have to get a particular kind of flour. I believe that's the secret of it.'

The ladies drank coffee and talked about the difficulties of certain kinds of home cookery.

'Miss Bolland was talking about you the other day, Mrs Beresford.'

'Oh?' said Tuppence. 'Really? Bolland?'

'She lives next to the vicarage. Her family has lived here a long time. She was telling us how she'd come and stayed here when she was a child. She used to look forward to it. She said, because there were such wonderful gooseberries in the garden. And greengage trees too. Now that's a thing you practically never see nowadays, not real greengages. Something else called gage plums or something, but they're not a bit the same to taste.'

The ladies talked about things in the fruit line which did not taste like the things used to, which they remembered from their childhood.

'My great-uncle had greengage trees,' said Tuppence.

'Oh yes. Is that the one who was a canon at Anchester? Canon Henderson used to live there, with his sister, I believe. Very sad it was. She was eating seed cake one day, you know, and one of the seeds got the wrong way. Something like that and she choked and she choked and she choked and she died of it. Oh dear, that's very sad, isn't it?' said Mrs Barber. 'Very sad indeed. One of my cousins died choking,' she said. 'A piece of mutton. It's very easy to do, I believe, and there are people who die of hiccups because they can't stop, you know. They don't know the old rhyme,' she explained. 'Hic-up, hic-down, hic to the next town, three hics and one cup sure to cure the hiccups. You have to hold your breath while you say it.'

CHAPTER 7

MORE PROBLEMS

'Can I speak to you a moment, ma'am?'

'Oh dear,' said Tuppence. 'Not more problems?'

She was descending the stairs from the book-room, brushing dust off herself because she was dressed in her best coat and skirt, to which she was thinking of adding a feather hat and then proceeding out to a tea she had been asked to attend by a new friend she had met at the White Elephant Sale. It was no moment, she felt, to listen to the further difficulties of Beatrice.

'Well, no, no, it's not exactly a problem. It's just something I thought you might like to know about.'

'Oh,' said Tuppence, still feeling that this might be another problem in disguise. She came down carefully. 'I'm in rather a hurry because I have to go out to tea.'

'Well, it's just about someone as you asked about, it seems. Name of Mary Jordan, that was right? Only they thought perhaps it was Mary Johnson. You know, there was a Belinda Johnson as worked at the post office, but a good long time ago.'

'Yes,' said Tuppence, 'and there was a policeman called Johnson, too, so someone told me.'

'Yes, well, anyway, this friend of mine – Gwenda, her name is – you know the shop, the post office is one side and envelopes and dirty cards and things the other side, and some china things too, before Christmas, you see, and –'

'I know,' said Tuppence, 'it's called Mrs Garrison's or something like that.'

'Yes, but it isn't really Garrison nowadays as keep it. Quite a different name. But anyway, this friend of mine, Gwenda, she thought you might be interested to know because she says as she had heard of a Mary Jordan what lived here a long time ago. A very long time ago. Lived here, in this house I mean.'

'Oh, lived in The Laurels?'

'Well, it wasn't called that then. And she'd heard something about her, she said. And so she thought you might be interested. There was some rather sad story about her, she had an accident or something. Anyway she died.'

'You mean that she was living in this house when she died? Was she one of the family?'

'No. I think the family was called Parker, a name of that kind. A lot of Parkers there were, Parkers or Parkinsons – something like that. I think she was just staying here. I believe Mrs Griffin knows about it. Do you know Mrs Griffin?'

'Oh, very slightly,' said Tuppence. 'Matter of fact, that's where I'm going to tea this afternoon. I talked to her the other day at the Sale. I hadn't met her before.'

'She's a very old lady. She's older than she looks, but I think she's got a very good memory. I believe one of the Parkinson boys was her godson.'

'What was his Christian name?'

'Oh, it was Alec, I think. Some name like that. Alec or Alex.'

'What happened to him? Did he grow up – go away – become a soldier or sailor or something like that?'

'Oh no. He died. Oh yes, I think he's buried right here. It's one of those things, I think, as people usedn't to know much about. It's one of those things with a name like a Christian name.'

'You mean somebody's disease?'

'Hodgkin's Disease, or something. No, it was a Christian name of some kind. I don't know, but they say as your blood grows the wrong colour or something. Nowadays I believe they take blood away from you and give you some good blood again, or something like that. But even then you usually die, they say. Mrs Billings – the cake shop, you know – she had a little girl died of that and she was only seven. They say it takes them very young.'

'Leukaemia?'

'Oh now, fancy you knowing. Yes, it was that name, I'm sure. But they say now as one day there'll maybe be a cure for it, you know. Just like nowadays they give you inoculations and things to cure you from typhoid, or whatever it is.'

'Well,' said Tuppence, 'that's very interesting. Poor little boy.'

'Oh, he wasn't very young. He was at school somewhere, I think. Must have been about thirteen or fourteen.'

'Well,' said Tuppence, 'it's all very sad.' She paused, then said, 'Oh dear, I'm very late now. I must hurry off.'

'I dare say Mrs Griffin could tell you a few things. I don't mean things as she'd remember herself, but she was brought up here as a child and she heard a lot of things, and she tells people a lot sometimes about the families that were here before. Some of the things are real scandalous, too. You know, goings-on and all that. That was, of course, in what they call Edwardian times or Victorian times. I don't know which. You know. I should think it was Victorian because she was still alive, the old Queen. So that's Victorian, really. They talk about it as Edwardian and something called "the Marlborough House set". Sort of high society, wasn't it?'

'Yes,' said Tuppence, 'yes. High society.'

'And goings-on,' said Beatrice, with some fervour.

'A good many goings-on,' said Tuppence.

'Young girls doing what they shouldn't do,' said Beatrice, loath to part with her mistress just when something interesting might be said.

'No,' said Tuppence, 'I believe the girls led very – well, pure and austere lives and they married young, though often into the peerage.'

'Oh dear,' said Beatrice, 'how nice for them. Lots of fine clothes, I suppose, race meetings and going to dances and ballrooms.'

'Yes,' said Tuppence, 'lots of ballrooms.'

'Well, I knew someone once, and her grandmother had been a housemaid in one of those smart houses, you know, as they all came to, and the Prince of Wales – the Prince of Wales as was then, you know, he was Edward VII afterwards, that one, the early one – well he was there and he was ever so nice. Ever so nice to all the servants and everything else. And when she left she took away the cake of soap that he'd used for his hands, and she kept it always. She used to show it to some of us children once.'

'Very thrilling for you,' said Tuppence. 'It must have been very exciting times. Perhaps he stayed here in The Laurels.'

'No, I don't think as I ever heard that, and I would have heard it. No, it was only Parkinsons here. No countesses and marchionesses and lords and ladies. The Parkinsons, I think, were mostly in trade. Very rich, you know, and all that, but still there's nothing exciting in trade, is there?'

'It depends,' said Tuppence. She added, 'I think I ought –'

'Yes, you'd best be going along, ma'am.'

'Yes. Well, thank you very much, I don't think I'd better put on a hat. I've got my hair awfully mussed now.'

'Well, you put your head in that corner where the cobwebs is. I'll dust it off in case you do it again.'

Tuppence ran down the stairs.

'Alexander ran down there,' she said. 'Many times, I expect. And he knew it was "one of them". I wonder. I wonder more than ever now.'

602 • AGATHA CHRISTIE

CHAPTER 8
···

MRS GRIFFIN

'I am so very pleased that you and your husband have come here to live, Mrs Beresford,' said Mrs Griffin, as she poured out tea. 'Sugar? Milk?'

She pressed forward a dish of sandwiches, and Tuppence helped herself.

'It makes so much difference, you know, in the country where one has nice neighbours with whom one has something in common. Did you know this part of the world before?'

'No,' said Tuppence, 'not at all. We had, you know, a good many different houses to go and view – particulars of them were sent to us by the estate agents. Of course, most of them were very often quite frightful. One was called Full of Old World Charm.'

'I know,' said Mrs Griffin, 'I know exactly. Old world charm usually means that you have to put a new roof on and that the damp is very bad. And "thoroughly modernized" – well, one knows what that means. Lots of gadgets one doesn't want and usually a very bad view from the windows of really hideous houses. But The Laurels is a charming house. I expect, though, you have had a good deal to do to it. Everyone has in turn.'

'I suppose a lot of different people have lived there,' said Tuppence.

'Oh yes. Nobody seems to stay very long anywhere nowadays, do they? The Cuthbertsons were here and the Redlands, and before that the Seymours. And after them the Joneses.'

'We wondered a little why it was called The Laurels,' said Tuppence.

'Oh well, that was the kind of name people liked to give a house. Of course, if you go back far enough, probably to the time of the Parkinsons, I think there *were* laurels. Probably a drive, you know, curling round and a lot of laurels, including those speckled ones. I never liked speckled laurels.'

'No,' said Tuppence, 'I do agree with you. I don't like them either. There seem to have been a lot of Parkinsons here,' she added.

'Oh yes. I think they occupied it longer than anyone else.'

'Nobody seems able to tell one much about them.'

'Well, it was a long time ago, you see, dear. And after the – well, I think after the – the trouble you know, and there was some feeling about it and of course one doesn't wonder they sold the place.'

'It had a bad reputation, did it?' said Tuppence, taking a chance. 'Do you mean the house was supposed to be insanitary, or something?'

'Oh no, not the house. No, really, the people you see. Well of course, there was the – the disgrace, in a way – it was during the first war. Nobody could believe it. My grandmother used to talk about it and say that it was something to do with naval secrets – about a new submarine. There was a girl living with the Parkinsons who was said to have been mixed up with it all.'

'Was that Mary Jordan?' said Tuppence.

'Yes. Yes, you're quite right. Afterwards they suspected that it wasn't her real name. I think somebody had suspected her for some time. The boy had, Alexander. Nice boy. Quite sharp too.'

BOOK 2

A LONG TIME AGO

Tuppence was selecting birthday cards. It was a wet afternoon and the post office was almost empty. People dropped letters into the post box outside or occasionally made a hurried purchase of stamps. Then they usually departed to get home as soon as possible. It was not one of those crowded shopping afternoons. In fact, Tuppence thought, she had chosen this particular day very well.

Gwenda, whom she had managed to recognize easily from Beatrice's description, had been only too pleased to come to her assistance. Gwenda represented the household shopping side of the post office. An elderly woman with grey hair presided over the government business of Her Majesty's mails. Gwenda, a chatty girl, interested always in new arrivals to the village, was happy among the Christmas cards, valentines, birthday cards, comic postcards, note paper and stationery, various types of chocolates and sundry china articles of domestic use. She and Tuppence were already on friendly terms.

'I'm so glad that the house has been opened again. Princes Lodge, I mean.'

'I thought it had always been The Laurels.'

'Oh no. I don't think it was ever called that. Houses change names a lot around here. People do like giving new names to houses, you know.'

'Yes, they certainly seem to,' said Tuppence thoughtfully. 'Even we have thought of a name or two. By the way, Beatrice told me that you knew someone once living here called Mary Jordan.'

'I didn't know her, but I have heard her mentioned. In the war it was, not the last war. The one long before that when there used to be zeppelins.'

'I remember hearing about zeppelins,' said Tuppence.

'In 1915 or 1916 – they came over London.'

'I remember I'd gone to the Army & Navy Stores one day with an old great-aunt and there was an alarm.'

'They used to come over at night sometimes, didn't they? Must have been rather frightening, I should think.'

'Well, I don't think it was really,' said Tuppence. 'People used to get quite excited. It wasn't nearly as frightening as the flying bombs – in this last war. One always felt rather as though *they* were following you to places. Following you down a street, or something like that?'

'Spend all your nights in the tube, did you? I had a friend in London. She used to spend all the nights in the tubes. Warren Street, I think it was. Everyone used to have their own particular tube station.'

'I wasn't in London in the last war,' said Tuppence. 'I don't think I'd have liked to spend all night in the tube.'

'Well, this friend of mine, Jenny her name was, oh she used to love the tube. She said it was ever so much fun. You know, you had your own particular stair in the tube. It was kept for you always, you slept there, and you took sandwiches in and things, and you had fun together and talked. Things went on all night and never stopped. Wonderful, you know. Trains going on right up to the morning. She told me she couldn't bear it when the war was over and she had to go home again, felt it was so dull, you know.'

'Anyway,' said Tuppence, 'there weren't any flying-bombs in 1914. Just the zeppelins.'

Zeppelins had clearly lost interest for Gwenda.

'It was someone called Mary Jordan I was asking about,' said Tuppence. 'Beatrice said you knew about her.'

'Not really – I just heard her name mentioned once or twice, but it was ages ago. Lovely golden hair she had, my grandmother said. German she was – one of those Frowlines as they were called. Looked after children – a kind of nurse. Had been with a naval family somewhere, that was up in Scotland, I think. And afterwards she came down here. Went to a family called Parks – or Perkins. She used to have one day off a week, you know, and go to London, and that's where she used to take the things, whatever they were.'

'What sort of things?' said Tuppence.

'I don't know – nobody ever said much. Things she'd stolen, I expect.'

'Was she discovered stealing?'

'Oh no, I don't think so. They were beginning to suspect, but she got ill and died before that.'

'What did she die of? Did she die down here? I suppose she went to hospital.'

'No – I don't think there were any hospitals to go to then. Wasn't any Welfare in those days. Somebody told me it was some silly mistake the cook made. Brought foxglove leaves into the house by mistake for spinach – or for lettuce, perhaps. No, I think that was someone else. Someone told me it was deadly nightshade but I don't believe *that* for a moment because, I mean, everyone knows about deadly nightshade, don't they, and anyway that's berries. Well, I think this was foxglove leaves brought in from the garden by mistake. Foxglove is Digoxo or some name like Digit – something that sounds like fingers. It's got something very deadly in it – the doctor came and he did what he could, but I think it was too late.'

'Were there many people in the house when it happened?'

'Oh, there was quite a lot I should think – yes, because there were always people staying, so I've heard, and children, you know, and weekenders and a nursery maid and a governess, I think, and parties. Mind you, I'm not knowing all about this myself. It's only what Granny used to tell me. And old Mr Bodlicott talks now and then. You know, the old gardener chap as works here now and then. He was gardener there, and they blamed him at first for sending the wrong leaves, but it wasn't *him* as did it. It was somebody who came out of the house, and wanted to help and picked the vegetables in the garden, and took them in to the cook. You know, spinach and lettuce and things like that and – er – I suppose they just made a mistake not knowing much about growing vegetables. I think they said at the inquest or whatever they had afterwards that it was a mistake that *anyone* could make because the spinach or the sorrel leaves were growing near the Digi – Digit-what-not, you see, so I suppose they just took a great handful of both leaves, possibly in a bunch together. Anyway, it was very sad because

Granny said she was a very good-looking girl with golden hair and all that, you know.'

'And she used to go up to London every week? Naturally she'd have to have a day off.'

'Yes. Said she had friends there. Foreigner, she was – Granny says there was some as said she was actually a German spy.'

'And was she?'

'I shouldn't think so. The gentlemen liked her all right, apparently. You know, the naval officers and the ones up at Shelton Military Camp too. She had one or two friends there, you know. The military camp it was.'

'Was she really a spy?'

'Shouldn't think so. I mean, my grandmother said that was what people *said*. It wasn't in the last war. It was ages before that.'

'Funny,' said Tuppence, 'how easy it is to get mixed up over the wars. I knew an old man who had a friend in the Battle of Waterloo.'

'Oh, fancy that. Years before 1914. People did have foreign nurses – what were called Mamoselles as well as Frowlines, whatever a Frowline is. Very nice with children she was, Granny said. Everyone was very pleased with her and always liked her.'

'That was when she was living here, living at The Laurels?'

'Wasn't called that then – at least I don't think so. She was living with the Parkinsons or the Perkins, some name like that,' said Gwenda. 'What we call nowadays an *au pair* girl. She came from that place where the patty comes from, you know, Fortnum & Mason keep it – expensive patty for parties. Half German, half French, so someone told me.'

'Strasbourg?' suggested Tuppence.

'Yes, that was the name. She used to paint pictures. Did one of an old great-aunt of mine. It made her look too old, Aunt Fanny always said. Did one of one of the Parkinson boys. Old Mrs Griffin's got it still. The Parkinson boy found out something about her, I believe – the one she painted the picture of, I mean. Godson of Mrs Griffin, I believe he was.'

'Would that have been Alexander Parkinson?'

'Yes, that's the one. The one who's buried near the church.'

CHAPTER 2
....

INTRODUCTION TO MATHILDE, TRUELOVE AND KK

Tuppence, on the following morning, went in search of that well-known public character in the village known usually as Old Isaac, or, on formal occasions if one could remember, Mr Bodlicott. Isaac Bodlicott was one of the local 'characters'. He was a character because of his age – he claimed to be ninety (not generally believed) – and he was able to do repairs of many curious kinds. If your efforts to ring up the plumber met with no response, you went to old Isaac Bodlicott. Mr Bodlicott, whether or not he was in any way qualified for the repairs he did, had been well acquainted for many of the years of his long life with every type of sanitation problem, bath-water problems, difficulties with geysers, and sundry electrical problems on the side. His charges compared favourably with a real live qualified plumber, and his repairs were often surprisingly successful. He could do carpentering, he could attend to locks, he could hang pictures – rather crookedly sometimes – he understood about the springs of derelict armchairs. The main disadvantage of Mr Bodlicott's attentions was his garrulous habit of incessant conversation slightly hampered by a difficulty in adjusting his false teeth in such a way as to make what he said intelligible in his pronunciation. His memories of past inhabitants of the neighbourhood seemed to be unlimited. It was difficult, on the whole, to know how reliable they might be. Mr Bodlicott was not one to shirk giving himself the pleasure of retailing some really good story of past days. These flights of fancy, claimed usually as flights of memory, were usually ushered in with the same type of statement.

'You'd be surprised, you would, if I could tell you what I knew about that one. Yes indeed. Well, you know, everybody thought they knew all about it, but they were wrong. Absolutely wrong. It was the elder sister, you know. Yes, it was. Such a nice girl, she seemed. It was the butcher's dog that gave them all the clue. Followed her home, he did. Yes. Only it wasn't her own home, as you might say. Ah well, I could tell you a lot more about *that*. Then there was old Mrs Atkins. Nobody knew as she kept a revolver in the house, but I knew. I knew when I was sent for to mend her tallboy – that's what they call those high chests, isn't it? Yes. Tallboys. Well, that's right. Well, there she was, seventy-five, and in that drawer, the drawer of the tallboy as I went, you know, to mend – the hinges had gone, the lock too – that's where the revolver was. Wrapped up, it was, with a pair of women's shoes. No. 3 size. Or, I'm not sure as it wasn't No. 2. White satin. Tiny little foot. Her great-grandmother's wedding shoes, she said. Maybe. But somebody said she bought them at a curiosity shop once but I don't know about that. And there was the revolver wrapped up too. Yes. Well, they said as her son had brought it back. Brought it back from East Africa, he did. He'd been out there shooting elephants or something of that kind. And when he come home he brought this revolver. And do you know what that old lady used to do? Her son had taught her to shoot. She'd sit by her drawing-room window looking out and when people came up the drive she'd have her revolver with her and she'd shoot either side of them. Yes. Got them frightened to death and they ran away. She said she wouldn't have anyone coming in and disturbing the birds. Very keen on the birds, she was. Mind you, she never shot a bird. No, she didn't want to do that. Then there was all the stories about Mrs Letherby. Nearly had up, *she* was. Yes, shoplifting. Very clever at it, so they say. And yet as rich as they make them.'

Having persuaded Mr Bodlicott to replace the skylight in the bathroom, Tuppence wondered if she could direct his conversation to any memory of the past which would be useful to Tommy and herself in solving the mystery of the concealment in their house of some treasure or interesting secret of whose nature they had no knowledge whatever.

Old Isaac Bodlicott made no difficulties about coming to do repairs for the new tenants of the place. It was one of his pleasures in life to meet as many newcomers as possible. It was in his life one of the main events to be able to come across people who had not so far heard of his splendid memories and reminiscences. Those who were well acquainted with them did not often encourage him to repeat these tales. But a new audience! That was always a pleasant happening. That and displaying the wonderful amount of trades that he managed to combine among his various services to the community in which he lived. It was his pleasure to indulge in a running commentary.

'Luck it was, as old Joe didn't get cut. Might have ripped his face open.'

'Yes, it might indeed.'

'There's a bit more glass wants sweeping up on the floor still, missus.'

'I know,' said Tuppence, 'we haven't had time yet.'

'Ah, but you can't take risks with glass. You know what glass is. A little splinter can do you all the harm in the world. Die of it, you can, if it gets into a blood vessel. I remember Miss Lavinia Shotacomb. You wouldn't believe . . .'

Tuppence was not tempted by Miss Lavinia Shotacomb. She had heard her mentioned by other local characters. She had apparently been between seventy and eighty, quite deaf and almost blind.

'I suppose,' said Tuppence, breaking in before Isaac's reminiscences of Lavinia Shotacomb could begin, 'that you must know a lot about all the various people and the extraordinary things that have happened in this place in the past.'

'Aw, well, I'm not as young as I was, you know. Over eighty-five, I am. Going on ninety. I've always had a good memory. There are things, you know, you don't forget. No. However long it is, something reminds you of it, you know, and brings it all back to you. The things I could tell you, you wouldn't believe.'

'Well, it's really wonderful, isn't it,' said Tuppence, 'to think how much you must know about what a lot of extraordinary people.'

'Ah no, there's no accounting for people, is there? Ones that aren't what you think they are, sometimes things as you wouldn't have believed in about them.'

'Spies, I suppose, sometimes,' said Tuppence, 'or criminals.' She looked at him hopefully . . . Old Isaac bent and picked up a splinter of glass.

'Here you are,' he said. 'How'd you feel if *that* got in the sole of your foot?'

Tuppence began to feel that the replenishing of a glass skylight was not going to yield much in the way of Isaac's more exciting memories of the past. She noticed that the small so-called green-house attached to the wall of the house near the dining-room window was also in need of repair and replacement by an outlay of money upon glass. Would it be worth repairing or would it be better to have it pulled down? Isaac was quite pleased to transfer himself to this fresh problem. They went downstairs, and outside the house walked round its walls until they came to the erection in question.

'Ah, you mean that there, do you?'

Tuppence said yes, she did mean that there.

'Kay-kay,' said Isaac.

Tuppence looked at him. Two letters of the alphabet such as KK really meant nothing to her.

'What did you say?'

'I said KK. That's what it used to be called in old Mrs Lottie Jones's time.'

'Oh. Why did she call it KK?'

'I dunno. It was a sort of – sort of name I suppose they used to have for places like this. You know, it wasn't grand. Bigger houses have a real conservatory. You know, where they'd have maidenhair ferns in pots.'

'Yes,' said Tuppence, her own memories going back easily to such things.

'And a greenhouse you can call it, too. But this here, KK old Mrs Lottie Jones used to call it. I dunno why.'

'Did they have maidenhair ferns in it?'

'No, it wasn't used for that. No. The children had it for toys mostly. Well, when you say toys I expect they're here still if nobody has turned them out. You see, it's half falling down, isn't it? They just stuck up a bit then they put a bit of roofing over and I don't suppose that anyone will use it again. They used to bring the broken toys, or chairs out here and things like that. But then, you see, they already had the rocking-horse there and Truelove in the far corner.'

'Can we get inside it?' asked Tuppence, trying to apply her eye to a slightly clearer portion of a pane of window. 'There must be a lot of queer things inside.'

'Ah well, there's the key,' said Isaac. 'I expect it's hanging up in the same place.'

'Where's the same place?'

'Ah, there's a shed round here.'

They went round an adjacent path. The shed was hardly worthy of being called a shed. Isaac kicked its door open, removed various bits of branches of trees, kicked away some rotting apples and, removing an old doormat hanging on the wall, showed three or four rusty keys hanging up on a nail.

'Lindop's keys, those,' he said. 'Last but one was as living here as gardener. Retired basket-maker, he was. Didn't do no good at anything. If you'd like to see inside KK –?'

'Oh yes,' said Tuppence hopefully. 'I'd like to see inside KK. How do you spell it?'

'How do you spell what?'

'I mean KK. Is it just two letters?'

'No. I think it was something different. I think it was two foreign words. I seem to remember now K-A-I and then another K-A-I. Kay-Kay, or Kye-Kye almost, they used to say it. I think it was a Japanese word.'

'Oh,' said Tuppence. 'Did any Japanese people ever live here?'

'Oh no, nothing like that. No. Not that kind of foreigner.'

The application of a little oil, which Isaac seemed to produce and apply quite quickly, had a wonderful effect on the rustiest of the keys which, inserted in the door and turned with a grinding noise, could be pushed open. Tuppence and her guide went in.

'There you are,' said Isaac, not displaying any particular pride in the objects within. 'Nothing but old rubbish, is it?'

'That's a rather wonderful-looking horse,' said Tuppence.

'That's Mackild, that is,' said Isaac.

'Mack-ild?' said Tuppence, rather doubtfully.

'Yes. It's a woman's name of some kind. Queen somebody, it was. Somebody said as it was William the Conqueror's wife but I think they were just boasting about that. Come from America, it did. American godfather brought it to one of the children.'

'To one of the –?'

'One of the Bassington children, that was. Before the other lot. I dunno. I suppose it's all rusted up now.'

Mathilde was a rather splendid-looking horse even in decay.

Its length was quite the length of any horse or mare to be found nowadays. Only a few hairs were left of what must once have been a prolific mane. One ear was broken off. It had once been painted grey. Its front legs splayed out in front and its back legs at the back; it had a wispy tail.

'It doesn't work like any rocking-horse I've ever seen before,' said Tuppence, interested.

'No, it don't, do it?' said Isaac. 'You know, they go up and down, up and down, front to back. But this one here, you see – it sort of springs forwards. Once first, the front legs do it – whoop – and then the back legs do it. It's a very good action. Now if I was to get on it and show you –'

'Do be careful,' said Tuppence. 'It might – there might be nails or something which would stick into you, or you might fall off.'

'Ah. I've ridden on Mathilde, fifty or sixty years ago it must have been, but I remember. And it's still pretty solid, you know. It's not really falling to bits yet.'

With a sudden, unexpected, acrobatic action he sprang upon Mathilde. The horse raced forwards, then raced backwards.

'Got action, hasn't it?'

'Yes, it's got action,' said Tuppence.

'Ah, they loved that, you know. Miss Jenny, she used to ride it day after day.'

'Who was Miss Jenny?'

'Why, she was the eldest one, you know. She was the one that had the godfather as sent her this. Sent her Truelove, too,' he added.

Tuppence looked at him enquiringly. The remark did not seem to apply to any of the other contents of Kay-Kay.

'That's what they call it, you know. That little horse and cart what's there in the corner. Used to ride it down the hill, Miss Pamela did. Very serious, she was, Miss Pamela. She'd get in at the top of the hill and she'd put her feet on there – you see, it's meant to have pedals but they don't work, so she'd take it to the top of the hill and then she'd let it begin to go down the hill, and she'd put the brakes on, as it were, with her feet. Often she'd end up landing in the monkey puzzle, as a matter of fact.'

'That sounds very uncomfortable,' said Tuppence. 'I mean, to land in the monkey puzzle.'

'Ah well, she could stop herself a bit before that. Very serious, she was. She used to do that by the hour – three or four hours I've watched her. I was doing the Christmas rose bed very often, you know, and the pampas grass, and I'd see her going down. I didn't speak to her because she didn't like being spoken to. She wanted to go on with what she was doing or what she thought she was doing.'

'What did she think she was doing?' said Tuppence, beginning suddenly to get more interested in Miss Pamela than she had been in Miss Jenny.

'Well, I don't know. She used to say sometimes she was a princess, you know, escaping, or Mary, Queen of What-is-it – do I mean Ireland or Scotland?'

'Mary Queen of Scots,' suggested Tuppence.

'Yes, that's right. She went away or something, or escaped. Went into a castle. Lock something it was called. Not a real lock, you know, a piece of water, it was.'

'Ah yes, I see. And Pamela thought she was Mary Queen of Scots escaping from her enemies?'

'That's right. Going to throw herself into England on Queen Elizabeth's mercy, she said, but I don't think as Queen Elizabeth was very merciful.'

'Well,' said Tuppence, masking any disappointment she felt, 'it's all very interesting, I'm sure. Who were these people, did you say?'

'Oh, they were the Listers, they were.'

'Did you ever know a Mary Jordan?'

'Ah, I know who you mean. No, she was before my time a bit, I think. You mean the German spy girl, don't you?'

'Everyone seems to know about her here,' said Tuppence.

'Yes. They called her the Frow Line, or something. Sounds like a railway.'

'It does rather,' said Tuppence.

Isaac suddenly laughed. 'Ha, ha, ha,' he said. 'If it was a railway, a line, a railway line, oh, it didn't run straight, did it? No, indeed.' He laughed again.

'What a splendid joke,' said Tuppence kindly.

Isaac laughed again.

'It's about time,' he said, 'you thought of putting some vegetables in, isn't it? You know, if you want to get your broad beans on in good time you ought to put 'em in and prepare for the peas. And what about some early lettuce? Tom Thumbs now? Beautiful lettuce, those, small but crisp as anything.'

'I suppose you've done a lot of gardening work round here. I don't mean just this house, but a lot of places.'

'Ah yes, I've done odd jobbing, you know. I used to come along to most of the houses. Some of the gardeners they had weren't any good at all and I'd usually come in and help at certain times or other. Had a bit of an accident here once, you know. Mistake about vegetables. Before my time – but I heard about it.'

'Something about foxglove leaves, wasn't it?' said Tuppence.

'Ah, fancy you having heard of that already. That was a long time ago, too. Yes, several was taken ill with it. One of them died. At least so I heard. That was only hearsay. Old pal of mine told me that.'

'I think it was the Frow Line,' said Tuppence.

'What, the Frow Line as died? Well, I never heard that.'

'Well, perhaps I'm wrong,' said Tuppence. 'Supposing you take Truelove,' she said, 'or whatever this thing's called, and put it on the hill in the place where that child, Pamela, used to take it down the hill – if the hill is still there.'

'Well, of course the hill is still there. What do you think? It's all grass still, but be careful now. I don't know how much of Truelove is rusted away. I'll have a bit of a clean-up on it first, shall I?'

'That's right,' said Tuppence, 'and then you can think of a list of vegetables that we ought to be getting on with.'

'Ah well, I'll be careful you don't get foxglove and spinach planted together. Shouldn't like to hear that something happened to you when you've just got into a new house. Nice place here if you can just have a little money to spend on it.'

'Thank you very much,' said Tuppence.

'And I'll just see to that there Truelove so it won't break down under you. It's very old but you'd be surprised the way some old things work. Why, I knew a cousin of mine the other day and he got out an old bicycle. You wouldn't think it would go – nobody had ridden it for about forty years. But it went all right with a bit of oil. Ah, it's wonderful what a bit of oil can do.'

CHAPTER 3

SIX IMPOSSIBLE THINGS BEFORE BREAKFAST

I

'What on earth –' said Tommy.

He was used to finding Tuppence in unlikely spots when he returned to the house, but on this occasion he was more startled than usual.

Inside the house there was no trace of her, although outside there was a very slight patter of rain. It occurred to him that she might be engrossed in some portion of the garden, and he went out to see if this might be the case. And it was then that he remarked, 'What on earth –'

'Hullo, Tommy,' said Tuppence, 'you're back a bit earlier than I thought you would be.'

'What is that thing?'

'You mean Truelove?'

'What did you say?'

'I said Truelove,' said Tuppence, 'that's the name of it.'

'Are you trying to go for a ride on it – it's much too small for you.'

'Well, of course it is. It's a child's sort of thing – what you had, I suppose, before you had fairy-cycles, or whatever one had in my youth.'

'It doesn't really *go*, does it?' asked Tommy.

'Well, not exactly,' said Tuppence, 'but you see, you take it up to the top of the hill and then it – well, its wheels turn of their own accord, you see, and because of the hill you go down.'

'And crash at the bottom, I suppose. Is that what you've been doing?'

'Not at all,' said Tuppence. 'You brake it with your feet. Would you like me to give you a demonstration?'

'I don't think so,' said Tommy. 'It's beginning to rain rather harder. I just wanted to know why you – well, why you're doing it. I mean, it can't be very enjoyable, can it?'

'Actually,' said Tuppence, 'it's rather frightening. But you see I just wanted to find out and –'

'And are you asking this tree? What is this tree, anyway? A monkey puzzle, isn't it?'

'That's right,' said Tuppence. 'How clever of you to know.'

'Of course I know,' said Tommy. 'I know its other name, too.'

'So do I,' said Tuppence.

They looked at each other.

'Only at the moment I've forgotten it,' said Tommy. 'Is it an arti –'

'Well, it's something very like that,' said Tuppence. 'I think that's good enough, don't you?'

'What are you doing inside a prickly thing like that?'

'Well, because when you get to the end of the hill, I mean, if you didn't put your feet down to stop completely you could be in the arti – or whatever it is.'

'Do I mean arti –? What about urticaria? No, that's nettles, isn't it? Oh well,' said Tommy, 'everyone to their own kind of amusement.'

'I was just doing a little investigation, you know, of our latest problem.'

'Your problem? My problem? Whose problem?'

'I don't know,' said Tuppence. 'Both our problems, I hope.'

'But not one of Beatrice's problems, or anything like that?'

'Oh no. It's just that I wondered what other things there might be hidden in this house, so I went and looked at a lot of toys that seem to have been shoved away in a sort of queer old greenhouse probably years and years ago and there was this creature and there was Mathilde, which is a rocking-horse with a hole in its stomach.'

'A hole in its stomach?'

'Well, yes. People, I suppose, used to shove things in there. Children – for fun – and lots of old leaves and dirty papers and bits of sort of queer dusters and flannel, oily stuff that had been used to clean things with.'

'Come on, let's go into the house,' said Tommy.

II

'Well, Tommy,' said Tuppence, as she stretched out her feet to a pleasant wood fire which she had lit already for his return in the drawing-room, 'let's have your news. Did you go to the Ritz Hotel Gallery to see the show?'

'No. As a matter of fact, I hadn't time, really.'

'What do you mean, you hadn't time? I thought that's what you went for.'

'Well, one doesn't always do the things that one went for.'

'You must have gone somewhere and done *something*,' said Tuppence.

'I found a new possible place to park a car.'

'That's always useful,' said Tuppence. 'Where was that?'

'Near Hounslow.'

'What on earth did you want to go to Hounslow for?'

'Well, I didn't actually go to Hounslow. There's a sort of car park there, then I took a tube, you know.'

'What, a tube to London?'

'Yes. Yes, it seemed the easiest way.'

'You have rather a guilty look about you,' said Tuppence. 'Don't tell me I have a rival who lives in Hounslow?'

'No,' said Tommy. 'You ought to be pleased with what I've been doing.'

'Oh. Have you been buying me a present?'

'No. No,' said Tommy, 'I'm afraid not. I never know what to give you, as a matter of fact.'

'Well, your guesses are very good sometimes,' said Tuppence hopefully. 'What have you been really doing, Tommy, and why should I be pleased?'

'Because I, too,' said Tommy, 'have been doing research.'

'Everyone's doing research nowadays,' said Tuppence. 'You know, all the teenagers and all one's nephews or cousins or other people's sons and daughters, they're all doing research. I don't know actually what they do research into nowadays, but they never seem to do it, whatever it is, afterwards. They just have the research and a good time doing the research and they're very pleased with themselves and – well, I don't quite know what does come next.'

'Betty, our adopted daughter, went to East Africa,' said Tommy. 'Have you heard from her?'

'Yes, she loves it there – loves poking into African families and writing articles about them.'

'Do you think the families appreciate her interest?' asked Tommy.

'I shouldn't think so,' said Tuppence. 'In my father's parish I remember, everyone disliked the District Visitors – Nosey Parkers they called them.'

'You may have something there,' said Tommy. 'You are certainly pointing out to me the difficulties of what I am undertaking, or trying to undertake.'

'Research into what? Not lawn-mowers, I hope.'

'I don't know why you mention lawn-mowers.'

'Because you're eternally looking at catalogues of them,' said Tuppence. 'You're mad about getting a lawn-mower.'

'In this house of ours it is historic research we are doing into things – crimes and others that seem to have happened at least sixty or seventy years ago.'

'Anyway, come on, tell me a little more about your research projects, Tommy.'

'I went to London,' said Tommy, 'and put certain things in motion.'

'Ah,' said Tuppence. 'Research? Research in motion. In a way I've been doing the same thing that you are, only our methods are different. And my period is very far back.'

'Do you mean that you're really beginning to take an interest in the problem of Mary Jordan? So that's how you put it on the agenda nowadays,' said Tommy. 'It's definitely taken shape has it? The mystery, or the problem of Mary Jordan.'

'Such a very ordinary name, too. Couldn't have been her right name if she was German,' said Tuppence, 'and she was said to be a German spy or something like that, but she could have been English, I suppose.'

'I think the German story is just a kind of legend.'

'Do go on, Tommy. You're not telling me anything.'

'Well, I put certain – certain – certain –'

'Don't go on saying certain,' said Tuppence. 'I really can't understand.'

'Well, it's very difficult to explain things sometimes,' said Tommy, 'but I mean, there are certain ways of making enquiries.'

'You mean, things in the past?'

'Yes. In a sense. I mean, there are things that you can find out. Things that you could obtain information from. Not just by riding old toys and asking old ladies to remember things and cross-questioning an old gardener who probably will tell you everything quite wrong or going round to the post office and upsetting the staff by asking the girls there to tell their memories of what their great-great-aunts once said.'

'All of them have produced a little something,' said Tuppence.

'So will mine,' said Tommy.

'You've been making enquiries? Who do you go to to ask your questions?'

'Well, it's not quite like that, but you must remember, Tuppence, that occasionally in my life I have been in connection with people who do know how to go about these sort of things. You know, there are people you pay a certain sum to and they do the research for you from the proper quarters so that what you get is quite authentic.'

'What sort of things? What sort of places?'

'Well, there are lots of things. To begin with you can get someone to study deaths, births and marriages, that sort of thing.'

'Oh, I suppose you send them to Somerset House. Do you go there for deaths as well as marriages?'

'And births – one needn't go oneself, you get someone to go for you. And find out when someone dies or read somebody's will, look up marriages in churches or study birth certificates. All those things can be enquired into.'

'Have you been spending a lot of money?' asked Tuppence. 'I thought we were going to try and economize once we'd paid the expense of moving in here.'

'Well, considering the interest you're taking in problems, I consider that this can be regarded in the way of money well spent.'

'Well, did you find out anything?'

'Not as quickly as this. You have to wait until the research has been made. Then if they can get answers for you –'

'You mean somebody comes up and tells you that someone called Mary Jordan was born at Little Sheffield-on-the-Wold or something like that and then you go and make enquiries there later. Is that the sort of thing?'

'Not exactly. And then there are census returns and death certificates and causes of death and, oh, quite a lot of things that you can find out about.'

'Well,' said Tuppence, 'it sounds rather interesting anyway, which is always something.'

'And there are files in newspaper offices that you can read and study.'

'You mean accounts of something – like murders or court cases?'

'Not necessarily, but one has had contact with certain people from time to time. People who know things – one can look them up – ask a few questions – renew old friendships. Like the time we were being a private detective firm in London. There are a few people, I expect, who could give us information or tell us where to go. Things do depend a bit on who you know.'

'Yes,' said Tuppence, 'that's quite true. I know that myself from experience.'

'Our methods aren't the same,' said Tommy. 'I think yours are just as good as mine. I'll never forget the day I came suddenly into that boarding-house, or whatever it was, Sans Souci. The first thing I saw was you sitting there knitting and calling yourself Mrs Blenkinsop.'

'All because I *hadn't* applied research, or getting anyone to do research for me,' said Tuppence.

'No,' said Tommy, 'you got inside a wardrobe next door to the room where I was being interviewed in a very interesting manner, so you knew exactly where I was being sent and what I was meant to do, and you managed to get there first. Eavesdropping. Neither more nor less. Most dishonourable.'

'With very satisfactory results,' said Tuppence.

'Yes,' said Tommy. 'You have a kind of feeling for success. It seems to happen to you.'

'Well, some day we shall know all about everything here, only it's all such years and years ago. I can't help thinking that the idea of something really important being hidden round here or owned by someone here, or something to do with this house or people who once lived in it being important – I can't just believe it somehow. Oh well, I see what we shall have to do next.'

'What?' said Tommy.

'Believe six impossible things before breakfast, of course,' said Tuppence. 'It's quarter to eleven now, and I want to go to bed. I'm tired. I'm sleepy and extremely dirty because of playing around with all those dusty, ancient toys and things. I expect there are even more things in that place that's called – by the way, why is it called Kay Kay?'

'I don't know. Do you spell it at all?'

'I don't know – I think it's spelt k-a-i. Not just KK.'

'Because it sounds more mysterious?'

'It sounds Japanese,' said Tuppence doubtfully.

'I can't see why it should sound to you like Japanese. It doesn't to me. It sounds like something you eat. A kind of rice, perhaps.'

'I'm going to bed and to wash thoroughly and to get all the cobwebs off me somehow,' said Tuppence.

'Remember,' said Tommy, 'six impossible things before breakfast.'

'I expect I shall be better at that than you would be,' said Tuppence.

'You're very unexpected sometimes,' said Tommy.

'*You're* more often right than *I* am,' said Tuppence. '*That's* very annoying sometimes. Well, these things are sent to try us. Who used to say that to us? Quite often, too.'

'Never mind,' said Tommy. 'Go and clean the dust of bygone years off you. Is Isaac any good at gardening?'

'He considers he is,' said Tuppence. 'We might experiment with him –'

'Unfortunately we don't know much about gardening ourselves. Yet another problem.'

CHAPTER 4

EXPEDITION ON TRUELOVE; OXFORD AND CAMBRIDGE

I

'Six impossible things before breakfast indeed,' said Tuppence as she drained a cup of coffee and considered a fried egg remaining in the dish on the sideboard, flanked by two appetizing-looking kidneys. 'Breakfast is more worthwhile than thinking of impossible things. Tommy is the one who has gone after impossible things. Research, indeed. I wonder if he'll get anything out of it all.'

She applied herself to a fried egg and kidneys.

'How nice,' said Tuppence, 'to have a different kind of breakfast.'

For a long time she had managed to regale herself in the morning with a cup of coffee and either orange juice or grapefruit. Although satisfactory so long as any weight problems were thereby solved, the pleasures of this kind of breakfast were not much appreciated. From the force of contrasts, hot dishes on the sideboard animated the digestive juices.

'I expect,' said Tuppence, 'it's what the Parkinsons used to have for breakfast here. Fried egg or poached eggs and bacon and perhaps –' she threw her mind a good long way back to remembrances of old novels – 'perhaps yes, perhaps cold grouse on the sideboard, delicious! Oh yes, I remember, delicious it sounded. Of course, I suppose children were so unimportant that they only let them have the legs. Legs of game are very good because you can nibble at them.' She paused with the last piece of kidney in her mouth.

Very strange noises seemed to be coming through the doorway.

'I wonder,' said Tuppence. 'It sounds like a concert gone wrong somewhere.'

She paused again, a piece of toast in her hand, and looked up as Albert entered the room.

'What is going on, Albert?' demanded Tuppence. 'Don't tell me that's our workmen playing something? A harmonium or something like that?'

'It's the gentleman what's come to do the piano,' said Albert.

'Come to do what to the piano?'

'To tune it. You said I'd have to get a piano tuner.'

'Good gracious,' said Tuppence, 'you've done it already? How wonderful you are, Albert.'

Albert looked pleased, though at the same time conscious of the fact that he *was* very wonderful in the speed with which he could usually supply the extraordinary demands made upon him sometimes by Tuppence and sometimes by Tommy.

'He says it needs it very bad,' he said.

'I expect it does,' said Tuppence.

She drank half a cup of coffee, went out of the room and into the drawing-room. A young man was at work at the grand piano, which was revealing to the world large quantities of its inside.

'Good morning, madam,' said the young man.

'Good morning,' said Tuppence. 'I'm so glad you've managed to come.'

'Ah, it needs tuning, it does.'

'Yes,' said Tuppence, 'I know. You see, we've only just moved in and it's not very good for pianos, being moved into houses and things. And it hasn't been tuned for a long time.'

'No, I can soon tell that,' said the young man.

He pressed three different chords in turn, two cheerful ones in a major key, two very melancholy ones in A Minor.

'A beautiful instrument, madam, if I may say so.'

'Yes,' said Tuppence. 'It's an Erard.'

'And a piano you wouldn't get so easily nowadays.'

'It's been through a few troubles,' said Tuppence. 'It's been through bombing in London. Our house there was hit. Luckily we were away, but it was mostly outside that was damaged.'

'Yes. Yes, the works are good. They don't need so very much doing to them.'

Conversation continued pleasantly. The young man played the opening bars of a Chopin Prelude and passed from that to a rendering of 'The Blue Danube'. Presently he announced that his ministrations had finished.

'I shouldn't leave it too long,' he warned her. 'I'd like the chance to come and try it again before too much time has gone by because you don't know quite when it might not – well, I don't know how

I should put it – relapse a bit. You know, some little thing that you haven't noticed or haven't been able to get at.'

They parted with mutually appreciative remarks on music in general and on piano music in particular, and with the polite salutations of two people who agreed very largely in their ideas as to the joys that music generally played in life.

'Needs a lot doing to it, I expect, this house,' he said, looking round him.

'Well, I think it had been empty some time when we came into it.'

'Oh yes. It's changed hands a lot, you know.'

'Got quite a history, hasn't it,' said Tuppence. 'I mean, the people who lived in it in the past and the sort of queer things that happened.'

'Ah well, I expect you're talking of that time long ago. I don't know if it was the last war or the one before.'

'Something to do with naval secrets or something,' said Tuppence hopefully.

'Could be, I expect. There was a lot of talk, so they tell me, but of course I don't know anything about it myself.'

'Well before your time,' said Tuppence, looking appreciatively at his youthful countenance.

When he had gone, she sat down at the piano.

'I'll play "The Rain on the Roof",' said Tuppence, who had had this Chopin memory revived in her by the piano tuner's execution of one of the other preludes. Then she dropped into some chords and began playing the accompaniment to a song, humming it first and then murmuring the words as well.

Where has my true love gone a-roaming?
Where has my true love gone from me?
High in the woods the birds are calling.
When will my true love come back to me?

'I'm playing it in the wrong key, I believe,' said Tuppence, 'but at any rate, the piano's all right again now. Oh, it is great fun to be able to play the piano again. "Where has my true love gone a-roaming?"' she murmured. '"When will my true love" – Truelove,' said Tuppence thoughtfully. 'True love? Yes, I'm thinking of that perhaps as a sign. Perhaps I'd better go out and do something with Truelove.'

She put on her thick shoes and a pullover, and went out into the garden. Truelove had been pushed, not back into his former home in KK, but into the empty stable. Tuppence took him out, pulled him to the top of the grass slope, gave him a sharp flick with the duster she had brought out with her to remove the worst of the cobwebs which still adhered in many places, got into Truelove, placed her feet on the pedals and induced Truelove to display his paces as well as he could in his condition of general age and wear.

'Now, my true love,' she said, 'down the hill with you and not too fast.'

She removed her feet from the pedals and placed them in a position where she could brake with them when necessary.

Truelove was not inclined to go very fast in spite of the advantage to him of having only to go by weight down the hill. However, the slope increased in steepness suddenly. Truelove increased his pace, Tuppence applied her feet as brakes rather more sharply and she and Truelove arrived together at a rather more uncomfortable portion than usual of the monkey puzzle at the bottom of the hill.

'Most painful,' said Tuppence, excavating herself.

Having extricated herself from the pricking of various portions of the monkey puzzle, Tuppence brushed herself down and looked around her. She had come to a thick bit of shrubbery leading up the hill in the opposite direction. There were rhododendron bushes here and hydrangeas. It would look, Tuppence thought, very lovely later in the year. At the moment, there was no particular beauty about it, it was a mere thicket. However, she did seem to notice that there had once been a pathway leading up between the various flower bushes and shrubs. Everything was much grown together now but you could trace the direction of the path. Tuppence broke off a branch or two, pressed her way through the first bushes and managed to follow the hill. The path went winding up. It was clear that nobody had ever cleared it or walked down it for years.

'I wonder where it takes one,' said Tuppence. 'There must be a reason for it.'

Perhaps, she thought, as the path took a couple of sharp turns in opposite directions, making a zigzag and making Tuppence feel that she knew exactly what Alice in Wonderland had meant by saying that a path would suddenly shake itself and change direction. There were fewer bushes, there were laurels now, possibly fitting in with the name given to the property, and then a rather stony, difficult, narrow path wound up between them. It came very suddenly to four moss-covered steps leading up to a kind of niche made of what had once been metal and later seemed to have been replaced by bottles. A kind of shrine, and in it a pedestal and on this pedestal a stone figure, very much decayed. It was the figure of a boy with a basket on his head. A feeling of recognition came to Tuppence.

'This is the sort of thing you could date a place with,' she said. 'It's very like the one Aunt Sarah had in her garden. She had a lot of laurels too.'

Her mind went back to Aunt Sarah, whom she had occasionally visited as a child. She had played herself, she remembered, a game called River Horses. For River Horses you took your hoop out. Tuppence, it may be said, had been six years old at the time. Her hoop represented the horses. White horses with manes and flowing tails. In Tuppence's imagination, with that you had gone across a green, rather thick patch of grass and you had then gone round a bed planted with pampas grass waving feathery heads into the air, up the same kind of a path, and leaning there among some beech trees in the same sort of summer-house niche was a figure and a basket. Tuppence, when riding her winning horses here, had taken a gift always, a gift you put in the basket on top of the boy's head; at the same time you said it was an offering and you made a wish. The wish, Tuppence remembered, was nearly always to come true.

'But that,' said Tuppence, sitting down suddenly on the top step of the flight she had been climbing, 'that, of course, was because I cheated really. I mean, I wished for something that I knew was almost sure to happen, and then I could feel that my wish had come true and it really *was* a magic. It was a proper offering to a real god from the past. Though it wasn't a god really, it was just a podgy-looking little boy. Ah well – what fun it is, all the things one used to invent and believe in and play at.'

She sighed, went down the path again and found her way to the mysteriously named KK.

KK looked in just the same mess as ever. Mathilde was still looking forlorn and forsaken, but two more things attracted Tuppence's attention. They were in porcelain – porcelain stools with the figures of white swans curled round them. One stool was dark blue and the other stool was pale blue.

'Of course,' said Tuppence, 'I've seen things like that before when I was young. Yes, they used to be on verandas. One of my other aunts had them, I think. We used to call them Oxford and Cambridge. Very much the same. I think it was ducks – no, it *was* swans they had round them. And then there was the same sort of queer thing in the seat, a sort of hole that was like a letter S. The sort of thing you could put things into. Yes, I think I'll get Isaac to take these two stools out of here and give them a good wash, and then we'll have them on the loggia, or lodger as he will insist on calling it, though the veranda comes more natural to me. We'll put them on that and enjoy them when the good weather comes.'

She turned and started to run towards the door. Her foot caught in Mathilde's obtrusive rocker –

'Oh dear!' said Tuppence, 'now what have I done?'

What she had done was to catch her foot in the dark blue porcelain stool and it rolled down on to the floor and smashed in two pieces.

'Oh dear,' said Tuppence, 'now I've really killed Oxford, I suppose. We shall have to make do with Cambridge. I don't think you could stick Oxford together again. The pieces are too difficult.'

She sighed and wondered what Tommy was doing.

II

Tommy was sitting exchanging memories with some old friends.

'World's in a funny way nowadays,' said Colonel Atkinson. 'I hear you and your what's-her-name, Prudence – no, you had a nickname for her, Tuppence, that's right – yes, I hear you've gone to live in the country. Somewhere down near Hollowquay. I wonder what took you there. Anything particular?'

'Well, we found this house fairly cheap,' said Tommy.

'Ah. Well, that's lucky always, isn't it? What's the name? You must give me your address.'

'Well, we think we may call it Cedar Lodge because there's a very nice cedar there. Its original name was The Laurels, but that's rather a Victorian hangover, isn't it?'

'The Laurels. The Laurels, Hollowquay. My word, what are *you* up to, eh? What are *you* up to?'

Tommy looked at the elderly face with the sprouting white moustache.

'On to something, are you?' said Colonel Atkinson. 'Are you employed in the service of your country again?'

'Oh, I'm too old for that,' said Tommy. 'I'm retired from all that sort of stuff.'

'Ah, I wonder now. Perhaps that's just the thing you say. Perhaps you've been told to say that. After all, you know, there's a good deal was never found out about all that business.'

'What business?' said Tommy.

'Well, I expect you've read about it or heard about it. The Cardington Scandal. You know, came after that other thing – the what-you-call-'em letters – and the Emlyn Johnson submarine business.'

'Oh,' said Tommy, 'I seem to remember something vaguely.'

'Well, it wasn't actually the submarine business, but that's what called attention to the whole thing. And there were those letters, you see. Gave the whole show away politically. Yes. Letters. If they'd been able to get hold of *them* it would have made a big difference. It would have drawn attention to several people who at the time were the most highly trusted people in the government. Astonishing how these things happen, isn't it? You know! The traitors in one's midst, always highly trusted, always splendid fellows, always the last people to be suspected – and all the time – well, a lot of all that never came to light.' He winked one eye. 'Perhaps you've been sent down there to have a look round, eh, my boy?'

'A look round at what?' said Tommy.

'Well, this house of yours, The Laurels, did you say? There used to be some silly jokes about The Laurels sometimes. Mind you, they'd had a good look round, the security people and the rest of them. They thought that somewhere in that house was valuable evidence of some kind. There was an idea it had been sent overseas – Italy was mentioned – just before people got alerted. But other people thought it might be still hidden there in that part of the world somewhere. You know, it's the sort of place that has cellars and flagstones and various things. Come now, Tommy, my boy, I feel you're on the hunt again.'

'I assure you I don't do anything of that kind nowadays.'

'Well, that's what one thought before about you when you were at that other place. Beginning of the last war. You know, where you ran down that German chap. That and the woman with the nursery rhyme books. Yes. Sharp bit of work, all that. And now, perhaps, they've set you on another trail!'

'Nonsense,' said Tommy. 'You mustn't get all these ideas in your head. I'm an old gaffer now.'

'You're a cunning old dog. I bet you're better than some of these young ones. Yes. You sit there looking innocent, and really I expect, well, one mustn't ask you questions. Mustn't ask you to betray State secrets, must I? Anyway, be careful of your missus. You know she's always one to stick herself forward too much. She had a narrow escape last time in the N or M days.'

'Ah well,' said Tommy, 'I think Tuppence is just interested in the general antiquity of this place, you know. Who lived there and where. And pictures of the old people who used to live in the house, and all the rest of it. That and planning the garden. That's all we're really interested in nowadays. Gardens. Gardens and bulb catalogues and all the rest of it.'

'Well, maybe I'll believe that if a year passes and nothing exciting has happened. But I know you, Beresford, and I know our Mrs Beresford, too. The two of you together, you're a wonderful couple and I bet you'll come up with something. I tell you, if those papers ever come to light, it'll have a very, very great effect on the political front and there are several people who won't be pleased. No indeed. And those people who won't be pleased are looked on as – pillars of rectitude at the moment! But by some they are thought to be dangerous. Remember that. They're dangerous, and the ones that aren't dangerous are in contact with those who *are* dangerous. So you be careful and make your missus be careful too.'

'Really,' said Tommy, 'your ideas, you make me feel quite excited.'

'Well, go on feeling excited but look after Mrs Tuppence. I'm fond of Tuppence. She's a nice girl, always was and still is.'

'Hardly a girl,' said Tommy.

'Now don't say that of your wife. Don't get in that habit. One in a thousand, she is. But I'm sorry for someone who has her in the picture sleuthing him down. She's probably out on the hunt today.'

'I don't think she is. More likely gone to tea with an elderly lady.'

'Ah well. Elderly ladies can sometimes give you useful information. Elderly ladies and children of five years old. All the unlikely people come out sometimes with a truth nobody had ever dreamed of. I could tell you things –'

'I'm sure you could, Colonel.'

'Ah well, one mustn't give away secrets.'

Colonel Atkinson shook his head.

III

On his way home Tommy stared out of the railway carriage window and watched the rapidly retreating countryside. 'I wonder,' he said to himself, 'I really wonder. That old boy, he's usually in the know. Knows things. But what can there be that could matter *now*. It's all in the past – I mean there's nothing, *can't* be anything left from that war. Not nowadays.' Then he wondered. New ideas had taken over – Common Market ideas. Somewhere, as it were *behind* his mind rather than *in* it, because there were grandsons and nephews, new generations – younger members of families that had always meant something, that had pull, had got positions of influence, of power because they were born who they were, and if by any chance *they* were not loyal, they *could* be approached, could believe in new creeds or in old creeds revived, whichever way you liked to think of it. England was in a funny state, a different state from what it had been. Or was it really always in the same state? Always underneath the smooth surface there was some black mud. There wasn't clear water down to the pebbles, down to the shells, lying on the bottom of the sea. There was something moving, something sluggish somewhere, something that had to be found, suppressed. But surely not – surely not in a place like Hollowquay. Hollowquay was a has-been if there ever was. Developed first as a fishing village and then further developed as an English Riviera – and now a mere summer resort, crowded in August. Most people now preferred package trips abroad.

IV

'Well,' said Tuppence, as she left the dinner table that night and went into the other room to drink coffee, 'was it fun or not fun? How were all the old boys?'

'Oh, very much the old boys,' said Tommy. 'How was your old lady?'

'Oh the piano tuner came,' said Tuppence, 'and it rained in the afternoon so I didn't see her. Rather a pity, the old lady might have said some things that were interesting.'

'My old boy did,' said Tommy. 'I was quite surprised. What do you think of this place really, Tuppence?'

'Do you mean the house?'

'No, I didn't mean the house. I think I mean Hollowquay.'

'Well, I think it's a nice place.'

'What do you mean by nice?'

'Well, it's a good word really. It's a word one usually despises, but I don't know why one should. I suppose a place that's nice is a place where things don't happen and you don't want them to happen. You're glad they don't.'

'Ah. That's because of our age, I suppose.'

'No, I don't think it's because of that. It's because it's nice to know there *are* places where things don't happen. Though I must say something nearly happened today.'

'What do you mean by nearly happened? Have you been doing anything silly, Tuppence?'

'No, of course I haven't.'

'Then what do you mean?'

'I mean that pane of glass at the top of the greenhouse, you know, it was trembling the other day a bit, had the twitches. Well it practically came down on my head. Might have cut me to bits.'

'It doesn't seem to have cut you to bits,' said Tommy, looking at her.

'No. I was lucky. But still, it made me jump rather.'

'Oh, we'll have to get our old boy who comes and does things, what's-his-name? Isaac, isn't it? Have to get him to look at some of the other panes – I mean, we don't want you being done in, Tuppence.'

'Well, I suppose when you buy an old house there's always something wrong with it.'

'Do you think there's something wrong with this house, Tuppence?'

'What on earth do you mean by wrong with this house?'

'Well, because I heard something rather queer about it today.'

'What – queer about this house?'

'Yes.'

'Really, Tommy, that seems impossible,' said Tuppence.

'Why does it seem impossible? Because it looks so nice and innocent? Well painted and done up?'

'No. Well painted and done up and looking innocent, that's all due to us. It looked rather shabby and decayed when we bought it.'

'Well, of course, that's why it was cheap.'

'You look peculiar, Tommy,' said Tuppence. 'What is it?'

'Well, it was old Moustachio-Monty, you know.'

'Oh, dear old boy, yes. Did he send his love to me?'

'Yes, he certainly did. He told me to make you take care of yourself, and me to take care of you.'

'He always says that. Though why I should take care of myself here I don't know.'

'Well, it seems it's the sort of place you might have to take care of yourself.'

'Now what on earth do you mean by that, Tommy?'

'Tuppence, what would you think if I said that he suggested or hinted, whatever way you like, that we were here not as old retired has-beens but as people on active service? That we were once more, as in the N or M days, on duty here. Sent here by the forces of security and order to discover something. To find out what was wrong with this place.'

'Well, I don't know if you're dreaming, Tommy, or if it was old Moustachio-Monty who was, if it was he who suggested it.'

'Well, he did. He seemed to think that we were definitely here on some kind of mission, to find something.'

'To find something? What sort of thing?'

'Something that might be hidden in this house.'

'Something that might be hidden in this house! Tommy, are you mad, or was he mad?'

'Well, I rather thought he might be mad, but I'm not so sure.'

'What could there be to find in this house?'

'Something that I suppose was once hidden here.'

'Buried treasure, are you talking about? Russian crown jewels hidden in the basement, that sort of thing?'

'No. Not treasure. Something that would be dangerous to someone.'

'Well, that's very odd,' said Tuppence.

'Why, have you found something?'

'No, of course I haven't found anything. But it seems there was a scandal about this place donkey's years ago. I don't mean anyone actually remembers, but it's the sort of thing that your grandmother told you, or the servants gossiped about. Actually, Beatrice has a friend who seemed to know something about it. And Mary Jordan was mixed up in it. It was all very hush-hush.'

'Are you imagining things, Tuppence? Have you gone back to the glorious days of our youth, to the time when someone gave a girl on the *Lusitania* something secret, the days when we had adventure, when we tracked down the enigmatic Mr Brown?'

'Goodness, that was a long time ago, Tommy. The Young Adventurers we called ourselves. Doesn't seem real now, does it?'

'No, it doesn't. Not a bit. But it was real, yes, it was real all right. Such a lot of things are real though you can't really bring yourself to believe it. Must be at least sixty or seventy years ago. More than that, even.'

'What did Monty actually say?'

'Letters or papers of some kind,' said Tommy. 'Something that would have created or did create some great political upheaval of some kind. Someone in a position of power and who oughtn't to have been in a position of power, and there were letters, or papers, or something that would definitely cook his goose if they ever came to light. All sorts of intrigues and all happening years ago.'

'In the time of Mary Jordan? It sounds very unlikely,' said Tuppence. 'Tommy, you must have gone to sleep in the train coming back, and dreamt all this.'

'Well, perhaps I did,' said Tommy. 'It certainly doesn't seem likely.'

'Well, I suppose we might as well have a look around,' said Tuppence, 'as we are living here.'

Her eyes passed round the room.

'I shouldn't think there would be anything hidden here, do you, Tommy?'

'It doesn't seem the sort of house where anything would have been likely to be hidden. Lots of other people have lived in the house since those days.'

'Yes. Family after family, as far as I can make out. Well, I suppose it might be hidden up in an attic or down in the cellar. Or perhaps buried under the summer-house floor. Anywhere.

'Anyway, it'll be quite fun,' said Tuppence. 'Perhaps, you know, when we haven't got anything else to do and our backs are aching because of planting tulip bulbs, we might have a little sort of look round. You know, just to think. Starting from the point: "If I wanted to hide something, where would I choose to put it, and where would it be likely to remain undiscovered?"'

'I don't think anything could remain undiscovered here,' said Tommy. 'Not with gardeners and people, you know, tearing up the place, and different families living here, and house agents and everything else.'

'Well, you never know. It might be in a teapot somewhere.'

Tuppence rose to her feet, went towards the mantelpiece, stood up on a stool and took down a Chinese teapot. She took off the lid and peered inside.

'Nothing there,' she said.

'A most unlikely place,' said Tommy.

'Do you think,' said Tuppence, with a voice that was more hopeful than despondent, 'that somebody was trying to put an end to me and loosened the glass skylight in the conservatory so that it would fall on me?'

'Most unlikely,' said Tommy. 'It was probably meant to fall on old Isaac.'

'That's a disappointing thought,' said Tuppence. 'I would like to feel that I had had a great escape.'

'Well, you'd better be careful of yourself. I shall be careful of you too.'

'You always fuss over me,' said Tuppence.

'It's very nice of me to do so,' said Tommy. 'You should be very pleased to have a husband who fusses about you.'

'Nobody tried to shoot *you* in the train or derail it or anything, did they?' said Tuppence.

'No,' said Tommy. 'But we'd better look at the car brakes before we go out driving next time. Of course this is all completely ridiculous,' he added.

'Of course it is,' said Tuppence. 'Absolutely ridiculous. All the same –'

'All the same what?'

'Well, it's sort of fun just to *think* of things like that.'

'You mean Alexander was killed because he knew something?' asked Tommy.

'He knew something about who killed Mary Jordan. *It was one of us* . . .' Tuppence's face lit up. 'US,' she said with emphasis, 'we'll have to know just all about US. An "US" here in this house in the past. It's a crime we've got to solve. Go back to the past to solve it – to where it happened and why it happened. That's a thing we've never tried to do before.'

CHAPTER 5

METHODS OF RESEARCH

'Where on earth have you been, Tuppence?' demanded her husband when he returned to the family mansion the following day.

'Well, last of all I've been in the cellar,' said Tuppence.

'I can see that,' said Tommy. 'Yes, I do see. Do you know that your hair is absolutely full of cobwebs?'

'Well, it would be of course. The cellar is full of cobwebs. There wasn't anything there, anyway,' said Tuppence. 'At least there were some bottles of bay rum.'

'Bay rum?' said Tommy. 'That's interesting.'

'Is it?' said Tuppence. 'Does one drink it? It seems to me most unlikely.'

'No,' said Tommy, 'I think people used to put it on their hair. I mean men, not women.'

'I believe you're right,' said Tuppence. 'I remember my uncle – yes, I had an uncle who used bay rum. A friend of his used to bring it him from America.'

'Oh really? That seems very interesting,' said Tommy.

'I don't think it is particularly interesting,' said Tuppence. 'It's no help to us, anyway. I mean, you couldn't hide anything in a bottle of bay rum.'

'Oh, so that's what you've been doing.'

'Well, one has to start somewhere,' said Tuppence. 'It's just possible if what your pal said to you was true, something *could* be hidden in this house, though it's rather difficult to imagine where it could be or what it could be, because, you see, when you sell a house or die and go out of it, the house is then of course emptied, isn't it? I mean, anyone who inherits it takes the furniture out and sells it, or if it's left, the next person comes in and *they* sell it, and so anything that's left in now would have belonged to the last tenant but one and certainly not much further back than that.'

'Then why should somebody want to injure you or injure me or try to get us to leave this house – unless, I mean, there was something here that they didn't want us to find?'

'Well, that's all *your* idea,' said Tuppence. 'It mightn't be true at all. Anyway, it's not been an entirely wasted day. I have found *some* things.'

'Anything to do with Mary Jordan?'

'Not particularly. The cellar, as I say, is not much good. It had a few old things to do with photography, I think. You know, a developing lamp or something like they used to use in old days, with red glass in it, and the bay rum. But there were no sort of flagstones that looked as though you could pull them up and find anything underneath. There were a few decayed trunks, some tin trunks and a couple of old suitcases, but things that just couldn't be used to put anything in any more. They'd fall to bits if you kicked them. No. It was a wash-out.'

'Well, I'm sorry,' said Tommy. 'So no satisfaction.'

'Well, there *were* some things that were interesting. I said to myself, one has to say something to oneself – I think I'd better go upstairs now and take the cobwebs off before I go on talking.'

'Well, I think perhaps you had,' said Tommy. 'I shall like looking at you better when you've done that.'

'If you want to get the proper Darby and Joan feeling,' said Tuppence, 'you must always look at me and consider that your wife, no matter what her age, still looks lovely to you.'

'Tuppence dearest,' said Tommy, 'you look excessively lovely to me. And there is a kind of roly-poly of a cobweb hanging down over your left ear which is most attractive. Rather like the curl that the Empress Eugenie is sometimes represented as having in pictures. You know, running along the corner of her neck. Yours seems to have got a spider in it, too.'

'Oh,' said Tuppence, 'I don't like that.'

She brushed the web away with her hand. She duly went upstairs and returned to Tommy later. A glass was awaiting her. She looked at it doubtfully.

'You aren't trying to make *me* drink bay rum, are you?'

'No. I don't think I particularly want to drink bay rum myself.'

'Well,' said Tuppence, 'if I may get on with what I was saying –'

'I should like you to,' said Tommy. 'You'll do it anyway, but I would like to feel it was because I urged you to do so.'

'Well, I said to myself, "Now if I was going to hide anything in this house that I didn't want anyone else to find, what sort of place would I choose?"'

'Yes,' said Tommy, 'very logical.'

'And so I thought, what places are there where one can hide things? Well, one of them of course is Mathilde's stomach.'

'I beg your pardon,' said Tommy.

'Mathilde's stomach. The rocking-horse. I told you about the rocking-horse. It's an American rocking-horse.'

'A lot of things seem to have come from America,' said Tommy. 'The bay rum too, you said.'

'Well, anyway, the rocking-horse did have a hole in its stomach because old Isaac told me about it; it had a hole in its stomach and a lot of sort of queer old paper stuff came out of it. Nothing interesting. But anyway, that's the sort of place where anyone might have hidden anything, isn't it?'

'Quite possibly.'

'And Truelove, of course. I examined Truelove again. You know it's got a sort of rather old decayed mackintosh seat but there was nothing there. And of course there were no personal things belonging to anyone. So I thought again. Well, after all, there's still the bookcase and books. People hide things in books. And we haven't quite finished doing the book-room upstairs, have we?'

'I thought we had,' said Tommy hopefully.

'Not really. There was the bottom shelf still.'

'That doesn't really need doing. I mean, one hasn't got to get up a ladder and take things down.'

'No. So I went up there and sat down on the floor and looked through the bottom shelf. Most of it was sermons. Sermons of somebody in old times written by a Methodist minister, I think. Anyway, they weren't interesting, there was nothing in them. So I pulled all those books out on the floor. And then I did make a discovery. Underneath, some time or other, somebody had made a sort of gaping hole, and pushed all sorts of things in it, books all torn to pieces more or less. There was one rather big one. It had a brown paper cover on it and I just pulled it out to see. After all, one never knows, does one? And what do you think it was?'

'I've no idea. First edition of *Robinson Crusoe* or something valuable like that?'

'No. It was a birthday book.'

'A birthday book. What's that?'

'Well, they used to have them. Goes back a long time. Back to the Parkinsons, I think. Probably before that. Anyway, it was rather battered and torn. Not worth keeping, and I don't suppose anyone would have bothered about it. But it *does* date back and one *might* find something in it, I thought.'

'I see. You mean the sort of thing people might have slipped something into.'

'Yes. But nobody has done that, of course. Nothing so simple. But I'm still going through it quite carefully. I haven't gone through it properly yet. You see, it might have interesting names in it and one might find out something.'

'I suppose so,' said Tommy, sounding sceptical.

'Well, that's one thing. That's the only thing in the book line that I came across. There was nothing else on the bottom shelf. The other thing to look through, of course, is the cupboards.'

'What about furniture?' said Tommy. 'Lots of things like secret drawers in furniture, and all that.'

'No, Tommy, you're not looking at things straight. I mean, all the furniture in the house now is *ours*. We moved into an empty house and brought our furniture with us. The only thing we found here from really old times is all that mess out in the place called KK, old decayed toys and garden seats. I mean, there's no proper antique furniture left in the house. Whoever it was lived here last took it away or else sent it to be sold. There's been lots of people, I expect, since the Parkinsons, so there wouldn't be anything left of theirs here. But, I *did* find something. I don't know, it may mean something helpful.'

'What was that?'

'China menu cards.'

'China menu cards?'

'Yes. In that old cupboard we haven't been able to get into. The one off the larder. You know, they'd lost the key. Well, I found the key in an old box. Out in KK, as a matter of fact. I put some oil on it and I managed to get the cupboard door open. And, well, there was nothing in it. It was just a dirty cupboard with a few broken bits of china left in it. I should think from the last people who were here. But shoved up on the top shelf there was a little heap of the Victorian china menus people used to have at parties. Fascinating, the things they ate – really the most delicious meals. I'll read you some after we've had dinner. It was fascinating. You know, two soups, clear and thick, and on top of that there were two kinds of fish and then there were two entrées, I think, and then you had a salad or something like that. And then after that you had the joint and after that – I'm not quite sure what came next. I think a sorbet – that's ice cream, isn't it? And actually after that – lobster salad! Can you believe it?'

'Hush, Tuppence,' said Tommy, 'I don't really think I can stand any more.'

'Well, anyway I thought it might be interesting. It dates back, you know. It dates back, I should think, quite a long time.'

'And what do you hope to get from all these discoveries?'

'Well, the only thing with possibilities is the birthday book. In it I see there is a mention of somebody called Winifred Morrison.'

'Well?'

'Well, Winifred Morrison, I gather, was the maiden name of old Mrs Griffin. That's the one I went to tea with the other day. She's one of the oldest inhabitants, you know, and she remembers or knows about a lot of things that happened before her time. Well, I think she might remember or have heard of some of the other names in the birthday book. We might get something from that.'

'We might,' said Tommy still sounding doubtful. 'I still think –'

'Well, what do you still think?' said Tuppence.

'I don't know what to think,' said Tommy. 'Let's go to bed and sleep. Don't you think we'd better give this business up altogether? Why should we want to know who killed Mary Jordan?'

'Don't you *want* to?'

'No, I don't,' said Tommy. 'At least – oh I give in. You've got me involved now, I admit.'

'Haven't *you* found out anything?' asked Tuppence.

'I hadn't time today. But I've got a few more sources of information. I put that woman I told you about – you know, the one who's quite clever about research – I put *her* on to a few things.'

'Oh well,' said Tuppence, 'we'll still hope for the best. It's all nonsense, but perhaps it *is* rather fun.'

'Only I'm not so sure it's going to be as much fun as you think,' said Tommy.

'Oh well. No matter,' said Tuppence, 'we'll have done our best.'

'Well, don't go on doing your best all by yourself,' said Tommy. 'That's exactly what worries me so much – when I'm away from you.'

CHAPTER 6

MR ROBINSON

I

'I wonder what Tuppence is doing now,' said Tommy, sighing.

'Excuse me, I didn't quite hear what you said.'

Tommy turned his head to look at Miss Collodon more closely. Miss Collodon was thin, emaciated, had grey hair which was slowly passing through the stage of recovering from a peroxide rinse designated to make her look younger (which it had not done). She was now trying various shades of artistic grey, cloudy smoke, steel blue and other interesting shades suitable for a lady between sixty and sixty-five, devoted to the pursuit of research. Her face represented a kind of ascetic superiority and a supreme confidence in her own achievements.

'Oh, it was nothing really, Miss Collodon,' said Tommy. 'Just – just something I was considering, you know. Just thinking of.'

And what is it, I wonder, thought Thomas, being careful this time not to utter the words aloud, that she can be doing today. Something silly, I bet. Half killing herself in that extraordinary, obsolete child's toy that'll come to pieces carrying her down the hill, and she'll probably end up with a broken something or other. Hips, it seems to be nowadays, though I don't see why hips are more vulnerable than anything else. Tuppence, he thought, would at this moment be doing something silly or foolish or, if not that, she would be doing something which might not be silly or foolish but *would* be highly dangerous. Yes, dangerous. It was always difficult keeping Tuppence out of danger. His mind roved vaguely over various incidents in the past. Words of a quotation came into his mind, and he spoke them aloud:

'Postern of Fate . . .
Pass not beneath, O Caravan, or pass not singing. Have
  you heard
That silence where the birds are dead, yet something pipeth
  like a bird?'

Miss Collodon responded immediately, giving Tommy quite a shock of surprise.

'Flecker,' she said. 'Flecker. It goes on:

"Death's Caravan . . . Disaster's Cavern, Fort of Fear."'

Tommy stared at her, then realized that Miss Collodon had thought he was bringing her a poetic problem to be researched, full information on where a certain quotation came from and who the poet had been who had uttered it. The trouble with Miss Collodon was that her research covered such a broad field.

'I was just wondering about my wife,' said Tommy apologetically.

'Oh,' said Miss Collodon.

She looked at Tommy with a rather new expression in her eye. Marital trouble in the home, she was deducing. She would presently probably offer him the address of a marriage advice bureau wherein he might seek adjustment in his matrimonial affairs and troubles.

Tommy said hurriedly, 'Have you had any success with that enquiry I spoke to you about the day before yesterday?'

'Oh yes. Not very much trouble in *that*. Somerset House is very useful, you know, in all those things. I don't think, you know, that there is likely to be anything particular that you want there, but I've got the names and addresses of certain births, marriages and deaths.'

'What, are they all Mary Jordans?'

'Jordan, yes. A Mary. A Maria and a Polly Jordan. Also a Mollie Jordan. I don't know if any of them are likely to be what you want. Can I pass this to you?'

She handed him a small typewritten sheet.

'Oh, thank you. Thank you very much.'

'There are several addresses, too. The ones you asked me for. I have not been able to find out the address of Major Dalrymple. People change their addresses constantly nowadays. However, I think another two days ought to get that information all right. This is Dr Heseltine's address. He is at present living at Surbiton.'

'Thanks very much,' said Tommy. 'I might start on him, anyway.'

'Any more queries?'

'Yes. I've got a list here of about six. Some of them may not be in your line.'

'Oh well,' said Miss Collodon, with complete assurance, 'I have to make things my line, you know. You can easily find out first just where you can find out, if that isn't a rather foolish way of speech. But it does explain things, you know. I remember – oh, quite a long time ago, when I was first doing this work, I found how useful Selfridge's advice bureau was. You could ask them the most extraordinary questions about the most extraordinary things and they always seemed to be able to tell you something about it or where you could get the information quickly. But of course they don't do that sort of thing nowadays. Nowadays, you know, most enquiries that are made are – well, you know, if you want to commit suicide, things like that. Samaritans. And legal questions about wills and a lot of extraordinary things for authors, of course. And jobs abroad and immigration problems. Oh yes, I cover a very wide field.'

'I'm sure you do,' said Tommy.

'And helping alcoholics. A lot of societies there are who specialize in that. Some of them are much better than others. I have quite a list – comprehensive – and some most reliable –'

'I'll remember it,' Tommy said, 'if I find myself shaping that way any time. It depends how far I get today.'

'Oh, I'm sure, Mr Beresford, I don't see any signs of alcoholic difficulties in you.'

'No red nose?' said Tommy.

'It's worse with women,' said Miss Collodon. 'More difficult, you know, to get them off it, as you might say. Men do relapse, but not so notably. But really, some women, they seem quite all right, quite happy drinking lemonade in large quantities and all that, and then some evening, in the middle of a party – well, it's all there again.'

In turn, she looked at her watch.

'Oh dear, I must go on to my next appointment. I have to get to Upper Grosvenor Street.'

'Thank you very much,' said Tommy, 'for all you've done.'

He opened the door politely, helped Miss Collodon on with her coat, went back into the room and said,

'I must remember to tell Tuppence this evening that our

researches so far have led me to impress a research agent with the idea that my wife drinks and our marriage is breaking up because of it. Oh dear, what next!'

II

What next was an appointment in an inexpensive restaurant in the neighbourhood of Tottenham Court Road.

'Well I never!' said an elderly man, leaping up from his seat where he was sitting waiting. 'Carroty Tom, on my life. Shouldn't have known you.'

'Possibly not,' said Tommy. 'Not much carrots left about me. It's grey-haired Tom.'

'Ah well, we're all that. How's your health?'

'Much the same as I always was. Cracking. You know. Decomposing by degrees.'

'How long is it since I've seen you? Two years? Eight years? Eleven years?'

'Now you're going too far,' said Tommy. 'We met at the Maltese Cats dinner last autumn, don't you remember?'

'Ah, so we did. Pity that broke up, you know. I always thought it would. Nice premises, but the food was rotten. Well, what are you doing these days, old boy? Still in the espionage-up-to-date do?'

'No,' said Tommy, 'I'm nothing to do with espionage.'

'Dear me. What a waste of your activities.'

'And what about you, Mutton-Chop?'

'Oh, I'm much too old to serve my country in that way.'

'No espionage going on nowadays?'

'Lots of it, I expect. But probably they put the bright boys on to it. The ones who come bursting out of universities needing a job badly. Where are you now? I sent you a Christmas card this year. Well, I didn't actually post it till January but anyway it came back to me with "Not known at this address".'

'No. We've gone to the country to live now. Down near the sea. Hollowquay.'

'Hollowquay. Hollowquay? I seem to remember something. Something in your line going on there once, wasn't there?'

'Not in my time,' said Tommy. 'I've only just got to hear of it since going to live there. Legends of the past. At least sixty years ago.'

'Something to do with a submarine, wasn't it? Plans of a submarine sold to someone or other. I forget who we were selling to at that time. Might have been the Japanese, might have been the Russians – oh, and lots of others. People always seemed to meet enemy agents in Regent's Park or somewhere like that. You know, they'd meet someone like a third Secretary from an Embassy. Not so many beautiful lady spies around as there used to be once in fiction.'

'I wanted to ask you a few things, Mutton-Chop.'

'Oh? Ask away. I've had a very uneventful life. Margery – do you remember Margery?'

'Yes, of course I remember Margery. I nearly got to your wedding.'

'I know. But you couldn't make it or something, or took the wrong train, as far as I remember. A train that was going to Scotland instead of Southall. Anyway, just as well you didn't. Nothing much came of it.'

'Didn't you get married?'

'Oh yes, I got married. But somehow or other it didn't take very well. No. A year and a half and it was done with. She's married again. I haven't, but I'm doing very nicely. I live at Little Pollon. Quite a decent golf-course there. My sister lives with me. She's a widow with a nice bit of money and we get on well together. She's a bit deaf so she doesn't hear what I say, but it only means shouting a bit.'

'You said you'd heard of Hollowquay. Was it really something to do with spying of some kind?'

'Well, to tell you the truth, old boy, it's so long ago that I can't remember much about it. It made a big stir at the time. You know, splendid young naval officer absolutely above suspicion in every way, ninety per cent British, rated about a hundred and five in reliability, but nothing of the kind really. In the pay of – well, I can't remember now who he was in the pay of. Germany, I suppose. Before the 1914 war. Yes, I think that was it.'

'And there was a woman too, I believe, associated with it all,' said Tommy.

'I seem to remember hearing something about a Mary Jordan, I think it was. Mind you, I am not clear about all this. Got into the papers and I think it was a wife of his – I mean of the above-suspicion naval officer. It was his wife who got in touch with the Russians and – no, no, that's something that happened since then. One mixes things up so – they all sound alike. Wife thought he wasn't getting enough money, which meant, I suppose, that *she* wasn't getting enough money. And so – well, why d'you want to dig up all this old history? What's it got to do with you after all this time? I know you had something to do once with someone who was on the *Lusitania* or went down with the *Lusitania* or something like that, didn't you? If we go back as far as that, I mean. That's what you were mixed up in once, or your wife was mixed up in.'

'We were both mixed up in it,' said Tommy, 'and it's such a very long time ago that I really can't remember anything about it now.'

'There was some woman associated with that, wasn't there? Name like Jane Fish, or something like that, or was it Jane Whale?'

'Jane Finn,' said Tommy.

'Where is she now?'

'She's married to an American.'

'Oh, I see. Well, all very nice. One always seems to get talking about one's old pals and what's happened to them all. When you talk about old friends, either they are dead, which surprises you enormously because you didn't think they would be, or else they're not dead and that surprises you even more. It's a very difficult world.'

Tommy said yes it was a very difficult world and here was the waiter coming. What could they have to eat . . . The conversation thereafter was gastronomic.

III

In the afternoon Tommy had another interview arranged. This time with a sad, grizzled man sitting in an office and obviously grudging the time he was giving Tommy.

'Well, I really couldn't say. Of course I know roughly what you're talking about – lot of talk about it at the time – caused a big political blow-up – but I really have no information about that sort of thing, you know. No. You see, these things, they don't last, do they? They soon pass out of one's mind once the Press gets hold of some other juicy scandal.'

He opened up slightly on a few of his own interesting moments in life when something he'd never suspected came suddenly to light or his suspicions had suddenly been aroused by some very peculiar event. He said:

'Well, I've just got one thing might help. Here's an address for you and I've made an appointment too. Nice chap. Knows everything. He's the tops, you know, absolutely the tops. One of my daughters was a godchild of his. That's why he's awfully nice to me and will always do me a good turn if possible. So I asked him if he would see you. I said there were some things you wanted the top news about, I said what a good chap you were and various things and he said yes, he'd heard of you already. Knew something about you, and he said, Of course come along. Three forty-five, I think. Here's the address. It's an office in the City, I think. Ever met him?'

'I don't think so,' said Tommy, looking at the card and the address. 'No.'

'Well you wouldn't think he knew anything, to look at him, I mean. Big, you know, and yellow.'

'Oh,' said Tommy, 'big and yellow.'

It didn't really convey much information to his mind.

'He's the tops,' said Tommy's grizzled friend, 'absolute tops. You go along there. He'll be able to tell you *something* anyway. Good luck, old chap.'

IV

Tommy, having successfully got himself to the City office in question, was received by a man of 35 to 40 years of age who looked at him with the eye of one determined to do the worst without delay. Tommy felt that he was suspected of many things, possibly carrying a bomb in some deceptive container, or prepared to hijack or kidnap anyone or to hold up with a revolver the entire staff. It made Tommy extremely nervous.

'You have an appointment with Mr Robinson? At what time, did you say? Ah, three forty-five.' He consulted a ledger. 'Mr Thomas Beresford, is that right?'

'Yes,' said Tommy.

'Ah. Just sign your name here, please.'

Tommy signed his name where he was told.

'Johnson.'

A nervous-looking young man of about twenty-three seemed like an apparition rising out of a glass partitioned desk. 'Yes, sir?'

'Take Mr Beresford up to the fourth floor to Mr Robinson's office.'

'Yes, sir.'

He led Tommy to a lift, the kind of lift that always seemed to have its own idea of how it should deal with those who came into it. The doors rolled open. Tommy passed in, the doors very nearly pinched him in doing so and just managed to slam themselves shut about an inch from his spine.

'Cold afternoon,' said Johnson, showing a friendly attitude to someone who was clearly being allowed to approach the high one in the highest.

'Yes,' said Tommy, 'it always seems to be cold in the afternoons.'

'Some say it's pollution, some say it's all the natural gas they're taking out of the North Sea,' said Johnson.

'Oh, I haven't heard that,' said Tommy.

'Doesn't seem likely to me,' said Johnson.

They passed the second floor and the third floor and finally arrived at the fourth floor. Johnson led Tommy, again escaping the closing doors by a mere inch, along a passage to a door. He knocked, was told to enter, held the door open, insinuated Tommy across the threshold, and said:

'Mr Beresford, sir. By appointment.'

He went out and shut the door behind him. Tommy advanced. The room seemed to be mainly filled by an enormous desk. Behind the desk sat a rather enormous man, a man of great weight and many inches. He had, as Tommy had been prepared for by his friend, a very large and yellow face. What nationality he was Tommy had no idea. He might have been anything. Tommy had a feeling he was probably foreign. A German, perhaps? Or an Austrian? Possibly a Japanese. Or else he might be very decidedly English.

'Ah. Mr Beresford.'

Mr Robinson got up, shook hands.

'I'm sorry if I come taking a lot of your time,' said Tommy.

He had a feeling he had once seen Mr Robinson before or had had Mr Robinson pointed out to him. Anyway on the occasion, whatever it had been, he had been rather shy about it because obviously Mr Robinson was someone very important, and, he now gathered (or rather felt at once) he was still very important.

'There's something you want to know about, I gather. Your friend, What's-his-name, just gave me a brief résumé.'

'I don't suppose – I mean, it's something perhaps I oughtn't to bother you about. I don't suppose it's anything of any importance. It was just – just –'

'Just an idea?'

'Partly my wife's idea.'

'I've heard about your wife. I've heard about you, too. Let me see, the last time was M or N wasn't it? Or N or M. Mm. I remember. Remember all the facts and things. You got that Commander chap, didn't you? The one who was in the English Navy supposedly but was actually a very important Hun. I still call them Huns occasionally, you know. Of course I know we're all different now we're in the Common Market. All in the nursery school together, as you might say. I know. You did a good bit of work there. Very good bit indeed. And so did your missus. My word. All those children's books. I remember. Goosey, Goosey Gander wasn't it – the one that gave the show away? Where do you wander? Upstairs and downstairs and in my lady's chamber.'

'Fancy you remembering that,' said Tommy, with great respect.

'Yes, I know. One's always surprised when one remembers something. It just came back to me at that minute. So silly, you know, that really you'd never have suspected it of being anything else, would you?'

'Yes, it was a good show.'

'Now, what's the matter now? What are you up against?'

'Well, it's nothing, really,' said Tommy. 'It's just –'

'Come on, put it in your own words. You needn't make a thing of it. Just tell me the story. Sit down. Take the weight off your feet. Don't you know – or you will know, when you're some years older – resting your feet is important.'

'I'm old enough already, I should think,' said Tommy. 'There can't be much ahead of me now except a coffin, in due course.'

'Oh I wouldn't say that. I tell you, once you get above a certain age you can go on living practically for ever. Now then, what's all this about?'

'Well,' said Tommy, 'briefly, my wife and I went into a new house and there was all the fuss of getting into a new house –'

'I know,' said Mr Robinson, 'yes, I know the sort of thing. Electricians all over the floor. They pick holes and you fall into them and –'

'There were some books there the people moving out wanted to sell. A lot of children's books, all sorts of things. You know, Henty and things like that.'

'I remember. I remember Henty from my own youth.'

'And in one book my wife was reading we found a passage underlined. The letters were underlined and it made a sentence when you put it together. And – this sounds awfully silly, what I'm going to say next –'

'Well, that's hopeful,' said Mr Robinson. 'If a thing sounds silly, I always want to hear about it.'

'It said, *Mary Jordan did not die naturally. It must have been one of us.*'

'Very, very interesting,' said Mr Robinson. 'I've never come across anything like that before. It said that, did it? Mary Jordan did not die a natural death. And who was it who wrote it? Any clue of that?'

'Apparently a boy of school age. Parkinson was the family's name. They lived in this house and he was one of the Parkinsons, we gathered. Alexander Parkinson. At least, anyway, he's buried there in the churchyard.'

'Parkinson,' said Mr Robinson. 'Wait a bit. Let me think. Parkinson – yes, you know there was a name like that connected with things, but you don't always remember who or what and where.'

'And we've been very keen to learn who Mary Jordan was.'

'Because she didn't die a natural death. Yes, I suppose that would be rather your line of country. But it seems very odd. What did you find out about her?'

'Absolutely nothing,' said Tommy. 'Nobody seems to remember her there much, or say anything about her. At least somebody did say she was what we'd call an *au pair* girl nowadays or a governess or something like that. They couldn't remember. A Mamselle or a Frowline, they said. It's all very difficult, you see.'

'And she died – what did she die of?'

'Somebody brought a few foxglove leaves in with some spinach from the garden, by accident, and then they ate it. Mind you, that probably wouldn't kill you.'

'No,' said Mr Robinson. 'Not enough of it. But if you then put a strong dose of digitalin alkaloid in the coffee and just made sure that Mary Jordan got it in her coffee, or in a cocktail earlier, then – then, as you say, the foxglove leaves would be blamed and it would all be taken to be an accident. But Alexander Parker, or whatever the schoolboy's name was, was too sharp for that. He had other ideas, did he? Anything else, Beresford? When was this? First World War, Second World War, or before that?'

'Before. Rumours passed down through elderly ancestors say she was a German spy.'

'I remember that case – made a big sensation. Any German working in England before 1914 was always said to be a spy. The English officer involved was one always said to be "above suspicion". I always look very hard at anyone who is above suspicion. It's all a long time ago, I don't think it's ever been written up in recent years. I mean, not in the way that things are occasionally for public enjoyment when they release a bit of stuff from the records.'

'Yes, but it's all rather sketchy.'

'Yes, it would be by now. It's always been associated, of course, with the submarine secrets that were stolen around then. There was some aviation news as well. A lot of that side of it, and that's what caught the public interest, as you might say. But there are a lot of things, you know. There was the political side to it, too. A lot of our prominent politicians. You know, the sort of chaps people say, "Well, *he* has *real* integrity." Real integrity is just as dangerous as being above suspicion in the Services. Real integrity my foot,' said Mr Robinson. 'I remember it with this last war. Some people haven't got the integrity they are credited with. One chap lived down near here, you know. He had a cottage on the beach, I think. Made a lot of disciples, you know, praising Hitler. Saying our only chance was to get in with him. Really the fellow seemed such a noble man. Had some wonderful ideas. Was so terribly keen to abolish all poverty and difficulties and injustice – things of that kind. Oh yes. Blew the Fascist trumpet without calling it Fascism. And Spain too, you know. Was in with Franco and all that lot to begin with. And dear old Mussolini, naturally, spouting away. Yes, there are always a lot of side-lines to it just before wars. Things that never came out and nobody ever really knew about.'

'You seem to know everything,' said Tommy. 'I beg your pardon. Perhaps that's rather rude of me. But it really is very exciting to come across someone who does seem to know about everything.'

'Well, I've often had a finger in the pie, as you might say. You know, come into things on the side-lines, or in the background. One hears a good deal. One hears a good deal from one's old cronies too, who were in it up to the neck and who knew the lot. I expect you begin to find that, don't you?'

'Yes,' said Tommy, 'it's quite true. I meet old friends, you know, and they've seen other old friends and there're quite a lot of things that, well, one's friends knew and you knew. You didn't get together just then but now you *do* hear about them and they're very interesting sometimes.'

'Yes,' said Mr Robinson. 'I see where you're going – where you're tending, you might say. It's interesting that you should come across this.'

'The trouble is,' said Tommy, 'that I don't really know – I mean, perhaps we're being rather silly. I mean, we bought this house to live in, the sort of house we wanted. We've done it up the way we want and we're trying to get the garden in some kind of shape. But I mean, I don't want to get tied up in this sort of stuff again. It's just pure curiosity on our part. Something that happened long ago and you can't help thinking about it or wanting to know why. But there's no point in it. It's not going to do anybody any good.'

'I know. You just want to *know*. Well, that's the way the human being is made. That's what leads us to explore things, to go and fly to the moon, to bother about underwater discoveries, to find natural gas in the North Sea, to find oxygen supplied to us by the sea and not by the trees and forests. Quite a lot of things they're always finding out about. Just through curiosity. I suppose without curiosity a man would be a tortoise. Very comfortable life, a tortoise has. Goes to sleep all the winter and doesn't eat anything more than grass as far as I know, to live all the summer. Not an interesting life perhaps, but a very peaceful one. On the other hand –'

'On the other hand one might say man is more like a mongoose.'

'Good. You're a reader of Kipling. I'm so glad. Kipling's not appreciated as much as he should be nowadays. He was a wonderful chap. A wonderful person to read nowadays. His short stories, amazingly good, they are. I don't think it's ever been realized enough.'

'I don't want to make a fool of myself,' said Tommy. 'I don't want to mix myself up with a lot of things which have nothing to do with me. Not anything to do with anybody nowadays, I should say.'

'That you never know,' said Mr Robinson.

'I mean, really,' said Tommy, who was now completely swamped in a cloud of guilt for having disturbed a very important man, 'I mean, I'm not just trying to find out things.'

'Got to try and find out things just to satisfy your wife, I suppose. Yes, I've heard of her. I've never had the pleasure of meeting her, I don't think. Rather wonderful person, isn't she?'

'I think so,' said Tommy.

'That's good hearing. I like people who stick together and enjoy their marriage and go on enjoying it.'

'Really, I'm like the tortoise, I suppose. I mean, there we are. We're old and we're tired, and although we've got very good health for our age, we don't want to be mixed up in anything nowadays. We're not trying to butt into anything. We just –'

'I know. I know,' said Mr Robinson. 'Don't keep apologizing for it. You want to know. Like the mongoose, you want to know. And Mrs Beresford, she wants to know. Moreover, I should say from all I've heard of her and been told of her, I should say she will get to know somehow.'

'You think she's more likely to do it than I am?'

'Well, I don't think perhaps you're quite as keen on finding out things as she is, but I think you're just as likely to get on to it because I think you're rather good at finding sources. It's not easy to find sources for something as long ago as that.'

'That's why I feel awful about having come and disturbed you. But I wouldn't have done it on my own. It was only Mutton-Chop. I mean –'

'I know who you mean. Had mutton-chop whiskers and was rather pleased with them at one time. That's why he was called that. A nice chap. Done good work in his time. Yes. He sent you to me because he knew that I am interested in anything like that. I started quite early, you know. Poking about, I mean, and finding out things.'

'And now,' said Tommy, 'now you're the tops.'

'Now who told you that?' said Mr Robinson. 'All nonsense.'

'I don't think it is,' said Tommy.

'Well,' said Mr Robinson, 'some get to the tops and some have the tops forced upon them. I would say the latter applies to me, more or less. I've had a few things of surpassing interest forced upon me.'

'That business connected with – Frankfurt, wasn't it?'

'Ah, *you*'ve heard rumours, have you? Ah well, don't think about them any more. They're not supposed to be known much. Don't think I'm going to rebuff you for coming here asking me questions. I probably can answer some of the things you want to know. If I said there was something that happened years ago that might result in something being known that would be – possibly – interesting nowadays, sometimes that would give one a bit of information about things that might be going on nowadays, that might be true enough. I wouldn't put it past anyone or anything. I don't know what I can suggest to you, though. It's a question of worry about, listen to people, find out what you can about bygone years. If anything comes along that you think might be interesting to me, just give me a ring or something. We'll find some code words, you know. Just to make ourselves feel excited again, feel as though we really mattered. Crab-apple jelly, how would that be? You know, you say your wife's made some jars of crab-apple jelly and would I like a pot. I'll know what you mean.'

'You mean that – that I would have found out something about Mary Jordan. I don't see there's any point in going on with that. After all, she's dead.'

'Yes. She's dead. But – well, you see, sometimes one has the wrong ideas about people because of what you've been told. Or because of what's been written.'

'You mean we have wrong ideas about Mary Jordan. You mean, she wasn't important at all.'

'Oh yes, she could have been very important.' Mr Robinson looked at his watch. 'I have to push you off now. There's a chap coming in, in ten minutes. An awful bore, but he's high up in government circles, and you know what life is nowadays. Government, government, you've got to stand it everywhere. In the office, in the home, in the supermarkets, on the television. Private life. That's what we want more of nowadays. Now this little fun and games that you and your wife are having, you're in private life and you can look at it from the background of private life. Who knows, you might find out something. Something that would be interesting. Yes. You may and you may not.

'I can't tell you anything more about it. I know some of the facts that probably nobody else can tell you and in due course I might be able to tell them to you. But as they're all dead and done with, that's not really practical.

'I'll tell you one thing that will help you perhaps in your investigations. You read about this case, the trial of Commander whatever-he-was – I've forgotten his name now – and he was tried for espionage, did a sentence for it and richly deserved it. He was a traitor to his country and that's that. But Mary Jordan –'

'Yes?'

'You want to know something about Mary Jordan. Well, I'll tell you one thing that might, as I say, help your point of view. Mary Jordan was – well, you can call it a spy but she wasn't a German spy. She wasn't an enemy spy. Listen to this, my boy. I can't keep calling you "my boy".'

Mr Robinson dropped his voice and leaned forward over his desk.

'*She was one of our lot.*'

BOOK 3

....
MARY JORDAN

'But that alters everything,' said Tuppence.

'Yes,' said Tommy. 'Yes. It was – it was quite a shock.'

'Why did he tell you?'

'I don't know,' said Tommy. 'I thought – well, two or three different things.'

'Did he – what's he like, Tommy? You haven't really told me.'

'Well, he's yellow,' said Tommy. 'Yellow and big and fat and very, very ordinary, but at the same time, if you know what I mean, he isn't ordinary at all. He's – well, he's what my friend said he was. He's one of the tops.'

'You sound like someone talking about pop singers.'

'Well, one gets used to using these terms.'

'Yes, but why? Surely that was revealing something that he wouldn't have wanted to reveal, you'd think.'

'It was a long time ago,' said Tommy. 'It's all over, you see. I suppose none of it matters nowadays. I mean, look at all the things they're releasing now. Off the record. You know, not hushing up things any more. Letting it all come out, what really happened. What one person wrote and what another person said and what one row was about and how something else was all hushed up because of something you never heard about.'

'You make me feel horribly confused,' said Tuppence, 'when you say things like that. It makes everything wrong, too, doesn't it?'

'How do you mean, makes everything wrong?'

'Well, I mean, the way we've been looking at it. I mean – what do I mean?'

'Go on,' said Tommy. 'You must know what you mean.'

'Well, what I said. It's all wrong. I mean, we found this thing in *The Black Arrow*, and it was all clear enough. Somebody had written it in there, probably this boy Alexander, and it meant that somebody – one of them, he said, at least, one of us – I mean he put it that way but that's what he meant – one of the family or somebody in the house or something, had arranged to bring about the death of Mary Jordan, and we didn't know who Mary Jordan was, which was very baffling.'

'Goodness knows it's been baffling,' said Tommy.

'Well, it hasn't baffled you as much as me. It's baffled me a great deal. I haven't really found out anything about her. At least –'

'What you found out about her was that she had been apparently a German spy, isn't that what you mean? You found out that?'

'Yes, that is what was believed about her, and I supposed it was true. Only now –'

'Yes,' said Tommy, 'only now we know that it wasn't true. She was the opposite to a German spy.'

'She was a sort of English spy.'

'Well, she must have been in the English espionage or security whatever it was called. And she came here in some capacity to find out something. To find out something about – about – what's his name now? I wish I could remember names better. I mean the naval officer or the Army officer or whatever he was. The one who sold the secret of the submarine or something like that. Yes, I suppose there was a little cluster of German agents here, rather like in N or M all over again, all busy preparing things.'

'It would seem so, yes.'

'And she was sent here in that case, presumably, to find out all about it.'

'I see.'

'So "one of us" didn't mean what we thought it meant. "One of us" meant – well, it had to be someone who was in this neighbourhood. And somebody who had something to do with this house, or was in this house for a special occasion. And so, when she died, her death wasn't a natural one, because somebody got wise to what she was doing. And Alexander found out about it.'

'She was pretending to spy, perhaps,' said Tuppence, 'for Germany. Making friends with Commander – whoever it was.'

'Call him Commander X,' said Tommy, 'if you can't remember.'

'All right, all right. Commander X. She was getting friendly with him.'

'There was also,' said Tommy, 'an enemy agent living down here. The head of a big organization. He lived in a cottage somewhere, down near the quay I think it was, and he wrote a lot of propaganda, and used to say that really our best plan would be to join in with Germany and get together with them – and things like that.'

'It is all so confusing,' said Tuppence. 'All these things – plans, and secret papers and plots and espionage – have been so confusing. Well, anyway, we've probably been looking in all the wrong places.'

'Not really,' said Tommy, 'I don't think so.'

'Why don't you think so?'

'Well, because if she, Mary Jordan, was here to find out something, and if she did find out something, then perhaps when *they* – I mean Commander X or other people – there must have been other people too in it – when *they* found out that she'd found out something –'

'Now don't get me muddled again,' said Tuppence. 'If you say things like that, it's very muddling. Yes. Go on.'

'All right. Well, when they found out that she'd found out a lot of things, well, then they had to –'

'To silence her,' said Tuppence.

'You make it sound like Phillips Oppenheim now,' said Tommy. 'And he was before 1914, surely.'

'Well, anyway, they had to silence Mary before she could report what she'd found out.'

'There must be a little more to it than that,' said Tommy. 'Perhaps she'd got hold of something important. Some kind of papers or written document. Letters that might have been sent or passed to someone.'

'Yes. I see what you mean. We've got to look among a different lot of people. But if she was one of the ones to die because of a mistake that had been made about the vegetables, then I don't see quite how it could be what Alexander called "one of us". It presumably wasn't one of *his* family.'

'It could have been like this,' said Tommy. 'It needn't have been actually someone in the house. It's very easy to pick wrong leaves looking alike, bunch 'em all up together and take them into the kitchen; you wouldn't, I think, make them really – I mean, not *really* – too lethal. Just the people at one particular meal would get rather ill after it and they'd send for a doctor and the doctor would get the food analysed and he'd realize somebody'd made a mistake over vegetables. He wouldn't think anyone had done it on purpose.'

'But then everybody at that meal would have died,' said Tuppence. 'Or everybody would have been ill but *not* died.'

'Not necessarily,' said Tommy. 'Suppose they wanted a certain person – Mary J. – to die, and they were going to give a dose of poison to her, oh, in a cocktail *before* the lunch or dinner or whatever it was or in coffee or something after the meal – actual digitalin, or aconite or whatever it is in foxgloves –'

'Aconite's in monkshood, I think,' said Tuppence.

'Don't be so knowledgeable,' said Tommy. 'The point is everyone gets a mild dose by what is clearly a mistake, so everyone gets mildly ill – but one person dies. Don't you see, if most people were taken ill after whatever it was – dinner or lunch one day and it was looked into, and they found out about the mistake, well, things *do* happen like that. You know, people eat fungus instead of mushrooms, and deadly nightshade berries children eat by mistake because the berries look like fruit. Just a mistake and people are ill, but they don't usually all die. Just one of them does, and the one that did die would be assumed to have been particularly allergic to whatever it was and so *she* had died but the others *hadn't*. You see, it would pass off as really due to the mistake and they wouldn't have looked to see or even suspected there was some other way in which it happened –'

'She might have got a little ill like the others and then the real dose might have been put in her early tea the next morning,' said Tuppence.

'I'm sure, Tuppence, that you've lots of ideas.'

'About that part of it, yes,' said Tuppence. 'But what about the other things? I mean who and what and why? Who was the "one of us" – "one of them" as we'd better say now – who had the opportunity? Someone staying down here, friends of other people perhaps? People who brought a letter, forged perhaps, from a friend saying "Do be kind to my friend, Mr or Mrs Murray Wilson, or some name, who is down here. She is so anxious to see your pretty garden," or something. All that would be easy enough.'

'Yes, I think it would.'

'In that case,' said Tuppence, 'there's perhaps something still here in the house that would explain what happened to me today and yesterday, too.'

'What happened to you yesterday, Tuppence?'

'The wheels came off that beastly little cart and horse I was going down the hill in the other day, and so I came a terrible cropper right down behind the monkey puzzle and into it. And I very nearly – well, I might have had a serious accident. That silly old man Isaac ought to have seen that the thing was safe. He said he *did* look at it. He told me it was quite all right before I started.'

'And it wasn't?'

'No. He said afterwards that he thought someone had been playing about with it, tampering with the wheels or something, so that they came off.'

'Tuppence,' said Tommy, 'do you think that's the second or third thing that's happened here to us? You know that other thing that nearly came down on the top of me in the book-room?'

'You mean somebody wants to get rid of *us*? But that would mean –'

'That would mean,' said Tommy, 'that there must be *something*. Something that's *here* – in the house.'

Tommy looked at Tuppence and Tuppence looked at Tommy. It was the moment for consideration. Tuppence opened her mouth three times but checked herself each time, frowning, as she considered. It was Tommy who spoke at last.

'What did he think? What did he say about Truelove? Old Isaac, I mean.'

'That it was only to be expected, that the thing was pretty rotten anyway.'

'But he said somebody had been monkeying about with it?'

'Yes,' said Tuppence, 'very definitely. "Ah," he said, "these youngsters have been in tryin' it out, you know. Enjoy pulling wheels off things, they do, young monkeys." Not that I've seen anyone about. But then I suppose they'd be sure that I didn't catch them at it. They'd wait till I'm away from home, I expect.

'I asked him if he thought it was just – just something mischievous,' said Tuppence.

'What did he say to that?' said Tommy.

'He didn't really know what to say.'

'It could have been mischief, I suppose,' said Tommy. 'People do do those things.'

'Are you trying to say you think that it was meant in some way so that I should go on playing the fool with the cart and that the wheel would come off and the thing would fall to pieces – oh, but that is nonsense, Tommy.'

'Well, it sounds like nonsense,' said Tommy, 'but things aren't nonsense sometimes. It depends where and how they happen and why.'

'I don't see what "why" there could be.'

'One might make a guess – about the most likely thing,' said Tommy.

'Now what do you mean by the most likely?'

'I mean perhaps people want us to go away from here.'

'Why should they? If somebody wants the house for themselves, they could make us an offer for it.'

'Yes, they could.'

'Well, I wondered – Nobody else has wanted this house as far as we know. I mean, there was nobody else looking at it when we were. It seemed to be generally regarded as if it had come into the market rather cheap but not for any other reason, except that it was out of date and needed a lot doing to it.'

'I can't believe they wanted to do away with us, maybe it's because you've been nosing about, asking too many questions, copying things out of books.'

'You mean that I'm stirring up things that somebody doesn't want to be stirred up?'

'That sort of thing,' said Tommy. 'I mean, if we suddenly were meant to feel that we didn't like living here, and put the house up for sale and went away, that would be quite all right. They'd be satisfied with that. I don't think that they –'

'Who do you mean by "they"?'

'I've no idea,' said Tommy. 'We must get to "they" later. Just *they*. There's *We* and there's *They*. We must keep them apart in our minds.'

'What about Isaac?'

'What do you mean, what about Isaac?'

'I don't know. I just wondered if he was mixed up in this.'

'He's a very old man, he's been here a long time and he knows a few things. If somebody slipped him a five pound note or something, do you think he'd tamper with Truelove's wheels?'

'No, I don't,' said Tuppence. 'He hasn't got the brains to.'

'He wouldn't need brains for it,' said Tommy. 'He'd only need the brains to take the five pound note and to take out a few screws or break off a bit of wood here or there and just make it so that – well, it would come to grief next time you went down the hill in it.'

'I think what you are imagining is nonsense,' said Tuppence.

'Well, you've been imagining a few things that are nonsense already.'

'Yes, but they fitted in,' said Tuppence. 'They fitted in with the things we've heard.'

'Well,' said Tommy, 'as a result of my investigations or researches, whatever you like to call them, it seems that we haven't learnt quite the right things.'

'You mean what I said just now, that this turns things upside down. I mean now we know that Mary Jordan wasn't an enemy agent, instead she was a *British* agent. She was here for a purpose. Perhaps she had accomplished her purpose.'

'In that case,' said Tommy, 'now let's get it all clear, with this new bit of knowledge added. Her purpose here was to find out something.'

'Presumably to find out something about Commander X,' said Tuppence. 'You must find out his name, it seems so extraordinarily barren only to be able to say Commander X all the time.'

'All right, all right, but you know how difficult these things are.'

'And she did find them out, and she reported what she had

found out. And perhaps someone opened the letter,' said Tuppence.

'What letter?' said Tommy.

'The letter she wrote to whoever was her "contact".'

'Yes.'

'Do you think he was her father or her grandfather or something like that.'

'I shouldn't think so,' said Tommy. 'I don't think that's the sort of way things would be done. She might just have chosen to take the name of Jordan, or they thought it was quite a good name because it was not associated in any way, which it wouldn't be if she was partly German, and had perhaps come from some other work that she had been doing for us but not for them.'

'For us and not for them,' agreed Tuppence, 'abroad. And so she came here as what?

'Oh, I don't know,' said Tuppence, 'we shall have to start all over again finding out *as what*, I suppose . . . Anyway, she came here and she found out something and she either passed it on to someone or didn't. I mean, she might not have written a letter. She might have gone to London and reported something. Met someone in Regent's Park, say.'

'That's rather the other way about, usually, isn't it?' said Tommy. 'I mean you meet somebody from whatever embassy it is you're in collusion with and you meet in Regent's Park and –'

'Hide things in a hollow tree sometimes. Do you think they really do that? It sounds so unlikely. It's so much more like people who are having a love-affair and putting love-letters in.'

'I dare say whatever they put in there was written as though they were love-letters and really had a code.'

'That's a splendid idea,' said Tuppence, 'only I suppose they – Oh dear, it's such years ago. How difficult it is to get anywhere. The more you know, I mean, the less use it is to you. But we're not going to stop, Tommy, are we?'

'I don't suppose we are for a moment,' said Tommy. He sighed.

'You wish we were?' said Tuppence.

'Almost. Yes. Far as I can see –'

'Well,' cut in Tuppence, 'I can't see you taking yourself off the trail. No, and it would be very difficult to get *me* off the trail. I mean, I'd go on thinking about it and it would worry me. I dare say I should go off my food and everything.'

'The point is,' said Tommy, 'do you think – we know in a way perhaps what this starts from. Espionage. Espionage by the enemy with certain objects in view, some of which were accomplished. Perhaps some which weren't quite accomplished. But we don't know – well – we don't know who was mixed up in it. From the enemy point of view. I mean, there were people here, I should think, people perhaps among security forces. People who were traitors but whose job it was to appear to be loyal servants of the State.'

'Yes,' said Tuppence. 'I'll go for that one. That seems to be very likely.'

'And Mary Jordan's job was to get in touch with them.'

'To get in touch with Commander X?'

'I should think so, yes. Or with friends of Commander X and to find out about things. But apparently it was necessary for her to come here to get it.'

'Do you mean that the Parkinsons – I suppose we're back at the Parkinsons again before we know where we are – were in it? That the Parkinsons were part of the enemy?'

'It seems very unlikely,' said Tommy.

'Well, then, I can't see what it all means.'

'I think the house might have something to do with it,' said Tommy.

'The house? Well, other people came and lived here afterwards, didn't they?'

'Yes, they did. But I don't suppose they were people quite like – well, quite like you, Tuppence.'

'What do you mean by quite like me?'

'Well, wanting old books and looking through them and finding out things. Being a regular mongoose, in fact. They just came and lived here and I expect the upstairs rooms and the books were probably servants' rooms and nobody went into them. There may be something that was hidden in this house. Hidden perhaps by Mary Jordan. Hidden in a place ready to deliver to someone who would come for them, or deliver them by going herself to London or somewhere on some excuse. Visit to a dentist. Seeing an old friend. Quite easy to do. She had something she had acquired, or got to know, hidden in this house.'

'You're not saying it's still hidden in this house?'

'No,' said Tommy, 'I shouldn't have thought so. But one doesn't know. Somebody is afraid we may find it or have found it and they want to get us out of the house, or they want to get hold of whatever it is they think we've found but that they've never found, though perhaps they've looked for it in past years and then thought it had been hidden somewhere else outside.'

'Oh, Tommy,' said Tuppence, 'that makes it all much more exciting, really, doesn't it?'

'It's only what we *think*,' said Tommy.

'Now don't be such a wet blanket,' said Tuppence. 'I'm going to look outside as well as inside –'

'What are you going to do, dig up the kitchen garden?'

'No,' said Tuppence. 'Cupboards, the cellar, things like that. Who knows? Oh, Tommy!'

'Oh, Tuppence!' said Tommy. 'Just when we were looking forward to a delightful, peaceful old age.'

'No peace for the pensioners,' said Tuppence gaily. 'That's an idea too.'

'What?'

'I must go and talk to some old age pensioners at their club. I hadn't thought of them up to now.'

'For goodness' sake, look after yourself,' said Tommy. 'I think I'd better stay at home and keep an eye on you. But I've got to do some more research in London tomorrow.'

'I'm going to do some research here,' said Tuppence.

CHAPTER 2

RESEARCH BY TUPPENCE

'I hope,' said Tuppence, 'that I'm not interrupting you, coming along like this? I thought I'd better ring up first in case you were out, you know, or busy. But, I mean, it's nothing particular so I could go away again at once if you liked. I mean, my feelings wouldn't be hurt or anything like that.'

'Oh, I'm delighted to see you, Mrs Beresford,' said Mrs Griffin.

She moved herself three inches along her chair so as to settle her back more comfortably and looked with what seemed to be distinct pleasure into Tuppence's somewhat anxious face.

'It's a great pleasure, you know, when somebody new comes and lives in this place. We're so used to all our neighbours that a new face, or if I may say so a couple of new faces, is a treat. An absolute *treat*! I hope indeed that you'll both come to dinner one day. I don't know what time your husband gets back. He goes to London, does he not, most days?'

'Yes,' said Tuppence. 'That's very nice of you. I hope you'll come and see our house when it's more or less finished. I'm always thinking it's going to be finished but it never is.'

'Houses are rather like that,' said Mrs Griffin.

Mrs Griffin, as Tuppence knew very well from her various sources of information which consisted of daily women, old Isaac, Gwenda in the post office and sundry others, was ninety-four. The upright position which she enjoyed arranging because it took the rheumatic pains out of her back, together with her erect carriage, gave her the air of someone much younger. In spite of the wrinkled face, the head of uprising white hair surmounted by a lace scarf tied round her head reminded Tuppence faintly of a couple of her great-aunts in past days. She wore bifocal spectacles and had a hearing aid which she sometimes, but very seldom as far as Tuppence could see, had to use. And she looked thoroughly alert and perfectly capable of reaching the age of a hundred or even a hundred and ten.

'What have you been doing with yourself lately?' enquired Mrs Griffin. 'I gather you've got the electricians out of the house now. So Dorothy told me. Mrs Rogers, you know. She used to be my housemaid once and she comes now and cleans twice a week.'

'Yes, thank goodness,' said Tuppence. 'I was always falling into the holes they made. I really came,' said Tuppence, 'and it may sound rather silly but it's something I just wondered about – I expect you'll think it's rather silly too. I've been turning out things, you know, a lot of old bookshelves and things like that. We bought some books with the house, mostly children's books years and years old but I found some old favourites among them.'

'Ah yes,' said Mrs Griffin, 'I quite understand that you must very much have enjoyed the prospect of being able to read certain old favourites again. *The Prisoner of Zenda*, perhaps. My grandmother used to read *The Prisoner of Zenda*, I believe. I read it once myself. Really very enjoyable. Romantic, you know. The first romantic book, I imagine, one is allowed to read. You know, novel reading was not encouraged. My mother and my grandmother never approved of reading anything like a novel in the mornings. A story book as it was called. You know, you could read history or something serious, but novels were only *pleasurable* and so to be read in the afternoon.'

'I know,' said Tuppence. 'Well, I found a good many books that I liked reading again. Mrs Molesworth.'

'*The Tapestry Room*?' said Mrs Griffin with immediate comprehension.

'Yes. *The Tapestry Room* was one of my favourites.'

'Well, I always liked *Four Winds Farm* best,' said Mrs Griffin.

'Yes, that was there too. And several others. Many different kinds of authors. Anyway, I got down to the last shelf and I think there must have been an accident there. You know, someone had banged it about a good deal. When they were moving furniture, I expect. There was a sort of hole and I scooped up a lot of old things out of that. Mostly torn books and among it there was this.'

She produced her parcel wrapped loosely in brown paper.

'It's a birthday book,' she said. 'An old-fashioned birthday book. And it had your name in it. Your name – I remember you told me – was Winifred Morrison, wasn't it?'

'Yes, my dear. Quite right.'

'And it was written in the birthday book. And so I wondered whether it would amuse you if I brought it along for you to see. It might have a lot of other old friends of yours in it and different things or names which would amuse you.'

'Well, that was very nice of you, my dear, and I should like to see it very much. You know, these things from the past, one does find very amusing to read in one's old age. A very kind thought of yours.'

'It's rather faded and torn and knocked about,' said Tuppence, producing her offering.

'Well, well,' said Mrs Griffin, 'yes. You know, everyone had a birthday book. Not so much after my time as a girl. I expect this may be one of the last ones. All the girls at the school I went to had a birthday book. You know, you wrote your name in your friend's birthday book and they wrote their name in yours and so on.'

She took the book from Tuppence, opened it and began reading down the pages.

'Oh dear, oh dear,' she murmured, 'how it takes me back. Yes. Yes indeed. Helen Gilbert – yes, yes of course. And Daisy Sherfield. Sherfield, yes. Oh yes, I remember her. She had to have one of those tooth things in her mouth. A brace, I think they called it. And she was always taking it out. She said she couldn't stand it. And Edie Crone, Margaret Dickson. Ah yes. Good handwriting most of them had. Better than girls have nowadays. As for my nephew's letters, I really can't read them. Their handwriting is like hieroglyphics of some kind. One has to guess what most of the words are. Mollie Short. Ah yes, she had a stammer – it does bring things back.'

'I don't suppose there are many of them, I mean –' Tuppence paused, feeling that she might be about to say something tactless.

'You're thinking most of them are dead, I suppose, dear. Well, you're quite right. Most of them are. But not all of them. No. I've still got quite a lot of people living, with whom I was, as they say, girls together. Not living here, because most girls that one knew married and went somewhere else. Either they had husbands who were in the Services and they went abroad, or they went to some other different town altogether. Two of my oldest friends live up in Northumberland. Yes, yes, it's very interesting.'

'There weren't, I suppose, any Parkinsons left then?' said Tuppence. 'I don't see the name anywhere.'

'Oh no. It was after the Parkinsons' time. There's something you want to find out about the Parkinsons, isn't there?'

'Oh, yes, there is,' said Tuppence. 'It's pure curiosity, you know, nothing else. But – well, somehow in looking at things I got interested in the boy, Alexander Parkinson, and then, as I was walking through the churchyard the other day, I noticed that he'd died fairly young and his grave was there and that made me think about him more.'

'He died young,' said Mrs Griffin. 'Yes. Everyone seems to

think it was sad that he should have done so. He was a very intelligent boy and they hoped for – well, quite a brilliant future for him. It wasn't really any illness, some food he had on a picnic, I believe. So Mrs Henderson told me. She remembers a lot about the Parkinsons.'

'Mrs Henderson?' Tuppence looked up.

'Oh, you wouldn't know about her. She's in one of these old people's homes, you know. It's called Meadowside. It's about – oh, about twelve to fifteen miles from here. You ought to go and see her. She'd tell you a lot of things, I expect, about that house you're living in. Swallow's Nest, it was called then, it's called something else, isn't it now?'

'The Laurels.'

'Mrs Henderson is older than I am, although she was the youngest of quite a large family. She was a governess at one time. And then I think she was a kind of nurse-companion with Mrs Beddingfield who had Swallow's Nest, I mean The Laurels, then. And she likes talking about old times very much. You ought to go and see her, I think.'

'Oh, she wouldn't like –'

'Oh, my dear, I'm sure she *would* like. Go and see her. Just tell her that I suggested it. She remembers me and my sister Rosemary and I do go and see her occasionally, but not of late years because I haven't been able to get about. And you might go and see Mrs Hendley, who lives in – what is it now? – Apple Tree Lodge, I think it is. That's mainly old age pensioners. Not quite the same class, you know, but it's very well run and there's a lot of gossip going there! I'm sure they'd all be quite pleased with visits. You know, anything to break the monotony.'

CHAPTER 3
TOMMY AND TUPPENCE COMPARE NOTES

I

'You look tired, Tuppence,' said Tommy as at the close of dinner they went into the sitting-room and Tuppence dropped into a chair, uttering several large sighs followed by a yawn.

'Tired? I'm dead beat,' said Tuppence.

'What have you been doing? Not things in the garden, I hope.'

'I have not been overworking myself physically,' said Tuppence, coldly. 'I've been doing like you. Mental research.'

'Also very exhausting, I agree,' said Tommy. 'Where, particularly? You didn't get an awful lot out of Mrs Griffin the day before yesterday, did you?'

'Well, I did get a good deal, I think. I didn't get much out of the first recommendation. At least, I suppose I did in a way.'

Opening her handbag, she tugged at a notebook of rather tiresome size, and finally got it out.

'I made various notes each time about things. I took some of the china menus along, for one thing.'

'Oh. And what did that produce?'

'Well, it's not names that I write down so much as the things they say to me and tell me. And they were very thrilled at that china menu because it seemed it was one particular dinner that everyone had enjoyed very much and they had had a wonderful meal – they hadn't had anything like it before, and apparently they had lobster salad for the first time. They'd heard of it being served after the joint in the richest and most fashionable houses, but it hadn't come their way.'

'Oh,' said Tommy, 'that wasn't very helpful.'

'Well, yes it was, in a way, because they said they'd always remember that evening. So I said why would they always remember that evening and they said it was because of the census.'

'What – a census?'

'Yes. You know what a census is, surely, Tommy? Why, we had one only last year, or was it the year before last? You know – having to say, or making everyone sign or enter particulars. Everyone who slept under your roof on a certain night. You know the sort of thing. On the night of November 15th who did you have sleeping under your roof? And you have to put it down, or they have to sign their names. I forget which. Anyway, they were having a census that day and so everyone had to say who was under their roof, and of course a lot of people were at the party and they talked about it. They said it was very unfair and a very stupid thing to have and that anyway they thought it was really a most disgraceful thing to go on having nowadays, because you had to say if you had children and if you were married, or if you were not married but did have children, and things like that. You had to put down a lot of very difficult particulars and you didn't think it was nice. Not nowadays. So they were very upset about it. I mean, they were upset, not about the old census because nobody minded then. It was just a thing that happened.'

'The census might come in useful if you've got the exact date of it,' said Tommy.

'Do you mean you could check up about the census?'

'Oh yes. If one knows the right people I think one could check up fairly easily.'

'And they remembered Mary Jordan being talked about. Everyone said what a nice girl she had *seemed* and how fond everyone was of her. And they would never have believed – you know how people say things. Then they said, Well, she was half German so perhaps people ought to have been more careful in engaging her.'

II

Tuppence put down her empty coffee cup and settled back in her chair.

'Anything hopeful?' said Tommy.

'No, not really,' said Tuppence, 'but it might be. Anyway, the old people talked about it and knew about it. Most of them had heard it from their elderly relations or something. Stories of where they had put things or found things. There was some story about a will that was hidden in a Chinese vase. Something about Oxford and Cambridge, though I don't see how anyone would know about things being hidden in Oxford or Cambridge. It seems very unlikely.'

'Perhaps someone had a nephew undergraduate,' said Tommy, 'who took something back with him to Oxford or Cambridge.'

'Possible, I suppose, but not likely.'

'Did anyone actually talk about Mary Jordan?'

'Only in the way of hearsay – not of actually knowing definitely about her being a German spy, only from their grandmothers or great-aunts or sisters or mothers' cousins or Uncle John's naval friend who knew all about it.'

'Did they talk about how Mary died?'

'They connected her death with the foxglove and spinach episode. Everyone recovered, they said, except her.'

'Interesting,' said Tommy. 'Same story different setting.'

'Too many ideas perhaps,' said Tuppence. 'Someone called Bessie said, "Well. It was only my grandmother who talked about that and of course it had all been years before her time and I expect she got some of the details wrong. She usually did, I believe." You know, Tommy, with everyone talking at once it's all muddled up. There was all the talk about spies and poison on picnics and everything. I couldn't get any exact dates because of course nobody ever knows the exact date of anything your grandmother tells you. If she says, "I was only sixteen at the time and I was terribly thrilled," you probably don't know *now* how old your grandmother really was. She'd probably say she was ninety now because people like to say they're older than their age when they get to eighty, or if, of course, she's only about seventy, she says she's only fifty-two.'

'*Mary Jordan*,' said Tommy thoughtfully, as he quoted the words, '*did not die naturally. He* had his suspicions. Wonder if he ever talked to a policeman about them.'

'You mean Alexander?'

'Yes – And perhaps because of that he talked too much. He *had* to die.'

'A lot depends on Alexander, doesn't it?'

'We do know when Alexander died, because of his grave here. But Mary Jordan – we still don't know when or why.'

'We'll find out in the end,' said Tommy. 'You make a few lists of names you've got and dates and things. You'll be surprised. Surprised what one can check up through an odd word or two here and there.'

'You seem to have a lot of useful friends,' said Tuppence enviously.

'So do you,' said Tommy.

'Well, I don't really,' said Tuppence.

'Yes, you do, you set people in motion,' said Tommy. 'You go and see one old lady with a birthday book. The next thing I know you've been all through masses of people in an old pensioners' home or something, and you know all about things that happened at the time of their great-aunts, great-grandmothers and Uncle

Johns and godfathers, and perhaps an old Admiral at sea who told tales about espionage and all that. Once we can figure a few dates down and get on with a few enquiries, we might – who knows? – get *something*.'

'I wonder who the undergraduates were who were mentioned – Oxford and Cambridge, the ones who were said to have hidden something.'

'They don't sound very like espionage,' said Tommy.

'No, they don't really,' said Tuppence.

'And doctors and old clergymen,' said Tommy. 'One could, I expect, check up on them, but I don't see it would lead one anywhere. It's all too far away. We're not near enough. We don't know – Has anybody tried anything more funny on you, Tuppence?'

'Do you mean has anyone attempted my life in the last two days? No, they haven't. Nobody's invited me to go on a picnic, the brakes of the car are all right, there's a jar of weedkiller in the potting shed but it doesn't even seem to be opened yet.'

'Isaac keeps it there to be handy in case you come out with some sandwiches one day.'

'Oh, poor Isaac,' said Tuppence. 'You are *not* to say things against Isaac. He is becoming one of my best friends. Now I wonder – that reminds me –'

'What does that remind you of?'

'I can't remember,' said Tuppence, blinking her eyes. 'It reminded me of something when you said that about Isaac.'

'Oh dear,' said Tommy and sighed.

'One old lady,' said Tuppence, 'was said to have always put her things in her mittens every night. Earrings, I think it was. That's the one who thought everyone was poisoning her. And somebody else remembered someone who put things in a missionary box or something. You know, the china thing for the waifs and strays, there was a label stuck on to it. But it wasn't for the waifs and strays at all, apparently. She used to put five pound notes in it so that she'd always have a nest egg, and when it got too full she used to take it away and buy another box and break the first one.'

'And spend the five pounds, I suppose,' said Tommy.

'I suppose that *was* the idea. My cousin Emlyn used to say,' said Tuppence, obviously quoting, 'nobody'd rob the waifs and strays or missionaries, would they? If anyone smashed a box like that somebody'd notice, wouldn't they?'

'You haven't found any books of rather dull-looking sermons, have you, in your book search in those rooms upstairs?'

'No. Why?' asked Tuppence.

'Well, I just thought that'd be a very good place to hide things in. You know, something really boring written about theology. An old crabbed book with the inside scooped out.'

'Hasn't been anything like that,' said Tuppence. 'I should have noticed it if there was.'

'Would you have read it?'

'Oh, of course I wouldn't,' said Tuppence.

'There you are then,' said Tommy. 'You wouldn't have read it, you'd have just thrown it away, I expect.'

'*The Crown of Success.* That's one book I remember,' said Tuppence. 'There were two copies of that. Well, let's hope that success will crown our efforts.'

'It seems to me very unlikely. Who killed Mary Jordan? That's the book *we'll* have to write one day, I suppose?'

'If we ever find out,' said Tuppence gloomily.

CHAPTER 4

POSSIBILITY OF SURGERY ON MATHILDE

'What are you going to do this afternoon, Tuppence? Go on helping me with these lists of names and dates and things?'

'I don't think so,' said Tuppence. 'I've had all that. It really is most exhausting writing everything down. Every now and then I do get things a bit wrong, don't I?'

'Well, I wouldn't put it past you. You have made a few mistakes.'

'I wish you weren't more accurate than I am, Tommy. I find it so annoying sometimes.'

'What are you going to do instead?'

'I wouldn't mind having a good nap. Oh no, I'm not going to actually relax,' said Tuppence. 'I think I'm going to disembowel Mathilde.'

'I beg your pardon, Tuppence.'

'I said I was going to disembowel Mathilde.'

'What's the matter with you? You seem very set on violence.'

'Mathilde – she's in KK.'

'What do you mean, she's in KK?'

'Oh, the place where all the dumps are. You know, she's the rocking-horse, the one that's got a hole in her stomach.'

'Oh. And – you're going to examine her stomach, is that it?'

'That's the idea,' said Tuppence. 'Would you like to come and help me?'

'Not really,' said Tommy.

'Would you be *kind* enough to come and help me?' suggested Tuppence.

'Put like that,' said Tommy, with a deep sigh, 'I will force myself to consent. Anyway, it won't be as bad as making lists. Is Isaac anywhere about?'

'No. I think it's his afternoon off. Anyway, we don't want Isaac about. I think I've got all the information I can out of him.'

'He knows a good deal,' said Tommy thoughtfully. 'I found that out the other day, he was telling me a lot of things about the past. Things he can't remember himself.'

'Well, he must be nearly eighty,' said Tuppence. 'I'm quite sure of that.'

'Yes, I know, but things really far back.'

'People have always *heard* so many things,' said Tuppence. 'You never know if they're right or not in what they've heard. Anyway, let's go and disembowel Mathilde. I'd better change my clothes first because it's excessively dusty and cobwebby in KK and we have to burrow right inside her.'

'You might get Isaac, if he's about, to turn her upside down, then we could get at her stomach more easily.'

'You really sound as though in your last reincarnation you must have been a surgeon.'

'Well, I suppose it is a little like that. We are now going to remove foreign matter which might be dangerous to the preservation of Mathilde's life, such as is left of it. We might have her painted up and Deborah's twins perhaps would like to ride on her when they next come to stay.'

'Oh, our grandchildren have so many toys and presents already.'

'That won't matter,' said Tuppence. 'Children don't particularly like expensive presents. They'll play with an old bit of string or a rag doll or something they call a pet bear which is only a bit of a hearthrug just made up into a bundle with a couple of black boot-button eyes put on it. Children have their own ideas about toys.'

'Well, come on,' said Tommy. 'Forward to Mathilde. To the operating theatre.'

The reversal of Mathilde to a position suitable for the necessary operation to take place was not an easy job. Mathilde was a very fair weight. In addition to that, she was very well studded with various nails which would on occasions reverse their position, and which had points sticking out. Tuppence wiped blood from her hand and Tommy swore as he caught his pullover which immediately tore itself in a somewhat disastrous fashion.

'Blow this damned rocking-horse,' said Tommy.

'Ought to have been put on a bonfire years ago,' said Tuppence.

It was at that moment that the aged Isaac suddenly appeared and joined them.

'Whatever now!' he said with some surprise. 'Whatever be you two doing here now? What do you want with this old bit of horse-flesh here? Can I help you at all? What do you want to do with it – do you want it taken out of here?'

'Not necessarily,' said Tuppence. 'We want to turn it upside down so that we can get at the hole there and pull things out.'

'You mean pull things out from inside her, as you might say? Who's been putting that idea into your head?'

'Yes,' said Tuppence, 'that's what we do mean to do.'

'What do you think you'll find there?'

'Nothing but rubbish, I expect,' said Tommy. 'But it would be nice,' he said in a rather doubtful voice, 'if things were cleared up a bit, you know. We might want to keep other things in here. You know – games, perhaps, a croquet set. Something like that.'

'There used to be a crookey lawn once. Long time ago. That was in Mrs Faulkner's time. Yes. Down where the rose garden is now. Mind you, it wasn't a full size one.'

'When was that?' asked Tommy.

'What, you mean the crookey lawn? Oh, well before my time, it was. There's always people as wants to tell you things about what used to happen – things as used to be hidden and why and who wanted to hide them. Lot of tall stories, some of them lies. Some maybe as was true.'

'You're very clever, Isaac,' said Tuppence, 'you always seem to know about everything. How do you know about the croquet lawn?'

'Oh, used to be a box of crookey things in here. Been there for ages. Shouldn't think there's much of it left now.'

Tuppence relinquished Mathilde and went over to a corner where there was a long wooden box. After releasing the lid with some difficulty as it had stuck under the ravages of time, it yielded a faded red ball, a blue ball and one mallet bent and warped. The rest of it was mainly cobwebs.

'Might have been in Mrs Faulkner's time, that might. They do say, you know, as she played in the tournaments in her time,' said Isaac.

'At Wimbledon?' said Tuppence, incredulous.

'Well, not exactly at Wimbledon, I don't think it was. No. The locals, you know. They used to have them down here. Pictures I've seen down at the photographer's –'

'The photographer's?'

'Ah. In the village, Durrance. You know Durrance, don't you?'

'Durrance?' said Tuppence vaguely. 'Oh, yes, he sells films and things like that, doesn't he?'

'That's right. Mind you, he's not the old Durrance, as manages it now. It's his grandson, or his great-grandson, I shouldn't wonder. He sells mostly postcards, you know, and Christmas cards and birthday cards and things like that. He used to take photographs of people. Got a whole lot tucked away. Somebody come in the other day, you know. Wanted a picture of her great-grandmother, she said. She said she'd had one but she'd broken it or burnt it or lost it or something, and she wondered if there was the negative left. But I don't think she found it. But there's a lot of old albums in there stuck away somewhere.'

'Albums,' said Tuppence thoughtfully.

'Anything more I can do?' said Isaac.

'Well, just give us a bit of a hand with Jane, or whatever her name is.'

'Not Jane, it's Mathilde, and it's not Matilda either, which it ought by rights to be, I should say. I believe it was always called Mathilde, for some reason. French, I expect.'

'French or American,' said Tommy, thoughtfully. 'Mathilde. Louise. That sort of thing.'

'Quite a good place to have hidden things, don't you think?' said Tuppence, placing her arm into the cavity in Mathilde's stomach. She drew out a dilapidated indiarubber ball, which had once been red and yellow but which now had gaping holes in it.

'I suppose that's children,' said Tuppence. 'They always put things in like this.'

'Whenever they see a hole,' said Isaac. 'But there was a young gentleman once as used to leave his letters in it, so I've heard. Same as though it was a post box.'

'Letters? Who were they for?'

'Some young lady, I'd think. But it was before my time,' said Isaac, as usual.

'The things that always happened long before Isaac's time,' said Tuppence, as Isaac, having adjusted Mathilde into a good position, left them on the pretext of having to shut up the frames.

Tommy removed his jacket.

'It's incredible,' said Tuppence, panting a little as she removed a scratched and dirty arm from the gaping wound in Mathilde's stomach, 'that anyone could put so many things or want to put them, in this thing, and that nobody should ever have cleaned it out.'

'Well, why should anyone clean it out? Why would anyone want to clean it out?'

'That's true,' said Tuppence. 'We do, though, don't we?'

'Only because we can't think of anything better to do. I don't think anything will come of it though. Ow!'

'What's the matter?' said Tuppence.

'Oh, I scratched myself on something.'

He drew his arm out slightly, readjusted it, and felt inside once more. A knitted scarf rewarded him. It had clearly been the sustenance of moths at one time and possibly after that had descended to an even lower level of social life.

'Disgusting,' said Tommy.

Tuppence pushed him aside slightly and fished in with her own arm, leaning over Mathilde while she felt about inside.

'Mind the nails,' said Tommy.

'What's this?' said Tuppence.

She brought her find out into the open air. It appeared to be the wheel off a bus or cart or some child's toy.

'I think,' she said, 'we're wasting our time.'

'I'm sure we are,' said Tommy.

'All the same, we might as well do it properly,' said Tuppence. 'Oh dear, I've got three spiders walking up my arm. It'll be a worm in a minute and I hate worms.'

'I don't think there'll be any worms inside Mathilde. I mean, worms like going underground in the earth. I don't think they'd care for Mathilde as a boarding-house, do you?'

'Oh well, it's getting empty at any rate, I think,' said Tuppence. 'Hullo, what's this? Dear me, it seems to be a needle book. What a funny thing to find. There's still some needles in it but they're all rusted.'

'Some child who didn't like to do her sewing, I expect,' said Tommy.

'Yes, that's a good idea.'

'I touched something that felt like a book just now,' said Tommy.

'Oh. Well, that might be helpful. What part of Mathilde?'

'I should think the appendix or the liver,' said Tommy in a professional tone. 'On her right-hand side. I'm regarding this as an operation!' he added.

'All right, Surgeon. Better pull it out, whatever it is.'

The so-called book, barely recognizable as such, was of ancient lineage. Its pages were loose and stained, and its binding was coming to pieces.

'It seems to be a manual of French,' said Tommy. '*Pour les enfants. Le Petit Précepteur.*'

'I see,' said Tuppence. 'I've got the same idea as you had. The child didn't want to learn her French lesson; so she came in here and deliberately lost it by putting it into Mathilde. Good old Mathilde.'

'If Mathilde was right side up, it must have been very difficult putting things through this hole in her stomach.'

'Not for a child,' said Tuppence. 'She'd be quite the right height and everything. I mean, she'd kneel and crawl underneath it. Hullo, here's something which feels slippery. Feels rather like an animal's skin.'

'How very unpleasant,' said Tommy. 'Do you think it's a dead rabbit or something?'

'Well, it's not furry or anything. I don't think it's very nice. Oh dear, there's a nail again. Well, it seems to be hung on a nail. There's a sort of bit of string or cord. Funny it hasn't rotted away, isn't it?'

She drew out her find cautiously.

'It's a pocket-book,' she said. 'Yes. Yes, it's been quite good leather once, I think. Quite good leather.'

'Let's see what's inside it, if there is anything inside it,' said Tommy.

'There's something inside it,' said Tuppence.

'Perhaps it's a lot of five pound notes,' she added hopefully.

'Well, I don't suppose they'd be usable still. Paper would rot, wouldn't it?'

'I don't know,' said Tuppence. 'A lot of queer things do survive, you know. I think five pound notes used to be made of wonderfully good paper once, you know. Sort of thin but very durable.'

'Oh well, perhaps it's a twenty pound note. It will help with the housekeeping.'

'What? The money'll be before Isaac's time too, I expect, or else *he'd* have found it. Ah well. Think! It might be a hundred pound note. I wish it were golden sovereigns. Sovereigns were always in purses. My Great-Aunt Maria had a great purse full of sovereigns. She used to show it to us as children. It was her nest egg, she said, in case the French came. I think it was the French. Anyway, it was for extremities or danger. Lovely fat golden sovereigns. I used to think it was wonderful and I'd think how lovely it would be, you know, once one was grown up and you'd have a purse full of sovereigns.'

'Who was going to give you a purse full of sovereigns?'

'I didn't think of anyone giving it to me,' said Tuppence. 'I thought of it as the sort of thing that belonged to you as a right, once you were a grown up person. You know, a real grown up wearing a mantle – that's what they called the things. A mantle with a sort of fur boa round it and a bonnet. You had this great fat purse jammed full of sovereigns, and if you had a favourite grandson who was going back to school, you always gave him a sovereign as a tip.'

'What about the girls, the grand-daughters?'

'I don't think they got any sovereigns,' said Tuppence. 'But sometimes she used to send me half a five pound note.'

'*Half* a five pound note? That wouldn't be much good.'

'Oh yes, it was. She used to tear the five pound note in half, send me one half first and then the other half in another letter later. You see, it was supposed in that way that nobody'd want to steal it.'

'Oh dear, what a lot of precautions everyone did take.'

'They did rather,' said Tuppence. 'Hullo, what's this?'

She was fumbling now in the leather case.

'Let's get out of KK for a minute,' said Tommy, 'and get some air.'

They got outside KK. In the air they saw better what their trophy was like. It was a thick leather wallet of good quality. It was stiff with age but not in any way destroyed.

'I expect it was kept from damp inside Mathilde,' said Tuppence. 'Oh, Tommy, do you know what I think this is?'

'No. What? It isn't money,' said Tuppence, 'but I think it's letters. I don't know whether we'll be able to read them now. They're very old and faded.'

Very carefully Tommy arranged the crinkled yellow paper of the letters, pushing them apart when he could. The writing was quite large and had once been written in a very deep blue-black ink.

'Meeting place changed,' said Tommy. 'Ken Gardens near Peter Pan. Wednesday 25th, 3.30 p.m. Joanna.'

'I really believe,' said Tuppence, 'we might have something at last.'

'You mean that someone who'd be going to London was told

to go on a certain day and meet someone in Kensington Gardens bringing perhaps the papers or the plans or whatever it was. Who do you think got these things out of Mathilde or put them into Mathilde?'

'It couldn't have been a child,' said Tuppence. 'It must have been someone who lived in the house and so could move about without being noticed. Got things from the naval spy, I suppose, and took them to London.'

Tuppence wrapped up the old leather wallet in the scarf she'd been wearing round her neck and she and Tommy returned to the house.

'There may be other papers in there,' said Tuppence, 'but most of them I think are perished and will more or less fall to pieces if you touch them. Hullo, what's this?'

On the hall table a rather bulky package was lying. Albert came out from the dining-room.

'It was left by hand, madam,' he said. 'Left by hand this morning for you.'

'Ah, I wonder what it is,' said Tuppence. She took it.

Tommy and she went into the sitting-room together. Tuppence undid the knot of the string and took off the brown paper wrapping.

'It's a kind of album,' she said, 'I think. Oh, there's a note with it. Ah, it's from Mrs Griffin.

'Dear Mrs Beresford, It was so kind of you to bring me the birthday book the other day. I have had great pleasure looking over it and remembering various people from past days. One does forget so soon. Very often one only remembers somebody's Christian name and not their surname, sometimes it's the other way about. I came across, a little time ago, this old album. It doesn't really belong to me. I think it belonged to my grandmother, but it has a good many pictures in it and among them, I think, there are one or two of the Parkinsons, because my grandmother knew the Parkinsons. I thought perhaps you would like to see it as you seemed to be so interested in the history of your house and who has lived in it in the past. Please don't bother to send it back to me because it means nothing to me personally really, I can assure you. One has so many things in the house always belonging to aunts and grandmothers and the

other day when I was looking in an old chest of drawers in the attic I came across six needle-books. Years and years old. And I believe that was not my grandmother but her grandmother again who used at one time always to give a needle-book to the maids for Christmas and I think these were some she had bought at a sale and would do for another year. Of course quite useless now. Sometimes it seems sad to think of how much waste there has always been.

'A photo album,' said Tuppence. 'Well, that might be fun. Come along, let's have a look.'

They sat down on the sofa. The album was very typical of bygone days. Most of the prints were faded by now but every now and then Tuppence managed to recognize surroundings that fitted the gardens of their own house.

'Look, there's the monkey puzzle. Yes – and look, there's Truelove behind it. That must be a very old photograph, and a funny little boy hanging on to Truelove. Yes, and there's the wistaria and there's the pampas grass. I suppose it must have been a tea-party or something. Yes, there are a lot of people sitting round a table in the garden. They've got names underneath them too. Mabel. Mabel's no beauty. And who's that?'

'Charles,' said Tommy. 'Charles and Edmund. Charles and Edmund seem to have been playing tennis. They've got rather queer tennis racquets. And there's William, whoever he was, and Major Coates.'

'And there's – oh Tommy, there's Mary.'

'Yes. Mary Jordan. Both names there, written under the photograph.'

'She was pretty. Very pretty, I think. It is very faded and old, but – oh Tommy, it really seems wonderful to see Mary Jordan.'

'I wonder who took the photograph?'

'Perhaps the photographer that Isaac mentioned. The one in the village here. Perhaps he'd have old photographs too. I think perhaps one day we'll go and ask.'

Tommy had pushed aside the album by now and was opening a letter which had come in the midday post.

'Anything interesting?' asked Tuppence. 'There are three letters here. Two are bills, I can see. This one – yes, this one is rather different. I asked you if it was interesting,' said Tuppence.

'It may be,' said Tommy. 'I'll have to go to London tomorrow again.'

'To deal with your usual committees?'

'Not exactly,' said Tommy. 'I'm going to call on someone. Actually it isn't London, it's out of London. Somewhere Harrow way, I gather.'

'What is?' said Tuppence. 'You haven't told me yet.'

'I'm going to call on someone called Colonel Pikeaway.'

'What a name,' said Tuppence.

'Yes, it is rather, isn't it?'

'Have I heard it before?' said Tuppence.

'I may have mentioned it to you once. He lives in a kind of permanent atmosphere of smoke. Have you got any cough lozenges, Tuppence?'

'Cough lozenges! Well, I don't know. Yes, I think I have. I've got an old box of them from last winter. But you haven't got a cough – not that I've noticed, at any rate.'

'No, but I shall have if I'm going to see Pikeaway. As far as I can remember, you take two choking breaths and then go on choking. You look hopefully at all the windows which are tightly shut, but Pikeaway would never take a hint of that kind.'

'Why do you think he wants to see you?'

'Can't imagine,' said Tommy. 'He mentions Robinson.'

'What – the yellow one? The one who's got a fat yellow face and is something very hush-hush?'

'That's the one,' said Tommy.

'Oh well,' said Tuppence, 'perhaps what we're mixed up in here is hush-hush.'

'Hardly could be considering it all took place – whatever it was, if there is anything – years and years ago, before even Isaac can remember.'

'New sins have old shadows,' said Tuppence, 'if that's the saying I mean. I haven't got it quite right. New sins have old shadows. Or is it Old sins make long shadows?'

'I should forget it,' said Tommy. 'None of them sounds right.'

'I shall go and see that photographer man this afternoon, I think. Want to come?'

'No,' said Tommy. 'I think I shall go down and bathe.'

'Bathe? It'll be awfully cold.'

'Never mind. I feel I need something cold, bracing and refreshing to remove all the taste of cobwebs, the various remains of which seem to be clinging round my ears and round my neck and some even seem to have got between my toes.'

'This does seem a very dirty job,' said Tuppence. 'Well, I'll go and see Mr Durrell or Durrance, if that's his name. There was another letter, Tommy, which you haven't opened.'

'Oh, I didn't see it. Ah well, that might be something.'

'Who is it from?'

'My researcher,' said Tommy, in a rather grand voice. 'The one who has been running about England, in and out of Somerset House looking up deaths, marriages and births, consulting newspaper files and census returns. She's very good.'

'Good and beautiful?'

'Not beautiful so that you'd notice it,' said Tommy.

'I'm glad of that,' said Tuppence. 'You know, Tommy, now that you're getting on in years you might – you might get some rather dangerous ideas about a beautiful helper.'

'You don't appreciate a faithful husband when you've got one,' said Tommy.

'All my friends tell me you never know with husbands,' said Tuppence.

'You have the wrong kind of friends,' said Tommy.

CHAPTER 5

INTERVIEW WITH COLONEL PIKEAWAY

Tommy drove through Regent's Park, then he passed through various roads he'd not been through for years. Once when he and Tuppence had had a flat near Belsize Park, he remembered walks on Hampstead Heath and a dog they had had who'd enjoyed the walks. A dog with a particularly self-willed nature. When coming out of the flat he had always wished to turn to the left on the road that would lead to Hampstead Heath. The efforts of Tuppence or Tommy to make him turn to the right and go into shopping quarters were usually defeated. James, a Sealyham of obstinate nature, had allowed his heavy sausage-like body to rest flat on the pavement, he would produce a tongue from his mouth and give every semblance of being a dog tired out by being given the wrong kind of exercise by those who owned him. People passing by usually could not refrain from comment.

'Oh, look at that dear little dog there. You know, the one with the white hair – looks rather like a sausage, doesn't he? And panting, poor fellow. Those people of his, they won't let him go the way he wants to, he looks tired out, just tired out.'

Tommy had taken the lead from Tuppence and had pulled James firmly in the opposite direction from the one he wanted to go.

'Oh dear,' said Tuppence, 'can't you pick him up, Tommy?'

'What, pick up James? He's too much of a weight.'

James, with a clever manoeuvre, turned his sausage body so that he was facing once more in the direction of his expectation.

'Look, poor little doggie, I expect he wants to go home, don't you?'

James tugged firmly on his lead.

'Oh, all right,' said Tuppence, 'we'll shop later. Come on, we'll have to let James go where he wants to go. He's such a heavy dog, you can't make him do anything else.'

James looked up and wagged his tail. 'I quite agree with you,' the wag seemed to say. 'You've got the point at last. Come on. Hampstead Heath it is.' And it usually had been.

Tommy wondered. He'd got the address of the place where he was going. The last time he had been to see Colonel Pikeaway it had been in Bloomsbury. A small poky room full of smoke. Here, when he reached the address, it was a small, nondescript house fronting on the heath not far from the birthplace of Keats. It did not look particularly artistic or interesting.

Tommy rang a bell. An old woman with a close resemblance to what Tommy imagined a witch might look like, with a sharp nose and a sharp chin which almost met each other, stood there, looking hostile.

'Can I see Colonel Pikeaway?'

'Don't know I'm sure,' said the witch. 'Who would you be now?'

'My name is Beresford.'

'Oh, I see. Yes. He did say something about that.'

'Can I leave the car outside?'

'Yes, it'll be all right for a bit. Don't get many of the wardens poking around this street. No yellow lines just along here. Better lock it up, sir. You never know.'

Tommy attended to these rules as laid down, and followed the old woman into the house.

'One flight up,' she said, 'not more.'

Already on the stairs there was the strong smell of tobacco. The witch-woman tapped at a door, poked her head in, said, 'This must be the gentleman you wanted to see. Says you're expecting him.' She stood aside and Tommy passed into what he remembered before, an aroma of smoke which forced him almost immediately to choke and gulp. He doubted he would have remembered Colonel Pikeaway apart from the smoke and the cloud and smell of nicotine. A very old man lay back in an armchair – a somewhat ragged armchair with holes on the arms of it. He looked up thoughtfully as Tommy entered.

'Shut the door, Mrs Copes,' he said, 'don't want to let the cold air in, do we?'

Tommy rather thought that they did, but obviously it was his not to reason why, his but to inhale and in due course die, he presumed.

'Thomas Beresford,' said Colonel Pikeaway thoughtfully. 'Well, well, how many years is it since I saw you?'

Tommy had not made a proper computation.

'Long time ago,' said Colonel Pikeaway, 'came here with what's-his-name, didn't you? Ah well, never mind, one name's as good as another. A rose by any other name would smell as sweet. Juliet said that, didn't she? Silly things sometimes Shakespeare made them say. Of course, he couldn't help it, he was a poet. Never cared much for Romeo and Juliet, myself. All those suicides for love's sake. Plenty of 'em about, mind you. Always happening, even nowadays. Sit down, my boy, sit down.'

Tommy was slightly startled at being called 'my boy' again, but he availed himself of the invitation.

'You don't mind, sir,' he said, dispossessing the only possible-seeming chair of a large pile of books.

'No, no, shove 'em all on the floor. Just trying to look something up, I was. Well, well, I'm pleased to see you. You look a bit older than you did, but you look quite healthy. Ever had a coronary?'

'No,' said Tommy.

'Ah! Good. Too many people suffering from hearts, blood pressure – all those things. Doing too much. That's what it is. Running about all over the place, telling everyone how busy they are and the world can't get on without them, and how important they are and everything else. Do you feel the same? I expect you do.'

'No,' said Tommy, 'I don't feel very important. I feel – well, I feel that I really would enjoy relaxing nowadays.'

'Well, it's a splendid thought,' said Colonel Pikeaway. 'The trouble is there are so many people about who won't let you relax. What took you to this place of yours where you're living now? I've forgotten the name of it. Just tell me again, will you?'

Tommy obliged with his address.

'Ah, yes, ah yes, I put the right thing on the envelope then.'

'Yes, I got your letter.'

'I understand you've been to see Robinson. He's still going. Just as fat as ever, just as yellow as ever, and just as rich or richer than ever, I expect. Knows all about it too. Knows about money, I mean. What took you there, boy?'

'Well, we had bought a new house, and a friend of mine advised me that Mr Robinson might be able to clear up a mystery that my wife and I found connected with it, relating to a long time back.'

'I remember now. I don't believe I ever met her but you've got a clever wife, haven't you? Did some sterling work in the – what is the thing? Sounded like the catechism. N or M, that was it, wasn't it?'

'Yes,' said Tommy.

'And now you're on to the same line again, are you? Looking into things. Had suspicions, had you?'

'No,' said Tommy, 'that's entirely wrong. We only went there because we were tired of the flat we were living in and they kept putting up the rent.'

'Nasty trick,' said Colonel Pikeaway. 'They do that to you nowadays, the landlords. Never satisfied. Talk about Daughters of the Horse Leech – sons of the horse leech are just as bad.

All right, you went to live there. *Il faut cultiver son jardin*,' said Colonel Pikeaway, with a rather sudden onslaught on the French language. 'Trying to rub up my French again,' he explained. 'Got to keep in with the Common Market nowadays, haven't we? Funny stuff going on there, by the way. You know, behind things. Not what you see on the surface. So you went to live at Swallow's Nest. What took you to Swallow's Nest, I'd like to know?'

'The house we bought – well, it's called The Laurels now,' said Tommy.

'Silly name,' said Colonel Pikeaway. 'Very popular at one time, though. I remember when I was a boy, all the neighbours, you know, they had those great Victorian drives up to the house. Always getting in loads of gravel for putting down on it and laurels on each side. Sometimes they were glossy green ones and sometimes the speckled ones. Supposed to be very showy. I suppose some of the people who've lived there called it that and the name stuck. Is that right?'

'Yes, I think so,' said Tommy. 'Not the last people. I believe the last people called it Katmandu, or some name abroad because they lived in a certain place they liked.'

'Yes, yes. Swallow's Nest goes back a long time. Yes, but one's got to go back sometimes. In fact, that's what I was going to talk to you about. Going back.'

'Did you ever know it, sir?'

'What – Swallow's Nest, alias The Laurels? No, I never went there. But it figured in certain things. It's tied up with certain periods in the past. People over a certain period. A period of great anxiety to this country.'

'I gather you've come in contact with some information pertaining to someone called Mary Jordan. Or known by that name. Anyway, that's what Mr Robinson told us.'

'Want to see what she looked like? Go over to the mantelpiece. There's a photograph on the left side.'

Tommy got up, went across to the mantelpiece and picked up the photograph. It represented an old-world type of a photograph. A girl wearing a picture hat and holding up a bunch of roses towards her head.

'Looks damn silly now, doesn't it?' said Colonel Pikeaway. 'But she was a good-looking girl, I believe. Unlucky though. She died young. Rather a tragedy, that was.'

'I don't know anything about her,' said Tommy.

'No, I don't suppose so,' said Colonel Pikeaway. 'Nobody does nowadays.'

'There was some idea locally that she was a German spy,' said Tommy. 'Mr Robinson told me that wasn't the case.'

'No, it wasn't the case. She belonged to us. And she did good work for us, too. But somebody got wise to her.'

'That was when there were some people called Parkinson living there,' said Tommy.

'Maybe. Maybe. I don't know all the details. Nobody does nowadays. I wasn't personally involved, you know. All this has been raked up since. Because, you see, there's always trouble. There's trouble in every country. There's trouble all over the world now and not for the first time. No. You can go back a hundred years and you'll find trouble, and you can go back another hundred years and you'll find trouble. Go back to the Crusades and you'll find everyone dashing out of the country going to deliver Jerusalem, or you'll find risings all over the country. Wat Tyler and all the rest of them. This, that and the other, there's always trouble.'

'Do you mean there's some special trouble now?'

'Of course there is. I tell you, there's always trouble.'

'What sort of trouble?'

'Oh, we don't know,' said Colonel Pikeaway. 'They even come round to an old man like me and ask me what I can tell them, or what I can remember about certain people in the past. Well, I can't remember very much but I know about one or two people. You've got to look into the past sometimes. You've got to know what was happening then. What secrets people had, what knowledge they had that they kept to themselves, what they hid away, what they pretended was happening and what was really happening. You've done good jobs, you and your missus at different times. Do you want to go on with it now?'

'I don't know,' said Tommy. 'If – well, do you think there is anything I could do? I'm rather an old man now.'

'Well, you look to me as though you've got better health than many people of your age. Look to me as though you've got better health than some of the younger ones too. And as for your wife, well, she was always good at nosing out things, wasn't she? Yes, good as a well-trained dog.'

Tommy could not repress a smile.

'But what is this all about?' said Tommy. 'I – of course I'm quite willing to do anything if – if you thought I could, but I don't know. Nobody's *told* me anything.'

'I don't suppose they will,' said Colonel Pikeaway. 'I don't think they want me to tell you anything. I don't suppose that Robinson told you much. He keeps his mouth shut, that large fat man. But I'll tell you, well, the bare facts. You know what the world's like – well, the same things always. Violence, swindles, materialism, rebellion by the young, love of violence and a good deal of sadism, almost as bad as the days of the Hitler Youth. All those things. Well, when you want to find out what's wrong not only with this country but world trouble as well, it's not easy. It's a good thing, the Common Market. It's what we always needed, always wanted. But it's got to be a real Common Market. That's got to be understood very clearly. It's got to be a united Europe. There's got to be a union of civilized countries with civilized ideas and with civilized beliefs and principles. The first thing is, when there's something wrong you've got to know where that something is and that's where that yellow whale of a fellow still knows his oats.'

'You mean Mr Robinson?'

'Yes, I mean Mr Robinson. They wanted to give him a peerage, you know, but he wouldn't have it. And you know what *he* means.'

'I suppose,' said Tommy, 'you mean – he stands for – *money*.'

'That's right. Not materialism, but he *knows* about money. He knows where it comes from, he knows where it goes, he knows why it goes, he knows who's behind things. Behind banks, behind big industrial undertakings, and he has to know who is responsible for certain things, big fortunes made out of drugs, drug pushers, drugs being sent all over the world, being marketed, a worship of money. Money not just for buying yourself a big house and two Rolls-Royces, but money for making more money and doing down, doing away with the old beliefs. Beliefs in honesty, in fair trading. You don't want equality in the world, you want the strong to help the weak. You want the rich to finance the poor. You want the honest and the good to be looked up to and admired. Finance! Things are coming back now to finance all the time. What finance is doing, where it's going, what it's supporting, how far hidden it is. There are people you knew, people in the past who had power and brains and their power and brains brought the money and means, and some of their activities were secret but we've got to find out about them. Find out who their secrets passed to, who they've been handed down to, who may be running things now. Swallow's Nest was a type of headquarters. A headquarters for what I should call evil. Later in Hollowquay there was something else. D'you remember Jonathan Kane at all?'

'It's a name,' said Tommy. 'I don't remember anything personally.'

'Well, he was said to be what was admired at one time – what came to be known later as a fascist. That was the time before we knew what Hitler was going to be like and all the rest of them. The time when we thought that something like fascism might be a splendid idea to reform the world with. This chap Jonathan Kane had followers. A lot of followers. Young followers, middle-aged followers, a lot of them. He had plans, he had sources of power, he knew the secrets of a lot of people. He had the kind of knowledge that gave him power. Plenty of blackmail about as always. We want to know what he knew, we want to know what he did, and I think it's possible that he left both plans and followers behind him. Young people who were enmeshed and perhaps still are in favour of his ideas. There have been secrets, you know, there are always secrets that are worth money. I'm not telling you anything exact because I don't know anything exact. The trouble with me is that nobody really knows. We think we know everything because of what we've been through. Wars, turmoil, peace, new forms of government. We think we know it all, but do we? Do we know anything about germ warfare? Do we know everything about gases, about means of inducing pollution? The chemists have their secrets, the Navy, the Air Force – all sorts of things. And they're not all in the present, some of them were in the past. Some of them were on the point of being developed but the development didn't take place. There wasn't time for it. But it was written down, it was committed to paper or committed to certain people, and those people had children and their children had children and maybe some of the things came down. Left in wills, left in documents, left with solicitors to be delivered at a certain time.

'Some people don't know what it is they've got hold of, some of them have just destroyed it as rubbish. But we've got to find out a little more than we do because things are happening all the time. In different countries, in different places, in wars, in Vietnam, in guerrilla wars, in Jordan, in Israel, even in the uninvolved countries. In Sweden and Switzerland – anywhere. There are these things and we want clues to them. And there's some idea that some of the clues could be found in the past. Well, you can't go back into the past, you can't go to a doctor and say, "Hypnotize me and let me see what happened in 1914," or in 1918 or earlier still perhaps. In 1890 perhaps. Something was being planned, something was never completely developed. Ideas. Just look far back. They were thinking of flying, you know, in the Middle Ages. They had some ideas about it. The ancient Egyptians, I believe, had certain ideas. They were never developed. But once the ideas passed on, once you come to the time when they get into the hands of someone who has the means and the kind of brain that can develop them, anything may happen – bad or good. We have a feeling lately that some of the things that have been invented – germ warfare, for example – are difficult to explain except through the process of some secret development, thought to be unimportant but it hasn't been unimportant. Somebody in whose hands it's got has made some adaptation of it which can produce very, very frightening results. Things that can change a character, can perhaps turn a good man into a fiend, and usually for the same reason. For money. Money and what money can buy, what money can get. The power that money can develop. Well, young Beresford, what do you say to all that?'

'I think it's a very frightening prospect,' said Tommy.

'That, yes. But do you think I'm talking nonsense? Do you think this is just an old man's fantasies?'

'No, sir,' said Tommy. 'I think you're a man who knows things. You always have been a man who knew things.'

'H'm. That's why they wanted me, wasn't it? They came here,

complained about all the smoke, said it stifled them, but – well, you know there's a time – a time when there was that Frankfurt ring business – well, we managed to stop that. We managed to stop it by getting at who was behind it. There's a somebody, not just one somebody – several somebodies who are probably behind this. Perhaps we can know who they are, but even if not we can know perhaps what the things are.'

'I see,' said Tommy. 'I can almost understand.'

'Can you? Don't you think this is all rather nonsense? Rather fantastic?'

'I don't think anything's too fantastic to be true,' said Tommy. 'I've learnt that, at least, through a pretty long life. The most amazing things are true, things you couldn't believe could be true. But what I have to make you understand is that *I* have no qualifications. I have no scientific knowledge. I have been concerned always with security.'

'But,' said Colonel Pikeaway, 'you're a man who has always been able to find out things. You. You – and the other one. Your wife. I tell you, she's got a nose for things. She likes to find out things and you go about and take her about. These women are like that. They can get at secrets. If you're young and beautiful you do it like Delilah. When you're old – I can tell you, I had an old great-aunt once and there was no secret that she didn't nose into and find out the truth about. There's the money side. Robinson's on to that. He knows about money. He knows where the money goes, why it goes, where it goes to, and where it comes *from* and what it's *doing*. All the rest of it. He knows about money. It's like a doctor feeling your pulse. He can feel a financier's pulse. Where the headquarters of money are. Who's using it, what for and why. I'm putting you on to this because you're in the right place. You're in the right place by accident and you're not there for the reason anyone might suppose you were. For there you are, an ordinary couple, elderly, retired, seeking for a nice house to end your days in, poking about into the corners of it, interested in talking. Some sentence one day will tell you something. That's all I want you to do. Look about. Find out what legends or stories are told about the good old days or the bad old days.'

'A naval scandal, plans of a submarine or something, that's

talked about still,' said Tommy. 'Several people keep mentioning it. But nobody seems to know anything really about it.'

'Yes, well, that's a good starting point. It was round about then Jonathan Kane lived in that part, you know. He had a cottage down near the sea and he ran his propaganda campaign round there. He had disciples who thought he was wonderful, Jonathan Kane. K-a-n-e. But I would rather spell it a different way. I'd spell it C-a-i-n. That would describe him better. He was set on destruction and methods of destruction. He left England. He went through Italy to countries rather far away, so it's said. How much is rumour I don't know. He went to Russia. He went to Iceland, he went to the American continent. Where he went and what he did and who went with him and listened to him, we don't know. But we think that he knew things, simple things; he was popular with his neighbours, he lunched with them and they with him. Now, one thing I've got to tell you. Look about you. Ferret out things, but for goodness' sake take care of yourselves, both of you. Take care of that – what's-her-name? Prudence?'

'Nobody ever called her Prudence. Tuppence,' said Tommy.

'That's right. Take care of Tuppence and tell Tuppence to take care of you. Take care of what you eat and what you drink and where you go and who is making up to you and being friendly and why should they? A little information comes along. Something odd or queer. Some story in the past that might mean something. Someone perhaps who's a descendant or a relative or someone who knew people in the past.'

'I'll do what I can,' said Tommy. 'We both will. But I don't feel that we'll be able to do it. We're too old. We don't know enough.'

'You can have ideas.'

'Yes. Tuppence has ideas. She thinks that something might be hidden in our house.'

'So it might. Others have had the same idea. Nobody's ever found anything so far, but then they haven't really looked with any assurance at all. Various houses and various families, they change. They get sold and somebody else comes and then somebody else and so they go on. Lestranges and Mortimers and Parkinsons. Nothing much in the Parkinsons except for one of the boys.'

'Alexander Parkinson?'

'So you know about him. How did you manage that?'

'He left a message for someone to find in one of Robert Louis Stevenson's books. *Mary Jordan did not die naturally.* We found it.'

'The fate of every man we have bound about his neck – some saying like that, isn't there? Carry on, you two. Pass through the Postern of Fate.'

CHAPTER 6

POSTERN OF FATE

Mr Durrance's shop was half-way up the village. It was on a corner site, had a few photographs displayed in the window; a couple of marriage groups, a kicking baby in a nudist condition on a rug, one or two bearded young men taken with their girls. None of the photographs were very good, some of them already displayed signs of age. There were also postcards in large numbers; birthday cards and a few special shelves arranged in order of relationships. To my Husband. To my Wife. One or two bathing groups. There were a few pocket-books and wallets of rather poor quality and a certain amount of stationery and envelopes bearing floral designs. Boxes of small notepaper decorated with flowers and labelled For Notes.

Tuppence wandered about a little, picking up various specimens of the merchandise and waiting whilst a discussion about the results obtained from a certain camera were criticized, and advice was asked.

An elderly woman with grey hair and rather lacklustre eyes attended to a good deal of the more ordinary requests. A rather tall young man with long flaxen hair and a budding beard seemed to be the principal attendant. He came along the counter towards Tuppence, looking at her questioningly.

'Can I help you in any way?'

'Really,' said Tuppence, 'I wanted to ask about albums. You know, photograph albums.'

'Ah, things to stick your photos in, you mean? Well, we've got one or two of those but you don't get so much of them nowadays, I mean, people go very largely for transparencies, of course.'

'Yes, I understand,' said Tuppence, 'but I collect them, you know. I collect old albums. Ones like this.'

She produced, with the air of a conjurer, the album she'd been sent.

'Ah, that goes back a long time, doesn't it?' said Mr Durrance. 'Ah, well now, over fifty years old, I should say. Of course, they did do a lot of those things around then, didn't they? Everyone had an album.'

'They had birthday books, too,' said Tuppence.

'Birthday books – yes, I remember something about them. My grandmother had a birthday book, I remember. Lots of people had to write their name in it. We've got birthday cards here still, but people don't buy them much nowadays. It's more Valentines, you know, and Happy Christmases, of course.'

'I don't know whether you had any old albums. You know, the sort of things people don't want any more, but they interest me as a collector. I like having different specimens.'

'Well, everyone collects something nowadays, that's true enough,' said Durrance. 'You'd hardly believe it, the things people collect. I don't think I've got anything as old as this one of yours, though. However, I could look around.'

He went behind the counter and pulled open a drawer against the wall.

'Lot of stuff in here,' he said. 'I meant to turn it out some time but I didn't know as there'd really be any market for it. A lot of weddings here, of course. But then, I mean, weddings date. People want them just at the time of the wedding but nobody comes back to look for weddings in the past.'

'You mean, nobody comes in and says "My grandmother was married here. I wonder if you've got any photographs of her wedding?"'

'Don't think anyone's ever asked me that,' said Durrance. 'Still, you never know. They do ask you for queer things sometimes. Sometimes, you know, someone comes in and wants to see whether you've kept a negative of a baby. You know what mothers are. They want pictures of their babies when they were young. Awful pictures, most of them are, anyway. Now and then we've even had the police round. You know, they want to identify someone. Someone who was here as a boy, and they

want to see what he looks like – or rather what he looked like
then, and whether he's likely to be the same one as one they're
looking for now and whom they're after because he's wanted
for murder or for swindles. I must say that cheers things up
sometimes,' said Durrance with a happy smile.

'I see you're quite crime-minded,' said Tuppence.

'Oh well, you know, you're reading about things like that every
day, why this man is supposed to have killed his wife about six
months ago, and all that. Well, I mean, that's interesting, isn't
it? Because, I mean, some people say that she's still alive. Other
people say that he buried her somewhere and nobody's found
her. Things like that. Well, a photograph of him might come in
useful.'

'Yes,' said Tuppence.

'She felt that though she was getting on good terms with Mr
Durrance nothing was coming of it.

'I don't suppose you'd have any photographs of someone called
– I think her name was Mary Jordan. Some name like that. But it
was a long time ago. About – oh, I suppose sixty years. I think
she died here.'

'Well, it'd be well before my time,' said Mr Durrance. 'Father
kept a good many things. You know, he was one of those –
hoarders, they call them. Never wanted to throw anything away.
Anyone he'd known he'd remember, especially if there was a
history about it. Mary Jordan. I seem to remember something
about her. Something to do with the Navy, wasn't it, and a
submarine? And they said she was a spy, wasn't she? She was
half foreign. Had a Russian mother or a German mother – might
have been a Japanese mother or something like that.'

'Yes. I just wondered if you had any pictures of her.'

'Well, I don't think so. I'll have a look around some time when
I've got a little time. I'll let you know if anything turns up. Perhaps
you're a writer, are you?' he said hopefully.

'Well,' said Tuppence, 'I don't make a whole-time job of it,
but I am thinking of bringing out a rather small book. You know,
recalling the times of about anything from a hundred years ago
down till today. You know, curious things that have happened
including crimes and adventures. And, of course, old photographs
are very interesting and would illustrate the book beautifully.'

'Well, I'll do everything I can to help you, I'm sure. Must be quite interesting, what you're doing. Quite interesting to do, I mean.'

'There were some people called Parkinson,' said Tuppence. 'I think they lived in our house once.'

'Ah, you come from the house up on the hill, don't you? The Laurels or Katmandu – I can't remember what it was called last. Swallow's Nest it was called once, wasn't it? Can't think why.'

'I suppose there were a lot of swallows nesting in the roof,' suggested Tuppence. 'There still are.'

'Well, may have been, I suppose. But it seems a funny name for a house.'

Tuppence, having felt that she'd opened relations satisfactorily, though not hoping very much that any result would come of it, bought a few postcards and some flowered notes in the way of stationery, and wished Mr Durrance goodbye, got back to the gate, walked up the drive, then checked herself on the way to the house and went up the side path round it to have one more look at KK. She got near the door. She stopped suddenly, then walked on. It looked as though something like a bundle of clothes was lying near the door. Something they'd pulled out of Mathilde and not thought to look at, Tuppence wondered.

She quickened her pace, almost running. When she got near the door she stopped suddenly. It was not a bundle of old clothes. The clothes were old enough, and so was the body that wore them. Tuppence bent over and then stood up again, steadied herself with a hand on the door.

'Isaac!' she said. 'Isaac. Poor old Isaac. I believe – oh, I do believe that he's dead.'

Somebody was coming towards her on the path from the house as she called out, taking a step or two.

'Oh, Albert, Albert. Something awful's happened. Isaac, old Isaac. He's lying there and he's dead and I think – I think somebody has killed him.'

CHAPTER 7

THE INQUEST

The medical evidence had been given. Two passers-by not far from the gate had given their evidence. The family had spoken, giving evidence as to the state of his health, any possible people who had had reason for enmity towards him (one or two youngish adolescent boys who had before now been warned off by him) had been asked to assist the police and had protested their innocence. One or two of his employers had spoken including his latest employer, Mrs Prudence Beresford, and her husband, Mr Thomas Beresford. All had been said and done and a verdict had been brought in: Wilful Murder by a person or persons unknown.

Tuppence came out from the inquest and Tommy put an arm round her as they passed the little group of people waiting outside.

'You did very well, Tuppence,' he said, as they returned through the garden gate towards the house. 'Very well indeed. Much better than some of those people. You were very clear and you could be heard. The Coroner seemed to me to be very pleased with you.'

'I don't want anyone to be very pleased with me,' said Tuppence. 'I don't like old Isaac being coshed on the head and killed like that.'

'I suppose someone might have had it in for him,' said Tommy.

'Why should they?' said Tuppence.

'I don't know,' said Tommy.

'No,' said Tuppence, 'and I don't know either. But I just wondered if it's anything to do with us.'

'Do you mean – what do you mean, Tuppence?'

'You know what I mean really,' said Tuppence. 'It's this – this place. Our house. Our lovely new house. And garden and everything. It's as though – isn't it just the right place for us? We thought it was,' said Tuppence.

'Well, I still do,' said Tommy.

'Yes,' said Tuppence, 'I think you've got more hope than

I have. I've got an uneasy feeling that there's something – something *wrong* with it all here. Something left over from the past.'

'Don't say it again,' said Tommy.

'Don't say what again?'

'Oh, just those two words.'

Tuppence dropped her voice. She got nearer to Tommy and spoke almost into his ear.

'Mary Jordan?'

'Well, yes. That *was* in my mind.'

'And in my mind, too, I expect. But I mean, what can anything then have to do with nowadays? What can the past matter?' said Tuppence. 'It oughtn't to have anything to do with – now.'

'The past oughtn't to have anything to do with the present – is that what you mean? But it does,' said Tommy. 'It does, in queer ways that one doesn't think of. I mean that one doesn't think would ever happen.'

'A lot of things, you mean, happen because of what there was in the past?'

'Yes. It's a sort of long chain. The sort of thing you have, with gaps and then with beads on it from time to time.'

'Jane Finn and all that. Like Jane Finn in our adventures when we were young because we wanted adventures.'

'And we had them,' said Tommy. 'Sometimes I look back on it and wonder how we got out of it alive.'

'And then – other things. You know, when we went into partnership, and we pretended to be detective agents.'

'Oh that was fun,' said Tommy. 'Do you remember –'

'No,' said Tuppence, 'I'm not going to remember. I'm not anxious to go back to thinking of the past except – well, except as a stepping-stone, as you might say. No. Well, anyway that gave us practice, didn't it? And then we had the next bit.'

'Ah,' said Tommy. 'Mrs Blenkinsop, eh?'

Tuppence laughed.

'Yes. Mrs Blenkinsop. I'll never forget when I came into that room and saw you sitting there.'

'How you had the nerve, Tuppence, to do what you did, move that wardrobe or whatever it was, and listen in to me and Mr What's-his-name, talking. And then –'

'And then Mrs Blenkinsop,' said Tuppence. She laughed too. 'N or M and Goosey Goosey Gander.'

'But you don't –' Tommy hesitated – 'you don't believe that all those were what you call stepping-stones to this?'

'Well, they are in a way,' said Tuppence. 'I mean, I don't suppose that Mr Robinson would have said what he did to you if he hadn't had a lot of those things in his mind. Me for one of them.'

'Very much you for one of them.'

'But now,' said Tuppence, 'this makes it all different. This, I mean. Isaac. Dead. Coshed on the head. Just inside our garden gate.'

'You don't think *that's* connected with –'

'One can't help thinking it might be,' said Tuppence. 'That's what I mean. We're not just investigating a sort of detective mystery any more. Finding out, I mean, about the past and why somebody died in the past and things like that. It's become personal. Quite personal, I think. I mean, poor old Isaac being *dead.*'

'He was a very old man and possibly that had something to do with it.'

'Not after listening to the medical evidence this morning. Someone wanted to kill him. What for?'

'Why didn't they want to kill us if it was anything to do with us,' said Tommy.

'Well, perhaps they'll try that too. Perhaps, you know, he could have told us something. Perhaps he *was* going to tell us something. Perhaps he even threatened somebody else that he was going to talk to us, say something he knew about the girl or one of the Parkinsons. Or – or all this spying business in the 1914 war. The secrets that were sold. And then, you see, he had to be silenced. But if *we* hadn't come to live here and ask questions and wanted to find out, it wouldn't have happened.'

'Don't get so worked up.'

'I am worked up. And I'm not doing anything for fun any more. This isn't fun. We're doing something different now, Tommy. We're hunting down a killer. But who? Of course we don't know yet but we can find out. That's not the past, that's Now. That's something that happened – what – only days ago, six days ago.

704 • AGATHA CHRISTIE

That's the present. It's here and it's connected with us and it's connected with this house. And we've got to find out and we're going to find out. I don't know how but we've got to go after all the clues and follow up things. I feel like a dog with my nose to the ground, following a trail. I'll have to follow it *here*, and you've got to be a hunting dog. Go round to different places. The way you're doing now. Finding out about things. Getting your – whatever you call it – research done. There must be people who know things, not of their own knowledge, but what people have told them. Stories they've heard. Rumours. Gossip.'

'But, Tuppence, you can't really believe there's any chance of our –'

'Oh yes I do,' said Tuppence. 'I don't know how or in what way, but I believe that when you've got a real, convincing idea, something that you know is black and bad and evil, and hitting old Isaac on the head *was* black and evil . . .' She stopped.

'We could change the name of the house again,' said Tommy.

'What do you mean? Call it Swallow's Nest and not The Laurels?'

A flight of birds passed over their heads. Tuppence turned her head and looked back towards the garden gate. 'Swallow's Nest was once its name. What's the rest of that quotation? The one your researcher quoted. Postern of Death, wasn't it?'

'No, Postern of Fate.'

'Fate. That's like a comment on what has happened to Isaac. Postern of Fate – *our* Garden Gate –'

'Don't worry so much, Tuppence.'

'I don't know why,' said Tuppence. 'It's just a sort of idea that came into my mind.'

Tommy gave her a puzzled look and shook his head.

'Swallow's Nest is a nice name, really,' said Tuppence. 'Or it could be. Perhaps it will some day.'

'You have the most extraordinary ideas, Tuppence.'

'Yet something singeth like a bird. That was how it ended. Perhaps all this will end that way.'

Just before they reached the house, Tommy and Tuppence saw a woman standing on the doorstep.

'I wonder who that is,' said Tommy.

'Someone I've seen before,' said Tuppence. 'I don't remember who at the moment. Oh. I think it's one of old Isaac's family. You know they all lived together in one cottage. About three or four boys and this woman and another one, a girl. I may be wrong, of course.'

The woman on the doorstep had turned and came towards them.

'Mrs Beresford, isn't it?' she said, looking at Tuppence.

'Yes,' said Tuppence.

'And – I don't expect you know me. I'm Isaac's daughter-in-law, you know. Married to his son, Stephen, I was. Stephen – he got killed in an accident. One of them lorries. The big ones that go along. It was on one of the M roads, the M1 I think it was. M1 or the M5. No, the M5 was before that. The M4 it could be. Anyway, there it was. Five or six years ago it was. I wanted to – I wanted just to speak to you. You and – you and your husband –' She looked at Tommy. 'You sent flowers, didn't you, to the funeral? Isaac worked in the garden here for you, didn't he?'

'Yes,' said Tuppence. 'He did work for us here. It was such a terrible thing to have happened.'

'I came to thank you. Very lovely flowers they was, too. Good ones. Classy ones. A great bunch of them.'

'We thought we'd like to do it,' said Tuppence, 'because Isaac had been very helpful to us. He'd helped us a lot, you know, with getting into the house. Telling us about things, because we don't know much about the house. Where things were kept, and everything. And he gave me a lot of knowledge about planting things, too, and all that sort of thing.'

'Yes, he knew his stuff, as you might say. He wasn't much of a worker because he was old, you know, and he didn't like stooping. Got lumbago a lot, so he couldn't do as much as he'd have liked to do.'

'He was very nice and very helpful,' said Tuppence firmly. 'And he knew a lot about things here, and the people, and told us a lot.'

'Ah. He knew a lot, he did. A lot of his family, you know, worked before him. They lived round about and they'd known a good deal of what went on in years gone by. Not of their own knowledge, as you might say but – well, just hearing what went on. Well, ma'am, I won't keep you. I just came up to have a few words and say how much obliged I was.'

'That's very nice of you,' said Tuppence. 'Thank you very much.'

'You'll have to get someone else to do a bit of work in the garden, I expect.'

'I expect so,' said Tuppence. 'We're not very good at it ourselves. Do you – perhaps you –' she hesitated, feeling perhaps she was saying the wrong thing at the wrong moment – 'perhaps you know of someone who would like to come and work for us.'

'Well, I can't say I do offhand, but I'll keep it in mind. You never know. I'll send along Henry – that's my second boy, you know – I'll send him along and let you know if I hear of anyone. Well, good day for now.'

'What was Isaac's name? I can't remember,' said Tommy, as they went into the house. 'I mean, his surname.'

'Oh, Isaac Bodlicott, I think.'

'So that's a Mrs Bodlicott, is it?'

'Yes. Though I think she's got several sons, boys and a girl and they all live together. You know, in that cottage half-way up the Marshton Road. Do you think she knows who killed him?' said Tuppence.

'I shouldn't think so,' said Tommy. 'She didn't look as though she did.'

'I don't know how you'd look,' said Tuppence. 'It's rather difficult to say, isn't it?'

'I think she just came to thank you for the flowers. I don't think she had the look of someone who was – you know – revengeful. I think she'd have mentioned it if so.'

'Might. Might not,' said Tuppence.

She went into the house looking rather thoughtful.

CHAPTER 8
REMINISCENCES ABOUT AN UNCLE
I

The following morning Tuppence was interrupted in her remarks to an electrician who had come to adjust portions of his work which were not considered satisfactory.

'Boy at the door,' said Albert. 'Wants to speak to you, madam.'

'Oh. What's his name?'

'Didn't ask him, he's waiting there outside.'

Tuppence seized her garden hat, shoved it on her head and came down the stairs.

Outside the door a boy of about twelve or thirteen was standing. He was rather nervous, shuffling his feet.

'Hope it's all right to come along,' he said.

'Let me see,' said Tuppence, 'you're Henry Bodlicott, aren't you?'

'That's right. That was my – oh, I suppose he was by way of being an uncle, the one I mean whose inquest was on yesterday. Never been to an inquest before, I haven't.'

Tuppence stopped herself on the brink of saying 'Did you enjoy it?' Henry had the look of someone who was about to describe a treat.

'It was quite a tragedy, wasn't it?' said Tuppence. 'Very sad.'

'Oh well, he was an old one,' said Henry. 'Couldn't have expected to last much longer I don't think, you know. Used to cough something terrible in the autumn. Kept us all awake in the house. I just come along to ask if there's anything as you want done here. I understood – as a matter of fact Mom told me – as you had some lettuces ought to be thinned out now and I wonder if you'd like me to do it for you. I know just where they are because I used to come up sometimes and talk to old Izzy when he was at work. I could do it now if you liked.'

'Oh, that's very nice of you,' said Tuppence. 'Come out and show me.'

They moved into the garden together and went up to the spot designated.

'That's it, you see. They've been shoved in a bit tight and you've got to thin 'em out a bit and put 'em over there instead, you see, when you've made proper gaps.'

'I don't really know anything about lettuces,' Tuppence admitted. 'I know a little about flowers. Peas, Brussels sprouts and lettuces and other vegetables I'm not very good at. You don't want a job working in the garden, I suppose, do you?'

'Oh no, I'm still at school, I am. I takes the papers round and I do a bit of fruit picking in the summer, you know.'

'I see,' said Tuppence. 'Well, if you hear of anyone and you let me know, I'll be very glad.'

'Yes, I will do that. Well, so long, mum.'

'Just show me what you're doing to the lettuces. I'd like to know.'

She stood by, watching the manipulations of Henry Bodlicott.

'Now that's all right. Yes, nice ones, these, aren't they? Webb's Wonderful, aren't they? They keep a long time.'

'We finished the Tom Thumbs,' said Tuppence.

'That's right. Those are the little early ones, aren't they? Very crisp and good.'

'Well, thank you very much,' said Tuppence.

She turned away and started to walk towards the house. She noted she'd lost her scarf and turned back. Henry Bodlicott, just starting for home, stopped and came across to her.

'Just the scarf,' said Tuppence. 'Is it – oh, there it is on that bush.'

He handed it to her, then stood looking at her, shuffling his feet. He looked so very worried and ill at ease that Tuppence wondered what was the matter with him.

'Is there anything?' she said.

Henry shuffled his feet, looked at her, shuffled his feet again, picked his nose and rubbed his left ear and then moved his feet in a kind of tattoo.

'Just something I – I wondered if you – I mean – if you wouldn't mind me asking you –'

'Well?' said Tuppence. She stopped and looked at him enquiringly.

Henry got very red in the face and continued to shuffle his feet.

'Well, I didn't like to – I don't like to ask, but I just wondered – I mean, people have been saying – they said things . . . I mean, I hear them say . . .'

'Yes?' said Tuppence, wondering what had upset Henry, what he could have heard concerning the lives of Mr and Mrs Beresford, the new tenants of The Laurels. 'Yes, you've heard what?'

'Oh, just as – as how it's you is the lady what caught spies or something in the last war. You did it, and the gentleman too. You were in it and you found someone who was a German spy pretending to be something else. And you found him out and you had a lot of adventures and in the end it was all cleared up. I mean, you were – I don't know what to call it – I suppose you were one of our Secret Service people and you did that and they said as you'd been wonderful. Of course, some time ago now but you was all mixed up with something – something about nursery rhymes too.'

'That's right,' said Tuppence. 'Goosey Goosey Gander was the one in question.'

'Goosey Goosey Gander! I remember that. Gosh, years ago, it was. Whither will you wander?'

'That's right,' said Tuppence. 'Upstairs, downstairs, in my lady's chamber. There he found an old man who wouldn't say his prayers and he took him by the left leg and threw him down the stairs. At least, I think that's right but it may be a different nursery rhyme I've tacked on to it.'

'Well, I never,' said Henry. 'Well, I mean, it's rather wonderful to have you living here just like anyone else, isn't it? But I don't know why the nursery rhymes were in it.'

'Oh there was a kind of code, a cypher,' said Tuppence.

'You mean it had to be sort of read and all that?' said Henry.

'Something of the kind,' said Tuppence. 'Anyway, it was all found out.'

'Well now, isn't that wonderful,' said Henry. 'You don't mind if I tell my friend, do you? My chum. Clarence, his name is. Silly name, I know. We all laugh at him for it. But he's a good chap, he is and he'll be ever so thrilled to know as we've got you really living amongst us.'

He looked at Tuppence with the admiration of an affectionate spaniel.

'Wonderful!' he said again.

'Oh, it was a long time ago,' said Tuppence. 'In the 1940s.'

'Was it fun, or were you ever so frightened?'

'Bits of both,' said Tuppence. 'Mostly, I think, I was frightened.'

'Oh well, I expect as you would be, too. Yes, but it's odd as you should come here and get mixed up in the same sort of thing. It was a naval gentleman, wasn't it? I mean as called himself an English commander in the Navy, but he wasn't really. He was a German. At least, that's what Clarence said.'

'Something like that,' said Tuppence.

'So perhaps that's why you come here. Because, you know, we had something here once – well it was a very, very long time ago – but it was the same thing, as you might say. He was a submarine officer. He sold plans of submarines. Mind you, it's only stories as I've heard people say.'

'I see,' said Tuppence. 'Yes. No, it's not the reason we came here. We just came here because it's a nice house to live in. I've heard these same rumours going about only I don't know exactly what happened.'

'Well, I'll try and tell you some time. Of course, one doesn't always know what's right or not but things aren't always known properly.'

'How did your friend Clarence manage to know so much about it?'

'Well, he heard from Mick, you know. He used to live a short time up by where the blacksmith used to be. He's been gone a long time, but he heard a lot from different people. And our uncle, old Isaac, he knew a good deal about it. He used to tell us things sometimes.'

'So he did know a good deal about it all?' said Tuppence.

'Oh yes. That's why I wondered, you know, when he was coshed the other day if that could be the reason. That he might have known a bit too much and – he told it all to you. So they did him in. That's what they do nowadays. They do people in, you know, if they know too much of anything that's going to involve them with the police or anything.'

'You think your Uncle Isaac – you think he knew a good deal about it?'

'Well, I think things got told him, you know. He heard a lot here and there. Didn't often talk of it but sometimes he would. Of an evening, you know, after smoking a pipe or hearing me and Clarrie talk and my other friend, Tom Gillingham. He used to want to know, too, and Uncle Izzy would tell us this, that and the other. Of course we didn't know if he was making it up or not. But I think he'd found things and knew where some things were. And he said if some people knew where they were there might be something interesting.'

'Did he?' said Tuppence. 'Well, I think that's very interesting to us also. You must try and remember some of the things he said or suggested some time because, well, it might lead to finding out who killed him. Because he was killed. It wasn't an accident, was it?'

'We thought at first it must have been an accident. You know, he had a bit of a heart or something and he used to fall down now and again or get giddy or have turns. But it seems – I went to the inquest, you know – as though he'd been done in deliberate.'

'Yes,' said Tuppence, 'I think he was done in deliberate.'

'And you don't know why?' said Henry.

Tuppence looked at Henry. It seemed to her as though she and Henry were for the moment two police dogs on the same scent.

'I think it was deliberate, and I think that you, because he was your relation, and I too, would like to know who it was who did such a cruel and wicked thing. But perhaps you do know or have some idea already, Henry.'

'I don't have a proper idea, I don't,' said Henry. 'One just hears things and I know people that Uncle Izzy says – said – now and then had got it in for him for some reason and he said that was because he knew a bit too much about them and about what they knew and about something that happened. But it's always someone who's been dead so many years ago that one can't really remember it or get at it properly.'

'Well,' said Tuppence, 'I think you'll have to help us, Henry.'

'You mean you'll let me sort of be in it with you? I mean, doing a bit of finding out any time?'

'Yes,' said Tuppence, 'if you can hold your tongue about what you find out. I mean, tell me, but don't go talking to all your friends about it because that way things would get around.'

'I see. And then they might tell the coshers and go for you and Mr Beresford, mightn't they?'

'They might,' said Tuppence, 'and I'd rather they didn't.'

'Well, that's natural,' said Henry. 'Well, see here, if I come across anything or hear anything I'll come up and offer to do a bit of work here. How's that? Then I can tell you what I know and nobody'd hear us and – but I don't know anything right at the moment. But I've got friends.' He drew himself up suddenly and put on an air clearly adopted from something he'd seen on television. 'I know things. People don't know as I know things. They don't think I've listened and they don't think I'd remember, but I know sometimes – you know, they'll say something and then they'll say who else knows about it and then they'll – well, you know, if you keep quiet you get to hear a lot. And I expect it's all very important, isn't it?'

'Yes,' said Tuppence, 'I think it's important. But we have to be very careful, Henry. You understand that?'

'Oh, I do. Of course I'll be careful. Careful as you know how. He knew a lot about this place, you know,' went on Henry. 'My Uncle Isaac did.'

'About this house, you mean, or this garden?'

'That's right. He knew some of the stories about it, you know. Where people were seen going and what they did with things maybe, and where they met people. Where there were hiding-places and things. He used to talk sometimes, he did. Of course Mom, she didn't listen much. She'd just think it was all silly. Johnny – that's my older brother – he thinks it's all nonsense and he didn't listen. But I listened and Clarence is interested in that sort of thing. You know, he liked those kind of films and all that. He said to me, "Chuck, it's just like a film." So we talked about it together.'

'Did you ever hear anyone talked about whose name was Mary Jordan?'

'Ah yes, of course. She was the German girl who was a spy, wasn't she? Got naval secrets out of naval officers, didn't she?'

'Something of that kind, I believe,' said Tuppence, feeling it safer to stick to that version, though in her mind apologizing to the ghost of Mary Jordan.

'I expect she was very lovely, wasn't she? Very beautiful?'

'Well, I don't know,' said Tuppence, 'because, I mean, she probably died when I was about three years old.'

'Yes, of course, it would be so, wouldn't it? Oh, one hears her talked about sometimes.'

II

'You seem very excited and out of breath, Tuppence,' said Tommy as his wife, dressed in her garden clothes, came in through the side door, panting a little as she came.

'Well,' said Tuppence, 'I am in a way.'

'Not been overdoing it in the garden?'

'No. Actually I haven't been doing anything at all. I've just been standing by the lettuces talking, or being talked to – whichever way you put it –'

'Who's been talking to you?'

'A boy,' said Tuppence. 'A boy.'

'Offering to help in the garden?'

'Not exactly,' said Tuppence. 'That would be very nice too, of course. No. Actually, he was expressing admiration.'

'Of the garden?'

'No,' said Tuppence, 'of me.'

'Of you?'

'Don't look surprised,' said Tuppence, 'and oh, don't sound surprised either. Still, I admit these *bonnes bouches* come in sometimes when you least expect them.'

'Oh. What is the admiration of – your beauty or your garden overall?'

'My past,' said Tuppence.

'Your past!'

'Yes. He was fairly thrilled to think I had been the lady, as he put it, who had unmasked a German spy in the last war. A false naval commander, retired, who was nothing of the kind.'

'Good gracious,' said Tommy. 'N or M again. Dear me, shan't we ever be able to live that down?'

'Well, I'm not very sure I want to live it down,' said Tuppence.

'I mean, why should we? If we'd been a celebrated actress or actor we'd quite like to be reminded of it.'

'I see the point,' said Tommy.

'And I think it might be very useful with what we're trying to do here.'

'If he's a boy, how old did you say he was?'

'Oh, I should think about ten or twelve. Looks ten but he's twelve, I think. And he has a friend called Clarence.'

'What's that got to do with it?'

'Well, nothing at the moment,' said Tuppence, 'but he and Clarence are allies and would like, I think, to attach themselves to our service. To find out things or to tell us things.'

'If they're ten or twelve, how can they tell us things or remember things we want to know?' said Tommy. 'What sort of things did he say?'

'Most of his sentences were short,' said Tuppence, 'and consisted of mainly "well, you know", or "you see, it was like this", or "yes, and then you know". Anyway, "you know" was always a component part of everything he said.'

'And they were all things you didn't know.'

'Well, they were attempts at explaining things he'd heard about.'

'Heard about from whom?'

'Well, not first-hand knowledge, as you'd say, and I wouldn't say second-hand knowledge. I think it might go up to third-hand, fourth-hand, fifth-hand, sixth-hand knowledge. It consisted also of what Clarence had heard and what Clarence's friend, Algernon, had heard. What Algernon said Jimmy had heard –'

'Stop,' said Tommy, 'that's enough. And what had they heard?'

'That's more difficult,' said Tuppence, 'but I think one can get round to it. They'd heard certain places mentioned or stories told and they were very, very anxious to partake of the joys of what we had clearly come to do here.'

'Which is?'

'To discover something important. Something that's well known to be hidden here.'

'Ah,' said Tommy. 'Hidden. Hidden how, where and when?'

'Different stories about all those three,' said Tuppence, 'but it's exciting, you must admit, Tommy.'

Tommy said thoughtfully that perhaps it was.

'It ties in with old Isaac,' said Tuppence. 'I think Isaac must have known quite a lot of things which he could have told us.'

'And you think that Clarence and – what's this one's name again?'.

'I'll remember it in a minute,' said Tuppence. 'I got so confused with all the other people he'd heard things from. The ones with the grand names like Algernon and the ones with the ordinary names like Jimmy and Johnny and Mike.

'Chuck,' said Tuppence suddenly.

'Chuck what?' asked Tommy.

'No. I didn't mean it that way. I think that's his name. The boy, I mean. Chuck.'

'It seems a very odd name.'

'His real name is Henry but I expect his friends call him Chuck.'

'Like Chuck goes the weasel.'

'Pop goes the weasel, you mean.'

'Well, I know that's correct. But Chuck goes the weasel sounds much the same.'

'Oh Tommy, what I really want to say to you is that we've got to go on with this, specially now. Do you feel the same?'

'Yes,' said Tommy.

'Well, I thought perhaps you did. Not that you've said anything. But we've got to go on with it and I'll tell you why. Mainly because of Isaac. Isaac. Somebody killed him. They killed him because he knew something. He knew something that might have been dangerous to somebody. And we've got to find out who the person was it would be dangerous to.'

'You don't think,' said Tommy, 'that it's just – oh, one of those things. You know, hooliganism or whatever they call it. You know, people go out and want to do people in and don't care who the people are, but they prefer them to be elderly and not to be able to put up any kind of a resistance.'

'Yes,' said Tuppence, 'in a way I do mean that. But – I don't think it was that. I think there *is* something, I don't know if hidden is the right word, there's something here. Something that throws light on something that happened in the past, something that someone left here or put here or gave to someone to keep here who has since died or put it somewhere. But something that someone doesn't want discovered. Isaac knew it and they must have been afraid he'd tell us because word's evidently going round now about us. You know, that we're famous anti-espionage people or whatever you call it. We've got a reputation for that sort of thing. And it's tied up in a way, you see, with Mary Jordan and all the rest of it.'

'Mary Jordan,' said Tommy, 'did not die a natural death.'

'Yes,' said Tuppence, 'and old Isaac was killed. We've got to find out who killed him and why. Otherwise —'

'You've got to be careful,' said Tommy, 'you've got to be careful of yourself, Tuppence. If anyone killed Isaac because he thought he was going to talk about things in the past that he'd heard about, someone may be only too pleased to wait in a dark corner for you one night and do the same thing. They wouldn't think there'd be any worry about it, they'd just think people would say: "Oh another of those things."'

'When old ladies are hit on the head and done in,' said Tuppence. 'Yes, quite so. That's the unfortunate result of having grey hair and walking with a slight arthritic limp. Of course I must be fair game for anyone. I shall look after myself. Do you think I ought to carry a small pistol about with me?'

'No,' said Tommy, 'certainly not.'

'Why? Do you think I'd make some mistake with it?'

'Well, I think you might trip over the root of a tree. You know you're always falling down. And then you might shoot yourself instead of just using the pistol for protection.'

'Oh, you don't really think I'd do anything stupid like that, do you?' said Tuppence.

'Yes, I do,' said Tommy. 'I'm sure you're quite capable of it.'

'I could carry a flick knife,' said Tuppence.

'I shouldn't carry anything at all,' said Tommy. 'I should just go about looking innocent and talking about gardening. Say, perhaps, we're not sure we like the house and we have plans for going to live elsewhere. That's what I suggest.'

'Who've I got to say that to?'

'Oh, almost anyone,' said Tommy. 'It'll get round.'

'Things always get round,' said Tuppence. 'Quite a place here for things getting round. Are you going to say the same things, Tommy?'

'Well, roughly. Say, perhaps, that we don't like the house as much as we thought we did.'

'But you want to go on, too, don't you?' said Tuppence.

'Yes,' said Tommy. 'I'm embroiled all right.'

'Have you thought how to set about it?'

'Go on doing what I'm doing at present. What about you, Tuppence? Have you got any plans?'

'Not quite yet,' said Tuppence. 'I've got a few ideas. I can get a bit more out of – what did I say his name was?'

'First Henry – then Clarence.'

CHAPTER 9

JUNIOR BRIGADE

I

Having seen Tommy depart for London, Tuppence was wandering vaguely round the house trying to single out some particular activity which might yield successful results. However, her brain did not seem to be full of bright ideas this morning.

With the general feeling of one returning to the beginning, she climbed up to the book-room and walked round it vaguely, looking at the titles of various volumes. Children's books, lots of children's books, but really one couldn't go any farther than that, could one? She had gone as far as anyone could already. By now she was almost certain that she had looked at every single book in this particular room; Alexander Parkinson had not revealed any more of his secrets.

She was standing there running her fingers through her hair, frowning and kicking at a bottom shelf of theological works whose bindings were nearly all of them scaling away from the books, when Albert came up.

'Someone as wants to see you downstairs, madam.'

'What do you mean by someone?' said Tuppence. 'Anyone I know?'

'I dunno. Shouldn't think so. Boys they are, mainly. Boys and a girl or two all in a hump. Spect they want a subscription for something or other.'

'Oh. They didn't give any names or say anything?'

'Oh, one of them did. Said he was Clarence and you'd know all about him.'

'Oh,' said Tuppence. 'Clarence.' She considered for a moment. Was this the fruit from yesterday? Anyway, it could do no harm to follow it up.

'Is the other boy here too? The one I was talking to yesterday in the garden?'

'Don't know. They all look much alike. Dirty, you know, and all the rest of it.'

'Oh well,' said Tuppence, 'I'll come down.'

When she had reached the ground floor she turned enquiringly to her guide.

Albert said, 'Oh, I didn't let them come into the house. Wouldn't be safe, I think. Never know what you might lose, these days. They're out in the garden. They said to tell you they was by the gold-mine.'

'They was by the what?' asked Tuppence.

'The gold-mine.'

'Oh,' said Tuppence.

'What way would that be?'

Tuppence pointed.

'Past the rose garden, and then right by the dahlia walk. I think I know. There's a sort of water thing there. I don't know if it's a brook or a canal or has once been a pond that has had goldfish in it. Anyway, give me my gumboots and I'd better take my mackintosh as well in case someone pushes me into it.'

'I should put it on if I was you, ma'am, it's going to rain presently.'

'Oh dear,' said Tuppence. 'Rain, rain. Always rain.'

She went out and came fairly quickly to what seemed to be a considerable deputation waiting for her. There were, she thought, about ten or twelve of assorted ages, mainly boys flanked by two long-haired girls, all looking rather excited. One of them said in a shrill voice as Tuppence approached:

'Here she comes! Here she is. Now then, who's going to

speak? Go on, George, you'd better talk. You're the one as always talks.'

'Well, you're not going to now. I'm going to talk,' said Clarence.

'You shut up, Clarrie. You know your voice is weak. It makes you cough if you talk.'

'Now look here, this is my show. I –'

'Good morning, all,' said Tuppence, breaking in. 'You've come to see me about something, have you? What is it?'

'Got something for you, we have,' said Clarence. 'Information. That's what you're after, isn't it?'

'It depends,' said Tuppence. 'What kind of information?'

'Oh, not information about nowadays. All long ago.'

'Historical information,' said one of the girls, who appeared to be the intellectual chief of the group. 'Most interesting if you're doing research into the past.'

'I see,' said Tuppence, concealing the fact that she did not see. 'What's this place here?'

'It's a gold-mine.'

'Oh,' said Tuppence. 'Any gold in it?'

She looked about her.

'Well, really, it's a goldfish pool,' explained one of the boys. 'Used to be goldfish in it once, you know. Special ones with lots of tails, from Japan or somewhere. Oh, wonderful it used to be. That was in old Mrs Forrester's time. That's – oh, that's ten years ago.'

'Twenty-four years ago,' said one of the girls.

'Sixty years ago,' said a very small voice, 'every bit of sixty years ago. Lots of goldfish there were. Ever so many. Said to be valuable, they was. They used to die sometimes. Sometimes they ate each other, sometimes they were just lying on top, floating about, you know.'

'Well,' said Tuppence, 'what do you want to tell me about them? There are no goldfish to see here now.'

'No. It's information,' said the intellectual girl.

A large outbreak of voices occurred. Tuppence waved her hand.

'Not all at once,' she said. 'One or two speak at a time. What's all this about?'

'Something perhaps you ought to know about where things

was hidden once. Hidden once and said to be very important.'

'And how do you know about them?' said Tuppence.

This provoked a chorus of replies. It was not very easy to hear everyone at once.

'It was Janie.'

'It was Janie's Uncle Ben,' said one voice.

'No, it wasn't. It was Harry, it was . . . Yes, it was Harry. Harry's cousin Tom . . . Much younger than that. It was his grandmother told him and his grandmother had been told by Josh. Yes. I don't know who Josh was. I think Josh was her husband . . . No, he wasn't her husband, he was her uncle.'

'Oh dear,' said Tuppence.

She looked over the gesticulating crowd and picked out a choice.

'Clarence,' she said. 'You're Clarence, aren't you? Your friend told me about you. You, well what do you know and what's it all about?'

'Well, if you want to find out you've got to go to the PPC.'

'Go to the what?' said Tuppence.

'The PPC.'

'What's the PPC?'

'Don't you know? Hasn't anyone told you? PPC is the Pensioners' Palace Club.'

'Oh dear,' said Tuppence, 'that sounds very grand.'

'It isn't grand at all,' said one boy of about nine. 'It isn't grand a bit. It's only old age pensioners saying things and getting together. Pack of lies, some people say they tell about things they knew. You know, knew in the last war and knew after it. Oh, all sorts of things they say.'

'Where is this PPC?' asked Tuppence.

'Oh, it's along at the end of the village. Half-way to Morton Cross, it is. If you're a pensioner you get a ticket for it and you go there and you have bingo and you have all sorts of things there. It's quite fun, it is. Oh, some of them are very old. Some of them are deaf and blind and everything else. But they all – well, they like getting together, you know.'

'Well, I should like to pay a visit to it,' said Tuppence. 'Certainly. Is there any particular time one goes there?'

'Well, any time you like, I suppose, but the afternoon would be a good time, you know. Yes. That's when they can say they've got a friend coming – if they've got a friend coming they get extra things for tea, you know. Biscuits sometimes, with sugar on. And crisps sometimes. Things like that. What did you say, Fred?'

Fred took a step forward. He gave a somewhat pompous bow to Tuppence.

'I shall be very happy,' he said, 'to escort you. Shall we say about half past three this afternoon?'

'Ah, be yourself,' said Clarence. 'Don't go talking like that.'

'I shall be very pleased to come,' said Tuppence. She looked at the water. 'I can't help being rather sorry that there aren't any goldfish any more.'

'You ought to have seen the ones with five tails. Wonderful, they was. Somebody's dog fell in here once. Mrs Faggett's, it was.'

He was contradicted. 'No it wasn't. It was somebody else, her name was Follyo, not Fagot –'

'It was Foliatt and it was spelt with a plain f. Not a capital letter.'

'Ah, don't be silly. It was someone quite different. It was that Miss French, that was. Two small ffs she spelt it with.'

'Did the dog drown?' asked Tuppence.

'No, he didn't drown. He was only a puppy, you see, and his mother was upset and she went along and she pulled at Miss French's dress. Miss Isabel was in the orchard picking apples and the mother dog pulled at her dress and Miss Isabel she come along and she saw the puppy drowning and she jumped right into this here and pulled it out. Wet through, she was, and the dress she was wearing was never fit for wearing again.'

'Oh dear,' said Tuppence, 'what a lot of things seem to have gone on here. All right,' she said, 'I'll be ready this afternoon. Perhaps two or three of you would come for me and take me to this Pensioners' Palace Club.'

'What three? Who's going to come?'

Uproar happened immediately.

'I'm coming . . . No, I'm not . . . No, Betty is . . . No, Betty shan't come. Betty went the other day. I mean, she went to the cinema party the other day. She can't go again.'

'Well, settle it between you,' said Tuppence, 'and come here at half past three.'

'I hope you'll find it interesting,' said Clarence.

'It will be of historical interest,' said the intellectual girl firmly.

'Oh, shut up, Janet!' said Clarence. He turned to Tuppence. 'She's always like that,' he said, 'Janet is. She goes to grammar school, that's why. She boasts about it, see? A comprehensive wasn't good enough for her and her parents made a fuss and now she's at grammar school. That's why she goes on like this all the time.'

II

Tuppence wondered, as she finished her lunch, whether the events of the morning would produce any sequel. Would anybody really come to escort her this afternoon and take her to the PPC? Was there any such thing really as the PPC or was it a nickname of some kind that the children had invented? Anyway, it might be fun, Tuppence thought, to sit waiting in case someone came.

However, the deputation was punctual to the minute. At half past three the bell rang, Tuppence rose from her seat by the fire, clapped a hat upon her head – an indiarubber hat because she thought it *would* probably rain – and Albert appeared to escort her to the front door.'

'Not going to let you go with just anyone,' he breathed into her ear.

'Look here, Albert,' whispered Tuppence, 'is there really such a place as the PPC here?'

'I thought that had something to do with visiting cards,' said Albert, who was always prone to show his complete knowledge of social customs. 'You know, what you leave on people when you're going away or when you're arriving, I'm not sure which.'

'I think it's something to do with pensioners.'

'Oh yes, they've got a sort of a place. Yes. Built just two or three years ago, I think it was. You know, it's just down after you pass the rectory and then you turn right and you see it. It's rather an ugly building, but it's nice for the old folk and any who like can go meeting there. They have games and things, and there's a lot of ladies goes and helps with things. Gets up concerts and – sort of – well, rather like, you know, Women's Institute. Only it's specially for the elderly people. They're all very, very old, and most of them deaf.'

'Yes,' said Tuppence, 'yes. It sounded rather like that.'

The front door opened. Janet, by reason of her intellectual superiority, stood there first. Behind her was Clarence, and behind him was a tall boy with a squint who appeared to answer to the name of Bert.

'Good afternoon, Mrs Beresford,' said Janet. 'Everybody is so pleased that you are coming. I think perhaps you'd better take an umbrella, the weather forecast was not very good today.'

'I've got to go that way anyway,' said Albert, 'so I'll come with you a short part of it.'

Certainly, Tuppence thought, Albert was always very protective. Perhaps just as well, but she did not think that either Janet, Bert or Clarence was likely to be a danger to her. The walk took about twenty minutes. When the red building was reached they went through the gate, up to the door and were received by a stout woman of about seventy.

'Ah, so we've got visitors. I'm so pleased you could come, my dear, so pleased.' She patted Tuppence upon the shoulder. 'Yes, Janet, thank you very much. Yes. This way. Yes. None of you need wait unless you like, you know.'

'Oh I think the boys will be very disappointed if they didn't wait to hear a little about what all this is about,' said Janet.

'Well, I think, you know, there are not so very many of us here. Perhaps it would be better for Mrs Beresford, not so worrying if there weren't too many of us. I wonder, Janet, if you would just go into the kitchen and tell Mollie that we are quite ready for tea to be brought in now.'

Tuppence had not really come for tea, but she could hardly say so. Tea appeared rather rapidly. It was excessively weak, it was served with some biscuits and some sandwiches with a rather nasty type of paste in between them with an extra fishy taste. Then they sat around and seemed slightly at a loss.

An old man with a beard who looked to Tuppence as though he was about a hundred came and sat firmly by her.

'I'd best have a word with you first, I think, my lady,' he said, elevating Tuppence to the peerage. 'Seeing as I'm about the oldest here and have heard more of the stories of the old days than anyone else. A lot of history about this place, you know. Oh, a lot of things has happened here, not that we can go into everything at once, can we? But we've all – oh, we've all heard something about the things that went on.'

'I gather,' said Tuppence, hastily rushing in before she could be introduced to some topic in which she had no interest whatever, 'I understand that quite a lot of interesting things went on here, not so much in the last war, but in the war before that, or even earlier. Not that any of your memories would go back as far as that. But one wonders perhaps if you could have heard things, you know, from your elderly relations.'

'Ah, that's right,' said the old man, 'that's right. Heard a lot, I did, from my Uncle Len. Yes, ah, he was a great chap, was Uncle Len. He knew about a lot of things. He knew what went on. It was like what went on down in the house on the quay before the last war. Yes, a bad show, that. What you call one of those fakists –'

'Fascists,' said one of the elderly ladies, a rather prim one with grey hair and a lace fichu rather the worse for wear round her neck.

'Well, fascist if you like to say it that way, what does it matter? Ah yes, one of those he was. Yes. Same sort of thing as that chap in Italy. Mussolini or something, wasn't it? Anyway, some sort of fishy name like that. Mussels or cockles. Oh yes, he did a lot of harm here. Had meetings, you know. All sorts of things like that. Someone called Mosley started it all.'

'But in the first war there was a girl called Mary Jordan, wasn't there?' said Tuppence, wondering if this was a wise thing to say or not.

'Ah yes. Said to be quite a good-looker, you know. Yes. Got hold of secrets out of the sailors and the soldiers.'

A very old lady piped up in a thin voice.

'He's not in the Navy and he's not in the Army,
But he's just the man for me.
Not in the Navy, not in the Army, he's in the
Royal Ar-till-er-rie!'

The old man took up his personal chant when she had got thus far:

> 'It's a long way to Tipperary,
> It's a long way to go,
> It's a long way to Tipperary
> And the rest of it I don't know.'

'Now that's enough, Benny, that's quite enough,' said a firm-looking woman who seemed to be either his wife or his daughter.

Another old lady sang in a quavering voice:

> 'All the nice girls love a sailor,
> All the nice girls love a tar,
> All the nice girls love a sailor,
> And you know what sailors are.'

'Oh, shut up, Maudie, we're tired of that one. Now let the lady hear something,' said Uncle Ben. 'Let the lady hear something. She's come to hear something. She wants to hear where that thing there was all the fuss about was hidden, don't you? And all about it.'

'That sounds very interesting,' said Tuppence, cheering up. 'Something *was* hidden?'

'Ah yes, long before my time it was but I heard all about it. Yes. Before 1914. Word was handed down, you know, from one to another. Nobody knew exactly what it was and why there was all this excitement.'

'Something to do with the boat race it had,' said an old lady. 'You know, Oxford and Cambridge. I was taken once. I was taken to see the boat race in London under the bridges and everything. Oh, it was a wonderful day. Oxford won by a length.'

'A lot of nonsense you're all talking,' said a grim-looking woman with iron-grey hair. 'You don't know anything about it, you don't. I know more than most of you although it happened a long time before I was born. It was my Great-Aunt Mathilda who told *me* and she were told by her Aunty Lou. And that was a good forty years before them. Great talk about it, it was, and people went around looking for it. Some people thought as it was a gold-mine, you know. Yes, a gold ingot brought back from Australia. Somewhere like that.'

'Damn silly,' said an old man, who was smoking a pipe with an air of general dislike of his fellow members. 'Mixed it up with goldfish, they did. Was as ignorant as that.'

'It was worth a lot of money, whatever it was, or it wouldn't have been hidden,' said someone else. 'Yes, lots of people come down from the government, and yes, police too. They looked around but they couldn't find anything.'

'Ah well, they didn't have the right clues. There are clues, you know, if you know where to look for them.' Another old lady nodded her head wisely. 'There's always clues.'

'How interesting,' said Tuppence. 'Where? Where are these clues, I mean? In the village or somewhere outside it or –'

This was a rather unfortunate remark as it brought down at least six different replies, all uttered at once.

'On the moor, beyond Tower West,' one was saying.

'Oh no, it's past Little Kenny, it was. Yes, quite near Little Kenny.'

'No, it was the cave. The cave by the sea front. Over as far as Baldy's Head. You know, where the red rocks are. That's it. There's an old smugglers' tunnel. Wonderful, it must be. Some people say as it's there still.'

'I saw a story once of an old Spanish main or something. Right back to the time of the Armada, it was. A Spanish boat as went down there. Full of doubloons.'

CHAPTER 10

ATTACK ON TUPPENCE

I

'Good gracious!' said Tommy, as he returned that evening. 'You look terribly tired, Tuppence. What have you been doing? You look worn out.'

'I am worn out,' said Tuppence. 'I don't know that I shall ever recover again. Oh dear.'

'What *have* you been doing? Not climbing up and finding more books or anything?'

'No, no,' said Tuppence, 'I don't want to look at books again. I'm off books.'

'Well, what is it? What have you been doing?'

'Do you know what a PPC is?'

'No,' said Tommy, 'at least, well, yes. It's something –' He paused.

'Yes, Albert knows,' said Tuppence, 'but it's not that kind of one. Now then, I'll just tell you in a minute, but you'd better have something first. A cocktail or a whisky or something. And I'll have something too.'

She more or less put Tommy wise to the events of the afternoon. Tommy said 'good gracious' again and added: 'The things you get yourself into, Tuppence. Was any of it interesting?'

'I don't know,' said Tuppence. 'When six people are talking at once, and most of them can't talk properly and they all say different things – you see, you don't really know what they're saying. But yes, I think I've got a few ideas for dealing with things.'

'What do you mean?'

'Well, there is a lot of legend, I think, going on about something that was once hidden here and was a secret connected with the 1914 war, or even before it.'

'Well, we know that already, don't we?' said Tommy. 'I mean, we've been briefed to know that.'

'Yes. Well, there are a few old tales still going around the village here. And everybody has got ideas about it put into their heads by their Aunt Marias or their Uncle Bens and it's been put into their Aunt Marias by their Uncle Stephens or Aunty Ruth or Grandmother Something else. It's been handed down for years and years. Well, one of the things might be the right one, of course.'

'What, lost among all the others?'

'Yes,' said Tuppence, 'like a needle in the haystack?

'I'm going to select a few what I call likely possibilities. People who might tell one something that they really *did* hear. I shall have to isolate them from everybody else, at any rate for a short period of time, and get them to tell me exactly what their Aunt Agatha or Aunt Betty or old Uncle James told them. Then I shall have to go on to the next one and possibly one of them might give me a further inkling. There must be something, you know, somewhere.'

'Yes,' said Tommy, 'I think there's something, but we don't know what it is.'

'Well, that's what we're trying to do, isn't it?'

'Yes, but I mean you've got to have some idea what a thing actually *is* before you go looking for it.'

'I don't think it's gold ingots on a Spanish Armada ship,' said Tuppence, 'and I don't think it's anything hidden in the smugglers' cave.'

'Might be some super brandy from France,' said Tommy hopefully.

'It might,' said Tuppence, 'but that wouldn't be really what we're looking for, would it?'

'I don't know,' said Tommy. 'I think it might be what I'm looking for sooner or later. Anyway, it's something I should enjoy finding. Of course it might be a sort of letter or something. A sexy letter that you could blackmail someone about, about sixty years ago. But I don't think it would cut much ice nowadays, do you?'

'No, I don't. But we've got to get some idea sooner or later. Do you think we'll *ever* get anywhere, Tommy?'

'I don't know,' said Tommy. '*I* got a little bit of help today.'

'Oh. What about?'

'Oh, about the census.'

'The what?'

'The census. There seems to have been a census in one particular year – I've got the year written down – and there were a good many people staying in this house with the Parkinsons.'

'How on earth did you find all that out?'

'Oh, by various methods of research by my Miss Collodon.'

'I'm getting jealous of Miss Collodon.'

'Well, you needn't be. She's very fierce and she ticks me off a good deal, and she is no ravishing beauty.'

'Well, that's just as well,' said Tuppence. 'But what has the census got to do with it?'

'Well, when Alexander said *it must be one of us* it could have meant, you see, someone who was in the house at that time and therefore you had to enter up their names on the census register. Anyone who spent the night under your roof, and I think probably there are records of these things in the census files. And if you know the right people – I don't mean I know them now, but I can get to know them through people I do know – then I think I could perhaps get a short list.'

'Well, I admit,' said Tuppence, 'you have ideas all right. For goodness' sake let's have something to eat and perhaps I shall feel better and not so faint from trying to listen to sixteen very ugly voices all at once.'

II

Albert produced a very passable meal. His cooking was erratic. It had its moments of brilliance which tonight was exemplified by what he called cheese pudding, and Tuppence and Tommy preferred to call cheese soufflé. Albert reproved them slightly for the wrong nomenclature.

'Cheese soufflé is different,' he said, 'got more beaten up white of egg in it than this has.'

'Never mind,' said Tuppence, 'it's very good whether it's cheese pudding or cheese soufflé.'

Both Tommy and Tuppence were entirely absorbed with the eating of food and did not compare any more notes as to their procedure. When, however, they had both drunk two cups of strong coffee, Tuppence leaned back in her chair, uttered a deep sigh and said:

'Now I feel almost myself again. You didn't do much washing before dinner, did you, Tommy?'

'I couldn't be bothered to wait and wash,' said Tommy. 'Besides, I never know with you. You might have made me go upstairs to the book-room and stand on a dusty ladder and poke about on the shelves.'

'I wouldn't be so unkind,' said Tuppence. 'Now wait a minute. Let's see where we are.'

'Where we are or where you are?'

'Well, where I am, really,' said Tuppence. 'After all, that's the only thing I know about, isn't it? You know where you are and I know where I am. Perhaps, that is.'

'May be a bit of perhaps about it,' said Tommy.

'Pass me over my bag, will you, unless I've left it in the dining-room?'

'You usually do but you haven't this time. It's under the foot of your chair. No – the other side.'

Tuppence picked up her handbag.

'Very nice present, this was,' she said. 'Real crocodile, I think. Bit difficult to stuff things in sometimes.'

'And apparently to take them out again,' said Tommy.

Tuppence was wrestling.

'Expensive bags are always very difficult for getting things out of,' she said breathlessly. 'Those basket-work ones are the most comfortable. They bulge to any extent and you can stir them up like you stir up a pudding. Ah! I think I've got it.'

'What is it? It looks like a washing bill.'

'Oh, it's a little notebook. Yes, I used to write washing things in it, you know, what I had to complain about – torn pillowcase or something like that. But I thought it would come in useful, you see, because only three or four pages of it had been used. I put down here, you see, things we've heard. A great many of them don't seem to have any point but there it is. I added census, by the way, when you first mentioned it. I didn't know what it meant at that time or what you meant by it. But anyway I did add it.'

'Fine,' said Tommy.

'And I put down Mrs Henderson and someone called Dodo.'

'Who was Mrs Henderson?'

'Well, I don't suppose you'll remember and I needn't go back to it now but those were two of the names I put down that Mrs What's-her-name, you know, the old one, Mrs Griffin mentioned. And then there was a message or a notice. Something about Oxford and Cambridge. And I've come across another thing in one of the old books.'

'What about – Oxford and Cambridge? Do you mean an undergraduate?'

'I'm not sure whether there was an undergraduate or not, I think really it was a bet on the boat race.'

'Much more likely,' said Tommy. 'Not awfully apt to be useful to us.'

'Well, one never knows. So there's Mrs Henderson and there's somebody who lives in a house called Apple Tree Lodge and there's something I found on a dirty bit of paper shoved into one of the books upstairs. I don't know if it was *Catriona* or whether it was in a book called *Shadow of the Throne*.'

'That's about the French Revolution. I read it when I was a boy,' said Tommy.

'Well, I don't see how that comes in. At any rate, I put it down.'

'Well, what is it?'

'It seems to be three pencil words. Grin, g-r-i-n, then hen, h-e-n and then Lo, capital L-o.'

'Let me guess,' said Tommy. 'Cheshire cat – that's a grin – Henny-Penny, that's another fairy story, isn't it, for the hen, and Lo –'

'Ah,' said Tuppence, 'Lo does you in, does it?'

'Lo and behold,' said Tommy, 'but it doesn't seem to make sense.'

Tuppence spoke rapidly. 'Mrs Henley, Apple Tree Lodge – I haven't done her yet, she's in Meadowside.' Tuppence recited quickly: 'Now, where are we? Mrs Griffin, Oxford and Cambridge, bet on a boat race, census, Cheshire cat, Henny-Penny, the story where the Hen went to the Dovrefell – Hans Andersen or something like that – and Lo. I suppose Lo means when they got there. Got to the Dovrefell, I mean.

'I don't think there's much else,' said Tuppence. 'There's the Oxford and Cambridge boat race or the bet.'

'I should think the odds are on our being rather silly. But I think if we go on being silly long enough, some gem of great price might come out of it, concealed among the rubbish, as you might say. Just as we found one significant book on the bookshelves upstairs.'

'Oxford and Cambridge,' said Tuppence thoughtfully. 'That makes me think of something. It makes me remember something. Now what could it be?'

'Mathilde?'

'No, it wasn't Mathilde, but –'

'Truelove,' suggested Tommy. He grinned from ear to ear. 'True love. Where can I my true love find?'

'Stop grinning, you ape,' said Tuppence. 'You've got that last thing on your brain. Grin-hen-lo. Doesn't make sense. And yet – I have a kind of feeling – Oh!'

732 • AGATHA CHRISTIE

'What's the Oh about?'

'Oh! Tommy, I've got an idea. Of course.'

'What's of course?'

'Lo,' said Tuppence. 'Lo. Grin is what made me think of it. You grinning like a Cheshire cat. Grin. Hen and then Lo. Of course. That must be it somehow.'

'What on earth are you talking about?'

'Oxford and Cambridge boat race.'

'Why does grin hen Lo make you think of Oxford and Cambridge boat race?'

'I'll give you three guesses,' said Tuppence.

'Well, I give up at once because I don't think it could possibly make sense.'

'It does really.'

'What, the boat race?'

'No, nothing to do with the boat race. The colour. Colours, I mean.'

'What *do* you mean, Tuppence?'

'Grin hen Lo. We've been reading it the wrong way round. It's meant to be read the other way round.'

'What do you mean? Ol, then n-e-h – it doesn't make sense. You couldn't go on n-i-r-g. Nirg or some word like that.'

'No. Just take the three words. A little bit, you know, like what Alexander did in the book – the first book that we looked at. Read those three words the other way round. Lo-hen-grin.'

Tommy scowled.

'Still haven't got it?' said Tuppence. 'Lohengrin, of course. The swan. The opera. You know, Lohengrin, Wagner.'

'Well, there's nothing to do with a swan.'

'Yes, there is. Those two pieces of china we found. Stools for the garden. You remember? One was a dark blue and one was a light blue, and old Isaac said to us, at least I think it was Isaac, he said, "That's Oxford, you see, and that's Cambridge."'

'Well, we smashed the Oxford one, didn't we?'

'Yes. But the Cambridge one is still there. The light blue one. Don't you see? Lohengrin. Something was hidden in one of those two swans. Tommy, the next thing we have to do is to go and look at the Cambridge one. The light blue one, it's still in KK. Shall we go now?'

'What – at eleven o'clock at night – no.'

'We'll go tomorrow. You haven't got to go to London tomorrow?'

'No.'

'Well, we'll go tomorrow and we'll see.'

III

'I don't know what you're doing about the garden,' said Albert. 'I did a spell once in a garden for a short time, but I'm not up in vegetables very much. There's a boy here that wants to see you, by the way, madam.'

'Oh, a boy,' said Tuppence. 'Do you mean the red-haired one?'

'No. I mean the other one, the one with a lot of messy yellow hair half down his back. Got rather a silly name. Like a hotel. You know, the Royal Clarence. That's his name. Clarence.'

'Clarence, but not Royal Clarence.'

'Not likely,' said Albert. 'He's waiting in the front door. He says, madam, as he might be able to assist you in some way.'

'I see. I gather he used to assist old Isaac occasionally.'

She found Clarence sitting on a decayed basket chair on the veranda or loggia, whichever you liked to call it. He appeared to be making a late breakfast off potato crisps and held a bar of chocolate in his left hand.

'Morning, missus,' said Clarence. 'Come to see if I could be any help.'

'Well,' said Tuppence, 'of course we do want help in the garden. I believe you used to help Isaac at one time.'

'Ah well, now and again I did. Not that I know very much. Don't say that Isaac knew much neither. Lot of talk with him, lot of talking saying what a wonderful time he used to have. What a wonderful time it was for the people who employed him. Yes, he used to say he was the head gardener to Mr Bolingo. You know, as lives farther along the river. Great big house. Yes, it's turned into a school now. Head gardener there, he said he used to be. But my grandmother says there isn't a word of truth in that.'

'Well, never mind,' said Tuppence. 'Actually, I wanted to turn a few more things out of that little greenhouse place.'

'What d'you mean the shed, the glass shed? KK, isn't it?'

'Quite right,' said Tuppence. 'Fancy your knowing the proper name of it.'

'Oh well, it was always used to be called that. Everybody says so. They say it's Japanese. I don't know if that's true.'

'Come on,' said Tuppence. 'Let's go there.'

A procession formed consisting of Tommy, Tuppence, Hannibal, the dog, with Albert abandoning the washing up of breakfast for something more interesting bringing up the rear. Hannibal displayed a great deal of pleasure after attending to all the useful smells in the neighbourhood. He rejoined them at the door of KK and sniffed in an interested manner.

'Hullo, Hannibal,' said Tuppence, 'are you going to help us? You tell us something.'

'What kind of a dog is he?' asked Clarence. 'Somebody said as he is the kind of dog they used to keep for rats. Is that so?'

'Yes, that's quite true,' said Tommy. 'He's a Manchester Terrier, an old English Black and Tan.'

Hannibal, knowing he was being talked about, turned his head, waggled his body, beat his tail with a good deal of exuberance. He then sat down and looked proud of himself.

'He bites, doesn't he?' said Clarence. 'Everyone says so.'

'He's a very good guard dog,' said Tuppence. 'He looks after me.'

'That's quite right. When I'm away he looks after you,' said Tommy.

'The postman said he nearly got bitten four days ago.'

'Dogs are rather like that with postmen,' said Tuppence. 'Do you know where the key of KK is?'

'I do,' said Clarence. 'Hanging up in the shed. You know, the shed where the flower-pots are.'

He went off and returned shortly with the once rusty but now more or less oiled key.

'Been oiling this key, Isaac must have,' he said.

'Yes, it wouldn't turn very easily before,' said Tuppence.

The door was opened.

The Cambridge china stool with the swan wreathed round it was looking rather handsome. Obviously Isaac had polished it up and washed it, with the idea of transferring it to the veranda when the weather was suitable for sitting out.

'Ought to be a dark blue one too,' said Clarence. 'Isaac used to say Oxford and Cambridge.'

'Is that true?'

'Yes. Dark blue Oxford and pale blue Cambridge. Oh, and Oxford was the one that smashed, was it?'

'Yes. Rather like the boat race, isn't it?'

'By the way, something's happened to that rocking-horse, hasn't it? There's a lot of mess about in KK.'

'Yes.'

'Funny name like Matilda, hasn't she?'

'Yes. She had to have an operation,' said Tuppence.

Clarence seemed to think this very amusing. He laughed heartily.

'My Great-Aunt Edith had to have an operation,' he said. 'Took out part of her inside but she got well.'

He sounded slightly disappointed.

'I suppose there's no real way of getting inside these things,' said Tuppence.

'Well, I suppose you can smash them like the dark blue one was smashed.'

'Yes. There's no other way, is there? Funny those sort of S-kind of slits around the top. Why, you could post things in there, couldn't you, like a post box.'

'Yes,' said Tommy, 'one could. It's an interesting idea. Very interesting, Clarence,' he said kindly.

Clarence looked pleased.

'You can unscrew 'em, you know,' he said.

'Unscrew them, can you?' said Tuppence. 'Who told you that?'

'Isaac. I've seen 'im do it often. You turn them upside down and then you begin to swing the top round. It's stiff sometimes. You pour a little oil round all the cracks and when it's soaked in a bit you can turn it round.'

'Oh.'

'The easiest way is to put it upside down.'

'Everything here always seems to have to be turned upside down,' said Tuppence. 'We had to do that to Mathilde before we could operate.'

For the moment Cambridge seemed to be entirely obstreperous, when quite suddenly the china began to revolve and very shortly afterwards they managed to unscrew it completely and lift it off.

'Lot of rubbish in here, I should think,' said Clarence.

Hannibal came to assist. He was a dog who liked helping in anything that was going on. Nothing, he thought, was complete unless he took a hand or a paw in it. But with him it was usually a nose in the investigation. He stuck his nose down, growled gently, retired an inch or two and sat down.

'Doesn't like it much, does he?' said Tuppence, and looked down into the somewhat unpleasant mass inside.

'Ow!' said Clarence.

'What's the matter?'

'Scratched myself. There's something hanging down from a nail on the side here. I don't know if it's a nail or what it is. It's something. Ow!'

'Wuff, wuff!' said Hannibal, joining in.

'There's something hung on a nail just inside. Yes, I've got it. No, it's slipping. Yes, here I am. I've got it.'

Clarence lifted out a dark tarpaulin package.

Hannibal came and sat at Tuppence's feet. He growled.

'What's the matter, Hannibal?' said Tuppence.

Hannibal growled again. Tuppence bent down and smoothed the top of his head and ears.

'What's the matter, Hannibal?' said Tuppence. 'Did you want Oxford to win and now Cambridge have won, you see. Do you remember,' said Tuppence to Tommy, 'how we let him watch the boat race once on television?'

'Yes,' said Tommy, 'he got very angry towards the end and started barking so that we couldn't hear anything at all.'

'Well, we could still see things,' said Tuppence, 'that was something. But if you remember, he didn't like Cambridge winning.'

'Obviously,' said Tommy, 'he studied at the Oxford Dogs' University.'

Hannibal left Tuppence and came to Tommy and wagged his tail appreciatively.

'He likes your saying that,' said Tuppence, 'it must be true. I myself,' she added, 'think he has been educated at the Dogs' Open University.'

'What were his principal studies there?' asked Tommy, laughing.

'Bone disposal.'

'You know what he's like.'

'Yes, I know,' said Tuppence. 'Very unwisely, you know, Albert gave him the whole bone of a leg of mutton once. First of all I found him in the drawing-room putting it under a cushion, then I forced him out through the garden door and shut it. And I looked out of the window and he went into the flower-bed where I'd got gladioli, and buried it very carefully there. He's very tidy with his bones, you know. He never tries to eat them. He always puts them away for a rainy day.'

'Does he ever dig them up again?' asked Clarence, assisting on this point of dog lore.

'I think so,' said Tuppence. 'Sometimes when they're very, very old and would have been better if they had been left buried.'

'Our dog doesn't like dog biscuits,' said Clarence.

'He leaves them on the plate, I suppose,' said Tuppence, 'and eats the meat first.'

'He likes sponge cake, though, our dog does,' said Clarence.

Hannibal sniffed at the trophy just disinterred from the inside of Cambridge. He wheeled round suddenly then and barked.

'See if there's anyone outside,' said Tuppence. 'It might be a gardener. Somebody told me the other day, Mrs Herring, I think it was, that she knew of an elderly man who'd been a very good gardener in his time and who did jobbing.'

Tommy opened the door and went outside. Hannibal accompanied him.

'Nobody here,' said Tommy.

Hannibal barked. First he growled again, then he barked and barked more loudly.

'He thinks there's someone or something in that great clump of pampas grass,' said Tommy. 'Perhaps someone is un-burying one of his bones there. Perhaps there's a rabbit there. Hannibal's very stupid about rabbits. He needs an awful lot of encouragement before he'll chase a rabbit. He seems to have a kindly feeling about them. He goes after pigeons and large birds. Fortunately he never catches them.'

Hannibal was now sniffing round the pampas grass, first growling, after which he began to bark loudly. At intervals he turned his head towards Tommy.

'I expect there's a cat in there,' said Tommy. 'You know what he's like when he thinks a cat is around. There's the big black cat that comes round here and the little one. The one that we call the Kitty-cat.'

'That's the one that's always getting into the house,' said Tuppence. 'It seems to get through the smallest chinks. Oh, do stop, Hannibal. Come back.'

Hannibal heard and turned his head. He was expressing a very high degree of fierceness. He gave Tuppence a look, went back a little way, then turned his attention once more to the clump of pampas grass and began barking furiously.

'There's something worries him,' said Tommy. 'Come on, Hannibal.'

Hannibal shook himself, shook his head, looked at Tommy, looked at Tuppence and made a prancing attack on the pampas grass, barking loudly.

There was a sudden sound. Two sharp explosions.

'Good Lord, somebody must be shooting rabbits,' exclaimed Tuppence.

'Get back. Get back inside KK, Tuppence,' said Tommy.

Something flew past his ear. Hannibal, now fully alerted, was racing round and round the pampas grass. Tommy ran after him.

'He's chasing someone now,' he said. 'He's chasing someone down the hill. He's running like mad.'

'Who was it – what was it?' said Tuppence.

'You all right, Tuppence?'

'No, I'm not quite all right,' said Tuppence. 'Something – something, I think, hit me here, just below the shoulder. Was it – what was it?'

'It was someone shooting at us. Someone who was hidden inside that pampas grass.'

'Someone who was watching what we were doing,' said Tuppence. 'Do you think that's it, perhaps?'

'I expect it's them Irish,' said Clarence hopefully. 'The IRA. You know. They've been trying to blow this place up.'

'I don't think it's of any political significance,' said Tuppence.

'Come into the house,' said Tommy. 'Come quickly. Come on, Clarence, you'd better come too.'

'You don't think your dog will bite me?' said Clarence uncertainly.

'No,' said Tommy. 'I think he is busy for the moment.'

They had just turned the corner into the garden door when Hannibal reappeared suddenly. He came racing up the hill very out of breath. He spoke to Tommy in the way a dog does speak. He came up to him, shook himself, put a paw on Tommy's trouser leg and tried to pull him in the direction from which he had just come.

'He wants me to go with him after whoever the man was,' said Tommy.

'Well, you're not to,' said Tuppence. 'If there's anyone there with a rifle or a pistol or something that shoots, I'm not going to have you shot. Not at your age. Who would look after me if anything happened to you? Come on, let's get indoors.'

They went into the house quickly. Tommy went out into the hall and spoke on the telephone.

'What are you doing?' said Tuppence.

'Telephoning the police,' said Tommy. 'Can't let anything like this pass. They may get on to someone if we're in time.'

'I think,' said Tuppence, 'that I want something put on my shoulder. This blood is ruining my best jumper.'

'Never mind your jumper,' said Tommy.

Albert appeared at that moment with a complete service of first aid.

'Well I never,' said Albert. 'You mean some dirty guy has shot at the missus? Whatever's happening next in this country?'

'You don't think you ought to go to the hospital, do you?'

'No, I don't,' said Tuppence. 'I'm quite all right but I want an outsize Band-Aid or something to stick on here. Put on something like friar's balsam first.'

'I've got some iodine.'

'I don't want iodine. It stings. Besides, they say now in hospitals that it isn't the right thing to put on.'

'I thought friar's balsam was something you breathed in out of an inhaler,' said Albert hopefully.

'That's one use,' said Tuppence, 'but it's very good to put on slight scratches or scars or if children cut themselves or anything like that. Have you got the thing all right?'

'What thing, what do you mean, Tuppence?'

'The thing we just got out of the Cambridge Lohengrin. That's what I mean. The thing that was hanging on a nail. Perhaps it's something important, you know. They saw us. And so if they tried to kill us – and tried to get whatever it was – that really would be something!'

CHAPTER 11

HANNIBAL TAKES ACTION

I

Tommy sat with the police inspector in his office. The police officer, Inspector Norris, was nodding his head gently.

'I hope with any luck we may get results, Mr Beresford,' he said. 'Dr Crossfield, you say, is attending to your wife.'

'Yes,' said Tommy, 'it isn't serious, I gather. It was just grazing by a bullet and it bled a good deal, but she's going to be all right, I think. There's nothing really dangerous, Dr Crossfield said.'

'She's not very young, though, I suppose,' said Inspector Norris.

'She's over seventy,' said Tommy. 'We're both of us getting on, you know.'

'Yes, yes. Quite so,' said Inspector Norris. 'I've heard a good deal about her locally, you know, since you came here to live. People have taken to her in a big way. We've heard about her various activities. And about yours.'

'Oh, dear,' said Tommy.

'Can't live down your record, you know, whatever it is. Good or bad,' said Inspector Norris in a kindly voice. 'You can't live down a record if you're a criminal and you can't live down your record if you've been a hero either. Of one thing I can assure you. We'll do all we can to clear things up. You can't describe whoever it was, I suppose?'

'No,' said Tommy. 'When I saw him he was running with our

dog after him. I should say he was not very old. He ran easily, I mean.'

'Difficult age round about fourteen, fifteen onwards.'

'It was someone older than that,' said Tommy.

'Not had any telephone calls or letters, demands for money or anything like that?' said the Inspector. 'Asking you to get out of your house, maybe?'

'No,' said Tommy, 'nothing like that.'

'And you've been here – how long?'

Tommy told him.

'Hmmm. Not very long. You go to London, I gather, most days of the week.'

'Yes,' said Tommy. 'If you want particulars –'

'No,' said Inspector Norris, 'no. No, I don't need any particulars. The only thing I should suggest is that – well, you don't go away too often. If you can manage to stay at home and look after Mrs Beresford yourself . . .'

'I thought of doing that anyway,' said Tommy. 'I think this is a good excuse for my not turning up always at the various appointments I've got in London.'

'Well, we'll do all we can to keep an eye on things, and if we could get hold of this whoever it is . . .'

'Do you feel – perhaps I oughtn't to ask this –' said Tommy – 'do you feel you know who it is? Do you know his name or his reasons?'

'Well, we know a good many things about some of the chaps around here. More than they think we know very often. Sometimes we don't make it apparent how much we do know because that's the best way to get at them in the end. You find out then who they're mixed up with, who's paying them for some of the things they do, or whether they thought of it themselves out of their own heads. But I think – well, I think somehow that this isn't one of our locals, as you might say.'

'Why do you think that?' asked Tommy.

'Ah. Well, one hears things, you know. One gets information from various headquarters elsewhere.'

Tommy and the Inspector looked at each other. For about five minutes neither of them spoke. They were just looking.

'Well,' said Tommy, 'I – I see. Yes. Perhaps I see.'

'If I may say one thing,' said Inspector Norris.

'Yes?' said Tommy, looking rather doubtful.

'This garden of yours. You want a bit of help in it, I understand.'

'Our gardener was killed, as you probably know.'

'Yes, I know all about that. Old Isaac Bodlicott, wasn't it? Fine old chap. Told tall stories now and then about the wonderful things he'd done in his time. But he was a well-known character and a fellow you could trust, too.'

'I can't imagine why he was killed or who killed him,' said Tommy. 'Nobody seems to have had any idea or to have found out.'

'You mean *we* haven't found out. Well, these things take a little time, you know. It doesn't come out at the time the inquest's on, and the Coroner sums up and says "Murder by some person unknown." That's only the beginning sometimes. Well, what I was going to say was it's likely someone may come and ask you whether you'd like a chap to come and do a bit of jobbing gardening for you. He'll come along and say that he could come two or three days a week. Perhaps more. He'll tell you, for reference, that he worked for some years for Mr Solomon. You'll remember that name, will you?'

'Mr Solomon,' said Tommy.

There seemed to be something like a twinkle for a moment in Inspector Norris's eye.

'Yes, he's dead, of course. Mr Solomon, I mean. But he *did* live here and he *did* employ several different jobbing gardeners. I'm not quite sure what name this chap will give you. We'll say I don't quite remember it. It might be one of several – it's likely to be Crispin, I think. Between thirty and fifty or so, and he worked for Mr Solomon. If anyone comes along and says he can do some jobbing gardening for you and *doesn't* mention Mr Solomon, in that case, I wouldn't accept him. That's just a word of warning.'

'I see,' said Tommy. 'Yes, I see. At least, I hope I see the point.'

'That's the point,' said Inspector Norris. 'You're quick on the uptake, Mr Beresford. Well, I suppose you've had to be quite often in your activities. Nothing more you want to know that we could tell you?'

'I don't think so,' said Tommy. 'I wouldn't know what to ask.'

'We shall be making enquiries, not necessarily round here, you know. I may be in London or other parts looking round. We all help to look round. Well, you'd know that, wouldn't you?'

'I want to try and keep Tuppence – keep my wife from getting herself too mixed up in things because – but it's difficult.'

'Women are always difficult,' said Inspector Norris.

Tommy repeated that remark later as he sat by Tuppence's bedside and watched her eating grapes.

'Do you really eat all the pips of grapes?'

'Usually,' said Tuppence. 'It takes so much time getting them out, doesn't it? I don't think they hurt you.'

'Well, if they haven't hurt you by now, and you've been doing it all your life, I shouldn't think they would,' said Tommy.

'What did the police say?'

'Exactly what we thought they would say.'

'Do they know who it's likely to have been?'

'They say they don't think it's local.'

'Who did you see? Inspector Watson his name is, isn't it?'

'No. This was an Inspector Norris.'

'Oh, that's one I don't know. What else did he say?'

'He said women were always very difficult to restrain.'

'Really!' said Tuppence. 'Did he know you were coming back to tell me that?'

'Possibly not,' said Tommy. He got up. 'I must put in a telephone call or two to London. I'm not going up for a day or two.'

'You can go up all right. I'm quite safe here! There's Albert looking after me and all the rest of it. Dr Crossfield has been terribly kind and rather like a sort of broody hen watching over me.'

'I'll have to go out to get things for Albert. Anything you want?'

'Yes,' said Tuppence, 'you might bring me back a melon. I'm feeling very inclined to fruit. Nothing but fruit.'

'All right,' said Tommy.

II

Tommy rang up a London number.

'Colonel Pikeaway?'

'Yes. Hullo. Ah, it's you, Thomas Beresford, is it?'

'Ah, you recognized my voice. I wanted to tell you that –'

'Something about Tuppence. I've heard it all,' said Colonel Pikeaway. 'No need to talk. Stay where you are for the next day or two or a week. Don't come up to London. Report anything that happens.'

'There may be some things which we ought to bring to you.'

'Well, hang on to them for the moment. Tell Tuppence to invent a place to hide them until then.'

'She's good at that sort of thing. Like our dog. He hides bones in the garden.'

'I hear he chased the man who shot at you both, and saw him off the place –'

'You seem to know all about it.'

'We always know things here,' said Colonel Pikeaway.

'Our dog managed to get a snap at him and came back with a sample of his trousers in his mouth.'

CHAPTER 12

OXFORD, CAMBRIDGE AND LOHENGRIN

'Good man,' said Colonel Pikeaway, puffing out smoke. 'Sorry to send for you so urgently but I thought I'd better see you.'

'As I expect you know,' said Tommy, 'we've been having something a little unexpected lately.'

'Ah! Why should you think I know?'

'Because you always know everything here.'

Colonel Pikeaway laughed.

'Hah! Quoting me to myself, aren't you? Yes, that's what I say. We know everything. That's what we're here for. Did she have a very narrow escape? Your wife, I'm talking about, as you know.'

'She didn't have a narrow escape, but there might have been something serious. I expect you know most of the details, or do you want me to tell you?'

'You can run over it quickly if you like. There's a bit I didn't hear,' said Colonel Pikeaway, 'the bit about Lohengrin. Grin-hen-lo. She's sharp, you know, your wife is. She saw the point of that. It seems idiotic, but there it was.'

'I've brought you the results today,' said Tommy. 'We hid them in the flour-bin until I could get up to see you. I didn't like to send them by post.'

'No. Quite right –'

'In a kind of tin – not tin but a better metal than that – box and hanging in Lohengrin. Pale blue Lohengrin. Cambridge, Victorian china outdoor garden stool.'

'Remember them myself in the old days. Had an aunt in the country who used to have a pair.'

'It was very well preserved, sewn up in tarpaulin. Inside it are letters. They are somewhat perished and that, but I expect with expert treatment –'

'Yes, we can manage that sort of thing all right.'

'Here they are then,' said Tommy, 'and I've got a list for you of things that we've noted down, Tuppence and I. Things that have been mentioned or told us.'

'Names?'

'Yes. Three or four. The Oxford and Cambridge clue and the mention of Oxford and Cambridge graduates staying there – I don't think there was anything in that, because really it referred simply to the Lohengrin porcelain stools, I suppose.'

'Yes – yes – yes, there are one or two other things here that are quite interesting.'

'After we were fired at,' said Tommy, 'I reported it at once to the police.'

'Quite right.'

'Then I was asked to go down to the police station the next day and I saw Inspector Norris there. I haven't come in contact with him before. I think he must be rather a new officer.'

'Yes. Probably on a special assignment,' said Colonel Pikeaway. He puffed out more smoke.

Tommy coughed.

'I expect you know all about him.'

'I know about him,' said Colonel Pikeaway. 'We know everything here. He's all right. He's in charge of this enquiry. Local people will perhaps be able to spot who it was who's been following you about, finding out things about you. You don't think, do you, Beresford, that it would be well if you left the place for a while and brought your wife along?'

'I don't think I could do that,' said Tommy.

'You mean she wouldn't come?' said Colonel Pikeaway.

'Again,' said Tommy, 'if I may mention it, you seem to know everything. I don't think you could draw Tuppence away. Mind you, she's not badly hurt, she's not ill and she's got a feeling now that – well, that we're on to something. We don't know what it is and we don't know what we shall find or do.'

'Nose around,' said Colonel Pikeaway, 'that's all you can do in a case of this kind.' He tapped a nail on the metal box. 'This little box is going to tell us something, though, and it's going to tell us something we've always wanted to know. Who was involved a great many years ago in setting things going and doing a lot of dirty work behind the scenes.'

'But surely –'

'I know what you're going to say. You're going to say whoever it was is now dead. That's true. But it tells us nevertheless what was going on, how it was set in motion, who helped, who inspired it and who has inherited or carried on with something of the same business ever since. People who don't seem to amount to much but possibly they amount to more than we've ever thought. And people who've been in touch with the same group, as one calls it – one calls anything a group nowadays – the same group which may have different people in it now but who have the same ideas, the same love of violence and evil and the same people to communicate with elsewhere and other groups. Some groups are all right but some groups are worse because they are groups. It's a kind of technique, you know. We've taught it to ourselves in the last, oh, say fifty to a hundred years. Taught that if people cohere together and make a tight little mob of themselves, it's amazing what they are able to accomplish and what they are able to inspire other people to accomplish for them.'

'May I ask you something?'

'Anyone can always ask,' said Colonel Pikeaway. 'We know everything here but we don't always tell, I have to warn you of that.'

'Does the name of Solomon mean anything to you?'

'Ah,' said Colonel Pikeaway. 'Mr Solomon. And where did you get that name from?'

'It was mentioned by Inspector Norris.'

'I see. Well, if you're going by what Norris said, you're going right. I can tell you that. You won't see Solomon personally, I don't mind telling you. He's dead.'

'Oh,' said Tommy, 'I see.'

'At least you don't quite see,' said Colonel Pikeaway. 'We use his name sometimes. It's useful, you know, to have a name you can use. The name of a real person, a person who isn't there any longer but although dead is still highly regarded in the neighbourhood. It's sheer chance you ever came to live in The Laurels at all and we've got hopes that it may lead to a piece of luck for us. But I don't want it to be a cause of disaster to you or to your missus. Suspect everyone and everything. It's the best way.'

'I only trust two people there,' said Tommy. 'One's Albert, who's worked for us for years –'

'Yes, I remember Albert. Red-haired boy, wasn't he?'

'Not a boy any longer –'

'Who's the other one?'

'My dog Hannibal.'

'Hm. Yes – you may have something there. Who was it – Dr Watts who wrote a hymn beginning, "Dogs delight to bark and bite, It is their nature to." – What is he, an Alsatian?'

'No, he's a Manchester Terrier.'

'Ah, an old English Black and Tan, not as big as a Dobermann pinscher but the kind of dog that knows his stuff.'

CHAPTER 13

VISIT FROM MISS MULLINS

Tuppence, walking along the garden path, was accosted by Albert coming down at a quick pace from the house.

'Lady waiting to see you,' he said.

'Lady? Oh, who is it?'

'Miss Mullins, she says she is. Recommended by one of the ladies in the village to call on you.'

'Oh, of course,' said Tuppence. 'About the garden, isn't it?'

'Yes, she said something about the garden.'

'I think you'd better bring her out here,' said Tuppence.

'Yes, madam,' said Albert, falling into his role of experienced butler.

He went back to the house and returned a few moments later bringing with him a tall masculine-looking woman in tweed trousers and a Fair Isle pullover.

'Chilly wind this morning,' she said.

Her voice was deep and slightly hoarse.

'I'm Iris Mullins. Mrs Griffin suggested I should come along and see you. Wanting some help in the garden. Is that it?'

'Good morning,' said Tuppence, shaking hands. 'I'm very pleased to see you. Yes, we do want some help in the garden.'

'Only just moved in, haven't you?'

'Well, it feels almost like years,' said Tuppence, 'because we've only just got all the workmen out.'

'Ah yes,' said Miss Mullins, giving a deep hoarse chuckle. 'Know what it is to have workmen in the house. But you're quite right to come in yourself and not leave it to them. Nothing gets finished until the owner's moved in and even then you usually have to get them back again to finish something they've forgotten about. Nice garden you've got here but it's been let go a bit, hasn't it?'

'Yes, I'm afraid the last people who lived here didn't care much about how the garden looked.'

'People called Jones or something like that, weren't they? Don't think I actually know them. Most of my time here, you know, I've lived on the other side, the moor side, of the town. Two houses there I go to regularly. One, two days a week and the other one, one day. Actually, one day isn't enough, not to keep it right. You had old Isaac working here, didn't you? Nice old boy. Sad he had to get himself done in by some of this violent guerrilla material that's always going about bashing someone. The inquest was about a week ago, wasn't it? I hear they haven't found out who did it yet. Go about in little groups they do, and mug people. Nasty lot. Very often the younger they are, the nastier they are. That's a nice magnolia you've got there. *Soulangeana*, isn't it? Much the best to have. People always want the more exotic kinds but it's better to stick to old friends when it's magnolias in my opinion.'

'It's really been more the vegetables that we're thinking about.'

'Yes, you want to build up a good working kitchen garden, don't you? There doesn't seem to have been much attention paid before. People lose their spirit and think it's better really to buy their vegetables, and not try and grow them.'

'I'd always want to grow new potatoes and peas,' said Tuppence, 'and I think French beans too, because you then can have them all young.'

'That's right. You might as well add runner beans. Most gardeners are so proud of their runner beans that they like them a foot and a half in length. They think that's a fine bean. Always takes a prize at a local show. But you're quite right, you know. Young vegetables are the things that you really enjoy eating.'

Albert appeared suddenly.

'Mrs Redcliffe on the telephone, madam,' he said. 'Wanted to know if you could lunch tomorrow.'

'Tell her I'm very sorry,' said Tuppence. 'I'm afraid we may have to go to London tomorrow. Oh – wait a minute, Albert. Just wait while I write a word or two.'

She pulled out a small pad from her bag, wrote a few words on it and handed it to Albert.

'Tell Mr Beresford,' she said. 'Tell him Miss Mullins is here and we're in the garden. I forgot to do what he asked me to do, give him the name and address of the person he is writing to. I've written it here –'

'Certainly, madam,' said Albert, and disappeared.

Tuppence returned to the vegetable conversation.

'I expect you're very busy,' she said, 'as you are working three days already.'

'Yes, and as I said it's rather the other side of the town. I live the other side of town. I've got a small cottage there.'

At that moment Tommy arrived from the house. Hannibal was with him, running round in large circles. Hannibal reached Tuppence first. He stopped still for a moment, spread out his paws, and then rushed at Miss Mullins with a fierce array of barking. She took a step or two back in some alarm.

'This is our terrible dog,' said Tuppence. 'He doesn't really bite, you know. At least very seldom. It's usually only the postman he likes to bite.'

'All dogs bite postmen, or try to,' said Miss Mullins.

'He's a very good guard dog,' said Tuppence. 'He's a Manchester Terrier, you know, and they are good guard dogs. He protects the house in a wonderful way. He won't let anyone near it or come inside and he looks after me very carefully. He evidently regards me as his principal charge in life.'

'Oh well, of course I suppose it's a good thing nowadays.'

'I know. There are so many robberies about,' said Tuppence. 'Lots of our friends, you know, have had burglars. Some even who come in in broad daylight in the most extraordinary way. They set up ladders and take window-sashes out or pretend to be window-cleaners – oh, up to all kinds of tricks. So it's a good thing to let it be known that there's a fierce dog in the house, I think.'

'I think perhaps you're quite right.'

'Here is my husband,' said Tuppence. 'This is Miss Mullins, Tommy. Mrs Griffin very kindly told her that we wanted someone who could possibly do some gardening for us.'

'Would this be too heavy work for you perhaps, Miss Mullins?'

'Of course not,' said Miss Mullins in her deep voice. 'Oh, I can dig with anyone. You've got to dig the right way. It's not only trenching the sweet peas, it's everything needs digging, needs manuring. The ground's got to be prepared. Makes all the difference.'

Hannibal continued to bark.

'I think, Tommy,' said Tuppence, 'you'd really better take Hannibal back to the house. He seems to be in rather a protective mood this morning.'

'All right,' said Tommy.

'Won't you come back to the house,' said Tuppence to Miss Mullins, 'and have something to drink? It's rather a hot morning and I think it would be a good thing, don't you? And we can discuss plans together perhaps.'

Hannibal was shut into the kitchen and Miss Mullins accepted a glass of sherry. A few suggestions were made, then Miss Mullins looked at her watch and said she must hurry back.

'I have an appointment,' she explained. 'I mustn't be late.' She bade them a somewhat hurried farewell and departed.

'She *seems* all right,' said Tuppence.

'I know,' said Tommy – 'But one can't ever be sure –'

'One could ask questions?' said Tuppence doubtfully.

'You must be tired going all round the garden. We must leave our expedition this afternoon for another day – you have been ordered to rest.'

CHAPTER 14

GARDEN CAMPAIGN

I

'You understand, Albert,' said Tommy.

He and Albert were together in the pantry where Albert was washing up the tea tray he had just brought down from Tuppence's bedroom.

'Yes, sir,' said Albert. 'I understand.'

'You know, I think you will get a bit of a warning – from Hannibal.'

'He's a good dog in some ways,' said Albert. 'Doesn't take to everyone, of course.'

'No,' said Tommy, 'that's not his job in life. Not one of those dogs who welcome in the burglars and wag their tails at the wrong person. Hannibal knows a few things. But I have made it quite clear to you, haven't I?'

'Yes. I don't know what I am to do if the missus – well, am I to do what the missus says or tell her what you said or –'

'I think you'll have to use a certain amount of diplomacy,' said Tommy. 'I'm making her stay in bed today. I'm leaving her in your charge more or less.'

Albert had just opened the front door to a youngish man in a tweed suit.

Albert looked up doubtfully at Tommy. The visitor stepped inside and advanced one step, a friendly smile on his face.

'Mr Beresford? I've heard you want a bit of help in your garden – just moved in here lately, haven't you? I noticed coming up the drive that it was getting rather overgrown. I did some work locally a couple of years ago – for a Mr Solomon – you may have heard of him.'

'Mr Solomon, yes, someone did mention him.'

'My name's Crispin, Angus Crispin. Perhaps we might take a look at what wants doing.'

II

'About time someone did something about the garden,' said Mr Crispin, as Tommy led him on a tour of the flower-beds and the vegetable garden.

'That's where they used to grow the spinach along this kitchen garden path here. Behind it were some frames. They used to grow melons too.'

'You seem to be very well aware of all this.'

'Well, one heard a lot you know of what had been everywhere in the old days. Old ladies tell you about the flower-beds and Alexander Parkinson told a lot of his pals about the foxglove leaves.'

'He must have been a rather remarkable boy.'

'Well, he had ideas and he was very keen on crime. He made a kind of code message out in one of Stevenson's books: *The Black Arrow*.'

'Rather a good one, that, isn't it? I read it myself about five years ago. Before that I'd never got further than *Kidnapped*. When I was working for –' He hesitated.

'Mr Solomon?' suggested Tommy.

'Yes, yes, that's the name. I heard things. Heard things from old Isaac. I gather, unless I've heard the wrong rumours, I gather that old Isaac must have been, oh, getting on for a hundred and did some work for you here.'

'Yes,' said Tommy. 'For his age he was rather wonderful, really. He knew a lot of things he used to tell us, too. Things he couldn't have remembered himself.'

'No, but he liked the gossip of the old days. He's got relations here still, you know, who have listened to his tales and checked up on his stories. I expect you've heard a good many things yourself.'

'So far,' said Tommy, 'everything seems to work out in lists of names. Names from the past but names, naturally, that don't mean anything to me. They can't.'

'All hearsay?'

'Mostly. My wife has listened to a lot of it and made some lists. I don't know whether any of them mean anything. I've got one list myself. It only came into my hands yesterday, as a matter of fact.'

'Oh. What's your list?'

'Census,' said Tommy. 'You know, there was a census on – I've got the date written down so I'll give it to you – and the people who were entered up that day because they spent the night here. There was a big party. A dinner-party.'

'So you know on a certain date – and perhaps quite an interesting date – who was here?'

'Yes,' said Tommy.

'It might be valuable. It might be quite significant. You've only just moved in here, haven't you?'

'Yes,' said Tommy, 'but it's possible we might just want to move out of here.'

'Don't you like it? It's a nice house, and this garden – well, this garden could be made very beautiful indeed. You've got some fine shrubs – wants a bit of clearing out, superfluous trees and bushes, flowering shrubs that haven't flowered lately and may never flower again by the look of them. Yes, I don't know why you'd want to go and move.'

'The associations with the past aren't terribly pleasant here,' said Tommy.

'The past,' said Mr Crispin. 'How does the past tie up with the present?'

'One thinks it doesn't matter, it's all behind us. But there's always somebody left, you know. I don't mean walking about but somebody who comes alive when people tell you about her or him or it or them. You really would be prepared to do a bit of –'

'Bit of jobbing gardening for you? Yes, I would. It would interest me. It's rather a – well, it's rather a hobby of mine, gardening.'

'There was a Miss Mullins who came yesterday.'

'Mullins? Mullins? Is she a gardener?'

'I gather something in that line. It was a Mrs – a Mrs Griffin, I think it was – who mentioned her to my wife and who sent her along to see us.'

'Did you fix up with her or not?'

'Not definitely,' said Tommy. 'As a matter of fact we've got a rather enthusiastic guard dog here. A Manchester Terrier.'

'Yes, they can be very enthusiastic at guarding. I suppose he thinks your wife is his business and he practically never lets her go anywhere alone. He's always there.'

'Quite right,' said Tommy, 'and he's prepared to tear anyone limb from limb who lays a finger on her.'

'Nice dogs. Very affectionate, very loyal, very self-willed, very sharp teeth. I'd better look out for him, I suppose.'

'He's all right at the moment. He's up in the house.'

'Miss Mullins,' said Crispin thoughtfully. 'Yes. Yes, that's interesting.'

'Why is it interesting?'

'Oh, I think it's because – well, I wouldn't know her by that name, of course. Is she between fifty and sixty?'

'Yes. Very tweedy and countrified.'

'Yes. Got some country connections, too. Isaac could have told you something about her, I expect. I heard she'd come back to live here. Not so very long ago, either. Things tie up, you know.'

'I expect you know things about this place that I don't,' said Tommy.

'I shouldn't think so. Isaac could have told you a lot, though. He knew things. Old stories, as you say, but he had a memory. And they talked it over. Yes, in these clubs for old people, they talk things over. Tall stories – some of them not true, some of them based on fact. Yes, it's all very interesting. And – I suppose he knew too much.'

'It's a shame about Isaac,' said Tommy. 'I'd like to get even with whoever did him in. He was a nice old boy and he was good to us and did as much as he could to help us here. Come on, anyway, let's go on looking round.'

CHAPTER 15

HANNIBAL SEES ACTIVE SERVICE WITH MR CRISPIN

I

Albert tapped on the bedroom door and in answer to Tuppence's 'Come in' advanced his head round the side of it.

'The lady as came the other morning,' he said. 'Miss Mullins. She's here. Wants to speak to you for a minute or two. Suggestions about the garden, I understand. I said as you was in bed and I wasn't sure if you were receiving.'

'The words you use, Albert,' said Tuppence. 'All right. I am receiving.'

'I was just going to bring your morning coffee up.'

'Well, you can bring that up and another cup. That's all. There'll be enough for two, won't there?'

'Oh yes, madam.'

'Very well, then. Bring it up, put it on the table over there, and then bring Miss Mullins up.'

'What about Hannibal?' said Albert. 'Shall I take him down and shut him up in the kitchen?'

'He doesn't like being shut up in the kitchen. No. Just push him into the bathroom and shut the door of it when you've done so.'

Hannibal, resenting the insult which was being put upon him, allowed with a bad grace Albert's pushing him into the bathroom and adjustment to the door. He gave several loud fierce barks.

'Shut up!' Tuppence shouted to him. 'Shut up!'

Hannibal consented to shut up as far as barking went. He lay down with his paws in front of him and his nose pressed to the crack under the door and uttered long, non-cooperative growls.

'Oh, Mrs Beresford,' cried Miss Mullins, 'I'm afraid I am intruding, but I really thought you'd like to look at this book I have on gardening. Suggestions for planting at this time of year. Some very rare and interesting shrubs and they do quite well in this particular soil although some people say they won't . . . Oh dear – oh no, oh, it's very kind of you. Yes, I would like a cup of coffee. Please let me pour it out for you, it's so difficult when you're in bed. I wonder, perhaps –' Miss Mullins looked at Albert, who obligingly drew up a chair.

'That be all right for you, miss?' he demanded.

'Oh yes, very nice indeed. Dear me, is that another bell downstairs?'

'Milk, I expect,' said Albert. 'Or might be the grocer. It's his morning. Excuse me, won't you.'

He went out of the room, shutting the door behind him. Hannibal gave another growl.

'That's my dog,' said Tuppence, 'he's very annoyed at not being allowed to join the party but he makes so much noise.'

'Do you take sugar, Mrs Beresford?'

'One lump,' said Tuppence.

Miss Mullins poured out a cup of coffee. Tuppence said, 'Otherwise black.'

Miss Mullins put down the coffee beside Tuppence and went to pour out a cup for herself.

Suddenly she stumbled, clutched at an occasional table, and went down on her knees with an exclamation of dismay.

'Have you hurt yourself?' demanded Tuppence.

'No, oh no, but I've broken your vase. I caught my foot in something – so clumsy – and your beautiful vase is smashed. Dear Mrs Beresford, what will you think of me? I assure you it was an accident.'

'Of course it was,' said Tuppence kindly. 'Let me see. Well, it looks as if it could be worse. It's broken in two, which means we shall be able to glue it together. I dare say the join will hardly show.'

'I shall still feel awful about it,' declared Miss Mullins. 'I know you must perhaps be feeling ill and I oughtn't to have come today, but I did so want to tell you –'

Hannibal began to bark again.

'Oh, the poor wee doggie,' said Miss Mullins, 'shall I let him out?'

'Better not,' said Tuppence. 'He's not very reliable sometimes.'

'Oh dear, is that another bell downstairs?'

'No,' said Tuppence. 'Albert'll answer it. He can always bring up a message if necessary.'

It was, however, Tommy who answered the telephone.

'Hullo,' he said. 'Yes? Oh, I see. Who? I see – yes. Oh. An enemy, definite enemy. Yes, that's all right. We've taken the countermeasures all right. Yes. Thank you very much.'

He dropped the receiver back, and looked at Mr Crispin.

'Words of warning?' said Mr Crispin.

'Yes,' said Tommy.

He continued to look at Mr Crispin.

'Difficult to know, isn't it? I mean, who's your enemy and who's your friend.'

'Sometimes when you know it's too late. Postern of Fate, Disaster's Cavern,' said Tommy.

Mr Crispin looked at him in some surprise.

'Sorry,' said Tommy. 'For some reason or other we've got in the habit of reciting poetry in this house.'

'Flecker, isn't it? "Gates of Baghdad" or is it the "Gates of Damascus"?'

'Come up, will you?' said Tommy. 'Tuppence is only resting, she's not suffering from any peculiar disease or anything. Not even a sneezing cold in the head.'

'I've taken up coffee,' said Albert, reappearing suddenly, 'and an extra cup for Miss Mullins wot's up there now with a gardening book or something.'

'I see,' said Tommy. 'Yes. Yes, it's all going very well. Where's Hannibal?'

'Shut him in the bathroom.'

'Did you latch the door very tight, because he won't like that, you know?'

'No, sir, I've done just what you said.'

Tommy went upstairs. Mr Crispin came just behind him. Tommy gave a little tap on the bedroom door and then went in. From the bathroom door Hannibal gave one more outspoken bark of defiance, then he leapt at the door from the inside, the latch gave, he shot out into the room. He gave one quick glance at Mr Crispin, then came forward and lunged with all his might, growling furiously, at Miss Mullins.

'Oh dear,' said Tuppence, 'oh dear.'

'Good boy, Hannibal,' said Tommy, 'good boy. Don't you think so?'

He turned his head to Mr Crispin.

'Knows his enemies, doesn't he – and your enemies.'

'Oh dear,' said Tuppence. 'Has Hannibal bitten you?'

'A very nasty nip,' said Miss Mullins, rising to her feet and scowling at Hannibal.

'His second one, isn't it?' said Tommy. 'Chased you out of our pampas grass, didn't he?'

'He knows what's what,' said Mr Crispin. 'Doesn't he, Dodo, my dear? Long time since I've seen you, Dodo, isn't it?'

Miss Mullins got up, shot a glance at Tuppence, at Tommy and at Mr Crispin.

'Mullins,' said Mr Crispin. 'Sorry I'm not up to date. Is that a married name or are you now known as Miss Mullins?'

'I am Iris Mullins, as I always was.'

'Ah, I thought you were Dodo. You used to be Dodo to me. Well, dear, I think – nice to have seen you, but I think we'd better get out of here quickly. Drink your coffee. I expect that's all right. Mrs Beresford? I'm very pleased to meet you. If I might advise you, I shouldn't drink *your* coffee.'

'Oh dear, let me take the cup away.'

Miss Mullins pressed forward. In a moment Crispin stood between her and Tuppence.

'No, Dodo dear, I wouldn't do that,' he said. 'I'd rather have charge of it myself. The cup belongs to the house, you know, and of course it would be nice to have an analysis of exactly what's in it just now. Possibly you brought a little dose with you, did you? Quite easy to put a little dose into the cup as you're handing it to the invalid or the supposed invalid.'

'I assure you I did no such thing. Oh, do call your dog off.'

Hannibal showed every desire to pursue her down the staircase.

'He wants to see you off the premises,' said Tommy. 'He's rather particular about that. He likes biting people who are going out through the front door. Ah, Albert, there you are. I thought you'd be just outside the other door. Did you see what happened, by any chance?'

Albert put his head round the dressing-room door across the room.

'I saw all right. I watched her through the crack of the hinge.

Yes. Put something in the missus's cup, she did. Very neat. Good as a conjuror, but she did it all right.'

'I don't know what you mean,' said Miss Mullins. 'I – oh dear, oh dear, I must go. I've got an appointment. It's very important.'

She shot out of the room and down the stairs. Hannibal gave one glance and went after her. Mr Crispin showed no sign of animosity, but he too left hurriedly in pursuit.

'I hope she's a good runner,' said Tuppence, 'because if she isn't Hannibal will catch up with her. My word, he's a good guard dog, isn't he?'

'Tuppence, that was Mr Crispin, sent us by Mr Solomon. Came at a very good moment, didn't he? I think he's been waiting his time to see what might be going to happen. Don't break that cup and don't pour any of that coffee away until we've got a bottle or something to put it in. It's going to be analysed and we're going to find out what's in it. Put your best dressing-gown on, Tuppence, and come down to the sitting-room and we'll have some drinks there before lunch.'

II

'And now, I suppose,' said Tuppence, 'we shall never know what any of it means or what it is all about.'

She shook her head in deep despondency. Rising from her chair, she went towards the fireplace.

'Are you trying to put a log on?' said Tommy. 'Let me. You've been told not to move about much.'

'My arm's quite all right now,' said Tuppence. 'Anyone would think I'd broken it or something. It was only a nasty scrape or graze.'

'You have more to boast about than that,' said Tommy. 'It was definitely a bullet wound. You have been wounded in war.'

'War it seems to have been all right,' said Tuppence. 'Really!'

'Never mind,' said Tommy, 'we dealt with the Mullins very well, I think.'

'Hannibal,' said Tuppence, 'was a very good dog there, wasn't he?'

'Yes,' said Tommy, 'he told us. Told us very definitely. He just leapt for that pampas grass. His nose told him, I suppose. He's got a wonderful nose.'

'I can't say my nose warned me,' said Tuppence. 'I just thought she was rather an answer to prayer, turning up. And I quite forgot we were only supposed to take someone who had worked for Mr Solomon. Did Mr Crispin tell you anything more? I suppose his name isn't really Crispin.'

'Possibly not,' said Tommy.

'Did he come to do some sleuthing too? Too many of us here, I should say.'

'No,' said Tommy, 'not exactly a sleuth. I think he was sent for security purposes. To look after you.'

'To look after me,' said Tuppence, 'and you, I should say. Where is he now?'

'Dealing with Miss Mullins, I expect.'

'Yes, well, it's extraordinary how hungry these excitements make one. Quite peckish, as one might say. Do you know, there's nothing I can imagine I'd like to eat more than a nice hot crab with a sauce made of cream with just a touch of curry powder.'

'You're well again,' said Tommy. 'I'm delighted to hear you feeling like that about food.'

'I've never been ill,' said Tuppence. 'I've been wounded. That's quite different.'

'Well,' said Tommy, 'anyway you must have realized as I did that when Hannibal let go all out and told you an enemy was close at hand in the pampas grass, you must have realized that Miss Mullins was the person who, dressed as a man, hid there and shot at you –'

'But then,' said Tuppence, 'we thought that she'd have another go. I was immured with my wound in bed and we made our arrangements. Isn't that right, Tommy?'

'Quite right,' said Tommy, 'quite right. I thought probably she wouldn't leave it too long to come to the conclusion that one of her bullets had taken effect and that you'd be laid up in bed.'

'So she came along full of feminine solicitude,' said Tuppence.

'And our arrangement was very good, I thought,' said Tommy. 'There was Albert on permanent guard, watching every step she took, every single thing she did –'

'And also,' said Tuppence, 'bringing me up on a tray a cup of coffee and adding another cup for the visitor.'

'Did you see Mullins – or Dodo, as Crispin called her – put anything in your cup of coffee?'.

'No,' said Tuppence, 'I must admit that I didn't. You see, she seemed to catch her foot in something and she knocked over that little table with our nice vase on it, made a great deal of apology, and my eye of course was on the broken vase and whether it was too bad to mend. So I didn't see her.'

'Albert did,' said Tommy. 'Saw it through the hinge where he'd enlarged it a crack so that he could look through.'

'And then it was a very good idea to put Hannibal in confinement in the bathroom but leaving the door only half latched because, as we know, Hannibal is very good at opening doors. Not of course if they're completely latched, but if they only look latched or feel latched he takes one great spring and comes in like a – oh, like a Bengal tiger.'

'Yes,' said Tommy, 'that is quite a good description.'

'And now I suppose Mr Crispin or whatever his name is has finished making his enquiries, although how he thinks Miss Mullins can be connected with Mary Jordan, or with a dangerous figure like Jonathan Kane who only exists in the past –'

'I don't think he only exists in the past. I think there may be a new edition of him, a re-birth, as you might say. There are a lot of young members, lovers of violence, violence at any price, the merry muggers society if there's anything called that, and the super-fascists regretting the splendid days of Hitler and his merry group.'

'I've just been reading *Count Hannibal*,' said Tuppence. 'Stanley Weyman. One of his best. It was among the Alexander books upstairs.'

'What about it?'

'Well, I was thinking that nowadays it's really still like that. And probably always has been. All the poor children who went off to the Children's Crusade so full of joy and pleasure and vanity, poor little souls. Thinking they'd been appointed by the Lord to deliver Jerusalem, that the seas would part in front of them so that they could walk across, as Moses did in the Bible. And now all these pretty girls and young men who appear in courts the whole time, because they've smashed down some wretched old age pensioner or elderly person who had just got a little money or something in the bank. And there was St Bartholomew's Massacre. You see, all these things *do* happen again. Even the new fascists were mentioned the other day in connection with a perfectly respectable university. Ah well, I suppose nobody will ever really tell us anything. Do you really think that Mr Crispin will find out something more about a hiding-place that nobody's yet discovered? Cisterns. You know, bank robberies. They often hid things in cisterns. Very damp place, I should have thought, to hide something. Do you think when he's finished making his enquiries or whatever it is, he'll come back here and continue looking after me – and you, Tommy?'

'I don't need him to look after me,' said Tommy.

'Oh, that's just arrogance,' said Tuppence.

'I think he'll come to say goodbye,' said Tommy.

'Oh yes, because he's got very nice manners, hasn't he?'

'He'll want to make sure that you're quite all right again.'

'I'm only wounded and the doctor's seen to that.'

'He's really very keen on gardening,' said Tommy. 'I realize that. He really did work for a friend of his who happened to be Mr Solomon, who has been dead for some years, but I suppose it makes a good cover, that, because he can say he worked for him and people will know he worked for him. So he'll appear to be quite *bona fide.*'

'Yes, I suppose one has to think of all those things,' said Tuppence.

The front door bell rang and Hannibal dashed from the room, tiger-style, to kill any intruder who might be wishing to enter the sacred precincts which he guarded. Tommy came back with an envelope.

'Addressed to us both,' he said. 'Shall I open it?'

'Go ahead,' said Tuppence.

He opened it.

'Well,' he said, 'this raises possibilities for the future.'

'What is it?'

'It's an invitation from Mr Robinson. To you and to me. To dine with him on a date the week after next when he hopes you'll be fully recovered and yourself again. In his country house. Somewhere in Sussex, I think.'

'Do you think he'll tell us anything then?' said Tuppence.

'I think he might,' said Tommy.

'Shall I take my list with me?' said Tuppence. 'I know it by heart now.'

She read rapidly.

'Black Arrow, Alexander Parkinson, Oxford and Cambridge porcelain Victorian seats, Grin-hen-lo, KK, Mathilde's stomach, Cain and Abel, Truelove . . .'

'Enough,' said Tommy. 'It sounds mad.'

'Well, it is mad, all of it. Think there'll be anyone else at Mr Robinson's?'

'Possibly Colonel Pikeaway.'

'In that case,' said Tuppence, 'I'd better take a cough lozenge with me, hadn't I? Anyway, I do want to see Mr Robinson. I can't believe he's as fat and yellow as you say he is – Oh! – but, Tommy, isn't it the week after next that Deborah is bringing the children to stay with us?'

'No,' said Tommy, 'it's this *next* weekend as ever is.'

'Thank goodness, so that's all right,' said Tuppence.

CHAPTER 16
THE BIRDS FLY SOUTH

'Was that the car?'

Tuppence came out of the front door peering curiously along the curve of the drive, eagerly awaiting the arrival of her daughter Deborah and the three children.

Albert emerged from the side door.

'They won't be here yet. No, that was the grocer, madam. You wouldn't believe it – eggs have gone up, *again*. Never vote for this Government again, *I* won't. I'll give the Liberals a go.'

'Shall I come and see to the rhubarb and strawberry fool for tonight?'

'I've seen to that, madam. I've watched you often and I know just how you do it.'

'You'll be a cordon bleu chef by the time you've finished, Albert,' said Tuppence. 'It's Janet's favourite sweet.'

'Yes, and I made a treacle tart – Master Andrew loves treacle tart.'

'The rooms are all ready?'

'Yes. Mrs Shacklebury came in good time this morning. I put the Guerlain Sandalwood Soap in Miss Deborah's bathroom. It's her favourite, I know.'

Tuppence breathed a sigh of relief at the knowledge that all was in order for the arrival of her family.

There was the sound of a motor horn and a few minutes later the car came up the drive with Tommy at the wheel and a moment later the guests were decanted on the doorstep – daughter Deborah still a very handsome woman, nearly forty, and Andrew, fifteen, Janet, eleven, and Rosalie, seven.

'Hullo, Grandma,' shouted Andrew.

'Where's Hannibal?' called Janet.

'I want my tea,' said Rosalie, showing a disposition to burst into tears.

Greetings were exchanged. Albert dealt with the disembarkation of all the family treasures including a budgerigar, a bowl of goldfish and a hamster in a hutch.

'So this is the new home,' said Deborah, embracing her mother. 'I like it – I like it very much.'

'Can we go round the garden?' asked Janet.

'After tea,' said Tommy.

'I want my tea,' reiterated Rosalie with an expression on her face of: First things first.

They went into the dining-room where tea was set out and met with general satisfaction.

'What's all this I've been hearing about you, Mum?' demanded Deborah, when they had finished tea and repaired to the open air – the children racing round to explore the possible pleasures of the garden in the joint company of Thomas and Hannibal who had rushed out to take part in the rejoicings.

Deborah, who always took a stern line with her mother, whom she considered in need of careful guardianship, demanded, 'What *have* you been doing?'

'Oh. We've settled in quite comfortably by now,' said Tuppence.

Deborah looked unconvinced.

'You've been doing things. She has, hasn't she, Dad?'

Tommy was returning with Rosalie riding him piggyback, Janet surveying the new territory and Andrew looking around with an air of taking a full grown-up view.

'You have been *doing* things.' Deborah returned to the attack. 'You've been playing at being Mrs Blenkinsop all over again. The trouble with you is, there's no holding you – N or M – all over again. Derek heard something and wrote and told me.' She nodded as she mentioned her brother's name.

'Derek – what could *he* know?' demanded Tuppence.

'Derek always gets to know things.'

'You too, Dad.' Deborah turned on her father. '*You've* been mixing yourself up in things, too. I thought you'd come here, both of you, to retire, and take life quietly – and enjoy yourselves.'

'That *was* the idea,' said Tommy, 'but Fate thought otherwise.'

'Postern of Fate,' said Tuppence. 'Disaster's Cavern, Fort of Fear –'

'Flecker,' said Andrew, with conscious erudition. He was addicted to poetry and hoped one day to be a poet himself. He carried on with a full quotation:

'Four great gates has the City of Damascus . . .
Postern of Fate – the Desert Gate . . .
Pass not beneath, O Caravan – or pass not singing.
Have you heard that silence where the birds are dead, yet something
*   pipeth like a bird?'*

With singularly apposite cooperation birds flew suddenly from the roof of the house over their heads.

'What are all those birds, Grannie?' asked Janet.

'Swallows flying south,' said Tuppence.

'Won't they ever come back again?'

'Yes, they'll come back next summer.'

'And pass through the Postern of Fate!' said Andrew with intense satisfaction.

'This house was called Swallow's Nest once,' said Tuppence.

'But you aren't going on living here, are you?' said Deborah. 'Dad wrote and said you're looking out for another house.'

'Why?' asked Janet – the Rosa Dartle of the family. 'I like this one.'

'I'll give you a few reasons,' said Tommy, plucking a sheet of paper from his pocket and reading aloud:

Black Arrow
Alexander Parkinson
Oxford and Cambridge
Victorian china garden stools
Grin-hen-lo
KK
Mathilde's stomach
Cain and Abel
Gallant Truelove.'

'Shut up, Tommy – that's *my* list. It's nothing to do with you,' said Tuppence.

'But what does it *mean*?' asked Janet, continuing her quiz.

'It sounds like a list of clues from a detective story,' said Andrew, who in his less poetical moments was addicted to that form of literature.

'It *is* a list of clues. It's the reason why we are looking for another house,' said Tommy.

'But I like it here,' said Janet, 'it's lovely.'

'It's a nice house,' said Rosalie. 'Chocolate biscuits,' she added, with memories of recently eaten tea.

'I like it,' said Andrew, speaking as an autocratic Czar of Russia might speak.

'Why don't *you* like it, Grandma?' asked Janet.

'I *do* like it,' said Tuppence with a sudden unexpected enthusiasm. 'I want to live here – to go on living here.'

'Postern of Fate,' said Andrew. 'It's an exciting name.'

'It used to be called Swallow's Nest,' said Tuppence. 'We could call it that again –'

'All those clues,' said Andrew. 'You could make a story out of them – even a book –'

'Too many names, too complicated,' said Deborah. 'Who'd read a book like that?'

'You'd be surprised,' said Tommy, 'what people *will* read – and enjoy!'

Tommy and Tuppence looked at each other.

'Couldn't I get some paint tomorrow?' asked Andrew. 'Or Albert could get some and he'd help me. We'd paint the new name on the gate.'

'And then the swallows would know they could come back next summer,' said Janet.

She looked at her mother.

'Not at all a bad idea,' said Deborah.

'*La Reine le veult*,' said Tommy and bowed to his daughter, who always considered that giving the Royal assent in the family was her perquisite.

CHAPTER 17

LAST WORDS: DINNER WITH MR ROBINSON

'What a lovely meal,' said Tuppence. She looked round at the assembled company.

They had passed from the dining table and were now assembled in the library round the coffee table.

Mr Robinson, as yellow and even larger than Tuppence had visualized him, was smiling behind a big and beautiful George II coffee-pot – next to him was Mr Crispin, now, it seemed, answering to the name of Horsham. Colonel Pikeaway sat next to Tommy, who had, rather doubtfully, offered him one of his own cigarettes.

Colonel Pikeaway, with an expression of surprise, said: 'I *never* smoke after *dinner*.'

Miss Collodon, whom Tuppence had found rather alarming, said, 'Indeed, Colonel Pikeaway? How *very, very* interesting.' She turned her head towards Tuppence. 'What a very well-behaved dog you have got, Mrs Beresford!'

Hannibal, who was lying under the table with his head resting on Tuppence's foot, looked out with his misleading best angelic expression and moved his tail gently.

'I understood he was a very *fierce* dog,' said Mr Robinson, casting an amused glance at Tuppence.

'You should see him in action,' said Mr Crispin – alias Horsham.

'He has party manners when he is asked out to dinner,'

explained Tuppence. 'He loves it, feels he's really a prestige dog going into high society.' She turned to Mr Robinson. 'It was really very, *very* nice of you to send him an invitation and to have a plateful of liver ready for him. He loves liver.'

'All dogs love liver,' said Mr Robinson. 'I understand –' he looked at Crispin-Horsham – 'that if I were to pay a visit to Mr and Mrs Beresford at their *own* home I might be torn to pieces.'

'Hannibal takes his duties very seriously,' said Mr Crispin. 'He's a well-bred guard dog and never forgets it.'

'You understand his feelings, of course, as a security officer,' said Mr Robinson.

His eyes twinkled.

'You and your husband have done a very remarkable piece of work, Mrs Beresford,' said Mr Robinson. 'We are indebted to you. Colonel Pikeaway tells me that *you* were the initiator in the affair.'

'It just happened,' said Tuppence, embarrassed. 'I got – well – curious. I wanted to find out – about certain things –'

'Yes, I gathered that. And now, perhaps you feel an equally natural curiosity as to what all this has been about?'

Tuppence became even more embarrassed, and her remarks became slightly incoherent.

'Oh – oh of course – I mean – I do understand that all this is quite secret – I mean all very hush-hush – and that we can't ask questions – because you couldn't tell us things. I do understand that perfectly.'

'On the contrary, it is I who want to ask you a question. If you will answer it by giving me the information I shall be enormously pleased.'

Tuppence stared at him with wide-open eyes.

'I can't imagine –' She broke off.

'You have a list – or so your husband tells me. He didn't tell me what that list was. Quite rightly. That list is *your* secret property. But I, too, know what it is to suffer curiosity.'

Again his eyes twinkled. Tuppence was suddenly aware that she liked Mr Robinson very much.

She was silent for a moment or two, then she coughed and fumbled in her evening bag.

'It's terribly silly,' she said. 'In fact it's rather more than silly. It's mad.'

Mr Robinson responded unexpectedly: '"Mad, mad, all the whole world is *mad*." So Hans Sachs said, sitting under his elder tree in *Die Meistersinger* – my favourite opera. How right he was!'

He took the sheet of foolscap she handed to him.

'Read it aloud if you like,' said Tuppence. 'I don't really mind.'

Mr Robinson glanced at it, then handed it to Crispin. 'Angus, you have a clearer voice than I have.'

Mr Crispin took the sheet and read in an agreeable tenor with good enunciation:

'Black Arrow
Alexander Parkinson
Mary Jordan did not die naturally
Oxford and Cambridge porcelain Victorian seats
Grin-Hen-Lo
KK
Mathilde's stomach
Cain and Abel
Truelove.'

He stopped, looked at his host, who turned his head towards Tuppence.

'My dear,' said Mr Robinson. 'Let me congratulate you – you must have a most unusual mind. To arrive from this list of clues at your final discoveries is really most remarkable.'

'Tommy was hard at it too,' said Tuppence.

'Nagged into it by you,' said Tommy.

'Very good research he did,' said Colonel Pikeaway appreciatively.

'The census date gave me a very good pointer.'

'You are a gifted pair,' said Mr Robinson. He looked at Tuppence again and smiled. 'I am still assuming that though you have displayed no indiscreet curiosity, you really want to know what all this has been about?'

'Oh,' exclaimed Tuppence. 'Are you really going to tell us something? How wonderful!'

'Some of it begins, as you surmised, with the Parkinsons,' said Mr Robinson. 'That is to say, in the distant past. My own great-grandmother was a Parkinson. Some things I learnt from her –

'The girl known as Mary Jordan was in our service. She had connections in the Navy – her mother was Austrian and so she herself spoke German fluently.

'As you may know, and as your husband certainly knows already, there are certain documents which will shortly be released for publication.

'The present trend of political thinking is that hush-hush, necessary as it is at certain times, should not be preserved indefinitely. There are things in the records that should be made known as a definite part of our country's past history.

'Three or four volumes are due to be published within the next couple of years authenticated by documentary evidence.

'What went on in the neighbourhood of Swallow's Nest (that was the name of your present house at that time) will certainly be included.

'There were leakages – as always there are leakages in times of war, or preceding a probable outbreak of war.

'There were politicians who had prestige and who were thought of very highly. There were one or two leading journalists who had enormous influence and used it unwisely. There were men even before the First World War who were intriguing against their own country. After that war there were young men who graduated from universities and who were fervent believers and often active members of the Communist Party without anyone knowing of that fact. And even more dangerous, Fascism was coming into favour with a full progressive programme of eventual union with Hitler, posing as a Lover of Peace and thereby bringing about a quick end to the war.

'And so on. A Continuous Behind the Scenes Picture. It has happened before in history. Doubtless it will always happen: a Fifth Column that is both active and dangerous, run by those who believed in it – as well as those who sought financial gain, those who aimed at eventual power being placed in their hands in the future. Some of this will make interesting reading. How often has the same phrase been uttered in all good faith: Old

B.? A traitor? Nonsense. Last man in the world! Absolutely trustworthy!

'The complete confidence trick. The old, old story. Always on the same lines.

'In the commercial world, in the Services, in political life. Always a man with an honest face – a fellow you can't help liking and trusting. Beyond suspicion. "The last man in the world". Etc., etc., etc. Someone who's a natural for the job, like the man who can sell you a gold brick outside the Ritz.

'Your present village, Mrs Beresford, became the headquarters of a certain group just before the First World War. It was such a nice old-world village – nice people had always lived there – all patriotic, doing different kinds of war work. A good naval harbour – a good-looking young Naval commander – came of a good family, father had been an admiral. A good doctor practising there – much loved by all his patients – they enjoyed confiding their troubles to him. Just in general practice – hardly anyone knew that he had had a special training in chemical warfare – in poison-gases.

'And later, before the Second World War, Mr Kane – spelt with a K – lived in a pretty thatched cottage by the harbour and had a particular political creed – not Fascist – oh no! Just Peace before Everything to save the world – a creed rapidly gaining a following on the Continent and in numerous other countries abroad.

'None of that is what you really want to know, Mrs Beresford – but you've got to realize the background first, a very carefully contrived one. That's where Mary Jordan was sent to find out, if she could, just what was going on.

'She was born before my time. I admired the work she had done for us when I heard the story of it – and I would have liked to have known her – she obviously had character and personality.

'Mary was her own Christian name though she was always known as Molly. She did good work. It was a tragedy she should die so young.'

Tuppence had been looking up to the wall at a picture which for some reason looked familiar. It was a mere sketch of a boy's head.

'Is that – surely –'

'Yes,' said Mr Robinson. 'That's the boy Alexander Parkinson. He was only eleven then. He was a grandson of a great-aunt of mine. That's how Molly went to the Parkinsons' in the role of a nursery governess. It seemed a good safe observation post. One wouldn't ever have thought –' he broke off, 'what would come of it.'

'It wasn't – one of the Parkinsons?' asked Tuppence.

'Oh no, my dear. I understand that the Parkinsons were not involved in any way. But there were others – guests and friends – staying in the house that night. It was your Thomas who found out that the evening in question was the date of a census return. The names of everyone sleeping under that roof had to be entered as well as the usual occupants. One of those names linked up in a significant manner. The daughter of the local doctor about whom I have just told you came down to visit her father as she often did and asked the Parkinsons to put her up that night as she had brought two friends with her. Those friends were all right – but later her father was found to be heavily involved in all that was going on in that part of the world. She herself, it seemed, had helped the Parkinsons in garden work some weeks earlier and was responsible for foxgloves and spinach being planted in close proximity. It was she who had taken the mixture of leaves to the kitchen on the fatal day. The illness of all the participants of the meal passed off as one of those unfortunate mistakes that happen sometimes. The doctor explained he had known such a thing happen before. His evidence at the inquest resulted in a verdict of Misadventure. The fact that a cocktail glass had been swept off a table and smashed by accident that same night attracted no attention.

'Perhaps, Mrs Beresford, you would be interested to know that history might have repeated itself. You were shot at from a clump of pampas grass, and later the lady calling herself Miss Mullins tried to add poison to your coffee cup. I understand she is actually a granddaughter or great-niece of the original criminal doctor, and before the Second World War she was a disciple of Jonathan Kane. That's how Crispin knew of her, of course. And your dog definitely disapproved of her and took prompt action. Indeed we now know that it was she who coshed old Isaac.

'We now have to consider an even more sinister character. The genial kindly doctor was idolized by everyone in the place, but it seems most probable on the evidence that it was the doctor who was responsible for Mary Jordan's death, though at the time no one would have believed it. He had wide scientific interests, and expert knowledge of poisons and did pioneering work in bacteriology. It has taken sixty years before the facts have become known. Only Alexander Parkinson, a schoolboy at the time, began having ideas.'

'*Mary Jordan did not die naturally*,' quoted Tuppence softly. '*It must have been one of us*.' She asked: 'Was it the doctor who found out what Mary was doing?'

'No. The doctor had not suspected. But somebody had. Up till then she had been completely successful. The Naval commander had worked with her as planned. The information she passed to him was genuine and he didn't realize that it was mainly stuff that didn't matter – though it had been made to sound important. So-called Naval plans and secrets which he passed to her, she duly delivered on her days off in London, obeying instructions as to when and where. Queen Mary's Garden in Regent's Park was one, I believe – and the Peter Pan statue in Kensington Gardens was another. We learned a good deal from these meetings and the minor officials in certain embassies concerned.

'But all that's in the past, Mrs Beresford, long, long in the past.'

Colonel Pikeaway coughed and suddenly took over. 'But history repeats itself, Mrs Beresford. Everyone learns that sooner or later. A nucleus recently reformed in Hollowquay. People who knew about it set things up again. Perhaps that's why Miss Mullins returned. Certain hiding-places were used again. Secret meetings took place. Once more money became significant – where it came from, where it went to. Mr Robinson here was called in. And then our old friend Beresford came along and started giving me some very interesting information. It fitted in with what we had already suspected. Background scenery, being set up in anticipation. A future being prepared to be controlled and run by one particular political figure in this country. A man with a certain reputation and making more converts and followers every day. The Confidence Trick in action once again. Man of Great Integrity – Lover of Peace. Not Fascism – oh no! Just something that looks like Fascism. Peace for all – and financial rewards to those who cooperate.'

'Do you mean it's still going on?' Tuppence's eyes opened wide.

'Well, we know more or less all we want and need to know now. And that's partly because of what you two have contributed – the operation of a surgical nature on a rocking-horse was particularly informative –'

'Mathilde!' exclaimed Tuppence. 'I *am* glad! I can hardly believe it. Mathilde's stomach!'

'Wonderful things, horses,' said Colonel Pikeaway. 'Never know what they will do, or won't do. Ever since the wooden horse of Troy.'

'Even Truelove helped, I hope,' said Tuppence. 'But, I mean, if it's all going on still. With children about –'

'It isn't,' said Mr Crispin. 'You don't need to worry. That area of England is purified – the wasps' nest cleared up. It's suitable for private living again. We've reason to believe they've shifted operations to the neighbourhood of Bury St Edmunds. And we'll be keeping an eye on you, so you needn't worry at all.'

Tuppence gave a sigh of relief. 'Thank you for telling me. You see, my daughter Deborah comes to stay from time to time and brings her three children –'

'You needn't worry,' said Mr Robinson. 'By the way, after the N and M business, didn't you adopt the child that figured in the case – the one that had the nursery rhyme books, Goosey Gander and all the rest of it?'

'Betty?' said Tuppence. 'Yes. She's done very well at university and she's gone off now to Africa to do research on how people live – that sort of thing. A lot of young people are very keen on that. She's a darling – and very happy.'

Mr Robinson cleared his throat and rose to his feet. 'I want to propose a toast. To Mr and Mrs Thomas Beresford in acknowledgement of the service they have rendered to their country.'

It was drunk enthusiastically.

'And if I may, I will propose a further toast,' said Mr Robinson. 'To Hannibal.'

'There, Hannibal,' said Tuppence, stroking his head. 'You've had your health drunk. Almost as good as being knighted or having a medal. I was reading Stanley Weyman's *Count Hannibal* only the other day.'

'Read it as a boy, I remember,' said Mr Robinson. '"Who touches my brother touches Tavanne," if I've got it right. Pikeaway, don't you think? Hannibal, may I be permitted to tap you on the shoulder?'

Hannibal took a step towards him, received a tap on the shoulder and gently wagged his tail.

'I hereby create you a Count of this Realm.'

'Count Hannibal. Isn't that lovely?' said Tuppence. 'What a proud dog you ought to be!'